A Gangsta Twist Saga

Books 1 & 2

Clifford "Spud" Johnson

www.urbanbooks.net

Urban Books, LLC
97 N18th Street
Wyandanch, NY 11798

ISBN 13: 978-1-60162-599-1
ISBN 10: 1-60162-599-5

First Trade Paperback Printing June 2014
Printed in the United States of America

10 9 8 7 6 5 4 3 2 1

Distributed by Kensington Publishing Corp.
Submit Wholesale Orders to:
Kensington Publishing Corp.
C/O Penguin Group (USA) Inc.
Attention: Order Processing
405 Murray Hill Parkway
East Rutherford, NJ 07073-2316
Phone: 1-800-526-0275
Fax: 1-800-227-9604

MAY - - 2014

Gangsta Twist 1

Chapter One

Once the flight reached it's cruising altitude, Taz watched as Keno reached under his seat, grabbed his carry-on bag, and pulled out his portable DVD player. Keno smiled at Taz as he inserted his *Scarface* DVD into his Toshiba SD-P2800. He loved that movie. Every time they went on a mission out of town, he repeatedly watched that DVD. Taz shook his head from side to side as he watched his partner plug his headphones into the DVD player.

Keno noticed him staring and asked, "Are you trying to watch *'Face* with me, dog?"

Taz shook his head no and said, "I'm chillin', fool. I'm thinking about what I'm going to get into when we get back home. I'm so fuckin' tired of the same ol' shit we be doing. Either it's the club or riding around town, flossin' and shit. I think I'm going out to Norman and spend some time with Tazneema. It's been way too long since I chilled with her."

"Yeah, that's straight, but tonight we're still going to the club and get our floss on. We gots to let the haters hate," Keno said with a smile on his face.

With a smile of his own, Taz said, "Yeah, I know." He sat back and reclined in his chair and started thinking about the mission they had just completed out in Seattle. As usual, everything went as planned. Hell, nothing ever went wrong whenever Won put something together. They had just successfully robbed some dope boys for over 1.5 million dollars, not including the jewelry and drugs that they took. Taz and his five comrades didn't fuck with drugs; all they took for themselves was the money. Won would look out for them with the jewels and keep the drugs for himself. That way, everyone would be happy, especially Taz and the crew. As long as they continued to maintain their strict and orderly ways, he didn't foresee any future problems with how they were earning their money.

It felt real good to be financially secure, but it felt even better to know that no matter what happened, it was highly unlikely that they would ever go back to broke. That was something that just simply could not happen. They were all millionaires. *Millionaires! Robbin' punk-ass dope boys has made us all fuckin' millionaires. Now, ain't that somethin'!* he thought as he closed his eyes.

As the plane was making it's final decent into Will Rogers Airport in Oklahoma City, one of the flight attendants lightly shook Taz and told him that he had to put his seat in the upright position for the landing. He opened his eyes, did as she had asked, and turned toward Keno.

Keno was smiling as he watched Al Pacino shooting up a bunch of Colombian hit men in his mansion. "Get 'em, 'Face! Don't go out by yourself, baby!" he said as if this was his first time ever watching the movie.

Taz tapped him on his shoulder, and Keno pulled the headphones out of the DVD. Taz told him, "Dog, turn that shit off. We're about to land."

"Hold the fuck up. It's almost over. You know this is my favorite part of the flick. 'Face is about to get smashed, but he's going out like a warrior, for real."

Taz stared at Keno briefly, shook his head again, and closed his eyes.

When their flight pulled up to the gate, Taz told Keno, "Call the others to make sure that they're on schedule."

Keno reached into his pocket, pulled out a thin cell phone, and started dialing. After a few seconds he asked someone on the other line, "Are y'all straight? . . . That's cool. We just got in too. We'll be at the house in about thirty to forty minutes. Have you gotten at Bo-Pete and Wild Bill yet? . . . Get at them and let them know everything is everything. By the time y'all make it in from Tulsa and they get in from Dallas, it'll be time to hit the club. So make sure y'all's gear is up to par. It's time to party, my nigga! . . . All right, I'll tell him. Out!" Keno closed his cell phone. "Bob and Red just got to Tulsa, and they're on their way in now. By the time we get to the house and get dressed and shit, Bo-Pete and Wild Bill should be there too. Dog, I hate all of this separate flying shit. Why we gots to get down like that every time we bounce?"

Taz frowned at Keno but remained silent as they left the plane. As they walked through the terminal, Taz noticed two of the three undercover airport security officers staring at them. He wasn't worried because all they had on them was a small amount of money. *Thanks to Won, we never have to worry about petty shit,* he said to himself as he led the way out of the airport.

Once they were outside, they climbed into one of the airport shuttle vans and rode in silence to the long-term parking area. After they were inside of Taz's all-black 2005 Denali, he answered Keno's question. "Dog, ever since we've been getting down, we've always maintained our discipline, right?"

"Yeah."

"So, why would you ask me some stupid shit? You know Won has it set up for us to move in sets of twos. That's how we move when we're at home, and that's how we move when we're on a mission. I swear, sometimes you just don't think before you run that mouth of yours! Bob was right. You be too damn anxious to get into shit. You need to relax a li'l, homey."

"Ain't that a bitch! That nigga Bob be just as anxious as I am. Shit, I ain't even talkin' about gettin' into shit. I was just thinking, like, damn! This shit always slows us down a little. Fuck! After we get paid, it's all about relaxing and having a good time, my nigga. You need to get off your ass and try it sometimes."

"What you talkin' 'bout, fool? I go out every time y'all go out."

"Yeah, I know. You go out with us, but you don't be trying to have a good time. All you do is post up and let a few bitches holla. But on the real, you don't be trying to holla back. It's like you're just passing the time, my nigga."

Taz knew Keno was right, but how could he explain that he just wasn't into that bullshit-ass club scene? How could he tell one of his lifelong friends that all he wanted to do was continue to make sure that their rental houses around the city were straight, and enjoy the fruits of their work by staying in his big-ass house and working out in his home gym? How could he explain how lonely he really was? Those were things that he kept close to his chest, because no one would ever understand the pain that he felt and lived with daily . . . *no one!* "Whatever, nigga! You just make sure that you get real fly tonight, 'cause I'm bustin' out the burgundy chinchilla."

Smiling, Keno said, "Oh, so we're sportin' the minks, huh? That's cool, 'cause I ordered a tight-ass creme chinchilla a few weeks ago. I've been waiting for it to get kind of chilly to sport that bitch. So it's on and poppin' tonight, nigga. You better be careful!"

"What are you talkin' 'bout now, fool?" Taz asked as he pulled into the circular driveway of Keno's mini-mansion.

"That chinchilla be making them hoes fiend, and you know you ain't with that much female attention." Keno started laughing as he got out of the truck. Taz smiled and gave him the finger as he pulled out of the driveway once he saw Keno go inside of his home.

By the time Taz made it to his home, Wild Bill, Bo-Pete, Red and Bob were all standing beside Bob's all-black Escalade. Bo-Pete's all-black Navigator was parked behind Bob's truck. They turned toward Taz as he jumped out of his truck.

"What up, fools? I'm glad to see y'all made it. Come on in so we can hit Won and check on everything," he said as he led the way into his 15,000-square-foot mini-mansion. Even though he stayed alone, he loved all of the space he had. Staying way out on the outskirts of the City made him feel secure. His whereabouts and safety were two things that were very important to him. But more importantly, he just loved being secluded.

Once they were inside, he led them to one of his two dens so they could all relax. Bob went to the bar and poured himself a shot of Rémy Martin, while Bo-Pete and Wild Bill pulled the cover back to Taz's pool table and started a game. Red turned on Taz's sixty-inch plasma screen and turned the channel to ESPN. Taz went upstairs to his bedroom and set his bag down.

He grabbed the phone and sent a text message to Won. After that, he walked back downstairs and rejoined his comrades.

The plushness of his home was so amazing that one would swear that a woman had decorated. The two dens were both identical; soft brown Italian leather sectional sofas, with a pool table in each, the same color as his furniture. Plasma screen televisions and the most sophisticated entertainment system money could buy gave his dens the feel as if one was in a high-tech arcade or something. The other ten rooms were just as tasteful, as were the four bathrooms, for that matter. Taz left no stone unturned when it came to his home. After all, he was a millionaire.

Just as Taz was about to speak, there was a loud knock at the front door. He sighed and said, "Man, go let that fool Keno in, please."

Red got up and went and let Keno inside. A minute later, he returned followed by Keno. Keno was dressed to impress. He had on a pair of creme-colored Azzure jeans with matching colored Timberland boots. You couldn't see his shirt because his creme-colored chinchilla mink was zipped all the way up. He smiled as he unzipped his coat and said, "What up, my peoples?"

"Damn, nigga! When you get that?" asked Bo-Pete.

Before Keno could answer him, Taz said, "He ordered it a few weeks ago. Now, sit down so we can take care of this shit. We need to get this out of the way." Taz sat down, flipped open his laptop, and quickly started tapping on the keys. After a few minutes of this he stopped, smiled, and said, "Now that's what I'm talkin' 'bout!"

"It's all there?" asked Red.

"Yep. Here, check your account," Taz said as he passed the small computer to Red.

Red quickly punched in his password and pulled up his account in the Cayman Islands. After a few minutes he, too, smiled and said, "Oh yeah! I'm loving that shit!"

After passing the laptop around, each member of the six-man crew saw that their accounts in the islands had an additional two hundred and fifty thousand dollars, profit from their short trip to Seattle. Not bad for twenty-four hours of work. Not bad at all.

Wild Bill closed the laptop and said, "Well, that's that. Let's go get something to eat before we hit the club. I'm hungry."

Laughing loudly, Bob said, "Nigga, for a li'l nigga, you always hungry. But I feel you, gee. I'm starving my damn self. That airline food ain't nothin' nice."

Taz's cell rang. He quickly flipped it open and said, "What up, Won?"

"What's up with you, Babyboy? I see y'all made it back safely."

"Yeah, we're good. How 'bout your end? You straight?"

"Always. Have you checked your accounts yet?"

"Yeah, we just finished. Everything is everything. Good lookin' on the jewels and shit."

"No problem. I tried to get y'all as much as I could for them. I'm glad you're satisfied. Now, check this. I'm on the move, so stay ready because you and the troops will definitely have to stay on standby for this next one. It could happen as soon as next week—possibly sooner."

"Don't trip. We got you. All we need is the call. As long as you set it up, we'll be ready," Taz replied confidently.

"I know, Babyboy. That's why you're my man. Now, tell them knuckleheads with you that I said enjoy, be merry, and most of all, be good! Out!"

Taz closed his phone and gave Won's message to the crew. They all laughed.

Taz then ran upstairs and changed into his gear for the night. He put on a pair of black Rocawear jeans and a black T-shirt; then he grabbed his black Timbs and his burgundy chinchilla. He stepped toward the bedroom mirror and smiled. The lights shined brightly against his one-hundred-and-fifty-thousand-dollar platinum and diamond fronts. He reached into his drawer and pulled out his Rolex, then his two-hundred-and-fifty gram platinum chain and put it around his neck. The diamonds in his Jesus piece sparkled in the lighting as he adjusted it around his neck. "Now that's what a nigga calls bling-bling!" he said aloud as he grabbed his wallet and went back downstairs. "Time to go clubbin'!"

Chapter Two

Sacha Carbajal stepped out of the office building of Johnson & Whitney, the law firm she was working for, feeling extremely excited. She had just been told by the partners that she was next in line for a partnership. Finally, after six years of hard work, it was about to happen for her. She smiled happily as she strolled toward her brand-new 2006 BMW 325i. She was on her way to the top, and it felt great! Once she was inside of her car, she pulled out her cell phone and called her best friend, Gwen.

Gwen answered her phone after the third ring. "Hello?"

"What it do, bitch?" yelled Sacha.

"What it do, ho? Did you get it?" asked Gwen.

"I think so, girl. I'll know for sure sometime next week. Mr. Whitney told me that I was definitely next in line, and as long as nothing drastic occurs, I should be a partner soon."

"I'm so happy for you, girl! Congratulations!"

"Save that shit for later. Nothing is written in stone yet, but I'm still feeling giddy all over. We need to go out tonight. Do you have any plans?"

"Nope. What, you want to hit Bricktown and hang out a little?"

"Uh-uh. I'm trying to kick it with my peoples tonight. Let's go to that club you told me about a couple of months back."

"Bitch, I know you ain't talking about Club Cancun, the same club that has nothing but hoochie hoes and wannabe ballers!" Gwen said sarcastically.

"All right, so I wasn't feeling it at first, but I'm in the mood to party with my peoples. I'm tired of hanging with the squares and those uppity-ass white people."

Laughing, Gwen said, "Now, ain't that something! Bitch, you're just as square as those uppity-ass white people! The only reason you still have a little hood left in your ass is because of me. Sometimes I think you've forgotten where you came from. But I ain't tripping. If you want to do the club, I'm with it. But we're going to have to go get some gear for tonight, 'cause I know you ain't got nothing in that uppity-ass closet of yours."

"Yeah, you're right. Meet me at Penn Square Mall in thirty, ho."

"Gotcha, bitch," Gwen said, and hung up the phone.

Gwen and Sacha had been best friends for over twenty years. They both graduated at the top of their classes in high school; then they went to Oklahoma State and graduated at the top of their classes there too. That's when their paths seemed to split. While Sacha went on to law school, Gwen got pregnant and had her son, Remel. Sacha tried her best to get Gwen to go back to school so she could follow her dreams, but the love bug had bitten her best friend too hard. Nothing anyone could say would deter Gwen from the love of her life. William had walked into Gwen's life and changed her forever.

Thinking back about the past almost caused tears to fill Sacha's eyes as she drove toward the mall. *Life just wasn't fair sometimes,* she thought as she remembered the day Gwen's life got turned completely upside down.

It had been raining all day and Gwen didn't feel like doing anything, so she had asked William to pick up Remel from day care after he got off of work. The rainy day had her in a funky mood, so she chose to sit back and relax a little. She began to doze off, and eventually fell asleep.

The next thing Gwen remembered was being awakened by banging at her front door. She got up groggily and went to see who was beating on her door like they were out of their damn minds. When she saw that it was her girl, Sacha, she smiled and opened the door. As soon as she saw Sacha's face, she knew that something was wrong. Her makeup was smeared, and she was shaking uncontrollably. "What's wrong, Sacha?" she asked as she brought her into her home and sat her down in her living room.

Tears rolled silently down Sacha's cheeks as she gathered the nerve to tell her best friend in the world that her son and husband were dead.

Sacha remembered Gwen's screams as if it were yesterday. She prayed to the Almighty that she'd never hear another person scream like that ever again. After calming Gwen down a little, she explained what had happened and how she came to be at the horrible scene.

William was pulling out of the driveway of the day-care center when he was hit head-on by a drunk driver. The drunk driver, William, and baby Remel all died instantly. Sacha was on her way home and just so happened to see everything. When she realized that William and Remel were inside of the car and Gwen wasn't, she remembered feeling slightly relieved. The guilt of that thought still haunted her to this very day. She jumped back into her car and drove as fast as she could to her best friend's home.

As Sacha pulled into the mall's parking lot, she smiled sadly as she thought about how her girl got herself back together from such a devastating loss. Gwen was never one to mope. As hard as it was for her, she got back on her feet, went back to school and got her bachelor's degree, as well as her master's. Her original goal was to be an attorney just like Sacha, but after losing her baby and the love of her life, she chose psychology as her major. She wanted to help people. She opened her own office and started helping others and healing herself all at the same time. She'd never blamed that drunk driver for taking her family away from her; she always blamed herself for being too lazy that day. She felt that if she had gone and picked up Remel like she always did, her family would be with her to this very day. She didn't use that as an excuse; she used that to motivate herself.

She was the most driven woman that Sacha had ever known, and it was her strength that helped Sacha continue on at Johnson & Whitney, Attorneys at Law. Many times she had considered quitting and joining another law firm because she felt as if her talents were being overlooked. But Gwen rode her hard and told her to never quit. "Stay down, girl. Everything

will be all right, and don't you give up on me, bitch!" Gwen
yelled at her every time she felt weak. And now, finally after
six years, the hard work was finally paying off, and Sacha
owed it all to her girl, the strongest woman alive. So, it was
only fitting that they spend the evening together, having a
good time.

As she got out of her car, she smiled as Gwen's thick-ass
strolled to meet her at the front of the Dillard's department
store in the mall. *She's living her life to the fullest after all
of the pain she's been through, damnit! I'm about to start
doing the same damn thing,* she said to herself as she stepped
toward her best friend.

"What's up, bitch? Come on, I got an idea of what we're
going to wear tonight," Gwen said as she pulled Sacha into the
mall.

"I don't need your ass picking out my clothes, ho. I know
what I like, and it damn sure ain't that hoochie shit you be
liking to wear."

"Humph! That's why your ass don't have a man now. Look
at you, with that power suit and power look. Bitch, you ain't
at court! Yo' wanna be Johnny Cochran-ass gots to loosen up.
Tonight, we're gonna let this city see exactly what you're working with. And I ain't talking about no slutty shit . . . well, a little
slutty . . . but with class, baby. Now, come on." Gwen took Sacha
into the Buckle, a small store in the mall, and led her straight to
a bunch of skimpy dresses.

Sacha stared at some of the dresses and started shaking her
head. "Uh-uh! I know you don't think you're about to get me
into any of that! Ho, you gots to be out of your fucking mind!
It's too damn cold to be wearing that type of shit, Gwen!"

"Would you shut the fuck up? It ain't that damn cold, bitch.
Look at this. Now tell me this ain't a fly-ass mini hookup,"
she said as she held up a one-piece Apple Bottoms skirt. It
was all black, with the words "Apple Bottoms" going across
the middle in gold lettering. "Bitch, if Melyssa can sport this
bitch, so can you. If you want to turn some heads tonight, then
this is the bad boy to do it in."

"Who said anything about turning some damn heads? All I want to do is go out and have some fun, and I don't need no damn man to do that."

"You see, that's what I'm talking about. Your ass is in denial. Has that square-ass nigga at your firm gotten up the nerve to get at you yet?"

"Who are you talking about? Clifford?"

"Who else could I be talking about, bitch? Stop playing with me!"

"Well, I still catch him peeking at me during meetings and stuff, but actually, I think he's lost interest."

"Good. That nerdy nigga ain't worthy anyway. But back to this. Get this skirt so we can go to Nine West and see if they have some tight pumps to match."

"You're really serious, huh?"

"You damn skippy! Now go try it on so we can see how it looks."

Sacha did as she was told. After putting on the skimpy dress, she couldn't deny it, she looked damn good. She came out of the dressing room and spun around slowly and asked Gwen, "How does it look?"

"Bitch, you already looked in the mirror! You know how good it looks, so I don't have to tell your ass!"

Sacha stood in front of the mirror outside of the dressing room, smiled, and said, "My legs are too thick for this."

"Shut the fuck up, bitch! Your legs are just right for that skirt. Go put your clothes back on so we can get you some pumps."

They both started laughing as Sacha went and changed back into her clothes. She couldn't argue and win with her girl, so she said to hell with it and bought the dress. They went to a few shoe stores and finally decided on a pair of black Prada pumps that matched the dress to a tee. Gwen bought herself a Coogi denim skirt with a matching top, and some colorful pumps by Jimmy Choo.

After getting all of their stuff together, they decided to go to Red Lobster for dinner. As they were being led to their table, Sacha noticed several different guys peeping at them. She knew she was looking tired, and she self-consciously tried to straighten herself out. She stood a little under five-five and weighed between 125 and 130 pounds. She was thick in all the right places. She had small hips, nice C-cup sized breasts, and an ass to make a grown man cry. But what made her stand out was the exotic look she possessed. She looked as if she had just flown in from the islands somewhere. Her skin tone was bronze-like. She looked as if she stayed in Florida or California somewhere. Her shoulder-length hair completed the island look she possessed. Even dressed in a navy blue pant suit, she still turned heads.

After they were seated, Gwen said, "Look at you, still turning heads wherever we go. I swear, sometimes I hate you, bitch!"

"You the one that got all the men in your life. Shit, how do you know the heads that are turning ain't looking at your hoochie mama hot ass?" They laughed as they gave their orders to the waiter.

After the waiter had left to go get them their salads, Gwen said, "We're going to do the damn thing tonight, bitch. And I swear, you're going to have the club shut the fuck down in that skirt."

"Whatever!"

"I'm serious, bitch. You gon' have every nigga on your ass."

"Whatever!"

Gwen sipped her water and shook her head as she stared at her best friend. Gwen knew she was no slouch when it came to men. Shit, she knew she could have any nigga she wanted for real. She just chose to fuck and go as she pleased. There was only one man who owned her heart, and he was in Heaven, so ain't no need trying to fake it. *It is what it is,* she thought as she continued to smile at her friend.

Gwen was the same height as Sacha, but thinner. She had that ghetto booty to make men's mouths water, but she was short in the breast department. Her little A-cups constantly frustrated her. She was dying to get a boob job, but was just too scared to go through with it. She knew that if she told Sacha about it, she would laugh her out of the house. But she was definitely eye candy. Her hazel eyes matched her light brown skin to perfection. God wasn't playing when he blessed her with her looks. But with William gone to Heaven, to her it was all moot.

After they finished their meal, Sacha smiled and said, "All right, girl, I'm about to head on home and take a hot bath so I can get ready for this wild night. I hope I don't look like no damn fool in this hoochie outfit you got me wearing."

"Trust me, bitch. The club and any nigga you want will be yours tonight."

They kissed each other on the cheek and parted ways.

Sacha made it home a little after eight p.m. She took her new clothes to her room and went and ran her bathwater. While the water was running, she checked a few e-mails from some of her clients. Since it was the weekend and she didn't have any court dates next week, she decided to put everything else on hold. She was focused on having a good time tonight. She stripped out of her pant suit, walked into her bathroom, and got into the steaming tub full of hot water. As she relaxed in the water, she smiled and said, "Time to go clubbin'!"

Chapter Three

The parking lot of Club Cancun was packed as Taz and the crew pulled into the parking lot. Keno was driving Taz's Denali, and he had the doors to the truck open as they pulled into the parking lot, followed by Bo-Pete, who was driving his truck, and Bob, who was bringing up the rear. Since Taz's Denali had a vertical door conversion kit, all eyes were on them as they parked.

The line to get inside was crazy long, but that didn't bother Keno as he stepped out of the truck and struck a pose for all of the ladies that were staring at them . . . oh, and for the haters also.

Taz climbed out of his truck, smiled, and said, "Damn, nigga! You love this shit, huh?"

After calmly zipping up his chinchilla, Keno said, "Dog, this town is ours, and it's only right that everyone knows it. Look at all of these window-shopping-ass bustas staring at us. Look at the hoes. I'm telling you, my nigga, this is *our* town!"

Bob, Red, Bo-Pete, and Wild Bill stepped next to the truck, and Keno asked them, "Are y'all ready?"

"You know it!" replied Bo-Pete.

"Then do you. You know the drill," Keno said as he fired up the purple haze.

Bo-Pete and Wild Bill walked straight toward the front door and were not bothered by the security as they entered the club.

Bo-Pete smiled at a few ladies as he passed them, and gave a soft nod to a few fellas from around the way. The confidence he possessed showed as he casually strolled into the club. Bo-Pete may be only five-eleven, but he felt like a king every time they went to the club. His chocolate brown skin was smooth as can be, and he knew he looked good. He felt that he made the clothes he wore look good, instead of the other way around. He kept his hair cut low and even all the way around, and sported a neat, well-kept goatee. His muscular frame spoke volumes to the women. They could tell that he always kept himself in tip-top condition.

Wild Bill, Bo-Pete's partner and road dog, was like the complete opposite of Bo-Pete. Bill's hair was extremely long. He kept it permed and combed to the back in a long ponytail. He was a short man, but just as muscular as Bo-Pete. He wore gold-rimmed glasses and if you paid close attention, you could tell that he was damn near blind. But he, too, possessed that confident stroll as he followed Bo-Pete into the club.

Inside of the club, Katrina and Paquita were having their normal conversation about who was doing what to whom, and what other females were wearing and whatnot. They both were regulars at the club, and were well known 'round-the-way girls. In other words, they were "hood rats."

". . . Girl, I'm telling you, I saw Latanya's scandalous-ass at the mall earlier, taking everything as if it was free. I mean, she wasn't even trying to be low! She's a bold bitch for real!" Paquita yelled excitedly.

"Shit, you know how that freak bitch get down. I don't know why your ass is shocked," replied Katrina as she straightened her too-tight, too-small miniskirt.

"Ooh, girl! Look who just came into the club!" Paquita said as she slung her micro-braids over her shoulder.

After taking a long look around the club and not noticing anyone of importance, Katrina asked, "Who, bitch? I don't see nobody."

"Over there by the front! It's Bo-Pete and Wild Bill!"

"So? What's so damn special about Bo-Pete and Wild Bill?"

"Girl, whenever you see them come into the club, that can only mean one thing."

"And what's that?"

Smiling broadly, Paquita said, "That means Taz is here!"

"Stop playing! Where he at?"

"Wait, and you'll see. Look, they're checking out the club to make sure that everything is straight for Taz to come in here. You know how he is about his surroundings."

"Nah, I don't know shit about it. But I do know that Taz is one fine-ass nigga, and sooner or later I'm gon' get me some of that dick," Katrina replied confidently.

"Well, bitch, you better get in line, 'cause damn near every bitch in this club has tried to get with him. You know I know my shit. And to my knowledge, ain't no ho in the City been successful. Oooh, ooh! I knew I was right, bitch! Look, there goes Red and Bob too. Watch. You see how Bo-Pete and Wild Bill went to the left of the club and posted up?"

"Yeah, so what?"

"Now Red and Bob are going to look around real quick. Then they're going to go to the right of the club. Then, I'll give it three to five minutes before we see Keno and Taz's fine-asses come in here. Taz is going to stand in the entrance and look around. Then, he's going to go to the bar and hold up two fingers, and Winky, the bartender, is going to pour him a double shot of that expensive-ass Courvoiser XO—you know, that three hundred a bottle type shit."

"Damn, bitch! How you know so much about Taz?"

"I told you, I know what I'm talkin' about! I've been about fuckin' that nigga since back in the day. I would have had action, too, if I wouldn't have done the goofy and started fucking with that whack-ass nigga Clarence. That's back when Taz was sociable. Ever since he . . . oh, never mind, bitch! What did I tell you? Here he comes now!"

At that moment, Paquita was right. Taz and Keno stood in the entranceway of the club and took a good look around until their eyes locked with Bo-Pete's and Wild Bill's, who were standing to their left. Then they let their eyes roam some more until they locked eyes with Red and Bob, who were posted up on the right side of the club. Then, Taz did exactly what Paquita said he would. He stepped to the bar and held up two fingers. Winky, the bartender, quickly poured Taz a double shot of XO into a brandy snifter and passed it to him. Taz sipped his drink and gave Winky a slight nod of his head.

Keno unzipped his chinchilla and smiled at a few ladies who were standing close to them.

Taz noticed how everybody was taking peeks their way, and he shook his head. *These broke mothafuckas are always hating. Look at all these soft-ass niggas! I swear, I don't know why I keep coming to this lame-ass spot,* he said to himself as he took another sip of his drink.

As if reading Taz's mind, Keno said, "Don't trip, my nigga. This may not be your scene, but for us, it is what it is. You straight? 'Cause I'm about to do me."

"Yeah, I'm good. Go on, 'Floss King'! Do you!"

Keno smiled as he took a quick look at his Presidential Rolex and said, "Yep, it's about that time."

As if they had been standing right by Taz and Keno and heard their conversation, Bo-Pete and Wild Bill went to the back bar and got themselves a drink, and Red and Bob had stopped a waitress and had her bring them both some Rémy Martin.

Bob's bald head was sweaty, so he wiped himself with a napkin. His decision to wear all black gave him a sinister look. His dark clothing and dark-skinned complexion made a few females around them a little nervous. But what really made Bob stand out was the knot on his forehead. It stood out about four inches and was an oval shape. People in the know knew never to play with Bob about his knot. But Taz and the crew clowned him about it all of the time. He was the same height as Bo-Pete, Taz, and Keno, but he was the wildest one out of the crew. Once that liquor got into him, he was going to start acting up. Red knew this, so he said, "Don't get too faded tonight, dog. I really don't feel like carrying your ass outta here."

"What's wrong, big boy? All those muscles and you worried about picking up your homeboy?"

"It ain't that, fool. That shit's embarrassing. Just don't over fucking do it," said Red as he lit up a Black & Mild cigar.

Red was the biggest in the crew. He stood between six-two and six-three, and he was the only light-skinned member. He kept his hair long and braided in tight French braids going toward the back of his head. To say he was muscular like Taz, Bo-Pete, and the rest of the crew would be an understatement. He was fucking huge! He could easily pass for Mr. Universe or some shit. He had muscles popping out of everywhere. His laid-back demeanor shocked those who got to know him, because you would swear he was one of those cocky, conceited niggas. Actually, he was the coolest member of the crew . . . except when he became angry. Then, watch out, 'cause all hell would break loose when that happened.

Back by the front bar, Taz stood and watched as Keno did his thing on the dance floor with a cute little female.

Keno, at five-eleven, was Taz's heart. No one knew Taz better, and Taz loved him like a brother. But for the life of him, Taz just couldn't figure out why Keno loved to floss so damn much. Yeah, it was cool sometimes, but every time they came out to play, Keno had to make sure that he shined the most. Though they were both the same height, they were completely different from each other. Where Taz was solid and thick, Keno was just as muscular but had a thinner lower body. Keno's hair was long and kept in braids like Red's, whereas Taz's hair was longer and kept in individual plaits.

What made Taz stand out the most were his eyes. His dark brown eyes could show you so much love, but at the snap of a finger they could show you much hate. You could read his every expression by looking into his eyes.

Keno's outgoing personality was irritating at times to Taz, but he loved him all the same. He chalked it up to Keno being the yin to his yang. Taz never let anyone too close, especially women. Keno, on the other hand, fell in love damn near every other day, and was very open about things, especially his personal life. That was definitely a no-no in Taz's book, and he had to constantly stay on Keno's ass about certain things. Taz was not going for any of that shit when it came to his personal life.

Katrina and Paquita finally built up enough nerve to approach Taz.

Taz smiled as they slowly came toward him. *I know these two crazy-ass hoes don't think they got a shot at the title! This is about to be some funny shit,* he told himself.

Once they were standing in front of him, Paquita took charge. "What's up, Taz? How ya been, baby?"

"Laid back. You know how I get down, 'Quita. What's up with you?"

"The same ol', same ol'. Just trying to make it out here in this cold, cold world."

"Is that right? What's up, Katrina? What, the cat got your tongue tonight?"

"Uh-uh. But you can have it if you want it, Taz."

Smiling, Taz asked, "Can I have *everything* I want?"

Stepping back slightly so that Taz could take a good look at her voluptuous figure, Katrina smiled and said, "It's yours for the taking, baby. You name it, you got it, Taz!"

He was sipping his drink as she said this, and he damn near spit a mouthful of his expensive cognac all over her. He caught himself and said, "I'll have to take a rain check on you this time, boo. You know I'm saving myself for that special lady."

"That's fucked up, Taz! Why you trying to clown a sista? You know I've been wanting to get with your fine-ass!" whined Katrina.

With a shrug of his shoulders, Taz smiled and said, "Baby, I guess it just ain't meant to be. Look, let me buy you two a drink or somethin', huh?"

"That's cool, but can you do me a favor, Taz, please?"

Sighing, he asked, "What is it, 'Quita?"

With a bright smile on her face, Paquita asked him, "Can you smile for me, Daddy?"

That got a smile out of him because he knew what she wanted to see. So, he smiled brightly and let her get a good look at the diamonds in his grille.

"Damn, baby! You the shit and you know it, huh?"

"Nah, 'Quita, I'm just good ol' Taz, baby girl. Look, y'all go on and tell Winky to give y'all whatever y'all want. And make sure you keep this 'tiger' out of trouble, 'Quita," he said, referring to Katrina.

"I will, Taz. Come on, girl. Let's go get our drink on."

As they were walking away, Katrina put an extra swish into her big hips, and Taz started shaking his head and laughing at the same time. He turned around to check and see what his partners were getting into and noticed the baddest female that he'd seen in a very long time. I mean, just by looking at her, he felt himself stir down below. *Who the fuck is that?* he asked himself as he watched the sexy female enter the club with another female. *Damn, she's sexy as hell!* he thought as he sipped his drink and continued to stare at her.

As Sacha and Gwen entered the club, Sacha could actually feel all of the eyes on her. *Oh, my God! Why did I let this girl talk me into wearing this hoochie outfit? I feel damn near naked!* she thought to herself as they found a table by the back bar. After they sat down, a waitress came to their table and asked if they wanted anything to drink. They both ordered apple martinis. While the waitress went to get them their drinks, they both took a look around the club.

Sacha could see a bunch of the fake wannabe ballers flossing around the club and acting like they owned the place. She also saw a few good-looking men here and there. As her eyes continued to scan the club, they stopped when they came to Taz. *Damn! Who's that fine-ass specimen of a man?* she asked herself as she took a real good look at Taz and what he was wearing. *Hmmm. A thug with taste, huh? Gots to be. He's wearing that chinchilla like it was made especially for him. Nice jewelry, expensive too. Not too much, but just enough. I like them braids too. Damn, that nigga is sexy!* she thought to herself as she turned back to face Gwen.

Gwen, who had followed her friend's eyes and saw the same thing that she had seen, said, "That is one bad man, bitch! You peep that chinchilla he has on?"

"Umm-hmm! He's definitely at the top of his game, ho. Probably the biggest dope dealer in the city. I'll probably be representing his ass in federal court one day." They both started laughing as the waitress came and set their drinks on the table.

While the ladies were sipping their drinks, Taz continued to watch them. *I gots to meet that broad. Ain't no way in hell I can let her leave this spot without me gettin' at her. But how? I don't get down like that. Shit! Bitches get at Taz. Taz don't get at bitches.* "Fuck it!" he said as he turned back toward the bar.

Someone came up behind him, tapped him lightly on his shoulder, and said, "Excuse me, Taz. Can I holla at ya for a sec?"

Taz turned around and faced a tall, brown-skinned brother with a few muscles showing under his white tee. "What up, dog? Do I know you?"

"Not personally, but you probably know my big brother, KK."

"Yeah, I remember him. Is he still on lock?"

"Yeah, he got twenty in the FEDs. I be looking out for him, though."

"That's straight. So, what's up?"

"Man, Taz, a nigga was trying to see how he could be down."

With a confused expression on his face, Taz asked, "Down with what, gee?"

"You know, down with you. I'm trying to eat big like you and your crew. I ain't no sucka nigga, and I'm vertical all the way, baby, straight up and down. I got a few traps around the way, and I'm moving shit. I just don't have no real plug, you know what I'm saying?"

"Hold the fuck up, youngsta! Are you talkin' 'bout some dope?"

"Yeah. Everyone knows you got the town on lock. I just want to be down."

Taz set his drink on the bar and said, "Check this, you li'l mark-ass nigga! I don't fuck with dope boys, nor do I fuck with dope, period! So, whoever told you that punk shit, you really need to check they ass, 'cause if you ever come near me again talking about some dope, I'm going to beat the fuck outta your punk-ass! Do . . . you . . . under . . . stand . . . me . . . D . . . Boy?" Taz said as he stabbed his index finger into the youngster's chest with each syllable to make his point.

The youngster was so shocked that he couldn't speak; he just turned and went to where his homeboys were seated. As soon as he sat down at his table, one of his homies asked him, "So, is he going to hook you up or what?"

"Yeah, he told me to get with him in a few weeks," lied the youngster. "But fuck that shit! We gots to eat. I ain't trying to be waiting on that nigga."

"But, nigga, I thought you said he has the town on lock," said his homey.

"So what? He ain't the only nigga in this town eating. Change the fuckin' subject, nigga."

Taz was so irritated now that his mood was borderline volatile. He turned and waved for Keno.

Keno saw him and quickly walked toward him. "What up, gee? You straight?"

"Nah, I'm ready to bounce."

"*What?* Dog, it's just starting to get crackin' in this bitch! Don't do me like that, baby!"

"I'm out. Tell them niggas that you'll be back. I want you to drop me off at the pad. I'm about to go out to Moore and lay it down for a minute. Since I'm going to spend the day with Tazneema tomorrow, I might as well be out that way."

"Nigga, go on with that shit! You want some ass, so you're going to your li'l chickie's pad. That's fucked up, dog, but I ain't trippin'. Let's roll so I can hurry up and get back to doing me."

After letting the others know that they were leaving, Taz took one last glance at the cutie in the Apple Bottoms outfit, shook his head sadly, and left. *If it's meant to be, I'll see her again,* he told himself as he followed Keno out of the club.

Keno drove like a madman all of the way out to Taz's home. Once he pulled into the driveway, he jumped out of Taz's truck and said, "I'm out, my nigga. I'll holla at you sometime tomorrow."

"That's straight," said Taz as he watched Keno jump into his Range Rover and pull out of his driveway. Taz then got into the driver's seat of his truck and slowly pulled out of his driveway. He grabbed his cell and made a call. As soon as the other line was answered, he said, "What's up, sexy? I'm on my way."

"Whatever, Taz. You know you don't have to call me every time you come out here. I was sleeping soundly."

"Sorry about that, baby. What, you don't want to see me tonight?"

"Stop being silly. I'm always ready to see you, baby. Now, hurry up," she said before hanging up the phone.

Twenty minutes later, Taz pulled into the driveway of a modest home on the southeast side of Oklahoma City. He jumped out of his truck and walked straight into the house. He knew Tari would have left the door unlocked for him as she always did. He walked through the house and made sure that there wasn't anyone lurking around.

"Taz, would you bring your ass in here! You know damn well there isn't anyone else in this house!" yelled Tari from the back bedroom.

He smiled as he walked into the bedroom. Tari was sitting at the edge of her bed, taking off her thong. "You know how I get down, Tari. You never know. One day you might decide to change the rules to the game."

Tari pulled her long blond hair into a ponytail and said, "Come get some of your pussy, Daddy." She sat back on her bed, opened her long legs, and said, "I'd never do anything to put you in harm's way, Taz. I'm here for you whenever you want me, baby. You know that."

As he walked slowly toward the bed, he said, "Yeah, I know, but I'll never change my ways, so stop trying to get me to, and continue to play your part."

"My part? That's all I'm doing, Taz? Playing a part?"

With his eyes softening slightly, he said, "You know what I mean, Tari. Everybody has a role to play in my life." He got on the bed with her.

"And what's my particular role, Mr. Taz?"

"You are my blue-eyed devil, and your role is to always be here to satisfy me," he said as he grabbed her hands to stop her from swinging at him. "I'm just clowning, baby. Come here."

Tari slid into his embrace and they shared a brief kiss. She pulled out of his embrace and said, "M—m—m! I kinda like playing this role, Daddy." She then slid down toward his manhood and put it into her mouth.

Taz smiled and said, "I do too, baby!"

Chapter Four

The next morning, Tari woke Taz and gave him breakfast in bed. Taz opened his eyes and said, "Damn, Tari! Why you always got to wake a nigga up so damn early?"

"Stop using that word, Taz! You know I hate that shit. Now, sit up so you can eat your breakfast. And to answer your question, you know I have to be at work early, and I'm not about to leave you without making sure that I've taken the very best care of you. Now eat!" After setting everything in front of him, she turned and went into the bathroom to finish getting ready for her shift at the hospital.

Taz smiled as he began eating his breakfast of pancakes, bacon, and orange juice. *For a white girl, Tari could cook her ass off*, he thought as he ate his food.

Tari came out of the bathroom fully dressed in her nurse's uniform. She was tall—almost six foot barefooted—and had a body that made sisters hate. She had curves in all the right places, as well as an ass that was just too damn phat. Her bright blue eyes and her sweet personality made Taz feel comfortable whenever he came over to her place. She was his escape from everyone. Whenever he felt the need to release some sexual energy, or whenever he felt the need to talk, her home was where he went. Tari was the only person who knew his personal dreams and his darkest nightmares. She was his confidante, lover, and friend all rolled into one beautiful package. Even though he knew that she wanted more out of their relationship, she accepted the fact that Taz just wasn't the type to ever love a woman the way she wanted to be loved.

"So, what are your plans for the day, lover boy?" Tari asked as she took the tray away from him and set it on the floor next to the bed.

"I'm going to go spend some time with Tazneema. It's been too long since we chilled together."

"That's good, but why do you do that to that darling little girl? You know she cherishes the ground you walk on, Taz."

"Come on with that shit, Tee! You know how I get down. Plus, she ain't no damn darling li'l girl. She's a grown-ass woman. You must have forgotten that she's now a freshman in college."

"I know how old she is, silly. You must have forgotten that she loves you more than anything in this world. Anyway, what do you have planned for her today?"

"Man, I don't know. I might take her to the mall and let her do her thing. After that, maybe lunch or some shit . . . whatever she wants to get into."

"Does she know that you're coming to spend the day with her?"

"Nope. I was going to, like, surprise her. Tari shook her head from side to side, and he asked, "What, you think I should call her and let her know I'm coming out there?"

"That would be wise. What if she already has plans, Taz? You never know what a young college student might have planned on a Saturday afternoon. I swear, sometimes you amaze me with your Neanderthal way of thinking!"

"My Neander-*what*? Gon' with that shit, Tee! I thought it would be cool if I popped up on her and surprised her, that's all."

Shaking her head no, Tari said, "No, you didn't. You think you're slick. You planned on popping up on her in hopes of catching her off guard. That way you might catch her doing something. Call her, Taz." Tari grabbed the cordless phone and placed it into his hands, then bent over and grabbed the tray that had held Taz's breakfast. Taz slapped her on her butt and smiled when she yelled, "Ouch!"

While Tari was in the kitchen, cleaning up, Taz did as he was told and gave Tazneema a call. She answered the phone on the second ring. "Hello?"

"What's up, baby girl? You straight?" he asked.

"Taz! I'm fine. What's up with you?"

"Just chillin'. How's the school thing coming along?"

"It's cool. I'm getting ready for the holidays. Mama-Mama wants me to come spend Christmas break with her, but I'd really rather go to Houston and spend the holidays with my roommate and her family. Do you think you could talk to Mama-Mama for me, Taz?"

"I don't know. You know how Mama-Mama is when she has her mind made up."

"But, Taz, it's going to be off the chain in Houston over the holidays. Ple—e—ease?"

"I'll see what I can do, but I ain't making no promises."

"Okay, just try real hard for me, okay?"

Laughing, he said, "Whatever, girl! But look, I was thinking about coming out that way and spending a li'l time with you today. Is that cool, or do you have plans already?"

"I was going to go to the mall with my roommate and finish up my Christmas shopping."

"Who is this damn roommate?"

"Her name is Lyla, and she's real cool, Taz."

"All right, this is what we'll do. I'm about to get up and get dressed. I should be out there in about thirty minutes. We'll go shopping and have some lunch. Cool?"

"That's cool, but make it an hour. We just got up about ten minutes ago. We kinda had a late night last night."

"Stop! I really don't need to be hearing any of that, especially if you plan on spending the holiday in H-Town."

"Oops! My bad! See you in an hour or so. Bye!" she said and quickly hung up the phone.

Taz started laughing as he hung up the phone.

Tari came back into the bedroom and asked, "What's so funny, baby?"

"That girl is something else. Now she wants to go spend the holiday in Houston with her roommate."

"What's wrong with that?"

"I don't have a problem with it, but I don't think Mama-Mama is going to go for it. 'Neema wants me to try to convince Mama-Mama to let her go."

"Mama-Mama will let her go if you okay it. You know she's a big old softy when it comes to you."

"Yeah, I know, but I'm wondering whether I should okay it or not."

"Why?"

"Do you really think it'll be wise to let 'Neema go running off to Houston, doing only God knows what?"

"Taz, Tazneema is eighteen years old. Technically, she doesn't need consent from you *or* Mama-Mama. She's legal now."

"Don't remind me! I feel old enough as it is!"

Tari smiled and said, "Ooh, my baby is feeling old now? You didn't act like an old man last night—or should I say this morning."

"I never feel old when I'm chillin' with you, baby. Come here," he said as he grabbed her and they shared a kiss.

After a minute or so, Tari pulled from his embrace and said, "Now, let me go. I have to go to work. Will I be blessed with your presence later on?"

"Ain't no tellin'. Don't wait up, though. I'll have to check and see what the boys are getting into later on. I'll hit you up when I know something."

"Okay. Bye, baby!" she said after giving him another quick kiss.

After Tari left, Taz got up and went into the guest room and grabbed some clothes out of the closet. He always kept a few outfits at Tari's. After taking a long hot shower, he got dressed and made himself a cup of coffee. As he sipped his coffee, he grabbed the phone and called Keno. "What up, fool? What you gettin' into today?" he asked when Keno answered the phone.

"Ain't shit. I just got up, nigga. I don't know what the fuck I'm doing later, but right now I'm about to go check on the house in the North Highlands."

"Which one?"

"The one on Eighty-third Street. The plumbing is tripping again. I'm about to call Al and have him meet me over there."

"What's up with the boys?"

"Ain't no tellin'. Bob got bent and started trippin' last night. Red had to carry that nigga up outta the club. Wild Bill came up with a bad bitch, so most likely he's still laid up with her.

Bo-Pete told me that he was going out to the south side to check on the houses over that way. What's up with you? You still going out to Norman?"

"Yeah, I'm about to bounce that way in a minute. Make sure you get at everybody and let them know to keep them phones open. Won may hit us at any given time."

"Don't trip. They know already. Hit me when you're through out that way."

"For sho'. Out!"

"Out!" Keno said and hung up.

Taz grabbed his keys and left the house. During the short drive out to the city of Norman, he was thinking about Tazneema. It seemed as if she was starting to get a little wild. He hoped and prayed that he would be able to calm her ass down. He knew that he had spoiled her too much, but hell, he really didn't have a choice. *Mama-Mama is just as much to blame as I am,* he thought to himself as he pulled in front of her apartment building. Eighteen years old, and she refused to live in the dorm building with the rest of the freshman females that attended the University of Oklahoma. Tazneema had to have her own apartment. Taz smiled as he remembered her begging him and Mama-Mama to let her move in with her roommate. Once Mama-Mama gave in, she knew Taz wouldn't object, and now look at her, wanting to spend the holiday out of town. *Ain't no way Mama-Mama is gon' go for that,* he thought as he climbed out of his truck.

When he made it to the front door, he could hear the music blasting from the other side. He shook his head and began to knock on the door. After about three minutes of waiting, he started banging on the door loudly. Finally, after another two minutes, a pretty little white girl opened the door and said, "Hi! You must be Taz. I'm Lyla. Please, come in. I'm sorry we didn't hear you. I was in the back room, and Tee is still in the shower."

Taz followed her inside and gave the living room a quick once-over. The apartment was neat and orderly. That made him feel a little bit better as he sat down on the sofa. He smiled at Lyla and asked, "So, how's school going for you two?"

"It's cool, but kinda boring because we have to go through the freshman thing and all . . . you know, silly pranks and whatnot."

Lyla was a small female but built nicely. She had firm breasts, and Taz could tell that she was trying her best to make him notice them. She sat at the dining room table and smiled seductively toward him as she talked. Her long brown hair fell past her shoulders, and he couldn't help but to think about Tari. He shook the thought off and asked, "Are you sure your parents won't mind having another mouth to feed over the holidays?"

"Mommy and Daddy both adore Tazneema. They met when we first moved in here. As a matter of fact, it was Mommy's idea to invite her. You are going to let her come, aren't you?"

"That's up to Mama-Mama. We'll have to wait and see. You better go on and get dressed. You're joining us, right?"

"Yeah, I'm ready, see?" she said as she turned around in her short little outfit. She was wearing a tiny pair of Baby Phat shorts, with a cut-off Baby Phat T-shirt showing off her nice abs. She was sockless in a pair of DKNY tennis shoes. Her slim legs looked very inviting to Taz. She noticed that he was staring at her legs and asked, "Taz, do you mind if we went out on a date?"

Taz smiled calmly and said, "A what? Lyla, baby, when you're able to buy liquor, holla at your boy. Until then, baby girl, look at me as your older brother."

"That sucks. You know I—"

"Girl, I know you ain't in here trying to get your mack on!" said Tazneema as she came into the room to give Taz a hug and a kiss on his cheek.

"Come on, Tee-Tee! You know how much I'm digging your brother."

Tazneema and Taz shared a smile with each other, and then Tazneema said, "Girl, stop! Taz is not about to waste his time on a li'l girl."

"Taz, do I look like a li'l girl to you?" Lyla asked as she did her li'l twirl for him again.

Once again, Taz took notice of her sexy legs and said, "Baby girl, you are tempting, but I have to stand on my word. So, get at me in, like, three more years and you just might have a shot."

Pouting slightly, Lyla said, "Well, hell! That's a bummer!"

They all laughed as the girls went and grabbed their purses.

Taz had a headache as he sat down outside one of the dressing rooms in the Gap store. It felt as if they had been in every store in the damn mall. He gave Tazneema and Lyla his Black Card, and those two little freshmen went crazy shopping. Shoes, shoes, and more shoes were their first purchases, and after that, they then started looking for clothes to match the shoes. He had made so many trips back to his truck, putting up their stuff, that he'd lost count. It was now close to noon and they hadn't even shown the least bit of slowing down.

He pulled out his cell and called Tari at work. As soon as she answered her cell, he said, "Help! These girls are killing me!"

Laughing, Tari said, "Aw-w-w! Poor baby! Where are you all at?"

"We're at the mall. These two crazy-ass girls are trying to buy everything in every fuckin' store! Please, talk to me and tell me something that will stop me from losing my mind!"

"Well, I wish I could, but as you well know, I'm currently at work right now, and I'm kinda busy. So, you're going to have to deal with this one solo, buddy, 'cause, I gots to go. Bye-e-e-e, boo!" she said and hung up the phone.

"Ain't that a bitch!" Taz said to himself as Lyla and Tazneema both came out of the dressing room wearing matching Gap jeans and tops.

"Tell me, Taz. Do you like how I look in these jeans?" asked Lyla as she did her twirl for him, showing her nice little booty.

Taz nodded his head and said, "You straight. But look, ladies. I'm getting tired of all of this shopping. Can we take a break and go have some lunch somewhere, please?"

They both started laughing. "All right, we can go get some Leo's Barbeque," said Tazneema.

"*What?* I ain't trying to go way back down to the City to get no damn Leo's!" said Taz.

"Taz, there's a Leo's out here in Norman. It's right down the street from here. See, we can go get something to eat, then come back here so I can finish doing my Christmas shopping."

"You mean to tell me that you're not finished yet?!"

Laughing, Tazneema said, "Uh-uh. I've gotten my stuff out of the way. Now I have to get gifts for you, Mama-Mama, and Lyla's parents. Come on, Taz. You said you wanted to spend the day with me."

He smiled and said, "Yeah, I did. I stuck my foot in my mouth this time, didn't I?"

Smiling brightly, Tazneema said, "Yep, you sure did!" She turned and went back into the dressing room to change back into her clothes.

Lyla, on the other hand, stayed and smiled at Taz with a sexy look on her face. "Taz, you know I've learned a lot of things since I've been in college."

Not really paying attention to the look in her eyes, Taz asked, "Yeah, like what?"

She stepped up to him and whispered into his ear, "Like how to please an older man."

Taz stepped back, smiled, and said, "Won't you ever give up?"

Smiling brightly, she said, "Not until I've gotten what I want. And, Taz, I *will* get what I want, sooner or later." She shook her small hips seductively as she, too, went back into the dressing room to change.

Taz shook his head and wondered if Tazneema was as horny as her roommate. *God, I hope she ain't!* he thought to himself as he sat back in the chair.

Chapter Five

What a relaxing weekend, thought Sacha as she walked into the office with a bright smile on her face. She spoke to a few other attorneys as she was headed toward her office. Just as she made it to her door, Clifford, another attorney who worked for Johnson & Whitney, stopped her. "How are you doing this morning, Sacha?" he asked with a smile on his face.

Damn! I almost made it! Sacha thought to herself as she turned around, smiled, and said, "Good morning, Cliff. I'm just fine. How about yourself?"

"I'm good. I heard the news about you becoming a partner soon. I guess congratulations are in order."

"Not yet, but hopefully soon," she said as she entered her office, hoping that he wouldn't follow her.

Her hopes were in vain. Clifford followed her into her office, closed her door, and said rather confidently, "Don't you think it's way past time for us to go out on a date, Sacha?"

"Was that a question or a statement, Cliff?"

Smiling, he said, "Both. I know you can tell that I'm interested. Won't you give a hardworking brother a chance?"

Sacha sat down behind her desk and once again took inventory of Clifford Nelson. He was a handsome man with a nice body. He stood a little over six foot and had very broad shoulders. He wasn't muscular like she liked her men, but he wasn't skinny either. He kept his hair cut low, nice and neat. Even though she liked nice trimmed goatees, his clean-shaven face was attractive.

Sacha had been wondering how long it was going to take for him to finally ask her out on a date. He had been eyeing her for some time now. He never made a suggestive comment toward her in the three years he'd been with the firm. Now that he had, she was unsure whether she wanted to go out with him. She thought about what Gwen had said to her repeatedly over the weekend, and decided to see if Cliff really wanted to play. God only knows how long it had been since she'd been on a date. She smiled and asked, "So, you want a chance, brother?"

"Definitely!"

"Okay, when and where?"

"You choose, because I want it to be the perfect date, and I don't want to stick my foot in my mouth and make a bad decision."

"Taking the safe way out, huh?"

"I feel it's best to be safe than sorry . . . for now. So, it's all up to you, lovely lady."

"What if I told you that I like for the man I date to have total control?"

Laughing, he said, "I wouldn't believe you. Don't forget, I've seen some of your work in the courtroom, Ms. Carbajal. There's no weakness in you."

"Why, thank you! But, just because I like my dates to have control doesn't mean I'm a weak woman. I like surprises, Cliff, so if you want to take me out for a pleasurable evening, you're going to have to make all of the decisions."

"Okay, that's fine, but don't say that I didn't give you the opportunity to choose."

"I won't."

"Good. Is Friday good for you?"

"Sure. What time?"

"Say about seven. That should give you enough time to unwind after work."

"Where are we going?" she asked with a smile on her face.

With a boyish grin, he said, "You said you like surprises, right?"

"Yes."

"So, you'll see Friday evening at seven. Have a nice day, Ms. Carbajal!" he said and turned and left her office.

Sacha started laughing as she watched Clifford's nice ass as he walked out of her office. "Not bad, Cliff . . . not bad at all!" she said aloud as she turned on her PC on her desk.

***

Clifford left Sacha's office feeling as if he'd just hit the lottery. *Yes! I knew my plan of patience would work. Sacha's too damn fine for me to have come at her any other way. Now all I have to do is impress the hell out of her fine-ass, and she'll be mine,* he thought to himself as he walked confidently to his office.

Friday came faster than Clifford expected it to. He was sitting down in his den, planning the finishing touches for his date with Sacha. It was ten after six, and he was already dressed and ready for the evening. He was wearing a pair of beige Dockers, a dark brown Lacoste shirt, and low-cut Polo boots.

He told Sacha to dress casually but comfortably for their evening together. He was going to take her out to dinner in Bricktown at his favorite Italian restaurant, and afterward he was going to take her to the Comedy Store for their late show. And, if everything went his way, they would have a pretty nice evening.

Even though he knew he wanted Sacha in his bed in the worst way, he knew that he would have to continue to be patient. Everything would happen in due time. First, he had to show her that he was everything she was looking for in a man: intelligent, secure financially, mature, and most of all, successful. He figured that was the type of man she was looking for. Not only was he sure of it, he was positive. She was about to be made a partner in one of Oklahoma City's highly successful law firms. She wouldn't settle for just any man, so he had to be on top of his game. He wasn't worried about losing his patience waiting for her to come around. He had plenty of women on his line to bide his time with while he was courting Sacha.

Thinking about that made him smile as he grabbed his cordless phone and made a quick call before he left to go pick her up. After a few rings the other line was answered. "Hello, Cory?" he asked.

"Hey, what's up, Cliff?"

"Nothing much. What's up with you?"

"Just relaxing a little, you know, sipping on a little Absolut Peach."

"Yeah? What are you going to be doing later on?"

"It depends on how much of this Absolut I consume."

Laughing, he said, "Well, if you're still able to function later, say around midnight, I'd love for you to come by and keep me company."

"Ummm, that sounds interesting. Would I be staying the night, or will I have to make a late-night departure?"

"You know I'd never forgive myself if I let you leave me too early."

"Whatever! You need to go on with that shit, playboy! You must have forgotten the countless times you had me get the fuck out after you've handled your business. But, since I don't have anything else planned for the night, I might as well see what kind of mood you're going to be in later on."

"What do you mean by that?"

"Come on, Cliff. You and I both know how you are. If you're in a freaky mood, I'll get broken off real proper like. If you're just horny, I'll get the kitty licked quickly and ran up in even faster."

Her bluntness cracked him up. He was laughing so hard that he damn near dropped the phone. After regaining his composure, he said, "Since you put it like that, I want to assure you that I'm going to be in that freak mode that you seem to desire. Is that cool with you?"

"Definitely, playboy! I'll see you later. Give me a call when you're ready for me."

"Most definitely, sexy. Bye!"

"See ya, playboy!" Cory said and hung up.

With a bright smile on his face, Clifford got up from his sofa, grabbed his wallet and keys, and left to go pick up his date for the evening.

As Clifford pulled into Sacha's driveway, he was impressed. She lived way out on the far north side of Oklahoma City, in a neighborhood called Camelot. Most of the homes were recently built, and the price range was close to three to four hundred thousand. *Yeah, she's doing damn good as far as ends are concerned,* he thought as he got out of his CLS 500 Mercedes.

He strolled confidently to her front door and rang her doorbell. He had already been shocked by her beauty from their first meeting, but when she opened the door, it was as if he had just met her for the first time. She was absolutely gorgeous! She was dressed as he requested, casually and comfortably. She made a simple outfit look as if it was made for Tyra Banks or something. She had on a pair of low-rise Apple Bottoms jeans and a black turtleneck wool sweater. Everything fit her so snugly that it seemed as if he could see her entire body. Her sexy shape made him feel a few twitches down below. He smiled and said, "Hello, Sacha! Are you ready for a very memorable evening?"

She returned his smile and said, "Most definitely, Cliff. Let me grab my purse and I'll be right with you."

She left him standing at her front door, which he thought was rude, but he didn't say anything as he waited for her to return. She came back within a few minutes and followed him outside to his car.

Clifford walked her to the passenger's side of the car and opened the door for her. Once she was inside of the car, he closed the door and got in on the other side. *Hmm! He definitely gets points for being a gentleman,* she thought to herself as she watched him get in the car. "So, where are we dining this evening?"

"I hope you like Italian food, because we're about to have one of the best Italian meals ever made in the City."

"Ummm, you must have read my mind. I was hoping you liked Italian food. That's one of my favorites. You still haven't told me where we're going, though."

"Ravio's out in Bricktown. Have you ever been there before?"

"No, I haven't, but they've received some nice reviews in the paper. I heard their veal is divine. And believe me, I love me some veal."

Love me some veal? Damn! She sounds as if she's straight from the eastside or some shit, he thought to himself. To her, he said, "That's great. I guess I'm starting off on the right foot, then, huh?"

Smiling, she said, "Yes, Cliff, you most definitely are."

After dinner, Clifford took Sacha to the Comedy Store, and they both enjoyed the up-and-coming comedians.

Now that their evening was coming to a close, Clifford realized just how lucky he was. Sacha was not only sexy as hell, but the intelligence she possessed was almost astonishing to him. Earlier, during their meal, they had several discussions on everything, from the war over in Iraq to the terrible state New Orleans was in after Hurricane Katrina. Sacha seemed so compassionate toward the hurricane victims that it was touching. She made him feel guilty for not donating more than he had already. She made him feel good all over, and he couldn't wait for the day when they would become intimate. His loins were actually burning for her at that very moment. *Hold on, big boy! Hold on!* he told himself as he pulled into her driveway. "Well, here we are. I hope you enjoyed this evening as much as I did, Sacha," Clifford said as he turned toward her.

Smiling sincerely, she said, "I really did, Cliff. The meal was excellent, and those comedians almost made me pee on myself, they were so funny! Thank you for a wonderful evening."

"I hope that this was the first of many wonderful evenings that we'll be able to share with each other, Sacha. I really want to get to know you better."

Smiling, she said, "I don't think that will be a problem, Cliff. Let's take it one day at a time and see where it leads us, okay?"

With a bright smile on his face, Clifford said, "That's fine with me."

Sacha leaned over and gave him a kiss on his cheek and said, "Give me a call tomorrow if you're not too busy. Maybe we can get into something."

"That sounds like a plan, then."

"Okay, bye! I'll talk to you tomorrow," she said and slid out of his car.

Clifford watched her as she walked toward her front door, and shook his head from side to side as he stared at her sexy walk. *She did those Apple Bottoms jeans proud with a body like that,* he thought as he watched her disappear into her home.

Once she closed her door, he started his car and pulled out of her driveway. As soon as he was out of Sacha's neighborhood, he grabbed his cell and quickly dialed Cory's number. When Cory answered, he said, "I'm on my way home now, babe. How long will it take for you to get there?"

"I'll be there in about twenty minutes. Is that cool, playboy?"

After a quick glance at his watch, he said, "Yeah, I guess that's cool. But hurry up, okay?"

Laughing loudly, Cory said, "Damn, playboy! Are you that horny tonight?"

"You better believe it! So hurry up, 'cause I promise you're going to love every bit of what I'm going to do to you. You wanted freaky-freaky, and that's exactly what I plan on giving you."

"Bye, playboy! 'Cause I'm walking out of the door right now!" she said and hung up the phone.

Chapter Six

Taz was pulling out of Tari's driveway when his cell rang. He flipped it open and saw that there was a picture of Michael Jordan slam-dunking the ball over Patrick Ewing of the New York Knicks. Taz smiled as he closed his cell because he knew it was on. That was Won's signal for them to get ready. Taz called Keno and told him to have everyone meet him at his place within the next thirty minutes. After he was finished talking with Keno, he called Tari at work and said, "Baby, I'm about to be out for a minute. I'm going to need you to make sure everything is straight at the house for me."

"No problem, Taz. Is there anything else?"

"Nah. Just feed the dogs and let them loose so they can roam around while I'm gone."

"How long this time?"

"Ain't no telling, so make sure you keep a line open just in case I need to holla."

"Don't I always? Bye, Mister! Oh, and Taz."

"What up?"

"Be careful."

"All the time, baby," he said and closed his cell phone. Whenever he went out of town, he always told Tari. She was the only person other than the crew that knew what he did for a living. She would make sure that his beloved Dobermans would be fed and taken care of while he was away. Even though he never expected to be gone longer than forty-eight hours, he never left the state without having her check on everything while he was gone. The trust and love he had for her was just as strong as the love he had for his homeboys—unbreakable.

Everything about Taz and the crew was timing. They were all disciplined in a military-type fashion. When it came to their missions, they remained prepared at all times.

Taz smiled as he pulled into his driveway and saw everyone there waiting for him. He jumped out of his truck and said, "Time to go to work, boys." They followed him as he entered his home. He led them to his den, and they watched as he grabbed his laptop computer and punched in several keys.

After about three minutes, he said, "All right, it's like this. Keno and I are bouncing outta DFW. Bo-Pete and Bill, y'all are out of here this time, so Red, you and Bob gots Tulsa. All three of our flights are to arrive at Atlanta's Hartsfield Airport within twenty minutes of each other. Catch a cab to the Sheraton off of Peach near downtown. As usual, the rooms will already be reserved, so give them your Barney, and everything should be good. Once me and Keno get in, I'll hit the front desk and check to make sure that y'all are in. Then, I'll leave a message for y'all to hit me up in my room. Once we all hook up, we'll then hook up with Won. Any questions?"

"Yeah. How do that fool Won be knowing what Barney we're going to be using?" asked Bob.

"He's made all of the arrangements, Bob. He's the one who takes care of getting us the fake IDs and shit. If it wasn't for him, we wouldn't have any Barneys. We'd be using our real hookups. Anyway, there will be a package left for me at the front desk when we check in. Knowing Won, that package most likely will have our instructions. So, it is what it is, gentlemen. Time to get paid. Let's do it." Taz stood and watched as everyone except Keno left his home. He checked a few more things on his laptop, turned it off, and said, "Since we have to make the ride out to Dallas this time, you're driving."

"That's cool, but you're driving back," Keno said as he followed Taz out of his home.

Once they were inside of Keno's Range Rover, Taz asked, "Do you have everything?"

"I repack my bag as soon as we make it back, dog. Everything I need is in the back."

"I hope you brought a different DVD this time. I'm tired of that damn *Scarface*."

Keno laughed and said, "Come on, dog, don't hate. You know you be loving *'Face*."

Taz moaned as he relaxed back in his seat. It was going to be another long-ass flight. *Damn!*

By the time Taz and Keno had checked into the Sheraton in downtown Atlanta, the sun was setting and the weather was nice and warm. Taz wished they could get to do some things while they were in the ATL, but he knew that was out of the question. They were there to handle their business, and that's exactly what they planned on doing.

After Taz and Keno entered their room, Taz called the front desk and asked for the room numbers of James Jenkins and Walter Johnson. The operator gave him the room numbers and asked if he would like to be connected to one of the rooms. He told her yes, and she transferred him to James Jenkins's room. James Jenkins was Red's alias.

Red answered the phone on the first ring and said, "What up?"

"Room 3923," Taz said and hung up the phone. He then called Walter Johnson's room, which was Wild Bill's alias. When the phone was answered, he once again said, "Room 3923." After hanging up the phone, he went to the dining room table and opened the package that was left for him at the front desk. Inside of the small package was a DVD and a brief typewritten note. After reading the note, he smiled and said, "Dog, this lick is worth a grip. Look." He passed the note to Keno.

Keno read it quickly, smiled, and said, "I'm loving those figures, my nigga."

Before Taz could reply, there was a soft knock at the door. He went and let the rest of the crew inside.

Wild Bill walked by him and said, "Damn, dog! It's a gang of hoes out here in the ATL! Bitches was choosing like a muthafucka at the airport when we got in. I'm tellin' you, dog, I'm going to have to bounce back this way sometime this summer."

Bo-Pete laughed and said, "Nigga, would you sit your blind-ass down so we can get to business? Worry about your dick on your time. I'm trying to make some money right now."

Taz laughed and passed Bo-Pete the note that was inside of the package. Then Bo-Pete passed it to Red, who in turn read it and passed it to Bob. After Bob was finished, he passed it to Wild Bill. Every last member of the six-man crew had smiles on their faces as they all stared at Taz.

Taz grabbed the DVD and went and inserted it into the DVD player sitting under the television in the hotel room. He turned it on, and the first thing that came onto the screen was a picture of Michael Jordan doing a reverse layup against A.C. Green of the Lakers.

After a full minute had passed, Won's voice could be heard. "I'm glad that you all made it safely. Taz, take a look under the bed in your room and you'll find everything you need necessary for this job. Make sure that everything is to your liking before you leave. If there are any problems, hit me on my cell immediately. As you all know, everything is timed down to the last minute. In exactly one hour, you are to leave your rooms and meet in the underground parking area. In the B-Section, you will see an all-black Ford Excursion, Georgia, plates 115 BHB. The doors will be unlocked and the keys will be inside of the glove box.

"You are then to proceed to a club located right off of Highway 75, exit right on Butner Avenue. That street will take you straight to the club. Once you have the club in your sights, drive one block past it and you'll see an alley. Make a left turn, and the alley will lead you right to the back entrance of the club. The back door of the club will be unlocked, but there will be one sentry to your immediate left. Once you enter the club, he must be secured.

"You'll then see the staircase leading to the upstairs office. There should be no more than four or five people inside of the office, but to be on the safe side, assume that there are five. Once you have entered the office and secured everyone, you will have ten to twelve minutes approximately to clean out the safe.

"Before I continue, Taz, one of y'all might want to write what I'm about to say down."

While there was a pause in Won's instructions, Taz quickly grabbed a pen and some writing paper out of the desk over by the bed. Just as he turned back toward the television, Won continued.

"Okay. Once you're in the office, to your right will be a wall with a yellow and brown sofa against it. There will be a thermostat at the left end of the sofa. That's where you'll go, and move the thermostat's knob to twenty degrees, then back to zero degrees, then to fifteen degrees, and lastly back to twenty degrees. Again, that's twenty degrees, back to zero degrees, fifteen degrees, and back to twenty degrees. Once you make that last turn, the wall will part like the Red Sea, and you'll see the rest.

"In your bag of goodies under the bed are backpacks for each one of you. The backpacks, as well as one ample-sized carryall bag for each, are for what's for me in the safe. The carryall bags are for the ends. Once you've cleaned everything out of the safe, double time it up outta there.

"There shouldn't be any need for violence, but you know how that goes. So have everything locked and cocked. Once you've made it safely back to the highway, head back to your rooms. When you've made it back to the hotel, leave everything inside the Excursion.

"I wasn't able to get you flights out tonight, so y'all are going to have to chill and relax for the rest of the evening. Here are your flight reservations."

The picture of Michael Jordan was replaced with flight reservations, which Taz quickly wrote down.

A minute passed before Won started speaking again. "You know the routine once you've made it back to the City. By the time you get home, check your accounts and give me a holla. Be safe, and remember, ten to twelve minutes tops. If you're in there any longer than that, be prepared to shoot your way up outta there. Be precise, be prepared, and most of all, be careful. Out!"

The television screen went blank, and Taz went over to the DVD player, popped out the DVD, and dropped it onto the floor. He then stepped on it with his Timberland boots. After crushing it, he picked up the pieces and went out onto the balcony of his room and threw them over the railing. After that, he came back into the room and said, "All right, we got about forty-five minutes to get ready. Let's do it."

Keno pulled three large bags out from under the bed and set them on top of the bed. In one bag were their weapons. Each member of the crew had a nine-millimeter Beretta with a silencer already attached to it. There were three magazines full for each, a bulletproof vest for each man, as well as several pairs of plastic hand restraints.

Bo-Pete and Wild Bill put their weapons, vests, and backpacks into their bags and set them down next to where they were standing. Red and Bob did the same, and so did Taz and Keno. Keno pulled out what looked like earplugs and gave one to every man in the hotel room. After each one of them had inserted the earplugs into their ears, they pulled out their cell phones and punched in a three-digit code. Keno then went into the bathroom and said, "Testing, 1, 2 . . . testing 1, 2!"

Back inside the room everyone said, "Good!"

Keno came back into the room, smiled, and said, "Ready!"

Taz checked the time and saw that they had thirty minutes before it was time for them to leave. "All right, go get changed and meet us at the truck in twenty."

Red, Bob, Bo-Pete, and Wild Bill left the room in single file.

Keno slipped out of his Sean Jean sweat suit and put on a pair of black army fatigue pants and a black, longsleeved T-shirt. As he was lacing up his black Tims, Taz started getting dressed, identically as Keno. They both put on their bulletproof vests and snapped them tightly on each other.

When they were finished, Taz said, "Time!" They smiled at each other briefly; then Taz led the way out of the room. They took the stairs to the parking area and met up with everyone inside of the Excursion. Once everyone was inside of the truck, Keno started the ignition and backed out of the parking space. The mission had begun.

Keno had no problem finding the club as he drove down Butner Avenue. He passed the club and made a left turn down the alley, just like Won had instructed on the DVD. He bypassed the back entrance of the club and made a U-turn onto the next street and returned back toward the club. That way, they were now facing the same way that they had come.

"Fa' sho'. I don't know the terrain that cool, so I figured, why risk it? At least this way I know all I have to do is go straight out the alley and bust a right, and we're on our way back to the hotel," Keno said confidently.

"Do you, baby. I'm always comfortable when you're behind the wheel," Red said as he once again checked his weapon. The only noise you heard inside of the Excursion was the click-clack of the chambers of the nine millimeters that everyone had inside their hands.

After their weapons were checked and the safety buttons were off, Taz said, "Red, you and Bob take the sentry to the left. Once he's secured, bring up the rear. We're not entering until we know y'all are on our ass."

"Gotcha'."

"When we hit the office, y'all know the drill. Two to the right, two to the left, and the last two posted at the door to watch our backs. When everything is secure, I'll hit the thermostat. Once the safe is open, Keno and I will fill up our bags and backpacks. Then, we'll switch with Bo-Pete and Wild Bill. Then they'll switch with Red and Bob. Time check."

They checked their watches and made sure that they were all on the exact same time. One minute off could cost one of them their lives.

They got out of the Excursion, with Red and Bob leading the way toward the back door of the club. Once they were in front of the door, Taz gave Red a nod of his head; then Red and Bob rushed into the club. Just like Won had told them, there was a security guard posted to their left. Red's nine millimeter was aimed directly at the security guard's head as he whispered, "Get the fuck on the ground or die!" The security guard was so scared that he couldn't move. Bob ran up to the guard and slapped him across his forehead. The guard fell to the ground, and Bob quickly restrained him with a pair of his plastic hand restraints. Once Red saw that Bob had the guard secured, he spoke softly and said, "We're good."

Taz heard Red and signaled for the rest to follow him as he entered the club. Taz, Keno, Bo-Pete, and Wild Bill slid past Red and Bob as if they weren't even there. They moved silently up the stairs toward the office. When they were right outside of the office, Taz looked over his shoulder and saw that Red and Bob were right behind Bo-Pete and Wild Bill. He inhaled deeply and slowly turned the doorknob. Once the door was slightly open, he rushed into the office with his gun drawn. "Get the fuck down! Get the fuck down, now!" yelled Taz.

There were four people inside of the office—three men and a female—who were stunned as they watched the six men rush in. They did as they were told and got onto the floor. Taz and Keno quickly put a pair of the hand restraints on two of the men, and Wild Bill and Bo-Pete did the same with the female and the other male in the room. Red and Bob stood at the door, covering them while they restrained everyone.

Red checked his watch and said, "One minute!"

Taz then quickly stepped toward the sofa. Once he was there, he moved the thermostat's knob to the numbers he memorized from Won's briefing. And just like Won had said, the walls parted like the Red Sea. Taz was stunned as he focused on all of the stacks of one-hundred-dollar bills inside of the wall safe. He was even more fascinated by all of the drugs.

Once again, Red's voice came into his ear. "Move, my nigga. We've been here three and a half minutes already." That snapped Taz out of his daze, and he snatched off his backpack and started piling as many of the kilos of cocaine he could into his backpack. Once his backpack was filled to capacity, he strapped it across his back and then started filling up his carry bag. Keno was right by his side, filling up his bags. They both finished at the same time and stepped away from the safe in one fluid motion.

As they moved toward the door, Wild Bill and Bo-Pete ran to the safe and started filling their bags. Red and Bob slid into the position that Wild Bill and Bo-Pete had just left from.

Now it was Taz's turn to watch the clock. He checked his watch and said, "Seven minutes, gentlemen." By the time Bo-Pete and Wild Bill had finished, they had been inside of the office for nine minutes. Red and Bob finished emptying the safe at the eleven-minute mark.

Taz spoke softly and said, "It's time to roll, baby. One minute left and it'll be time for some gunplay." They then ran out of the office just as quickly as they had come in.

As they were descending the stairs, they heard the female that was upstairs start screaming. That gave them an extra pep in their steps as they broke out of the back door and back into the alleyway.

Once they were all inside of the Excursion, Keno started the truck and pulled away smoothly. When he made the right turn back onto Butner Avenue, he noticed several black SUVs as they pulled up in front of the club. Armed men were exiting the SUVs and running into the club. Keno smiled and said, "It's all about the timing, baby!"

Taz relaxed in his seat and said, "You know it! Once again, that fool Won did the damn thang."

"Man, how the fuck does he be knowing all of this shit?" asked Wild Bill from the backseat of the Excursion.

"Ain't no tellin', my nigga. And to tell you the truth, I don't really give a fuck, just as long as he continues to be on point. I'm good," Taz said with a satisfied smile on his face.

"I know that's right, gee!" Wild Bill said as he opened his carry bag and smiled at all of the Benjamin Franklins that were stacked on top of each other.

They made it back to the hotel without incident. Keno locked the doors to the truck, and they went back to their rooms. After they had changed their clothes, they met back up in Taz's and Keno's room. They were relaxing and sipping on some of the liquor out of the minibar of Taz's room when Bob said, "Damn, my nigga! How much dope do you think was in that safe?"

"Dog, I'm not knowing. It had to be over a hundred bricks," said Bo-Pete.

"I know, huh? How much chips you think we took?" asked Red.

"We're clearing two million apiece, so it had to be twelve tickets or more," said Taz as he turned the channel on the television.

"You know what, though? That nigga Won is a muthafucka! You know he be having us watched, right?" asked Keno.

"How do you know that?" asked Wild Bill.

"How else would that fool be able to have that DVD in here done, and be able to tell us that we have one hour to be here and there? He has to be having us peeped at. He would have to know what time we arrived here and shit. Yeah, he knows when we'll touch down at the airport and shit, but how does he know exactly when we've made it to the hotel and shit? That's one smooth nigga, dog. I love fuckin' with that fool."

Taz smiled but didn't say anything as he continued to watch the television. He knew that they were watched whenever they went on a mission for Won. That's how he got down. Won would never leave anything to chance; every move he made was calculated. He'd taught Taz that a long time ago. *Yeah, my man will always be on top of his game. That's why we are all on top of the pile,* he thought as he continued to watch television.

The next morning, Taz and Keno checked out of the hotel and caught a cab to the airport. They were scheduled for a ten a.m. flight back to Dallas Fort Worth, while Red and Bob's flight had already departed for Tulsa International. Wild Bill and Bo-Pete's flight back to Oklahoma City wasn't due to depart until noon, so they had decided to run to Lenox Square Mall to do a little shopping before they left.

Keno and Taz boarded their flight, and as soon as they were seated, Keno pulled out that damn DVD player and put in that damn *Scarface* DVD. Taz shook his head and said, "I swear, I'm going to take that muthafucka and break it in half before our next trip, Keno! I hate that fuckin' movie now!"

Keno smiled and said, "Don't hate, nigga. You know you love some *'Face.*"

Taz laughed as he closed his eyes. He was glad they were on their way home. Mission completed.

It was a little after ten p.m. when the crew had made it out to Taz's home. They went through their usual routine and checked the laptop to make sure that their financial gains were intact. And as usual, they were. They each had made two million dollars for their day spent in the ATL.

Taz's cell rang, and when he answered it, Won said, "Another job well done, Babyboy."

"You know it, Won. As long as you give it to us raw, we'll handle the rest."

"I know that's right! Have you checked y'all's accounts yet?"

"Yeah, it's all good."

"All righty then. I don't anticipate anything anytime soon, so you know the routine. Enjoy, be merry, and most of all be good! Out!"

"Hold up a minute, Won. Bob has a question for you real quick."

"Put him on."

Taz passed his cell to Bob and sat down and watched as Bob spoke to Won.

Bob accepted the phone, smiled, and said, "What up, Won?"

"What's poppin', Babyboy?"

"Dog, I love how you do your thing and all, but I've been real curious about something ever since we've been fuckin' with you."

"Speak your mind, baby."

"How the fuck do you be knowing the shit you be knowing?"

Won started laughing, then said, "I know what needs to be known, Babyboy, because I'm always on top of my game. Always. Is there anything else?"

"Yeah, I got one more question for you, big homey. Why do they call you 'Won'?"

That made Won start laughing harder than before. After he regained his composure, he said, "A long time ago I was in the game, and I played it with so much vigor that I knew one day I was going to win it. After I did in fact win the game, I changed my name to 'Won'."

"Because you had 'won' the game?"

"Exactly!"

"So, what was your name before you won the game?"

Won started laughing again. Afterward he simply said, "Win!" And then the line went dead in Bob's ear.

Bob gave the phone back to Taz and said, "Well, I guess that's that. Y'all know what time it is now, huh?"

Taz said, "Yep."

And in unison, they all said, "It's time to go clubbin'!"

Chapter Seven

Sacha was relaxing in her bedroom, wondering what Clifford had in store for their evening together. For the past three weeks, they'd spent almost every evening doing something, whether it was going out to dinner, taking long walks down by the river, walking downtown, going to the movies, or just chilling with each other at either of their homes. She felt comfortable with him, but still there seemed to be something missing. She just couldn't put her finger on it yet. *Maybe I should go on and give him some. God knows I want to,* she thought to herself as she got off of her bed and went into the living room. She plopped onto her sofa and concluded that having sex with Clifford would definitely propel their relationship to the next level. She smiled as she grabbed her cordless phone and gave Clifford a call.

Clifford answered the phone on the first ring. "Hello, pretty lady!" he said before Sacha could speak.

"Hey, Cliff. Were you busy?"

"Not really. I just got out of the shower. I was about to call you and see if you wanted to go down to Bricktown and get into something."

"Actually, I was thinking about just chilling out tonight. Why don't you come over here and keep me company?" she asked in a seductive tone.

Not noticing the tone in her voice, Clifford said, "That's cool. How about I stop at Blockbuster and pick up a few movies?"

"I have a better idea. Why don't you stop at the liquor store and pick us up a bottle of wine? That way when you get here, we'll be able to set this evening off properly. What'd you say about that, handsome?"

Once again not realizing that what he'd been so patiently waiting for was within his grasp, he said, "If it makes you happy, Sacha, I'm here to please. I'll be there in thirty to forty-five minutes."

"That's fine. That'll give me just enough time to get nice and sexy for you. Bye!" she said and hung up the phone.

Clifford hung up the phone feeling really good with the progress he'd made with Sacha. *She's going to be the future Mrs. Nelson. I can feel it,* he thought as he quickly started to get himself dressed.

Sacha went back into her bedroom and chose a sexy black and emerald skirt with a thin black lace top. Her matching black bra and thong completed the look she desired. *If I'm going to give him some, I'm going to make this night one he's never going to forget,* she thought as she went into her bathroom to take a shower.

Clifford arrived at Sacha's home right on time. He was dressed casually, as usual, in a pair of khakis and a long sleeved Polo shirt. While he waited for Sacha to come let him inside of her home, he checked to make sure that he had everything. He did as she requested, and stopped at the liquor store and bought an expensive bottle of Chablis. He also made a quick stop at Blockbuster and rented two DVDs for them to watch. Just being able to spend quality time like this with her made him feel as if there was indeed a perfect world.

Sacha opened the door with one hand and had the other on her hip. The three-inch heels by Giorgio Armani made it seem as if she almost stood eye to eye with Clifford. She smiled seductively and said, "Hi, handsome! Come on in." She turned and led the way into the living room. She could feel Clifford's eyes all over her was she walked. Tiny goose bumps were all over her body as she thought about what she was actually about to do. *Damn! I'm more excited than I thought I'd be,* she thought as she sat down on the sofa.

Clifford followed her into the living room and said, "You never did tell me what you wanted me to rent, so I got us *Diary of a Mad Black Woman* and *Batman Begins*. Is that cool?" he asked as he set the DVDs and the bottle of wine on the coffee table.

No, this nigga didn't! I know he can see what I'm wearing. He can't possibly think I'm trying to watch some damn DVDs! Or is he just nervous? Yeah, that's it. Cliff's a li'l scared. That's so cute! she thought as she slid next to him on the sofa and said, "Baby, I'm not really in the mood to watch any movies. Why don't we open up that bottle of wine and listen to some music and chill?"

"That's cool, baby, but I really want to check out this *Diary of a Mad Black Woman.* Alton down in Entertainment told me that it was definitely worth watching."

Is this man serious? Hold up! He is! She watched as Clifford got up from the sofa and went toward her entertainment center, where her television and DVD player were located. She watched amazingly as he inserted the DVD into the DVD player. *Uh-uh! This ain't even happening!* She got up and said, "Cliff, come here for a minute."

He turned around and faced her and said, "Yeah, babe?"

"Do you like what I have on?"

As if noticing what she was wearing for the first time, he said, "Oh, that's sexy, Sacha. I like how your toenails are painted the same color green as your skirt."

"Emerald."

"Huh?"

"I said, emerald. My toenails are emerald, not green."

"My bad. They still look nice."

"Thanks!" she said sarcastically. She sat back down and watched as Clifford went back to turning on the television. *Uh-uh! Not me! Not tonight! If this clown-ass nigga really wants to watch this movie, he's going to be on his own!* she thought to herself as she stood up and said, "Cliff, I'm not in the mood to watch any movies. Let's do something else instead."

He turned toward her and asked, "Like what, Sacha?"

"Let's go to the club and hang out."

"The club? Which one? Birdies down in Bricktown, or that one by the Comedy Store?"

"Neither. Let's go to Club Cancun or to Rhea's."

"What? I know you're not serious! You want to go to one of those 'hood clubs?"

"'Hood clubs? I want to go out and have a good time with my peoples, not a bunch of corny fakes. Is there something wrong with that, Cliff?"

For the first time this evening he seemed to be aware of Sacha and her tone of voice. If he'd only paid closer attention, he would have had his wildest fantasies about her come true. But since he didn't, he was now wondering what had gotten into her. "You mean to tell me that you'd actually be comfortable in a place like that Club Cancun?"

"I'm comfortable whenever I'm around my people."

"Your people? Sacha, what's gotten into you tonight? I thought we were going to chill out and watch some movies."

Shaking her head from side to side, she said, "You know what? Forget it. I'm not in the mood to sit in this house tonight, Cliff. I'm going out. The only question I have for you is, am I going out alone or not?"

"Are you serious?"

"As a heart attack. So, what's your answer?"

Smiling, he said, "Well, I guess we're going to the club!"

Smiling brightly, Sacha said, "That's right, baby! We're about to go clubbin'!"

Club Cancun was packed, as usual, when Clifford and Sacha finally made it inside. They got lucky and found an empty table close to the bar. After they were seated, Sacha asked, "Are you going to have a drink with me, Cliff?"

"Sure. I don't do the heavy stuff, but I'll sip on a glass of wine," he said as he waved at a waitress as she was headed toward the bar.

After ordering a glass of white wine for himself and an apple martini for Sacha, he sat back and took a better look around the club. He noticed several old acquaintances and smiled. *If Sacha only knew!* he thought to himself with a slight smile on his face. *There are some hot, looking females inside of the club. I might have to come back here and check this scene out again,* he thought just as their drinks arrived.

As he sipped his glass of wine, he noticed how Sacha seemed to fit right in at this type of club. That didn't really sit well with him. *She's a top-notch type of lady. No way was she supposed to fit in with a 'hood crowd like this,* he thought as he stared at some of the obvious-looking thug drug dealer types that had passed their table. *Then again, at least she's a little versatile. Maybe that's a good thing.*

Sacha smiled at Clifford and said, "I like their choice of music here. They're not all caught up on that straight hip-hop. They mix it real smooth with R&B. Then they seem to know right when to slow it up for ya. I hope you'll get out there and dance with me before we leave."

"I wouldn't consider myself a gentleman if I didn't, Sacha," he said with a satisfied smile on his face. *Maybe this wasn't a bad idea, after all,* he thought to himself as he took another sip of his drink.

At the opposite side of the bar, Paquita and Katrina were taking inventory of everyone inside of the club. "Girl, that's that broad who had that skimpy-ass Apple Bottoms mini on a few weeks ago," Paquita said as she pointed toward Sacha.

"I wonder who's that fine-ass nigga she's with," said Katrina.

"She's cute. I like how she keeps her hair. I wonder who does her weave."

"Probably Stacey over at Images. You know she's the best in the City."

"Bullshit! Javon does the tightest weaves in the City, bitch. Shit, look at my shit," Katrina said as she patted her micro-braids.

"Yeah, you clownin', bitch, but I'm doin' the damn thing with this new look Javon gave me," Paquita said as she shook her extra long blond weave job. Before Katrina had a chance to speak, Paquita said, "Ooh, bitch! There goes Bo-Pete and Wild Bill!"

Turning toward the front entrance of the club, Katrina smiled and said, "Damn! That means that Taz is on his way! You know what, bitch? I think I'm going to get at that nigga Keno tonight. I'm feelin' that nigga too."

"Well, you go on and do you. I'm not going to stop until I get me some of that fine-ass nigga Taz. He's not going to keep shaking me," Paquita said confidently.

The both of them turned and watched as Wild Bill and Bo-Pete entered the club and walked toward the right of the bar. Five minutes later, Red and Bob came into the club and went and posted up on the far left side of the club. A few minutes after that, Keno and Taz walked inside of the club as if they were royalty.

Keno smiled as they stepped toward the bar. Winky, the bartender, passed Taz his normal drink and smiled after Taz gave him a slight nod of his head. Taz saw Paquita and Katrina staring at them and whispered to Keno, "Dog, why don't you break one of them hoes off so they can get off a nigga's nuts?"

"Who, them rats to the right? Nigga, you gots to be outta your fuckin' mind! Don't get me wrong Katrina is definitely fuckable. But that other one is on some other shit. Plus, she's all yours, big boy. Look how she's staring at your ass!" Keno started laughing as Taz turned and saw Paquita smiling at him from ear to ear.

"Oh, God, let me make it through the night!" he prayed silently as his sipped his Courvoisier XO. As he turned and gave a slight nod toward Red and Bob, then toward Wild Bill and Bo-Pete, he smiled as he watched his crew break loose like a bunch of horny niggas fresh out of prison. He shook his head and started to take another sip of his drink when he saw Sacha sitting at a table with Clifford. He smiled at the square-looking guy she was with and said, "I guess it was meant to be, sexy. I'm not letting you get away from me tonight."

Sacha looked away from Cliff and directly at Taz, as if she had heard the statement he'd just made. She smiled at him and thought, *Oh, my God! That's that sexy somethin'-somethin' I saw the last time I was here. Come on, babe. Don't stare at me like that. You're getting me wet!* She shook herself slightly, turned back toward Clifford, and said, "Do you want to have that dance now, Cliff?"

"Let's do it, sexy," Clifford said as he got up from the table. He grabbed her hand and led her out onto the dance floor.

Taz watched amused as Sacha and Clifford started dancing. He knew she was feeling him because of the nervous glances she kept shooting his way. *I know you want me, boo, and I'm going to make damn sure you know I want you,* he thought to himself as he turned back toward the bar and asked, "Winky, which waitress is working the section to my right?"

Winky smiled and said, "That's Mikki's section, Taz. What's up? Is everything okay?"

"Yeah, everything's straight. Tell Mikki to come get at me when she comes back to the bar."

"Gotcha, Taz," the bartender said, and went back to making someone a drink.

Taz resumed his staring game with Sacha. *Damn, she's fine! She's wearing the hell out of that skirt. She's got class too. I can tell. And that long-ass hair gots to be real. Ain't no way that's a weave,* he thought as he continued to stare at her.

Keno came back to the bar, saw how his homey was staring at Sacha, and said, "Well, I'll be damn! You got your sights locked on that ass, huh?"

Taz smiled and said, "Dog, that's one bad broad. I gots to holla."

"Do you, nigga. What, you gon' let that square cat stand in your way?"

Taz recognized the challenge in his homey's voice, smiled, and said, "Since when have I ever let someone stop me from doing what I want to do?"

"Now that's what I'm talkin' 'bout! My nigga Taz is back in the game! I think I'll drink to that!" Keno said, and he downed the rest of his glass of Hennessy.

The waitress Mikki came up to Taz and asked, "You wanted to see me, Taz?"

"Yeah, I did. What's up, Mikki? How you been?"

"I'm good. Just trying to finish up with school and stuff. I'm trying to get the hell out of the City."

"Is that right? Where you trying to move to?"

"Anywhere, just as long as I'm out of Oklahoma."

Laughing, he said, "I know that's right. But check this out. I need to know what that couple is drinking over there at that table," he said as he pointed toward Sacha and Clifford's table.

Mikki smiled and said, "The female is drinking an apple martini, and the guy has a white wine."

"Do me a favor and take them another round of drinks for me. Make sure it's after they're back and seated. Let the female know that they're from me," he said as he gave Mikki a hundred-dollar bill.

"Taz, why you got to be giving me this big-ass bill? You know Winky's gon' be whining when he sees this."

"Don't trip, Mikki. Keep the change for yourself. Maybe that can help out a li'l."

Smiling brightly, Mikki said, "Thank you Taz! You're so sweet!" She gave him a quick kiss on his cheek and hurried to go do what he'd told her to.

Taz watched as Sacha and Clifford finished dancing. He smiled when he saw Mikki go to their table and give them their drinks. When she pointed toward Taz at the bar, Sacha smiled and raised her drink in thanks. Clifford, on the other hand, frowned and turned his attention back toward Sacha. Taz laughed and said, "Old boy, you're way out of your league on this one."

To say Clifford was agitated would be putting it way too mildly. He was pissed off. "How dare that clown send you a drink over here! I should go over there and have a word with his ass!"

Sacha smiled and said, "Come on, Cliff. He bought the both of us a drink. Why are you tripping?"

"Why am I tripping? I'm tripping because he has blatantly disrespected me. He's trying to get at you on the cool."

"By buying us a drink, he's trying to get at me? Cliff, that's absurd. And even if he is, so what? I'm here with *you!* You should take his gesture as a compliment and stop hating."

That comment irked the hell out of Clifford; he was ready to leave now. "Sacha, it's getting late. Maybe we should leave now."

"Leave? I'm not ready to leave. We haven't been here an hour yet. Come on, don't let that guy ruin our evening. The night's still young, and we have plenty more of it to enjoy. So relax."

Shaking his head no, Clifford said, "Nah, for real, I'm ready to go, Sacha."

Sacha didn't like the tone of his voice, so she said, "Well, I'm not, Cliff. I came out to enjoy myself, and that's exactly what I plan on doing."

"Let's not go through this, Sacha. I said I'm ready to go!"

"And I said I'm not!"

"Don't make me do something I know I'll regret!"

She laughed and said, "Cliff, you're a grown-ass man. You can do whatever you want to. Whether you'll regret it or not is solely on you. I'm a big girl, so if you want to leave, then leave. I'm quite sure I won't have a problem finding a way back home." She turned and shot a seductive smile toward Taz to add emphasis to her statement. That statement hit Clifford right where she figured it would . . . his pride.

"I'm sure you wouldn't! Maybe that thug you seem to be so fascinated by would love to take you home! Wait! I didn't mean that, Sacha. Can't we just leave? I'm no longer enjoying this place."

She couldn't believe how much Clifford sounded like a child. *And to think I was just about to give the li'l baby some ass! Whoa!* she thought. "Cliff, if you want to leave, then I think you should. Like I've already told you, I'm a big girl. I'll be fine." She sipped her drink and said, "As a matter of fact, I think you *should* leave. I'm no longer enjoying your company."

"What? Come on, Sacha. It's not that serious."

"Yes, Cliff, it is. You're trying to ruin a perfectly good evening, and I refuse to let you. So, why don't you just leave?"

"Don't push me, Sacha, 'cause I won't have a problem bouncing up out of this place without you."

She started laughing so hard that she thought she was going to pee on herself. Once she regained her composure, she said, "Have a nice evening, Cliff!" She stood and left him sitting at the table by himself. She put an extra sway in her walk as she passed Taz on her way toward the restroom.

Taz watched and smiled when he saw Clifford storm out of the club. *The first part of my mission has now been completed. Now on to phase two. Taz, do you, boy! Do you!* He turned toward Winky and ordered himself another glass of XO.

By the time Sacha came out of the bathroom, she saw that Clifford had gone, and that sexy-ass, thug-looking guy was boldly sitting at her table. *So, you think you got it like that, huh, Mr. Smooth? Let me see what you're really working with.* She went back to her table. Once she was standing in front of Taz, she said, "Excuse me, but this is my table."

"I know. Since your date shook you, I thought I'd come keep you company."

"Shook me? What makes you think that he shook me?" she asked as she sat down in her seat.

"Come on, sexy. Ain't no need for game playin'. I saw how he got heated behind the drinks I sent y'all. I didn't mean to interrupt your evening with that squ—uh—guy."

"Is that right? So, what were your intentions when you sent those drinks over to us?"

Staring directly into her sexy brown eyes, he said, "I wanted to get your attention."

"And why is that? You did notice I was with someone, didn't you?"

Taz laughed and said, "Of course! I sent him a drink, too, didn't I?"

Sacha couldn't help herself from laughing. *This cutie is something else,* she thought as she took a sip of her drink. "Well, since you've run my date away, can I at least know your name?"

"My name is Taz."

"Taz . . . hmm . . . I like that. My name is Sacha, Taz."

"Sacha . . . hmm . . . I like that too. Now that the introductions are out of the way, I have a question for you, Sacha."

"What's that, Taz?"

"Will you let me take you back out on that dance floor so we can get our groove on a li'l?"

Smiling, Sacha said, "I don't have a problem with that."

Taz stood up, took one of Sacha's small hands in his, and led her onto the dance floor.

Keno was talking to Bob when he noticed Taz slow dancing with Sacha. "Look, nigga! Taz is back in the game, dog!"

Bob turned and stared in disbelief at what he was seeing and said, "Now ain't that a bitch! What's gotten into that nigga?"

Keno smiled and said, "Fool, if you can't see that he done cracked a bad bitch, then you're one blind muthafucka!"

Out on the dance floor, Taz couldn't believe that he was actually dancing with this sexy-ass woman. She felt so good in his arms that he wanted to hold her like this all night long. *Slow down, nigga! You don't even know this broad!* he thought to himself as she held on tightly to his broad shoulders.

Sacha, on the other hand, was just as mesmerized by Taz as he was by her. *I know he's some sort of thug, but he sure as hell smells good,* she thought as she inhaled deeply and savored the smell of his Vera Wang for men.

The slow song came to an end and the DJ switched to some "Laffy Taffy" by D4L, and they started shaking all around the dance floor together, having a real good time.

Paquita and Katrina couldn't believe what they were seeing. "Bitch, Taz don't dance! How the fuck did that stuck-up-looking bitch get him out there?" yelled Paquita.

"I don't know, girl, but look at him! I've never seen Taz smile like that. He's digging that bitch."

"I hate that ho! Where the fuck did she come from any fuckin' way?"

"I don't know, girl, but it looks like he's finally chosen someone."

"That's fucked up!"

"Bitch, why you trippin'?"

"'Cause he didn't choose me!" Paquita said with a hurt expression on her face.

"That's the way the game is, girl. Come on. Let's go get a drink," Katrina said as she led her homegirl toward the bar.

After five or six songs, Taz and Sacha were sweating and tired. He led her back to her table and signaled Mikki to bring them some more drinks. After Mikki had brought their orders and left, he said, "I can't remember the last time I've actually been out on a dance floor. That shit was kinda fun."

"You're kidding, right? You dance too damn good for that."

"I'm serious. I'm not really into this club scene shit."

"So, why do you come to the club then?"

"My homies like to come and unwind here. They're into it more than I am. Usually, I just get me a drink and chill in front of the bar."

"I noticed that the last time I was here. You had a real serious look on your face. You were looking as if you didn't want to be bothered by anyone."

"Yeah, I'm like that at times."

Smiling, she said, "Well, you're sure not like that tonight. What changed?"

Taz sipped his XO and simply said, "You."

Chapter Eight

By the time the club started letting out, Taz had found out through their conversation what Sacha did for a living, as well as confirmed that this was definitely a woman that he wanted to get to know better. "I hope that you'll let me take you to go get some breakfast or something," he asked.

"Or something?" Sacha asked with a raised eyebrow.

Smiling sheepishly, Taz said, "Come on, you know what I mean. I'm really feeling you, and I kinda don't want this night to end right now. Let's go get some Denny's or something."

"I'd prefer IHOP."

"I ain't trippin'. Whatever you want is fine with me."

Before he could continue, Keno, Bo-Pete, Wild Bill, Bob, and Red came to their table. Keno smiled and said, "You ready to shake this spot, gee?"

"Nah, I'm good. Look, Red, take Keno back to my spot so he can get his truck. I'm about to go have breakfast with this lovely lady."

Red laughed and said, "Well, it's about time, dog."

"Whatever! Excuse my rudeness, Sacha. These are my homeboys, Red, Bob, Bo-Pete, Wild Bill, and this clown right here is Keno."

Sacha smiled at the crew and said, "Hello, gentlemen."

They all said their hellos and smiled, but Bob just couldn't help himself. He had to say something slick. "So, you're the one who has finally been able to get this old fuddy-duddy interested in someone, huh?"

She smiled at Bob and said, "If you say so."

Before their conversation could get any deeper, Taz said, "All right, clowns. Y'all can bounce."

"You sure, gee?" asked Keno.

"Yeah, I'm good. I'll get with y'all at the gym in the morning."

Keno smiled and said, "Yeah, we'll see you at the gym in the morning." Keno and the rest of the crew all started laughing as they left the club.

Taz waited until they were out of the club and said, "Come on, let's go get our eat on."

Sacha smiled as she stood up from the table. She liked what she had seen so far in Taz. *Be careful, girl! You know he's into something illegal,* she warned herself as they were headed toward the exit.

Once they made it outside of the club, Taz led her toward his all-black Denali and pulled out his keys. He hit a button and his alarm chirped twice and the doors to his truck made a "whoosh" sound and opened vertically. Sacha smiled and said, "Men and their toys!"

After Taz made sure that Sacha was safely inside the truck, he went around the other side and climbed in himself. He started the truck and said, "Yeah, you know how it is. We have to have all the go-go gadgets and whatnot. Life wouldn't be that much fun if men couldn't play with their toys."

"Uh-hmm, whatever! I know you have a sound system in this toy of yours. Would you turn on some music, please?"

Taz smiled and said, "Anything to please a lady." He then said, "What would you like to listen to?"

"What do you have?"

"Whatever you want to listen to, I have it."

"Is that right?"

"Yep, that's right."

I got something for this slickster! she told herself. "Okay, I'd like to listen to that new single by Alicia Keys, 'Unbreakable'."

"Yeah, I like that one too," Taz said with his smile still in place. Then he focused as he pulled his truck out of the club parking lot.

I knew he was just fronting. That's a shame. I really didn't think he was the fake type. Oh, well, at least I'll get me some breakfast out of his ass. Then I'll call Gwen and have her come pick me up from IHOP. I'm not letting this thug know where I live, Sacha thought to herself as she relaxed back in her seat.

Once Taz had slid his truck into traffic, he said, "CD number three, track number one, volume level four, mids three, and highs four, please."

Sacha stared at him as if he'd lost his mind.

A second later, the song "Unbreakable" by Alicia Keys started playing on Taz's sound system. He turned toward Sacha, shrugged his shoulders slightly, and said, "More toys, huh?"

Sacha started laughing and said, "Oh, my God! How much did you pay for something like that?"

"A li'l bit of nothin'. I let Keno talk me into getting that voice-activated system. It's pretty cool, huh?"

"It sure is. Play another song for me, Taz."

"What do you wanna hear?"

"Anything. I just want to see you do that again."

He smiled and said, "So, you *are* impressed by my toys. I guess that's a good thing." His cell phone started ringing and he said, "Excuse me for one minute, Sacha." He flipped opened his cell and said, "What up, Red?"

"Nothin' much, my nigga. Just wanted to make sure that your new girlfriend was treating you all right."

"Fuck you!"

"Aw-w-w, come on, dog. Don't be like that. Tell me, will she be at the gym with you in the morning? I mean, the gym is at your house and all."

Before Taz could reply, he heard Bob in the background telling Red to ask Taz if she had a friend. Taz shook his head and said, "Tell that nigga I said I'll find out for him after I finish eating. Now, can I go please? I am on a date!"

Red started laughing and said, "You know we love this shit, gee. It's been way too long since you really enjoyed yourself. I hope she's the one, my nigga. I really do."

Taz turned toward Sacha and told Red, "I do too, homey. Out!" After he closed his phone, he said, "My homey Bob wants to know if you have a friend."

"Bob was the darker one with the lump on his head, right?"

Taz started laughing and said, "Yeah, that's him."

"Hmm . . . I might. My girl Gwen loves her men dark skinned. Hey, what happened to my other request?"

"Oh, I forgot. Here you go. CD number seven, track six, volume level seven, mids two, and highs three please." It was quiet inside of the truck as his automated sound system changed CDs as it was told to. Then, all of a sudden, Fifty Cent's "Just a Li'l Bit" started playing.

Sacha started laughing and said, "I like it! I like it!"

Taz smiled as he drove on toward IHOP.

By the time they arrived at the restaurant, Sacha had made him play six different songs. She was really impressed with his voice command system.

They entered the restaurant hand in hand, and Taz noticed several people in the crowded restaurant take notice of them. *I hate this part of the game. All of these clowns are going to try and be all up in my business,* Taz thought as he walked straight toward a waitress and said, "Table for two, please."

The waitress stared at Taz as if he was crazy and said, "Sir, there's about a twenty-minute wait. Please give me your name and I'll call you when your turn has come up."

Taz grinned and said, "Tell your manager that Taz said he needs a table for two." He then turned and winked at Sacha.

Sacha stared at him and said, "So you got it like that, huh?"

"I guess we're about to find out."

The waitress Taz had spoken with came back, followed by the manager. When the manager saw Taz, he smiled and said, "Right this way, Taz. I thought Sheila was playing with me when she said your name. How have you been? It's been a while."

"The same ol', same ol'. Staying busy and stuff," Taz replied as they followed the manager as he led them to the back of the restaurant. Once they were seated, Taz said, "Thanks, Donald. I know how busy you are at this time of the morning."

"No problem, Taz. Anything for you, you know that. I'll have another waitress come take your orders in a few minutes."

"That's cool." Taz waited until the manager was out of earshot and asked, "Did that impress you?"

Sacha laughed and turned her small right hand from side to side, saying, "Just a li'l bit."

"Well, I see that you're hard to impress, so I'm going to have to step up my game."

"Don't do that, Taz. Just be yourself. I'm quite sure that will impress me more than enough," she said as she opened up her menu.

I can't believe that I'm actually having breakfast with a broad like this. Shit, what the fuck am I doing? Taz asked himself as he stared at Sacha.

Sacha saw him staring, put down her menu, and asked, "So, tell me something about you that I'd never believe."

"What?"

Smiling, she said, "Tell me something interesting about yourself, Taz."

"Interesting? To be honest, there's really nothing interesting about me. I'm your average businessman. I work out a lot to try and stay in shape, and tend to my businesses the best I can."

"What exactly are some of your businesses?"

"I do a li'l bit of this and a li'l bit of that."

"Uh-uh, slick. That's too evasive. Have you forgotten that I told you I'm an attorney? You've got to come better than that."

Laughing, he said, "A'ight, but can I ask you a question first?"

"Go ahead."

"What kind of businesses do you think I have?"

"To be completely honest with you, you look like a very successful drug dealer to me."

Taz laughed and said, "Well, at least you said 'successful.' But why a brother have to sell drugs?"

"Look at yourself. You got the nice expensive clothing, the high-priced diamonds in your ears. Your grille looks more expensive than that rapper guy, Baby. Your truck has the big, big chrome rims, and the extra loud automated sound system. And, on top of everything else, you got the mean-looking macho crew. Everything about you screams drugs."

With his smile still in place Taz shook his head slowly and said, "First of all, I've never sold drugs in my life. And to tell you the truth, I despise the people who do. I'm a successful businessman, and my crew, as you called them, are my closest friends. We've been together for a very long time. Thugs, yeah, maybe, but it is what it is. We've never forgotten our beginnings and we never will. Just because we made it financially doesn't mean that we have to dress and act all goody-goody. Or do we have to maintain a certain look for certain people?"

"Not really, but—"

"But what? We work for ourselves. Therefore, we don't have to answer to anyone but us."

"Okay, okay, dang! So, what kind of businesses are you all involved in?"

"You're nosy, aren't ya?"

"I'm just trying to get to know the man I'm having breakfast with," she said with a smile on her face.

"Real estate and small food chains."

Sacha started laughing so hard that she almost choked. "Come on, handsome! You got to come better than that! Don't forget, you're talking to an attorney."

Slightly irritated yet amused, Taz said, "So, you're calling me a liar? Let me tell you something, boo. I'm not the type to go around bragging about my accomplishments. That's just not my style. But, as you obviously noticed, I'm a li'l on the flashy side. I'm a thirty-six-year-old man who is set financially for the rest of my life. All I have is a high school diploma from John Marshall, but I've been blessed with enough business sense to make all of the right moves with my money. So have my homies. Answer this for me, do you think we were able to get this table without a wait just because I'm the big kingpin of the town?"

Smiling, she said, "Maybe. You know the ballers get special treatment wherever they roll."

"True." Staring directly into Sacha's lovely eyes, Taz said, "I like what I see in you so far, Sacha, and I hope you will give me the opportunity to get to know you better. But before I go any further, it is a must that you believe me, as well as in me. I am not a drug dealer. I've never dealt with drugs in my life, and neither have any of my homeboys."

The tone in his voice made her feel that his words were honest, but what really convinced her was the look in his brown eyes. "The eyes never lie. . . . Well, most times they don't," she said. She raised her glass of water to her lips, sipped, and said, "I believe you, Taz. You can't blame me for asking, can you?"

"Nah, I don't. I just want that understood before we go any further."

"What makes you think we'll go any further than this breakfast?"

Smiling, he said, "Like you said, the eyes never lie."

"What's that supposed to mean?"

"You're diggin' me just as much as I'm diggin' you. I can see it in your eyes." Before she could respond, Donald, the manager of IHOP, came back to their table and said, "Sorry about the wait, Taz, but you know how it is after the club lets out. Sheila's running around like crazy back there. Let me take you guys' order."

"That's cool, Donald. What are you having, Sacha?"

"I'll have the Denver omelet and hash browns."

"That sounds good. I'll have the same, Donald. Add a side of bacon and sausage for me also. Will orange juice be cool, boo?"

Blushing slightly, she said, "Yes, that'll be fine."

"A carafe of orange juice, too, Donald."

"Coming right up, Taz."

Before Donald left to go fill their order, Taz stopped him and asked, "Donald, how do this month's profits look? Better than last months, I hope."

Smiling brightly, Donald said, "Everything's great, Taz. I think we're having our best month this year. I sure hope you don't open up another place and cause me more competition."

Taz smiled at Donald and said, "Now, you know that might just be a good idea, Don. I bet that'll keep you on your toes."

"Ah, Taz, you're killin' me!" They both laughed as Donald left to go fill their orders.

Sacha had a smirk on her face as she said, "Show-off!"

"What?"

"You know what, slick! I told you I believed you, Taz!"

"I had to make sure. Like you said, you are an attorney."

"What's that supposed to mean?"

"You need proof beyond a reasonable doubt."

"I'm goin' to get you for that one, slick!" she said with that sexy smile on her face.

"I hope so, boo! I hope so!"

Chapter Nine

Over the next few weeks, Taz and Sacha had become inseparable. Whenever she wasn't at work, she was with him. They enjoyed each other's company tremendously. Sacha found herself daydreaming about Taz whenever they weren't together. She loved the way he took charge when they went anyplace. His strength was a complete turn-on to her. And those eyes! Taz's brown eyes made her heart skip a beat whenever he stared at her.

"I'm telling you, Gwen, I think I'm falling in love."

"Bitch, please! How long have you been dating this Taz? Two weeks?"

"Ho, it'll be a month this Saturday. And I want you to meet him this weekend, so don't make any plans, okay?"

"Whatever! You said he had a crew, huh? Are any of them worth me giving the time of day?"

"Maybe. There are five of them you can choose from. Knowing your whorish ass, you'll be able to pick one or two."

"You got that right, bitch! Look, I have a client coming over. Let me call you later on."

"All right, ho, but if I don't answer the phone, it's because I'm giving Taz some of my goodies tonight."

Laughing, Gwen said, "It's about time you knocked the dust off that coochie, bitch! Bye!"

Sacha was laughing as she hung up the phone. She went into her bathroom and climbed into the tub. Tonight was the night she was going to let Taz take their relationship to the next level. *I hope he doesn't pull that same shit Clifford pulled on me.* The thought of Clifford and how he completely missed a golden opportunity amused the hell out of her. *Thanks to his ass, I got me some Taz!* she said to herself as she let the bubbles in her bath consume her body. "Fuck Calgon! Taz, take me away!" she laughed aloud.

Clifford was lying back on Cory's bed, thinking about Sacha. It had been almost a month since the incident at the club. Ever since, Sacha had made it a point to avoid him. *Damn, I fucked up! How in the hell am I ever going to get back in good with her? All because of that damn wannabe-ass thug nigga. Fuck!* he thought to himself as he watched Cory come back into the bedroom from her bathroom. Her slim frame was cool, but she was a straight slouch compared to Sacha.

Cory smiled as she climbed onto the bed and said, "Smile, baby. It can't be that bad."

"What? What are you talking about?"

"You look as if you've lost your best friend, baby."

"Nah, I just got a lot on my mind, that's all."

"Well, maybe I can get your mind on something else," she said as she slid down toward his manhood and put it inside of her mouth.

"Yeah, you just might," Clifford said as he closed his eyes while she did her thing.

Taz was dressed in a pair of light gray Dickies and a plain white tee. He climbed out of his truck and smiled as he walked toward Sacha's front door. *I can't believe how patient I'm being with this broad. I know I could have fucked the first night if I'd wanted to, but instead I chose to play the patient game with her. Why? That's the million-dollar fucking question,* he thought to himself as he knocked on the door.

Sacha came to the door dressed like the "Eye Candy" of the month in *XXL* magazine. She had on a matching bra and panties set covered with a sheer top. Her curvy figure was looking so enticing that it took all of Taz's self-control not to grab her and start making love to her right there in the doorway.

She smiled and said, "I hope you didn't have any plans for us tonight, baby, 'cause as you can see, I have plans for you all night long."

He smiled as he entered her home and said, "Nah. I thought we were going to watch a flick or something, but I see you're tryin' to make your own flick tonight, huh?"

Smiling seductively, she said, "That's right, baby. I want to see if we can make our own magic on the big screen tonight. Now, come here and kiss me, baby." As they shared a long kiss, Sacha couldn't believe that she was being this straightforward. This was completely out of character for her. But she didn't care; all she cared about at that moment was making love to Taz. He had shown her that he could be patient, and she respected that so much, even though she knew that he could have had her that very first night. That thought got her even wetter than she already was. She stepped out of his embrace and said, "Come." She then led him into her bedroom, which was dark except for the three scented candles she had burning.

Taz stopped her and said, "Boo, are you really ready?"

"I've been ready, Taz. Tonight's the night, baby." She sat on her bed and watched as he slowly began to undress. Watching him taking off his clothes got her so hot that she didn't even realize that she had let her right hand slip between her legs. She fondled herself while he took off his clothes.

Taz smiled as he watched her playing with her pussy. *This is one bad-ass female! Damnit, man, it's about to be on!* he said to himself as he stepped to her. "Come here, baby. Let me taste some of that."

She pulled her hand from her sex, put two of her fingers inside of his mouth, and asked, "How does that taste, baby? Is it good? Tell me it tastes good, baby."

Taz sucked her fingers and said, "Mmm! You're just as sweet as I thought you'd be." He then scooped her into his arms and gently laid her onto her bed. He climbed on top of her and began to methodically lick her entire body. When he made it to her toes, he began to suck each one, one at a time.

Sacha moaned as her right hand found it's way back to her pussy. She was on fire from Taz's every touch.

Taz was so hard he felt as if he was about to explode. *I have to get inside of this pussy like now!* he said to himself as he slid back toward her face. They kissed each other passionately until Taz just couldn't take it any longer. He rolled off of her and reached for his wallet.

Sacha smiled as she took the condom he grabbed out of his wallet and opened the wrapper. She then pushed him onto his back and began sucking his dick. Her mouth was so warm and wet!

Damn! I done died and went to heaven! thought Taz as he watched her suck on him. He didn't know when or how she had done it, but somehow she had slid the condom onto his dick while she was sucking him off. The next thing he knew, she was straddled on top of him, riding him as if her life depended on it. He reached up with both of his hands and began to squeeze each of her nipples. They grew hard instantly from his touch. Sacha's hair was all over the place as she continued to ride him harder and harder. Taz didn't think he would be able to hold off any longer. He wanted to be on top when he came, so he pulled her close to him and started kissing her as he rolled on top of her without ever coming out of her sex. He mounted her and took complete control. Through all of this, Sacha remained silent, which he appreciated. He really wasn't with all of that yelling and screaming shit, so it shocked the hell out of him when he heard all of the noise that he was making. "Damn, baby! This pussy is so good . . . it's so good! Is it mine, boo? Tell me it's mine! Tell! Me! It's! Mine!" he screamed.

"It's yours, Taz! It's all yours, baby! It's all yours!" Sacha yelled as she wrapped her legs around his waist and used her vaginal muscles to grip his dick harder. It had been so long since she had had sex that she was extremely tight. Taz was filling her completely, and she was in ecstasy. "Cum with me, baby! Can you do that for me?" she panted. "Cum with me, baby! Let's make this special. Cum! With! Me! Taz!"

"I'm cummin', baby! I'm cummin'!" he screamed as he unloaded his sperm into the condom he was wearing.

Spent, he rolled off of her and sighed. Sacha was still feeling a few aftershocks of their lovemaking as she lay there, still slightly trembling. After a few minutes, she seemed to regain her bearings. She turned toward Taz and knew right then and there that she was in love. She wiped the sweat off of his forehead, smiled, and said, "Get up, baby. I'm not finished with you yet."

She then pulled him to the end of the bed so that his feet were on the floor. She got in front of him and started sucking his dick with so much vigor that Taz felt as if he was going to cum again that fast. Once she had him nice and hard again, she put her feet onto his thighs and turned her body so that her back was against his chest. Using her legs for leverage, she slid herself onto his dick and began to ride him real slow at first, then faster and faster.

All Taz could do was lay back on the bed and watch in amazement as she rode him like she was a sex maniac.

This time when she came, he came also. "Oh! Taz! I'm! Cumming! It feels so go-o-o-od, baby! It feels so-o-o-o good!"

"Ride that dick, baby! Ride that dick!" he screamed.

"Is it mine, Taz? Is it all mine?"

Just as he started to cum, he screamed, "Yeah, boo, it's yours! It's all yours!"

They both fell back onto the bed, completely spent. They were so caught up with their lovemaking that neither of them realized that their second round of sexing was without a condom.

Chapter Ten

The next morning, Sacha got up to find Taz gone. She groggily climbed out of her bed and went to the bathroom, where she was surprised to see Taz soaking in the bathtub. She smiled and said, "Good morning, baby. How long have you been up?"

"Good morning. I got up a li'l after six. I don't like to sleep late. Plus, I knew you would be getting up early to go to work."

Sacha sat down on the toilet and started relieving herself. After she was finished, she smiled and said, "I'm sorry, I couldn't hold that much longer."

Taz laughed and said, "I ain't trippin'. After all, this is your spot."

"Speaking of spots, Mr. Taz, when am I going to be invited to yours? We've been seeing quite a bit of each other, and I don't even know where you live. Don't tell me that you have a wife and kids somewhere stashed on me. I wouldn't take too kindly to that, mister."

Taz climbed out of the tub, wrapped a towel around himself, and said, "Nah, baby, nothin' like that is goin' on in my life. It's all about you, Sacha."

The look in his eyes told her that he was telling the truth. For some reason, she felt that his eyes seemed to speak volumes to her. She smiled and said, "Good. So, when am I going to get to make love to you in your bedroom?"

He laughed and said, "Whenever you want to, baby. I'm about to go get my workout on, and then I'll be free for the rest of the day. What's on your agenda today? Any court appearances?"

"Nope. I have to go to the county jail and visit a client at ten. After that, my day is done. Are we on for some lunch, then heart-stopping sex or what?" she asked with that sexy smile of hers.

"How about the heart-stopping sex, then lunch?"

Laughing, she said, "Either way is fine with me, Mister Taz."

"That's cool. Now, come here and give me a hug." They shared a tight hug and then a passionate kiss. "I'm digging you more than I expected, Sacha," Taz said as he pulled himself from their embrace.

Staring into his eyes, she asked, "Is that good or bad, baby?"

Smiling, he responded, "It's definitely good. I never thought I could feel this strongly for a woman so quickly."

"Why is that?"

"My past just wouldn't let me love easily."

"Love? Are you telling me that you're in love with me?"

He returned her stare briefly, then nodded his head yes. "I fell in love with you the first time I laid my eyes on you, boo. But I refused to let my emotions override my intellect. I knew that if I ever saw you again, you were going to be mine. That's why when I saw you at the club again, I didn't hesitate. That clown you were with didn't have a chance. I was going after what I wanted."

As she pulled Taz out of the bathroom, she said, "You're so damn cocky sometimes! I wish I could say the same, but I wasn't sure about you or your intentions until after I got to know you."

"Yeah, I know. You thought I was Nino Brown."

She punched him lightly on his arm and said, "I'm serious, Taz. I have to be careful. You know I could be disbarred if I got involved with a criminal. But, when we made love last night, I realized that I don't give a damn if you're on the Ten Most Wanted list by the FBI. All I want is for you to love me as much as I love you."

Smiling, he asked, "Love? So, are you telling me that you love me, Sacha?"

"Yes, Taz, I love you."

"I love you, too, Li'l Mama."

"Li'l Mama? Where'd that come from?"

"My mother always told me that she will always be my Big Mama, and any other woman who ever comes into my life will be my Li'l Mama. Now that it's official that you're my woman, you're now my Li'l Mama. So, I guess I have to call Mama-Mama and set up a time for you two to meet."

"Mama-Mama?"

"That's my mother."

"Oh, okay. When will I get to meet her?"

"I'll give her a call after I finish working out this morning. Call me after you come from the county jail, and we'll see then."

"Taz, it's a quarter to eight. I don't have to be at the county jail until ten."

"And I told you I have to go work out. I'm meeting my niggas at the gym in a hour."

Smiling seductively, she said, "Well, that means we still have some time to kill." She pulled him close to her and said, "There are a few more things I didn't get to show you last night."

Smiling, he asked, "And what's that, Li'l Mama?"

She pulled him onto the bed and said, "You'll see!"

By the time Taz made it home, the entire crew was parked in his driveway.

Keno smiled as he watched Taz get out of his truck. "Damn, my nigga! Is she really like that? You look like you've been in a fuckin' marathon or some shit."

Taz smiled and said, "Yeah, dog, she's like that!"

They went inside of Taz's home, and Taz said, "Y'all go on downstairs and start warming up. I'll be down after I change." He went upstairs to his bedroom and quickly changed into a pair of sweatpants and a wife-beater. Once he was changed, he went downstairs and joined his homies.

Bob was stretching, while Red and Wild Bill were loosening up their joints by curling one of Taz's curl bars without any weights on it. Bo-Pete and Keno were taking turns warming up their joints by bench-pressing light weight.

Taz's built-in gym was equipped with everything one could imagine. There were over several hundred pounds of free weights. He had dumbbells, shoulder machines, squat machines, even a built-in Olympic-sized swimming pool, not to mention a sauna room and Jacuzzi. He had spent over three hundred thousand dollars on everything. To him, it was money well spent, because he had all the luxuries of a regular gym inside of his home.

"All right, you clowns, let's do this," Taz said as he began to stretch and get loose.

They had a set routine that they did Monday thru Friday. They would start by doing five sets of twenty-five reps with the curl bars. Then they would do some work with the dumbbells. Afterward, they would head to the bench press and do ten sets of twenty reps on the bench. Finally, they would jump into the pool and swim fifty laps. Since they were all over thirty, it was a must that they kept themselves in tip-top shape. And though they had different characteristics physically, they were some very strong men.

After they had finished their workout, Taz told Keno that he was having lunch with Sacha, and that he planned on taking her over to meet Mama-Mama.

"Is that right? Damn, gee! You're really serious about, her huh?"

"Yeah, dog, I love her."

Wild Bill was sipping on a bottled water and damned near spit a mouthful all over Bob's face. "You're *what?* Damn, nigga, you just met the broad!"

"So what? I know when I'm loving a female, nigga. I'm not like your li'l ass. I don't fall in and out of love every other week."

Bob started laughing and said, "I'm happy for you, my nigga. I hope she's been looking for a homegirl for me."

"Bob, she's a attorney, gee. I don't think she has any fuckin' 'homegirls'," Taz said sarcastically.

"Well, one of her colleagues, then," Bob said with a smile.

"You're a fuckin' clown, nigga, you know that?"

"Don't pay that nigga any attention, homey. Do you. I'm happy for your ass. It's about time you really started living again," Red said seriously.

"I have a question, though. What you gon' do about Tari now that you're all in love and shit?" asked Bo-Pete.

"That, my nigga, is a very good question," Taz said as his sipped his bottled water.

Sacha decided to stop at the office before she went to go visit her client in the county jail. She was feeling extremely giddy as she walked down the hallway toward her office. The smile she had on her face quickly turned to a frown when she saw Clifford coming toward her. He stopped her and said, "Hello, Sacha."

"Good morning, Cliff. How are you?"

"Fine. You're looking stunning this morning."

"Thanks. Could you excuse me? I'm kind of pressed for time. I have to be at County in about twenty minutes," she said as she checked the time on her Rolex.

"Sacha, I know I made a complete ass of myself at the club that night. I hope you can forgive me for my childish behavior."

"Cliff, that's the past. Let's just leave it there, okay?"

Smiling brightly, he said, "Exactly! So, when do you think we could get together and start from scratch?"

She gave him a look as if to ask whether he was serious. When she saw that he was, she said, "Well, Cliff, I'm seeing someone now, and it looks as if it's getting pretty serious."

"Serious? Come on, Sacha! It's barely been a month since we were at the club. How could it be that serious?"

Sighing heavily, she said, "It'll be a month this Saturday, Cliff. And believe me, it is serious, so let it go, okay? Look, like I said, I'm running late. Bye, Cliff," she said as she went inside of her office and grabbed a few of her notes on her new client.

After Sacha was led into the visiting room of the county jail, she sat down at the small table and pulled out her files and started reviewing them. Her new client was being held without bail by the DEA for distribution of crack cocaine. He obviously had plenty of money, since he was able to afford her as an attorney. She figured the best thing she could do for him was to get him to plea out and hope for the best deal possible, especially since he was caught on tape making a direct drug transaction with an undercover agent.

One of the sheriffs came into the visiting room with her client in handcuffs. After cuffing one of his hands to the small table, the sheriff left them alone inside the visiting room.

"Hello, Mr. Surefield. How are you doing today?"

"I'm hangin' in there. Do you think you'll be able to get me a bail, ma'am?"

"I don't think so, but I'll try when we go to your bail hearing next week."

"*Next week?* Why do we have to wait so damn long?"

"First off, your court date has been set for Tuesday, Mr. Sure-field. That's only six days away. And secondly, that's how these things go. Now, tell me, have you ever been in any trouble like this before?"

"Nah, this is my first case. How much time do you think I'm gon' get?"

"That's kind of difficult to say at this point. You do know that you were caught on tape selling crack cocaine to an undercover officer."

"Yeah, I know. You can't tell me what I'm lookin' at?"

"Since this is your first arrest, you might be lucky enough to get ten years."

"*Ten years?* Fuck that shit! I ain't tryin' to do no damn ten years! You gots to get me a better deal than that!"

"Mr. Surefield, the only way we can get you a better deal than that will be for you to tell the DEA something that will want to make them help you out."

"So, in order for me to get less than a dime, I got to tell somethin', huh? Fuck that shit! I ain't no snitch!"

"I understand, Mr. Surefield."

"Call me Tony."

"Okay, Tony. Let's go over everything for the record. You sold two ounces of crack cocaine to an undercover agent on November 10th, 2005. You were unlucky enough to be caught up in a DEA sting operation. Since you sold more than fifty-two grams of crack, that puts you in the ten to life penalty range."

"Ten to life? I thought you said I was lookin' at ten years!"

"I did. But the federal system doesn't work exactly like that."

"You need to break this shit down for me, ma'am."

"Your deal will most likely be, like I said, ten years to life. But since this is your first arrest, your numbers on the federal guidelines should be relatively low—category one to be exact. It's the decision of the U.S. assistant attorney on exactly how low your numbers will be down the category. If they want to, they could push for more time. It all depends."

"On what?"

"On you, Mr.—excuse me—Tony."

"So, once again you're tellin' me that I should tell them something?"

"No, I'm not telling you to tell them anything, Tony. That decision has to be made by you, and you only. What I am telling you is that you're looking at doing some time, either way. The final decision is solely up to you. If you'd like, I'll speak with the U.S. assistant attorney who has your case, and see what he's actually talking about."

"Yeah, you do that, 'cause if I gots to tell somethin' to get under a dime, then so be it."

Damn! I thought you weren't going to snitch, Sacha thought to herself. To her client, she said, "That's fine, Tony. I'll get right on it, and I'll see you Tuesday in court."

"If I tell somethin', will that help me get a bail?"

"It might. Like I said, it's all up to the U.S. assistant attorney."

"Okay. When you speak with him, make sure that you let him know that I gots a lot to tell. Okay?"

"I'll do that. You do understand that my fee is still the same either way?"

"Yeah, I got your chips. Don't trip on that shit."

"Whom shall I contact for payment?"

"My big brother KK's wife will be getting at you later on today."

"That's fine. Have her take the check to my office and leave it with the receptionist if I'm not there. Well, I guess that's all for now, Tony. I'll give the assistant attorney a call and see exactly where we're at. I'll know more when we get to court Tuesday. If you need to speak with me, give me a call at the office. You can call collect if you have to."

"Thanks."

After they had shaken hands, Sacha gathered her things and put them inside of her leather briefcase and called for the sheriff. She watched as Tony was led back into the county jail. *It's a shame that these young brothers get themselves caught up like this. Now he's about to get more young brothers caught up in the system just because he can't do all of the time he's about to get. This shit is so crazy,* thought Sacha as she left the visiting room.

Clifford was sitting at his desk, steaming. *How could that bitch do me like that? That's some cold-ass shit! After all of the time and energy I've put into her, she's just going to up and get involved with someone else. That's cold!* he said to himself as he stared at the picture he and Sacha had taken in front of the Oklahoma City Bombing memorial. *She's too damn special to lose like that. I'm going to have to find a way to get her away from whomever she's seeing. I have to!* He put the picture back inside of his desk drawer.

Once Sacha was outside of the county jail, she pulled out her cell phone and quickly called Taz. He answered his cell after the third ring. "What up, Li'l Mama?"

She smiled and said, "Hi, baby! Are you through getting your muscles all worked up?"

"Yeah, we just finished. Where are you?"

"I'm leaving County now. I'm going to go back to the house and change into something comfortable. What do you have planned for us?"

"After I take a quick shower, I'm going to give Mama-Mama a call and see if she's busy. If she isn't, I'm going to see if she'd mind cooking us lunch. More than likely she'll tell me to hurry up and get over there. So, I'll give you a call after I get at her. Then I'll come scoop you up."

"That's fine, baby. After we leave from your mother's, are we going to your house to do the nasty some more?"

Laughing, Taz said, "Damn, Li'l Mama! You're a straight sex fiend, huh?"

"I am now! See you in a li'l bit, baby."

Laughing loudly, Taz said, "A'ight then, Li'l Mama."

Chapter Eleven

Sacha stepped out of her home, dressed casually in a pair of brown corduroy pants and a tan sweater. Since it was slightly chilly outside, she hoped she was dressed appropriately to meet Taz's mother.

Taz smiled as he watched Sacha walk toward his truck. "That's one sexy-ass lady!" he said aloud as he continued to stare at her.

Once Sacha was inside of the truck and comfortable, she said, "Hi, baby. Did you have a nice workout?"

"Yeah, it was cool. I got at Mama-Mama. She's expecting us to be there in about twenty minutes."

"That's fine. Do I look okay, baby?"

"You're on point, Li'l Mama. I like those boots you got on. They're tight."

Blushing slightly, she said, "Thanks. I've been having these bad boys for a minute now. I've been waiting for a reason to wear them. I hope your mom will like me. I'm kinda nervous."

"Nervous about what? Baby, you've already impressed the hell outta me, and that's all that matters. I love Mama-Mama, but nothin' and no one will ever change how I feel about you. So relax, 'cause she's goin' to love you, anyway," Taz said seriously as he pulled out of her driveway.

"I hope you're right."

Taz pulled into the long driveway of his mother's home out in the city of Spencer. Spencer is considered the country, since it's about twenty minutes outside of Oklahoma City, and is mostly a rural area with lots and lots of land. Taz's mother's home was a large ranch-style house with plenty of flowers in the front.

Sacha smiled and said, "Oh, I love your mother's flower garden! I wish I had the time to do something like that in front of my house."

"If you'd like, I could come over when I find some time and hook yours up just like it."

"You'd do that?"

"Yep. Why do you look so surprised? I got skills, Li'l Mama," he said as he pushed a button on the door panel and both of their doors opened with a whoosh.

Mama-Mama was standing in her doorway when Taz and Sacha stepped out of the truck. She smiled as she watched her loving child. Finally, after all of these years, he was bringing a girl home for her to meet. *Thank you, Jesus, for letting this boy finally start to live again!* Mama-Mama thought to herself as she stepped out of the doorway. "Well, well, it's about time I got to see my man child! For a minute there, I thought you done forgot about Mama-Mama," she said as she gave Taz a tight hug.

After they finished hugging each other, Taz stepped back and said, "You need to gon' with that, Mama-Mama. You know I be busy and stuff. Anyway, Mama-Mama, this is Sacha. Sacha, this is my mother, Mama-Mama."

Sacha stepped forward, extended her hand, and said, "I'm pleased to meet you, Mrs.—"

Mama-Mama slapped her hand down, gave Sacha a tight hug, and said, "Girl, you gon' with that Mrs. stuff! You call me 'Mama-Mama' just like everybody else, hear?"

Laughing, Sacha said, "Sure, Mama-Mama."

"Good. Now, y'all come on inside so we can sit down and eat. After lunch, we can gets to know each other better."

As they followed Mama-Mama into the house, Taz grabbed Sacha's hand and whispered, "See, I told you! Mama-Mama loves you."

Sacha smiled but remained silent as they went inside. Once they were inside, she smiled because Mama-Mama's home was so comfortable looking. She had a beige sectional in her living room, with a huge glass coffee table sitting in front of it. The house made her think of something out of that old TV show, *Dallas*. It was homey looking as well as expensive. *I bet Taz made sure that Mama-Mama remained well taken care of,* she thought as she stepped to the mantel over the fireplace and stared at some of the pictures that were sitting there. There were pictures of Taz when he was in high school, looking funny in his football uniform. Then there were some of Taz, Mama-Mama, and another little girl who Sacha assumed was Taz's little sister, because they could pass as twins, except that she could see that she was much younger than Taz.

Taz plopped himself onto the sofa and watched Sacha as she was looking at the pictures of him and his family. *Yeah, she's definitely going to be in my life for a long time.*

After a few more minutes, Mama-Mama yelled from the kitchen, "Y'all come on back here! The food's ready now!"

Sacha turned and asked, "Where's your little sister, Taz?"

He smiled and said, "She goes to OU. She lives out by the campus in Norman."

"That's nice. You know you two could pass as twins."

"Yeah, that's what everybody tells me. Come on, before Mama-Mama starts tripping."

"Tripping about what, boy?" Mama-Mama asked, standing in the doorway of the kitchen.

"Nothin'."

"Humph! Y'all come on now before I gets upset and gets my switch!"

They all laughed as they went into the kitchen.

Mama-Mama sat her large frame down and said, "Taz, have you spoken to Tazneema lately?"

Taz was reaching across the table, grabbing himself one of Mama-Mama's buttered rolls, and said, "Yeah, I talked to her a few weeks ago. Why? Is something wrong?"

"Did you know that she wants to go spend the holidays with some white folks way out in Houston?"

"Yeah, she told me. I really don't see nothin' wrong with it, Mama-Mama. She's been doing real good in school, so you might as well let her have some fun."

"Humph! You know how them youngstas are now these days. Especially out there in Houston."

"Come on, Mama-Mama! What do you know about what's goin' on in Houston?"

"Boy, you think I don't know about how they be out there sippin' on that syrup?" The shocked look on both Sacha's and Taz's face answered her question. "Just like I thought. Y'all be thinkin' 'cause I'm an old woman, I don't be knowin' what's goin' on. Well, you're both wrong."

Laughing, Taz asked, "Mama-Mama, what do you know about syrup?"

"Miss Jones's son lives out there in Houston, and he told her all about that there 'lean' they be drankin' down there. She told me it's codeine and pop they be mixing and stuff. I'm not having my baby out there gettin' mixed up with all of that stuff, ya hear me, Taz?"

"Yes, ma'am. But I doubt if 'Neema would get caught up with any of that stuff. You need to have more faith in her, Mama-Mama."

"Faith my ass! Now pass me the corn, boy."

As Taz did as she told him to, she turned toward Sacha and said, "Now, tell me something about yourself, Sacha. I already knows you're a lawyer, so you can skip that part."

Sacha laughed nervously and said, "Well, I was born in the City. I grew up in Bethany. After I graduated from Putnam North, I went to Oklahoma State and studied law. I'm an only child, and both of my parents now live in Florida."

"Florida? What made them want to move way out that way?"

"After they retired, my mom talked my father into it. They seem to love it out there, because I hardly ever get to see them anymore."

"You mean to tell me that they don't come to visit or nothin'?"

"That's right."

"And you don't go out to visit them neither?"

"Well, with my job it's kind of difficult to find the time. But I was hoping to go out there this summer."

"That sounds like a lovely idea. You need to make sure that you take this knucklehead out there with you. That way, he can meet your folks. They gon' need to meet their new son-in-law," Mama-Mama said, and she stuffed a piece of the tender brisket she made inside of her mouth.

Taz almost choked on the corn he had in his mouth. Sacha laughed as she watched him. "Mama-Mama! You know you need to quit it!" Taz said and smiled.

"Boy, this is the first woman that you've brought to this house in I don't know how long. And I can tell by the way the both of you look that y'all done fell in love with each other. So don't be tryin' to play like Mama-Mama don't know what she be talkin' 'bout. 'Cause I do!"

"It hasn't even been a whole month since we've been goin' out, Mama-Mama."

"So what, Taz? That ain't squat. Ain't no time limit on love, boy. Look at the both of y'all. If y'all ain't in love with each other, my name ain't Mama-Mama."

They laughed some more and continued to eat the big lunch that Mama-Mama prepared for them.

After spending a couple of hours chatting with Mama-Mama, Taz said, "Well, Mama-Mama, it's time for us to be going. Do you need anything before we leave?"

"Mama-Mama's just fine, boy. I want you to know that I don't agree with that Houston stuff, but I'm gon' go on and let that girl go. But if somethin' crazy happens, I'm gon' blame it all on *you*, Taz!"

Smiling, Taz shook his head and said, "All right, Mama-Mama." He then stepped to her and gave her a tight hug and a kiss on her cheek and said, "I love you, Mama-Mama."

"I love you, too, boy. Now, gon' and get out my way so I can give my daughter-in-law a hug."

They laughed as Sacha stepped into Mama-Mama's warm embrace and gave her a hug. "It was really nice meeting you, Mama-Mama. I hope we can come and do this again real soon," Sacha said sincerely.

"Girl, you're welcome in this home anytime . . . anytime, ya hear?"

"Yes, ma'am," replied Sacha.

Taz turned toward Sacha and said, "Here, Li'l Mama. Go on out to the truck. I need to holla at Mama-Mama for a sec."

Sacha took the keys from Taz, waved good-bye to Mama-Mama, and went and got inside of Taz's truck.

After she was out of the house, Taz asked, "Mama-Mama, do you like her?"

"She's perfect for you, Taz. That girl loves you, boy."

"Yeah, I know."

"The question is, do you love her?"

"Yeah, Mama-Mama, I do."

"What you gon' do about that white girl?"

Sighing heavily, he said, "I'm gon' have to keep it real with her. Tari knows everything about me. I've never kept any secrets from her, and I'm not about to start now."

"You know you gon' break that girl's heart, don't you?"

Nodding his head yes, he asked, "But what else can I do, Mama-Mama?"

"Nothin' I guess. Follow your heart, boy. I guess that's all you can do."

Smiling, he said, "That's exactly what I'm doing! All right then, let me go. Oh, and don't worry about 'Neema. She'll be all right."

"Speaking of 'Neema, does Sacha—"

"One thing at a time, Mama-Mama . . . one thing at a time," Taz said as he gave his mother another hug and left her home.

Taz climbed inside of his truck and said, "You were a hit. She loves you."

Smiling brightly, Sacha said, "That's good. I really like your mom, Taz. She's so down to earth."

"Yeah, Mama-Mama's gon' always keep it real. Well, since you're now in with my Mama-Mama, all you have to do now is impress 'Neema."

"Your sister?"

Before he could answer her question, his cell rang. He flipped it open and saw a picture of Michael Jordan shooting a fadeaway jump shot over Joe Dumars of the old Detroit Pistons. He closed his phone and said, "Shit!" He reopened his phone and quickly dialed Keno's cell number. When Keno answered his cell, Taz said, "Dog, I just got hit by Won. Call the others and meet me at my spot. I'm out in Spencer, and I'm on my way there now."

"I'm on it, my nigga," said Keno, and he hung up the phone.

Taz turned toward Sacha and said, "Look, Li'l Mama. I gots to bounce outta town. I'm goin' to need you to do me a favor, okay?"

"Is something wrong, baby?"

"Nah. I just need you to take my truck to your pad for me, 'cause I'm not gon' have enough time to take you back to your spot. I'll most likely be gone for a day or two. I'll hit you when I know for sure."

"That's no problem, Taz, but is everything okay? You seem kind of bent out of shape."

"Everything is everything, Li'l Mama. I just gotta take care of some business and I'm on the clock."

Sacha didn't respond as she watched as Taz drove toward his house.

Oh, my God! I know this isn't this man's home! Sacha said to herself as Taz pulled into the circular driveway of his mini-mansion. He stopped his truck in front of his four-car garage, grabbed the remote control and pressed one of it's buttons. All four doors of the garage opened slowly, and Sacha gasped as she saw Taz's 2005 S Class 600 Mercedes-Benz in one stall. In the other stall he had an all-chrome Softail Harley-Davidson, and in the last stall there was a brand-new convertible Bentley Azure. *What the fuck?* Sacha shook her head to make sure she wasn't dreaming. When she realized what she was staring at wasn't a dream, she said, "Taz, baby, what are—"

"Look, Li'l Mama, I ain't got time for questions right now. I gots to go get ready to get up outta here. I kinda got an idea of what's goin' on in that beautiful head of yours. Don't trip. I'll explain everything when I get back. Just trust me, okay?"

"Okay, Taz, but you definitely have some explaining to do, mister."

He smiled, gave her a quick kiss, and said, "Fa' sho! Now, let me go. I'll give you a call later on this evening if I can. If not, I'll call you sometime in the morning. I love you, Sacha."

"I love you, too, Taz."

They shared a quick kiss, and Taz jumped out of his truck and went inside of his home through the garage.

Sacha climbed over and got comfortable in the driver's side of his truck. After she adjusted the seat, she put the Denali in reverse and backed out of the driveway. As she turned onto the street, she stared in disbelief at what looked like a small fleet of all-black trucks driving past her and pulling into Taz's driveway: Keno's all-black Range Rover, Red's all-black Tahoe, Bo-Pete's all-black Navigator, Wild Bill's all-black Durango, and Bob's all-black Escalade. "Yeah, you're going to be explaining your ass off when you get back, Taz!" Sacha said as she drove away from his home.

Inside of Taz's house, the crew was waiting for Taz to let them know where they were going to now. Taz was sitting down in his den, tapping on the keys of his laptop. After about five minutes of this, he closed the laptop and said, "A'ight, it's like this. We're on our way to Chi-Town, boys. Keno and I are bouncing up outta Tulsa in two hours. Bo-Pete, you and Wild Bill are bouncin' up outta DFW, and Red, you and Bob gets to bounce up outta the City. The mission is set to go down tomorrow night, so we'll be spending at least a day out there. We're staying at the Courtyard Marriott in downtown Chicago. Our Barneys are intact so your rooms will be reserved. I'll hit y'all when we get in, and then we'll find out everything else. Any questions?"

"Yeah. What's the figures on this one?" asked Wild Bill.

"Oh, I forgot. Hold up," Taz said as he reopened the laptop and quickly tapped it's keys. After a few minutes of this, he smiled and passed the laptop to Wild Bill. Wild Bill smiled as he passed the laptop to Red. After the laptop had been passed to every member of the crew, Taz said, "Let's go earn our chips!"

Chapter Twelve

Later on that evening, Sacha was on the telephone with Gwen, explaining to her what she had seen earlier at Taz's home. "Girl, I'm telling you, that man has a fucking mansion! And the cars! Ho, he gots a damn Bentley!"

"Bitch, you lying!" yelled Gwen.

"I swear! What's the name of those loud-ass old type motorcycles them white boys be riding?"

"What, a Harley?"

"Yeah, ho, he even has one of those in his four-car garage."

"Four-car garage! Damn, he's got it like that, huh?"

"Yep. Oh, and did I mention the brand-new 600 Benz?"

"Stop it, bitch! You gone too damn far with that."

"I ain't lying. I'm telling you, Gwen, Taz is living large! My only question now is, how in the hell did he get it like that?"

"Didn't he tell you he owned a few restaurants and stuff?"

"Yeah, but ain't no way in hell can a nigga get money like he has with a few IHOPs and some rental houses."

"Why not? Shit, he might own way more than you think. Bitch, stop tripping out. I ain't never seen a woman who's mad 'cause she done found out the man she's in love with is rich. You are one silly bitch," said Gwen as she started laughing.

"Ho, I'm serious! You know I can't get caught up with no nigga who's into some illegal shit. I'd get disbarred. Ain't no man worth me losing my career over. I've worked too damn hard to let some shit like that happen to me."

"I hear you, Sacha, but didn't he tell you that he wasn't into anything illegal?"

"Yeah, but—"

"And you believed him, right?"

"Yeah, but—"

"But my ass, bitch! You're loving that man, so once he gets back, you ask him again just to satisfy your curiosity. Also, stress the fact that you can't risk being involved with someone who is into any illegal shit. If his answers are still the same after that, then you will have two choices to make. One, you believe him and move on with what y'all are trying to build, or two, you stop it right there and tell him that you just can't take the chance on him. It's as simple as that, Sacha," Gwen said seriously.

Before Sacha could speak, there was a click on her phone letting her know that there was another call coming in. "Hold on for a minute, ho," she said, and she clicked over to the next line. "Hello?"

"What up, Li'l Mama? You miss me yet?" asked Taz.

"Hey, Taz. Where are you?"

"Not too far. But check this out. I'll be back Friday evening. Do you want to get into anything particular, or do you wanna just chill at my spot?"

Sighing, she said, "Taz, we need to talk first."

"Hold up, Li'l Mama. I know you're out there thinking all types of shit, but I want you to think back to that time when we were at my IHOP. Remember what I told you what was a must for me, baby? Do you?" he urged.

Sacha thought back to that night for a minute and said, "Yes, I do, Taz."

"What was it?"

She smiled and said, "You said that it was a must that I believe you as well as in you."

"And do you?"

"Yes, but—"

"No buts, Li'l Mama. Do you or don't you believe me?"

"I do, Taz. I really do."

"Then don't trip off of any of the li'l shit. And believe me, all that you've seen so far is just that li'l shit. I told you from the beginning that I'm set financially for the rest of my life, so there's no reason for you to be letting your mind get you to trippin' out, thinking I'm *Scarface* and shit." He laughed, and then continued, "That's what you're doing, aren't you?"

Laughing herself, Sacha said, "I couldn't help it, baby. You know I can't risk ruining my career being involved with someone who's into some shady shit."

"I understand that, Li'l Mama, and you should know that I would never, and I mean *never*, put you or your career at risk. But look, I gots to bounce. I'll try to call you back later, after I finish handling my business."

"Taz, where are you?"

Laughing, he said, "Taking care of my business, Li'l Mama. I'll talk to you later. Now, tell me you love me before I bounce."

Smiling and blushing as if he was in the same room with her, she said, "I love you, baby."

"Good. I love you, too, Li'l Mama," he said and hung up the phone.

Sacha clicked back to Gwen and said, "Ho that was Taz."

"I figured that shit 'cause you was taking too damn long. The only reason I waited was because I wanted to know what he told your ass."

"He just reminded me of something he told me when we first met."

"And what was that, bitch?"

Smiling, she said, "That I should always believe in him, because he would never put me at risk."

"Do you?"

"Yeah, ho, I do. I love him, and my heart is telling me that he wouldn't do anything to jeopardize me or my career."

"Look at it this way. If he does, at least he has enough money to take care of your ass!" They both started laughing.

Clifford arrived at the office early in hopes of catching Sacha when she first came to work. He just couldn't get her out of his system. He wanted to be with her so badly that it actually hurt. *I have to convince her to give me another shot,* he thought to himself as he went into his office.

Sacha arrived at work in a really good mood. All was well, and she was in love! When she saw Clifford talking to one of the partners in front of her office, she almost stopped and went in the other direction. *I'm really starting to get tired of this nigga,* she thought as she held her head high and strolled confidently toward them.

"Good morning, gentlemen," she said once she was in front of Clifford and Mr. Whitney.

"Good morning, Sacha," they replied in unison.

"And a good morning it is, Sacha. I was just telling Clifford here that we're going to announce you becoming a partner at our annual Christmas party next week," Mr. Whitney said with a smile on his face.

Sacha beamed and said, "Really?"

"Yes, really. You will officially be a partner on the second day of the New Year. So, why not announce it at our party at the Westin's ballroom? So, you know the rules. Dress to impress, 'cause we're all going to have a real good time."

"Thank you, Mr. Whitney! Thank you so much!" she said sincerely.

"You've earned it, Sacha. You're one of the best attorneys in this entire firm."

"Congratulations, Sacha. This couldn't be happening to a sweeter person," Clifford said with a smile on his face.

"Thanks," she said flatly. "Well, if you two will excuse me, I have a court date in twenty minutes, and I have a few calls to make before I leave."

"Sure. Go get 'em, tiger!" Mr. Whitney said as he left her alone with Clifford.

Sacha went inside of her office, followed by Clifford. She went and sat behind her desk and quickly grabbed the phone. Even though she didn't have any calls to make, she dialed the number to her home, hoping that he would get the hint and leave her be, but her hopes were in vain. Clifford sat down in one of the leather chairs on the opposite side of her desk and waited patiently for her to finish. After letting her phone go to her voicemail, she finally hung up and asked, "Is there something that I can do for you, Cliff?"

Smiling, he said, "As a matter of fact, there is, Sacha. Could you please let me take you out Friday to celebrate your partnership?"

Sighing heavily, she said, "Cliff, look. We've been here before. Why do you insist on making this more difficult that it already is? I told you that I'm involved with someone, and it's serious. Can't you respect that and let it be?"

"To be completely honest with you, Sacha, no, I can't. I know that we were on our way to building something special, and I just can't get you or that night out of my mind. I really care about you. Can't you see that?"

"Yes, I do, Cliff. But you have to understand that what is done is done. Neither of us can go back and change what happened that night."

"I understand that, but can we at least try to move past that? Let me take you out to dinner Friday evening, Sacha. Come on, it's just a meal between colleagues."

Shaking her head no, she said, "I have plans for Friday, Cliff. As a matter of fact, I'm going to the same club that started all of this."

"You mean to tell me that you've become a regular at that ghetto-ass establishment? Come on, Sacha, that's really not your style."

"Humph! It may not be *your* style, but my man and I seem to enjoy ourselves whenever we're there."

"Your man?"

"Excuse me, Cliff, but I'm running late. I have to be in court in a few minutes." She grabbed her briefcase and left her office with Clifford standing in her doorway, mad as hell. *Let that one simmer for a minute, fool!* she thought as she left the office building on her way toward the courthouse.

Mission complete, thought Taz as he sat back in Keno's Range Rover for the ride back to the City. As usual, their job was smooth and easy. Won had done it again. *Now that the crew is four hundred thousand dollars richer, it is once again time to go clubbin',* he thought as he grabbed his cell and called Sacha. He frowned as he heard her voicemail pick up, and he left a quick message: "I'm back, baby. Give me a holla when you get this message. I'm trying to be with you tonight. I miss you. Bye!"

Keno smiled and said, "Damn, my nigga! You're in love for real, huh?"

"Looks that way, dog. She's the real thing, homey, and I'm not letting her get away from me."

"I feel you, gee. Do your thang, boy!" They both laughed as Keno drove them back to Oklahoma City.

By the time Sacha made it home, she was dead tired. For the last two days, she had been in and out of court, and back and forth from the courthouse to the county jail. Her client, Tony Surefield was starting to get on her nerves with his snitching-ass.

She slid off her shoes and went into her bedroom. After getting comfortable on her bed, she grabbed the phone and gave Gwen a call. "What's up, ho? I hope you haven't changed your mind about going to the club tonight," she asked as soon as Gwen answered the phone.

"That depends, bitch."

"On what?"

"On whether or not your man and his homies are back from their business trip. I'm trying to get me one of those rich-ass niggas for myself. Ain't no need in you having all of the damn fun, bitch!"

They both started laughing. Sacha said, "Ho, you're crazy for real. I haven't heard from Taz since last night. But he did tell me that he'd be back sometime this evening and that he would meet us at the club. So, I guess it's on."

"That's what I'm talking about! Bitch, I'm going all out tonight. Wait until you see what I'm wearing."

Laughing, Sacha said, "Oh, my God! I know you're about to be on some hoochie shit for real."

"Nah, bitch, it's all about classy and fine tonight. Wait, you'll see."

"Whatever! All right, girl, I'll be over to pick your ass up around ten. Cool?"

"Cool," said Gwen, and she hung up the phone.

After hanging up the phone with Gwen, Sacha got up and went to her closet. "I might as well get sexy for my baby," she said aloud as she began to pick out what she was going to wear to the club.

The rest of the crew made it to Taz's house a little after nine p.m. They went inside and completed their ritual of checking their accounts. After seeing that everything was in order, they waited for Won's phone call. And as usual, he was right on time.

"What's up, Babyboy?" asked Won when Taz answered his cell phone.

"The same ol' same, O.G."

"Y'all checked them accounts yet?"

"Yeah, everything is everything."

"Good. Nothing's going to go down for the rest of the year, so you know how it goes. Enjoy, be merry, and most of all, be good! Out!"

Taz laughed as he told the crew what Won had said. "Now, I guess we can bounce on to the club so y'all clowns can do y'all's thang. I doubt if I stay too long, though. Sacha's going to bring my truck, so I'll be bouncin' up outta there with her."

"Damn, you sprung-ass nigga! You can't even kick it with your boys for a li'l while?" asked Bo-Pete.

"Nigga, I'll chill for a minute, but I'm trying to get my freak on with my broad. I ain't tryin' to be all up in the bunk-ass club, lookin' at you niggas all night."

"Whatever, dog! Come on, let's bounce. There's hoes to catch and liquor to drink," Keno said as he stood up.

"I'm with you, my nigga," said Bob as he, too, got to his feet.

When they arrived at the club, Taz smiled when he saw his truck parked in his usual parking space. *It's good to see that the security at the club let Sacha park my shit where it normally sits,* he thought as he got out of Keno's Range Rover.

Bob parked his Escalade next to Bo-Pete's Navigator and climbed out of his truck. "Dog, I'm telling you, tonight I'm patching the baddest bitch in da club. I'm trying to go get my freak on somethin' awful," Bob said as he walked toward the entrance of Club Cancun.

"Whatever, clown! I'm tellin' yo' ass, I ain't with that carryin' you shit tonight, fool."

"The only person who's going to be carrying Bob tonight, is a bitch, nigga!"

Inside of the club, Katrina and Paquita were both busy hating on Gwen and Sacha. "I can't believe that bitch gots the nerve to be all up in here like she's the shit!" said Paquita.

"I know, girl. And look at her friend. She thinks she's flyer than a muthafucka in that mink wrap she gots on," added Katrina.

At their table, Sacha and Gwen both knew that they were looking especially fly. Their outfits spoke volumes to everyone around them. Several different guys came by and offered to buy them drinks, and they politely declined as they waited for Taz and his crew.

Sacha was dressed in a long, formfitting black Prada dress and red and black Prada pumps, while Gwen was just as sexy looking in a beige and brown suede jumpsuit and a dark brown chinchilla fur wrapped around her shoulders. Her brown Manolos set the outfit off completely.

"Bitch, where the hell is your man and his homies? 'Cause if they don't get their asses here soon, I'm gon' start choosing some of these fine-ass youngstas up in this spot."

Sacha smiled and said, "They'll be here, ho. Relax."

Back by the bar, Katrina smiled and said, "Girl, there goes Bo-Pete and Wild Bill."

"So? I ain't feelin' that nigga Taz no more. I don't give a fuck about his entrance and shit," Paquita said as she sipped her glass of E&J.

"What? You mean to tell me that my girl has finally given up? Bitch, say it ain't so!"

"Don't get me wrong. I'm still diggin' that nigga, but I'm just not gon' be all on his dick, even though you know I'd love to."

They both smiled and watched as Bo-Pete and Wild Bill entered the club and went and posted up in their normal spot. And just like always, Red and Bob followed about five minutes later and went to their normal spot. Then, finally, Keno and Taz came into the club.

Paquita's smile turned to a frown quickly when she noticed how Taz's eyes lit up when he spotted Sacha sitting at the table with Gwen. "I hate that bitch!"

Katrina didn't say anything. She just smiled at her homegirl and shook her head.

After Taz stepped to the bar and accepted the drink that Winky held out for him, he casually strolled over to Sacha and Gwen's table, followed by Keno. Once there, he said, "Damn, Li'l Mama! You're looking edible!"

Sacha smiled and said, "Hi, baby!" She stood, and they shared a long kiss, as if they were alone somewhere instead of in a jam-packed club. She pulled from Taz's embrace and said, "Whew! Do I get that every time you come back from a business trip?"

Taz smiled and said, "You better believe it! Now, introduce me to your friend."

"Oh, I'm sorry. Taz, this is Gwen. Gwen, this is my man, Taz."

Taz smiled and shook hands with the slim goody sitting in front of him and said, "Hello! I've heard a lot about you, Ms. Gwen."

Smiling herself, Gwen said, "And I've heard some fine things about you, Mr. Taz. And please, call me Gwen. That Ms. shit makes me feel old." They both started laughing.

"Excuse me, but I think you've forgotten about your homey, fool!" Keno said with a fake frown on his face.

Taz laughed and said, "My bad, dog! Ladies, this is my right-hand man, Keno. Keno, this is Sacha, my boo, and her friend, Gwen."

Keno shook hands with them and said, "It's nice to meet you both. Even though I've already met Sacha, your boo, it's still a pleasure."

"As you can see, he's a smart-ass, but I still love his ass," Taz said as he sat down next to Sacha.

"Well, y'all can excuse me. I see someone who wants to get better acquainted with me," said Keno as he left them to go chase a high yellow female with long hair, and a booty as big as Buffy the Body's.

Gwen frowned and said, "He's cute, but a li'l too cocky for me. Where's the rest of your homies, Taz? If I'm not mistaken, I was told that there were five of them."

"Damn, it's like that, huh?" asked Taz.

"Yep, it's like that," Gwen replied confidently.

Taz said, "All right then. Over there to the left are my niggas Bo-Pete and Wild Bill. See the real short one and the dark-skinned one standing right there?" He pointed to where Bo-Pete and Wild Bill were standing. "And over there to the far right are my niggas Red and Bob. The bigger one out of the two is Red, and the guy standing right next to him is Bob. So, those are your choices, Gwen. Which one would you care to meet first?" Taz asked with a smile on his face.

"Hmm, let me see. I love me some dark chocolate, so it's either going to be Bo-Pete or Bob," said Gwen as she looked back and forth from Bob to Bo-Pete. After about two minutes of deliberating, she said, "I want to meet Bob. He looks exciting."

Sacha and Taz both laughed and in unison said in a loud voice, "*Bob!*"

"That's right, bitch, Bob. I bet that nigga is packin'!"

Taz damn near spit out his drink when she said that. He wiped his face and waved over to Bob and signaled for him to come and join them.

Bob had a smile on his face as he came to the table. "What's up, my nigga? Hello, ladies."

"Dog, You seem to have been chosen by this pretty lady right here. Gwen, this is my nigga Bob. Bob, this is Gwen."

Gwen smiled wickedly and asked, "Tell me, Bob. How did you get that sexy-looking knot on your forehead?"

Bob smiled and said, "You like the knot, huh?"

"Umm-hmm! Love it!"

"Well, let's shake these two lovebirds for a minute so I can give you the history of the knot," Bob said as he winked at her.

As she got to her feet, Gwen smiled and said, "I'm with you, sexy."

Taz and Sacha were laughing so hard that tears were falling from their eyes as they watched Bob lead Gwen toward another table.

"Well, I'll be damn! She chose Bob! Of all niggas, she chose one of the freakiest niggas around!"

"Is that right? Well, I think Bob might have met his match tonight, 'cause my girl puts the capital F in the word *freak!*" They both started laughing some more. "Now, tell me, where were you, Taz? You never did tell me where you had to go and why."

He smiled at her and said, "I was in Chi-town, Li'l Mama. And like I told you, I went to take care of some business."

"For some of your properties?"

"You're not going to give up, are you?"

"Look, I trust you, baby. I really do. I just have to be certain that everything is on the up-and-up with you, that's all."

"I can dig that, but check this out. My business is complex and yet simple at the same time. Simple, because all I do in this state is make sure that my rental houses are in order and everything is straight. As for the IHOPs and the Popeyes chicken restaurants, my managers take care of them, so it's an easy process with them. I sign the checks and pay my taxes. I own close to fifty homes throughout the City. I even own a couple in your neighborhood. My yearly income in this state alone is close to two hundred thousand a year. So you see, Li'l Mama, I've never lied to you. I just chose not to speak on that shit 'cause I'm not with the braggin' and shit."

"Okay, I can understand that. I guess that's the simple part. But what about the complex part, Taz?"

Staring at her seriously, he said, "That, my love, is none of your business. Please don't press me about it, Sacha. Just try your best to understand what I'm about to say. If I tell everybody my business, I won't have any business at all."

Smiling as she shook her head from side to side, she said, "That's just too damn slick, Mister Taz."

"Nah, Li'l Mama, that's just keeping it real with you. So, like I said before, don't you worry about me ever putting you or your career in jeopardy, because that will never happen. Cool?"

"Yeah, we cool. Can I ask you one more thing, babe?"

Laughing, he said, "Anything baby . . . anything at all!"

"How many rooms do you have in that big-ass house of yours?"

He laughed even harder than he did about Gwen and Bob. After regaining his composure, he said, "That, my love, you'll find out later on. If you'd like, we can make love in every one of them when we get to my spot."

"That, Mister Taz, is something that I definitely would like to do!"

He smiled at her and said, "Yeah, I bet you would, with your horny-ass!"

"You know it! You done got it started, so you better be prepared for it."

"As long as I stay ready, I'll never have to get ready, Li'l Mama."

"Good."

Clifford couldn't believe his eyes. Sacha and her best friend, Gwen, were chillin' out with those wannabe thug-ass niggas. "Ain't that a bitch! She done chose a nigga that's most likely going to be in federal prison before the summer's over. I can't believe this shit!" he said aloud as he sipped his drink. He had decided earlier to come to the club and see for himself exactly what type of nigga Sacha had chosen over him. And now as he stood in the back of the club and watched her, he just couldn't accept this shit. He set his drink down and stormed toward Sacha and Taz's table. He stepped straight to them and said, "What's up, Sacha?"

Sacha looked up and saw Clifford standing over her with a mean mug look on his face. She smirked and said, "What's up, Cliff?"

"So, this is your man?" he asked while pointing toward Taz.

Sacha smiled and said, "Yes, he is. What do you want, Cliff? As you can see, I'm enjoying my evening with my man, and you're interrupting us."

"Interrupting you! Ain't that a bitch! Come on, Sacha. I know you're not going to go out like that."

Before Sacha could respond, Taz felt that enough was enough. *It's time for this chump to be checked,* he thought as he stood up from the table and said, "Look, dog. Ain't no need for any drama tonight. My girl has told you what time it is, so you need to get to steppin'."

"Fuck you, nigga! I ain't going nowhere until we can get a better understanding out of this shit! And the 'we' I'm referring to is Sacha and myself! Not you, fool!"

Taz couldn't believe what he had just heard. He shook his head slowly from side to side and asked, "Are you sure you're trying to go that route, nigga? 'Cause if you are, I want you to remember that this was your call," he said menacingly.

"Like I said, fuck you!" Clifford yelled. He turned his attention back toward Sacha and said, "Sacha, I really think we should leave this place so we can go somewhere and talk."

"*What?* Cliff, haven't you been hearing what I've repeatedly told you? This is my man, not you, so leave me the fuck alone!"

Her words were like a knife going straight inside of his chest. The pain was unbearable. Clifford didn't realize that he was reaching for Sacha's arm until he felt Taz's right hand on his forearm. "If you touch my girl, you're going to regret it, fool!" Taz said as he shoved Clifford away from the table.

Keno and Red were both talking to some females on the other side of the club when they noticed Taz's confrontation with Clifford. They quickly left the females they were conversing with and went to Taz's side. So did Bo-Pete, Wild Bill, and Bob, who had left Gwen out on the dance floor when he saw Taz shove Clifford.

Clifford saw that Taz's homeboys had him surrounded, and smiled. "Just like I thought. You ain't no man, nigga. You need your boys with you in order to help your soft-ass fight. You're coward-ass nigga!"

Taz smiled and said, "That's funny, clown. But my niggas are here for *your* safety, nigga, 'cause they're the only ones who could stop me from serving your soft ass. Why don't you go on and bounce, dog? You're way out of your league," he said calmly.

Before Clifford could respond, Sacha said, "I don't know what the fuck's gotten into you, Cliff, but you really need to check yourself because you are way out of line. So, would you please leave us alone before someone gets hurt?"

Clifford was confused, hurt, and mad as hell, but he was no one's fool. He stared at Taz and his crew, smiled and said, "Yeah, I'll leave you alone, Sacha." He turned and faced Taz and said, "But I'm going to see you again when you don't have your boys, partna. Then we'll see how good your hands really are."

Taz was laughing as he watched Clifford leave the club.

Without a word being said, Keno and Red returned to the ladies that they were talking to before they had gone to Taz's side. Bo-Pete and Wild Bill went back by the bar where they had been standing before the commotion, and Bob grabbed Gwen's hand and said, "Come on, baby, they're playin' our song!" Gwen smiled and let Bob lead her back out on the dance floor.

Taz sat back down and asked, "What's up with that clown, Li'l Mama?"

"I honestly don't know, baby. We were going out for awhile, that is, until I met you and I told him that it was over. But I guess he can't accept it."

"He has no choice. And if he gets in my way again, he's going to get hurt."

"Come on, Taz, he's not worth it, baby," Sacha said as she grabbed ahold of Taz's hand. But as she looked into his dark brown eyes, she knew that if Cliff ever caused any more drama, he was in some serious trouble. She could tell that Taz was not a man to be fucked with.

Taz calmed himself, smiled, and said, "So, are you ready to shake this spot, baby? We do have some rooms at my pad that need to be touched, don't we?"

Sacha blushed and said, "Yes, we do, baby. I'm ready if you are."

Taz turned and waved toward Red and Keno. They came over to their table, and Keno said, "What's up, my nigga?"

"Dog, I'm out. Go holla at Bob and see if he's going to take Gwen home or what."

Red turned and went to go talk to Bob, and Keno said, "Dog, you might not want to leave just yet. Look who just came into the club."

Taz turned and frowned when he saw Tazneema and Lyla walking toward the bar. "Now how in the hell did they get in here? They ain't even twenty-one!" he said to himself louder than he intended to.

"Come on, nigga. Since when did you have to be twenty-one to get into any club in the City?" Keno pointed out honestly.

"Yeah, I know, huh? Man, go get her ass and bring her over here for me, gee."

"Gotcha," said Keno as he went over toward the bar.

"Who are you guys talking about, Taz?" Sacha asked as she tried to see who they were talking about.

Before Taz could answer her, Gwen and Bob came to their table and sat down. Bob smiled and said, "Sacha, I guess I owe you one, 'cause I think I'm in love!" They all started laughing.

Gwen shook her head and said, "Uh-uh, nigga! You ain't in love . . . yet. Wait 'til I put this thang on your ass! Then, you'll be in love!"

Taz shook his head and laughed. "So, I guess you're going to go on and take Gwen home for us, then, huh?"

"Nah, my nigga, I ain't taking her home. She's coming home with me!"

Taz stared at Bob as if he'd lost his mind. They normally didn't get down like that until after they were sure the females they were fucking with were straight. That usually took at least a month or so. That's why it had taken Taz so long to let Sacha know where he lived. Caution was a must with them. Taz was shocked at Bob's words, but he felt comfortable that Gwen was all good, so he didn't speak on it.

Keno brought Tazneema and Lyla over to the table and said, "Taz, guess who I've found?"

Taz turned and smiled at Tazneema and said, "So, you're hangin' in clubs now, huh?"

"I'm grown, Taz," Tazneema said with a smile on her face.

"Hi, Taz. I told your sister that you might be up in here, but she said that the club wasn't your thing," Lyla said, smiling at him.

Taz smiled and said, "Don't worry about it. It ain't no thang. 'Neema, I want you to meet someone. Sacha, this is Tazneema. 'Neema, this is Sacha."

Sacha smiled and said, "It's nice to meet you, Tazneema."

After they had shaken hands, Tazneema said, "Please, call me 'Neema." She stared at Sacha briefly and realized just like Mama-Mama had that they were in love with each other. It was written all over both of their faces. She smiled and said, "Ooh, she's your girlfriend!"

Taz started laughing and said, "Yeah, she's my Li'l Mama. Do you approve?"

Smiling brightly, she said, "Yeah, she's cool. But what about Tari? Oops! I mean . . . you . . . you know what . . . I . . . never mind. Look, I'm about to go over and get me something to drink, okay?"

With a frown on his face, Taz said, "Yeah, you go on and do that. Oh, before you go, I spoke with Mama-Mama. You can go spend the holidays with Lyla and her family."

"For real? Thank you, Taz!" She gave him a hug and a kiss on his cheek, said good-bye to Sacha, and led Lyla toward the bar.

Sacha, who had caught what Tazneema had said, was frowning at Taz, who was trying to avoid eye contact with her. He looked up at Keno and said, "Dog, I'm goin' to need you to stay until the club lets out. Keep an eye on her for me, gee."

"Don't trip, dog. You know we got her. Go on and do you. See ya later, Sacha," Keno said as he left them alone.

Sacha tapped Taz lightly on his hand and asked, "Who's Tari, Taz?"

Taz sighed and said, "Somebody that you're about to meet. Come on."

Chapter Thirteen

When Taz and Sacha left the club, neither of them saw Clifford watching them from inside of his car as they climbed inside of Taz's truck. "Gotcha!" Clifford said as he quickly wrote down Taz's license plate number. Once they pulled out of the parking lot of the club, he smiled and started his car and went home feeling confident again about his and Sacha's future together.

Sacha was silent as she listened to Taz talk to someone on his cell phone. "Wake up, girl. I told you I'm on my way."

"Taz, why do you insist on waking me every time you choose to come over here?" whined Tari. "I do work, you know."

"Yeah, I know, but I need you to be up when I get there. I'm bringing someone for you to meet. And it . . . it's kind of important."

That statement grabbed Tari's attention. She sat up in her bed and asked, "A woman, Taz?"

He sighed and said, "Yeah."

Her tone changed to a more businesslike one when she said, "Okay, I'll be up by the time you get here. Good-bye."

After hanging up with Tari, Taz felt like his heart was going to pop outside of his chest. He couldn't remember the last time that he was this nervous. *Man, she's hot! I can tell,* he thought as he turned onto the highway, headed toward the city of Moore.

Sacha noticed that Taz was uncomfortable, and that made her all the more curious, but she chose to remain silent as long as he did.

After about twenty minutes or so, Taz said, "We're almost there. I'd rather have to say this once, because this shit is kinda hard for me, Li'l Mama. And please, don't trip out. This is something that I've been dreading since I realized how deeply I care about you. I've never lied, Li'l Mama, I just didn't exactly come completely clean with you. I hope that this won't hurt us or get in the way of our future," he said as he pulled into Tari's driveway.

"Well, I guess we're about to find out, Taz," Sacha replied with more attitude than she intended to.

Tari was standing at her front door as she watched Taz and Sacha get out of his truck. *Well, I'll be! He's finally found someone he can really love. Now ain't that somethin'!*

Taz stepped onto Tari's porch with Sacha's hand in his and said, "What's up, Tee?"

"It's late, Taz. Come on inside so we can get this over with." Tari turned her back to them and went back inside of her house. She was smiling as she entered her home—smiling because of how nervous Taz looked. She couldn't remember the last time she had seen him look so cute. *Ahh, my baby is nervous because he thinks he's going to hurt my feelings! That's so special!* she thought to herself. She turned and motioned for them to have a seat on her sofa and said, "I'd offer you both something to drink, but I have a feeling that Taz really wants to get whatever off of his chest. So, the floor is yours, babe." She sat down on the floor in front of her floor model sixty-inch big-screen television.

Taz got to his feet and said, "Tari, this is Sacha, and Sacha, this is Tari. I really don't know how to say this shit without it upsetting either of you, so I'm just gon' spit it out." Turning toward Tari, he said, "Tee, I love this woman, and if she lets me, I want to be with her for the rest of my life."

Before Tari could respond, he turned toward Sacha and said, "Li'l Mama, Tari's been my friend, my confidante, as well as my lover, for a very long time. She will always be a major part of my life . . . always. But since we've hooked up, I've realized that it's you that I want in my life in that very special way. I love you, Li'l Mama. Now, I'll take a seat and let the both of you rip me apart," he said as he went and sat down next to Sacha, praying that this soap opera shit worked out in his favor.

Tari and Sacha smiled at one another. Sacha spoke first. "Tari, I want you to know that it is a pleasure to meet you. I have no ill feelings toward you or your relationship with Taz. I love him just as deeply, and if you are a major factor in his life, then I want you to know that you will mean just as much to me."

Intelligent, pretty, and sincere. I like that, Taz. I really do. You done good, babe. You done damn good! Tari said to herself. She smiled and said, "Thank you for that, Sacha. I do love this man, and I know for a fact that I always will. I don't know why he's so damn nervous, but I think it's so cute that he is. That shows me that he cares for me just as much as I've always figured he did. I've waited for years for this day to come. I've always known that I was not the woman for him. I am surprised that it has finally happened, though. For a minute there I thought our relationship, however strange it is, might just be able to make it. But now, I see the love you have for each other in the both of your eyes. I feel so happy for the both of you."

Taz sighed in relief, and Sacha smiled.

Tari continued, "I have only one thing to say to you, Sacha, and please don't take offense, because I'm speaking from my heart here. Don't ever hurt this man, whatever you do. Don't you ever cause him any pain. Because if you do, then you will see how unruly a white woman can be."

Sacha smiled and said, "Well, that's something that I'm really not looking forward to." They both laughed, and then Sacha said, "I respect everything you've said, Tari, and I give you my word that I'll love this man with all of my heart as long as he'll let me. And I'll never, and I mean *never,* hurt him." Turning toward Taz, she said, "But if you ever keep anything from me that is as important as this is, I might break your neck, mister!"

They all laughed, and Taz felt the tension leave his body in waves. He smiled at the both of them and said, "I love you two more than you both will ever know. Thank you, Tari, for not trippin' the fuck out on me. And thank you, Li'l Mama, for understanding. I didn't know how to tell you about Tari without pissing you off. That's why I had been procrastinating."

"So, what made you decide to get it over with?" asked Tari.

Before he could answer Tari's question, Sacha said, "His little sister let it slip at the club earlier."

Tari and Taz stared at each other momentarily, and then Tari said, "Ahh, so you've had the pleasure of meeting Tazneema, I see."

"Yes, I have, and she seems like a very sweet girl. She looks so much like this joker that they could pass for twins."

Taz smiled and said, "Well, I guess we'll be getting outta here now, Tee. I know you gots to get some rest for work in the morning."

"Yeah, I do. Umm, excuse me, Sacha, but could I have a moment alone with Taz before y'all leave?"

"Sure. I'll be in the truck, baby. And once again, it was very nice meeting you, Tari."

"Same here, girl. Don't worry, we'll be seeing a lot of each other." Tari waited for Sacha to leave her home before she spoke. After the front door was closed, she said, "Love is a wonderful thing, isn't it?"

"Yeah, I guess it is. But to tell you the truth, I never thought it was for me. That is until I met Sacha. I'm tellin' you, Tee, the first time I laid eyes on her I knew that she was the one."

"That's good, baby. I meant what I said earlier, that if she ever hurts you, I'm going to hurt her something awful."

Taz laughed and said, "I don't think she'll ever get down like that, Tee. But it's good to know that you still got my back."

"Always. How much have you told her about your lifestyle?"

"Not much."

Laughing, she said, "Yeah, I can tell."

"She knows about the IHOPs, the rental houses, as well as the Popeye spots. But that's about it."

"Everything that's in the dark will sooner or later come to the light, Taz. If you love her, you're going to have to trust her."

"I know. But she's a lawyer. She can't afford to know what my real bread and butter is, at least not right now."

"True. Don't wait too long on telling her everything that's vital in your life, Taz. Or you'll risk losing her. It's been way too long since you've been able to love like this, so don't fuck it up," Tari said seriously.

"I won't. Now, give me a kiss so I can get the fuck up outta here," he said as he wrapped his arms around her waist and they shared a quick kiss.

"Damn! I guess that means you can't even come and break me off from time to time, huh?" Before he could answer, she smiled and said, "Don't worry about me, boy. I'm going to be all right."

Staring directly into Tari's eyes, he said, "I know, 'cause I'm always going to make sure that you're straight. Always. I don't think we're doing any traveling for the rest of the year, so everything is everything. I'll get at ya before we do bounce, though."

Tari yawned and stretched and said, "All right. I hope my babies like Sacha, 'cause if they don't, she's in some big trouble, and so are you, for that matter." They both started laughing as Tari walked Taz to the door.

When Taz got inside of the truck, he smiled and said, "That lady is truly something special."

"I can tell that you two are really close. How long have you been . . . you know?"

He smiled and said, "From the days when I just didn't give a fuck."

"What's that supposed to mean, baby?"

Taz smiled and said, "Nothin'. I guess it's time for us to go touch those rooms, huh?" he asked, hoping she would let it go.

Smiling seductively, Sacha said, "Yes, I guess it is."

They arrived at Taz's home a little after three in the morning. During the drive back toward the City, Sacha decided that they'd better stop and get something to eat, so they had a quick breakfast at a local Waffle House.

Now that they were at home, Taz was excited. He was excited because his life finally seemed to have a purpose again; excited about being able to make love to a woman other than Tari at his home; and excited to actually feel alive again. *Damn! And it feels real good!* Taz thought as he showed Sacha around his home.

By the time they made it downstairs to the gym area, Sacha felt as if she was watching the *Lifestyles of the Rich and Famous* television show. *This nigga is living larger than I thought,* she said to herself as she dipped her foot into the Olympic-sized swimming pool. She frowned for a moment and said, "I thought you told me that you went to a gym when you worked out."

Smiling, he said, "I did. I just didn't tell you that it was inside of my home."

She punched him lightly on his arm and said, "All right, mister, what else do you have in store for me?"

He grabbed her by her slender arms, pulled her close to him, and said, "First, you have to meet two more of my special loved ones. And after that, it's time for some of the wildest lovemaking you've ever had in your life."

Smiling, Sacha said, "I'm ready whenever you are, baby. Now, who are these two other special loved ones?"

Taz smiled and said, "Whether you believe me or not, they've been watching you ever since we came into the house."

"What are you talking about?"

He smiled and said, "Heaven and Precious, come meet Li'l Mama."

Taz's two prized Dobermans came trotting out of the gym area as if they had been a part of the gym equipment. They had been observing their master and guest from a distance when they had first entered the house. Taz had them trained especially for stealth and stalking tactics. They were trained to kill at the slightest sign of danger to Taz, and anyone he deemed friendly. Both Heaven and Precious stopped in front of Sacha and raised their wet noses toward her hands.

Sacha was fascinated yet terrified. She couldn't believe that these dogs had been watching them the entire time they had been inside of the house. She reached down and patted them both on their heads and said, "Hey, Heaven! Hey, Precious!"

Taz laughed and said, "Heaven is on your left, and Precious is on the right."

"Oh, I'm sorry," she said as she turned to her left and said, "I'm sorry, Heaven." Then to her right she said, "Forgive me, Precious." She then rubbed both of them gently under their chins.

The Dobermans seemed to like Sacha, because the both of them began licking her hands and tried their best to keep her attention.

Taz smiled and said, "Well, it looks like you're a hit. Now that that's out of the way, are you ready to do the damn thang?"

Sacha looked toward Taz and said, "Whenever you are, lover! Whenever you are!"

Taz shook his head and said, "Protect us, Heaven. Protect us, Precious." Both of the Dobermans' ears became alert as they trotted out of the room. Taz said, "Come on, Li'l Mama. We're completely safe now, so let's go play!"

"Let the games begin!"

Chapter Fourteen

Sacha smiled when she opened her eyes the next morning. She smiled because she saw Precious and Heaven sitting by the door, alert and aware of their surroundings. *Taz didn't play around when it came to his safety,* she thought as she climbed out of his bed.

She went into the restroom and turned on the shower. While she was showering, she was trying to figure out a way to ask Taz to accompany her to the firm's Christmas party next week. She loved him so much, and she wanted her coworkers to meet him. Shit, she wanted the world to know about her and Taz! *But damn, Taz's platinum grille and all of the flossy diamonds he wore are just a bit much,* she thought as she lathered herself with a scented bar of Taz's soap. She made up her mind by the time she finished her shower. Taz was her man, and the grille and the diamonds were a part of him. "I love everything about that man, so who gives a fuck what my coworkers will think?" she said aloud as she wrapped herself in one of Taz's big fluffy, towels.

When she stepped back into the bedroom, Taz was still sleeping soundly. She smiled as she dropped the towel and climbed back in bed with him. She shook him lightly and said, "Taz, wake up, baby."

Taz had been awake ever since she first climbed out of his bed. He was so content with her being in his bed that it didn't make any sense. He opened his eyes, smiled, and said, "Good morning, sexy. How long you been up?" He played with a few strands of her wet hair.

"About twenty minutes. I just finished taking a quick shower."

"I can tell. Your hair is still wet."

"Baby, I need to ask a favor of you, okay?"

As he sat up in the bed, he asked, "What's up, Li'l Mama?"

"Well, next week the firm is having our annual Christmas party, and I'd really like for you to come with me. You see, the partners are going to announce my partnership, and I . . . well . . . It would mean a lot to me if you were there with me."

Smiling, Taz said, "I don't have a problem with that. When is it exactly, so I can make sure that I'm free?"

"Next Friday. It's going to be a real dressy-dressy type of an affair."

With a raised eyebrow he asked, "What's dressy-dressy mean, Li'l Mama?"

"You know, suit and tie stuff. You can do a suit and a tie, can't you?"

Taz smiled and said, "Yeah, I can clean up when I want to. Don't worry, Li'l Mama. I'll make sure we leave your peers with a positive impression."

"What do you mean by that?"

"Look, I know you were nervous about asking me to join you next week. It's written all over your face. And then you're probably worried about what your peers are going to think of you bringing a guy like myself to your party. But don't trip, Li'l Mama. Like I told you before, I'd never do anything to jeopardize your career. And I meant that. In fact, you'll be surprised at exactly how much I mean it."

"What's that supposed to mean, mister?" she asked, relieved that he wasn't offended.

"You'll see. Now, let me get up. The homies should be arriving any minute for our workout."

"Y'all work out on the weekends too?"

"Not really. Today is our running day. We're going to go run a few miles. Then we'll come back and chill out. Do you have any plans for the day?"

"Not really. I was going to call Gwen and see if she wanted to get into anything."

"That's cool. After I run, I was going to go check on a few of my rental houses. Then the rest of the day I was hoping we could chill out."

"That's fine with me."

"Have I told you that I loved you this morning?"

With a mock pout on her face, she said, "No, you haven't, Taz."

Smiling, he said, "Damn, I love it when you stick that bottom lip out like that! Come here, baby!" They shared a deep kiss for a full minute. Taz pulled away from her face and said, "I love you, Li'l Mama."

"I love you, too, baby," she said, and they started kissing each other again.

Bo-Pete and Wild Bill pulled up to Taz's home, followed by Keno. Just as they were getting out of their trucks, Red, Bob, and Gwen pulled into the driveway.

"What the fuck is this?" asked Keno when he saw Gwen getting out of Red's Tahoe, followed by Bob.

Bob smiled and said, "What up, niggas? Y'all ready to get y'all's run on this morning?"

Wild Bill smiled and said, "Nigga, we might not be doing no damn running after Taz sees that you've brought a fuckin' guest."

"Shut the fuck up, li'l man! I just got off of the phone with him. He knows I brought my baby with me. She's hooking up with Sacha."

"Is that right? So, Sacha's inside, huh?" asked Keno.

"Yep. So I guess you guys better get used to us being around, 'cause we're going to be here awhile. Ain't that right, babe?" asked Gwen.

Smiling from ear to ear, Bob answered, "You damn skippy!"

"Damn, she must have really put that thang on that nigga!" said Bo-Pete with a smile on his face. They all were laughing as they went inside of Taz's home.

Taz, who had opened the door for them, asked, "What's so damn funny, clowns? What's up, Gwen? I see my nigga has made a good impression."

"Yes, indeed. Where's my girl Taz?" she asked as she looked around his spacious home.

"Here I am, girl. Come on up here so they can go on and get their run on. Baby, I'm going to take Gwen home. Then, after I change, I'll be back, okay?"

"Yeah, that's cool. Do you want to take the truck or what?" asked Taz.

Smiling mischievously, she said, "I'd rather take the Benz."

Taz laughed loudly and said, "Well, take it then. The keys are on the dresser, next to my jewelry." Turning toward his homies, he said, "All right, clowns, let's go do this."

Gwen gave Bob a kiss and said, "Give me a call after you're finished, lover. You know we gots some more work to put in later on."

"Without a doubt, baby girl," said Bob. They quickly shared a kiss.

The rest of the crew was laughing and clowning with Bob as they went back outside.

Sacha led Gwen upstairs to the bedroom and showed her around a little. "Damn, this nigga is living large! Look at the size of this place!" yelled Gwen.

"What's up with Bob? How's his place look?" asked Sacha as she sat down on the bed.

"It's real nice, bitch. Real nice. But it's nothing as fancy as this. Bob's more laid back, but you can tell he's got plenty of loot. He has expensive black paintings all around the place. And the bed! Bitch, the bed is the biggest bed I've ever seen!"

"You mean it's bigger than this one?" Sacha asked as she patted Taz's bed. "This is a California king-sized bed. This is, I think, the biggest they come."

"Nah, bitch, that there bed is small compared to my babe's. I'm telling you, bitch, when I say huge, I mean huge!"

"What! Come on, let's go downstairs so I can show you the rest of the house."

Gwen followed Sacha as she gave her the same tour of the house that Taz had given her the night before. By the time they made it to the gym, Gwen was completely speechless.

Sacha was smiling, because during the entire time she was showing Gwen around the house, Gwen hadn't noticed once that they were being followed by Heaven and Precious. Hell, the only reason why she knew it was because she'd spotted them coming out of the bathroom as they left the bedroom to go downstairs. *Damn, they're good!* she thought as she led Gwen toward the pool and Jacuzzi. "You like, ho?"

"I like! I like, bitch! Taz is the fucking man!"

They both started laughing. "Before we leave, I have to show you something. Now please, whatever you do, don't freak the fuck out on me, okay?"

"What are you talking 'bout, bitch?"

"Just relax, and watch." Sacha turned toward the gym, where she had watched Heaven and Precious enter after they had made it to the pool, and said, "Heaven and Precious, come and meet my friend Gwen."

Gwen's eyes damn near popped out of their sockets when she saw Heaven and Precious come trotting out of the gym. Once they were at her side, she stood frozen and scared shitless.

Sacha saw how nervous she was and laughed. "Girl, go on and pet them. They won't hurt you."

Gwen rubbed and softly petted the deadly Dobermans on top of their heads and watched, horrified, as they began to rub their wet noses on her hands. "O-okay, Sacha! Tell them to go bye-bye now, okay?"

Sacha smiled and said, "Protect us, Heaven. Protect us, Precious." Both of the Dobermans' ears rose at Sacha's command as they turned and trotted out of the room.

"Bitch, I done seen it all!"

They both laughed as they left and went back upstairs.

Chapter Fifteen

It was the night of Sacha's firm's Christmas party, and Taz was late. She couldn't believe that he would do this to her! Sacha was a nervous wreck as she paced back and forth in her living room. Here she was, dressed to fucking kill in a tight, formfitting Versace dress and matching Versace pumps, and Taz was fucking late! "I'm gon' kill him! I swear God, I'm going to kill him!" she screamed as she stormed back into her bedroom.

Just as she was coming back into the living room, there was a knock at her door. All of Sacha's anger evaporated when she opened the front door and saw Taz standing in front of her, looking like dapper don himself. He was dressed elegantly in a tailor-made Armani suit and black alligator shoes. The silk peach shirt and peach tie complemented his black suit perfectly. But what shocked her the most was his smile. When he smiled, she damn near felt faint. His diamond and platinum grille had been replaced with one of the most beautiful smiles she had ever seen. His white teeth seemed to sparkle, they were so bright.

"Damn, Li'l Mama! Are you going to let me in, or are you just going to stare at me all damn evening? We do have a party to attend, don't we?" he asked with that gorgeous smile of his.

"Baby, when you said you cleaned up good, you weren't lying!"

"I guess I should take that as a compliment, then, huh?"

Nodding her head yes, she said, "Yes, you should. Let me go get my purse. Then we can go, okay?"

"All right. I'll be outside in the car. I brought the Azure, or would you have preferred the Six?"

Smiling brightly, she said, "You know I would've preferred the Six, but the Azure is cool too. Ain't nothing wrong with pulling up somewhere in a Bentley."

Taz laughed and said, "Go on and get your stuff. I'll be in the car."

Once Sacha came and got inside of the car, Taz asked her, "Didn't you tell me that that clown nigga who was gettin' at you also worked at the same firm as you?"

"Shit! He does! Baby, I didn't even think about that. Please don't let Cliff ruin this evening for me. If he says anything, just ignore him, okay?"

"I can't make any promises, Li'l Mama. But as long as that fool stays out of arms reach of me, he won't get the shit smacked out of his soft-ass. That's about the best I can do for you."

Smiling, she said, "Fair enough."

Taz pulled the Bentley Azure in front of the valet parking at the Westin Hotel in downtown Oklahoma City. One of the young valets came and opened the door for the both of them. Taz stepped quickly around the car, and they entered the hotel with their arms linked together.

Sacha had a huge smile on her face as they entered the ballroom. Here she was, about to officially become a partner. All of her dedication and hard work had finally paid off. To make everything even sweeter, she had her man, Taz, by her side. This was definitely going to be a night to remember. She led Taz toward a table that she saw was reserved for them. After they were seated, she said, "Thank you for coming with me tonight, baby. This really means a lot to me."

"Don't trip, Li'l Mama. Tonight's your night to shine. I'm just glad that you have let me be a part of it."

Before he continued, a tall, immaculately dressed brother came to their table and said, "Mr. Good? How are you doing, sir?"

Taz looked up from his seat, smiled, and said, "Edward! How are you?" He stood, and they both shook hands. "I'm sure you know Sacha here."

"Oh, yes, she's one of the most talked about people at the firm nowadays. Good evening, Sacha."

"Hello, Edward," Sacha said as she glanced at Taz with a puzzled look on her face.

Edward noticed the look and said, "Don't tell me that Sacha doesn't know that you're one of the firm's most prized clients, Mr. Good."

Taz laughed and said, "Come on, Edward. I wouldn't go so far as to say one of the most prized clients."

"I don't see why not. Hell, I make a nice chunk maintaining all of your finances, Mr. Good. And I'm quite sure when Mr. Whitney and old man Johnson find out that you're here with Sacha, they'll be delighted." They all laughed. "Well, I'll leave you two now. I saw you when you two came in and thought I'd come say hello. Oh, congratulations on your partnership, Sacha. You deserve it."

"Thank you, Edward. Don't worry. Your turn is coming."

Smiling, he said, "I sure hope so. See you guys later."

After Edward had left their table, Sacha smiled at Taz and said, "One of Whitney & Johnson's most prized clients? Humph! I should have known. You are just too damn slick, Mister Taz!"

Taz started laughing and said, "Baby, it's a small town we live in. How was I to know that you worked for the law firm that I let handle most of my business? Are you mad at me, Li'l Mama?"

"No, I'm not mad. I just wish you would have told me. Taz, you make me sick sometimes, with all of your little secrets!"

"Secrets? Uh-uh. Remember what I told you about my business?"

"Uh-huh. If you tell me all of your business, you won't have any business at all. Bullshit!"

They both started laughing as a waiter approached them and asked them if they would like anything to drink. Taz ordered an XO for himself and an apple martini for Sacha.

While they were waiting for their drinks, several attorneys from Whitney & Johnson came over to their table and spoke to both Sacha and Taz. Sacha was shocked to learn that the firm she worked for handled all of Taz's business affairs, everything from the trust fund he had set up for Tazneema to his will. But what shocked her most was when Mr. Whitney and Mr. Johnson came over to their table and told them that they were extremely happy to see that they were an item. *My man is not only richer than I could have ever imagined, he's completely legal! Thank you, Lord!* she thought to herself as she accepted her drink from the waiter.

Taz was sipping his drink when he almost spit it all over Sacha's expensive dress. He set his glass on the table, wiped his mouth, smiled, and said, "Well, I'll be damn! Why didn't you tell me they were coming, Li'l Mama?"

Sacha smiled and said, "Bob made me promise not to. He wanted to surprise you." They both watched as Bob led Gwen toward their table.

"What's up, my brother? How are you this evening?" asked Bob, who was dressed just as clean as Taz was in a brown, tailor-made suit by Christian Dior. His Italian loafers completed the elegant but casual look he was sporting. Gwen was looking gorgeous herself, in a tan dress with her hair hanging past her shoulders.

Taz couldn't front. They were looking real good this evening. After they were seated, Taz said, "So, I see she's a keeper, huh?"

"Yeah, my nigga, she's here to stay," Bob replied confidently.

Sacha couldn't believe her eyes. Her girl Gwen was actually blushing. *Shit, I haven't seen her act like this since William,* she thought to herself as she continued to stare at her best friend. She smiled and then said, "You know what? This has turned out to be even better than I hoped it would be. My girl's all in love, and I'm in love. Shit, that's a wonderful thing!"

"Hold up, Sacha. Where is all of this all in 'love' shit coming from? I'm just loving your girl's sex game, that's all," Bob said with a serious expression on his face.

Sacha's face fell flat when she heard this. She turned toward Gwen to see what her reaction to that statement was going to be. Gwen smiled and said, "Bitch, don't pay that nigga no mind. He's just as gone for me as I am for his black sexy-ass!"

They all started laughing as Bob smiled and winked his eye at Sacha. "Gotcha!" he said.

Nodding her head, she said, "Yeah, you did, and I will get you back for that one, Bob!"

The evening was going smoothly, and they were having a real nice time chitchatting back and forth with each other.

After dinner was served, Mr. Whitney and Mr. Johnson announced to everyone that Sacha was now a partner of the firm. She received a standing ovation from all of her peers, as well as their family members who had joined them tonight. *It feels really good to finally be appreciated,* she thought as she stood and waved her hands to everyone in thanks. *This night just couldn't be more perfect,* she thought as she sat back down.

Taz was so proud of his girl that he just wanted to grab her and hug her tight. But he knew that was just a little too much emotion for him to be showing out in public. Since he had been kicking it with Sacha, she brought out feelings inside of him that he'd completely forgotten about. It felt so good to be able to love again. But he knew that he had to be careful. He wasn't going to let this love end like his last love affair. He'd die before he let that happen to him again.

Just as it seemed the night was coming to an end, Clifford made his appearance inside of the ballroom, accompanied by Cory. They made an excellent-looking couple. Cory was looking good, dressed in a gown by Donna Karan, and Clifford was dressed neatly in a suit by Sean Jean. When Clifford saw Sacha, he went directly to her table and said, "Congratulations, Sacha."

Sacha smiled nervously and said, "Thank you, Cliff."

Clifford smiled at Taz and said, "So, the thug can clean up. How nice." Before Taz could move an inch, Clifford said, "I hope you all have a wonderful evening." Then he quickly stepped toward Mr. Whitney's table.

"That was close, Li'l Mama . . . real close," Taz said seriously.

Sacha smiled and said, "He didn't come within arms reach, baby."

"As long as he doesn't, then we're good."

"What are y'all talkin' 'bout?" asked Bob.

"Nothin', fool. Relax."

"Are you good, homey?"

"Yeah, everything is everything. Don't trip, dog. Let's enjoy the rest of the evening." And enjoy they did.

Taz had Sacha out on the dance floor, song after song, dancing and laughing as if they didn't have a care in the world. Bob was right alongside them with Gwen in his arms. Everything was wonderful until Clifford came out on the dance floor with Cory and got a little too close to Taz. Taz turned and saw that it was Clifford who had just bumped into them and said, "Li'l Mama, it looks like this clown wants to play, after all."

"Come on baby, let's go. I'm getting kind of tired, anyway."

"You sure?"

"Yes, I'm positive," she said as she led Taz off of the dance floor. Gwen and Bob came to the table, and Sacha told them, "Thank you both for coming tonight. I really enjoyed your company. Me and my baby are about to—as he would say—shake this spot. Are you two good or what?"

"Oh, God, Taz! Do you hear how you got my girl talking? I think you've become a bad influence on her!" Gwen joked.

Smiling, Taz said, "Nah, if anything, she's became a bad influence on me. All she wants to do is go home so she can try to freak me crazy!"

"Taz! You know you need to quit that! But I am going to love you a long time tonight, mister!" Sacha said, and they all started laughing.

"Well, since y'all are about to bounce, I don't see no reason for us to still be here, baby. Let's shake this spot and go do the damn thing ourselves," Bob said with a smile on his face.

"I'm with that, sexy. Tonight's the night I plan on doing some freaky things with the knot."

"Is that right?"

"Yep!"

"What you got planned for the knot tonight, baby?"

"You'll see. Now come on, let's get outta here," said Gwen.

"Don't let her take all of your energy, my nigga. We do have to get our run on in the morning," Taz said with a laugh.

"Don't trip, gee. I gots this," Bob replied as he followed Gwen out of the ballroom.

"Well, baby, why don't you go on and say your good-byes and stuff, and I'll ease on by the door and wait for ya."

"Okay, baby. I'll be right there," Sacha said. She went to go say good-bye to Mr. Whitney and Mr. Johnson.

Taz left the ballroom and stood outside in the lobby as he waited for Sacha to get finished. A few people who he knew at the firm walked past him and said goodnight. When he saw Clifford walk out of the ballroom, he said to himself, "If this clown-ass nigga tries me, it's on!"

Clifford was holding on to Cory's hand as they were leaving the ballroom. When he saw Taz standing in the lobby alone, he smiled and said to himself, "Now, let's see what you're really working with." He turned toward Cory and said, "Cory, go on ahead and wait for me outside by the valet. I need to talk to someone real quick."

"All right, baby, but don't take too long. I'm in the mood to get real freaky tonight."

"Don't worry. I won't," he replied, and he watched her walk away down the lobby. Once she was out of sight, he stepped toward Taz and said, "I think I remember telling you that I was going to see what you were working with whenever I got a chance at you without your boys around to protect your punk-ass."

Taz smiled, took a quick look around, and said, "Well, it looks like tonight is the night you were referring to." *Now, come a few inches closer, nigga. That's right. Step into arms reach, you bitch!* Taz thought to himself as he watched Clifford move into his arms reach.

Sacha saw Clifford and Taz talking, quickly said good-bye to one of her coworkers, and hurried over to Taz's side. Just as she made it there, she heard Clifford tell Taz that he wasn't worth ruining a good suit. But he would definitely have his chance at him again one day. That infuriated her. "Damnit, Cliff! Why won't you leave us the fuck alone? I'm telling you, I'm getting sick and tired of this shit! And if I have to, I swear, I'm going to file a complaint with both Mr. Whitney and Mr. Johnson!"

"Sacha, I'm just trying to stop you from making the worst mistake of your life. This guy is a fucking loser!" Clifford said as he poked his index finger into Taz's chest.

Taz smiled as he stared into Sacha's eyes. He gave her a slight shrug of his shoulders and said, "Arms reach, Li'l Mama!" Then with the speed of a boxer, he slapped the shit out of Clifford. He hit Clifford with so much power that the blow knocked him to the floor. "Now, be a man and show me that you're not all talk, you bitch-ass nigga! I've tried to be civil, but if it's gangsta shit you want, so be it!" Taz said as he towered over Clifford.

Clifford was trying to scoot away from Taz so that he could get to his feet.

Sacha came and stood next to Taz and said, "Come on, baby, don't do this. He's not worth it."

This gave Clifford the opportunity to get to his feet. He was so mad and embarrassed that he was literally shaking. "You wanna be thug-ass nigga! What, you gon' let a bitch stop you now?"

"*Bitch!* Cliff, you done lost your fucking mind! Beat the shit out of this nigga, baby!"

Taz smiled as he stepped a little closer to Clifford. Just as he was about to swing, Mr. Whitney, Edward, and Mr. Johnson all came running over to stop them from fighting. "What the hell is going on over here?" yelled Mr. Whitney.

Taz took a step back and said, "I'm sorry about this, Lee, but this guy has been asking for this for a minute now."

"That's bull, sir! He just assaulted me!" yelled Clifford.

"Is that true, Taz? If so, I want to know why," asked Mr. Johnson.

"Yeah, it's true, Jeff. This guy is interested in Sacha, and since she doesn't want to be bothered, he has issued several threats to me. Tonight was the last time that I was going to stand for any of them."

Before he could continue, Sacha said, "Mr. Whitney, sir, I don't know what's gotten into Cliff, but he needs to understand that Taz and I are together, and that there is absolutely no chance for us getting together. He's been acting extremely childish throughout the past few weeks."

"Clifford, this is a complete shock. But you have been assaulted, so if you want to press charges, the choice is yours. But I want you to know, and I'm confident that I'm speaking for both Mr. Johnson and myself here, that Taz is a very special client of the firm. He's been conducting business with us for years now. Some very good business. I think you should think about that before you make your decision."

"If he does press charges against Taz, I will file harassment charges against him, sir!" Sacha added vehemently.

Clifford realized that this situation had gotten out of control. The threat that Mr. Whitney had given him was crystal clear. Taz was special, and he was not. "No, sir, I don't feel that any of that will be necessary. I want to apologize to you, Sacha, for my behavior. I will not bother either of you again."

Smiling, Edward said, "I bet you won't! I saw how Taz slapped the mess out of you!"

"That'll be enough of that, Edward! All right then, so, Mr. Taz, do you have anything that you'd like to say to Clifford here?" asked Mr. Whitney.

Taz smiled and said, "Nope."

"Come on, Taz, let's put an end to this issue, okay?" asked Mr. Johnson.

"Look, Jeff. This clown has been bothering me ever since he found out about Sacha and me. Now, he has said it's over and he'll stop. If that's the case, then so be it. But I will not apologize for my actions tonight. He pushed this issue, not me. And to be completely honest, I wouldn't give a damn if he pressed charges against me or not. He's very lucky that all he's received is a fuckin' slap. Make sure he stays away from me in the future, Jeff, 'cause the next time, I'm goin' to hurt him." He then turned toward Sacha and asked, "You ready to bounce, Li'l Mama?"

Sacha stared at Taz for a moment, then said, "Yes, we should be going. Good evening, Mr. Whitney, Mr. Johnson, Edward. It's definitely been memorable." She gave Clifford a frown as she grabbed Taz's hand and let him lead her out of the hotel.

Mr. Whitney smiled and said, "Clifford, you better make sure that you stay away from that man. He's one not to be messed with."

"That's right, Clifford. Not only does he spend close to fifty thousand dollars a year with the firm, he's a dangerous man," warned Mr. Johnson.

Clifford was so embarrassed that he was speechless. He said good evening to them all and went and caught up with Cory at the valet. Just as he made it outside, he saw Sacha and Taz climbing into Taz's Bentley. *Before it's all said and done, I'll get the both of you back for this night. Believe that!* he thought to himself.

Chapter Sixteen

The holidays flew by, and the New Year had started out strong for both Taz and Sacha. They were in love, and loving every minute of it. They became inseparable. And, they weren't the only ones. Bob and Gwen's affair seemed to have turned into something special also. Bob was becoming more and more interested in Gwen. They spent all of their spare time with each other too.

Gwen had shocked the both of them when she told Bob all about the loss of her beloved William, and her only child, Remel. Bob was touched deeply by what she had told him, especially when she told him that she thought she'd never be able to love again, that is, until she had met him.

For the first time in his life, Bob was in love, and it felt strange, but good at the same time. He had had a few flings over his lifetime, but nothing as serious as this one. Gwen gave him the impression that she wanted to ride for the long haul, and if that was the case, he was ready to accept her with open arms.

Bob pulled into Gwen's driveway with a smile on his face. Today was the day he was going to ask her to move into his place with him. He told his boys of his decision, and they all seemed to be very happy for him, especially Taz. Taz had told him that it was time for all of them to start settling down. None of them were getting any younger. Every member of the crew had everything that they ever wanted, but only Bob and Taz had found the one love of their lives. *"The game is starting to come to an end, so it's time that we all start preparing for it."* These words that Taz spoke stuck deep within Bob. His mind was made up. If Gwen moved in with him, he was going to ask her to marry him within six months. He was definitely in love.

When Gwen came outside and got inside of Bob's truck, she said, "Hey, you! How was your day?"

"It was straight. It's better now that I'm here with you. Let's go get our grub on somewhere. I gots some things I want to talk to you about."

"That's fine. Where do you want to go eat at, babe?"

"It don't matter. You choose."

"Let's get some fish from Bob Davis's, and then come back here and chill."

"I'm with that," Bob said as he started to pull out of her driveway. Once he had started driving down her street, his cell rang. He grabbed the phone and said, "What up?"

"Dog, Taz just got the word from Won. Meet us at the house in thirty," said Keno.

"Damn! All right, gee, out!" After closing his cell phone, he made a U-turn and told Gwen, "Baby, some shit has come up. I gots to bounce outta town. I shouldn't be no longer than a day or so."

"Where are you going, babe?"

"To be honest, I don't even know yet. I'll find out in a li'l bit. Once I do, I'll give you a holla and let you know what's what. Cool?"

"Yeah, I'm cool. But I am curious as to why you have to up and leave all of a sudden. But I ain't tripping, as long as it's not for some other female."

Bob smiled as he pulled back into her driveway and said, "Baby, you are the only woman I'm seeing. Fuck, you are the only woman that I want to see! Believe that! And when I get back, we'll have that talk I wanted to have with you tonight."

"About what, babe?"

Bob stared into Gwen's sexy brown eyes and simply said, "Us. Now, let me roll. Business gots to be handled." He gave her a tender kiss and watched as she climbed out of his truck and went back inside of her home. Once her door was closed, he pulled out of her driveway and punched it toward Taz's house. *Time to go to work!*

The crew was assembled inside of Taz's den, watching as he was tapping the keys on his laptop. After a few minutes, he closed the laptop and said, "Okay, boys, it's like this. We're on our way to L.A. Everything is set to go down in the morning. Me and Keno are leaving from here this time. Bob, you and Red are bouncing out of Tulsa, and Bo-Pete, you and Bill got Fort Worth this time. Once y'all touch down at LAX, take a shuttle to the Budget Rent A Car spot right by the airport. Keno and I will already be there to pick y'all up. It's a timed op, so be ready because we're moving right from there. We should be back here sometime late tomorrow night. The pay for this one is a ticket apiece. Any questions?"

The room remained silent, as no one said a word.

"All right then, my niggas, let's roll!" Taz stood up and told Keno, "I'll drive this time, clown. And you better not bring that damn *Scarface* DVD!"

Keno laughed and said, "Dog, it's going to be a long flight out to Cali. What else am I goin' to watch?"

Taz smiled and said, "Here," as he gave Keno a DVD.

Keno opened the case, smiled, and said, "I can do this. Yeah, I can fuck with me some Fifty Cent. Where the fuck did you get this from? This shit just came out a couple of months ago."

"My nigga Big O hooked me up. You know that old nigga be having the hookups on bootlegs and shit. When he told me that he had *Get Rich or Die Tryin'*, I was like yeah, this might stop you from watching that old-ass *Scarface*."

Keno started laughing as he put the DVD inside of his carry bag. As they all were leaving Taz's home, he said, "Yeah, I'm gon' get into this one, but I'm still watching me some *'Face!*"

Taz shook his head and said, "I just can't win fuckin' with you, can I?"

"Nope. Now come on, let's go get this money!"

Taz and Keno's flight arrived in Los Angeles a little after midnight. Since the rest of the crew wasn't due to arrive for several more hours, they went and checked into the Best Western Suites, where Won had a room already reserved for them. Once they were inside, Taz pulled out the DVD that was given to him by the manager when they had checked in. He quickly inserted the DVD and smiled when he saw a picture of Michael Jordan gliding through the air with a basketball gripped tightly in the palm of his hand. After about thirty seconds, Won's deep voice started speaking:

"Glad that y'all made it safely, boys. Now pay attention, 'cause like I told you, everything about this one is on the clock. The rest of the crew should be there by eight a.m. They should be at the Budget no later than nine. So, after you scoop them up, you are to get onto the 405 Freeway South and head out to Long Beach. Get off on the Carson Street exit and drive exactly one mile. You will see some apartments to your left and an auto body shop to your right. Park the truck over in the apartment's parking lot. Strap up and wait for a blue Mazda 626 to pull up. Once you spot the Mazda, start making your move across the street. A thick older lady should get out of the car and head toward the front of the body shop. Once she reaches inside of her purse to grab her keys, you should be on her. Take her inside and lead her to the back of the shop. After she's secure, two of you go straight inside of the office located on the far left of the building. There's a safe under the desk. The combo is twenty-one to the left, eleven to the right, and ninety-nine back to the left. There should be approximately six million dollars in that safe. After the chips are secure, go back with the others and prepare yourselves, because this is where it's going to get tricky.

"Within ten minutes after you guys have entered the shop, two carloads of mean-ass brothers will be coming in. Force may have to be used, because these ain't no pootbutts. They're straight killas, so handle them as such. If need be, do what has to be done. All of your weapons are silenced for that purpose. One of the gentlemen will be carrying a case full of work. That's what has to be snatched next. After retrieving the case, secure everyone and get the fuck out.

"You are to then proceed back to the Budget rental spot and drop off the truck with everything you've acquired still inside of the truck. Your return flights are already reserved. You leave on the same flights you arrived on. Each of your flights departs between twelve and twelve-thirty. You should all be back home no later than ten p.m. Your weapons and everything you will need for this mission are under the bed. Be precise, be prepared, and most of all, be careful. Out!"

The television screen went blank, and Taz and Keno went and got their tools for their mission. They made sure that each and every weapon was loaded and ready to fire. After that, they got the gym bags and plastic hand restraints in order for everyone else. Since they still had some time before they went to go pick up Bob, Red, Bo-Pete, and Bill, they decided to relax and get some sleep.

Taz called downstairs at the front desk and gave them a seven a.m. wake-up call for him. After he hung up the phone, he picked up his cell and called Sacha. Even though he knew that it was after two in the morning back in Oklahoma, he still wanted to hear her voice. When she answered the phone, he said, "Hey, Li'l Mama, I'm sorry I woke you."

"That's okay, baby. Is everything all right?"

"Yeah, everything's straight. I just wanted to hear your voice before I laid it down."

Smiling, she asked, "Where are you this time, baby?"

"I'm in L.A. I should be back tomorrow evening sometime."

"L.A.! Oooh, I wish I was with you! I could do some serious damage in those malls out there."

"Is that right? Well, I guess I'm going to have to get you back out here soon, so you can do all the damage you'd like."

"For real? Baby, you're so damn good to me. When can we go, Taz?"

Taz laughed and said, "Whenever you have the time, Li'l Mama. Now, go on and get some rest. I'll give you a call when I know exactly what time I'll be in tomorrow."

"All right, baby. Love you!"

Smiling, he said, "Love you too! Bye."

Keno was lying on the other twin bed in the room and said, "Damn, my nigga! It must really feel good to have someone to love again, huh?"

Taz smiled as he closed his eyes and said, "Yeah, my nigga, it does."

Keno and Taz pulled their rented Ford Expedition into the Budget rental parking lot just as the Budget shuttle van from the airport pulled in. Bo-Pete and Wild Bill were the first to climb out of the van. They saw the Expedition and stepped quickly toward the truck. By the time they were inside, Red and Bob stepped out of the van and went and joined the rest of the crew.

Keno pulled out of the parking lot and headed toward the 405 Freeway. While they were riding, Taz filled everyone in on how the mission was supposed to go down. After he was finished, Wild Bill asked, "Do you think we'll have to smoke any of those fools?"

"Ain't no tellin', so make sure that you're prepared to do whatever, feel me?"

"Don't trip, my nigga. If they make a wrong move, they're outta there," Wild Bill said seriously.

"I know that's right, homey!" added Red.

The rest of the ride was done in silence as they all prepared themselves for what had to be done. They were completely focused. None of them were scared, but their adrenaline was pumping big-time. *Time to go to work!*

Keno got off of the 405 on Carson Street and drove directly to the apartments that Won told them about. He parked the truck, and everyone inside began to check and recheck their weapons.

Keno pulled out a Black and Mild cigar and was about to light up until Taz stopped him and said, "No time for that, my nigga. There's the blue Mazda now. "Let's go!"

They climbed out of the truck slowly, looking both ways to make sure that there wasn't too much attention being paid to their movements. Once Taz felt that everything was good, he gave them all a nod of his head, and they quickly ran across the street.

The old lady who had climbed out of the Mazda 626 never had a chance. Just as she stuck her key into the front door of the auto body shop, Keno grabbed her by the back of her neck and said, "Don't turn around. Just keep doing what you were doing and you'll be fine, lady. Open the door nice and slow. Then step on inside." She did as she was told, and they all entered the auto body shop behind her.

Once they were inside, everything went on autopilot. Keno led the lady to the back of the shop and quickly put a pair of the hand restraints on her wrists and legs. Taz stood watch while Red, Bob, Bo-Pete, and Wild Bill went inside of the office. Red and Bob stood at the door of the office as Bo-Pete and Wild Bill went and opened the safe. Once their bags were filled and the safe was completely empty, all four of them came out of the office and stepped quickly to the back of the shop.

Taz checked his watch and figured that they had maybe three minutes tops before the killas arrived. He smiled and said, "All right, the easy part's over with. Y'all get ready, 'cause it's almost time for us to earn our chips."

"You are some dumb young fuckers! Do you actually know who you're fucking with? You won't live a month after this, you damned fools!" screamed the restrained lady.

Keno smiled and said, "Don't worry about us, Ma. You need to be worrying about your boys, 'cause if they act up, not only will they lose all of that dope, but their lives are as good as bye-bye!" He smiled when he noticed the lady's reaction to his words. She shook her head slowly and said, "You all are still some walking dead men."

Bob, who had gone to the front of the shop to keep a lookout, suddenly turned around and said, "They're here!"

Taz gave Keno a nod, and they stepped to the right side of the shop with their weapons drawn. Bo-Pete and Wild Bill were on the other side of the shop, crouched low with their weapons aimed at the front door. Red stayed at the back with his hands wrapped around the old lady's mouth so she wouldn't be able to warn her peoples.

Since the auto body shop's lights were off and the room was somewhat dark, Taz felt comfortable that the advantage was theirs as he watched as two men came strolling through the front door, followed by three more. Once they were inside, one of the men said, "Why didn't Dee turn on the fuckin' lights?"

"Because she's a li'l tied up at the moment, gee," said Taz as he stepped in front of the first two who had entered the shop. He pointed his silenced weapon at their heads and continued, "Now, get down on the floor slowly."

The three men who had come in behind the first two tried to reach for their weapons, but Wild Bill and Bo-Pete stopped them. "Go on and pull out, nigga! You'll be dead with your gun in your hand," Wild Bill said as he put the barrel of his nine-millimeter to the side of one of the guys' head.

With a smile on his face, Bo-Pete had the other two held at gunpoint. "Make it happen, Captain! It's all on you. You want to live or die?"

All three of the men raised their hands in the air slowly.

"That's what I thought! Now, get your asses on the fuckin' floor!" yelled Bo-Pete.

Once they had them all on the ground and restrained, Taz had Keno and Bob take them to the back of the shop with Dee. Red watched with an amused smile on his face as the captives were led toward him.

"All right then, let's grab the work and shake this spot," Taz said as they sat all of the men down on the floor next to Dee.

One of the first two men who had come inside of the shop was staring real hard at Taz. *These fools are about to smoke us. How the fuck did they get onto us? This shit ain't right. Somethin' just ain't right. They ain't got on no masks or nothin'. Damn! They is goin' to smoke our asses!* he thought as he continued to stare at Taz.

Taz noticed him staring and said, "Don't trip, gee. Y'all gon' live. We gots what we came for." Then he gave him a big smile so he could see his platinum and diamond grille.

Some country niggas! Hell nah! You fools are dead! the man thought to himself as he watched in disbelief.

"Dog, go and get the truck. As soon as you're in front, blow the horn twice," Taz instructed Keno.

"Gotcha." Keno ran out of the shop and got the truck. By the time he blew the truck's horn twice, the crew was standing at the door, looking over their shoulders at the men and lady that they had secured in the back of the shop. They stepped out of the shop one at a time with a smile on their faces as they each climbed inside of the Expedition. They didn't have to kill anyone, and they were all one million dollars richer.

Taz came out of the shop and was about to climb inside of the truck when he noticed someone staring at him from inside of a red Escalade. He opened the door to the Expedition and asked, "What kind of car did those clowns pull up in, Bob?"

"That Escalade, my nigga. Why? What's up?"

"Fuck!" Taz screamed as he slammed the door and walked back inside of the shop. After he closed the door, he saw the guy inside of the truck talking to someone on his cell phone. "Damn, he gots to die!" Taz said as he opened the door to the shop quickly and charged the red Escalade with his pistol in hand.

The driver was so caught up with his phone call that he didn't even get a chance to yell. Seven bullets from Taz's silenced nine-millimeter crashed through the windshield of the Escalade, killing the driver instantly.

Taz opened the passenger's side of the truck, reached across and pulled the slumped driver over to him to make sure that he was dead. When he saw the three holes in his face, he grimaced and let the dead body fall back against the headrest. He closed the door and walked back to the Expedition. Once he was inside of the truck, he calmly said, "Let's roll out."

Chapter Seventeen

Sacha was sitting at her desk. Her intercom buzzed, and her receptionist told her that she had a call. "Hello, This is Sacha Carbajal. How may I help you?"

"Hello, ma'am, this is Tony Surefield. I just wanted to let you know that I'm out, and it looks like I won't be needing your services, after all."

"I see. So I assume that you were able to work a deal out with the U.S. assistant attorney, Mr. Surefield."

"Yeah, something like that."

"Okay, then, you better make sure that you keep your nose clean out there."

"I will, and thanks for your help anyway though."

"That's what you paid me for, Mr. Surefield. Have a nice day."

"You too," he said and hung up.

After Sacha hung up the phone with her client, she said, "Snitch!" Then she went back to reading the file on her upcoming trial.

Clifford was sitting in his office when he got a call from someone from his past. "Long time, C-Baby!" said the voice on the other line.

When Clifford heard his old nickname, he asked "Who is this?"

"Come on, my nigga, don't tell me you done forgot about your boy!"

Clifford couldn't help but smile when he asked, "Do-Low?"

"What's good, C-Baby?"

"When did you get out the pen?"

"Two days ago. I got your number from your moms. I need you, C-Baby. I need you bad."

"Look, I don't go by C-Baby any longer, Do-Low. You know that was a long time ago. I go by my government name now."

"Yeah, I know. But check it out, dog. We need to talk. You know about old times and shit. Come on, man, let's get together and kick it a li'l bit."

"What's up? You need some money or something?"

"Man, my problems are way worse than ends, my nigga. I'm dying, C—I mean Clifford. I got that thang, dog."

"What thang? What the hell are you talking about, Do-Low?"

"HIV, man. I got that package," Do-Low said seriously.

"How the fuck did you get that shit? I know you didn't go out backward when you was in the pen."

"Hell nah! You know I ain't on that fag shit, fool. Remember when I got blasted back in '94?"

"Yeah."

"They had to give me a blood transfusion during surgery while I was down. I got called to take our yearly HIV test, and I tested positive. That was two years ago. This shit is starting to kick in on me now, dog. My days are numbered, and I'm not trying to go out without being able to leave something for my shorties, dog. Feel me?"

In a somber voice, Clifford answered, "Yeah, I feel you. How are your kid's anyway?"

"Man, they're big! Dionne is ten now, and she's almost as tall as her mother is. And the twins, man, they're the spitting images of me, gee," he said excitedly.

"That's cool. Yeah, that's real cool. Listen, I got a few things to take care of real quick. Give me a number and I'll get back at you in an hour or so." After writing Do-Low's number down, Clifford said, "Don't worry, dog. I'm going to make sure that you'll be able to look out for your seeds."

"Is that right? Come on, don't bullshit me C—I mean Clifford."

Smiling as he thought about Taz and Sacha, Clifford said, "You know me, Do-Low. I'd never play with you like that. Now, let me go so I can handle my business. I'll get at you in one hour."

"A'ight then, Clifford. One!"

"Yeah, later," Clifford said and hung up. "A nigga with nothing to lose. Perfect! Just fucking perfect!" he said aloud as he went back to work.

It had been a long time since Taz had actually had to use his weapon. It felt strange, but at the same time exciting. *Damn, this is some crazy-ass shit!* he thought as he relaxed in his seat as their flight prepared to depart out of LAX.

After their flight was airborne, Keno smiled as he inserted his *Scarface* DVD into his portable DVD player. Just before he plugged in his headphones, he asked Taz, "Are you all right, my nigga?"

"Yeah, I'm good. I'd be better if I didn't have to look at that old-ass movie again. I thought you were going to watch Fifty."

"I watched it when we left the City. It was cool, but gee, that shit just wasn't gritty enough for me. 'Face is a damn fool."

Taz laughed and said, "Whatever! Damn, dog! Bob slipped on us today. He was supposed to be on point with that clown in the truck."

"Yeah, I was thinking about that. What's up?"

"Nothin'. I'll get at him when we get back."

"Yeah, you need to, 'cause if that love-struck-ass nigga's gon' be slippin' like that on us, it's time for his ass to get the fuck out."

Taz closed his eyes and said, "I know, gee. I know."

After Clifford dropped Do-Low back off at his apartment, he sat in his car and thought about what he had just done. He was going to pay Do-Low fifty thousand dollars to take Taz's life for him. But he had to make it look as if it was a random robbery attempt. That way, Sacha would never link him to it. "I'll play the good, supportive friend with her for a few months. Then we'll gradually get closer. Then, everything will be good," he said to himself as he started his car and pulled out of the apartment complex.

***

Sacha and Gwen had just finished having dinner when both of their cell phones began to ring at the same time. Sacha smiled when she saw that it was Taz who was calling her. Gwen smiled also when she noticed that it was Bob who was calling her. After speaking to Taz for a few minutes, Sacha hung up her phone and waited for Gwen to finish talking to Bob.

When Gwen finally got off of her cell, Sacha said, "Damn, ho! He must have been telling you some real good shit. It took your ass long enough."

Smiling, Gwen said, "Yeah, bitch, he told me that he has something serious to talk to me about. I'm meeting him at his place in a couple of hours. I'm going to go home and get changed, and grab me some gear for tomorrow, 'cause I got a feeling it's going to be a real long night."

"What do you think he wants to talk about? I remember when you told me he said something about y'all getting closer and stuff."

"I think he wants me to move in with him."

"Stop lying! Ho, are you going to do it if he asks you to?"

"I might. Bitch, I'm sick and tired of being all by myself. It would feel real good to be able to wake up with someone every morning."

"I know that's right! But you have to remember, sometimes there will still be mornings when you'll wake up by yourself. You know how often they be going out of town."

"I know. What do they be doing when they leave?"

"I've tried my best to get Taz to tell me, but he just won't do it. No matter how mad I act, he refuses to tell me. He always comes with that 'it's my business' shit, or 'don't worry, Li'l Mama. It ain't nothin',"' she said as she tried to imitate Taz's voice.

"Do you think they're into some shady shit?"

"To be completely honest, no, I don't. Taz has shown me that he's legit, and I won't question him on it again. You know they're still caught up with their thug images and shit, so I've chosen to ignore that shit. The jewelry, the fancy cars, the gangsta shit, that's just who they are. I love Taz, and no matter what, I'm going to support him. As long as he's safe and I'm happy. Regarding his business affairs, no matter how sneaky they may seem, I'm rolling with my nigga."

"I hear you, bitch. But still, they could at least put our minds at ease."

"As far as I'm concerned, Taz has done just that. Don't worry about that shit, girl. I don't."

"Well, that's you. Bob and I are going to discuss this later on, and I'm going to make it a point to let him know that I want to know exactly what is going on. And believe me, bitch, he's going to tell me."

"Whatever! Come on, ho. Let's get out of here. I'm ready to see my man."

Taz and the rest of the crew were all seated in his den. They had just finished checking their accounts. After Taz got off of the phone with Won, he closed his cell and said, "All right, I guess everything is everything. Won wants us to stay ready, 'cause we might be bouncing as quickly as next week, so you know what it is. Stay ready so you won't have to get ready."

Bob stood and said, "All right then, my niggas, I'm out. I'm about to go get with Gwen and chill for the rest of the night. What's up for the weekend? Are we clubbin' or what?"

"It's whatever with me, dog. You know now that you and Taz are all in love and shit, y'all might not be able to come hang with us," Red said with a smile on his face.

"Fuck you, clown!"

They were all laughing as they filed out of Taz's home.

Taz stopped Bob before he had a chance to get into his truck and said, "Dog, let me holla at you for a minute."

Bob climbed into his truck and asked, "What's up, homey?"

"Tell me something. Do you feel that you're ready to get out of the game we're playing?"

"As long as we're safe and the chips are chunky, I'm in it to win it, gee."

"That's what I'm talkin' 'bout. But, dog, you slipped on us back in L.A. One of us could have gotten twisted."

"I was thinking about that shit on the flight back. I didn't pay attention once I saw the truck stop and saw the fools climb out. That was my bad, dog. It won't happen again, Taz."

"It can't happen again, Bob. I love you, dog, but before I let you put either of us in a jam like that again, I'll have to shake you, gee. We've been too strong for too long, my nigga. Ain't no room for getting sloppy now."

"I got you, dog."

"Do you? Is what you're feeling for Gwen causing you to slip, my nigga? This is some real shit, so I'm giving you some real talk. 'Cause we won't ever have this conversation again, gee. So don't take offense to my words. Feel every one of them."

Bob sat back in his seat and thought about what Taz had just told him. He smiled and said, "I ain't mad at ya, Taz. I love you and the rest of the homies as if we were all brothers. I fucked up in Cali, and like I said, it won't happen again. Thank you for catching my back, dog. And to answer your question, yeah, I love that broad. Dog, it's been a long time since a nigga has been able to feel some real love from a female. For once it ain't about the chips I got or the car I'm rollin' in. Dog, she's into me and I'm into her. It's real, dog . . . real as it can get. As a matter of fact, I'm about to meet her at my pad and ask her to move in with me."

Taz smiled and said, "That's cool, dog. I'm feeling just as deeply for Sacha as you are for Gwen, but I will never, and I mean never, let my thoughts or love for her interfere with the work that we do. So, make sure that you stay on your square, my nigga." Taz closed the door to Bob's truck, turned, and went back inside of his home.

By the time Bob pulled into his garage, Gwen was already parked in his driveway. He smiled as he climbed out of his truck, and his girl ran into his arms. "I've missed you so much, baby!" Gwen said as she kissed him passionately.

Bob pulled from her embrace, scooped her into his arms, and said, "I've missed you too. Let me take you inside so I can show you exactly how much." He then carried her into his

home and straight to the bedroom. He dropped her onto his
bed and started laughing when she threw her purse at him.
"Ouch!"

"Don't get it twisted, nigga. I ain't with that rough shit!"

"I was just playin'! Damn!" He smiled as he sat next to her
on the bed and said, "Check this out, baby. How would you
feel if I asked you to move in with me?"

Smiling, she said, "That depends."

"On what?"

"On whether or not you're asking me, babe."

"Okay, let's do this then. I'm tired of being alone, and I love
having you around me. I love everything about you, Gwen.
You bring some balance into this crazy-ass life of mines. Will
you move in with me, baby?"

"What about my house? What am I going to do with it?"

"You own it, right?"

"Yep."

"Well, rent it out. That way, you'll have some more income
coming in, even though money will be the least of your
concerns."

"Who's going to fix shit when something goes wrong over
there?"

"Come on with that shit, Gwen. You know I'll make sure
everything is straight. I love you, Gwen, and I want you to be
with me. Let's do this for a while and see how things fall."

"What if they don't fall the way you expect them to?"

"I seriously doubt that will happen."

"But what if it does, babe? Then what?"

"Then, you can move back in and everything will be everything."

"I don't know, Bob. Don't you think that we're moving kind
of fast here?"

"Baby, I don't give a damn about nothing but you. I love
you, and I want to be with you. I want to wake up and see you
sleeping in our bed. I want to spend the rest of my life with
you, Gwen. Let's start with this, and once we've kicked it for a
minute, let's make it official."

"Are you asking me to marry you, Bob?"

"You damn skippy! I love you and I want you to be wifey."

With a smile on her face, Gwen said, "All right, babe, we can do this. I'll move in with you, and then we'll see if this is as special as we both seem to think. But I have a question that I want to ask you first."

"What's up?"

"I'm curious as to why you always have to go out of town so unexpectedly. What's up with the trips and shit, babe?"

"It's business, baby, that's all. We be having to go take care of certain things."

"So, why is it always a different place?"

"Look, you have to understand that our business ventures are spread all over the place. We're a team, and it takes all of our manpower to be able to deal with everything we have on our plates."

Shaking her head slowly, Gwen asked, "What exactly do y'all be doing out of town, Bob?"

"It depends. Sometimes there's business meetings that we have to attend, or sometimes we have to go look at several different sites that we're trying to acquire—business shit, baby. Now, what's up? Are you moving in with me or what?"

This slick, sexy-ass nigga of mines thinks he has all of the answers. Humph! He's forgotten that I'm a fucking psychiatrist. I'll let him off the hook for now, but sooner or later I'm going to find out exactly what the fuck they're into, she said to herself. She smiled at Bob and said, "Yeah, babe, we can do it. I love you, and I want to be with you just as much as you want to be with me." She took off her blouse and said, "Now, come here and let me show you how much I love you."

"Now, that's what I'm talkin' 'bout!" he said as he slid into her arms.

Chapter Eighteen

Taz and Sacha had spent the entire day together shopping. Now that they were finally finished, all Taz wanted to do was to go back to his house and relax and chill. But Sacha was in the mood for more. "Baby, we should go out to the club tonight," she said as she climbed inside of Taz's truck.

"For what? To look at the same old tired-ass niggas and shit? Nah, I'm good with that one, Li'l Mama," he said as he turned on the ignition.

Pouting, she said, "Come on, baby, it'll be fun. We haven't been out in a while. I'll call Gwen, and get her and Bob to go, and we'll have a nice evening."

"Why can't you just have them come on over to the house so we could chill out there?"

"'Cause that's no fun, baby! Let's go out and have some fun and drink and stuff," Sacha whined.

Taz sighed as he pulled out of the parking lot of the mall, and said, "If you want to go out that bad, I ain't trippin', Li'l Mama. But I'm going to have to see what Keno, Red, Bo-Pete, and Wild Bill are gettin' into. I never go to the club without all of my niggas with me."

"Why?"

"Security reasons, Li'l Mama. Beef never dies."

"What do you mean by that?"

"Let's just say that there are some people in this town that don't love Taz. And for that reason, I never go to any clubs without my niggas."

"But what if they don't want to go out?"

"Then neither am I."

"So, you're telling me that if your boys don't want to go out, then you're not going to go out with me?"

"Don't make this out to be somethin' against you, Li'l Mama, 'cause it ain't. It's just how I get down. Please don't try to make me go against the way I've been living for years."

"But that's so unfair, Taz!"

"Not really, baby, 'cause I don't really want to go to the club, anyway. The only reason why I gave in was because it seemed like you had your heart set on going out tonight."

"Anyway, go on and call Keno and the rest of your niggas, 'cause I'm trying to go out, and I want my man with me," she said sarcastically.

Taz smiled but said nothing as he grabbed his cell and called Keno. When Keno answered his cell, he said, "What up, dog?"

"What's good, my nigga?" replied Keno.

"Ain't shit. Just finished doing some shopping with Sacha. I'm on my way to the pad now. What you got planned for tonight?"

"Not much as of right now. I was thinking about rollin' by the club later on to see what was poppin'. What's with you?"

"Sacha wants to hit the club, so I was checkin' to see if y'all wanted to roll."

"I'm with it. It don't seem like there's much else to get into tonight. I'll get at Red and 'em, and I'll get back at you by the time you get to the pad."

"That's straight. Oh, and Sacha thanks you."

"For what?"

"Never mind, my nigga. I'll tell you about it later. Out!"

Sacha was just about to say something slick when for the second time that day she noticed that there was a black Altima following them. She turned a little in her seat so she could get a clear view in the rearview mirror on the side of Taz's truck. When she saw the Altima slow down a little and let a few cars get in front of it, she was positive that they were being followed. "Taz, I think someone has been following us."

"What? What are you talkin' 'bout Li'l Mama?" he asked as he checked his rearview mirror.

"About three cars back is an all-black Altima. I could have sworn I seen that same car as we left Crossroads Mall a few hours ago. I just noticed it again as we pulled out of Penn Square."

"Are you sure?"

"Positive."

"Okay, let's see then," Taz said as he accelerated. His truck gave a slight lurch as the speed increased from forty-five miles per hour to sixty quickly. He made a left turn onto May Avenue and slowed down a little as they came close to Sixty-third Street. "Don't look over your shoulder, Li'l Mama, but tell me, do you still see the car you was talkin' 'bout?"

Sacha checked the rearview mirror again and said, "Yep, about two cars back."

Taz slowed down and pulled into the parking lot of a Blockbuster Video store and hopped out of his truck. As he strolled slowly toward Blockbuster, he saw the black Altima pull into the parking lot of Ted's Mexican restaurant across the street. Taz turned around and stepped quickly back to the truck. Once he was back inside, he started the truck and said, "You're right, Li'l Mama. It looks like we do have a tail. Now, let's see who the fuck this is following us."

"H—how are you going to do that, baby?" she asked nervously.

"Don't trip, Li'l Mama. Everything is going to be all right," Taz said confidently as he picked up his cell and quickly dialed. A few seconds later he said, "Check this out, Won. I done picked me up a tail, O.G."

"Is that right? How long have you had it?"

"I'm not knowing exactly. At least a few hours."

"And you're just now getting at me?"

"Shit, I just figured it out."

"You're slippin', Babyboy. Can you get me the license plate number?"

"Yeah, I got 'em. GVM 214, Oklahoma tags." He had locked it into his memory as he walked back toward his truck when they were in the Blockbuster parking lot.

"All right, take 'em around the City for a li'l ride while I get on it. I'll hit you back in a minute."

"That's straight."

"Are you alone?"

"Nah, I got my boo with me."

"Your *what?* Since when did you have a fuckin' boo, Baby-boy?"

Laughing, Taz said, "Don't you think we could get into that a li'l later, O.G.? This does need to be handled."

"My bad, Babyboy! Out!" Won said and hung up.

After Taz had closed his phone, Sacha asked, "Who is Won, baby?"

"A real good friend of mine." Before Sacha could ask him another question, he reopened his cell and called Keno back. When Keno answered his phone, Taz quickly told him about his tail and said, "I'm waiting on Won to get back at me now. After that, I'll hit you and we'll see what's what."

"How are we going to put something down when you got Sacha with you?" asked Keno.

"Don't trip. If we have to put a demo down, I'm going to go drop her back off at the mall. Then, I'll have Red or Bo-Pete come scoop her up while we handle this shit. For now, just stand by, my nigga."

"Gotcha," Keno said before hanging up.

After listening to what Taz had just told Keno, Sacha's heart rate seemed to increase rapidly. "Baby, what are you planning on doing?"

Taz stared at her briefly and said, "Whatever I have to do, Li'l Mama."

His comment was made so coldly that Sacha felt like she didn't even know the man that was sitting next to her.

Taz's cell rang just as he was getting onto the highway. "Talk to me, O.G."

"Babyboy, are you doing anything outta the normal out there?"

"Nah, why?"

"Are you sure?"

"Yeah, I'm sure. What's up?"

"You got the suits on your ass. That's a government vehicle. Now tell me, what the fuck's going on?"

"I'm tellin' you, O.G., I ain't doing shit! You know I don't get down like that. For what, some crumbs? This is some straight bullshit, Won!" Taz yelled with panic in voice.

"Calm down, Babyboy! Just relax. Go on and head to the house, and give me a call when you get there. We'll figure this shit out and put a stop to whatever the fuck is going on."

"Nah, fuck that, O.G.! I gots me a lawyer with me right fuckin' now, and I'm about to see what the fuck is crackin'! Exactly who the fuck is this? DEA or the FEDs?"

"The FEDs."

"All right, cool. I'll hit you back in a li'l bit."

"What the fuck are you about to do, Babyboy?"

"What needs to be done. Out!" Taz turned toward Sacha as he pulled off of the highway and said, "Li'l Mama, those are federal agents following us. Why? I do not know. But I'm about to find the fuck out. I need you to represent me. Are you cool with that?"

"You know I am, baby, but business hours are over. How are you going to get in contact with anyone?"

"Sit back and watch," he said confidently as he drove toward the headquarters of the FBI in Oklahoma City.

Taz pulled his truck into the parking lot of 50 Penn Place Mall. He smiled when he saw the shocked expression on the face of the driver of the black Altima as they passed by him on their way into the mall. Fifty Penn Place was not only an exclusive mall, but it also held the offices of the FBI.

Taz led Sacha to the elevator, and they quickly rode it to the third floor. When they stepped off of the elevator, Taz went straight to the receptionist's desk and said, "I'd like to speak to the duty officer, please."

"May I ask your name and reason, sir?" asked the receptionist.

"My name is Taz Good, and I'm here to find out exactly why your fucking federal agents have been following me!"

"Please, calm down, sir! There's no need for profanity."

"Fuck you! Get the fuckin' duty officer out here right fuckin' now!" he screamed.

The shocked receptionist quickly picked up the phone and called someone. A minute after she had hung up the phone, two white federal agents came into the waiting area.

"What seems to be the problem, Silvia?" asked one of the agents.

"This gentleman has come in here demanding to see you, sir. He seems to be very upset about someone following him."

The duty officer stepped toward Taz and said, "Hello, sir. My name is Agent Frank Johns. I'm the duty officer for today. How may I be of assistance?"

Taz took a deep breath to calm himself and said, "Look. I just figured out that I'm being followed by one of your agents, and I want to know why. I do not indulge in any form of illegal activity, so there should be no reason for this bullshit!"

"Please, calm down, sir! Maybe there's some misunderstanding. How do you know that it's one of our agents that is following you?"

Taz smiled and said, "Because I'm a nigga that is not to be fucked with. I have friends in very high fuckin' places. That's how I know. I had the license plate checked, and it came back to you all. So, like I said, I want to know why you got your people following me!"

"You need to watch your mouth, young man!" the other agent said to Taz.

"Man, fuck you! I'm grown! I have my attorney here with me just in case y'all want to try some bullshit. But I want some answers. And if I don't get them, I promise you that on Monday morning, there's going to be a lot of media in this bitch, 'cause I'm going to use everything in my power to put on a show this city hasn't seen since the muthafuckin' bombing in '94!"

Agent Johns stared at Taz briefly, and for some reason he took Taz's threats seriously. *This guy is too damn confident. He's not bluffing,* he thought to himself. "Please, come into my office so we can see if we can figure this out."

They followed the agents back into the inner offices of the FBI.

Sacha couldn't believe that Taz was talking to these people that way. She was excited both by how her man was checking these people and at the fact that he was showing no sign of fear whatsoever. She was actually getting turned on by his tirade.

After they were seated in Agent Johns's office, Sacha said, "My name is Sacha Carbajal. I work for Whitney & Johnson, and as you've already been told, I'm representing Mr. Good here."

"That's fine, Miss Carbajal. If you two would give me a moment, I need to contact my superiors. Hopefully we'll be able to find something out." Agent Johns then made a few phone calls and spoke to a couple of different people. After about ten minutes, he finally hung up with his last call and said, "Mr. Good, may I ask what you do for a living?"

Taz looked across at Sacha, and she gave him a nod of her head, giving him her consent to answer the question.

"I'm part owner in several small food chains here in Oklahoma City. I own over forty homes here, also."

"And that is your main source of income, sir?"

Taz smiled and said, "That's my only income."

"Have you ever been arrested, Mr. Good?"

"Nope."

"I see. Okay, here it is, sir. We have received information that you're involved in drugs. We admit that we have checked you and your background thoroughly, and you are clean. At least it looks that way. But the information we received came from a valuable witness, so we had to take it seriously. I've been told by my superior to inform you that we are backing off of this part of the investigation, and that you have our word that for now you will not be followed by anyone from our offices."

Sacha started to speak, but Taz interrupted her. "So, you're telling me that someone told you I was a dope boy?"

"Yes, sir, that's exactly what I'm telling you."

"And you believed him just because he's a valuable snitch? Y'all gots to be outta your fuckin' minds!"

"Come on, Taz. Calm down. There's no need to get too crazy. They're backing off for now, and that's all that matters. I'll check into this deeper on Monday. At least we've accomplished something out of this trip," Sacha said wisely.

Taz, whose thoughts were on who could have been telling the FEDs that he was a drug dealer, wasn't really paying any attention to her. He was too busy wracking his brain. After a few minutes, he snapped back to reality and said, "All right, I can accept that. But I'm telling you, I've never in my life sold any fuckin' dope. And if you really check deep into my past, you'll know why. I despise dope boys and anyone who deals with them."

"And why is that, if I may ask?" asked Agent Johns.

Taz smiled at Sacha, and then turned toward the federal agent and said, "You're the FBI, man. Figure it out. Come on, Li'l Mama, let's bounce."

As Sacha and Taz left the agents' office, Agent Johns told his partner, "He's as clean as a whistle, Tom."

"What makes you think so?"

"Too confident . . . too fuckin' confident."

"Yeah, I can tell. Did you catch what he called his attorney when they left?"

"What, the Li'l Mama thing? Yeah, I caught it. Not only is he confident, he has some very good taste, too."

"That's right. She's a looker."

Both of the federal agents started laughing as they resumed their duties for the evening.

By the time Taz had dropped Sacha off at her house and made it to his, he had explained everything that had just happened to Won and Keno. Won laughed and told him that he didn't have anything to worry about. Since everything was bullshit, he should maintain his composure and keep to his normal every-day routine.

Keno, on the other hand, was a little spooked. "What if they get into our business with Won?" he asked.

Taz didn't have an answer for that, so he left it up to Won.

Won smiled into the receiver and said, "Listen. Don't worry about our business. Everything is everything. As a matter fact, we won't be doing anything for at least a month or so, so relax, Keno! It's all good!"

"I hear you, O.G. I had to ask, you know?" said Keno.

"Yeah, I know. All right, you two, be good. I'm out!" Won said and hung up the phone.

Taz pressed the button and cut the line to the speakerphone they were talking to Won on and said, "Dog, I really wasn't feeling the club at first, but now I am. Go get changed and get back over here. We needs to get to that club tonight, for real."

Keno smiled and asked, "All black?"

Taz stared at him for a moment, then said, "Call the homies. All black!"

Chapter Nineteen

Taz was dressed in a pair of black Sean Jean jeans, black T-shirt, and black Timb boots. Keno, Red, Bob, Bo-Pete, and Wild Bill were dressed almost exactly as Taz. The only difference was that they had on other urban designer gear. But it was still all black.

When they made their entrance inside of Club Cancun, it seemed as if everyone inside of the club could feel the dangerous vibes coming from them.

Katrina and Paquita were standing by the bar as Taz came in and accepted his drink from Winky, the bartender.

Paquita watched him as he downed his drink quickly. "Girl, something is wrong with Taz. He never downs his entire drink like that. Shit, look at how all of them are dressed. Something's going to go down tonight."

"I know, girl, I've never seen Keno look so damn mean. Look how they're mean mugging all of the niggas in the club," said Katrina.

"Ain't that some shit? And those scary-ass niggas ain't even trying to make eye contact with them. I've heard some way-out-ass stories about Taz and Keno, but I've never actually seen them in action."

"Well, come on. Let's go get a table, 'cause from the way they're looking, we're going to see their work tonight," Katrina said, and they left the bar.

Taz scanned the club over and over, trying his best to make eye contact with any and every male inside. He was hoping to catch someone's eye to see if he could spot some fear. He was confident that if the guy who had told the FEDs anything about him was in the club, he would be able to tell if they made eye contact. Even if he didn't spot anyone, someone inside the club was going to get a beat down tonight. Tonight was statement night: *Do not fuck with Taz!* It was wrong and Taz knew that, but he was in a real fucked-up mood, and the only way he was going to feel better was if he got to put his hands on one of these soft-ass, wannabe thug-ass niggas.

Keno came to Taz's side and said, "Here comes your girl, dog."

"Damnit! I told her to stay her ass at home. It's time for this broad to get checked!" Taz waited as Sacha and Gwen came over to where they were standing, and said, "Sacha, why are you here?"

With a defiant look on her face, she said, "To make sure that you don't do anything that you might regret later on."

Her words had the exact effect on him that she had hoped for. She saw how his eyes softened a little. He smiled and said, "Thanks, Li'l Mama. I really appreciate that. But you have to understand something about me. When my mood becomes dangerous, there is nothing and no one that can stop me from doing what needs to be done. No one, Li'l Mama, not even you."

Before Sacha could respond, Tony Surefield, her client, walked up to them and said, "Hey, Ms. Carbajal! What you doing up in this piece?"

Sacha smiled and said, "How are you doing, Mr. Surefield?"

"Tony. Call me Tony."

"Okay, Tony. I'm here with my boyfriend, trying to have a good time. Taz, this is Tony. Tony, this is my boyfriend, Taz."

Taz stared directly at Tony for a few seconds, then said, "Yeah, I remember you. KK's li'l brother, right?"

"Yeah, that's right," Tony said as he quickly lowered his eyes.

Well, I'll be damned! It was that easy! This bitch-ass nigga is the one, Taz said to himself. He turned toward Sacha and said, "Excuse me, baby. Let me have a word with Tony for a minute."

Sacha noticed how timid Tony was acting, and knew instantly that her client was the person who had snitched on Taz. *Oh, God! Don't let Taz hurt that man!* she prayed silently. She knew better than to try and talk to Taz, so she told him that she'd be by the bar, and quickly walked away.

After Taz was sure that Sacha was out of earshot, he turned back toward Tony and said, "Dog, I heard you got scooped up by them peoples. You straight?"

"Y—yeah, I'm good. It wasn't nothin' but some bullshit. H—how did you find out about that?"

Taz hadn't heard anything. He just wanted to see if Tony had been in contact with any form of law enforcement. Now, he was absolutely positive that it was this clown-ass nigga who put them onto him. But, why? That was the question he was going to find out. "Dog, it ain't too much that goes on in the City that I don't know about. But I am curious, though. How the fuck did you get out? I know the FEDs didn't give you a bond. They don't get down like that too often . . . unless you told them somethin'."

"N—nah, I ain't get down like that. Th—the case was so w— weak that they th—threw it ou—out," Tony stuttered.

"Is that right? Check this out, gee. Do you have a problem with how I got at you the last time?"

"Nah, Ta—Taz, I understood you, gee. You don't get down. I was wrong for even gettin' at you like that."

"If that's the case, then tell me why the fuck you told the FEDs you have been dealing with me, you bitch-ass nigga!" Before Tony could respond, Taz hit him so hard on his nose that blood splashed everywhere. Tony dropped to the floor as if he was hit with a sledgehammer. Several people in the club came over and watched the action. Tony got to his feet and swung wildly at Taz, who easily sidestepped his wild punch. Taz smiled and said, "Calm down, Tony! You don't want to hurt yourself, do you?"

"Fuck you, nigga! I ain't no snitch, and I don't go for no nigga calling me one!" yelled Tony as he wiped his bleeding nose.

"So, I'm lying on you, Tony? You're calling me a liar, nigga? The only reason why you got socked in the fuckin' nose and not served properly is because of your brother, nigga! So, don't stand there and call me a liar, you coward-ass nigga!" Taz said with venom in his voice. "Now, what else did you tell them, Tony? I need to know every fuckin' lie you told them peoples, nigga. And if you don't tell me, as God as my witness, I'm catching a murder charge tonight!"

Before Tony could respond, four of his homeboys came over to his side. This seemed to give him some courage, because he smiled and said, "Like I told you, nigga, I ain't no fuckin' snitch. I ain't never even fucked with your ass, so how could I tell them anythin' about you?"

Taz smiled and held up his hands to stop the security from interrupting them. He focused on Tony and his little crew and said, "I knew you were a dumb-ass nigga. I just didn't expect for you to be crazy." He then turned toward Bo-Pete and said, "Dog, I want y'all to smash these niggas with Tony, so that he can see that they have no win what-so-fucking-ever with us."

Bo-Pete's response to Taz's words was his fist swinging. He dropped the first guy he hit with a hard left; then he charged the next guy who was backing away from him and caught him with a series of vicious blows to his face. Before either of Tony's remaining two homeboys could react, Wild Bill and Red were all over them. Red slapped the hell out of one of the guys and dropped him as if he had hit him as hard as Taz had hit Tony in the nose. Wild Bill, though small, was hitting just as hard as his comrades. He showed his strength as he hit one of the guys with a kidney shot that would make old Iron Mike proud.

Bob, who was standing next to Keno, said, "Dog, fuck all this shit! Let's take this nigga somewhere so he can tell us what we need."

Taz smiled and said, "Nah, we don't have to do that, do we, Tony? You're going to tell everyone in this club exactly what you told the FEDs about me. Aren't you?" Taz stared Tony directly in his eyes, and once again asked, "Aren't you, Tony?"

Tony hesitated briefly and simply gave him a nod of his head yes.

With all of the commotion going on, the owner of the club had the lights turned on and the music turned off, so everyone in the club had heard what Taz had said to Tony.

"Now, get to talkin', bitch-ass nigga!" Keno said with contempt.

Tony turned toward his homeboys who were busy trying to tend to the wounds that Bo-Pete, Red, and Wild Bill had inflicted on them. He sighed heavily and said, "Man, I told them that I was plugged in with you, and that you were going to hook me up with some major weight."

Before he could say another word, someone in the crowd yelled, "You fuckin' snitch! Kill his ass, Taz!"

Taz ignored the comment and said, "What else?"

"That's it. They told me that they were going to put someone on you, and that they were going to bury you."

"So, that's all you told them about me, Tony?"

"Yeah, man, that's it, I swear."

"So, you want me to believe that all you said was that you were going to get hooked up by me, and they let you off on a FED beef? Come on, nigga! I guess you are ready to die!"

"I'm serious, Taz. That's all I said about you."

Taz paused for a moment, then said, "Okay, so who else did you tell on, nigga?"

Tony stared at Taz, pleading with his eyes, and said, "Come on, Taz! Don't do me like that, dog!"

"I'm not your dog, snitch! It's been too many niggas like you puttin' a black eye in the game. That's why most of you dope boys are so fuckin' soft. Y'all ain't layin' these snitches down. So now, everyone is tellin' they asses off." He then stepped back from Tony, turned slightly so that he was facing the onlooking crowd, and said, "You see? This is how the game got punked in the City, 'cause of niggas like this coward. If I was a dope boy, he'd be dead! I know y'all be on some hating shit, but it is what it is. So, I have a question for you dope boys in here that have dealt with this nigga. What are y'all gon' do about him?" Taz started laughing as he stepped up to the owner of the club and said, "I'm sorry about this drama, Big Tim. I had to clear the air, you know?"

"I ain't tripping, Taz. You know I know how you and your boys get down."

"Good lookin'. Now here, take this and let everyone know that the drinks are on me for the rest of the night," Taz said as he passed Big Tim over four thousand dollars in one-hundred-dollar bills. "If that don't cover it, let me know when I come back next time and I'll take care of it."

Smiling brightly, Big Tim said, "Gotcha, Taz!" He then gave the DJ a wave of his hand to signal him to turn the music back on. The lights dimmed, and D4L's "Laffy Taffy" started playing loudly through the speakers.

Taz stepped toward a frowning Sacha and asked, "Are you all right, Li'l Mama?"

"That was my client you just humiliated, Taz!"

"Your client? You mean to tell me that you knew that he told the people on me?"

"Don't be stupid! But even if I did, I wouldn't have been able to tell you."

"Yeah, I know attorney-client privacy and shit. I ain't trippin', Li'l Mama. It's all but a memory now."

"You think? Humph! Let me see. Have you ever heard of obstruction of justice, assault, and a host of other felonies you have just committed? Taz, I'd be very surprised if the FEDs weren't at your home first thing in the morning."

Taz smiled and said, "You think? At least I'll have the upper hand on them, Li'l Mama."

With a smirk on her face, she asked, "And how's that?"

"I'll already have my attorney present."

She punched him on his arm and said, "Ooh, you make me sick with your damn arrogance sometimes!"

"You love me?"

With a smile on her face, she answered, "With all of my heart."

He returned her smile and said, "Good. Now, let's go enjoy the rest of this evening."

Clifford and Do-Low stood at the back of the club and witnessed Taz's show with his homeboys. Do-Low frowned and told Clifford, "That nigga really thinks he's the shit, huh? I can't wait to serve that fool."

"Yeah, he does. Do you think he'll give you problems?"

"Did you just hear what I said? You know how I get down. It ain't no thang," Do-Low replied confidently.

"Good. When do you think you're going to take care of him?"

"If the time presents itself, I'm going to do it tonight."

"He has his boys with him now. I don't think that'll be wise."

"The night's still young, dog. You never know how things are gonna fall. Let's just wait and see," Do-Low said as he sipped his drink.

Bob and Gwen were sitting at a table, laughing and sipping their drinks, when Taz and Sacha came and joined them.

"Damn, bitch! Did you see how these tough guys handled their business? We got some straight gangstas in our lives, huh?"

After taking a seat, Sacha said, "Yeah, ho, we got us some real ones."

"Well, I'm glad to hear that our gangsta impresses y'all. I feel a whole lot better now knowing that," Taz said sarcastically.

Before either of the ladies could reply with a smart remark, Bob said, "Looks like our girl is really into clubbin' all of a sudden."

Taz turned and followed Bob's gaze toward Tazneema and Lyla and said, "Damn! What's with this girl?"

"Who are you talking about, baby?" asked Sacha.

Taz sighed and said, "Tazneema."

"Let her have some fun, baby. Your sister is still young."

He stared at Sacha for a minute, then shook his head. She just wouldn't be able to understand if he really told her why he was so concerned with Tazneema being in the club. He glanced toward Bob and noticed that he was following Tazneema's movements around the club. Bob gave him a slight nod, as if saying "Don't worry about it."

Keno saw Tazneema when she had entered the club also. He stepped over to her quickly and said, "Hey, baby girl! What you doing hangin' out in this dump?"

"Hi, Uncle Keno. Me and Lyla were bored and decided to come have a drink and chill out for a little while," said Tazneema.

"That's cool. If you need somethin', holla at me. Taz is sitting over there. You might want to go holla at him," Keno said as he pointed to where Taz was seated.

"Okay," replied Tazneema, and she gave him a kiss on his cheek and led Lyla toward Taz's table. When she made it to the table, she smiled and said, "Hey, Taz! What ya doing?"

Taz smiled and said, "Just chillin' a li'l bit. What it do?"

"Just came to hang out for a li'l while. We were bored, with nothing else better to do, so we came up here to chill too."

"How was your trip to H-town? Did you have fun?"

"Yeah, it was straight. Lyla's parents were real sweet. We had a really nice holiday."

"That's cool. Did you like your gift?"

"Did I! Thank you, Taz! You know I've been wanting that Dell notebook for the longest. Mama-Mama told me that it was too expensive. How did you talk her into letting you get it for me?"

Taz smiled at that and said, "You're not the only one who has a li'l pull with Mama-Mama. I just told her that you needed something like that to help you with your schoolwork. I knew she wouldn't trip out if I said something like that." They both laughed for a minute; then he said, "Well, go on and do you. Make sure that you—"

"I know! Be good! Bye, y'all!" she said as she grabbed Lyla's arm and quickly left them.

Sacha smiled and said, "You're very protective of your li'l sister, huh, baby?"

Bob and Taz exchanged quick glances with each other; then Taz answered, "Yeah. Next to Mama-Mama, she's all I got."

Sacha pouted and asked, "What about me?"

"You know what I mean, Li'l Mama."

She smiled, and they all started laughing again.

"Damn, my nigga! Look at that bad-ass young broad that just left that fool's table. That li'l bitch is right!" said Do-Low.

"I know," replied Clifford as he watched Tazneema as she led a white girl toward the bar. *She may be young, but she sure in the in hell is ready,* Clifford thought as he sipped his drink and focused back on Taz and Sacha. Just watching Sacha clinging to Taz drove him crazy. He hoped and prayed that Do-Low would be able to handle that fool as soon as possible. The sooner the better.

After another hour or so, Taz could tell that Sacha had gotten her club fix for the evening. Her eyes were a little glassy, and she had yawned at least twice in the past fifteen minutes. "Are you ready to shake this spot, Li'l Mama?"

Sacha smiled and said, "Yeah, baby, I'm getting kind of tired."

He stood and said, "Let me go get at my niggas real quick."

Sacha watched as he went and had a few words with Keno, Red, Wild Bill, and Bo-Pete. Gwen and Bob were still on the dance floor, acting like they didn't have a care in the world. Sacha smiled as she watched her best friend enjoy herself. *I'm so happy for her. She deserves all of the happiness she can get,* she thought as she finished the rest of her apple martini.

"I'm outta here, my nigga. What ya gon' do?" Taz asked Keno.

"I don't know about them, but I'm gon' chill until it lets out. I ain't got nothin' else to do," said Keno as he scanned the club for a victim for the night. His eyes stopped on Katrina and Paquita. He smiled and said, "As a matter a fact, I think I'm going to get with one of those rats for the night."

Taz laughed and said, "Don't tell me that you're slummin' tonight, my nigga!"

"Nah, I'm just in the mood for some of that good old-fashioned 'hood pussy! No strings, and no 'Can we get together again' shit. And that bitch Katrina is thicker than Thelma, so I'm tryin' to hit that tonight."

"That's on you, fool. What about y'all? Y'all straight?"

"I'm good," replied Red.

"Me too," added Wild Bill.

"Shit, ain't nothin' else to do. Might as well finish the night up here," said Bo-Pete.

"All right then, I'm out. Keep an eye on baby girl for me, huh?"

"Gotcha," they all replied in unison.

Taz left his homeboys and went over to the bar, where Tazneema and Lyla were standing. "I'm about to bounce, baby girl. Give me a holla tomorrow. Maybe we can do lunch or somethin'."

"Okay."

"Lyla, you make sure that you take care of her, ya hear?"

"Don't worry about it, Taz. I got her back," Lyla said with a smile on her face.

Taz smiled and said, "All right, you two. You be—"

"Good! We know, Taz!" replied Tazneema.

"All right, smart-ass!" he replied affectionately. He gave her a kiss on her cheek and a brief hug, and went back to his table.

After Taz was back seated, Sacha said, "Gwen and Bob are staying, baby, so I guess we can go on and leave."

"Good. Let's go," he said as he stood up from the table.

"They're leaving, my nigga, and it looks like that nigga ain't taking his boys with him. I got him, gee," Do-Low said as he quickly stepped away from Clifford.

Clifford's heartbeat increased dramatically as he watched Do-Low leave the club right before Taz and Sacha did. *That nigga is about to die tonight, and soon Sacha will be all mines!* he thought to himself as he noticed that pretty young lady that Taz had spoke to before he left the club walk by him. She smelled so sweet that he had to speak. He reached out and gently grabbed her arm and said, "Hello, beautiful!"

Tazneema smiled and said, "Hi!"

"Since you already have a drink in your hand, I won't offer to buy you one. But I would be honored to buy you another one when you're finished with that one."

Tazneema stared at Clifford for a moment and then said, "Okay, maybe I'll let you do that." She stepped away, giggling with Lyla.

Damn! How did she get all that ass in them jeans? Clifford asked himself as he sipped his drink.

As Taz and Sacha stepped toward Taz's truck, they were completely unaware of Do-Low leaning against the front of his car, which was parked right next to the truck. Taz reached inside of his pocket, pulled out his keys, and hit the alarm button, which deactivated his alarm, as well as opened the doors of his truck.

Once the doors were open, Do-Low made his move. He pulled out a chrome 45-caliber pistol, pointed it at the couple, and said, "Don't move, tough nigga! You know what this is!"

Sacha gasped and fell back into Taz's arms. Taz wished she hadn't, because now he couldn't grab his nine-millimeter that he had in the small of his back. *Damn!* he thought as he gently pulled Sacha next to him. He wasn't about to let this clown hurt her. He'd die first. "Check this out, homey. If it's chips you want, don't trip. I got plenty for you right here," Taz said as he lightly patted his right pocket.

"You damn right I want the chips, nigga! The jewels too. Run everything, fool! One wrong move and your bitch gets it first!"

Taz took his platinum chain from around his neck and gave it to Do-Low. He then gave him his two diamond pinky rings. "Look, my nigga, I gots to reach in my pocket for these ends, so relax. I'm not trying to trip on you or do anything stupid."

"Whatever, nigga! Just run the ends 'fore you get blasted!" Do-Low said nervously as he quickly looked over his shoulder.

Mistake! Major fuck-up! Taz took that split second when Do-Low looked over his shoulder to push Sacha aside. He pulled out his weapon and shot Do-Low twice. The first bullet tore through Do-Low's face, and the second one caught him square in his chest. Do-Low fell flat on his back, dead as a doorknob.

Sacha screamed and ran into Taz's arms. He held on to her tightly as the security and a lot of people came running out of the club.

When Keno and Bo-Pete came outside and saw that Taz had his gun in his hand, they both pulled out their weapons and were by Taz's side immediately. "What the fuck happened, my nigga?" asked Keno.

Taz, who was still holding on to Sacha, said, "This fool tried to fuckin' rob us, gee! He slipped and took a look over his shoulder, and I nailed his ass."

"Are you all right, my nigga?" asked Bo-Pete.

"Yeah, I'm good. Look, get her out of here, dog. I'm going to be stuck dealing with the police and shit. She's seen enough."

"N—no, I'm fine, baby. I'm a witness to this so I need to stay," Sacha said shakily.

"Are you sure, baby?"

"Yes, I'm sure."

"All right then, go on back inside of the club while I get with these clowns first," Taz said as he pointed to some of the police officers as they were headed their way.

Gwen and Bob came outside, and Bob had Gwen take Sacha back inside of the club. He then went and joined his homeboys.

Wild Bill and Red were the last to come outside, and when they saw the body lying next to Taz's truck, they stared at each other briefly and then shook their heads at each other. They went and joined the rest of the crew to find out what the fuck had gone down.

The police had the entire club parking lot roped off. It was a crime scene now, and they weren't letting anyone leave for the moment.

The homicide detective took Taz's statement as well as his weapon. He sent his partner inside of the club to go get Sacha. After he received a similar statement from her, he told Taz that they were going to have to take him down to the station for further questioning.

"Whatever, man. Just let her go. I ain't trippin' off this shit. This was self-defense all the fuckin' way."

"We have Ms. Carbajal's statement, so she's free to leave. We'll get in contact with you if we need anything else, ma'am," the homicide detective said as he led Taz toward his car.

"Uh-uh! I'm his attorney, and I'd like to accompany him if I may."

"There's really no need, ma'am. We just want to make sure that his weapon is legal, and ask a few more questions, that's all. It's all pretty clear that this is an open-and-shut case."

"Well, if that's the case, you won't mind me accompanying him."

The homicide detective sighed and said, "Whatever you like, ma'am."

As they were walking toward the unmarked police vehicle, Taz saw Tazneema staring at him with a look of horror on her face. He stopped and called Keno.

Keno ran over to him and said, "What's up, my nigga?"

Taz pointed toward Tazneema and Lyla and said, "Get them the hell outta here. Now!"

"Gotcha, gee," Keno said and stepped over to Tazneema and Lyla.

Taz saw the tears in her eyes, and his heart felt as if it had stopped. *Damn! This is some fucked-up shit. Two bodies in less than two months.* He shook his head sadly as he watched as Keno led Lyla and Tazneema to their car.

What he didn't notice was Clifford as he stood there the entire time and watched in disbelief as the coroner covered up Do-Low's body with a sheet. The hatred he had for Taz had just been multiplied by 100.

Chapter Twenty

It had been a few weeks since the incident at Club Cancun, and Tazneema was still a little shaken by it. Even though she knew that Taz had done what he had to do, it still bothered her that he murdered that man in the parking lot.

On a brighter side of things, she was excited about her upcoming date with a guy she met that same night. She was excited because this was the first date that she'd been on in a long time. Usually, Taz wouldn't let her go out with any guys. With everything going on with him, she decided not to tell or ask him for his permission to go out tonight with Clifford. Clifford had asked for her telephone number that night at the club, and she willingly gave it to him because she thought he was so cute. She didn't expect to hear from him, but she was happy when he called her. She was even happier when he asked her out on a date.

So, here she was, all dressed up and ready to go. She couldn't remember the last time that she had been this excited. She chose her clothes carefully. She didn't want to be too dressy, but she wanted to show Clifford that she had class, so she went with a linen pantsuit and matching beige pumps. Her long hair was tied in a ponytail because there just wasn't much she could do with it other than to let it hang loosely past her shoulders. Even though her linen pants fit her loosely, she smiled when she noticed how they still displayed her thin waistline and fat booty. "All men love the booty!" she said to herself as she went into the living room to wait for Clifford to arrive.

Clifford smiled as he pulled into Tazneema's apartment complex. *Yeah, not only am I going to fuck this clown's sister,*

I'm going to make her love me, he thought as he climbed out of his Mercedes.

That night at the club was a sad night for Clifford, but he still found something positive out of it. When he realized that Tazneema was related to Taz, he couldn't stop himself from smiling. Even though he was hurt behind losing Do-Low the way that he did, he still felt that it was better for him than suffering with AIDS and dying with no dignity. At least this way, he died the way he lived, in the streets. Clifford smiled when he remembered how excited he became when he heard Sacha's friend tell her boyfriend that someone should make sure that Taz's sister was okay. *His sister! Ain't that something! She's going to be mine, and ain't nothing that nigga gon' be able to do to change that after I get finish with her ass,* he thought to himself as he knocked on Tazneema's front door.

Tazneema jumped when she heard the knock. She took a deep breath and told herself to calm down as she went and answered the door. She opened the front door and said, "Hi!"

"Hello, beautiful! Are you ready?" asked Clifford.

"Yep," she said as she stepped out of the apartment with her purse in hand.

As they walked toward Clifford's car, he asked, "Do you have a special place you like to dine, or will I have the pleasure of choosing this evening?"

"I'm not picky. You choose, Cliff."

"Well, how about we do some Bricktown? I know a nice Italian restaurant that has the best veal in the City."

"That's fine."

Clifford opened the car door for her and closed it behind her after she was comfortable. He went and got inside of the car, thinking about how big and firm her ass was. He thought, *Man, I'm loving her already!* He then pulled out of the apartment complex.

Taz couldn't believe that that fool had actually tried to rob him, even though the shooting had been a few weeks ago. He just couldn't understand what would have made that clown think he could get away with some shit like that. This shit was crazy!

He went into his bedroom, changed clothes quickly, and called Sacha. When she didn't answer her phone, he decided to give Tazneema a call. After not getting an answer from her house, either, he dialed her cell phone.

"What's up, Taz?" she asked when she answered the phone.

"Nothin' much. What's up with you? Are you busy?"

"Kinda. I'm eating right now."

"All right. I didn't really want anything. I just wanted to make sure that you were straight, you know, with what happened at the club and all."

"Oh, yeah, I'm fine. I was worried about you, but I figured I'd wait for you to call. Are you okay?"

He laughed and said, "You know me. I'm good. Go on and finish eating. I'll get at you tomorrow or somethin'."

"Okay, bye, Taz," she said and hung up the phone.

"I need a break from this town. Fuck this shit!" he said aloud as he called Won. As soon as Won answered his phone, Taz asked him, "Do you think we have enough time for me to take a li'l vacation, O.G.?"

"As a matter a fact, you do. I thought it was going to get hectic for us, but my plans got screwed a li'l. Where are you planning on going, Babyboy?" asked Won.

"After all this drama, I was thinking about bringing my boo your way for a few days, and chill out in the sun, ya know what I'm sayin'?"

"That's cool. Come on out here and show her Hollywood and shit. I'm kinda curious as to what she's like, anyway. She has to be something special if she's captured your heart."

Taz smiled at that and said, "She is O.G., she is. All right, let me get at her and I'll get back at you."

"That's straight. How's Mama-Mama and 'Neema doing?"

"They're good. I'll make sure I let them know you asked about them."

"All right then, out!" Won said.

After Taz got off of the phone with Won, he called Keno and told him that they had a break coming, and that he should let the others know what was up. He also told him that he was going to take a quick trip out to California with Sacha. "I need a break, dog. That shit at the club got me kinda trippin'."

"Why is that? That nigga brought that on himself, my nigga."

"Yeah, I know, but that fool should have known better. Every nigga in this town knows I'm not to be fucked with."

Keno laughed and said, "Well, for what I've heard, that clown was fresh out the pen."

"Is that right?"

"Yeah. And guess what?"

"What?"

"I heard the nigga had AIDS. You really did that clown a favor, my nigga. You took him out before that shit kicked in on his ass."

Taz laughed and said, "You're sick, fool!"

Keno laughed also and said, "Maybe, but it's the truth. You saved that coward-ass nigga some misery, gee."

"Yeah, I feel you. Let me roll. I gots to get at Sacha and see if she'll be able to take a few days off."

"How long are you goin' to be out that way?"

"Three or four days tops. I want to let her get her shopping on and shit. Then we'll just sightsee and kick it a li'l."

"Go on, dog, and get your mind right, my nigga," Keno said before he hung up the phone.

After Taz hung up the phone, he called Sacha on her cell and got her voicemail. He left her a message telling her to call him back as soon as possible.

After that, he went into his backyard and watched Heaven and Precious as they ran around the yard. As he watched his beloved Dobermans, he thought about what Keno had just told him. *Maybe I did do some good by smokin' that nigga. At least he won't have to go through all of that shit that comes along with AIDS,* he thought to himself. The ringing of his cell phone snapped him back to reality. "Hello."

"Hi, baby. I got your message. Is everything okay?" asked Sacha.

"Yeah, everything's good. I wanted to see if you could take some time off this week."

"Why? What's going on?"

"I wanted to take you out to Cali for three or four days."

"For real?"

He laughed and said, "Yeah, for real. So, can you go or what?"

She smiled into the receiver and said, "Baby, I'm a partner now. Hell, yeah, I can go! Plus, I don't have anything that pressing on my schedule, anyway."

"All right then, this is what I want you to do. Go home and pack a light suitcase. Then head on over here. I'll make the arrangements while you're getting ready. I think it's a flight out of Will Rogers that leaves a li'l after nine. If not, I'll check with Tulsa. That way, we'll be able to get out of here as soon as possible."

"Okay, baby, I'll be there no later than an hour or so."

"I said a *light* bag, Sacha!"

"I know, but I still have to make sure I have everything I need, baby."

"Sacha . . ."

"All right, dang! You can't even let a girl be a girl!"

"Whatever! I love you, Ms. Carbajal!"

"I love you too! Bye!"

Taz hung up the phone and called Tari. "What's up, sexy lady?"

"Damn, it's been a long time, stranger," Tari said as she smiled into the receiver. She had been missing Taz's voice something terrible, and now that he called, she felt as if they were still together.

"I know. I'm down bad for not checkin' in on you, but I've been caught up a li'l. A lot of shit has been goin' on."

"Is that an apology, Mr. Taz?"

He smiled and said, "Yeah, it is. Do you accept it?"

"You know I do. Now, what's up?"

"Shit. I'm about to take a trip to the West Coast, so I'm goin' to need you to come take care of your babies and shit. Is that cool?"

"You know it is. But since things are different now, I'm going to have to charge you for my services."

He laughed and said, "Is that right?"

"Yep."

"All right then, what's your price?"

"Dinner."

"Dinner?"

"Yep. Dinner and a movie."

"Come on, Tee, you know I don't really be playin' the movies and shit."

"That's my price. Take it or leave it."

"All right, Tee, you got that."

"As soon as you get back?"

"As soon as I get back."

"Good. Now, have a safe trip, and make sure that you call me as soon as you get back to this city, Mr. Taz."

"I will, baby. Bye," he said as he hung up the phone. He stood up and called for Heaven and Precious to come on in. He turned and went back inside of his house, followed by his dogs, so he could make his and Sacha's reservations for their flight to sunny California.

After dinner was over, Clifford took Tazneema for a walk down by the River Walk. They strolled casually hand in hand as Tazneema told Clifford all about herself. She felt so comfortable that she didn't even realize that she had just told him everything about herself . . . well, almost everything.

"So, how do you like going to OU?" asked Clifford.

"It's cool, but it's nothing like I thought it would be. I would have rather went to an all-Black college, but Taz and Mama-Mama would have both had babies if I would have tried that."

"Taz, that's your older brother, right? The guy at the club that night?"

Tazneema smiled sadly and said, "I'd rather forget that night."

"Oh, I'm sorry, beautiful. I forgot."

"It's okay." She glanced at her watch and said, "Well, it's getting kind of late, and I do have classes in the morning."

"All right, let me get you on home, then," Clifford said as they walked toward the parking lot.

Clifford walked Tazneema to her front door and said, "I want you to know that I had a wonderful time with you this evening, Tazneema."

"Call me 'Neema, Cliff. I'd prefer that."

He smiled and said, "Okay, 'Neema. I hope you'll give me another opportunity to take you out again."

She smiled brightly and said, "Sure. You name the time and place. I really like you, too, Cliff."

"Good. I'll give you a call in a day or so, when I'll have a grip on my schedule, okay?"

"That's fine," she said as she got on her tiptoes and kissed Clifford softly on his lips. "Good night, Cliff."

"Good night, beautiful," he said as he watched her go inside of her apartment. As he walked back to his car, he had a huge smile on his face. Phase one of his plans had just been accomplished.

"Damn, baby, don't stop! Oh, damnit, Taz! Don't you stop!" screamed Sacha as she bit her bottom lip. Taz was riding her like a bronco. Their lovemaking was so intense that it felt as if neither of them had had sex in years. "Ooh! I'm! Cumming! Taz! I'm cumming!"

"Me too, baby! Me to-o-o-o!" screamed Taz as they reached their climax simultaneously. Taz slid off of her and fell back onto the bed, out of breath.

They had arrived in Los Angeles late the night before. Since it was so late, they went and got a room and fell fast asleep.

Sacha had woken Taz up with one of the best blowjobs he had ever had in his entire life. That was around seven in the morning, and now it was after nine and they had just finished.

"Damn, Li'l Mama! You done fucked up your day of shoppin' now, 'cause I don't feel like doin' nothin' but staying in this damn bed all day."

Shaking her head no, Sacha climbed out of the bed and said, "Uh-uh! You better get yourself up. We got some shopping to do. You can rest while I take a shower. After I'm finished, then you'll come take yours. Then we're out of here, mister."

He smiled and asked, "Why can't I take one with you?"

She returned his smile and said, "Because then neither of us would get finished." She ran into the shower, laughing.

An hour later, they were riding in a rented convertible BMW. Taz figured that Sacha would have wanted a convertible so they would be able to enjoy the weather, and his assumption was correct. Sacha couldn't keep still. Everywhere they went, she kept oohing and aahing. She was like a kid on a field trip. He smiled at her as he drove toward the Lakewood Mall.

Sacha had seen a pamphlet that indicated where all of the malls were, and she said that she wanted to go to the Lakewood Mall first. They had a store called BeBe's that she wanted to go to. When they arrived at the mall, she went ballistic; she bought something in almost every store they went into.

Taz didn't mind. It was kind of funny to him as he watched her do her thing. He just pulled out his Black Card and paid for everything she wanted. This was her time, and he was happy just to see that beautiful smile of hers. *This is what life's all about,* he thought as he lugged all of Sacha's bags.

"Oh, baby, let's go into that Zales jewelry store. I want to buy you something."

"Come on, Li'l Mama! You know I don't need no more jewels. I got damn near every new piece that's out," he said with a cocky smile on his face.

"Humph! Well, you don't have everything, mister. Come on," she said as she led him inside of the jewelry store. They went to the counter, and Sacha started looking at all of the different types of rings, bracelets and platinum chains the store had to offer. Her eyes grew wide when she saw a platinum bracelet with huge, canary-yellow diamonds inside of it. "That's it!" she yelled excitedly. "Excuse me, sir. May I see this bracelet right here, please?"

The jeweler came to the counter and grabbed the bracelet she had requested. She smiled as she held it in her hand. "Do you like that, ma'am? It's a new design from Jacob the Jeweler. We just got it in yesterday," said the jeweler.

"I love it! See, baby, you don't have any colored diamonds. This is nice. Let me see how it'll look on your wrist," she said as she grabbed Taz's arm and put the bracelet on him. Shaking her head yes, she said, "Yep, I knew it. That's the bomb, baby!"

As Taz stared at the bracelet, he had to admit that it was pretty tight. He asked the jeweler, "How much?"

"Five thousand eight hundred, sir."

Before Taz could say anything, Sacha spotted a pair of canary-yellow diamond earrings and asked, "How much are those earrings right there?"

"Those are eight hundred and twenty-five dollars a pair, ma'am," replied the jeweler.

"Okay, what will you do for me if I got the bracelet and a pair of earrings?"

The jeweler smiled and simply said, "You wouldn't want to just stop with the bracelet and earrings, ma'am. You'd have to complete the set with this." He then reached back under the counter and grabbed a small pinky ring with the same colored canary-yellow diamonds inside of it and said, "Now, this ring is thirty-five hundred dollars. As you can see, they have the same flawless canary-yellow colored diamonds inside. If you were to buy the bracelet, earrings, and this ring, I'd give them all to you for nine thousand dollars even. After taxes, it'll be around eleven thousand or so. The total price without my discount would be closer to thirteen thousand dollars for everything, so I'm saving you close to two thousand dollars."

Sacha smiled and said, "We'll take it!"

Taz started to say something, but she stopped him and said, "This is my gift to you, Taz, so please don't try to stop me." Then to the jeweler she said, "Could you please size my man for me, and we'll come back in an hour or so to pick everything up?"

The jeweler smiled and said, "No problem, ma'am!"

After the jeweler had gotten Taz's ring size, Sacha led Taz into yet another store. *Damn! This girl ain't playin', and this is just the first mall on her list,* he thought to himself as he shook his head and watched his girl continue to go wild with her shopping spree.

Finally after another hour or so inside of the mall, Sacha was ready to leave. "Let's go pick up your stuff from Zales, baby. Then we can go get us something to eat. I want to go to that soul food place called Aunt Kizzy's Kitchen. The brochure I read said it was one of the best soul food places in L.A."

"I'm with it, Li'l Mama, 'cause you're killin' me with all of this damn shopping!"

She laughed and said, "Will you come on, boy?"

As they were leaving the Zales jewelry store, Taz saw three guys staring at them. He didn't mind, because he knew that Sacha was a bad-ass female, so he took their stares as a compliment. But as they passed the three men, recognition snapped in both Taz's and one of the guys' eyes. Taz kept his cool and smiled as they walked by them. *Damnit! Of all places, I had to come to a fuckin' mall and bump into one of those clowns. Fuck!* he thought to himself as he walked toward the mall exit. *Think, nigga! You know you can't go outside. They'll move on you then.* He took a look over his shoulder and saw that the three guys were following them. He turned to Sacha and said, "Look, baby, let's go back into that Sam Goody's for a minute. I almost forgot that Keno asked me to see if I could find him some mixed CDs. That nigga loves West Coast rap," he lied.

"Okay, baby, but let's hurry, okay? I'm starving."

He smiled and said, "All right." He then led her into the record store and started browsing as if he was really looking for CDs to buy. But, in actuality, he was trying to buy some time so he could figure a way out of this shit. The same guys he had robbed over a month ago were waiting right outside of the Sam Goody record store. He knew he was in some deep shit. He had killed one of their comrades, so he knew they had murder on their minds. He had no other choice but to call Won and see if he would be able to get him out of this mess. He didn't have a weapon, so basically he had no win whatsoever.

He stepped away from Sacha and pulled out his cell and quickly dialed Won's number. When Won answered the phone, he said, "O.G., you ain't gon' believe this shit, but I'm out here at the Lakewood Mall, and I done bumped into someone I met about a month in a half ago."

"Ah shit! Say it ain't so, Babyboy! Say it ain't so!"

"They're on me, O.G., and I'm strapless."

"Why in the hell did you go to the Lakewood Mall? Out of all of the fuckin' malls, you chose the one that's maybe ten minutes tops from where the work was put in."

"Dog, how the fuck would I know that shit? I'm from fuckin' Oklahoma!"

"All right, listen. You can't leave that mall 'cause they will do you."

"You think I don't know that shit? Tell me something I don't know, O.G.!"

"Stay close by security or some shit while I get someone out there to take care of this shit. Where is your car parked?"

"It's by JCPenny."

"What you driving?"

"A black convertible Beamer."

"A'ight, stay safe for as long as you can. Once my people are in position, I'll hit you back. Out!" Won said and hung up.

Taz closed his cell, stepped back next to Sacha, and said, "Check this out, Li'l Mama. Let's go to the food court and get something to hold us off for a li'l bit."

"But I thought we were going to get some Aunt Kizzy's, baby!" she whined.

"We will, but not right now. Now, come on," he said as he grabbed her hand with his free hand.

Once they had stepped out of this record store, one of the guys that had been following them said, "I never forget a face, cuz, and I damn sho' wouldn't forget a grille like yours!"

Taz stopped, let go of Sacha's hand and said, "Excuse me? Are you talkin' to me?"

"You know who I'm talkin' to, cuz. And you already know what time it is, so ain't no need to be tryin' to play dumb and shit, cuz."

Taz gave Sacha a confused expression and said, "Come on, Li'l Mama. These fools are trippin'."

The guy who did all of the talking said, "Yeah, we're trippin', cuz, but the best is yet to come."

Taz took a look over his shoulder and saw that the group of men resumed following them. Sacha saw that Taz was uncomfortable and asked, "Is everything all right, baby?"

Taz smiled at her and said, "Yeah, everything is everything, Li'l Mama."

They went to the food court, and Taz bought them a burger and some french fries from Wendy's. While they sat and were eating their food, Taz noticed the men that were following them had taken a seat about four or five tables away. They stared and smiled deadly looking smiles at him. One of them even went as far as taking his index finger and sliding it against his throat, indicating that Taz was a dead man. Taz shook his head and kept on eating his food.

Just as they finished eating, Taz's cell rang. "Hello."

"Head on out to your car. You know there won't be any way to do this without your girl getting up on it?"

Taz looked across the table at Sacha, sighed, and said, "Yeah, I know. I'll deal with that later."

"Okay, then do you, and hit me back when you're on your way. Out!"

Taz closed his cell and said, "Come on, Li'l Mama, it's time to go."

By now Sacha had figured out that something serious was going on. Taz's tone with her was just how it had been that night at the club. Someone was about to get hurt. She could see it in his eyes.

Out in the parking lot, Taz took a quick look to his right and smiled as he saw the opening doors of an all-black Lincoln Navigator that had just pulled up. He said, "Yeah, homey, I'm ready!"

Before the guy could reply, four gigantic men jumped out of the Navigator with automatic rifles in their hands. "Get your fuckin' hands in the air, now!" one of the huge men yelled as they stepped closer to the three men. The man who had given the order then told his partners, "Get them niggas in the truck." Two of the four big men then went and shoved the three guys toward the Navigator. Once they were secure inside of the truck, the obvious leader of the big men turned toward

Taz and said, "It's all good, homey. You can go on and shake this spot. We gots this now."

Taz stepped to him, shook his hand, and said, "Thanks."

"Don't thank me. Thank your man, Won," he said as he turned and climbed back inside of the truck.

Taz followed him to the Navigator, peeped into the window, and said to the three captives, "It's been real, gentlemen, but as the saying goes, you can't win 'em all!" Then he started laughing as he walked toward Sacha and the BMW. As the Navigator pulled away, he heard the one guy who had been doing all of the slick talking yell, "Fuck you, cuz!"

Taz just smiled as he climbed into the BMW.

Chapter Twenty-one

Sacha remained silent during the entire ride back to their hotel, but as soon as they entered their suite at the Marriott, she went ballistic. "Damnit, Taz! I want to know what the hell just went on back there, and I want to know right damn now!" She plopped herself onto the bed, folded her arms across her chest, and glared at him.

Taz sighed and said, "You're not goin' to let this go, are you, Li'l Mama?"

Her answer to his question was an even harder glare.

He shook his head slowly and asked, "All right, what do you want to know? Why that shit went down at the mall, or why it happened in the first place?"

"Don't play with me, Taz! I want to know everything! Why that shit happened, what happened to the men that got put in that Navigator, and why the hell any of this shit happened in the first fucking place! But most of all, I want to know exactly what it is that you do when you go out of town. Because, I got a funny feeling all of the shit that happened today revolves around your trips."

"You're right," Taz said as he sat down on the bed next to her. "You have to understand that the life I lead is not a normal one, and you may not understand the things I'm about to tell you. So please, don't judge what I do, because I never meant for you to find out. You've pushed my hand, and I'm about to give it to you raw, only because I love you, and I don't want to lose you, Li'l Mama."

"I love you, too, Taz, and I have the right to know exactly what my man is involved in. Don't worry about me. Just keep it real with me, baby."

Taz took a deep breath and then went into detail about how he became involved in robbing people in other states. After about thirty minutes, he finished and said, "And that's everything."

"So, you mean to tell me that you've acquired millions from doing this stuff for Won?"

"Yeah. Seventeen point five to be exact. That's not counting the cars, my home, the jewelry, or the homes I own in the City. That's a completely different income."

"And the rest, are they in the same position as you are financially?"

"Yeah. We split everything six ways. You can never speak on any of this to them, because we've always sworn to never let anyone know our business. The only other woman who knows what I do is Tari, and that's because Won introduced us a long time ago."

"All right, I understand. But tell me, were those guys at the mall going to kill us?"

"They were going to try."

She sat there on the bed still and quiet for a moment. Then she asked, "What happened to them, baby? Are they dead now?"

Taz put his arms around her shoulders and said, "Don't worry about them, Li'l Mama. You're safe, so that's all that matters to me."

She put her head onto his shoulders and said, "*We're* safe. That's all that matters to *me*."

"So, you're not going to leave me now that you've found out what I do?"

"I love you, Taz, and I mean that more and more every time I say those words. As long as your work doesn't affect mine, I will try my best not to let it bother me. But I know I'll be a nervous wreck every time you leave town from now on."

"You see, that's one of the reasons why I didn't want you to know about my business. But don't trip, because every time we get down, it's planned to the tee, and it's a cakewalk."

"How long do you think that will last, baby? Nothing lasts forever."

"Yeah, I know, but you don't know how Won gets down."

"I want to meet him, baby. I want to meet this spectacular man who saved our lives this afternoon."

Taz smiled and said, "That's funny, 'cause he wants to meet you too. Come on, let's go get something to eat at that Aunt Kassy's you was talkin' 'bout. Then we'll see what we can do about you meeting Won."

"Aunt *Kizzy's*, Taz!"

He laughed and said, "Oh, my bad! Come on, Li'l Mama."

Back in Oklahoma City, Tazneema had just gotten off of the phone with Clifford. They arranged to meet at the Red Lobster down in the City. She was so excited that she couldn't take the smile off of her face.

"Damn, girl! Why do you have that goofy-ass smile on your face?" asked Lyla.

"'Cause I'm meeting Cliff at the Red Lobster in an hour, and I'm happy as hell about it," Tazneema replied.

"Have you asked him if he has any attorney friends for me yet?"

"Your name has only come up once, and that was when I told him that you are my roommate. Wait until I see if this is going to go anywhere. Damn, you act like you're desperate or something."

"I'm not desperate. I'm just horny, girl! These little college boys out here act as if they're scared to talk to a nice-looking white girl like myself," Lyla said as she pranced in front of Tazneema.

Tazneema laughed and said, "If they only knew that you were a borderline nymphomaniac!"

"I know, huh? Maybe I should go pick a few players on the football team and invite them over for an all-night orgy. I'll bet I'd get their attention then!" Lyla said and busted out laughing.

"I know you're clowning, but then again, I'm afraid that you might actually be serious."

Lyla smiled and said, "You never know!" as she went into her bedroom.

***

Taz and Sacha were enjoying their meal at Aunt Kizzy's soul food restaurant when a tall older man approached their table. "Well, well! Look at my Babyboy! What it do?" asked Won.

Taz stood, and both men embraced each other tightly. "What's up, O.G.? Damn, you lookin' better and better every time I see you, old-timer!"

Won laughed and said, "Old-timer, huh? I'd run circles around you in any sport you name, Babyboy. I'm in the best shape of my life."

Taz laughed and said, "I can tell. Well, O.G., this here is my Li'l Mama. Sacha, I'd like you to meet Won. Won, this is Sacha."

Won reached out and shook hands with Sacha and said, "It is truly a pleasure to meet you, Sacha."

"Likewise, Mr. Won."

"Please, call me Won. That mister stuff ain't for us. You're now a part of this joker's life, so that makes us family."

Sacha smiled and said, "Okay, Won."

"That's better," Won said as he sat down at their table. "So, are you enjoying your stay in sunny, sunny land?"

"Oh, yes! It's been exciting, to say the least. I can't wait to see what's going to happen next in this wild and crazy town," Sacha said as she stared at Taz.

Taz smiled and said, "I put her up on everything, O.G."

Won raised his eyebrows and asked, "Everything?"

"Yep. Everything."

Won started laughing and said, "Well, I'll be damn! You really *are* in love then, aren't ya? That's good . . . that's real good, Babyboy." Won then turned his attention toward Sacha and said, "Since you already know what's what, I'd like to apologize for today's li'l. . . ah . . . festivities. That was something that was never to have happened. It was unexpected, and I apologize to you for it."

"There's really no need for apologizing, Won. After all, you did save us."

Won turned back toward Taz and said, "Yeah, I did, huh? I've been saving this guy here for a real long time now, but that's another story. Tell me, can you really accept what he does for a living?"

"Honestly, no. But I have no other choice if I want to continue to be a part of his life. I love him, and I will always have my man's back."

Won chuckled and said, "Oh, you're impressing me more and more, lovely lady."

Sacha stared at Won as she sipped her drink, and smiled. *This is one powerful man,* she thought to herself as she watched Won and Taz share words with one another. She took in his six-three frame and his conservative style of dress and wondered how many people he had killed or had had killed in his lifetime. His salt-and-pepper, short haircut gave him a sense of respectability, and his eyes were so warm looking she felt as if he could be her uncle or something. All in all, she felt comfortable around him, and that was all that mattered, because she could tell that Taz was really close to him.

"Sacha! Sacha!"

"Uh-huh? Oh! Excuse me, I must have been daydreaming."

"Well, I'm glad your back, Li'l Mama. Won wants to know if we'd like to join him out on his yacht tomorrow."

"Yacht? You mean as in boat?"

Won laughed and said, "Exactly, lovely lady. I have her docked out on Marina del Rey, not too far from here, actually. If you'd like, we could take her out and take a li'l ride out on the Pacific."

"I'd love to! I've never been on a yacht before."

"Well, it's settled then. I'll come pick the both of you up around noon." Won stood and asked Taz to step outside with him for a moment. "He'll be right back, lovely lady. I need to discuss a li'l somethin'-somethin' with him real quick."

"No problem, Won. I know business will be business. Plus, I haven't finished this scrumptious meal yet. Bye!" she said and started back eating her food.

After they had stepped outside of the restaurant, Taz asked, "What do you think?"

"She's definitely a keeper, Babyboy. I'm proud of you. But tell me, why did you tell her everything?"

"She wouldn't have it any other way. And I didn't exactly tell her everything. I told her enough, though . . . more than I thought I'd ever tell anyone."

"So, I guess it's safe to say that you trust her, huh?"

"With my life, O.G. . . . with my life!" Taz answered seriously.

"Okay, then, that's good enough for me. Now, check this out. We'll be ready to move most likely next Friday or Saturday. I'll know for sure by the time you leave. So make sure that the knuckleheads are ready."

Taz smiled and said, "They're always ready to get money."

"Yeah, I know. All right then, I'll see y'all tomorrow around noon. Out!" Won said as he walked quickly toward his car.

Taz smiled as he walked back into the Aunt Kizzy's Kitchen to finish dining with his Li'l Mama.

After dinner at Red Lobster, Clifford took Tazneema back to his place. They listened to some of his CDs and shared a bottle of white wine.

Tazneema was enjoying herself so much that she'd lost track of the time. When she glanced at her watch and saw that it was almost midnight, she said, "Oh, my! I didn't know it had gotten this late. I have a class at nine. I should be going home now."

Clifford got up from the sofa and said, "I'm sorry, Tazneema. I've been having so much fun with you that I didn't pay any attention to the time. Come on, let me walk you to your car."

Once they were outside in Clifford's driveway, Tazneema said, "Thank you for another wonderful evening, Cliff."

"No problem, Tazneema . . . no problem at all."

She grabbed his hand and said once again, "Please, call me, 'Neema. Everyone who's close to me calls me that."

Clifford smiled and asked, "Am I close to you, 'Neema?"

Her answer to his question was a long passionate kiss. When she pulled from his embrace, he said, "I guess that answers that question!"

She smiled at him and said, "Yep, I guess it does." She climbed into her car and said, "Cliff, I've never been in a serious relationship, so I really don't want to rush into anything. But I want you to know that I like you. I like you a lot. Please be patient with me, okay?"

Clifford bent his head so that his face was inside of the window of her car and said, "We have all the time in the world, 'Neema. I'd never rush you into anything."

"Thank you. Thank you so much for saying that. I promise you, once I'm ready, I'll be ready."

He smiled and asked, "What's that supposed to mean?"

She smiled seductively and said, "It means that when I'm ready to lose my virginity, you're going to be the one to take it. Bye!"

He was at such a loss for words that all he could do was nod his head as he watched her pull out of his driveway. *Well, I'll be damn!* he thought to himself as he watched her drive off down the street.

Chapter Twenty-two

Ever since their trip to the West Coast, Sacha and Taz's relationship seemed to have blossomed. Not only had they become closer, it felt as if they had become somewhat of a team. When it came time for Taz and the crew to take their trips, Sacha made sure that she kept herself busy so that she wouldn't have time to worry about Taz. She knew that if she didn't, she would drive herself crazy. She stayed at the house and enjoyed Heaven and Precious's company while Taz was away. A couple of times when Tari had come over to feed the Dobermans, they had sat and chatted with each other. The more Sacha got to know Tari, the more she liked her. They got along fine, and her life with Taz just couldn't get any better.

"What's up, Li'l Mama?"

"Hi, baby! Where are you?"

"I'm on my way in from Tulsa. I should be home in about forty-five minutes or so. You straight?"

"I am now. I've just finished for the day. I'll be at the house by the time you get there."

"That's cool. We have to take care of some things, but it shouldn't take that long."

"I know, I know, the last part of the business stuff. Don't worry about me. After I kiss that face of yours, I'll go back upstairs until you all are finished."

Taz laughed and said, "Damn! How did I get so lucky to catch a female like you?"

"I don't know. I guess God was smiling on you that night at the club," she said, and they both started laughing.

"I guess you're right. All right then, baby, out!" he said and closed his cell phone.

"Love is truly a wonderful thing, ain't it, my nigga?" asked Keno.

Taz smiled and said, "Fuck you, nigga!"

Keno smiled as he drove Taz's truck toward Oklahoma City.

Sacha went directly to Taz's home and took a quick shower. After she was finished, she fed the dogs and went outside and watched them as they ran around the yard. As she watched them, she grabbed the cordless phone and called Gwen. "What's up, ho?" she asked when Gwen answered the phone.

"Nothing much, bitch. I'm sitting here bored as fuck. I'll sure be glad when my man comes home. I'm horny, and I want something inside of this kitty other than this plastic-ass vibrator."

"Ho, you nasty!"

"Uh-uh, bitch! Like I said, I'm horny!"

"Well, all that should be taken care of in a little while. They're on their way back now. I spoke to Taz about thirty minutes ago, and he said he'll be here within the hour."

"That's what I'm talking about! Bitch, let me go. I need to go take me a long hot bath so I can set the scene for this freak show."

"Damn, ho! You can't chill out and talk for a minute?"

"Bitch, haven't you heard me? I'm horny! Bye!" Gwen yelled and hung up the phone on Sacha.

Sacha shook her head from side to side as she set the phone next to her. *Gwen is happy, I'm happy, and everything and everyone in my life is happy. That is a true blessing!*

She called for the dogs to come on inside. Heaven and Precious obeyed her command and followed her back inside of the house. After refilling their water bowls, she went upstairs and pulled out her sexy little Vickie's Secret outfit she had bought while Taz was out of town. "Humph! Gwen's not the only one who's horny!" she said aloud as she started taking off her clothes.

About twenty minutes later, Taz and Keno pulled into the driveway, and Bob and Red pulled up right behind them. By the time they had made it into Taz's den, Wild Bill and Bo-Pete had entered the house.

Taz went upstairs to speak with Sacha real quickly before he made the call to Won. When he walked into his bedroom and saw Sacha lying on his bed in a short, sheer red nightgown, his eyes almost bulged out of their sockets. "Wha—what's poppin', Li'l Mama?"

Sacha turned toward him while lying on the bed so he could see that her outfit was crotchless, and said, "Nothing, baby. I'm just waiting for you to finish your business, so you can come take care of 'your business'!"

He smiled and said, "I know that's right! Keep it hot for me, Li'l Mama. I'll be back up here as fast as I can." He stepped to her and gave her a quick kiss with a little tongue, then said, "You know you're in trouble for this, right?"

She smiled wickedly and said, "I hope so!"

Taz laughed as he went back downstairs and into the den. "All right, dogs, let's check this shit," he said as he opened his laptop and checked his account. After passing the laptop around, he said, "It looks like we're quickly approaching 30 tickets, my niggas."

"I know that's right! But I'm trying to get a hundred of them bitches for me," said Bo-Pete.

"As long as we keep fuckin' with that nigga, Won, I don't see why we won't be able to get it, gee," Bob said with a smile on his face.

"Stay down, my nigga. Just stay down," said Red.

Taz's cell rang, and when he answered it, Won said, "I'm glad to see that y'all made it back okay. Have you checked the accounts yet?"

"Yep. And everything is everything, O.G.," answered Taz.

"Good. Now check this out. It's almost time for the big finale, so get plenty of rest, and make sure that y'all are prepared for a three-week trip."

"*Three weeks?*"

"Yeah, three weeks. When this is over, each and every one of you will have 200 million in those accounts of yours."

"Two hundred! Ain't that some shit!"

"What are you talking about, Babyboy?"

"Bo-Pete was just saying that he was tryin' to get a hundred tickets, and now you're talkin' 'bout two!"

"That's right. So tell Bo-Pete don't worry about a thang. It's all gravy, baby. You know how it is. Make sure you tell them knuckleheads I said enjoy, be merry, and most of all, be good! Out!"

Taz laughed and told everyone what Won had just told him. After he finished, he said, "Now, if y'all would excuse me, I have something very important to tend to."

Wild Bill laughed and said, "Come on, y'all. Let's bounce. That nigga is ready to get his fuck on." They all laughed as they filed out of the den.

Once they were outside, Taz told them, "Since it's the middle of the week, let's skip a workout. We'll hook up the day after tomorrow."

"Go on, you soft-ass nigga! We know you're not going to have any more energy after Sacha gets through with your ass!" yelled Bo-Pete.

Taz's response was his middle finger as he walked back inside of his house. Once he closed the front door, he bolted up the stairs toward his bedroom, screaming, "Here I come, Li'l Mama!"

Bob knew that something was up when he walked into his house and saw that all of the lights had been dimmed. He smiled as he stepped toward his bedroom. When he opened the door and saw Gwen sitting on the edge of his bed, completely naked, he said, "Damn, baby! Who you waitin' on?"

She smiled and responded, "Who the fuck you think? Sacha called and told me that you were on your way home, so I decided to get ready."

With a grin on his face, he asked, "Ready for what?"

"Ready to get real fucking freaky, baby! Now, come here!"

Bob stepped up to her and dropped straight to his knees. Without any hesitation, he started eating out her sex as if he was a starved man.

Gwen fell back on the bed with her small feet planted firmly on the floor, while Bob enjoyed her exquisite taste. She moaned softly as his tongue went deeper inside of her love walls. "O-o-o-o-h, baby! Let me feel the knot, baby! Let me feel the knot!"

Bob knew what she wanted, and he smiled as he pulled his tongue out of her sex and replaced it with the tip of the knot on his forehead. He applied just the right amount of pressure onto her clit and drove Gwen over the top.

"O-o-o-o-h, Bobbaby! Bobbaby, that's it . . . that's it . . . that's it! I'm cumming baby! I'm cumming baby!" she screamed at the top of her lungs. Her orgasm hit her so hard that all of her words ran together.

After Gwen's trembling seemed to stop, Bob got up from between her legs, climbed on top of her, put his forehead toward her face, and said, "Now taste yourself for me, baby. Lick the knot and taste that sweet-ass pussy of yours."

Gwen smiled as she did as she was told. She licked Bob's forehead and enjoyed the tangy taste of her love juices.

Bob pulled away from her after she was finished, and took off his clothes quickly. Once he was undressed, he climbed back on top of her and started sucking her small breasts.

When his mouth touched her breasts, Gwen flinched slightly and said, "Uh-uh, baby. Come here. Put that dick in my mouth first. I want to taste *you* now."

Bob ignored her and shook his head while he continued to suck each of her nipples. The feeling felt so damn good that she relented and let him continue. She was so wet and hot that she felt as if she was going to cum again just from him sucking on her breasts.

Bob sensed this, pulled away from her ,and said, "You want this dick now, baby?"

"Yes! Yes! Give it to me, Daddy!"

Bob shook his head no and said, "Not until you answer a question for me."

"What is it, baby?" she panted as she squirmed and closed her legs tightly.

"Why do you tense and flinch every time I suck or play with your titties?"

"Yo—your imagining things, baby. Stop tripping and give it to me, Bob. Come on, baby, give it to me, please!" she begged.

Bob climbed off of the bed, shaking his head no again, and said, "Nope, you ain't gettin' this dick until you answer my question."

Gwen narrowed her eyes and said, "Stop playin', nigga! You better get your ass on this bed and come fuck this hot-ass pussy!"

Bob started laughing and said, "You know what? I think I'm going to go on and make me something to eat. I'm kinda hungry."

Gwen sighed and said, "Damnit, Bob! Don't you do me like that! Come on, baby. Give me what I need, please!"

"Not until you answer my question. What's with you and your titties?"

Gwen frowned and said, "They're too damn small! I hate them! Ever since I turned eighteen, I've hated them. Now, are you satisfied?"

He smiled and said, "They may be small, but they're just right for me, baby!" He climbed back on top of her and gave her the ride of her life.

As soon as Taz ran into the bedroom, he jumped onto the bed and started kissing Sacha all over her body. He started at her toes, then slowly worked his way higher. When he reached her pussy, he slid his tongue onto her clit and worked it over feverishly.

Sacha felt as if she was in heaven as she held on to Taz's hair while he pleasured her. She came hard and screamed, "Ooh, yes! Oh! Yes! Yes! Yes, Taz! Yes!"

Taz smiled as he raised himself on top of her and slowly slid himself inside of her piping hot sex. With long, slow strokes, he slowly gained momentum as his strokes increased rapidly. Before too long, he was banging inside of her as if his life depended on it. The bed shook and rocked for the next twenty minutes.

By the time he reached his second orgasm, Sacha was in complete ecstasy. "My God! Oh! My! God! Taz! Baby! Don't!

Stop! Please! God! Don't! Stop!" she screamed as she scratched his back with her fingernails and bit his shoulders. She felt as if his manhood was touching her deep inside of her stomach.

"Is it mines, baby? Huh? Is it mines?" asked Taz as he continued to pound away.

"Yes, baby! It's yours!" she screamed over and over again.

Upon hearing her answer his question, Taz felt his testicles tighten, and he surged forward with newfound energy. "If it's mine, then cum with me, baby! Cum with me!" he screamed as he unloaded what seemed like a gallon of his sperm inside of Sacha's pussy.

Sacha's orgasm was just as intense. She felt as if she couldn't breathe as her body rocked and trembled with so much force that she felt light-headed after her orgasm had subsided.

After taking a few minutes to recuperate, Sacha said, "Damn, that was intense! Where did you get all of that energy from, baby?"

Taz smiled lazily and said, "You did it to me, Li'l Mama. I was cool until I saw you all sexy lookin' in that li'l hookup you were wearing. Shit, after that it was a wrap!"

"If I knew that's what got you going, then I would have spent more money in Vickie's Secrets the other day. But don't you worry. I'm going to be spending a lot of money with them real damn soon!"

They both started laughing and held each other until they fell asleep in each other's arms.

By the time Bob and Gwen had finished sexing, they were both starving. Bob got up and took a quick shower, then went into the kitchen and made them both some breakfast. He fried some eggs and bacon, and popped a few slices of bread into the toaster for them. While they were eating their meal, he asked, "Baby, if you don't like the size of your titties, why won't you get some implants?"

"I've given it some thought, but I always chicken out. Plus, those fuckers cost a grip."

"Do you want me to get them for you, baby? 'Cause if you do, I'll give you the chips. Hell, I'll even go with you to get them done."

"You would? Oh, baby, that's so sweet!"

"What size are you going to want to get?"

Gwen smiled and said, "I want to go from an A-cup to at least a C-cup. That way, I won't look too crazy, you know, coming from something so small to something nice and right."

"Baby, I don't have a fuckin' clue 'bout no cups. Give me an example or some shit."

"Around the same size as Sacha's, Bob."

"Oh, okay, that's straight. So, when do you want to do it?"

"You're the one paying for them, so it's on you."

"Okay, this is what we're going to do. Since Taz don't want to work out in the morning, let's check and see if we can find someone here in the city that can do it. If everything works out, we'll set it up in the morning. And if we don't find anyone out here, we'll check out in Dallas. I know it doesn't take that long. I was watching that talk show *Tyra*, and she said that they basically have drive-thru spots for that shit nowadays."

Gwen smiled and said, "Thank you, baby, for being so good to me. I love you, Bob!"

Bob smiled and said, "As long as you're happy, baby, I'm the happiest man in this fuckin' world."

"Let's go back into the bedroom so I can make sure that you're completely happy tonight."

"I'm with that, baby!" he said as he got up from the table and followed her back into the bedroom.

Chapter Twenty-three

Clifford had decided that after a month of seeing Tazneema, he was in love. She was young, but she was perfect for him. He found himself thinking about her constantly all during the day. Whenever he had the time, he made sure that he gave her a call. And if he missed her, he would leave long sweet messages on her voicemail on her cell phone or on her answering machine at home. They went out to eat almost every other night. She was so energetic that she seemed to have breathed new life into him. All thoughts of Taz and revenge were gone. *Taz has Sacha, and he is happy. I have Tazneema, and I'm equally as happy. So, why not let bygones be bygones?* he thought as he pulled into Tazneema's apartment complex. He jumped out of his car and went to the front door.

Tazneema heard the knock at the door and smiled. "Right on time, as always!" she said as she went and answered the door. "Hi, Cliff! Come on in. I'll be ready in a minute."

"Hello, beautiful! Man, you're looking extremely sexy tonight. What's up? Have I forgotten something important?"

"What makes you say something like that?" she asked with a smile on her face.

"Come on, baby. You're looking too damn good tonight just to go back to my place and have dinner. Something's going on inside of that pretty head of yours. What is it?"

She smoothed down her dress and simply said, "You'll see!"

By the time they made it to Clifford's house, dinner was ready. He had put two steaks in his Crock-Pot and had been slow cooking them the entire day. When he got home from work, he put two potatoes into the oven and let them bake as he went out to Norman to pick up Tazneema. He prepared a quick salad, and dinner was served. They ate in Clifford's dining room and listened to some soft, soothing music by the great Luther Vandross.

The meal was perfect, the mood was nice, and Tazneema felt that the time was right for her to give that special something to her man. But first, she had to be sure that Clifford was in fact her man.

Clifford was clearing the table when she asked him, "Cliff, do you consider us a couple now, or are we still just friends?"

He smiled and said, "I'd love to say that we're a couple, but you wanted me to take it slow with you, so I've held back on asking you, 'Neema."

"Thank you for that. Thank you for respecting my wishes, Cliff. I want you to know that means an awful lot to me. I've fallen in love with you, and I want us to take this a step further this evening."

"Wha—what do you mean by that, 'Neema?" he asked as he set the plates he had in his hands down onto the dining room table.

Tazneema stood up from the table, stepped into Clifford's arms, and said, "I want you to have me tonight, baby. I want you to have my virginity, tonight."

"Are you sure, 'Neema? There's really no need to rush into this. I can wait as long as you want me to, baby."

She smiled and said, "You've waited patiently enough, Cliff. Tonight's the night it goes down." She stepped out of his embrace and slid the thin shoulder straps of her dress off of her slim shoulders, and let her dress fall to the floor. Her firm breasts stood at attention as she wiggled out of her black thong. She stood right in front of him completely naked and said, "Do you want me, baby? If so, come and get me, because I'm yours."

Clifford's dick was so hard that it felt as if it was about to burst out of it's skin. He took a deep breath and said, "Yes, beautiful, I want you. I want you now, and I want you for as long as you'll be mine."

They kissed slowly and hungrily. The passion between them was like a wildfire, getting hotter and hotter. Clifford scooped her into his arms, took her into his bedroom, and gently laid her down onto his bed. He took off his clothes and quickly joined her. He was so excited that he felt as if he was about to cum on himself any minute. *Calm down, boy! Calm down!* he thought, and reminded himself that this going to be Tazneema's first time. He wanted it to be a good memory, not a bad one. He kissed her earlobes, her neck; then he slid down to her breasts and put each one into his mouth one at a time.

Her erect nipples ached as he sucked them gently, then bit them lightly, causing her to shake all over. Her body trembled in anticipation of the next step. She was so wet that she felt as if she had peed on herself. She had heard plenty of stories about how the first time was always the worst time, and right then, she couldn't believe any of that, because Clifford was being so gentle with her that she felt like she was floating.

Clifford smiled as he slid down toward her pussy and started licking her all over it. She was shaved down there, so her smooth skin glistened as his tongue roamed all over her sex. He located her clit and started lightly nibbling on it.

Tazneema gasped and held her breath as feelings she had never felt before rocked through her entire body. "O-o-o-o-o-oh, that feels so good, baby!" she moaned as Clifford munched lightly on the sweetest taste he'd tasted in a very long time. *Eighteen years young, and the sweetest pussy in the world!*

When he felt Tazneema start to shake and shiver, he knew that her first orgasm was nearing, so he flicked his tongue faster and faster across her clit.

"Cliff! Oh, my God! Cliff, I'm cumming! I'm cumming!" she screamed.

Clifford let what felt like a small flood gush all over his face. He enjoyed her sexy aroma as he continued to lick all over her pussy. He pulled away from her and smiled when he saw how beautiful her face was. She was practically glowing as she blushed deeply. He reached into the nightstand drawer next to his bed and pulled out a condom. He tore it open and gently put it on. He then climbed on top of her and said, "Baby, you're nice and wet so it shouldn't hurt you that much. But there is going to be some discomfort for a minute. If I start hurting you, tell me, so I can take it nice and slow."

Tazneema was so caught up in the moment that all she could do was nod her head yes.

Clifford smiled as he slid himself inside of her. When he felt resistance, he pushed a little harder. *Damn! She wasn't lying! She is a virgin!* That excited him so much that he'd forgotten about what he had just told her and shoved harder than he had intended to. Tazneema screamed, and he came with so much force that he became dizzy. He never slowed his stroke as he continued to ease in and out of her.

As the pain somewhat subsided, Tazneema became more and more excited. *It did hurt, but it feels so-o-o-o good now!* she thought as she wrapped her legs around Clifford's waist and bucked back into his dick. This encouraged him to turn it up a little as he increased his pace. Now, they were both bucking back and forth and sexing each other like their lives depended on the outcome of their journey.

Tazneema felt that tingle again, and this time she was prepared for it . . . at least she thought she was. When her next orgasm hit her, it was just as intense as her first one was. She screamed out Clifford's name over and over and he penetrated deeper inside of her. By the time his own orgasm hit him, he was yelling just as loudly as she was.

Finally, their noisy lovemaking came to a halt, and they fell asleep in each other's arms, sated.

Taz was working out inside his gym by himself when he got the call from Won. He closed his camera phone and called Keno. "It's time to put in work, gee. Call the others," he said before hanging up. He then went upstairs and jumped into the shower.

By the time he finished, Sacha had come into the bedroom and was lying on the bed, watching television. He grabbed his clothes and quickly got dressed. While he was dressing, she tried her best to remain calm, but every time he went out of town she felt like that would be the last time she would ever see him again. That thought alone drove her insane. She didn't know what she'd do if she ever lost that man. She was in love, and her love was forever. "So, this is the three-week trip, baby?" she asked.

"Nah, Li'l Mama, that shit got put on hold. I should be back in a day—two tops."

She breathed a sigh of relief and, as calmly as she could, said, "Oh, all right. I'll make sure that everything is taken care of on this end, baby."

He smiled and said, "Yeah, I know you got me, you big old phony!"

"What are you talking about, baby?" she asked innocently.

"Don't even try to fake it, Li'l Mama. I saw how you were looking at me as I got dressed. I know you be worried about a nigga. I hate that I have to put you through this, but it's what I do."

The sincerity in his voice touched her heart deeply. She took a deep breath and said, "I know, Taz, and I will not try to stop you from doing you. Just please, be careful, baby. I'd die without you. I mean that."

He stepped over to her, kiss her, and said, "I know, Li'l Mama . . . I know. And I give you my word, ain't nothin' gon' happen to me. Every move we make is calculated to the very last detail. I don't slip, baby. Never have, and I never will. Now, let me bounce. The boys should be here any minute."

"Okay, baby. I love you, Taz."

"I love you, too, Li'l Mama," he said and went downstairs to wait for the crew.

After everyone was inside the den, Taz explained the mission. Bo-Pete and Wild Bill were due to leave Tulsa in the next two hours. Red and Bob's flight was scheduled to leave Dallas/Fort Worth later on that night. Keno and Taz were flying out of Will Rogers Airport in forty-five minutes. Their destination was Houston. Once they all arrived in Houston, the details for the mission would be given to them by Won via DVD, as usual. This mission was going to make them all six million dollars richer. That put smiles on all of their faces as they filed out of the house.

Sacha hated what she was doing, but she couldn't resist the urge to listen in on Taz's conversation. After she had heard him tell everyone that they were going to be making six million dollars each, she put her hand over her mouth in fear that she would give herself away. She went back upstairs, closed the bedroom door, and watched as they all pulled out of Taz's driveway. "Six million dollars apiece! That's 18 million dollars! Who in the hell are they going to rob for that much money?" she asked herself aloud.

Taz and Keno arrived at Houston's Hobby Airport a little after ten p.m. Bo-Pete and Wild Bill would be arriving within the next twenty to thirty minutes. Since Red and Bob flew out of Dallas, they weren't due to arrive until close to midnight.

Taz drove their rented Ford Excursion to the Double tree Hotel in downtown Houston. He parked the truck, and they entered the hotel. After getting their room key, Taz asked the hotel clerk, "Do you have a package for me?"

"Yes, I do, sir. I was given strict instructions that you were to ask for it before I gave it to you," said the clerk.

"No, problem. Thanks," Taz said as he stepped away from the counter. As they stepped inside of the elevator, he told Keno, "Damn, my nigga! Six tickets! This shit is gettin' wilder and wilder, huh?"

"Nah, gee, it ain't gettin' wilder. We're gettin' richer!"

They both laughed as they stepped off of the elevator and went into their room.

Once they were inside of the room, Taz quickly inserted the DVD and listened to what Won had to tell them. Like always, a picture of the great Mike came onto the screen. After about thirty seconds, Won's voice came through the speakers of the television:

"Good evening, gentlemen. I trust all is well. As you already know, this is a money getter for you all, so pay close attention, because tonight you will be dealing with a whole lot of the greenbacks. Under your bed are the tools that you'll need for this mission. Your weapons of choice are there, as well as six army surplus duffel bags. Once everyone has arrived, you are to go down to the underground parking garage and get inside of the dark blue Tahoe. Taz and Keno are to drive this vehicle by themselves. The others are to follow in the rental that you already have.

"You are then going to take Texas Avenue to Main Street. After making a right on Main, I want you to take Main Street all of the way into North Houston. You'll know you're at your destination when you see a Platinum Jewelry store to your right on the corner of Main and Dewater Avenue. Pull around behind the jewelry store and park your vehicles. Then, proceed to the back entrance of the jewelry store. The doors will be unlocked, and the alarms will already be deactivated. Once you are inside, there will be six safes lined against the far wall. From right to left, the combinations are as follows . . ."

There was a pause while Keno and Taz both grabbed a pen and a piece of the hotel stationery. Just as they sat back down, Won continued:

"The first combination is fifty-four to the right, sixty-one to the left, and nineteen to the right. The next one is three to the right, twenty-six to the left, then seventy-one to the right. The next one is two to the right, nineteen to the left, and seventy to the right. The next one is eleven to the right, twenty-nine to the left, and fifty to the right. The next one is ten to the right, fourteen to the left, and sixty-nine to the right. And the last one is seven to the right, five to the left, and forty-seven to the right.

"You all are to enter together and proceed straight to your designated safes. Once you get them open, take all of it's contents and fill each of your duffel bags. This is a timed op, so make sure that you're out of there within ten minutes after you enter. The alarms will reset at exactly two a.m. I expect for you to be in and out of there in no more than eight minutes, tops. If by chance you do stay inside over ten minutes, be prepared for heavy hostilities. Once the alarm is tripped, it will take no more than two minutes for the war to begin. This is what we're trying to avoid, so make sure that all watches are synchronized exactly. No room for error is allowed.

"After you have emptied the safes, you are to head back to the hotel and leave all of the bags inside of your room. Then, take your rental back to the airport and head back to the City in the Tahoe. I'll be in contact with you no later than four p.m.

tomorrow afternoon. Do not try to contact me. Check your accounts by noon, and everything should be completed. Once again, do not try to contact me, because I will be dark for the time being."

"Good luck, gentlemen!"

The television screen then went blank.

Taz smiled and said, "In and out, just like that!" He snapped his fingers.

"I can dig it, my nigga! Damn, look at the fuckin' size of these bags! I can see why we're gettin' broken off so much for this shit. That nigga Won is gon' make a killin' tonight," said Keno.

"Yeah, and so are we," Taz said as he started to check and recheck their weapons.

As Taz drove toward the jewelry store, his mind was on Sacha. *Damn! Maybe it's time to get out of this shit. I can't be havin' my Li'l Mama stressed the fuck out every time I do me. Am I being selfish or what? Just hold me down a li'l more, Li'l Mama, and I promise, I'm gone make everything all right,* he thought to himself as he pulled in back of the jewelry store. He parked the Tahoe and climbed out, followed by Keno. They met the rest of the crew at the back door as they checked their watches. It was one forty-five a.m. exactly. They had ten minutes to get the money, and fifteen minutes total to be in and out of the store.

Taz took a deep breath and entered the store, followed by his homeboys. They were each designated a safe. Taz went to the first safe; Keno went to the next one, followed by Bob, who went to the third. Wild Bill went to the fourth, Bo-Pete went to the fifth one, and Red to the last safe.

When Keno had his safe open, he smiled and said, "Damnit, man! Look at all of these fuckin' chips!"

"Nigga, we ain't got time for lookin'! Clean that muthafucka out so we can get the fuck out!" whispered Red.

Each safe was filled to it's capacity with nothing but money. Taz couldn't believe his eyes as he quickly filled his bag. When he finished, he checked the time and said, "Seven minutes, gentlemen! How we lookin'?"

"I'm done," said Red.

"Me too," said Bob.

"Almost," said Bo-Pete.

"Done," said Keno.

"Got it," said Wild Bill.

"Good. Let's get the fuck outta here," Taz said as he led the way out of the jewelry store.

They made it back to the trucks without difficulty and departed just as quickly as they came. Mission completed.

Taz smiled as Keno drove them back to Oklahoma City in the Tahoe that Won had arranged for them. Bo-Pete and Wild Bill were in the back of the truck, sleeping, while Bob and Red watched Keno's damn *Scarface* DVD on the screen that was mounted on the seat's headrest. After they had dropped off the duffel bags full of money, they quickly stashed their weapons back under the bed and departed from the Doubletree.

Now that they were safely out of Houston and headed back home, Taz had to call Sacha. Even though it was close to four in the morning, he wanted to let her know that he was all right and on his way back home.

Sacha answered the phone on it's first ring. "Hello."

"What's up, Li'l Mama? What you doing up this late?" asked Taz.

"I was going over some files for my trial in the morning. How are you?"

"I'm good."

"Where are you?"

He laughed and said, "On the highway. I'm on my way home. I should be there by the time you're leaving to go to work."

Sacha smiled a relieved smile and said, "That's good. So, I guess everything went accordingly?"

"Always. I told you, Li'l Mama, every single move is calculated to a tee."

"Thank God! Good night, baby. I have to get some sleep, and now that I know you're all right, I'll be able to sleep peacefully."

"I know. That's why I called. I love you, Li'l Mama!"

"I love you, too, baby!"

After Taz closed his cell, he smiled as he relaxed back in his seat.

Red said, "You know what was the only fucked-up thing about this mission, dog?"

Taz turned around in his seat and asked, "What was that, gee?"

"We gots to drive all the way back out to fuckin' Dallas to get my truck!"

Bob started laughing and said, "*We* ain't got to do a mutha-fuckin' thang, partner! *Your* ass is on your own!"

They all started laughing as Keno drove on.

Chapter Twenty-four

Tazneema stepped out of the shower and walked into Clifford's bedroom with a towel wrapped around her. She smiled when she saw that he had left a note for her on his pillow. She let her towel fall to the floor as she quickly went to the bed and opened the letter.

Good morning, beautiful!
I'm sorry that I had to run off, but I was afraid that if I stayed and waited for you to finish your shower, I wouldn't have been able to make it to work this morning. (Smile!) No, seriously, I have a nine o'clock meeting that I can't be late for. I hope I'll see you this evening.
I really wish you would give some deep consideration on moving in with me. I love it when I open my eyes and the first sight I see is your lovely face. I know it'll be difficult for you with school and all, but for me, please give it some thought.
Bye, for now. Give me a call when you get out of class.
Love always, Cliff.

"Ooh, that's so sweet!" she said and began to get dressed.
Ever since their first night of lovemaking, Tazneema made it a point that Clifford made love to her at least twice every other day. She may have been a late starter, but now she considered herself a veteran. She had even given Clifford some head, and that was something that she thought she would never do. She smiled as she thought back to how excited Clifford's face looked the first time she had sucked his dick. Seeing him so happy made her feel even prouder of the fact that she could satisfy him. She was in love, and she wanted the world to know it. She knew that she would catch hell from Taz

and Mama-Mama, but so what? *This is my life, and it's about time I started living it my way,* she thought to herself as she finished getting dressed. She had a man now, and they were just going to have to accept that fact.

Taz was breathing heavily as he climbed out of his swimming pool. He had just completed forty laps, and he was tired. He chose to push himself today, because he knew that any day now Won would be summoning them for the upcoming three-week mission. The thought of getting close to two hundred million was enough incentive for him. He didn't want to stress the crew, but something in the back of his head told him to make sure that he was on top of his game. Even though he trusted Won with his life, something about this next mission just didn't sit right with him.

He thought back to Won's words a few weeks ago, when he had told him that it was almost time for the finale. *Finale . . . finale to what?* he asked himself as he finished drying himself off.

He went upstairs to his bedroom and decided to give Mama-Mama a call. After speaking with his mother for a few minutes, he hung up and called Tari at work. "What up, Tee? You busy?"

"Not really, Taz, How are you?"

"I'm good. Look, can we get together after you get off? I really need to holla at you about some things."

"Sure. Do you want me to come over, or do you want to meet me someplace?"

"Yeah, let's meet at the Olive Garden, on me."

She laughed and said, "Oh, but of course! Tell me, is everything still going okay with you and Sacha?"

"Yeah, we're good. What I want to talk to you about doesn't concern her. It's more about Won."

"I see. All right then, I'll see you there around six?"

"That's good. And thanks, Tee."

"Don't thank me, joker. You know I'll always be there for you when you need me."

He smiled into the receiver and said, "Yeah, I know. Bye."

After he hung up the phone, he went and took a shower, still wondering exactly what the fuck he was tripping for. Won had never let him down before, so there was no reason for him to be second-guessing him now . . . or was there?

Tazneema called Clifford right after she left her last class for the day. "Hi, baby! What ya doing?" she asked as soon as Clifford answered his cell phone.

"Nothing much. I've just finished arranging a few meetings with some new clients, that's all. Just another boring day at the office. How about you? How was your day?"

"The same. I've just left my last class for the day, and I'm starving. Are you cooking tonight, or are we going out to eat?"

"Whatever you want, beautiful, you know that," he said sincerely.

She smiled and said, "Okay, I want some of your special pork chops and rice, with some buttered mixed vegetables."

"So be it! What time should I be expecting you?"

"I'm going to go get changed and pack me a light bag. Then I'm going to go see Mama-Mama for a little bit. Then I'll be there. So, be expecting me around seven. Is that okay?"

"You know it is, baby. I'll see you then."

"Okay, bye!" she said and pressed the END button on her cell. She jumped into her car, as happy as can be. *It feels real good having someone special to share your life with,* she thought as she drove toward her apartment complex.

"Damn! Baby, I'm loving them new knockers!" Bob yelled excitedly.

"Come on, baby, don't play with me. Do you really like them? They don't look too big, do they?" asked Gwen as she stared down at her chest.

"I wouldn't tell you they looked tight if they didn't look tight. I can't wait to get them inside of my mouth."

She smiled as she continued to stare at her breasts. Bob had remained true to his word and paid the seventy-five hundred dollars it had cost for her new breast implants. It took three and a half hours, and now here she was with a brand-new look. They had driven down to Dallas earlier that morning with a noon appointment. Now that they were finally finished, she couldn't wait to get back home. She wanted to know what Sacha thought about her new chest size. She was happy as hell that Bob seemed to love them, but she really needed to know what her girl thought, 'cause if Sacha didn't like them, she was coming back and getting them reduced immediately. She didn't want to look foolish to her best friend. Sacha's judgment was very important to her.

Ever since she had dropped out of college, she had always felt as if she had become inferior to Sacha. Once she went back to school and had gotten her degree, she thought she had leveled the playing field between them, but somehow over the years, she never overcame the insecurity she felt around Sacha. Even though she loved her as a sister, she just couldn't rid herself of those feelings.

"Come on, baby, let's get back to the City. I can't wait to show off my girl's new titties!"

"Bob, I'm still sore. It's going to be some time before I can go out. I can't even wear a bra yet."

"Don't trip, baby. You don't need no damn bra, anyway. Look how firm them thangs are. Shit, you're standing at attention, baby, and I want to show them joints off!" Bob said and started laughing.

Gwen laughed also and said, "You're crazy, nigga!" But with renewed confidence, she said, "If you want to show me off, baby, who am I to try and stop you? Come on, let's go home."

They left the doctor's office hand in hand, and with smiles on both of their faces.

Taz smiled as he watched Tari coming toward his table. *She's still one sexy white broad,* he thought, standing as she sat down. "What's up, Tee?" he asked after he had taken his seat again.

"Nothing much, really. You know, the same ol' same. What's up with you? That's the question."

"I've been doing a lot of thinking lately, and it's like I'm confused and shit."

"About what?"

"Everything."

Tari laughed and said, "Please, be a little more specific."

Taz then told her of his doubts about the upcoming mission, and how he had never doubted Won before, and how strongly he felt for Sacha. "Basically, this shit is all about her, I guess. Won has never given me a reason to ever doubt him, but now I am. He's made us all millions, and now just because I done fell in love, I'm starting to doubt my nigga. This shit is crazy. You know how I get down. I'm always cautious. But now that I have Sacha in my life, I'm spooked that something might jump off backward, and I'll lose everything."

Tari smiled at her friend, her ex-lover, and said, "Love is a bitch, baby. But answer this for me. Do you still trust Won?"

"With my life," he said seriously.

"Do you want to stop doing you?"

"I've been thinking about it a lot lately."

She shook her head and asked again, "Do you want to stop?"

"Sacha becomes a nervous wreck every time I go out of town."

"What? She knows what you do?" Tari asked incredulously.

He smiled and nodded yes. "Yeah, we kinda got into a jam when we were in L.A., and Won had to bail us out," he said and told Tari all about what had happened when he and Sacha were in Los Angeles.

"Damn! This is deeper than I thought. Okay, but back to my question. Do you want to stop? Not because of Sacha, but because of you. This all revolves around your decisions, Taz. It's all about what you want. Either you do or you don't. When you can answer that question, everything else will fall right into place for you."

"Damn, how did you get to be so fuckin' smart?"

"I've been in this game a long time, Babyboy," she said, trying her best to impersonate Won's deep voice.

Taz laughed and said, "Yeah, I guess you have, huh?" He then waved for a waitress to come so they could order.

After the waitress had taken their orders, Tari said, "You need to hurry and find that answer, baby. All of you guys' lives will be at stake until you do. Don't take the chance by putting off what needs to be known."

Taz stared directly into her eyes and said, "I won't."

Chapter Twenty-five

Tazneema and Clifford were relaxing at Clifford's home, trying to see what they were going to get into for the weekend. It was Friday night, and Lyla had pitched a fit with Tazneema for leaving her to go be with Clifford. "I'm sorry girl, but that's how it is when you have a man in your life," Tazneema had told Lyla as she grabbed her overnight bag and left the apartment. Now, as she sat cuddled with Clifford, she felt as if everything in her life was just perfect.

She had finally built up the nerve to inform Mama-Mama about Clifford, and it wasn't as bad as she thought it would be. Mama-Mama was pretty cool about it. Her only concern was the age difference, but then she even took that kind of easily.

Tazneema smiled at Clifford and said, "You know you're going to have to meet Mama-Mama this weekend, don't you?"

He smiled and asked, "This weekend? I thought it would be in a couple of weeks."

"Nope. I told her that we would either come by tomorrow for lunch, or we'd be there for sure for Sunday dinner. So, which one is it going to be, baby?"

"Let's do lunch tomorrow."

"Are you sure?"

"Yes. It would be better for me. You know how I like to get my rest on Sundays before I start a new workweek. So, call Mama-Mama and find out what time she would want us to come over."

Tazneema smiled and said, "I don't have to do that. Mama-Mama will have everything ready, anyway. As long as we're there before four, we'll be on time for lunch."

"What do you mean by that?"

Tazneema laughed and said, "Mama-Mama prepares her meals for the day early in the morning, every morning. Her lunch for tomorrow will be ready by seven or eight a.m., so don't worry. Everything will be fine."

"Do you think she'll like me?" Clifford asked with a smile on his face.

Tazneema turned so that their faces were inches apart and said, "I love you, Cliff, and, baby, that's all that matters."

He smiled and said, "I love you, too."

After Taz and Keno had entered the club, Taz saw Katrina and Paquita, smiled, and asked Keno, "Did you ever hit that broad Katrina, gee?"

"Nah, nigga. You fucked that up that night, remember? You was on that murder shit that night."

"That's right. I forgot about that shit! I can't front, dog. She's over there lookin' kinda tight tonight."

Keno casually gave a glance toward Katrina and Paquita and saw that Katrina was indeed looking pretty damn good. He turned back toward Taz and asked, "You straight?"

Taz smiled and said, "Yep. I'm good."

"All right, I'll holla. She's mine tonight, my nigga," Keno said confidently as he started walking toward Paquita and Katrina's table.

"Go get 'em, tiger!" Taz said as he watched Keno go do his thing. He then gave a slight nod toward Bob and Red, then to Bo-Pete and Wild Bill. They dispersed from their normal spots and started mingling with the rest of the club goers. He then leaned against the bar and sipped his drink as he waited for Sacha and Gwen to arrive.

As Sacha pulled Taz's 600 Benz into Club Cancun's parking lot, she smiled when she saw Keno's, Red's, and Bo-Pete's trucks all parked side by side.

"Damn! I don't see why they wouldn't let us just ride with them. This shit don't make no sense," said Gwen as she checked her makeup in a compact mirror she held in her hand.

"That's just how they do things, ho. There isn't any need for you to be tripping, so relax."

"Relax? Bitch, I *am* relaxed! My titties are still so damn sore that I'm just a little irritable."

Sacha smiled and said, "But they look good, ho. I still can't believe you did that crazy-ass shit. What made you do it?"

Gwen, who was happy as ever that Sacha really seemed to be impressed by her bold decision to get her breasts enlarged, smiled and said, "I've always wanted bigger breasts, but I was scared to do it in the past. Bob convinced me when he realized that I was a little insecure about my chest. So I said, 'Fuck it! Why not?' and went down to Dallas and just did it. You like them for real, bitch?"

Sacha started laughing and said, "Ho, I didn't say that I like them. What, you thinking I'm on some pussy now? I think they fit you perfectly, if that's what you mean." They both laughed as they stepped toward the entrance of the club.

The line to get inside of the club was wrapped around the other side of the building, but that didn't bother Sacha, as she walked straight to the front and told the security guard, "I'm meeting Taz." The guard smiled at her as he stepped aside and let her and Gwen enter the club. Sacha heard a few females say something slick, but she paid no attention to them as she led her best friend into the club. *Being Taz's woman has all types of little perks,* she thought to herself.

When Taz saw Sacha and Gwen enter the club, he smiled and waved for them to come and join him by the bar. As they were walking toward him, his smile turned into a look of shock as he noticed how big Gwen's breasts were.

Sacha stepped into his arms, gave him a kiss on his cheek. and said, "Close your mouth, baby. You act like you never seen any titties before."

He frowned slightly at Sacha's jibe and said, "Damn, Gwen! When you get them thangs?"

Gwen smiled brightly and said, "Last week. You like?"

"I wouldn't answer that question if I was you, Taz," Sacha said with a smile on her face.

Taz laughed and said, "You're looking real good tonight, Gwen."

"Thank you. Now, I'll leave you two lovers to do y'all for a minute. I see my boo smiling at me over there, so I gots to go. Get us a table or something, bitch. And you already know what I want to drink," she said as she went and joined Bob, who was at the back of the club, chilling out.

Sacha shook her head and said, "That girl is something else!"

"That, she is," Taz said, and he turned around and ordered two apple martinis for the two women. After he had given Winky the order, he turned back to Sacha and said, "So, when are you going to go get yours done?"

She slanted her eyes to mere slits and said, "You better start smiling to let me know that you're clowning, Mister Taz!"

Taz laughed and said, "You already know. You're just perfect just the way you are, baby. Ain't no need to try to improve perfection."

She smiled and said, "That's better. For a minute there I thought I was going to have to show a side of me that you're really not trying to see." They both started laughing as Winky gave Taz the apple martinis.

"Stop playin', Keno! You know damn well you ain't always wanted to holla at me. You think you can tell me anything and I'd go for it. You need to stop that weak shit and come better than that!" Katrina said confidently, and sipped her glass of hypnotic that Keno had bought for her.

"Nah, on the real, boo, you know a nigga be caught up on some other shit. But every time I be gettin' ready to holla at ya, it's like you either have a nigga all on you already, or some shit comes up and gets in my way. But I'm tellin' you, ain't nothin', and I mean nothin' stoppin' me from gettin' at you tonight."

Katrina smiled and said, "Is that right?"

"You better believe it, boo."

"Damn, Keno! What's up with your homeboy Red? He always comes to the club with y'all, but he don't be trying to get at nobody. What, he already gots somebody or somethin'?" asked Paquita.

Keno stared at Paquita for a moment and thought about dissing her, but he thought better of it, because he knew that she was Katrina's girl. Katrina was looking too damn good tonight, dressed in a blue and gold silk dress by Duro Olowu and a pair of blue strapped stilettos by Alessandro Dell'Acqua. Her long legs were looking so tempting to him that he decided to see if Red would play with him tonight. "Nah. See, my nigga just be on some laid-back time. What, you tryin' to holla?" he asked with a smile.

"You damn straight! That big, red, sexy-ass nigga needs a bitch like me in his life," Paquita said as she stared over to where Red was standing.

"All right, I'll be right back. I'm goin' to see if he'll come rock your world."

"Whateva!" yelled Paquita, and she and Katrina started laughing.

Keno stepped over to Red and said, "Check this out, my nigga. I need your help."

Red shook his head no and said, "Don't say what the fuck I think you're going to say, dog. 'Cause ain't no way I'm going to go over there and fuck with you and them rats."

"Come on, my nigga! Just entertain the bitch for me for a li'l bit. Once I know for sure that Katrina's going to bounce with me, then you can shake that broad. Come on, nigga. She ain't that fuckin' bad. She's thicker than a muthafucka. And, you never know, she might be down for the freaky-freaky thang."

Red smiled and said, "You think she'll be down for whatever, huh?"

"Come on, my nigga, look at that broad! She's answering that question herself right now. Look!" Keno said as he turned and pointed toward Paquita. She was staring at them, licking her lips with a seductive look in her eyes.

She may not be the prettiest female inside of the club, but she wasn't the ugliest, Red thought to himself as he smiled at her. After taking a deep breath and draining the rest of his drink, he said "Fuck it, nigga! Come on. But you're going to owe me for this one!"

Keno laughed as they strolled toward Katrina and Paquita, and said, "As long as I owe you, nigga, you'll never be broke!"

***

After Sacha and Taz had joined Bob and Gwen at the table that Bob had a waitress get for them, they proceeded to have a good time by getting nice and drunk. Bob and Gwen went back and forth out on the dance floor, while Taz and Sacha danced very little but drank a lot.

"Damn, Li'l Mama! You trying to get faded, huh?" asked Taz.

Sacha smiled at her man and said, "I'm enjoying myself, baby, that's all."

"I feel you, but at the rate you're going, you won't be enjoying much tomorrow."

She smiled, shrugged her shoulders slightly, and said, "Oh well! At least I know I'll be well taken care of, right?"

Taz grinned and said, "Always, Li'l Mama . . . always."

Bob and Gwen came back to the table and sat down. "Damn, girl! I ain't goin' back out there with your wild ass. You act like you trying to wear a nigga out before I can get your ass home and tap that thang!" Bob said, and he sipped his drink.

"Humph! You know damn well I'm going to be having your ass begging me to stop when we get home, nigga, so stop frontin' for Taz," Gwen said as she smiled lovingly at Bob.

"You two really need to quit that shit. Both of y'all are some straight characters," Taz said. He then noticed a little commotion over by where Keno and Red were standing. He got to his feet and said, "Bob, the homies are getting into somethin'. Come on."

Bob stood and followed Taz over to where Keno and Red were.

"Oh, shit! Here we go again!" Sacha said as she watched the men leave.

"Come on, my nigga. Ain't no need for any bullshit tonight. My nigga didn't know that this was your girl," explained Keno.

"I ain't his damn girl, Keno! I just got a baby by that broke-ass nigga! He thinks just 'cause he just got out the pen that he can come home and run me. Fuck him!" yelled Paquita.

Just as it seemed as if everything was going smoothly with the four of them, Paquita's baby daddy, Bump, had to come into the club, tripping. Once he saw Paquita all up under Red, he rushed right up to her and snatched her out of Red's big arms.

Red's first instinct was to start beating the shit out of Paquita's kid's father, but he was able to control that sudden urge.

"Nah, you check this out, partna. This bitch has my seed at home all by himself, when she should have her rat-ass at the house taking care of him. I don't give a fuck who she fucks with, gee, but she's gon' respect me and take proper care of my seed!" yelled the angry father.

"I respect your mind, gangsta, so go on and chill, and I give you my word she'll go on and check on your seed. We're not trying to have all of this drama up in here tonight," Keno said wisely.

"Fuck you, Bump! My sister is at my house, watching my son! You ain't never done shit for him any fuckin' way! I don't see how your bitch-ass has the nerve to come up in here and try to run shit! Yeah, he's your seed, but that's all! You ain't no damn daddy! You a fuckin' wannabe-ass dope dealer, you broke-ass muthafucka!"

Before Keno could calm Paquita down, Bump slapped her so hard that she fell to the floor instantly.

"Come on, dog. Leave her alone," said Red.

Bump turned toward Red and was about to say something, but Taz stepped up and said, "What up, Bump? Back to your old antics again, huh?"

Bump focused on Taz, smiled, and said, "What up, Taz? Dog, it's been a minute, huh?"

"Yeah, It's been a minute. Why don't you let me buy you a drink or somethin'? Ain't no need for this shit, dog."

Shaking his head no, Bump said, "Nah, Taz, this bitch needs to be checked, and I'm goin' to make sure that she gets checked thoroughly."

Taz saw that Red was upset, and he knew that he had to get Bump out of the way before Red hurt him. "I can't let you do that, Bump. As you can see, Paquita is chillin' with my nigga Red here. So, why don't you let her make it tonight, huh?"

"Fuck this bitch, Taz, and fuck your nigga too!" yelled Bump.

Before Bump could say another word, Red stepped in front of him and punched him as hard as he could right between his eyes, and Bump fell to the floor, dazed. "Now, get the fuck up and show me how much you want to get down, you clown-ass nigga!" Red said angrily.

Taz helped Bump to his feet and said, "I told you to let this go tonight, Bump. Now, the rest of this shit is on you. As you can see, my nigga ain't for no bullshit. So, are you tryin' to see him or not?"

Bump saw the fire blazing in Red's eyes and knew that he had no win with him. He shook his head no and said, "Nah, this bitch ain't worth it." Then like a whipped dog, he turned and left the club.

Paquita smiled and said, "Thank you, Red! Thank you for checking that nigga for me!"

Red smiled and said, "Don't trip. Now, tell me. How are you going to repay old Red for lookin' out for you?"

Paquita stepped close to him and whispered something into his ear. After she finished, Red asked, "For real?" She shook her head yes, and he said, "I'm wit' that!"

Keno started laughing and said, "Damn, nigga! What did she say she's gon' do to your ass?"

"That's none of your business, Keno! You just worry about what you've gotten yourself into with me!" Katrina said with a smile on her face.

Keno smiled brightly and said, "No doubt, Ma!"

"Well, since everything is everything, me and Bob can go rejoin our girls. Be good, niggas," Taz said as he left the group.

Bo-Pete and Wild Bill went back to where they had been standing and resumed talking to a few females.

When Taz and Bob had sat back down at their table, Sacha asked Taz, "Is everything okay, baby?"

"Yeah, everything is straight."

"Damn! Can y'all ever go to the club without getting into some shit?" asked Gwen.

Bob started laughing and said, "It don't look like it, huh?"

They all started laughing and went on to enjoy the rest of their evening.

Chapter Twenty-six

Clifford and Tazneema arrived at Mama-Mama's home a little after noon. Mama-Mama was impressed immediately by Clifford's good looks, as well as his manners. She led them into the dining room and began to ask him all kinds of questions—everything from where he was born to what his religious beliefs were. By the time she finished questioning him, she was satisfied that Tazneema had picked a winner.

Mama-Mama smiled as she watched how Tazneema fussed over Clifford, making sure that his glass stayed filled with Mama-Mama's homemade lemonade, to keeping his plate full until he was completely stuffed. *She sure knows how to treat her man,* Mama-Mama thought to herself as she continued to watch their interaction. *My God! That boy Taz is going to have a fit when he finds out about this mess!* "So, when are you going to introduce Clifford here to Taz? You know Taz is going to want to meet him as soon as he finds out about you two's relationship," Mama-Mama said seriously.

"You know how busy Taz is, Mama-Mama. I don't see why I have to rush and bother him about something so minor."

"So minor? Humph! You go on with that mess, 'Neema! You give Taz a call as soon as you can, and just gon' and get it out of the way. I'm sure he's going to get along just fine with Clifford here."

At the second mention of Taz's name, Clifford once again realized that the odds of Taz liking him were like a trillion to one. *Shit! I don't even like him, so I can't blame the fool!* To Mama-Mama he said, "I really enjoyed lunch, ma'am. I can't remember the last time I enjoyed a meal this good."

"Why, thank you, Cliff! But you stop with that 'ma'am' mess and call me Mama-Mama like everybody else does, hear?"

Clifford smiled and said, "Yes, Mama-Mama."

"That's better."

"Excuse me, Mama-Mama. I'm about to go call Taz and see if he's busy," Tazneema said as she got up from the table.

"All right, girl, you go on and do that. We'll be in here getting better acquainted," said Mama-Mama as she smiled at Clifford.

Tazneema went into her old bedroom and grabbed the phone. As she was dialing Taz's number, she saw how her hands were shaking lightly. Once the phone started ringing, she took a deep breath and told herself that everything was going to be all right. As soon as Taz answered the phone, she said, "What's up, Taz?"

"Ain't nothin'. What's up with you, 'Neema?"

"Nothing. I'm over here having lunch with Mama-Mama."

"Yeah? What she cook?"

"The usual."

"That much, huh?"

"You know it! Fried catfish, rice, mac and cheese, her homemade corn bread, pies, and—"

Laughing, Taz said, "Enough! You're making me hungry up in here. I get the point!"

"So, what are you getting into today?"

"I really don't have much to do. I was going to take Sacha out to get something to eat in a minute. Other than that, I was goin' to chill out around the house. Why, what's up? You got somethin' on your mind?"

"Kinda. I think we need to have a talk."

"You think?"

"You know what I mean, Taz."

Taz laughed and said, "No, I don't, 'Neema. What do you want to talk to me about?"

"I'd rather talk about it in person, Taz. Could you come over here after you finish having lunch with Sacha?"

"Yeah, I could do that. We'll be over there in an hour or so."

"Okay. I'll tell Mama-Mama. Bye!"

***

After Taz hung up his phone, he turned toward Sacha and said, "'Neema wants to talk to me about something, and I got a funny idea it will have something to do with a nigga."

"What are you talking about, baby?" Sacha asked as she stretched and climbed out of the bed.

"'Neema was too damn nervous while we were talkin' just now. She says she has somethin' that she wants to talk to me about, and that she would rather do it in person."

"So, what makes you think it has something to do with a man?"

"'Cause I know 'Neema. Whenever she thinks I'll be real upset with her, she gets real nervous and wants to talk to me with Mama-Mama around. She thinks I won't go off too bad 'cause of Mama-Mama."

Sacha laughed and said, "Smart young lady. I think I'll remember that the next time I have something I need to say to you that might piss you off."

"But what 'Neema doesn't realize is that not even Mama-Mama can keep me off of her ass," Taz said with a smile on his face.

Sacha's only reply to that was, "Oh!"

Taz laughed and said, "Go get dressed, girl. After we get something to eat, we're going out to Mama-Mama's."

She smiled and said, "Okay, Daddy."

He started laughing as he watched her enter the bathroom.

Just as Sacha and Taz had finished their meal at Leo's Barbeque, Taz's phone beeped to let him know that he had an incoming picture. He opened his cell and saw a picture of Michael Jordan holding up three fingers, indicating the Chicago Bulls' third NBA title. Taz closed his phone and said, "Shit!"

Sacha stared at him for a moment and then said, "It must be that time."

"Looks like it," Taz said as he reopened his phone and called Keno. When Keno answered his phone, Taz said, "Time to rock, my nigga. This is the one. Get at the others and meet me at the pad."

"Gotcha," said Keno.

Taz quickly paid for their meal and led Sacha out to his truck. They rode back to his house in silence. When he pulled into the garage, he told Sacha, "Look, Li'l Mama, when this trip is over, I'm gettin' at Won and lettin' him know that I'm done with this shit."

"Don't tell me that, Taz, just because you know it's what I want to hear. You don't have to do that, baby. I love you, and I'm not going anywhere. You know that."

"Yeah, I know it. Just like you should know that I would never tell you anything like this if I didn't mean it. It's over with, Li'l Mama. I'm ready to settle down and really enjoy some of this paper I've made. I want to go see the world, I want to relax and live for once, and I want to do that all with you. I want you in my life forever!"

"Are . . . are you asking me what I think you're asking me, Taz?"

"I know this isn't the most romantic moment I could come up with, but yeah, will you marry me, Li'l Mama?" he said as he pulled a ring box out of his back pocket and passed it to Sacha.

She opened the box, and her eyes bulged as if they were about to pop out of their sockets. She stared amazingly at an eight-carat solitaire diamond, mounted in all platinum. She was so stunned that she couldn't find her voice. All she did was nod her head yes over and over.

With a smile on his face, Taz said, "I guess your answer is yes, then, huh, Li'l Mama?"

"Yes! Yes! Yes!" she screamed.

He reached across the seat, gave her a hug and a kiss, and said, "I really hate to ruin this moment, but I gots to get ready. Keno and 'em should be here in a minute."

"I know. Come on, let's get inside so I can help you get yourself ready."

They climbed out of Taz's truck and walked hand in hand inside of his home.

The crew was assembled in Taz's den, waiting for Won's call. When the call came, Taz asked him, "Is this the one, O.G.?"

"Yeah, this is the one that's going to get us where we need to be, so pay close attention.

"First off, your flights are all arranged, as usual. Taz, you and Keno are leaving out of Tulsa in two hours. Bo-Pete and Wild Bill are leaving out of the City in about an hour or so. Red and Bob got Dallas/Fort Worth again. I know they left this way before, but it shouldn't be a problem, because it's completely a different terminal. You guys' destination is Detroit. Everything will be set up inside your room, as always. You are to proceed to the Westin, located inside of the Renaissance Building in downtown Detroit, after you land. Each of your flights will land an hour behind each other.

"Once you all make it to your room, sit down and review the DVD that Taz will pick up once he checks into the hotel. Taz, don't look at the DVD until everyone has arrived. This is very important, because once again, everything about this one is timed. After you review the DVD, get strapped and head on out. As soon as this mission is over, you will be on a flight to your next destination, gentlemen.

"For the next three weeks, your stamina will be put to the ultimate test. Whenever you have the chance to rest, make sure that you take advantage of the opportunity. You will see as the days progress exactly what I'm talking about.

"After the initial flights out to Detroit, all of you will then be flying together on the same flights. After the last mission, you will then fly back the way you flew to Detroit.

"That's about it for now. If you have any questions along the way, Taz, you know how to get at me. Like I told you before, this is a two-hundred-million-dollar mission. After each mission, the money will be added to your accounts. Good luck! Out!" Won said before he hung up the phone.

Taz turned off the speakerphone button and sat down next to Keno.

"It looks like this is it, my niggas, the one we've been waiting for. Are y'all ready?" asked Keno.

"You damn skippy!" replied Wild Bill.

"Fuckin' right!" yelled Bo-Pete.

"Let's do this!" said Bob.

"I been ready!" added Red.

And finally, Taz said, "Yeah, let's go get this fuckin' money." He stood up, and they all filed out of his home.

Once again, Sacha was in her hiding spot, listening to the entire conversation that had just taken place. She went to the front door and watched as the man she loved and his friends climbed into their vehicles on their way to get two hundred million dollars. As they pulled out of the driveway, she went into Taz's den and poured herself a straight shot of his XO and quickly downed it. As it burned her throat, she stared at her engagement ring and said, "Two hundred million dollars! Well, I'll be damn!"

As Taz and Keno headed toward Tulsa, Taz remembered that he had forgotten to call Tazneema. He pulled out his cell phone and called Mama-Mama's house. When Mama-Mama answered the phone, he said, "Hey, Mama-Mama! What you doing?"

"Waiting on your butt, boy! What you think I'm doing?" she scolded.

"I'm sorry about this, Mama-Mama, but I have to go out of town."

"Well, why didn't you tell 'Neema about that when y'all spoke earlier?"

"'Cause something just came up. I was on my way out there when I got the call. Tell 'Neema that we'll talk about whatever she has to talk about when I get back."

"I'll do no such thing! You tell her yourself!" she screamed and dropped the phone.

A minute or two later, Tazneema got on the line, sounding relieved as she asked, "Is everything all right, Taz?"

"Yeah, everything is good. I just got to bounce out of town for a minute, though. So, we're going to have to postpone our li'l chat. Is that all right, or do you want to tell me what you have to tell me now?"

"Uh-uh. I'll wait until you get back."

"Is everything all right, 'Neema?"

"Yes, everything is fine, Taz, for real. It's just that I need to tell you some things that have been going on in my life, and I'd rather do it face-to-face."

Not wanting to be distracted during this upcoming mission, he said, "All right, we'll talk as soon as I get back, okay?"

"All right. Bye, Taz!"

"Bye!" He turned toward Keno and said, "'Neema has a boyfriend."

"*What?* Nah, not our favorite li'l virgin!"

"She hasn't come out and told me yet, but I know her, gee. Her nervousness has damn near confirmed it."

"Do you think she's lost her . . . you know?"

Taz sighed and said, "God, I hope not!"

Back at Mama-Mama's house, Tazneema and Clifford were preparing to leave. "I'd like you to know that it was truly a pleasure having such a delicious meal made by you, Mama-Mama," Clifford said sincerely.

Mama-Mama smiled and said, "Why, thank you, Cliff. Now, you make sure this girl brings you back over again real soon, hear?"

"I wouldn't let her talk me out of coming back over here if she tried!" He then gave Mama-Mama a brief hug and went outside to wait for Tazneema.

After Clifford had walked out of the house, Mama-Mama said, "I like him, 'Neema. I like him a lot. He's respectable and shows that he was brought up in a loving home. You done good, girl. You done real good."

"But what do you think Taz is going to say when he finds out about him?"

"Don't you worry about that boy none. He'll be bent out of shape for a li'l bit, but he'll be all right. Hell, he told me himself a while ago that you're grown now, and to let you start making grown-up decisions. You're a grown woman now, and much as I hate to admit it, he was right. I trust you and your judgment, and so will he."

Tazneema smiled as she gave Mama-Mama a hug and a kiss on her cheek, and said, "I love you, Mama-Mama!"

"I know, baby, and Mama-Mama loves you too. Now, gon' on with your man."

As Tazneema walked out of the house, Mama-Mama watched with pride as she got inside of Clifford's car and pulled out of her driveway. "That boy Taz is going to pitch a fit about this one!" she said as she shook her head sadly and went back into her favorite room of her house . . . the kitchen.

Chapter Twenty-seven

Forty-five minutes after Taz and Keno had arrived at their room at the Westin in Detroit, Bo-Pete and Wild Bill had joined them. They all sat around the suite, checking and rechecking their weapons as they waited for Red and Bob to arrive. As usual, all of their weapons came equipped with silencers, and even though they hardly ever had to use them, Taz felt comforted that they had them. He wasn't trying to kill anyone, but he knew that anything could go down, and they're Golden Rule was that as long as they stayed ready, they would never have to get ready. After they had finished making sure that their weapons were in proper order, they started talking about the upcoming mission.

"Why do you think that nigga Won is breaking us off this much fuckin' money?" asked Bo-Pete.

"Obviously because it's going to be a huge fuckin' take," replied Wild Bill.

"For real, I don't even give a fuck. Just as long as shit goes as smooth as it normally does, I'm wit' it," Keno said from the other side of the room.

"Yeah, I feel you, 'cause after this one, I think I'm out of this shit," said Taz.

"Yeah? You ready to lay it down, huh, homey?" asked Keno.

"Might as well, my nigga. We gots enough chips to last us a lifetime. Why push our luck?"

"I know that's right, but what the fuck are we going to do after we give up this shit?" asked Wild Bill with a smile on his face.

"I don't know about y'all, but I'm taking Sacha and marching her down that aisle, gee. And after that, I'm going to take me one hell of a long vacation. See the world and shit."

"That's straight, dog. I might not have a wifey yet, but I'm about to get on the fucking hunt and find me one, 'cause that shit you talkin' 'bout sounds real damn good to me," Keno said with a smile.

Before anyone could say another word, there was a knock at the door. "Go let them fools in so we can get this shit started," Taz said from across the room.

After Keno had let Red and Bob in, Taz pulled out the DVD and inserted it into the DVD player located under the television inside of their room. A picture of Michael Jordan shooting a fadeaway jumper over Karl Malone of the Utah Jazz came onto the screen as soon as Taz had turned on the DVD. A minute later, Won's voice came over the speakers:

"Glad that y'all made it safely. Now, it's time to go to work. You are to leave your hotel and take Jefferson Boulevard to the corner of East Grand Boulevard, make a right turn on Grand and take that all the way to Mack. On the corner of East Grand and Mack, you're going to see a funeral home, Swanson's Funeral Home, to be exact. You are to make a right turn onto Mack, and then pull into the back of the funeral home. The back door will be unlocked, and you are to proceed inside and go directly into the funeral director's office.

"Once you're inside of the office, move the funeral director's desk and you'll see a floor safe. The combination is sixteen to the right, sixteen to the left, and sixteen back to the right. There will be a substantial amount of drugs as well as money. As usual, the ends are yours and the narcotics are mine.

"After each of you has filled your bags, then proceed into the chapel of the funeral home. There will be an open casket sitting right in front of the altar. Go directly to it, lift the pillows inside of it, and you will see some more money and drugs. After you have emptied the casket, you are then to head back to your room and leave all of what you've just acquired inside of your suite.

"Each of you is then to catch a cab back to Detroit Metro, check in at the flight counter, and get your tickets for your flight to Indianapolis. There will be a day's break before the next op, so make sure that you take this time to get some rest.

When you get there, there will be a rental waiting for you reserved under Taz's Barney. Take that and drive to the W out in downtown Nap. Your instructions will be there as normal.

"Good luck, gentlemen! Out!"

After the screen had gone blank, Taz said, "Let's get to work!"

"Oh! Cliff! Give it to me, baby! Give it to me!" screamed Tazneema as she pulled Clifford as far as she could inside of her sex.

Clifford was amazed at how horny Tazneema was. As soon as they had gotten back to his place, the first thing she did was to take off all of her clothes and began ripping Clifford's off of him. Once she had him naked, she dropped to her knees and started giving him some of the best head he had ever received. After she let him come inside of her mouth, she led him into his bedroom, and that's where they stayed for the last two and a half hours.

After cumming way too many times, Clifford said, "Come on, 'Neema, you're killing me!"

Panting and almost out of breath, Tazneema said, "Come on, baby. One more time, 'k?"

Shaking his head no, Clifford said, "I can't do it, baby. I'm worn out. I have no more strength."

"Do you want me to suck it some more?"

"No!" he screamed as he jumped off of the bed and ran into the bathroom.

Tazneema laughed and yelled, "Come on, baby! I want some more!"

"I'm not coming out of this bathroom until you promise to let me get some sleep! You've turned into a sex maniac, and I can't take it!"

She laughed some more and said, "Okay, I promise. But you're going to have to give me some in the morning. Deal?"

Clifford opened the door to the bathroom and said, "Deal. Now, please go to sleep."

"'Kay," she said with a satisfied smile on her face.

***

Taz drove their rented SUV toward the funeral home. *Detroit's East Side is a wicked-looking place at night,* he thought as he made the left turn off of Jefferson and onto East Grand Boulevard. When he spotted Swanson's Funeral Home on the corner of Mack, he said, "All right, my niggas, it's time." He made a right turn onto Mack and then made a left turn into the back of the funeral home.

As soon as the SUV came to a complete stop, they all jumped out of the truck and headed straight toward the back door. Just like Won had told them, the door was unlocked. What Won didn't tell them was that as soon as they entered the back of the funeral home, they would come face-to-face with several dead bodies with plastic bags over their heads.

"Oh, shit! This is some creepy-ass shit!" Keno said as he followed Taz out of the preparation room.

"Don't pay that shit no mind, dog. We got a job to do, so let's do it," Taz said as he led the way into the funeral director's office.

Once they were inside of the office, Taz and Keno moved the funeral director's desk to the side so Wild Bill could open the safe. Red, Bob, and Bo-Pete stood by the door, making sure that there weren't any more surprises. Once Wild Bill had the safe open, he started filling up his bag. After he finished, he stepped aside so that Taz could start filling up his bag. After Keno had filled his bag, he said, "It's empty, gee."

"Good. Now, come on so we can get at that casket and get the fuck out," Red said as he led the way into the funeral home's chapel. Red opened the door to the chapel and saw the casket. He shook his head and said, "Dog, this is some morbid shit, for real."

"Come on, scary-ass nigga," said Bob as he went to the casket and pulled back the pillows that were inside of it. Just like Won had told them on the DVD, the casket was filled with money and drugs. Bob started packing kilo after kilo of cocaine into his bag. Once he had his bag filled, he stepped back so that Red could fill his. Bo-Pete came right behind Red and finished emptying the casket. After his bag was full and the casket was completely empty, he turned and gave Taz a nod of his head.

"Let's bounce," Taz said as he led the way out of the funeral home. When they had made it safely back inside of the SUV, Taz smiled and said, "God bless the dead!"

As they pulled out of the funeral home's parking lot, Red said, "You are one sick nigga!"

Every one of them laughed, and Taz said, "Maybe, but I'm also on my way to being one rich, sick nigga!" They all laughed again as Taz drove them back to the Westin. Mission completed.

Sacha couldn't sleep. Ever since Taz had left, she just couldn't stop herself from thinking about all of that money he was about to get. "This shit is like the movies. Whenever someone tries to stop doing wrong so they can live happily ever after, something always goes wrong. Please, God, don't let that be the case with Taz. Please!" she begged as she tried to get some rest.

Taz and the crew were on their way to the airport when he remembered that he hadn't called Sacha to let her know that everything was okay. He pulled out his cell and gave her a call. When she answered the phone, he said, "Hey, Li'l Mama! What you doin'?"

"Trying to get some sleep, but for some reason I can't keep my eyes closed. How are you?"

"I'm good. Everything is everything. I'm in a cab now on my way to another spot. I'll give you a call tomorrow, after I get up, okay?"

"All right, baby. I love you."

"Yeah, I love you too," he said and closed his cell.

"Dog, can I ask you a question?" asked Keno.

"What's up, gee?"

"Does Sacha know how we get down?"

Taz sighed heavily and said, "Yeah, gee, she does. I put her up on it after that shit went down out in Cali. I know I broke one of our rules, but I couldn't find another way out of it without exposing our hand. I even introduced her to Won."

"Ain't that a bitch! *We've* never even met that nigga, but your broad has. That's some cold shit, my nigga."

"Look, this is the last quarter of the game any fuckin' way, so why does it really matter?"

"It matters because you broke a rule, gee, a rule that we all swore we'd never break for anyone," Keno said seriously. "Just because you're in love doesn't justify your fuckup, my nigga."

"You're right, dog, and I apologize for my weakness for Sacha. But I love her, and whatever it takes to keep her sane I'm goin' to do it. After all of that shit went down in L.A., I had a decision to make, and I made it for my girl. I've asked her to be wifey, dog, 'cause she's the one. She's the one, my nigga," he said as he sat back and rode the rest of the cab ride to the airport in silence.

Chapter Twenty-eight

Monday morning, Sacha got out of bed feeling good. Ever since she had spoken to Taz the night before, she felt confident that everything was going to be okay. As she got dressed for work, her thoughts of Taz put a smile on her face. "Damn, I love that man!" she said aloud as she grabbed her briefcase and left for work.

Clifford saw Sacha as she walked inside of the office. He stepped quickly toward her and said, "Excuse me, Sacha. Can I have a word with you?"

Sacha glanced at her watch and said, "Could you make it kind of quick? I'm due in court in twenty minutes."

"Sure. I just wanted to tell you that I'm sorry for the way I behaved a while back. I was really hurt that I'd lost the opportunity to get close to you."

Sacha frowned at that statement and chose to remain silent.

"Anyway, I hope you will accept my apology, because it is definitely a sincere one. I've moved on with my life and I'm quite happy. I don't want to have any bad blood between us."

Sacha smiled and said, "Apology accepted, Cliff. I'm glad that you've moved on and that you're happy. That makes the both of us, see?" she said as she showed off the monstrous diamond ring Taz had given her.

"Wow! That's nice. So, you're taking the next step, huh?"

"Yes. We haven't set a date yet, but it most likely will be sometime this summer."

"Congratulations, Sacha. I'm happy for you. Well, I won't take up any more of your time. Have a nice day," he said as he turned and went into his office.

As soon as he closed the door to his office, he clenched his fist together tightly. "I hate that nigga! I can't believe that she's actually going to marry that wannabe-ass thug! Fuck!" he said aloud as he stepped toward his desk. After sitting down, he started wondering why in the hell was he so upset. He had Tazneema. He meant every word that he had just told Sacha. He was happy and had moved on with his life. But the thought of her marrying that nigga Taz irked him to no end. All of the old anger and passion he had had for Sacha came storming back tenfold. He shook his head sadly and said, "It just wasn't meant to be." He then grabbed some cases from his briefcase and started his workday.

"Damn, dog! We've been in this bitch over twenty-fo'. Why the fuck Won ain't got at us yet?" asked Red.

"Ain't no tellin', my nigga. Relax. When it's time to go to work, he'll holla," Taz said as he grabbed his cell and called Sacha. After getting her voicemail, he left her a quick message and closed his cell phone. Just as he had gotten off of his bed, his cell started ringing. He checked the caller ID and saw that it was Won. He smiled and said, "Looks like you done talked that nigga up, Red. This is Won right here. "What's up, O.G.?" he asked when he answered his cell.

"Everything is everything, Babyboy. I assume y'all have watched the DVD already, huh?"

"Oh yeah, we're ready whenever you are."

"Good. This is another day op. You are to move in approximately thirty minutes after we kill this call. You already have the directions, so you know where you're going. After everything is handled, come back to your room and drop off everything. I have already made y'all some reservations on a two o'clock flight out of Nap to Denver, Colorado. When you get to Denver, catch a shuttle bus to the Hertz Rental, and there will be a SUV already reserved for you. You are then to drive to the Doubletree Hotel on MLK and Monaco. After you're checked in, pick up your package and head on up to your room. You will be moving to your next op within an hour after you have checked into the hotel. Good luck. We won't speak again until you're out of Denver. Out!"

Taz closed his cell and said with a smile, "Time to get money, y'all!"

Sacha smiled as she listened to Taz's message on her voicemail. *He's so considerate,* she thought as she saved the message. Now that she was through with court, she had the rest of the day to herself. She didn't want to go back to Taz's big house all by herself, so she decided to call Gwen and see what she was up to.

Gwen answered her cell phone in a hushed tone. "Hello!" she whispered.

"Ho, what's wrong with you?" asked Sacha.

"I'm with a client, and we're watching a seminar on drunken drivers. Can I call you back in a little while?"

"Sure. I didn't want anything, really. Just wanted to see if you wanted to hang a little bit."

"Okay, I'll be out of here in an hour. I'll give you a call on your cell. Bye!"

Since Gwen was busy, Sacha decided to head on to her house. When she made it home, she smiled and said, "Damn! It feels as if I haven't been here in ages!" She walked around her living room, smiling. She was so happy. She knew that pretty soon she would no longer be living in this home anymore. Instead of this thought making her feel sad, she was elated. "I guess I'm going to have to contact a Realtor soon," she said as she went into her bedroom, feeling giddy about all of her and Taz's future plans together.

As Taz pulled out of the beauty shop's parking lot, he smiled and said, "Damn! It seems as if this shit is gettin' easier and easier."

"I know, huh? Those suckas was slippin' somethin' awful," added Keno.

They had just finished their mission in Indianapolis, and now they were headed back to their room so they could drop of their illegally gotten gains. Won had been exactly on the money again. His information about the beauty shop they had just finished robbing was perfect. Even though they had had to get a little physical with two of the men that were inside of the shop, the job still went off without a hitch.

"Denver, Colorado, here we come!" Taz yelled as he pulled into the parking lot of their hotel.

By the time Gwen had made it over to Sacha's house, Sacha had packed three suitcases full of her clothes. "Damn, bitch! What you doing, moving in with that nigga?" asked Gwen as she set her purse onto Sacha's dining room table.

Shaking her head yes, Sacha smiled as she stuck out her left hand so Gwen could see her engagement ring. "Does this answer your question, ho?"

Gwen's eyes grew wide when she saw the sparkling diamond ring on Sacha's wedding finger. She smiled and said, "That nigga done stepped up his game, I see. Congratulations, bitch! I'm so happy for you!"

"Ho, I can't lie. I never thought Taz was the marrying type, but when he asked me and I looked into those sexy-ass brown eyes, I knew he was serious. He loves me, Gwen, and I love him so much that it hurts to even think of my life without him in it. This is definitely the real thing."

"I know. I can see it in the both of you guys' eyes. Whenever we're together, I see how you two be looking at each other. I knew after the first day that I saw you two that your relationship was going to blossom into something real special. This shit is just perfect. You have found your soul mate, and so have I."

"*What?* Don't tell me you and Bob are planning on jumping that broom too!"

"Bitch, you're so late! When I moved in with him, he told me that he wanted to see if what we had was real, and if everything worked out the way he hoped it would, we would do the damn thing sometime this year. And so far, everything has been going just as we both had hoped for. So, you're not the only one who'll be changing their last name this year."

Sacha hugged Gwen and said, "Ho, I'm so happy for you! You know you deserve all of the happiness in the world."

"Yeah, I do, 'cause I've sure had enough pain. But come on with this corny shit. Our men are out of town, doing God knows what, and we're sitting here being all mushy-mushy and shit. Let's go on over to Taz's house and get blitzed off of some of that expensive-ass liquor he has behind that bar."

Sacha laughed and said, "I'm with that! Come on!"

Taz and the crew arrived in Denver right on schedule. After picking up their rented SUV, Taz gave Keno the directions to their hotel. While Keno drove, Taz called Sacha. "What you doing, Li'l Mama?" he asked as soon as Sacha answered the phone.

"Nothin'," Sacha answered with a slight slur in her voice.

"Nothin', huh? Sounds to me like you're doing somethin'."

"Uh-uh. Gwen and I are just chilling, baby. How are you? Is everything everything?"

Taz started laughing and said, "Yeah, I'm straight. Have you been drinking, Li'l Mama?"

"A li'l."

"What have you been drinking? Apple martinis?"

"Nope. Some of your XO."

"*What?* Now you know damn well your system ain't used to nothin' like that. What's gotten into you, Li'l Mama?"

"Nothin'."

"Somethin' must have, 'cause you're over there trippin'."

"No, I'm not, baby. Me and Gwen are just relaxing by the pool, sippin' on some of your good stuff. You're not mad at me, are you?"

He laughed again and said, "Nah, I ain't mad at ya. This shit is kinda funny, really. Check it out, though. I'm going to call you later, after my business is finished, okay? No, better yet, I'm just gon' call your drunk-ass in the morning, before you go to work. I bet you won't have a problem gettin' any sleep tonight."

"I hope not."

"Tell me, how much of my XO have you two been drinkin'?"

Sacha grabbed the bottle of liquor out of Gwen's hand, saw that it was almost empty, and said, "Almost all of this bottle, baby."

"Sacha, take your ass upstairs and get in the bed! Tell Gwen I said that you two don't need to be down there by the pool! That shit is gon' kick in and lay the both of y'all down!" Taz said sternly.

"Uh-uh, baby. We know what we doing. We used to get drunk all the time when we was back in school."

"Do what I told you, Li'l Mama. Go upstairs now for me, okay?"

"All right, baby, I will."

"Do it while I'm still on the phone with you."

"Come on, Gwen. Taz wants us to take this party upstairs to the bedroom," Sacha said as she got to her feet.

"Ask Taz is my baby with him."

"Baby, Gwen wants to—"

"I heard her, Li'l Mama. Yeah, he's here. Go on and give the phone to her drunk ass," Taz said, and he passed the phone to Bob in the backseat of the SUV.

Bob accepted the phone from Taz and said, "Hello."

"Hi, you sexy-ass Black man! What'cha doin'?" asked Gwen.

"Taking care of some business. What's up with you?"

"Missing you."

"I guess that's a good thing then, huh?"

"You know it! Baby, did you know that Taz asked Sacha to marry him?"

"Yeah, he told us the other day. Why?"

"I was just wondering, that's all. Did you know that he bought her a big-ass diamond ring?"

"Nah, he didn't tell us that. What's up? You ready for yours yet?"

Gwen smiled as she sat down on Taz's bed and said, "You got that right, buddy!"

Bob laughed and said, "Don't trip. I gots you. Have you and Sacha taken y'all drunk asses upstairs yet?"

"Yep, we're in the room now."

"Good. Go on and spend the night, 'cause I know you are in no shape to be doing any driving. I'll get at you in the morning, okay?"

"All right, baby. Love you!"

"Yeah, I love your crazy ass too. Give the phone back to Sacha. Taz wants to holla at her."

"Okay. Bye!"

When Sacha got back on the phone, Taz said, "All right, Li'l Mama, I'm outta here. I'll get at you tomorrow."

"Okay, baby. Be careful, Taz."

"I will, Li'l Mama."

"I love you!"

Taz smiled at that and said, "I love you, too!"

Chapter Twenty-nine

After a week of traveling and doing what they did best, Taz was starting to understand why Won had told them that this trip would be the ultimate test of their stamina. All of the flying that they were doing was starting to catch up to them. After they had left Denver, they drove to Colorado Springs and completed a mission there. After that, they flew to Memphis, where they took care of a quick mission worth a couple of million dollars. After leaving Memphis, they drove to a small town near Nashville, Tennessee, called Madison. They drove into the town and checked into the local Days Inn. After they had their rooms, Taz called Won as he was instructed to do back when they were in Colorado Springs. Won gave him the details to the next mission and told him that they had a flight to catch in five hours out of Memphis.

After Taz hung up the phone with Won, he went and checked under the bed and grabbed their weapons. *For the life of me, I don't know how this fool be doing this shit,* he thought as he pulled the duffel bag containing their guns and the rest of their equipment out from under the bed.

"All right, my niggas, it's like this. We are to drive over to this house off of Lovell Street. It's about ten minutes from here. We park the truck down the street from 307 B Lovell Street and walk the rest of the way. This is a home invasion raid, and it's all about in and out. No one is inside of the house, so it should go pretty smooth. There are two safes in the bedroom. Keno and I will go hit it while y'all watch our backs. We're getting a ticket for this one 'cause there is a lot of drugs there. Once we come out with the chips, Red, you, Bob, Wild Bill, and Bo-Pete will then go in the back and grab the work. Me and Keno will be standing point while y'all are handling your business. After everything is everything, we'll then close the door and casually walk back to the truck. The street is dimly lit, so there shouldn't be a problem. Come on, let's do this."

Tazneema and Clifford were having the time of their lives. They spent a weekend down in Dallas, shopping and wandering around the city. Clifford even took her to Six Flags out in Dallas/Fort Worth.

Tazneema felt as if she was on cloud nine. No one in her short life had ever shown her this much attention. Even though Taz had always been there for her, he just wasn't the type to spend a lot of quality time with a person. She understood that, and she had never complained. She loved Taz, and no matter what happened, she always would. Being with Clifford showed her an entirely different side of life, and she was loving it. "Baby, when we get back home, I've decided to move in with you."

Clifford smiled and said, "Are you sure, 'Neema?"

"Positive. I love you, Cliff, and I want to be with you as much as I can, every single day."

"Have you spoken with Taz or Mama-Mama about this?"

Shaking her head no, she said, "I don't have to. This is my decision, and my decision only. I don't need their approval."

He smiled and said, "Well then, let's get our butts back to the city then, 'cause we got some moving to do!" They laughed as Clifford started packing his bags.

As Taz parked the truck, he noticed how dark Lovell Street was and said, "That nigga Won wasn't lying. This street is dark as fuck. Come on, let's get this over with." He killed the ignition and jumped out of the truck.

As they walked down the street, they noticed that the street was damn near deserted. There were only a few houses on each side of the street. Taz scanned the houses until he saw the one he was looking for. "Three-oh-seven B Lovell Street.

That's it right there, gee. The door should be unlocked, so we won't have to worry about making any noise kickin' it in," he said as he led the way toward the house.

"Shit, it wouldn't matter any fuckin' way. Ain't nobody around this bitch to hear us if we did have to kick it in," said Bo-Pete.

Taz stepped onto the porch and turned the doorknob to see that it was in fact locked. "Fuck! It's locked!"

"Kick the bitch in, dog, so we can do this shit and get the fuck out of here," urged Keno.

Taz gave a nod of his head, pulled out his weapon, and kicked the door hard right by the doorknob. The thin door busted open easily, and they all rushed inside with their guns drawn.

The first thing that Taz saw was a small lady sitting down at the dining room table. *Oh, shit!* he thought as he raised his gun, pointed it toward her, and said, "Be quiet, ma'am, and you will not be hurt. Now, is there anyone else in here with you?"

The small-framed lady shook her head no.

"Okay, then. Watch her, dog," Taz instructed as he led Keno into the back room. After moving some clothes out of his way, Taz spotted the safe concealed inside the closet. He quickly opened the safe and started filling up his duffel bag. After his bag was full, he stepped to the next safe and opened it also. He smiled when he saw all of the kilos of cocaine stacked neatly inside of it. After Keno's bag was full, they went back into the front and stood watch over the lady while Red, Bob, Wild Bill, and Bo-Pete went to the back room to retrieve the narcotics.

While they were standing watch, Keno stared at Taz and raised his eyebrows as if asking, what the fuck is going on? Taz's answer was a shrug of his shoulders, indicating that he didn't have a fucking clue.

A few minutes later, Red came back into the room, followed by Bob, Bo-Pete, and Wild Bill.

Taz said, "All right, ma'am, I'm goin' to need you to get on the floor. I give you my word that you will not be harmed. Just do as I ask."

For the first time during the entire incident the small lady spoke. "I'm not worried, son. Y'all done got what y'all came for. I know you ain't gon' do me nothin'. You better watch out, though, 'cause the boys be watchin' this house from across the street!"

Taz tried his best not to show any surprise in his voice when he asked, "What boys, ma'am?"

"Them boys who's puts those drugs in my house."

"Are you sure?"

"Positive."

"This changes shit, gee. Go get the truck and pull up in front of the house, K. Go with him, BP. You too, WB," Taz ordered, using the crew's initials instead of their names.

Keno, Bo-Pete, and Wild Bill walked out of the house with their weapons inside of their hands, cocked and ready, while Taz, Red ,and Bob stood at the door, watching the house directly across the street. All of the lights in the house were off, so Taz couldn't tell whether anyone was inside or not. It seemed as if it was taking Keno and the rest forever to come back with the truck, when in fact it had only been a couple of minutes. When Taz heard the horn blow, he turned and stepped out of the house, followed by Bob and Red. They jumped inside of the truck and sighed as Keno sped away from Lovell Street.

Mission completed, but Won has some fucking questions to answer! thought Taz as he relaxed a little.

By the time they had made it to Norman, Tazneema was asleep. Clifford shook her gently and said, "We're here, baby. Why don't you go on inside and get some rest? After I get off tomorrow, I'll come back and we can get your things."

"Okay, baby. I didn't know I'd be this tired. All I want to do is go to bed. Are you sure that you don't want to spend the night with me here?"

He smiled and said, "Yeah, I'm sure. Plus, it'll be nice getting a good night's sleep without worrying about being attacked in my sleep!"

Tazneema smiled and said, "Okay, I see how you are then! But wait until I move in. You're never going to get any sleep!" They laughed with each other, then shared a passionate kiss. "I love you, Cliff!"

"I love you, too, 'Neema. Now go on. I'll talk to you tomorrow."

"Bye!" Tazneema said, and she went into her apartment. After changing clothes, she went into the bedroom and pulled out the pregnancy test she had bought while they were in Dallas. She knew she was late for her period, and she was terrified of the results of the test she was about to take. "Please, God, don't let it be! Taz will kill me!" she prayed as she began to urinate onto the pregnancy test.

After waiting for the amount of time written on the instructions, Tazneema took a deep breath to see if she was in the blue or the pink. The blue would indicate that she was not pregnant, and the pink would indicate that she was. She stared at the test with a weird look on her face as tears slowly slid down her face. The test results were in the pink. *Damn!*

As soon as they were on the highway out of Madison, Taz pulled out his cell and called Won. When Won answered the phone, Taz quickly told him what had happened at the house on Lovell Street. After he was finished, Won asked, "Did you hurt her?"

"Nah, I tied her up and left the restraints kind of loose so she could easily slip out of them after we were gone."

"Good thinking. Damn! That was not suppose to happen!"

"Who the fuck you tellin'? You damn right that shit wasn't supposed to have happened! Don't tell me that you're finally slippin' on us, O.G."

"Nah, Babyboy, I'm on it. But like I've always told y'all, you will have to be ready for anything at any given time. As long as you are, if any surprises come up, y'all will be able to handle it."

"True, but you got us so damn comfortable with how we get down that we really ain't expectin' shit like this to pop off."

"I feel you. Go on and hit your next destination. Give me a call when you touch. I'm gonna make damn sure that everything is on point for this next one," Won said seriously.

"I hope so, O.G. I hope so!" Taz closed his cell phone.

Chapter Thirty

"Where are you now, baby?" asked Sacha as she tapped her fingers on top of her desk.

"In Baton Rouge."

"Louisiana?"

"Yeah."

"How long will you be there?"

Sighing, he said, "I'm not sure yet, Li'l Mama. What's with all of these questions? I was just callin' to let you know everything is everything. Damn!"

"Well, excuse me for caring! Bye, Taz!" she yelled and hung up the phone in his face.

Taz stared briefly at his cell before closing it. He got off of the bed and went into the bathroom of his and Keno's hotel room. They had made it to Baton Rouge early that morning, and to say they were tired would have been an understatement. The entire crew was completely exhausted. Taz had called Won after they arrived at the hotel. After retrieving the DVD, they sat and listened to Won's instructions with weary eyes. They all smiled when they heard Won say that the first of their two missions in Louisiana wouldn't be until late that night. That meant that they could get some much-needed rest. Even though they got to doze a little during their flights and brief road trips, there was nothing like getting some good old-fashioned sleep in a comfortable bed.

Everyone was in their rooms, sound asleep, at that moment—everyone except Taz. He couldn't stop thinking about how fucked up things had been in Madison. *What if they would have killed that old lady? What if the guys she had warned them about would have come out blasting?* These questions were running through his mind constantly.

He chose to call Sacha to try and keep his mind off of the Lovell Street mission. *And look what happened with that!* he thought as he smiled. *I done pissed my Li'l Mama off.* He grabbed his cell and called Sacha back. As soon as she answered the phone, he said, "I'm sorry, Li'l Mama. I'm tired as fuck, and I didn't mean to snap at you."

Sacha smiled and said, "I understand, baby. I can't help it if I'm overly concerned about your well-being."

"I know. But look, I really need to get some rest, so I'll give you a holla later on, okay?"

"All right, bye, Taz."

"Bye, Li'l Mama." He got back into bed and closed his eyes. As he finally started to fall asleep, his last thoughts were on Won. He hoped and prayed that he kept shit together. It was too fucking late in the game for mistakes.

Tazneema smiled as she unloaded the last of her stuff inside of Clifford's house. Clifford smiled at her and said, "Home, sweet home, baby!"

"You said it, mister! Now come here, because I have something to discuss with you." Clifford sat down next to her on the couch. "Cliff, what I'm about to say to you doesn't have to affect our relationship negatively. No matter what decision we make, I'm still going to love you. Do you understand?"

"Not really. Can you be a little bit more specific, 'Neema?"

She took a deep breath and said, "I'm pregnant." She stared at Clifford briefly, then continued. "I want to have this child, but if you're not ready, then I understand, and I have no problem with getting an abortion. I'm happy as long as I have you in my life. I would never do anything to hurt you, but more importantly, I want you to know that I never want to lose you. So, what you think?" she asked nervously.

Clifford smiled at her and said, "I love you, Tazneema Good, and I can't wait for our child to be born!"

Her face lit up as she asked, "For real?"

Nodding his head yes, he said, "For real. I don't know why you would think that I'd want you to have an abortion. I love you, and no matter what, I want us to be together also."

They hugged one another for a full minute, and Tazneema pulled from his embrace and said, "I'm going to have to tell Taz. He's not going to like this at all, but I'm sure after he meets you and sees what kind of man you are, you two will hit it off just fine. Taz can be hard sometimes, but he's a big softy when it comes to me."

"I hope you're right, 'cause your brother seems to be a little intimidating, from what I've heard about him."

Tazneema smiled and said, "Don't worry. I'll take care of him. Now as for Mama-Mama, that's another story."

"Oh, God!" Clifford said as he slapped his forehead.

They both laughed and gave each other another hug.

"Bitch, have you talked to Taz?" asked Gwen.

"Yes, I spoke with him earlier. What's up?"

"I've been trying to call Bob all damn day and he's not answering his phone."

"From what Taz told me, they were pretty tired, and they were getting some rest. Maybe Bob has his phone turned off," Sacha said logically.

"Uh-uh. If it was turned off, it would go straight to his voicemail. That nigga bet' not be up to no bullshit."

"Ho, go on with that silly talk. Bob is handling his business with Taz and the others. You don't have shit to worry about."

"How come all of the sudden you're not worried about what they be doing when they go out of town? Do you know something I don't?"

Sacha smiled and said, "Maybe I do . . . and maybe I don't!"

"So, it's like that, huh? We're keeping secrets from each other now, bitch?"

"Come on, Gwen. You know that if I knew something that was important, I'd put you up on it. I trust Taz, and I know he's legitimate, so I've stopped worrying myself about their business. And you should too. Bob loves you and you love him. Everything is just how it should be." Sacha felt bad for lying to her best friend, but she had promised Taz that she would never tell anyone of his secrets, especially Gwen, because if she said anything about it to Bob, he would have to answer to the rest of the crew for betraying them. So, here she was, lying to her best friend in the entire world for her man, her fiancé, the man she was planning to spend the rest of her life with.

Taz was just getting out of bed when his cell phone started ringing. "Hello," he said groggily when he answered it.

"I hope y'all got some rest, Babyboy, 'cause it's time to get busy. Have you already checked out the DVD?"

"Yeah, we took care of that as soon as we got here."

"Good. After you finish this op, you are to take the truck you have and head to Shreveport, check into any hotel you want to, and get some rest. Your next op will be early in the morning. Give me a call once you've made it there and I'll then give you the information for what needs to be handled out there."

"So, we need to keep the equipment with us from this last mission?"

"Nah. I don't want y'all making that drive dirty. Once you get at me, I'll have everything set up. Someone most likely will be bringing you what you need."

"All right, that's cool. Anything else?"

"This is the last leg of this mission, Babyboy. After y'all are finished in Louisiana, y'all will be flying out east to finish the last two ops."

"Good, 'cause this shit is starting to wear on a nigga's nerves. Mistakes can happen when we're this fuckin' tired, O.G. I've been staying on top of everybody, but still, all of this flying is tiring a nigga out," Taz said seriously.

"Hold on, Babyboy. This ride is coming to an end. Remember what I told you a long time ago, when we first started this shit?"

Taz smiled and said, "Yeah, you told me that when everything is everything, I would be rich and you would be in the position of power. And, as long as you had the power, I would have the power."

"That's right. My position of power has gotten stronger and stronger over these last few years. We're almost there. Just a little bit longer and everything I told you back in the day will become a reality. So, make sure you handle this shit for me, Babyboy."

"I got you."

"Out!" Won said and hung up.

Taz woke Keno and told him to call the others and wake them while he took a quick shower. It was time to go back to work.

After work, Sacha went over to Taz's house to relax. She smiled as she pulled into the driveway and saw Tari's Altima parked by the garage. She climbed out of her BMW and went inside.

Tari was out back, watching Heaven and Precious run around the yard. When she saw Sacha come outside, she smiled and said, "Hey, girl! How are you doing today?"

"I'm fine. How about yourself?"

"I'm all right. I had the day off today, so I came to spend some time with my babies. I didn't want them to think that I've forgotten about them."

"Those dogs are so spoiled. When I first started coming over here, they never showed themselves. But now, as soon as they smell my scent, they're all over me," Sacha said affectionately as she watched Precious and Heaven out in the yard.

"That's a good thing, though, 'cause if they didn't like you, you and Taz's relationship would have been doomed!" They both started laughing.

"Have you spoken to Taz lately?" Sacha asked as she slipped off her pumps.

"A couple of weeks ago, before he left, we met and had a talk."

"A talk? About what?"

Tari smiled and said, "You, what he does when he goes out of town, and Won."

"Whoa!"

"Those were my thoughts too. He doesn't know whether or not he wants to get out of the game he's been playing for so long. He's giving it some serious thought now because of you. But he's still unsure."

"He told you that?"

"Yep. I know how he thinks. Better yet, I know firsthand how Won thinks, and I know that even if Taz does decide to stop doing his thing, Won is going to try his very best to deter him from stopping. Won has something heavy up his sleeve, and Taz is a major part of his plans."

"What makes you think that Won won't let Taz stop?"

Tari shrugged her shoulders slightly and said, "I know Won, and I know the things that they've been doing for all these years are for a reason."

"What's the reason?"

"That's something that Taz and I have never been able to figure out. Won is the only person who can answer that question for you. And I highly doubt if he ever will."

Sighing heavily, Sacha said, "Taz asked me to marry him before he left, and he told me that he was going to get at Won and let him know that it's over and he wants out."

"Taz has always been his own man, to a degree. You have to understand that Won has done so much for Taz and never asked for anything in return. All he ever wanted for Taz was for him to be successful. Taz is financially secure for the rest of his life, and it's all because of Won. If and when Taz chooses to tell Won that he wants out, I'm 99.9 percent sure that Won will use whatever tactics he can come up with to keep Taz in the game."

"But why? If Taz wants to stop, why won't Won let him?"

Tari smiled sadly and said, "Because he gets to win!"

"Win what?" Sacha asked with a confused look on her face.

"Only Won knows the answer to that question, Sacha."

"That's so unfair!"

"That's how it is."

"So, are you telling me that no matter what, Won won't let Taz get out?"

"No, I'm not saying that at all. What I am saying is that when Won is ready for Taz to get out, he'll let him out. But only after he has accomplished whatever it is that he's after. And, baby, believe me when I tell you this. People don't just call him 'Won' for nothing."

"What's that supposed to mean?"

Tari stared at Sacha briefly and simply said, "He always, and I mean always, has to win."

Chapter Thirty-one

Everything seemed to be back to normal. The missions in both Baton Rouge and Shreveport, Louisiana, went according to plan and without any problems.

As Taz drove their rented SUV out of Louisiana toward Dallas, he once again felt comfortable with their chances of completing these last two missions.

"So, we're flying out of Dallas/Fort Worth, on our way to the East Coast, huh?" asked Bob.

"Yep. These are the last two missions," Taz said as he smiled at Keno, who was sleeping next to him in the passenger seat.

"Good. I'm tired of this shit, dog. All I want to do is get back to town and chill the fuck out."

"Stop whining, nigga. You ain't gone be tired when you see all of them chips in your account. You gots to work to get paid, fool," Red said with a smile on his face.

"Yeah, and the more we work, the more we get paid!" yelled Wild Bill from the back of the truck.

Bo-Pete smiled and said, "That's cold, though. We're so close to home and we gots to head the other fuckin' way."

"Yeah, I know. But don't trip, 'cause when we come back, we will be able to do whatever the fuck we want to," Taz said wisely.

Keno opened his eyes, scratched his two-day-old stubble, and said, "Nigga, we already can do whatever the fuck we want!"

Taz laughed and said, "I know, huh?"

Keno shook his head from side to side and said, "Bo-Pete, pass me my bag so I can put 'Face in the DVD. It's time for me to get motivated."

***

Tazneema and Clifford went to Tazneema's doctor and confirmed what she already was certain of. She was nine weeks pregnant. Her doctor gave her a prescription for some vitamins and told her to make sure that she watched what she ate.

After they left the doctor's office, Clifford felt as if he was on cloud nine. He was about to be a father! He was in love with Tazneema, and he didn't give a damn whether or not Taz accepted it or not. There was no way in the world he was going to let Taz interfere with his child being born. "So, since I have the rest of the day off, is there anything special you'd like to do, 'Neema?" he asked as he pulled out of the parking lot.

Tazneema smiled sheepishly and said, "I want to go home and do it, Cliff. I'm horny."

"Damn, baby! Don't you ever think about anything else other than sex?"

"I'm still making up for lost time. Remember, I started late."

He smiled and said, "Okay, okay! But first we're going to go somewhere and get something to eat. I'm not about to let you wear me out on an empty stomach."

Tazneema smiled and said, "Thank you, baby. You're so good to me. And because of you being so good to me, I'm going to be extremely good to you as soon as we get home."

Clifford slapped his forehead with the palm of his left hand and said, "Oh my God!"

"Girl, why haven't you called that nigga?" asked Paquita as she sat down on Katrina's sofa.

"I didn't want him to think I was sweatin' his ass or nothin' like that. Plus, I wanted to see if he would get back at me first."

"Well, now that you've seen that he ain't, you need to be gettin' at his ass."

"Damn, bitch! Why you all up in mines any fuckin' way?"

"'Cause I want to see what's up with Red's big, sexy yellow-ass. He hasn't gotten back at me either. I want to know if I impressed him or not."

"What did your freaky-ass do with him, anyway?"

"Bitch, I ain't given you my secrets. That's for me and my baby, Red, only."

Katrina started laughing and said, "You and your baby, Red! Ain't that a bitch! What happened to you wanting Taz?"

"Taz is in love. You can see it in his eyes. I'm trying to get in where I fit in. I want Red to have that same kind of look that Taz has. You feel me?"

"Yeah, I feel you."

Shaking her head no, Paquita said, "Nah, you ain't feelin' me."

"What are you talkin' 'bout, bitch? I said I feel you, didn't I?"

"If you're really feelin' me, you'd be on the phone, dialing Keno's number right now."

Katrina didn't respond to her best friend. Instead, she picked up her phone, smiled, and started dialing Keno's cell phone number.

Once they arrived at JFK in New York, Taz led the crew through the crowded airport terminal. Since this was their first time on the East Coast, Won had told them that there would be too much traffic for them to try and maneuver through in a rental, so he told them to catch a cab to their hotel.

When they arrived at the Midtown Marriott, they quickly checked into their reserved rooms. After putting their bags in their room, they met back up with Taz and Keno inside of their room on the tenth floor.

Taz pulled out the DVD and inserted it into the television's DVD player. A picture of Michael Jordan came onto the screen, showing the Great Mike slam-dunking the ball over Charles Barkley. A minute later, Won's voice came over the speakers:

"I know by now y'all are tired and about ready to get back home. Don't trip. The Big Apple is your last stop. But first, you have to do a quickie out in Jersey.

"Downstairs you have an SUV waiting for you that is to be used for this mission, as well as the one out in Brooklyn after you finish with Jersey."

As they sat and listened to Won explain their last two missions, Taz was thinking about Tazneema. He quickly shook her out of his mind and paid attention to what Won was saying on the DVD.

After the DVD went blank, Taz turned off the television and said, "All right, let's get this shit over with."

Keno reached under the bed and pulled out their equipment. Once again, it was time to go to work.

"Are you busy, Mama-Mama?" asked Tazneema.

"Girl, even if I was, it wouldn't matter none. You know I always have time for you. What's wrong?"

"Nothing. I just want to talk to you, that's all."

"About what?"

"A lot of things."

"Well, talk then, girl."

"I'd rather do it in person, but my schedule is kind of hectic right now. I'll give you a call later in the week and see when I can make it down to your house."

Concerned, Mama-Mama asked, "Are you feeling all right, 'Neema?"

Tazneema smiled and said, "Yes, I'm fine, Mama-Mama. Don't worry about me. I'm A-okay. I'll talk to you later, 'kay?"

"All right, baby. Bye now," Mama-Mama said before hanging up. "Humph! That girl done got herself into some trouble. I can feel it in my bones," she said aloud as she went back to work on the homemade biscuits she was baking.

By the time Taz and the crew had made it back to their rooms, it was close to midnight. That meant that it was close to eleven back in Oklahoma City. Taz sat down on the bed in their room and called Sacha. When she answered his phone, he smiled and said, "What's up, Li'l Mama?"

"Hi, baby. How are you doing?"

"I'm good. I'll be home within the next two days."

"For real?"

He laughed and said, "Yeah, for real. You miss me?"

"Now you know that's a silly question. Of course I miss you. I've been missing you ever since you first left me."

"How much do you miss me?"

"A lot."

"How much is a lot?"

"What are you talking about, Taz?"

Taz saw that Keno had fallen fast asleep, so he took his cell and went into the bathroom, closed the door, and said, "I said, how much is a lot?"

"A whole lot."

"Have you been horny since I've been gone, Li'l Mama?"

Sacha lowered her voice as if she wasn't alone and whispered, "Yes, extremely horny, baby."

He smiled and asked, "What you got on right now, Li'l Mama?"

"One of your wife-beaters."

"That's it?"

"Mmmm, hmm."

"You wanna do somethin' for me, Li'l Mama?"

"What's that, baby?"

"Play with it for me. I want to listen to you while you make yourself cum. Can you do that for me, Li'l Mama?"

She giggled like a schoolgirl and asked, "You want to have phone sex with me, baby?"

"Yeah, I want you to cum for me, baby."

"What are you going to do for me in return?"

"What you want, Li'l Mama?"

"I want you to stroke that big thang of yours while I stroke my kitty."

"I'm way ahead of you, Li'l Mama. I'm strokin' him already," he said as he continued to stroke his manhood with his right hand.

"Is it nice and hard for me, baby?"

"Yeah, it's hard, baby . . . it's real hard. Is my pussy nice and wet?"

"Yes! It's wet, baby! It's real wet," she said as she let her fingers manipulate her clitoris.

"You want this dick, don't ya?"

"Ooooh, yes, baby, I want it bad! Do you want this kitty?"

"You know I do, baby. I want it so bad it hurts," he said as his right hand started stroking himself faster and faster. "I'm almost there, baby! I'm almost there!" he panted.

"Oooh, me too, baby! Me too!" she screamed into the receiver.

"Cum with me, Li'l Mama. Let's cum together as if I was with you."

"I'm ready, baby! I'm ready!" she screamed.

"Me too, baby! Me too!" he yelled as he skeeted his semen all over his right hand.

Sacha moaned loudly as she gushed a large amount of her love juices all over Taz's sheets. After a minute of recuperation, she said, "Are you still there, baby?"

"Ye—yeah, I'm here, Li'l Mama. Damn, I've made a mess!" he said, and they both started laughing.

"That was crazy. I've never done anything like that before."

"To tell you the truth, me neither. It was cool, but nothin' beats the real thing."

"I know that's right, so hurry up and get your ass back home!"

He laughed and said, "Don't worry about a thang, Li'l Mama. I got one more mission to complete, and I'm on my way home for good."

"For good?"

"That's right, Li'l Mama, for good."

She laughed and said, "I can't wait!"

Chapter Thirty-two

"Damn! I told you I've been out of town, baby! Why you trippin' on me like that?" asked Keno with a smile on his face.

"'Cause you said you were goin' to get me the next day," Katrina whined.

Keno sighed and said, "Check this out, boo. I'll be back in town in a day or so. I give you my word that as soon as I hit the city, I'll give you a holla and we'll hook up. Cool?"

Katrina smiled into the receiver and said, "All right, Keno."

"Look, I gots to bounce. I'll talk to you soon."

"Wait! Paquita wants to know if Red is with you."

"Yeah, he's with me, but he's not in my room right now. I'll tell him to give her a call when he has time."

"All right, baby. Be good."

Keno laughed and said, "I'm always good, boo, even when I'm being bad!"

"I know. That's why I'm diggin' you so much."

"I know that's right! Bye, boo," Keno said and hung up the phone. He turned toward Taz, who had a smile on his face, and said, "Don't even start, nigga."

Taz started laughing, raised his hands in the air as if surrendering, and said, "I don't want any problems, my nigga. It's just good to see that you've finally found someone that's able to hold your attention, playa."

Keno smiled and said, "Fuck you! Yeah, I'm feelin' Katrina a li'l, but that don't mean she's about to be wifey or no shit like that. I'm goin' to take it nice and slow and see if she's really worthy to be with a nigga, ya know what I'm sayin'?"

"That's the best thing, dog. Now, let's get some rest. It's on in the morning. Once we finish this last one, we can head on back to town and start living for once."

"So, this is the last one for real, then, huh?"

Taz nodded his head yes and said, "I'm gon' get at Won when we get back and let him know that this mission was our last one."

"Do you think he's goin' to trip out?"

"I doubt it. But if he does, so what? We ain't sign no lifetime contract with this shit. Nothin' lasts forever, and I'm tryin' to get out while everything is everything."

"I'm with you, dog. Whatever way you choose to go, I'm rollin' with my nigga."

"I know, gee. I know," Taz said as he got onto his bed and closed his eyes.

Sacha woke up the next morning feeling extremely happy. Taz was finishing up his last job, and then he was coming back home so they could start living a normal life together. That was a blessing from God, and she thanked Him silently as she started getting dressed for work.

Clifford had already left for work by the time Tazneema had awakened from a very comfortable night's sleep. She felt so secure when she was with Clifford that it was as if she was living with her knight in shining armor.

She stretched as she got out of the bed, and then ran to the bathroom and started throwing up. After she had finished, she wiped her mouth with a face towel, smiled, and said, "My first time having morning sickness!" While she was brushing her teeth, she thought about having to tell Taz that she was pregnant. "Damn, he's going to go ape on me! I just hope Mama-Mama will be on my side, 'cause if she's not, then I know I'm going to have hell convincing Taz to let me have this baby. Damn!" she said and rinsed the Colgate from her mouth.

Clifford was in his office, finishing up with a client, when he was interrupted by his secretary. "Excuse me, Mr. Nelson, but you have a call on line one."

"Thank you, Marcette. Put it through." He then thanked his client and quickly walked him to the door of his office. He came back to his desk and answered his call. "Clifford Nelson. How may I help you?"

"Hi, baby. You busy?"

He smiled and said, "I'm never too busy for you, 'Neema. You know that."

"I didn't want anything. I just wanted to tell you that I had my first case of morning sickness this morning, before I left the house."

"Are you all right? Do you want to go see the doctor?"

"No, and calm down before you have a heart attack. It was nothing really. I'm fine. As a matter of fact, I'm on my way to school now."

"Are you sure, 'Neema? Something might be wrong with the baby!"

"Don't worry, Cliff. If I thought it was something that serious, I would be calling you from the doctor's office now, instead of from my car on my way to class. I should be done by lunchtime. Do you want to meet somewhere, or are you tied up today?"

"Sorry, baby, but I have to be in court at one, and I have a lot of paperwork here that needs to be taken care of. I don't think I'll be eating any lunch at all today. Let's go somewhere and have dinner later, okay?"

"That's fine. All right, I'll talk to you later. Bye."

"Bye, baby," he said and hung up the phone with a smile on his face.

By the end of her workday, Sacha was exhausted. For some reason she felt as if she was completely drained. That puzzled her, because she didn't do anything differently than she normally did.

When she made it back to Taz's house, she went and changed into her swimsuit, went downstairs, and got into the shallow end of the swimming pool. As she sat in the water, she smiled as she watched Heaven and Precious as they slowly walked around the pool, staring at her. *It feels so good to be protected and loved,* she thought as she watched the Dobermans as they continued to watch over her.

Just as she started to swim around in the pool a little, she had a queasy feeling in her stomach. She stopped, stood up in the pool, and grabbed her stomach. After her queasiness had subsided, she stepped out of the pool and went back upstairs to the bedroom. She went into the bathroom and splashed some water onto her face. Something was wrong, and she didn't know what it was.

She went back into the bedroom and climbed onto the bed. While she was resting, a thought came into her head and she smiled. "No, it can't be!" she yelled excitedly as she jumped out of the bed quickly and threw on a pair of shorts and a shirt. She grabbed her car keys and quickly left the house, feeling extremely excited.

Won woke Taz up early and said, "It's on for in the morning, Babyboy. After we finish talking, I want you to go downstairs and grab that bag that's in the backseat of the truck. You are to use them for this mission, because there's going to be a few people there, and they may be strapped."

"What are you talking 'bout, O.G.?" asked Taz sleepily.

"Vests. Y'all need to wear them for this mission."

"*What?* We ain't never needed no vests before. What's up with that, Won?"

"Safety measures, Babyboy. That's all. This is going to be an easy op, but then again, it's a dangerous one simply because there will be guards on point. But they'll be in front, and y'all are coming in from the back and the element of surprise is on your side. I would prefer for you to wear them just in case something goes down. At least this way y'all will have more protection."

"All right, I ain't trippin' or nothin'. That just threw me for a loop."

"I understand. Now listen. You are going to this clothing store called BB's. It's located in the Fulton Street strip mall. You

are to take Forty-second Street to the FDR, and take the FDR to
the Brooklyn Bridge and exit in downtown Brooklyn on Fulton
Street. Once you get on Fulton Street, drive around back behind
the strip mall and park in back of the store. You will know it
when you see it, because there will be a sign on the back door.
Y'all are then to proceed into the back and empty both safes.
The combinations are twenty-nine to the right, forty-one to
the left, and sixty-seven to the right. Both of the safes have the
same combo, so that should save time for y'all. One of them is
full of drugs, and the other is full of money.

"While you are emptying the safes, three of you should be on
point by the door that leads into the front of the store. Like I told
you, there will be armed guards in front. As long as you use your
stealth abilities, you should be in and out without a problem. But
if it has to go down, then you know how to handle your business.

"Now, what I'm about to suggest is optional. Y'all can do it
the way I just suggested, or you can go in and rush the front
and secure everyone, and then handle your business. The
choice is yours, Babyboy.

"Once y'all are out of there, proceed straight back to your
hotel and leave everything inside of the room. Y'all's flights
are already reserved for a noon flight out of JFK. When you
make it back to the city, check your accounts and give me
a holla. This one puts y'all well over two hundred million,
Babyboy."

Taz smiled and said, "I'm fuckin' with that!"

"All right then, do you. I'll holla at ya when you make it back
to the city. Out!" Won said and hung up the phone.

After Taz hung up the phone with Won, he woke Keno and
told him that he'd be right back. He then took the elevator
down to the underground parking area and grabbed the bag
out of the truck with the bulletproof vests in it that Won had
told him about. After that, he went back to his room and ran the
mission down to Keno.

"Damn, it's like that, huh? So, how we gone put it down?
Won's way, or secure the spot first?"

"I think we should do it Won's way. What do you think?"

"It really don't matter to me, dog. Let's get at the homies
and see what they think."

"All right, wake them niggas up and let's go get something to eat. We have the rest of the day to come up with how we're going to put it down, anyway,"

"That's cool. I wanted to go to Jay-Z's 40/40 Club, anyway. They say the food's expensive as fuck, but I ain't trippin'. I am a fuckin' millionaire too."

Taz started laughing and said, "I know that's right! And we might bump into B. She might choose a playa like you over the Jiggaman."

With a serious look on his face, Keno said, "Damn, gee! I didn't think about that shit. If Beyoncé is in the spot, she's definitely going to see that a nigga like me has way more flavor than that nigga Jay."

Taz shook his head but said nothing as he continued to unpack the bulletproof vests for their upcoming mission.

Chapter Thirty-three

Sacha's hunch turned out to be correct. She was pregnant. When she left Taz's house, she went to Walgreens and bought a pregnancy test. She then sped right back to the house and took the test. When she saw that the test came back positive, she was elated. "Yes!" she screamed as she ran into the bedroom and grabbed the phone. Her hands trembled as she dialed Taz's cell number. As soon as he answered the phone, she said, "I know you told me not to call you unless it's really important, baby, but I have something that I just have to tell you."

"Is everything all right, Li'l Mama?" asked Taz as he stepped away from the table. Taz and the crew were enjoying an expensive lunch at the 40/40 Club. He didn't want to disturb the others, so he stepped away and went and stood by the bar.

Sacha smiled and said, "Yes, everything is just perfect, baby. I have the most wonderful news for you. I'm pregnant!"

Taz was silent for a moment; then he asked, "Are you sure?"

"Positive. I just finished taking a pregnancy test, and it came out positive. I'm pregnant, Taz! I'm really pregnant!"

Taz smiled and said, "Damn! We're having a baby boy!"

"Whoa! Hold up there, mister! What makes you think it's going to be a boy?"

He smiled and said, "It has to be. It has to be!"

"I'm glad that you're as excited about this as I am. I was kind of worried that you might not want to have any children."

"Baby, I love kids, and I want to have plenty more, if it's all right with you."

"Three will be just fine. I don't think I could do more than that. But who knows? I love you, baby!"

"I love you, too, Li'l Mama! Look, I gots to go, 'cause we have something to take care of. When I get back, we'll sit down and talk about kids more thoroughly, 'cause I have some things that I need to tell you about."

"Like what, Taz?"

"I can't get into that right now. Don't trip. We'll talk when I get back."

"That will be tomorrow, right?"

"Yes, it should be. Now, let me bounce, okay?"

"All right, Taz. I love you!"

"I love you, too, Li'l Mama!" As he went back to the table to join the others, his only thought was, *Damn, we having a baby!*

After Sacha got off the phone with Taz, she called Gwen and said, "Guess what, ho?"

"What, bitch?"

"I'm pregnant!"

"Ooh, bitch, stop lying!"

"I just found out, ho."

"Are you keeping it?"

"Hell yes! Why wouldn't I?"

"Have you told Taz?"

"I just got off the phone with him, and he's just as excited as I am about the baby."

"I'm so happy for you, bitch! Congratulations!" Gwen said sincerely.

"I wish you could come over and have a drink with me, but I guess I can't be doing any more drinking for a while."

"You might not can drink, but that doesn't stop me from drinking! I'm on my way, ho. Get the XO out! I'll celebrate for the both of us!" Gwen yelled as she hung up the phone.

Sacha started laughing as she went downstairs and grabbed another bottle of Taz's expensive liquor.

By the time the crew had made it back to their rooms, they all decided to take it in early. Taz had explained to them the details for their next mission, and they were ready. More than ready, really. They just wanted to hurry up and finish the job so they could get back home. They agreed to do the job the way Won had suggested, but if anything got crazy, they were prepared for whatever.

"All right then, my niggas, go get some rest. We're out at five in the morning," Taz said before he got into his bed.

Keno walked the rest of the crew to the door with his cell phone in his hand and closed it behind them. He smiled at Taz as he dialed a number on his phone. "What's up, boo? What'cha doin'?" he asked when Katrina answered her phone.

Taz shook his head from side to side as he started to doze off to sleep.

The next morning, Taz got up at twenty minutes to four a.m. He took a shower and got himself prepared mentally for what had to be done. After he finished getting dressed, Keno went and took himself a shower. By the time he was finished, the rest of the crew had come into the room. Keno threw on his clothes, strapped on his bulletproof vest, and said, "I'm ready."

"Let's go to work," Taz said as he led the crew out of the hotel room.

They got into their SUV, and Taz drove them down Forty-second Street. He followed Won's precise instructions, and twenty-five minutes after they had departed from the hotel room, he had them parked behind BB's clothing store in the Fulton strip mall.

Taz took a deep breath and said, "This is it, my niggas. Keep your eyes open and stay alert for any surprises. We should be in and out of this bitch in less than ten, but if there are any surprises, don't hesitate to do you. Our lives depend on how we watch each other's backs. Y'all ready or what?"

"You know I'm ready, my nigga," said Keno.

"I'm here," said Red.

"Let's get this fucking money!" yelled Wild Bill.

"It is what it is, my nigga," said Bo-Pete.

And finally, Bob said, "I was born for this shit, dog."

Taz gave a slight nod of his head and said, "Let's go!"

They all jumped out of the SUV and went to the back of the store.

Just as Won had told them, the door was unlocked. Taz turned the doorknob and opened the door slowly. Once the door was open, he led the way inside. He went straight to the safes, followed by Keno and Wild Bill. Red, Bo-Pete, and Bob stood by the door, watching the front entrance into the store from the back room.

Just as Taz opened the first safe, Red yelled, "Bob, watch yourself!"

A tall, dark-skinned man came walking through the door that led from the front of the store. When he heard Red yell at Bob, he quickly pulled out a gun and started shooting.

Bob's reaction was a tad slow as he shot his silenced weapon twice. He hit his target twice in his chest, but during the process, he got shot in his stomach. He fell to the ground and moaned as he tried to remain focused on the door that the armed man had come through.

Red ran to Bob's side and said, "Hold on, my nigga! Hold on!"

Keno had his safe open and was busy cleaning it out as Bo-Pete and Red pulled Bob to the back door. Just as they had him close to the door, three more men came running into the back room, firing semiautomatic weapons at the crew.

Wild Bill turned just in time and started spitting fire with his silenced weapon. He caught one of the men with a bullet to his face, while Red and Bo-Pete finished the other two.

Taz and Keno never stopped filling up their duffel bags. Once they were finished, Taz said, "Red, Keno, get Bob to the truck. Bo-Pete, Wild Bill, come with me." His face was grim as he led them toward the front of the store. He opened the door cautiously and saw a woman on the phone, screaming to someone on the other end. "Someone's in the back with the shit! They're shooting the fucking place up! Get someone here quick!" she shouted.

Those were her last words, because Taz shot her from fifteen feet right between her eyes. He turned back and said, "Let's get the fuck outta here!" They then ran back the way they had come and climbed into the SUV. As soon as they were from behind the strip mall, Taz noticed several different types of cars speeding to the front of the store. Keno was in the backseat trying to calm Bob down, while Taz drove.

Taz pulled out his cell and quickly dialed Won's number. It took several rings before he answered. "Dog, the shit went haywire! Bob is hit!" Taz yelled frantically.

"Calm down, Babyboy! Calm down!" Won said calmly.

Too fucking calm for Taz's taste, he said, "What the fuck you mean, calm down? My mans is hit!"

"Where are you now?"

"I'm back on the Brooklyn Bridge! We gots to take Bob to a hospital, O.G.! He's bleeding like a muthafucka!"

"No! That's the last thing you want to do. Just stay on the same route that you came on. Someone will be calling you in less than five minutes."

"What the fuck are you talkin' 'bout? I gots to get Bob to a fuckin' hospital!"

"Don't panic on me now, Taz. Just trust me," Won said, and he hung up the phone.

Taz dropped the phone on his lap and yelled, "Hold on, my nigga! You're going to be all right!"

"All right, dog . . . all right, dog," Bob said weakly from the back of the truck.

"Damn, dog! Where the fuck is your vest?" asked Keno as he held Bob in his lap.

Bob winced from the pain in his stomach and said, "I . . . I forgot to put it on, my nigga."

Keno stared at Bo-Pete, and Red shook his head in disgust but said nothing.

Taz's cell started ringing and he quickly answered it. "Yeah?"

"Check this out, God. This is Magoo from the Bronx. Are you on the FDR yet?"

"Yeah."

"All right, son, stay on the FDR until you get uptown. Then, cross over to the Major Deegan and get off at 149th Street. You'll see some projects—the Patterson Projects. I'll be parked out front. Don't worry about your mans. By the time you touch down, a doctor will be on deck for you, son."

"Cool. How long will it take for me to get to you?"

"If you're already on the FDR, it should be no more than ten to twelve minutes."

"All right, I'll see you in a minute. Thanks."

"Don't thank me. You know who to thank. One!" Magoo said and hung up.

Taz turned around and yelled, "Hang on, my nigga! We're taking you to get some help now! You're goin' to be all right!"

Bob's eyes were closed, but he heard everything that Taz had said, because he shook his head slightly.

"Come on, Bob, baby! Open your eyes for me, gee! You can't close your eyes, dog!" Keno screamed.

Bob opened his eyes and weakly said, "I'm tired, my nigga. I'm real tired."

Shaking his head no, Keno screamed, "Think about Gwen, nigga! Keep your eyes open for her, dog!"

Bob smiled slightly, opened his eyes, and said, "I hear you, gee. I hear you."

Taz got off of the FDR on 149th Street and pulled in front of the Patterson Projects just like the guy Magoo had told him to. Magoo was standing in front of his red Cadillac Escalade as they pulled behind it. After Taz had parked the SUV, he jumped out of the truck and stepped up to Magoo and asked, "You Magoo?"

"Yeah, son."

"All right then, what now?"

Magoo turned his head and gave a slight nod. Three young Puerto Ricans with red bandannas on their heads came from behind a parked car and went straight toward the crew's SUV. "Don't trip, my nigga. I gots your man, Blood. He's in the good hands of some of the Bronx's best Damus. Y'all gots to get outta here now though, Blood. Won told me to tell you to stick to the script."

Shaking his head no, Taz said, "Nah, we can't leave my nigga."

"Everything is all good. My niggas are taking him upstairs to one of our joints. A doctor is up there, and he'll make sure that your man is good. We got the painkillers and everything, son, so don't worry. We gots him," Magoo said confidently as he turned and followed his three young homies who carried Bob into the building.

Taz stepped back to the SUV and told the rest of the crew, "Won wants us to keep rollin', but I'm not sure if we should leave the homey. Magoo said he got Bob, and everything is goin' to be good. But we don't know this nigga, dog."

"If Won says we should keep with the program, I think we should go on and bounce. I don't think he'd say that unless he trusted this fool," Keno said wisely. "Come on, gee. We gots to keep some trust in Won."

"What if he's wrong, dog? What if something happens to Bob and we never see our nigga again?"

"Then we come back out here to the Bronx and look at every nigga in these fuckin' projects! And then we look at Won's ass too!" Red said angrily.

Taz sighed and said, "All right, let's bounce."

They climbed back inside of the SUV and went back to their hotel. After dropping everything off inside of Taz and Keno's room, the crew got back into the SUV and drove straight to JFK to wait for their flight back to Oklahoma City. They came into the Big Apple six deep but left one crew member short. *Damn!*

Chapter Thirty-four

Sacha and Gwen were still at Taz's house. Gwen had gotten so drunk the night before that she decided to stay over with Sacha. They stayed up late into the night, talking about their futures with their men. Sacha was so excited about her pregnancy that all she could think about was what room they were going to change into the baby's room in Taz's home. They laughed and joked until they both fell asleep.

The next morning, when Sacha woke up, she called in and told her secretary that she wasn't coming into the office, and to make sure that she rescheduled anything that she had on her calendar. After that was taken care of, she then took a shower and went downstairs to make some breakfast for her and Gwen. While she was making breakfast, Taz called. "Hi, baby. Is everything all right?" she asked him as she scrambled some eggs.

"Nah, Li'l Mama, shit is kinda fucked up. But we're good. I should be home in a few hours, though. You straight?"

"Yes, I'm fine. What's wrong, Taz? You don't sound too good. Are you feeling okay?"

"Yeah, I'm straight. We'll talk more when I get there. I just wanted to let you know that everything is everything. I gots to go now, okay?"

"Okay, baby. I love you."

"Love you too," he said and boarded the flight back home.

After Sacha hung up the phone with Taz, she finished cooking breakfast and took the food upstairs to where Gwen was still asleep. As she climbed the stairs, she wondered what was going on with Taz. She hoped and prayed that everything was okay. She couldn't take it if things weren't as perfect as they had been. She just couldn't take it!

***

Since they were all flying back the way they originally flew out, Red was the only one who flew alone. It felt strange to him as he sat in his seat without his partner, Bob, with him. *Please let him make it, God. Please!* Red prayed as he tried to close his eyes and get some rest on his long flight into Dallas/ Fort Worth.

Keno and Taz got comfortable as their flight to Tulsa International prepared to depart from JFK. They had watched as Red boarded his flight, and Bo-Pete and Wild Bill as they got onto the plane that would be taking them back to the City. Now that they were on their way back, Taz was thinking about everything that had gone down earlier that morning. "That shit was whack from the gate, dog."

"I know. But we had to do what we had to do," replied Keno.

"What the fuck was Bob thinking about by not protecting himself properly?"

"Ain't no tellin', gee. Look, don't stress yourself. He's going to be all right, my nigga."

"And how in the fuck do you know that?"

"I can feel it, homey. I can feel it in my bones. So relax."

Shaking his head no, Taz said, "Nah, gee, fuck that!"

As soon as their flight was airborne, Taz picked up the Skyphone from the seat in front of him and swiped his credit card. Once he received a dial tone, he called Won's cell. When Won answered the phone, Taz said, "What's what with Bob, O.G.?"

"Where are you, Babyboy?"

"We're on our way back to the house. We're in the air right now."

"Good. Listen, I don't really want to talk too long on this type of line. Give me a call as soon as you get back and we'll talk some more."

"All right. So, what's up with the homey?"

"He's all right. He had to have surgery, and it looks like he'll be wearing a shit bag for a few months. Other than that, everything is good. He should be able to be moved within a few days. I'm arranging for transport for him now. I should have something definite for you by the time you get back to the house."

"All right then. That's all I needed to know for now. I'll holla." Taz hung up the phone and returned it to the back of the seat in front of him. He turned and told Keno, "It looks like you were right, my nigga. Bob's straight. He had surgery and he's going to have to have a shit bag for a few months, but other than that, he's going to be good."

Keno smiled and said, "I knew it! I knew it, dog! Now that's what I'm talkin' 'bout!"

Taz smiled and said, "Yeah, I know." As he sat back in his seat, he gave a heavy sigh of relief and thanked God. His prayers had been answered.

It was a little after seven p.m. when the rest of the crew made it to Taz's house.

Sacha was full of smiles when she saw Taz and Keno walk in the front door. Taz gave her a hug and a kiss and said, "We have some loose ends to take care of, so you're going to have to excuses me for a li'l bit, Li'l Mama."

She smiled and said, "I understand. Gwen is still upstairs, so I'll go up and kick it with her until you're finished."

"Gwen? Why is she still here?"

"She got too drunk last night, so she spent the night with me, and this morning she was still out of it, so she's been sleeping it off."

"All right. But check this out. As soon as she wakes up, bring her down to the den. I need to talk to her about somethin'."

Sacha stared into Taz's brown eyes, and she knew instantly that something was wrong. Her heart skipped a beat as she asked, "Is everything all right with Bob, baby? Please, tell me everything is all right with Bob."

Taz shook his head and said, "He's fine, Li'l Mama, but he was shot in the stomach early this morning."

Before Taz could finish giving Sacha the details, Gwen, who was standing at the top of the stairs and had heard what Taz had just said, screamed the loudest scream that Taz had ever heard in his entire life. "No-o-o-o-o!" She fainted right where she stood.

Taz, Sacha, and Keno ran to the stairs and grabbed her before she had a chance to tumble down the steps. Taz carried her back upstairs into his bedroom, while Sacha went into the bathroom and ran some cool water onto a face towel. She then came into the bedroom and placed the cool towel across Gwen's face. While she was doing this, she explained some of Gwen's past to Taz and Keno.

"Damn, that's cold!" Taz said as he thought about his past and how much he and Gwen had in common. "Look, when she gets up, explain to her that Bob's going to make it, and I'll try and get a way for them to speak to each other before the night's up. Right now, I need to go downstairs and finish up things."

"Okay, baby. I got this. Go on and handle your business."

Taz and Keno went downstairs to the den and made the call to Won. Bo-Pete, Wild Bill, and Red came inside and sat down as they waited for Won's return call. Taz's cell rang a few minutes later, and he answered by pressing the speakerphone button. "What's up, O.G.?"

"I just got off the phone with Magoo. He has Bob secure at one of his spots. Here's the number, 'cause I know y'all want to holla at your boy: 212-252-9869. You might want to wait until the morning to give him a holla. He was sleeping soundly when I was speaking with Magoo."

"That's good lookin', O.G. You don't know how good that sounds to our ears."

"Tell me something. Why didn't Bob have his vest on?"

"I wish I could answer that one, O.G. I slipped on that one, because I should have made sure that everyone was ready. I take full responsibility for that shit," Taz said seriously.

"Nah, fuck that shit! It's my fault. I'm his partner, and I should have made sure that my nigga was ready," Red said angrily.

"It's no one's fault but Bob's, really, but I understand where y'all are coming from. Have you checked your accounts yet?" asked Won.

"Yeah, I did before I called you. Everything is everything."

"Good. It looks as if everything will be put on hold until Bob gets back on his feet, so I'll set things back for a minute."

"Nah, O.G., we're done. This shit is starting to get too crazy. We're out. Might as well while we're on top of the game," Taz said sincerely.

"Out? Babyboy, we're at the final stages of everything I've been working toward for the last five years. This shit ain't over yet. I understand that y'all are hurt by what went down with Bob, but it ain't over with yet."

"It is for us, O.G. We're done."

Won started laughing and said, "I'm going to let you go for now, Babyboy. But keep this in your head at all times. As a matter of fact, I want all of you to keep this in your heads. Don't ever think you're running shit in this, 'cause you ain't. I'm the head nigga. Always have been, and I always will be. So this shit ain't over until I say it's over. Relax and chill, and do whatever it is y'all be doing during our downtime. But as soon as Bob is ready to go again, we'll finish what we've started. Out!"

After Won hung up the phone, Taz stared at the rest of the crew and said, "I always hoped that it would never have to come to this, but it looks like we're going to have to go on one last mission, after all."

"I feel you, my nigga. That nigga Won has to be touched," Wild Bill said from the other side of the room.

"Exactly!" replied Bo-Pete.

"Definitely!" said Red.

"He's outta there!" said Keno.

Sacha and Gwen came into the den and joined the crew. After Gwen was seated, Taz explained that Bob had been shot, and that he had a number for her to call once Bob was able to get some more rest.

"Thank you, Taz! Thank you so much! But can you please tell me exactly what the fuck is going on with y'all? I have the right to know, don't I?"

Taz stared at the rest of the crew, and each one of them gave him a nod yes, so he told her exactly what it was that they did when they went out of town. He also explained in detail what had happened out in New York. "That's everything, Gwen. All of it. We're finished now, though. Our money is straight, and there will be no more missions for us."

"Are you lying to me, Taz?"

Taz shook his head no and said, "Nah, I'm givin' it to you 100. We're out."

Before Gwen or Sacha could say anything else, Taz's cell phone started ringing. When he answered it, Tazneema said, "Taz, I need to speak to you. Please tell me that you're back in town."

"Yeah, I'm at home now. What's up, 'Neema?"

"Could you come out to Mama-Mama's house? I'm over here now, and we have some serious things to talk about."

Taz sighed and said, "Can't this wait until tomorrow, 'Neema? I have a lot of shit on my plate, and I'm tired as hell right now."

"No! I need you, Taz. Can't you see that?" she screamed and dropped the phone.

Mama-Mama picked the receiver up from the floor and said, "Taz Good, you get your ass over to this house right now! Do you hear me?"

"Yeah, Mama-Mama, I hear you," he said and closed his cell. He turned toward everyone and said, "I gots to go out to Mama-Mama's house. Somethin's goin' on with 'Neema."

"Do you want us to roll with you, dog?" asked Bo-Pete.

"Nah, y'all go on and get some rest. I'll get at y'all in the morning. Sacha, do you want to roll with me?"

"Yes. Let me go get my purse."

"What about you, Gwen? You straight?"

"Yeah, I'll be all right. I'm going home to try and get some more sleep, 'cause that XO of yours ain't no punk." They all started laughing. Then she said, "Seriously, I'm fine. I want to be well rested when I speak with Bob in the morning."

"All right then, I guess I'll get at y'all later, then," Taz said and left the den.

After everyone had gone, Taz and Sacha climbed into his truck, and Taz sped out of his driveway. "Is everything all right with Tazneema, baby?" Sacha asked.

"She seems real upset, so I guess not, Li'l Mama," Taz said as he turned onto Sixty-third Street.

They made the twenty-five-minute drive out to Mama-Mama's home in less than fifteen minutes. As soon as the truck stopped in Mama-Mama's driveway, Taz hopped out of it and marched directly inside of the house. Sacha followed him, praying that this wouldn't get ugly. When Taz opened the door, he saw Tazneema sitting on the couch, being consoled by Mama-Mama. He took a deep breath and asked, "What's wrong, 'Neema? Why are you crying?"

Tazneema raised her head off of Mama-Mama's lap, smiled sadly, and said, "I'm pregnant, Taz."

Taz was so stunned by her news that he was speechless. He just stood there staring at her as her words kept repeating themselves over and over inside of his head.

Sacha had come inside of the house just as Tazneema told Taz that she was pregnant. She knew then that this was definitely going to be an ugly scene. She grabbed Taz's right hand and said, "Calm down, baby. Please don't get too crazy right now. More than anything, Tazneema needs your support, not your anger."

Taz shook his head, took a deep breath, and asked, "By who?"

A defiant look came into Tazneema's eyes as she said, "His name is Clifford, and he's a very nice, respectable man, Taz. Ask Mama-Mama."

Taz glared at Mama-Mama and asked, "So, you've met him?"

"Yes, I met him a while back."

"And you didn't tell me about this, Mama-Mama?"

"It wasn't much to tell. 'Neema brought him over to meet me, and I cooked them both a meal."

"But why didn't you tell me about this?"

"Don't you raise your voice at me in my own house, Taz! It wasn't my place to tell you. I told 'Neema that she had to tell you. She called you and asked you to come over, but you had to go out of town. So don't you be blamin' me about this mess, boy!"

Turning his attention back toward Tazneema, he said, "You're too young to be havin' any kids, 'Neema."

"I'm eighteen years old, Taz! I'll be nineteen later this year! I'm grown, and you can't make this decision for me!"

Taz shook his head and said, "The decision's been made, and you are goin' to have an abortion."

"Taz, you should—"

"Hold what you got, Li'l Mama!" he said angrily. "Let me deal with this in my way. Please, don't get in my way right now."

"Taz, if 'Neema wants to have this child, you have no right not to let her," Mama-Mama said as she got up from the couch.

Taz's head was spinning so badly that he felt a little dizzy as he went and sat down next to Tazneema. After getting his bearings together, he said, "Okay, you're right. Where is this clown at? I want to meet him."

"He's not a clown, Taz! He's my man!" Tazneema screamed.

"Your what? Raise your voice to me again like that, 'Neema, and I swear I'll—"

"Taz! Don't you dare threaten that there girl!" screamed Mama-Mama.

"I think everyone needs to take a deep breath and calm down. There will be no way to resolve this intelligently with this much anger in the air," Sacha said wisely.

"All right. Now, where is this Clifford at? I want to talk to him. Do I have that right, Mama-Mama?"

"Watch yourself, boy! You're not that grown! I'll still pop you upside your head!"

Taz smiled at that and said, "I'm sorry, Mama-Mama. You know I'll never disrespect you. But this has to be dealt with accordingly."

"He's on his way over now. He should be here any minute," Tazneema said as she wiped her nose on the sleeve of her blouse.

"How long have you been messing with this guy, 'Neema?" asked Taz.

"Ever since that night you shot that guy at the club."

"Shot? Club? Boy, I thought your crazy days were behind you! What the hell have you been gettin' into out there?" screamed Mama-Mama.

"It was self-defense, Mama-Mama. A dude at the club tried to rob me and Sacha, so I shot him."

"Lord! Taz, you know this stuff is going to have to stop one day. You can't keep on living this crazy life you've been living. It's bad enough this girl's moth—"

"I know, Mama-Mama . . . I know," Taz said, cutting Mama-Mama off.

Before anyone could say another word, Sacha heard a car pull into the driveway. "I guess that's your boyfriend now," she said, and she stepped to the door so she could get the first look at Tazneema's boyfriend. She gasped and felt as if she had been hit in the stomach by a two-by-four when she saw Clifford getting out of his Mercedes-Benz. She shook her head a few times to make sure she wasn't seeing an illusion. When she focused on Clifford as he walked up to the front door, she said, "Oh my God!"

Taz got up from his seat and asked, "What's wrong, Li'l Mama?"

Sacha was speechless. All she could do was point toward the door.

When Clifford walked through the front door, Taz's eyes grew as wide as saucers as he yelled, "Oh, hell nah! I know God damn well this ain't the nigga that has gotten you pregnant, 'Neema! Please, baby girl! Tell me this ain't the nigga!"

With a confused expression on her face, Tazneema got up from the couch and said, "Yes, that's Cliff, and he's my man, Taz."

Before Taz could speak, Clifford said, "Look, Taz. I know this looks kind of crazy, but ever since I meet 'Neema, I've been in love with her."

"Nigga, if you don't shut the fuck up, I swear to God, I'll blast you right here in my mother's fuckin' living room! You know damn well you don't love her! You're just trying to do this shit to get back at me for taking Sacha away from your sorry-ass!"

"*What?* What are you talking about, Taz?" asked Tazneema.

"Baby girl, this clown-ass nigga you've been callin' your man don't fuckin' love you! He used to be all caught up with Sacha until she dumped his ass for me! Can't you see? This nigga is just trying to get back at me! Just like I've always told you, you have to stay out of the way, 'cause niggas out there would one day try to use you as a tool against me. And that's exactly what this nigga is doing. He don't love you, 'Neema! He's been using you!"

"That's not true! We've been living together for the last two weeks. I know this man. I share a home with him. He does love me, Daddy! He does!" screamed Tazneema.

"*Daddy?*" Clifford and Sacha yelled out at the same time.

Taz smiled and said, "Yeah, nigga! Daddy! 'Neema's my daughter, you punk muthafucka! My fuckin' seed, fool! So, do you really think I'm goin' to let you get away with this shit? Huh? Do you?" yelled Taz.

Clifford said, "Listen, Taz. It doesn't matter that she's your child. What does matter is that we both love her and want nothing but the very best for her. And I'm willing to do whatever it takes to prove that to you. I know you don't like me, and I know you think it's some type of conspiracy going on here, but you are wrong. I love Tazneema, and I'd die for her!"

Taz grinned and said, "Nigga, you don't know how true those words you just spoke are!"

"Taz! Watch yourself, boy!" Mama-Mama threatened.

Shaking his head no, Taz said, "Nah, Mama-Mama. This is my baby, and you know that ever since MiMi was killed, I swore that nothing and no one would ever hurt my baby. This nigga has got to go, one way or the other!"

Clifford knew that this could possibly turn into something ugly, and that's why he came prepared. He stepped back toward the door, pulled out a chrome .380 pistol, and said, "Look, Taz. I don't want any problems with you, but there is no punk in me. I'm not letting you take the woman I love away from me."

Taz stared at the small-caliber gun in Clifford's hand, smiled, and said, "So, you ready to play gangsta, nigga? You gots me twisted if you think you will ever have a child by my seed, fool. So, if you gone bust your gun, you needs to get to bustin', 'cause as far as I'm concerned, you are already a dead man!"

"If I lose 'Neema and my child, I might as well be dead, because she's all that I have," Clifford said as he raised his pistol and aimed it directly at Taz's face.

Taz smiled as he glared at Clifford and said, "Go on, coward-ass nigga! Do it! *Do it!*"

Clifford was so scared that he was literally shaking.

Mama-Mama was so shocked at what was happening that she felt as if she was going to faint.

Sacha, on the other hand, was neither scared nor shocked. She was flat-out angry. "Damnit, Cliff! This isn't the way to go about handling this! Put that fucking gun down!"

"No! He took you, and I accepted that. But he's not taking my 'Neema away from me! I'll kill his ass before I let him do that to me!"

With her hands in the air, pleading, Tazneema begged, "Please, baby! Don't hurt my daddy! If you kill him, it won't do anything but hurt us both. I'll lose my father, and I'll lose you, too, 'cause you're going to go to jail. Put the gun down, baby. Please!"

Shaking his head no, Clifford said, "I love you, 'Neema. You have to believe me. But your father will never let us live our lives. Look at him. Look at how he's staring at me now. Can't you see the hatred, baby? Can't you see it?"

"That's right, nigga. Pump yourself up to do it. Don't let no female stop you, you coward. You're right. I'm never going to let you take my seed away from me. Do you hear me, coward? Never!"

Tazneema screamed, "No-o-o-o-o!" and pushed her father out of the way just as Clifford pulled the trigger on his weapon. The small pop hit Tazneema in her upper torso, and she fell to the ground.

Taz got off of the floor and stared in disbelief at his daughter lying there unconscious. He stepped to her and cradled her in his arms as tears streamed down his face.

Mama-Mama fainted, and Sacha ran to her to see if she was all right.

Clifford stood in the doorway, speechless. "Lord, God, what have I done?" he said to himself as he turned and ran out of the house.

Sacha screamed for Taz to call an ambulance, but he couldn't hear her. He was in too much pain.

Author's Note

This is my first attempt at writing a two-part book. I hope that the readers are feeling this story so far. I guarantee that you won't be disappointed in *Gangsta Twist 2*. I will answer all of the unanswered questions, such as: What is Won really up to, and why? And what happened to Tazneema's mother, and why? This will also give the readers a better understanding as to why Taz does the things that he does where Tazneema is concerned.

The twists have just begun, so hold on for a few until I can get back to the lab and bring it all together for you all.

I want to thank every homie who has let me use their name for creative purposes. I hope I haven't upset anyone too badly by how I displayed their character. Remember, gee, it's just fiction. All make-believe! (Smile!)

So, once again, please stay tuned for the next installment of *Gangsta Twist*.

ONE LOVE,

SPUD

Gangsta Twist 2

Chapter One

Taz, Sacha, and Mama-Mama were sitting in the waiting area of the emergency room at Mercy Hospital. Taz sat dazed as he stared at the wall without saying a word to anyone. Sacha sat next to him, trying her best to console and comfort her man, while Mama-Mama, Taz's mother, was on the other side of the room silently praying.

Taz couldn't believe that fool, Cliff, had actually shot his child. His daughter Tazneema was currently in surgery fighting for her life all because of his arrogance. *If I hadn't chosen to goad Clifford on, my child wouldn't be inside of that damn operating room,* Taz thought as he continued to stare at the wall.

"Please say something, baby. You're really scaring me," Sacha told Taz as she gently rubbed his back.

Taz turned toward his fiancée, smiled sadly and said, "I'm here, Li'l Mama, but I'm damn sure not all right. This shit is killin' me."

"I know, baby . . . I know. But Tazneema is going to be okay. You have to keep the faith, baby."

"Faith? *Faith?* Faith is for Mama-Mama, Li'l Mama, not me. All my life I've vowed to protect that girl. When I lost her mother because of my cocky-ass attitude, I swore to never let anything ever happen to my baby girl. And years later, look what the fuck I've done. Once again, my cockiness has gotten another loved one hurt. I'm tellin' you, Li'l Mama, I'm a cursed man. You really might want to take some time and think again about marrying a nigga like me!" he said angrily.

"That's nonsense, boy, and you damn well know it!" screamed Mama-Mama from across the room. "God has a plan for us all. It is not your fault what happened today. It's that damned Cliff's!

So don't you dare beat yourself up behind this, Taz. And sure as I know God is good, He's not going to take my grandbaby away from me."

When Taz saw tears streaming down his mother's face, he quickly got to his feet and went and held her in his arms. As they were hugging, he said, "I can't lose her, Mama-Mama! She's all of MiMi I got left. I can't lose my baby girl!" he cried.

"She's gon' be all right, baby. She's gon' be all right," Mama-Mama said as she held on tightly to her only child.

After Taz seemed to have regained some of his composure, he sat back down in his seat and resumed staring at the wall.

Sacha, still confused about everything, had a lot of questions running through her mind. *This may not be the right time, but I need some answers,* she thought to herself. Then to Taz she said, "Do you feel like talking, baby? It might help a little."

"Talk about what, Li'l Mama? How I'm gon' murder Cliff? Do you really want to talk about somethin' like that? 'Cause that's the only thing that's on my mind right now, other than my baby girl."

She knew not to even go there with him, so she said, "You're right. I don't want to talk about any of that nonsense. Why don't you tell me about MiMi?"

Taz stared at Sacha's beautiful face for a moment, and once again gave her that sad smile and said, "All right, Li'l Mama. I should have told you this story a long time ago, but for some reason I chose to keep it to myself. If you're goin' to be caught up in my cursed life, you might as well know the entire story." He shook his head from side to side as he began:

"What seems like a million years ago, I was a wild youngsta with a two-year-old daughter. MiMi was my everything. We'd been in love with each other ever since we were in junior high school. I guess the first sign of my curse was when I messed that girl's life up."

"Would you please stop with that 'cursed' stuff? You are not a cursed man, Taz. God!" Sacha said sternly.

"Whatever! Anyway, I got her pregnant when we were in the tenth grade, and she had to miss the rest of our tenth grade year as well as our eleventh because of the baby. She had plans on becoming a doctor. She actually wanted to be a brain surgeon. I used to laugh at her, but I could tell by the determined look in those beautiful brown eyes that she was going to accomplish every single goal that she had set for herself. And I fucked it all up. Once Tazneema was born, her family flipped out on her and refused to give us any help. They actually put her out! Can you believe that shit? I was so mad that for a minute I thought about doin' somethin' to them. But, as usual, Mama-Mama came to my rescue and let MiMi move in with us." Taz smiled at that memory and continued.

"Since Mama-Mama had spoiled me so much, I had no choice but to drop out of school so I could get my hustle on. I couldn't let my mother be the breadwinner for me and my family. I would have felt less of a man. Even though I was just a seventeen-year-old, I had to step up to the plate. So, like everybody else in the city was doin' in the late eighties, I started slangin' rocks. But somethin' about being a dope boy just wasn't cool with me. I was small time, and I didn't like the fact that I was destroying my people. So I quit the dope game after a few months and got some of my closest friends together and formed the crew."

Sacha smiled and said, "The crew, as in Keno, Bob, Bo-Pete, Red, and Wild Bill?"

"Yeah. My plan was simple. Since a bunch of dudes from Texas and Cali were coming to the city, gettin' rich off of the dope game, I came up with the smart-ass idea that we should just sit back and let those niggas make the money. Then we would come in and jack them for their easily earned dividends. With the li'l money I had from the game, I bought us some guns, and we quickly put my plan into effect. We was jackin' every nigga we even thought had some money. We were young, and murder was something that I never even gave a thought about. Can you believe that shit? Here I was, robbing niggas for a living and I wasn't even thinkin' about takin' a nigga's life. Young, dumb and arrogant as hell. Yep, that was me.

"Anyway, after a year of this, we had came up pretty damn good. We all had cars, and we even had our own apartments. I saved a nice chunk of change so MiMi could enroll in college. I was determined to help her become a brain surgeon. As far as I was concerned, she wasn't goin' to fail because of me. She was proud of me, yet she hated what I was doin' in them streets. She understood though, because hell, I didn't know much of anything else. All I had was my high school diploma, and that wasn't shit. See, after I dropped out of school, MiMi made me promise her that I would go back so I could get my diploma. I kept my word and went back to school, but I was still robbing any and everybody with chips.

"Everything was goin' just fine, until the day my stupidity finally caught up with me. Some Crips from California set up shop on the East Side, and as usual, they were slippin'. You see, niggas come out here from out of town and think since we're from Oklahoma we're some straight country suckas. And to tell you the truth, most of them dope boys in the city are exactly that . . . suckas. All they want to do is get plugged in with Cali niggas and try their best to be just like them. That's how we got all of this damn gang-bangin' in the city now. Anyway, once we found out where them Crips niggas was gettin' money at, we quickly came up with a plan to get at them fools. The lick went just as smoothly as the rest of them had. But, you see, I was so cocky that I never anticipated any retaliation from any of our victims. That's why we never wore any ski masks over our faces. After all, most of the niggas we were jackin' weren't from here anyway.

"A couple of weeks after that particular jack, the word around town was that those Cali niggas were lookin' for me and my crew. I was confident that no one knew where any of us lived, so we decided to lay low for a minute until those clowns got tired. That was my second mistake. It took them a Li'l over a month, but somehow they finally found out where my apartment was. I was at the store gettin' some fish and shrimp for MiMi, because she loved her some seafood," he remembered fondly. "By the time I came back to the apartment building, I heard my daughter crying. I ran up the stairs as fast as I could because I knew that something was wrong. When I made it to my apartment, I saw that the door had been kicked in. I dropped the bags I was holding and ran inside of the apartment with no gun or nothin'. All I was thinkin' about was MiMi and my baby girl.

"The first thing I noticed when I entered the apartment was Tazneema crying. For some reason, that's what I remember most about that day; the way my baby girl was crying. When I saw MiMi lying on the floor with three bulletholes in her chest, I screamed as I ran and held her dead body in my arms.

"After a few minutes, a strange calm came over me. I gently laid my MiMi back on the floor, grabbed my daughter out of her bassinet and took her into the bedroom and fed her a bottle so she could calm down. I then grabbed the phone and called Keno, and told him what had happened. After I hung up with him, I called Mama-Mama and told her that she had to hurry up and get over to my apartment before the police did, so she could take 'Neema over to her house.

"By the time Mama-Mama had come and left, the crew had arrived just before the police did. They asked me all types of fuckin' questions. For a minute I thought they thought I did that stupid shit. When the homicide detective told me that I was going to have to go downtown to the police station for more questioning, I lost it. I told them that they could all go to hell 'cause I wasn't goin' any fuckin' where. My girl was dead, and those niggas had to die. You see, I wasn't prepared for murder before, but after they took my MiMi from me, my murder game became the most vicious that Oklahoma City had ever seen. Not only did I get those Cali Crip niggas, but almost every other jack we put down after MiMi's murder resulted with a murder being committed. I didn't give a fuck about anything anymore. All of the money I made I gave to Mama-Mama for 'Neema. I kept what I needed for survival, but I had to make sure that Mama-Mama was straight financially, because I knew I was walking around on borrowed time. My niggas rode with me, and we all made a pact that, no matter what happened, if anything happened to any one of us, the rest of the crew would ride until we were either dead or in jail for the rest of our lives. So murder was my game, and that was the only thing that kept me sane. If I didn't kill someone at least twice a month, I started to feel as if I had somehow betrayed MiMi. That's how twisted my thinking had become. MiMi was my everything, and without her in this world with me I didn't give a damn about anyone other than 'Neema, Mama-Mama, and my niggas."

"What stopped you from that insane mission you were on?"

Taz smiled and simply answered, "Won. He came into my life because a friend of his had heard about this crazy-ass crew in the city, robbin' and killin' everything in their way. This friend then set up a meet for me and Won. That was the day that Won gave me a brand-new way of thinking."

"What did he say at that meeting, baby?"

"He told me that it was time for me to stop killing and to start living for my seed."

"So, Won is the reason that you stopped killing and robbing people?"

Taz thought about Sacha's question for a moment, and then said, "Yes and no. You know what we do, so you know that I've never stopped doin' my thang. But the senseless killings stopped. The only time I've had to take a life since then was to ensure the safety of me and the crew—not counting that time that fool tried to jack me and you at the club. My anger has subsided over the years, Li'l Mama, but believe me, the hatred is still in my heart. I lost the woman of my dreams, and I will never be able to have her back. That pain still lingers deep within me, and I honestly feel that it will never go away completely."

"That's natural, baby. You were deeply in love, and that love got cut short. But, Taz, you have to stop this madness. You can't let what Cliff has done turn you back into that monster you once were. It'll ruin you this time, baby," Sacha wisely said.

Taz shook his head slowly and said, "If God wants that fool to remain breathing, He has to spare my baby's life. 'Cause if 'Neema dies, so will Cliff. That's real talk, Li'l Mama."

Sacha stared deeply into her fiancé's eyes, and knew that he meant every word of what he had just told her. Before she could say anything, the crew finally arrived.

Keno was the first to enter the waiting room. He walked straight up to Taz and asked, "How is she, dog? Why the fuck didn't you call us as soon as you got here? Who did this shit?"

Taz got to his feet and said, "First off, calm down, my nigga. 'Neema's still in surgery. We're waiting for the doctors to finish up with her now. Her nigga Cliff shot her. He was trying to blast me, and 'Neema pushed me out of the way and took the hit for me, dog. Some straight movie shit, for real. I didn't call y'all 'cause I haven't even been thinkin' straight, *gee*. That's my bad."

"Who is this nigga? 'Cause he gots to go!" Bo-Pete said vehemently.

Taz smiled and said, "Remember that nigga that used to try to holla at Sacha? He somehow got 'Neema to fall in love with him. Not only did they become involved with each other, the nigga got my baby girl pregnant!"

"*What?* Come on, *gee*! That's some straight up soap opera shit," Red said as he stepped closer to Taz.

"Yeah, I know, but it is what it is, dog."

"All right, *gee*. Where can we find this clown-ass nigga? You stay down with Mama-Mama and wifey while we go handle this nigga real quick like," Wild Bill said in a deadly tone.

Mama-Mama, who had been silent through all of this, stepped over to them and said, "You will do no such thing, Billy! I want each one of you to sit down and wait this out here with Taz, Sacha, and myself. Do you understand me?"

Keno gave Mama-Mama a hug and said, "Mama-Mama, you know we love you and 'Neema as if we were all family. We can't let this clown get away with this. We gots to go."

Tears fell slowly from Mama-Mama's eyes as she said, "Keno, you boys have been family to me for a very long time. Just because we're not blood-related doesn't mean a thing to me. Out of all of these years, have I ever asked any of you for anything? Have I?

"No, ma'am," Keno answered with his head bowed.

"Well, I'm asking y'all for something now. Will y'all please leave this alone, at least for the time being? My heart wouldn't be able to take it if anything else happened to someone I care for. Please, baby. Y'all sit down and help us through this rough time like families are supposed to. Please!"

Red, Keno, Wild Bill and Bo-Pete each took turns hugging Mama-Mama and reassuring her that they would stay and do as she asked them to. They all sat down and resumed waiting for the doctors to come and tell them whether or not Tazneema was going to live or die.

The room became silent, until Taz's cell started ringing. He pulled his phone off of his belt clip, checked the caller ID and answered it. "What's up, O.G.?"

"What's up, baby boy? Look, I was out of line the last time we spoke. This shit is really getting hectic for me. You have to understand that everything we've been doing is for a very important reason."

"Yeah, I feel you, O.G., but right now I got a lot of shit on my plate. That shit with you is like way on the back burner, for real."

"What's up out that way, Babyboy?" Won asked curiously.

"'Neema got shot."

"*What?* When did this happen? And why in the hell haven't you called me?" Won screamed.

"My mind is on a million and one different things right now, O.G. I can't think straight enough to take a piss, let alone think about callin' you and lettin' you know what's what."

"I understand, Babyboy. Look, I'll be on the next thing smoking. I should be there some time tomorrow. How is she?"

"She's in surgery now. We're all here waiting and praying that everything goes her way."

"How's Mama-Mama?"

"You already know how she gets down, O.G. She's put everything in God's hands."

"Is Tari there?"

"Nah. Shit, I haven't told her either, and she works in this fuckin' place."

"So, y'all are at Mercy?"

"Yeah."

"All right, let me get my flight shit together. We'll talk some more when I get into town."

"All right, O.G."

"Your boy Bob will be flown into town in a couple of days. Magoo has everything set up out east. By the time I get there I'll have all of the details."

"That's cool. At least something is goin' like it's supposed to."

"Hold your head, Babyboy. Everything is going to be all right."

"I hope you're right, O.G. I hope you're right. Out!" Taz said, and closed his phone.

Keno stared at Taz with raised eyebrows and asked, "What's he talkin' 'bout?"

"Bob's straight, and he should be home in a day or so."

"That's cool. That's it?"

"Basically," Taz answered as he reopened his phone and dialed Tari's home number. When he didn't get an answer, he left a message quickly explaining what happened to Tazneema over at Mama-Mama's house earlier. After he was finished, he turned toward Sacha and asked, "Are you straight, Li'l Mama? Why don't you go on back to my spot and get some rest. I'm not tryin' to have you gettin' sick on me or nothin'."

Sacha shook her head no and said, "If you think I'd leave your side right now, you're out of your mind, Mr. Good. I'm going to be standing right next to you when they come out here and tell you that 'Neema is going to be just fine."

Taz smiled that sad smile and said, "Okay." He sat back down and started thinking again about how he was going to kill that nigga, Cliff.

"Taz, tell me some more about what happened to you and the crew after you hooked up with Won."

"You really want to know it all, huh?"

"Yep."

"All right. After meeting Won, he took me out to L.A., where he gave me what he likes to call my complete makeover. He taught me a lot of things about the game, and how wrong I was playin' it."

"Like what?"

"Everything. But the most important lesson to me was to make sure that I never shit in my own backyard."

Sacha smiled and asked, "Meaning?"

"Meaning, never do dirt in the city you live in. That has been a rule that I've sworn never to break. That's why I told you that you would never have to worry about any of my actions puttin' you in any jeopardy. Other than that, everything else was basic common sense really. He told me that I should get healthy and maintain a strict habit of exercising. In order to be thorough, he wanted me and the crew to be trained properly."

"Trained? Trained for what?"

"In order for us to be effective in what we do, we had to be able to be as fluid as possible. By it being six of us, we had to become accustomed with each other's moves, and be able to watch each other's backs so we would always be able to maintain our safety during missions. So, for one year after our meeting, me and the crew worked out seven days a week, and went to the shooting range daily to get familiar with various types of weapons. We went out to the country and practiced all types of simulated jack moves and stuff like that. Won told me to call him back when I felt that we were ready."

"Ready for what?"

"To get rich! I called him a year later and told him that we were in fact more than ready. After that, everything is pretty much history. I kept my word to Won, and in return he kept his word with me. He made each of us richer than we could have ever imagined. We stuck to the script he laid out for us, and everything fell into place just like he said it would. I owe that man my life, Li'l Mama. He's been like a father to me. But enough is enough. I want out. I'm ready to live my life with you and put all of this shit behind me now."

Sacha smiled at that comment and said, "Have you told Won that you want to quit?"

"Yeah, and he told me that we're not finished yet. We're almost there, but not yet."

"What is that supposed to mean, Taz?"

"Right now, Li'l Mama, all I'm worried about is my seed. Everything else has to hold up. Won's comin' out here tomorrow, so I guess we'll talk more about that shit then."

"He can't make you keep doing something that you no longer want to do, Taz."

"Don't worry about that, Li'l Mama. No man has ever made me do somethin' that I didn't want to do, and I ain't gonna let that shit start now."

Before Sacha could respond, Tari came running into the waiting area with her face flushed a deep crimson. She stepped straight up to Taz and asked, "How is she?"

"I don't know. We've been waiting here for hours and no one has came and told us shit," Taz said seriously.

"I'll be back in a minute," Tari said as she stormed right back out of the waiting area without saying a word to anyone else in the room.

Taz smiled and said, "Tee is 'bout to go the fuck off!"

Keno smiled and said, "I bet she finds out somethin' for us."

"They done fucked up! That white girl is 'bout to go on the warpath for real!" Red said from the other side of the room.

"Red! Watch your mouth boy!" yelled Mama-Mama.

"Sorry, Mama-Mama," Red said sheepishly.

Everyone laughed, and for a minute the tension inside of the room seemed to have eased up a little . . . just a little.

Ten minutes after Tari had left the waiting area, she came back with a smile on her face. That smile made Taz's heart rate increase dramatically as he stood and stared at her. He was so nervous that he could barely speak as he whispered, "How is she, Tee?"

"She's all right, Taz. She's all right. The doctor is on his way here now so he can tell you exactly what's been going on. But he did confirm for me that she is okay, and that she should make a full recovery."

Mama-Mama clapped her hands together loudly and screamed, "Thank you, Jesus! I Thank You, Lord! I knew You would keep Your gracious hands on my grandbaby! I knew it!"

Taz was feeling so numb that all he could do was stand there and smile. Tari put her arms around him, and they shared a tight hug. "My God! What the hell happened, Taz?" she whispered into Taz's ear.

Taz pulled himself from her embrace and said, "Later. I'll explain everything later on. Right now, I need to see my baby girl."

A doctor came into the waiting area, stepped toward Mama-Mama and said, "Hello, ma'am. Are you a relative of Tazneema Good?"

"Yes, yes, I am. She's my granddaughter. And this young man right here is her father," Mama-Mama said as she pointed toward Taz.

Taz shook the doctor's hand and asked, "Can I see my baby, sir?"

The doctor shook his head no and said, "I'm sorry, Mr. Good, but not tonight. Tazneema is going to be just fine, but she's been heavily sedated and she won't come out of it until early in the morning. We had to remove the bullet out of her back because it traveled much faster than we had originally anticipated. She's going to have a nasty scar, but she'll definitely make a one hundred percent recovery. I suggest that you all go on home and get some much-needed rest. Come back bright and early, and I'm positive Tazneema will be in a much better state than she is now."

"Thank you, doctor! Thank you so very much!" Taz said, relieved. He then turned toward everyone inside of the waiting area and said, "Come on, y'all. Let's bounce. You heard the man. My baby girl is gon' be all right!"

"I know that's right, my nigga! Let's get to the crib so we can kill some of that liquor of yours. I don't know about y'all, but my ass needs a drink!" yelled Bo-Pete.

Mama-Mama grabbed her purse from her seat and said, "I'm spending the night at your house, Taz. I want to be here with you bright and early in the morning."

"Okay, Mama-Mama. Anything you say."

"Shoot! I think I'll have me a strong dose of whatever y'all gon' be drinkin' too!"

Everyone started laughing as they filed out of the waiting area. Everything was going to be all right, or was it?

Chapter Two

Clifford parked his CLS 500 Mercedes in the parking lot of the Oklahoma City Police Department and turned off the ignition. He couldn't believe what he had done. He shot the woman he was in love with. Even though it wasn't intentional, he knew it was still his fault for trying to shoot Taz. "God, help me!" he said aloud as he stepped out of his car and walked inside of the police station. He went to the front desk and asked a police officer, "Who do I speak with about a shooting?"

A small overweight police officer asked him, "Where did this shooting take place, sir?"

"Out in Spencer."

"And how long ago did this happen?"

"About thirty minutes ago."

"Do you know the person who did the shooting, and was anyone shot?"

"Yes, on both accounts. My girlfriend, Tazneema Good, was shot, and I am the person who shot her," Clifford said somberly.

"Would you please have a seat, sir, while I get a detective for you to speak with."

Clifford gave the officer a nod of his head and went and sat down in one of the chairs in the hallway. While he was waiting for a detective, his mind was steady racing. *Was Tazneema all right? And if she was, was their child going to be able to survive this type of trauma?* These were the questions running through his mind as he patiently waited for the detective. *Please, God, let her be all right! I don't care what happens to me, just let 'Neema and our baby be all right!* he prayed silently.

After a few minutes, a slim brown-skinned detective came from behind the closed doors, walked directly up to Clifford and said, "Hello, sir, my name is Detective Bean. Would you step this way, please?"

Clifford stood and followed the detective to an office. Once they were inside the office, Detective Bean motioned for Clifford to have a seat while he went and sat down behind his desk. "Now, I've been told that you have some information about a shooting. Why don't you tell me about it."

Clifford sighed heavily and said, "About forty-five minutes ago, I accidentally shot my girlfriend, Tazneema Good. I went over to her grandmother's home out in Spencer, so I could be introduced to who I once thought was my girlfriend's brother. But it turned out that the person I thought was her brother was actually her father. His name is Taz Good. Taz and I have a mutual dislike for one another."

"Wait a minute. I thought you said that you went over there to meet him."

"I did. You see, it's like this, we already knew one another. Taz got involved with a woman that I was kind of involved with." He sighed again and continued. "To make a long story short, the woman decided to leave me alone and mess with Taz. Ever since then, Taz and I had a slight beef with one another. Anyway, I met his daughter, and we became very close—so close in fact that she's pregnant with my child. She didn't know that I knew Taz, and she wanted us to meet each other. When I got to her grandmother's home and Taz saw who I was, he went ballistic. He started yelling at me and Tazneema, talking about how I didn't care about her, and how I was trying to get back at him for taking Sacha away from me. He was very irate and was not trying to hear anything either Tazneema or I had to say. He even went so far as to threaten me."

"What did he say?"

"He told me that he would kill me before he let me be with Tazneema."

"Okay. What happened next?"

"I took his threats literally and felt like my life was in danger. I pulled out my weapon. I pointed it at Taz and told him that I loved Tazneema. He smiled and tried his best to get me to shoot him."

"What exactly did he say to you?"

"He told me to go ahead and shoot him 'cause, if I didn't, he was going to kill me."

"And?"

"Tazneema yelled for me not to do it, but I was scared and I feared that Taz would in fact live up to the threats he was making. So, I pulled the trigger. Just as I did, Tazneema screamed and pushed her father out of the way. By doing so, she was hit instead of her father. I don't know where the bullet hit her, but I watched as she fell to the floor. Taz got off of the floor and grabbed her in his arms while I turned and ran outside to my car."

"And then you came straight here to the station?"

"Yes, sir. I know that I've committed a crime, and I had no other choice but to come and turn myself in."

Detective Bean nodded his head for a moment and said, "I respect that, sir. For the record, please give me your full name."

"Clifford Nelson."

"Place of employment?"

"I'm an attorney for the firm of Whitney & Johnson here in the city."

"An attorney? Well, I guess my next question won't need to be answered. Since you're an attorney, is it safe to assume that you have no criminal record?"

"That's correct."

"Since you've come and turned yourself in to the authorities, I'm going to try my best to make this situation as bearable as I can for you, Mr. Nelson."

"Thank you, Detective."

"Excuse me for a moment while I go speak with my captain. You can help yourself to some coffee if you'd like. It's not the best in the world, but it's strong and hot," Detective Bean said as he pointed toward his coffee pot on a small table behind his desk.

"No, thank you. I don't drink coffee."

"All right. I'll be back in a few," said the detective as he came from behind his desk and left his office. While on his way toward his captain's office, Detective Bean stopped at another detective's desk and said, "Wally, have we received any calls from any hospitals concerning a shooting within the last hour or so?"

"Yeah, we got two. One of them was from Mercy, and the other one was from St. Anthony's. What's up?"

"Do me a favor and check and see if the victim at either of the hospitals is a female by the name of . . ." he pulled out his notes that he had taken while Clifford was telling his story, found Tazneema's name and continued, "A Tazneema Good. If it is, make sure that you get right back at me, okay?"

"Gotcha, Frank."

Detective Bean then stepped briskly toward the captain's office and knocked on his door. After being told to come inside, he opened the door and entered his superior's office. He quickly told the captain what Clifford had told him, and asked, "So, what do you think? Should I book him now or what, sir?"

"Book him for what? We don't have any grounds to actually arrest him yet. Wait until you can confirm whether or not this Tazneema woman has actually been shot. Then we'll go from there," said the captain.

"Gotcha, sir," Bean said as he turned and left the captain's office.

As Bean was walking back to his office, the detective that he had asked to check on any shootings stopped him. "Looks like there is a Tazneema Good over at Mercy, Frank. Gunshot wound to her upper torso," he said.

"Has anyone been sent over there yet?"

"She's still in surgery. The nurse I spoke with told me that they didn't know how long she'd be in the operating room."

"Thanks, Wally," Detective Bean said as he made an about face and went back toward the captain's office. He once again knocked on the captain's door, and was told to enter. Bean stuck his head inside of the door and said, "We have confirmation on Tazneema Good, sir. One gunshot wound to her upper torso."

"How is she?

"She's still in surgery."

"All right, read Mr. Nelson his rights and let him go."

"Let him go?" Detective Bean asked, shocked.

"That's what I said. He's not a runner. He'll be okay."

"Are you sure, Cap?"

"Trust me, I know what I'm doing. Let him know that after we get a statement from Ms. Good, he'll be hearing from us."

"But what if she dies, sir?"

"Then he'll definitely be hearing from us. Give him the not-to-leave-town speech and let him go, Frank."

"All right, sir." Detective Bean closed the office door and went back to his own office. As soon as he stepped inside, he said, "I'm going to have to read you your Miranda Rights, Mr. Nelson."

"So, I'm being arrested?" Clifford asked nervously.

"Not at the moment. We have confirmed that Tazneema Good has indeed been shot. She's currently in surgery over at Mercy Hospital."

"Do you know how she's doing?"

"Not at the moment. After I've finished reading you your Miranda Rights, you'll be free to go. I have a complete statement from you, so once we interview Ms. Good you'll most likely be hearing from us."

"I understand," Clifford said somberly. He sat back in his seat and listened as the detective read him his Miranda Rights. After the detective was finished, Clifford asked him, "How much time do you think I'm facing, Detective?"

"Honestly, it all depends."

"On what?"

"On whether or not Ms. Good lives or dies. If she lives, then you're looking at a shooting with intent charge. Since this is your first arrest, a judge may be lenient. You might come out of this with some probation and community service because of the unique circumstances of this situation—that is, if things went exactly the way you say they did. But if she dies, then it could mean a lot of time, Mr. Nelson."

"I understand. But what I don't understand is, why are you all letting me go home now? I could run away if I chose to."

Detective Bean smiled and said, "We don't think you're the running type, Mr. Nelson. After all, you did come and inform us of your crime. But, for the record, let me tell you that it would be in your best interest not to leave town," Bean said sternly.

"I won't, Detective," Clifford said as he got out of his seat.

"Go on home and try to take it easy. We'll contact you after we've had a chance to speak with Ms. Good."

"Okay. Thank you, Detective," Clifford said, and left the detective's office. As he walked out of the police station, he gave a sigh of relief. He was happy as hell to still be a free man. *If I was still the same man I used to be, I might not have come and turned myself in to the authorities*, he thought as he climbed inside of his car. *At least I'm not going to jail tonight*, he thought as he started his car and pulled out of the parking lot of the police station.

Chapter Three

The next morning, Taz, Sacha and Mama-Mama got up early and went straight to the hospital. When they arrived, two nurses escorted them to Tazneema's room. Tazneema was lying in her hospital bed sleeping when they entered her room. Taz smiled when he saw that his baby was breathing on her own without any medical equipment. *She's going to be all right,* he thought as he stepped closer to the bed. He bent over and kissed her on her forehead and said, "You're going to be all right, baby girl. You're going to be all right!"

Tazneema slowly opened her eyes, smiled and said, "Hi, Taz."

Tears welled in Taz's eyes as he said, "What's up? How are you feeling?"

"Tired."

"Yeah, you're going to have to stay off your feet for a minute," he said as he wiped his eyes.

Tazneema saw Mama-Mama standing beside Sacha and said, "Hi, Mama-Mama."

Mama-Mama came to the bed, grabbed Tazneema's hand and said, "Hey, baby!"

Tazneema waved at Sacha and said, "Well, it looks as if the whole gang's here, huh. I feel kinda important."

"You are important," Sacha said as she stepped up to the bed and stood next to Taz. "You gave us all quite a scare, young lady."

"I know, but I'm fine." Tazneema turned her head toward Taz and asked, "What happened to Cliff? You haven't done anything to him, have you?"

Taz's smile turned into a frown as he said, "Nah, not yet."

"Please don't do anything to him, Taz. He was scared. You pushed him into trying to shoot you."

"So, you're sayin' this is *my* fault?" Taz asked angrily.

"What I'm saying is, there isn't any reason for you to hurt him. I'm all right, and we should let this all go."

"Don't worry yourself 'bout any of that stuff right now, 'Neema. You need to be getting some rest so you can hurry up and get back on your feet. Taz ain't gon' be doin' nothin to that boy," Mama-Mama said sternly. She gave Taz the eye. "Ain't that right, boy?"

"Yes, Mama-Mama," Taz answered without looking in her direction.

Before Tazneema could speak again, there was a knock at the door, and Keno, Bo-Pete, Red and Wild Bill all entered the room, each holding a dozen red roses in their hands.

Keno smiled and said, "Look at my niece, all laid up looking all pretty like."

Tazneema smiled brightly and said, "Stop it, Uncle Keno! I'm a mess! Look at my hair!"

Keno laughed and said, "You look pretty damn good to me, baby girl."

"Watch your mouth, Keno!"

"Sorry, Mama-Mama," replied Keno.

Bo-Pete set his flowers on the counter and asked, "Are you feeling okay, 'Neema?"

"Yes, I'm fine. Just a little tired."

"That's cool."

Each one of her play uncles went and gave her a light kiss on her cheek and told her how much they all loved her. Taz took a step back while his homeboys showed his daughter some love. Sacha grabbed his hand and watched silently as the crew spoke with Tazneema.

After a few minutes, a nurse came into the room and said, "Tazneema needs to take her medication. Afterward, it's going to make her drowsy, so it would be better if you all left for a little while so she could get some rest."

"No problem, ma'am," Taz said as he stepped back next to the bed and gave Tazneema a kiss and said, "We'll be back a little later, baby girl."

"Okay, Taz," Tazneema said, and she said good-bye to everyone else inside the room.

As they all filed out of the room, Taz noticed a police officer speaking with a nurse at the nurses' station. *I wondered how long it would be before they would be gettin' at 'Neema,* he said to himself.

When they had made it to the nurses' station, Taz stopped and said, "Excuse me, officer, but are you here to speak with my daughter, Tazneema Good?"

"Yes, sir, I am. But I've just been told that I won't be able to interview her until later on this afternoon," replied the police officer.

"Yeah, she's just taken her medication. I can answer any questions that you have for her. I was there when everything happened."

"That's a start. Could we go somewhere and talk, sir?"

"Taz. My name is Taz Good."

"Okay, Mr. Good. Can you step over into the waiting room and answer a few questions for me?"

"No problem," Taz said as he followed the police officer.

Once they made it to a row of chairs, they both took a seat and the police officer said, "Tell me what exactly happened, Mr. Good."

Taz started from the beginning, and finished with how he had taunted Clifford. "You see, it's all my fault. If I wouldn't have kept pushing and taunting that fool, my baby girl wouldn't be laid up in this damn hospital."

"So, what you're telling me is that neither you nor your daughter are going to press charges against Mr. Nelson?" asked the police officer.

"That's correct. We want to put this incident behind us so we can move on with our lives," lied Taz.

"I understand. Mr. Nelson came down to the station yesterday after the shooting occurred and confessed to everything. From what I've been told, everything you have just told me matches exactly with what he told our detective. While I'm waiting to speak with your daughter, I'll give the lead detective a call and inform him of what you've told me. He may decide not to arrest Mr. Nelson."

"That's straight. If there's anything else that you need from me, I can be reached at my home anytime," Taz said, and gave the police officer the number to his home as well as his cell phone number.

Sacha, who had been listening to the entire interview, knew Taz was lying through his teeth. *You think you're so damn slick, Mr. Good! I'm not letting you commit another murder, mister!* she thought as she watched Taz shake hands with the police officer. After they had gotten into the elevator, Sacha said, "Keno took Mama-Mama home. She said she had a headache, and she was going home to get some rest. She's going to meet us back here later on, baby."

"That's cool. I'm kinda still faded from last night too. That XO don't be playin'."

Sacha smiled and said, "Don't I know it! I'm still feeling it from that time me and Gwen killed that bottle."

They stepped off of the elevator and into the lobby on the first floor, and were walking toward the exit when Sacha asked, "Why did you lie to that policeman, Taz? You know damn well that you have plans on doing something to Cliff."

"Why would you ask me a question that you already know the answer to, counselor? I don't want that clown-ass nigga in jail. He has to pay for this shit! And you know damn well I'm goin' to be the one to make him pay!"

"Even though your daughter is still in love with him?"

"What? Are you outta your mind? 'Neema's not goin' to fuck with that nigga no more! He shot her!"

Sacha smiled, shook her head from side to side and said, "I saw and heard all of the compassion on her face and in her voice. She's still in love with him, Taz. Why do you think she said what she said? She's still going to be with him, baby."

Taz shook his head violently and said, "No, she won't! 'Cause he won't be around for her to be with him!"

"So, you're going to cause her further anguish by killing the man she loves? How do you think she's going to feel about you after you murder the love of her young life, Taz?"

Taz stopped, stared directly into his fiancée's eyes and said, "To be totally honest with you, Li'l Mama, I don't give a fuck!

That nigga is a dead man walkin'!" He then stormed out of the lobby of the hospital.

Sacha was so upset with Taz that she didn't say a word to him as they drove back to his home.

Taz pulled into the circular driveway of his mini-mansion, jumped out of his truck and went inside of his home. He was greeted by his beloved dobermans, Precious and Heaven. His dogs sensed that their master was in a foul mood because they instantly became alert. Each gave a low growl deep in their throats, awaiting the command from Taz to kill something. Taz noticed them, smiled and said, "Relax, girls. Everything is good. Go play, you two." Both Dobermans quickly obeyed their master's command and silently ran off into the large home. Taz went inside of one of his dens and poured himself a drink from his bar.

Sacha followed him into the den, sat across from him on his sectional sofa and said, "I've made an appointment to go see the doctor. Do you want to come with me?"

"When is it?"

"Tuesday at nine a.m."

"Yeah, I'll go. How far along do you think you are?"

She smiled and said, "I don't have a clue. Maybe a month or so."

"That's cool. Look, Li'l Mama. I've got a lot on my mind right now. Not only do I have this shit with Cliff to deal with, but I still got issues with Won to clear up. So I'm goin' to need you to give me some space for a minute."

"Space? What the fuck do you mean by space, Taz?"

He smiled, held his hands up and said, "Hold up, Li'l Mama! Not like that! I mean I don't need you tryin' to make me feel guilty and shit. I can't have you in my way tryin' to fuck up my train of thought and shit. You have to understand that I'm goin' to do me, regardless. You can't stop me from doin' whatever I feel in my heart is the right thing to do. Do you understand what I'm sayin'?"

"Yes. I just don't want you to do something that you might regret later on, baby."

"I know, Li'l Mama, but you're goin' to have to trust me and my decisions."

"I do, and I will, baby."

"Good. Now come here and give me some love," Taz said as he grabbed her and gave her a tender kiss.

After a full minute of kissing each other, Sacha pulled from Taz's embrace and said, "I'm going to head on home so I can get some more of my clothes. Why don't you get some rest before you go back up to the hospital? You look like you need a few more z's."

Taz smiled and said, "Yeah, I could use a li'l rest. But first I gots to make a few calls. Hold up though. What do you mean you got to get some more clothes from your house? What, you movin' in with a nigga or some shit?"

She playfully slapped Taz on his face and said, "You got a problem with that, Mr. Taz?"

With a bright smile on his face, he said, "Hell nah!" They both laughed and shared another kiss.

After Sacha left, Taz went upstairs and took a shower. After he finished, he was putting on a pair of shorts when his cell started ringing. "Hello."

"What's up, Babyboy?" asked Won.

"What's up, O.G.?"

"I'm in town. Tari's taking me over to Mercy to see 'Neema. She already told me that she was straight, but I want to see her for myself, you know?"

"Yeah, I feel you. I was about to lay it down for a minute. A nigga's straight drained."

"Go on and get you some rest. I'll come by there in a couple of hours. After we leave the hospital, I'm going to have Tari take me to see a few people. Then I'll be by there. Call everyone and have them at your house around one. We need to talk so y'all can understand everything that's going on."

"All right, I'll holla at you later then," Taz said, and closed his cell phone.

By the time Sacha had finished packing a few bags, she felt as if she was going to pass out. She sat down on her bed, grabbed the telephone and called her best friend, Gwen.

When Gwen answered her phone, Sacha said, "What it do, ho? What you doing?"

"Sitting here waiting on Bob to call me back. He promised me he'd call me back before he left."

"Left?"

"Yeah, bitch, he's on his way home. Some guy named Magoo is driving him back to the city."

"Why are they driving all of the way back from New York?"

"Bob told me that it would be safer that way. Obviously something bad went down and they're trying to stay low-key. Hell, bitch, I don't know! You know more about this shit than I do."

"Whatever! After you talk to Bob, give me a call, ho. I'm about to finish packing my stuff, then I'm going back over to Taz's."

"Oh, so you're moving in, huh? 'Bout time, bitch!"

Laughing, Sacha said, "Fuck you, ho!" and hung up the phone. She was happy for her best friend, Gwen. She had endured far too much pain in her life, and she deserved to be happy. Ever since she lost her son and her husband in a terrible car accident, her life was kind of just coasting along. Even though she'd got herself back together by going back to school and getting her degree in physcology, Sacha could tell that her girl still wasn't really happy. Gwen put up a good front though. One could never tell how badly she was actually hurting. But all of her pain seemed to have been eased once she met Taz's homeboy, Bob. Sacha knew every time she saw them together that her best friend had once again found love, and that was a true blessing from God.

But then out of nowhere, tragedy struck again. Bob was shot in his stomach during Taz and the crew's last robbery out in New York. When Gwen found out, she fainted, and Sacha knew in her heart that if Bob didn't pull through, her best friend wasn't going to be able to move on with her life this time around. Thank God that Bob had made it. Now everything can get back to normal. *Normal! Ain't that some shit! Ain't nothing normal about the way Taz, Bob, and the rest of that damn crew is living. This shit has got to stop!* Sacha said to herself as she got back up to finish packing her things.

***

Keno, dressed in a pair of Ecko sweat pants and matching Ecko T-shirt, came into Taz's home and sat down in the den as he watched Taz pour himself a drink from his bar. Keno's long hair was braided in four French braids going toward the back of his head. Though he was the same height as Taz—five foot eleven, and just as muscular—he gave off an entirely different type of vibe. He was always vibrant and upbeat, where Taz was more quiet and low-key. They had been best friends for what seemed like forever. That's why Keno could tell that Taz had something heavy on his mind. "Damn, nigga! It's barely after twelve and you're drinkin'! What's with that?" he asked him.

"My daughter is layin' in the fuckin' hospital tryin' to heal up from being shot, and you ask me what's up with me havin' a drink? Kill that shit, nigga!" Taz said as he came from behind the bar.

"Come on, my nigga! This is Keno you're talkin' to! I know you better than you know yourself, fool. Now, what the fuck is really good?"

Taz smiled and said, "Fuck you! Nah, on the real, I'm worried about what Won is goin' to get at us about in a li'l bit. I want out, dog. The time is right for us to shake this shit and live the right way for once."

"So, let the nigga know that we want out."

Shaking his head no, Taz said, "It's not that simple, gee. We owe that nigga for everything he has done for us. I just can't see me shaking him, especially if he really needs me."

"If that's the case, then why are you trippin'?"

"I told you, I want out."

"But you just said—"

"I know what I just said, nigga! Damn! This shit is confusing enough, dog. I don't need you questioning me over and over."

"Questioning you? Nigga, this shit ain't just about you and your loyalty to that nigga. We are a crew, and all decisions are made together. No one in this crew calls the shots, remember?"

"Yeah, I know. How do you feel about this shit then?"

Keno smiled and said, "Nigga, I gots over two hundred million dollars in the bank. How the fuck do you think I feel? It's whatever with me, dog. We can quit and I'll be straight, or we can keep it rollin' too. I really don't give a fuck."

"If you don't give a fuck, then why are you talkin' 'bout the crew and decision-making and shit?"

"'Cause that's how it has always been. The others might not feel the same way as I do. You're goin' to have to bring it to the table, and then we'll all decide together, like we have always done."

"You're right, gee," Taz said as he went to let the others inside of his home. When he opened the door, he smiled at Bo-Pete, Red and Wild Bill and said, "Right on time, my niggas! We were just talkin' 'bout y'all."

As they entered the house, Red said, "I hope y'all were talkin' some good shit, 'cause I ain't in the mood for no bullshit. Business has to be handled, dog. When are we goin' to get that coward-ass nigga, Cliff?"

Taz didn't answer Red's question until they were all inside of the den. "That nigga is a dead man walkin', gee. You already know that. But right now, we have to figure out how and what we're goin' to do with Won."

"What you mean by that, dog? I thought it was already understood. He's outta there, right?" asked Bo-Pete.

"He should be here in a li'l bit. He wants to get at us and explain everything. I feel we should hear him out before we make any decisions. We owe him that much at least. Y'all know what he's done for us. I really don't want to just cross him out of the game like that," Taz said seriously.

"I feel you, gee, but he can't expect us to stay in the game just because he wants us to. If we feel the need to get out, we have that right," Wild Bill said.

"You're right, Bill. Is that how you feel, dog? Do you want out?"

"Dog, for real, it's whatever with me. I'm rollin' with y'all either way."

Taz smiled and asked, "What about you, Red?"

"If y'all want to smash Won, then so be it. If y'all want to keep rollin' with him, then so be it. I'm riding with my niggas."

Before Taz could ask Bo-Pete the same question, Bo-Pete said, "I feel exactly the same way, my nigga."

"All right then, this is what I feel we should do. Let's hear him out. Then we'll make our decision. If y'all are feelin' what he's talkin' 'bout, give a nod after he's finished. If we all agree, then we'll roll with it."

"And if we ain't feelin' what he's talkin' 'bout, then what?" asked Keno.

"He dies," Taz said with deadly simplicity.

"Right here?" asked Wild Bill.

"Right fuckin' here!" Red said in a tone just as deadly as Taz's.

Twenty minutes after the crew had made their decision, Won and Tari came over to Taz's home. After they were situated inside of the den, Won said, "It's a pleasure to finally be able to meet each one of you in person. We've been dealing with each other for so long, I feel as if each one of you are members of my family." Won stood close to six foot four inches, with a short salt-and-pepper hair cut. He looked dapper, dressed casually in a pair of black slacks with a black-and-gray sweater on. His warm brown eyes stared at each man in the room for a few seconds before he continued. "Y'all have made a tremendous amount of money over the past fifteen years. That was my plan from the beginning. You were all to become millionaires. That part of my plan has been accomplished. Now, we're at the last phase of all of this."

"Which is?" Red asked with a little attitude in his voice.

Won smiled and said, "For me to get what I've been wanting for a very long time. But before I go into that, I need to explain a few things. I've been a part of what me and my associates call 'The Network' for the past twenty-five years. The Network consists of ten council members. Each member of the council controls certain areas around the country. What I mean by 'control' is all illegal activities, such as drugs, gambling, prostitution . . . everything. Over these last past fifteen years,

I have used my inside connections to weaken seven members of the council. My purpose for doing this was to elevate my position. My goal is to become the top man of the council, and run as well as control the entire Network."

"So that's what you was talkin' 'bout when you said you will soon have the position of power?" asked Taz.

Won smiled and said, "Exactly, Babyboy! Like I was saying, I have weakened several members of The Network's council without revealing my hand. Every time y'all complete a mission, I gain more and more strength. The reason why I gave y'all all of the money was to keep my promise in making y'all richer beyond your wildest dreams, but also to hurt the other council members' pockets. By hurting them financially, I used the drugs that I kept from every mission to help them maintain their status in the council. You see, I'm not trying to completely axe them out of the council. I just want to be confident that when the time comes for me to make my move, they will feel obligated to stand, by my side."

"A slow power move, huh?" asked Bo-Pete.

"Exactly. There are two members of The Network that I have never been able to get a good line on as far as their business is concerned. Because of this, I had to make sure that I successfully weakened everyone around them. Thanks to y'all, I've done exactly that. Now, it's time for the final two missions to be completed. Pitt, a man out of Northern California is our first target. I will have the details for you within a week or so. All I can say right now is that he's not to be underestimated, 'cause he's no fool. As a matter a fact, I feel he has already figured out that I had something to do with the robberies that have taken place over the years."

"Why is that?" asked Wild Bill.

"Shit went wrong when there weren't supposed to be any problems. I think Pitt made the call and tipped certain people off. Because of that, Bob was shot and shit went haywire, even though the mission was still completed. Anyway, I've finally gotten inside of Pitt's camp, and I'm confident that this mission will go smoothly. Know this, if I didn't think it could go down smoothly, I would never put any of you in harm's way. Like I said, I look at each of you as a member of my family."

"All right, what about the last mission?" asked Keno.

"Cash Flo' is the other member of The Network that I haven't been able to get close to. I know for a fact that he's close to retiring and handing over his position and part of The Network over to Pitt. After we put a nice dent in Pitt's pocket, Cash Flo' is to be terminated."

"So, you're askin' us to kill for you now?" asked Red.

Won shook his head from side to side and said, "No, I just want you to accompany the person who's going to take Cash Flo's life for me."

"And who is that?" asked Taz.

Won held up his hands and said, "I'll get to that in a moment. I understand that things are hectic now, with 'Neema being shot and Bob out of commission, but we are going to have to be ready to move on Pitt as soon as I get the call. Like I said, it should be within a week or two, tops."

"Dog, we're a six-deep crew. We ain't movin' without Bob," Bo-Pete said seriously.

"Yeah, so it's a no-go if we ain't got our man with us," added Wild Bill.

Won stared at Taz for a minute then said, "I understand. I pretty much figured as much. Magoo and Bob are on their way here as we speak. They should make it into the city some time tomorrow evening. But I know Bob won't be in any shape to handle up. So I've found a replacement for him."

"A replacement? Fuck that shit! We don't need no new nigga in our mix! It's either Bob or nothin'!" Red stated angrily.

Taz held up his hand to calm Red down and said, "Hold up, gee. Let's hear him out. Who's this replacement, O.G.?

Won smiled and said, "The same person who's going to take out Cash Flo' for me."

"And who the fuck is that?" asked Keno, agitated.

Before Won could say a word, Tari got to her feet and said, "Me!"

Chapter Four

Clifford was so relieved that he felt as if he was going to pass out. He had just been informed by Detective Bean that he was not going to be brought up on charges for shooting Tazneema. No one was pressing charges, so he was going to be able to remain a free man. His heart hurt when he found out that he had lost his child, but at least Tazneema was alive and doing well.

He tried numerous times to speak with her, but Mama-Mama refused to let them talk to each other. Once when he called the hospital he actually heard Tazneema tell Mama-Mama that she wanted to speak with him, and that made him feel real good inside. He could hear the love in her voice, and he was now confident that she still wanted him. He was also confident that if they didn't press any charges against him, it was because Taz had other plans for him. He would have to deal with that whenever the time came. The most important thing to him at that moment was getting in contact with the woman he loved.

He walked into his office, and before he had a chance to sit behind his desk, his secretary buzzed in on the intercom and told him that Mr. Johnson and Mr. Whitney wanted to see him as soon as possible in Mr. Whitney's office. He set his briefcase down and quickly stepped out of his office. When he made it to Mr. Whitney's office, his secretary told him that he could go right in. He took a deep breath and opened the door to Mr. Whitney's office. Once he was inside the office, his heart felt as if it was about to burst, it was beating so hard. Clifford smiled nervously as he stared at Mr. Whitney and Mr. Johnson, the two head partners of the firm, and one of the newest partners, Ms. Sacha Carbajal.

"Have a seat, Clifford," Mr. Whitney said in a tone that could mean only one thing to Clifford.

I'm outta here, he thought as he did as he was instructed to.

"Clifford, we've received some very disturbing news about you," Mr. Johnson said as he glared at him. "And we want you to know that though you are a very competent attorney, there is no room at this firm for a person who cannot control his emotions."

"I understand, sirs, but if you would let me explain—"

With both of the partners of the firm shaking their heads no, Mr. Whitney continued. "I don't feel that there's an explanation good enough to make us believe that you are still worthy to work for us here at Whitney and Johnson, Clifford. So we have no other choice but to terminate you immediately."

"Please don't make this any more difficult than it already is, Clifford," added Mr. Johnson. "We expect you to have your office cleared out as soon as possible."

"That's it? Just like that I'm out of here? I can't believe this! I don't know what you've been told, sirs, but there are certain factors to this situation that you two need to know about!" Clifford yelled as he glared at Sacha.

Sacha met his glare with one of her own as she said, "Both Mr. Johnson and Mr. Whitney have spoken with a Detective Bean of the Oklahoma City Police Department. They are well informed of your criminal behavior. We also have a copy of the statement you gave Detective Bean, so there isn't anything else to be said. You're very lucky that the Good family chose not to press any charges against you."

"Come on! You know damn well why they didn't press any charges against me. For one, Tazneema would never press charges because she loves me! And, two, your damn thug-ass boyfriend is planning on taking my life! Did you tell the bosses that? You spiteful li'l bitch!"

"Clifford! That is enough! I will not tolerate that kind of language inside my office!" yelled Mr. Whitney. "Now, you are to get your things and be out of this office building immediately! If not, then we will have someone assist you! Am I understood, Mr. Nelson?"

"Man, fuck you and this firm!" Clifford screamed as he stormed out of Mr. Whitney's office. When he made it back to his office he called for his secretary to come in and told her, "Do me a favor, Kathy. Pack all of my stuff up for me and have it sent down to the front security desk. I'll come back and get it later on."

"Wha—what happened, Mr. Nelson?" she asked.

Clifford smiled sadly and said, "Oh, nothing. I just got canned."

Back inside of Mr. Whitney's office, Mr. Johnson was telling Sacha, "I hope that young lady will not be seeing Clifford any longer. He's obviously a dangerous individual."

"Only time will tell, sir. But I do think Cliff was right. She's still in love with him, so you know how that goes," Sacha said with a slight shrug of her slender shoulders.

"What about Taz? Do you think he was right when he said Taz was planning to hurt him?" asked Mr. Whitney.

"I can assure you, gentlemen, that Taz has no plans to do anything to Cliff. He's very angry at him, but he's no fool. If something was to happen to Cliff, Taz knows that he would be the prime suspect. I've spoken with him repeatedly, and he understands that it's best to try and put this unpleasant incident behind him and his family."

"I hope you're right, Sacha," Mr. Johnson said as he got out of his chair.

I do too, Sacha thought to herself as she followed Mr. Johnson out of Mr. Whitney's office.

Taz was sitting next to Tazneema's bed, trying his best to figure out his daughter's way of thinking. "Can't you understand that that nigga is no fuckin' good, 'Neema?" he yelled.

"Why can't you understand that I love that man?" Tazneema yelled right back.

Before the yelling match could continue any further, Won said, "Look, baby boy. Maybe you should let this go for now.

There's no need to further frustrate 'Neema while she's in here recovering."

Tazneema smiled and said, "Thank you, Uncle Won, 'cause he's gettin' on my last nerves. My head hurts enough as it is."

Taz stood and said, "Whatever! But I'm standin' on my word, 'Neema. Stay the fuck away from that clown!" he yelled as he left the hospital room.

When the door closed behind Taz, Won said, "Don't worry about him, 'Neema. It'll pass. Just give him some time."

"I don't know, Uncle Won. You know how stubborn he is."

"Yeah, I know, but I also know how stubborn you are too."

She smiled and said, "You better believe it!"

Won bent over and gave her a kiss on both of her cheeks and said, "Get some rest. We'll come back and check on you later on, okay?"

"Okay. Bye, Uncle Won."

"Bye, sweetie," Won said, and turned and left the room. When he caught up with Taz at the elevator bank, he said, "You need to learn how to control your emotions, Babyboy. I thought I taught you better than that."

"I know, O.G., but when it comes to my baby girl, I can't help it. She really wants to be with that nigga! After he fuckin' shot at me! *Me!* Her fuckin' Daddy!"

"Calm down. She's not going to be with that fool. You know I wouldn't let that happen."

"What do you mean by that?"

As they stepped into the elevator, Won said, "I'll take care of that nigga when the time's right. Right now, if he came up missing, you'd be caught the fuck up. We can't afford that, so let's just chill and finish what we gots to finish."

Taz shook his head and said, "Nah. After everything is everything, I'm goin' to be the one that takes out that clown-ass nigga, O.G. Me, not you."

"All right, but only after we're done."

"Whatever! Tell me something. How in the hell did you get Tari involved in all of this shit?"

Won smiled and said, "Tari has been on my team for a very long time. Believe it or not, you two share a similar story. She lost her parents when she was young, so she took to the streets to survive. The same person who introduced us, introduced me to her. I took her out West, cleaned her up and put her back into school. By the time she graduated high school, she told me she wanted to become a nurse, so I sent her to nursing school. From time to time she was called upon to handle certain things for me. And just like you, she's very thorough. Don't underestimate her, Babyboy. She's a stone-cold killer. I sent her back to the City and introduced you two because I knew you needed a woman to take your mind off of MiMi from time to time. I also knew that you would never fall in love with her, and I thought she would never fall in love with you, but there I was wrong. That girl would give her life for you if you asked her to."

Taz smiled and said, "Yeah?"

"That's right."

They stepped into the lobby of the hospital, and Taz said, "I have always loved Tee. I just never felt the kind of love like I have for Sacha."

"She knows that, and she respects Sacha tremendously. All she cares about is your well-being. When I asked her, would she help me out for this mission, she said she would, on one condition."

"What was that?"

Won smiled again and said, "As long as this be the last time that I ever asked you to do something dangerous for me again."

"What?"

"You heard me. She's doing this so that I can let you live the rest of your life happily."

"So, you're tellin' me that she's doin' this crazy shit for me?"

"You got it, Babyboy."

"Damn!"

Clifford drove around for hours, thinking about what the fuck he was going to do with his life now. He knew for a fact that Mr. Whitney and Mr. Johnson were going to do their best to fuck him over, so getting employed by another firm in the city was definitely going to be out of the question. He couldn't believe that bitch Sacha went out of her way to make sure he lost his job. *That bitch is going to pay—her and her punk-ass nigga!* he thought as he continued to drive aimlessly around the city.

After a few hours of driving around, he found himself rolling through his old stomping grounds. He smiled as he saw some young Crips hanging on the corner of Twenty-third Street and Lottie Avenue. They started throwing up their Hoover Crip gang sign—thumb in between the index and middle finger of their left hand—as he rolled past them. He shocked himself as he instinctively returned the Hoover gang sign back to the youngsters hanging on the corner. Throwing up the Hoover sign made a lot of memories come storming back inside of his head. He remembered how he and Do-Low used to be some of the hardest Crips in Oklahoma City. *Do-Low . . . Damn! That punk-ass nigga Taz killed a lifelong friend!* he thought as he rolled through his old neighborhood. If he hadn't tried to have Do-Low kill Taz, his homeboy would still be alive. Even though Do-Low had been dying slowly of AIDS, he still didn't deserve to be shot dead in the parking lot of some damn club. The hatred Clifford had for Taz was steadily intensifying.

He smiled when he saw someone from his past. He quickly parked his Mercedes, jumped out of the car and said, "What's up, cuz? What's that 107 Hoover Crip like?"

A short, stocky brother dressed in a pair of blue Dickies with a matching blue Dickies shirt on said, "What the fuck! What's up, cuz? What the hell yo' rich ass doing in the 'hood?"

"Shit done got fucked up for me, cuz. You know how it goes. When everything else fails, a nigga still gots the set. What's up with you, H-Hop? How you been?"

"Ain't shit. The same old shit. You know how it is out here, trying to make some ends and shit. Damn, C-Baby! You got the tight Benz and shit. Can't too much be goin' wrong for yo' ass."

"Yeah, my paper is straight for now, but I just got fired from my job."

"I thought you was a big-time lawyer and shit,"

Clifford started laughing and said, "Yeah, kinda. But that's old news. I'm not anymore."

"So, what you gon' do now? I know you ain't tryin' to come back to the block."

"Why not? What, an O.G. ain't welcome back in his 'hood, nigga?"

"Cuz, it's a new day out here. I honestly don't think you'd be able to keep up with these young niggas. Shit, I barely can, and you know I'm still 107's top killa."

Clifford laughed and said, "Is that right? You mean to tell me that these youngstas are out here wildin' like that?"

"You fuckin' right! They tryin' to smoke somebody every fuckin' day! Cuz, I'm out here tryin' my best to stay down for the set, but I got kids to feed so they are my first priority, ya feel me?"

"Yeah, I feel you. Where are you on your way to now?"

"I was about to go holla at the li'l homey to see if cuz has my ends yet. What, you tryin' to meet some of these new niggas from the Groove?"

With a shrug of his shoulders, Clifford replied, "Why not? I don't have shit else to do."

"All right then, come on. Them niggas is gon' trip the fuck out when they see us pull up in that tight-ass Benz," H-Hop said as he started walking toward Clifford's car.

Clifford made the short drive deeper into 107 Hoover Crip's turf, and parked his Mercedes in front of a small group of teenagers dressed in a mixture of orange and blue. As they climbed out of the Benz, H-Hop smiled and said, "What's up, cuz?"

Several of the teenagers responded by yelling out, "Hoover Crip!" or "Ain't nothin' smoother than Hoover over here, cuz!"

H-Hop and Clifford smiled at each other as they walked toward the backyard of the vacant home that they had parked in front of. A few of the teenagers standing out front followed them.

Once they made it to the back, Clifford saw another familiar face. He smiled and said, "Damn, cuz! You still around this bitch?"

A tall, skinny brother with a light-skinned complexion smiled and said, "Look at this shit! It's a fuckin' Hoover legend and shit! What up, C-Baby? What it do, cuz?"

Clifford smiled and said, "My nigga, Astro! You ain't changed at all I see, cuz."

"Yeah, you know how it is. Got a li'l older and shit, but still doin' my thang. What the fuck you doin' around the 'hood? Last time I seen you, you was at Do-Low's funeral."

"Just came through with H-Hop to holla at y'all for a minute. It's been too long, and I wanted to make sure that you young bucks was maintaining this Hoover Groove."

Astro laughed and said, "Is that right? One thang's for sho', big homey. You ain't even gots to worry about how we gets down out here. Every nigga in the city knows how we handle ours."

One of the teenagers who had followed H-Hop and Clifford into the backyard stepped up and said, "Cuz, who the fuck is this old nigga?"

Astro frowned because he knew that Li'l Bomb was a young hothead not to be taken lightly. "Cuz, this is the big homey, C-Baby. He's one of the first Hoovers in the city. When the big homies came out here from Cali, they put him on first to help start the set," Astro said as he fired up a Newport.

"What up, cuz? I'm Li'l Bomb," said the teenager who couldn't have been more than fifteen—sixteen years old, tops.

Clifford extended his hand and said, "What's up, cuz? They call me C-Baby."

After shaking hands, Li'l Bomb asked, "So, you're a gee from the set, huh?"

"You better believe it, loco!"

"Cuz, just 'cause you're a gee don't mean shit to me or any of my niggas. We're runnin' the set now, loc. And to be honest with you, cuz, I don't think you gots what it takes to be a 107 Hoover in the twenty-first century!"

A few other young Hoovers had came and stood next to Li'l Bomb as he spoke. Clifford noticed this, and he knew it was his time to either leave or check these youngsters and let them know he was still in fact an original gangster from 107 Hoover

Crips. "Let me tell you somethin', li'l nigga. Since when does a killa forget how to kill? Don't get it twisted, cuz. Just 'cause I haven't been around in a minute doesn't mean that I've lost my heart, loc."

Li'l Bomb smiled and simply said, "Prove it."

"What?"

"I said prove it, cuz. If you're still that gee you claim to be, come and put some work in with me and the homies."

"Li'l nigga, I ain't gots to prove shit to no young-ass niggas like y'all! I've put in mines long before you li'l niggas were even thought of."

"Just like I thought. A has-been-ass Hoover comin' around here talkin' that O.G. shit, but ain't gonna bust a grape on skates. Come on, cuz. Let's let this old nigga chop it up with H-Hop and Astro. We gots some work to put in," Li'l Bomb said as he turned to leave the backyard.

"Hold up, cuz! I like how you seem to have leadership qualities. The set has always needed that. So, this is what I'm goin' to do. Go get the straps and come back and scoop me. But it's goin' to be just you and me, loc. We don't need your li'l fans to roll with us," Clifford said with a sarcastic smile on his face.

"You ain't sayin' shit, cuz! I'll be right back!" Li'l Bomb yelled as he left the backyard to go get some weapons for himself and Clifford to use.

"C-Baby, I don't think you should fuck with that nigga, Li'l Bomb. That nigga is a straight fool wit' it," Astro said as he lit up a blunt of some very strong-smelling weed.

"Fo' real, cuz. That nigga gots bodies all over the fuckin' city," added H-Hop.

"Damn, cuz! What's with you niggas? Ain't shit changed, and I'm gon' show this young nigga that once a Hoover, always a Hoover! These niggas are gon' always give me my props around this bitch, whether I come around here every day or not! I've earned mines."

Even though Clifford was still dressed in a pair of slacks and a long-sleeved buttoned-up shirt, he was ready to go kill some of his enemies with Li'l Bomb. For some strange reason, he wasn't nervous, nor was he worried about the fact that he was about to go commit a murder . . . or possibly murders. He felt just like he used to feel back in the days when he was one of the hardest Hoover Crips in the city. The only difference now was that he wasn't about to go put in work with any of his old crew. They were either all dead or locked up in prison somewhere. H-Hop and Astro were two of the few left from his old wrecking crew.

Cliff took a deep breath and rotated his broad shoulders so that he could loosen himself up a little. His six foot frame was solid, and he was still in pretty good shape for a man his age.

Suddenly, common sense seemed to have slapped him in his face. *What the fuck am I doing? I may have lost my job, but I haven't lost my fuckin' mind! I can't be doing no shit like this!* he thought to himself as he stared at Astro and H-Hop.

Before he could speak his mind, Li'l Bomb came back into the backyard carrying a large duffel bag in his hand. He walked up to him and set the bag in front of him and said, "All right, cuz, choose your shit."

Clifford watched as Li'l Bomb unzipped the bag and pulled out several handguns. There were 9 mm pistols, Tech-9 semi-automatic pistols, as well as an AK-47. *What the fuck am I going to do now?* he asked himself. *Fuck it! I done got myself caught up in this shit now. I can't lose face to this li'l nigga of the Pepsi generation.* He bent toward the bag and chose two of the nine-millimeters and asked, "All right, who we blastin'?"

Li'l Bomb smiled and said, "Some of those Prince Hall niggas. Who else?"

"I thought since they redid that projects those niggas weren't around no more."

"Nah, cuz. Them mark-ass niggas are still around. You just have to know where to look. And, believe me, cuz, I know right where they be at," Li'l Bomb replied confidently. "Come on, let's go!"

Clifford couldn't believe he was actually falling for some peer pressure from a fucking baby. *This has got to be the craziest shit in the world,* he thought as he followed Li'l Bomb. They climbed inside of a '77 Cutlass Supreme that was obviously stolen, because Li'l Bomb started the ignition with a screwdriver. Once they were on their way, Clifford tried his best to calm his nerves. *Everything is going to be all right. You know how to put in work, nigga. It's just like riding a bike,* he thought as he took a quick glance at the baby driving the car he was inside of. *Fuck it! It's too late now!*

Li'l Bomb parked the Cutlass and said, "Come on, cuz. We're walkin' from here."

"Walkin'? Li'l nigga, you trippin'! Where the fuck them fools at?"

"They're right down the street, cuz. I don't do drive-bys, loc. I like to be up close and personal. I gotta make sure that I gets my man. Now, are you comin' or what?"

"Lead, li'l nigga. I'm right on your bumper, cuz," Clifford said as he followed Li'l Bomb.

Li'l Bomb smiled as he led the way toward their enemies. About halfway down the street from where he had parked the stolen Cutlass, there were about seven teenagers and a few older people dressed in all blue and standing in front of an apartment complex. Li'l Bomb stopped and said, "There they go, cuz. Since you're dressed like a fuckin' goody-goody, this is what we should do. Walk up and ask them niggas, do they have any work. Once they relax a li'l after figuring out you ain't 'one time,' start blastin' they ass. After you put yours in, break back to the car."

"What the fuck are you goin' to be doing while I'm handlin' mines?"

"Watchin'."

"Watching? Cuz, you gots me fucked up if you think I'm puttin' this work in by myself!"

"Chill out, loc. Once you've handled your business, I'm comin' behind you to play the clean-up man. I don't like leavin' witnesses when I put in work, cuz," Li'l Bomb said menacingly.

Damn! This li'l nigga is heartless, Clifford thought to himself. But to Li'l Bomb he said, "Whatever, cuz. Now watch how a gee does it." He cocked both of his guns and made sure that a live round was inside of the chambers. He then casually walked toward the group of people standing in front of the apartment building.

Once he made it in front of the group, he said, "Man, can I get somethin' for forty?"

Two of the young gang members looked him over for a full minute before one of them asked, "You a police, nigga?"

Shaking his head no, Clifford said, "Nah, man, I'm just tryin' to get some work for me and this freak bitch I got. So, can I get somethin' for forty or what?"

The two young men smiled at one another. "Yeah, I gots you right here, cuz. Where the money at, though?" asked the young man who seemed to be in charge.

Clifford stared at them for a moment then said, "Right here, cuz," as he pulled out his weapons and started firing at them simultaneously. He hit the two youngsters in their upper torsos then he turned his aim toward the others and started shooting at them.

Once both of his guns were empty, he turned and started running as fast as he could back toward the stolen getaway car. He was back inside of the car when he heard Li'l Bomb doing his cleanup. The sound of that AK-47 was loud as ever to Clifford as he waited for Li'l Bomb to finish handling his business. After what felt like forever but in actuality was just a couple of minutes, Li'l Bomb came running back to the car.

He climbed inside of the Cutlass, smiled and said, "Now, that's what I'm talkin' 'bout, cuz!" He started the car and drove off as calm as ever, as if they didn't have a care in the world. Once he had the car out into traffic, he turned toward Clifford and said, "You still a down nigga, O.G. I gots love for you, C-Baby."

Clifford smiled and said, "You better, loc!" They both started laughing as they went back to their 'hood.

Clifford leaned his head back on the seat and let what he had actually done sink in. *I've just committed murder again. I thought this part of my life was over with. I guess not, 'cause now that I've done it again, I'm ready for some more bodies. Taz and his crew are about to feel the wrath of an O.G. Hoover Crip,* he thought to himself with a smile on his face.

Chapter Five

Taz and Sacha walked into Tazneema's hospital room to see her. Mama-Mama and Tazneema's best friend, Lyla, were laughing about something. "What's so funny?" Taz asked as he stepped up to Mama-Mama and gave her a hug.

"This here crazy li'l white girl was tellin' me and 'Neema about how she wants to be a stripper! Can you believe her, Taz? A stripper! Her parents done paid all of this money for her to get a good education at OU, and she's talkin' 'bout becoming a stripper!"

Taz laughed and said, "Lyla, I know you're playin', right?"

Lyla, who was a small woman but built nicely, frowned at Taz. Her long, brown hair hung loosely past her shoulders as she sat down and crossed her long, slim legs. She was definitely a pretty young lady. Taz couldn't deny that fact. Lyla smiled and said, "Of course, I'm serious, Taz. It's not like I want to make a career out of it or anything like that. It's something that I want to try, though. It seems exciting to me."

"Come on, Lyla. You can't be serious," Tazneema said as she sat up on her bed.

"I don't see why not. I'm an adult, and I can do whatever I want to," she replied stubbornly.

Before Lyla could continue with her tirade, Tari entered the room with a huge smile on her face. "Guess who's getting ready to be cleared to go home tomorrow?" She gave Mama-Mama, Sacha and Taz a hug.

"Stop playing, Tari! Please tell me you're playing!" Tazneema said anxiously.

"I'm serious. The doctor told me a few minutes ago that he didn't see any reason for you to remain here. As long as you agree to stay off of your feet for a few more weeks, he's going to let you go home in the morning."

"Well, he won't have to worry about that none. She's comin' home with me, and ain't no way I'm gon' let her be on her feet!" Mama-Mama yelled happily.

"I know that's right, Mama-Mama!" Tari said with a smile on her face. She turned toward Taz and said, "We need to talk. It's kind of important."

Taz nodded, turned toward Tazneema and said, "Excuse me for a minute, y'all. I'll be right back."

Sacha smiled and said, "Don't you be trying to steal my man, Tari! I got my eyes on you, girl!"

Tari laughed and said, "He's too damn old for me now, girl. I got my sights set on a teeny bopper!"

They both started laughing as Taz followed Tari out into the lobby. She led him toward some chairs by the elevator bank, sat down and said, "We're moving in the morning. Won got the call he was waiting for last night. He wants us to be at your house in thirty minutes."

"Damn!"

"What's wrong?"

"I haven't had time to get at Sacha yet."

"Get at her about what? She already knows what's what, doesn't she?"

"Yeah . . . kinda."

"What you mean, kinda, Taz?"

"I promised her that I was done with this shit. I never told her about our decision to finish this shit up for Won."

Tari smiled and said, "You're going to be in some big trouble, sir."

"I know. Fuck!"

"Listen. Just tell her that there's something that we have to take care of, and that I'm going with you. She'll never think I'm going to be doing something wild with y'all."

Shaking his head no, he said, "Nah, I'm not goin' to lie to my Li'l Mama. I gots to keep it one hundred with her at all times."

"You sure?"

"Yeah, I'm sure."

Tari stared at Taz, her friend, her ex-lover, and said, "We have to get this hit over with, Taz."

"I know. But tell me something. Why are you so damn worried about Won letting me go?"

"'Cause I love you, stupid! I want you to have the happiness you've been looking for. You deserve it."

"But what about you? You deserve some happiness too."

"As long as you're happy, baby, then so am I."

He stared deeply into Tari's blue eyes and saw the love she had for him in them. *Damn! This girl really does love a nigga. If only I could have loved her the way she wants me to,* he thought.

Tari's long blonde hair was pulled tightly in a ponytail. She was looking extremely good in her nurse's uniform. For a white girl, she was packing some major ass . . . an ass that would make some sistas feel bad. She stood close to six foot barefoot, and was definitely one sexy-ass lady.

"I wish we could have—"

"Stop that shit, Taz. It is what it is. Everything happens for a reason, baby. I know you love me, and I know you're not in love with me. That's life. What matters most to me is that you're safe. Let's get this shit over with so we can move on and live happily ever after," Tari said with a smile on her face.

"You sure?"

"Yep!"

"You know it's gon' be hard workin' with you, right?"

"Don't worry 'bout me. I can handle my own. I'm a big girl, see?" She got out of her seat and slapped herself on her behind.

"Yeah, I see all of that ass you got, but ass has nothin' to do with what we're about to get into," he said seriously.

"Maybe you're right, but you never know what the power of a big ass can do for you."

Taz smiled and said, "You're crazy, girl! Look, let me go get at Sacha then I'll round up the crew so we can all get on point."

"All right. You know Bob made it home last night, huh?"

"Is that right?"

"Yep. Won told me before I left for work this morning."

"Cool. I'll holla at the nigga before we bounce."

"I'll see you in a little bit," she said as she turned and quickly hopped inside one of the elevators before the doors closed.

Taz went back inside of Tazneema's room and told her, "Baby girl, I want you to make sure that you do everything that Mama-Mama tells you, okay?"

"Since when has she not done everything that I tell her to, boy?" asked Mama-Mama.

"Come on, Mama-Mama. You know what I mean."

Tazneema could tell that Taz had something on his mind and asked, "Is everything all right, Taz? You look kinda funny."

"I'm good. I have to go out of town for a day or so to tie up some loose ends and stuff," he said as he cut his eyes in Sacha's direction.

"Don't worry, Taz. I'll be okay."

"I know, but I want you to know that I don't want you talkin' to that nigga Cliff, 'Neema."

"Taz," she whined.

"I mean it, 'Neema. I'm your father, and I expect for you to obey my wishes on this shit."

Before Tazneema could say a word, Lyla yelled, "Her father? How? When? Wait a minute! You're her *what*?"

Everyone inside of the room started laughing, except for Lyla. After the laughter had subsided a little, Tazneema said, "Taz is my daddy, Lyla, not my brother. Everyone thinks he's my big brother, so we let people think what they want."

"But, Tee-Tee, why didn't you tell me? I'm your roommate and best friend. I've actually been flirting with your father! Ugggh! That's like so gross!"

"Why, thank you, Lyla!" Taz said with a smile on his face.

"I didn't mean it like that, Taz. I just—"

Taz held up his hand and said, "I know, I know. I was just clownin'. But, look, I gots to go get ready. I'll give y'all a call to see how everything is when I get to where I'm goin', okay?"

"Okay, Taz. I love you."

"I love you too, baby girl. Please do as I asked you to."

"I will."

After giving Mama-Mama and Lyla a brief hug, Taz grabbed Sacha's hand and led her out of the room. Before he could say a word, she said, "Take me to my house, Taz. I think I'm going to stay there while you're out of town."

"You're that mad, huh, Li'l Mama?"

"What the fuck do you think?"

"I'm gon' keep it real with you, Li'l Mama. After we finish this mission, there will be one more, and then it's over with."

She laughed in his face and said, "You know what's so crazy about all of this shit, Taz? You actually believe that shit Won is hand-feeding your ass. You're never going to be through with this shit! Won's not going to let you. And you're not even man enough to say no to the big man! I'm telling you, Taz, you really need to think. 'Cause if you don't start using your head, you're going to lose everything you got. And I'm not just talking about me, I'm talking about everything!"

After Taz dropped Sacha off at her home, he drove back to his house and started to pack his bags. After he was finished, he grabbed the phone and called Bob's house.

Gwen answered on the second ring, sounding as happy as ever. "Hello!"

"What's good, Gwen? Where's my nigga at?" Taz asked with a smile on his face.

"He's right here, Taz. Hold on a sec."

Bob accepted the phone from Gwen and said, "What it do, my nigga?"

"Ain't shit. What's with you, dog? You good?"

"Yeah, I'm straight. Still a li'l sore and shit, though."

"Damn, dog! Why you didn't vest up like you was supposed to?" Taz asked seriously.

"I tripped the fuck out, gee. I mean, I didn't think about it until we were already on our way to do us. By then, I was like, fuck it! Everything is goin' to be everything, so I didn't say shit to y'all."

"That shit is crazy! You know better, dog. Where's that nigga Magoo at? I want to thank him for lookin' out for your crazy-ass."

"After he dropped me off, he said he was on his way to go get with Won. He said something about meeting up at your spot. What's up with that, my nigga?"

"We're almost to the finish line, dog. We got two more things to take care of. Then it's a done deal."

"How are y'all goin' to handle up? I won't be able to roll for at least a couple more weeks," Bob said with a hurt sound in his voice.

Bob's cracking voice damn near broke Taz down. "Don't worry about it, dog. We can handle it. Your lucky-ass gets to retire a li'l earlier than us," he said, trying to make Bob feel a little better.

"Fuck that shit! We're a six-deep crew! We trained for it always to be that way! And, no matter what, we don't move unless we all move!"

Taz took a deep breath and said, "Look, gee. We on the clock, and we don't have the time to wait until you can get back on your feet. So, it is what it is right now."

"So that nigga Magoo's taking my place, huh?"

"Fuck, no! You know damn well we don't know that nigga like that."

"Then who is it, Taz? Don't lie to me, my nigga."

Taz took another deep breath and said, "Tari."

Bob burst into laughter and said, "Now, ain't that somethin'! I done got replaced by a bitch! A white bitch at that!"

Bob's comment about Tari pissed Taz off, but instead of getting into it any further with him, Taz said, "Look, we're about to bounce. I just wanted to holla at ya to make sure that you're straight. We'll get over there to see you when we get back."

"Whatever, dog," Bob said sadly, and hung up the phone.

After Taz hung up the phone, he grabbed his bag and went downstairs to the den. He poured himself a drink from the bar and said, "Damn! It seems like all of my peoples are salty at me right now. I can't do any shit good at the moment."

There was a knock at his front door just as he finished draining his glass. He went to let the crew in. Keno, Bo-Pete, Red, Wild Bill and Tari filed inside of his house, and followed him back inside of the den.

"Have you gotten at Bob yet?" asked Wild Bill as he sat down on the sectional sofa.

"Yeah."

"Did you tell him?" Red asked with a smile on his face.

"Yeah."

Red started laughing and said, "I know that nigga is pissed the fuck off!"

Taz smiled and said, "That's puttin' it real mild like, dog."

"Aww, poor Bob's mad 'cause I get to play with his li'l friends!" Tari said playfully.

"It don't matter. This shit is almost over any fuckin' way," Keno said as he leaned against Taz's pool table.

Before anyone could respond, Won and Magoo knocked at Taz's front door. After Taz brought them inside of the den, Won said, "All right, peoples, this is how it goes down. Pitt runs the Bay Area out in Cali. His strength in the game comes from the heroin and the ya-yo. After y'all arrive out in Oakland, you will then go check into the Marriot Courtyard, located in downtown Oakland. Your rooms will already be reserved, as usual.

"Downstairs in the underground parking lot will be a blue Navigator parked for y'all. Your weapons will be inside of Taz's room under the bed, with all of the equipment you normally use.

"After y'all strap up, you are to drive to east Oakland. Take Main Street all the way into the East Side of town. Once you make it to Shaw Boulevard, you are to make a left turn, and on your immediate right, there will be a bail bondsman's office. Bypass it and bust a U-turn down the street.

"Once you have seen that everything is clear, you are to park behind the bondsman's office and go in from the rear. The back door will be unlocked, and the alarm will have already been tripped. Once you're inside, you'll see four safes. Combination are as follows . . ."

Won stopped and waited for Taz as he pulled out a pen and a pad so he could write the numbers down. When he saw that Taz was ready, he continued.

"The combination to the safe on the far left side of the room is three to the right, twenty-six to the left, and seventy-one to the right. The safe right next to it is forty-nine to the right, sixty-one to the left, and ninety-nine to the right. The next one is fifty-two to the right, fifteen to the left, and sixty-six to the right, and the last safe, which will be placed at the far right of the room, is thirty-three to the right, seventy-seven to the left, and eighty-four to the right. Each safe will contain at least twenty or more kilos of cocaine and heroin. If there is any money inside of any of them, it's yours.

"After you've emptied the safes, get back to your rooms and drop everything off. Your return flights are scheduled for early the next morning out of SFO out in San Francisco.

"Though this should be a smooth op, I still want y'all to be on your toes and sharp as ever. That nigga, Pitt is a smart nigga, and he may be trying to anticipate my moves. I doubt it though, but yet and still, I want y'all to be very careful. Any questions?"

"Yeah. How long are we gonna have to wait until we can handle that other nigga you told us about?" asked Keno.

"Once Pitt's spot is hit, I'm sure the shit is going to hit the fan. A lot of accusations will be flying, but with no proof behind them, everything will be good. Cash Flo' will then announce that he plans to back Pitt with his end of The Network. But that won't be enough, because I will have the position I need to challenge him. At that point, Pitt will know that I'm the one been making the power move. Knowing him, he's going to raise hell 'cause he is a ride-type nigga, and a damn fool once he becomes angry. But, like I said, it will be too late for him to do anything. When I get word of the meet that will take place, I'll notify y'all so you can then fly out and take care of Cash Flo'. That way, he will never be able to announce that he's supporting Pitt. I expect the meet to take place within thirty days after you finish this mission."

"Where?" asked Bo-Pete.

"I won't know that until twenty-four hours before the meeting. Most likely it will either be in Waco, Texas, or the West Coast. But I can't be certain of that just yet. Y'all will have to be on standby. Cash Flo's home base is the West, but he's down South around my way too. He's touchable because he's old school. He has a few bodyguards, but they won't be able to handle y'all." Won checked his watch and said, "Y'all have to get going. Your flight leaves in forty minutes out of Will Rogers."

"We're all flying together?" asked Red.

"Yep. There's no need for the normal routine. This is an in-and-out. Hit me up when you get back. If there are any chips, I will split it evenly between y'all and deposit it into your accounts in the islands."

Taz came from behind his bar, stared at Tari and asked her, "You ready for this, Tee?"

She stood up, smiled and said, "Let's go to work!"

Chapter Six

Tazneema, Lyla, Mama-Mama and Won were all sitting inside of Mama-Mama's living room, laughing at Lyla and her antics. Lyla was so determined to become a stripper that she actually came up with a stage name for herself. She told everyone inside the room that she wanted to be called "White Chocolate."

After Tazneema stopped laughing, she asked her, "Why in the heck did you choose a name like that?"

Lyla smiled slyly and said, "Because I'm white, obviously, and I just loves me some chocolate!"

"Oh, my Lord!" Mama-Mama said as she slapped her palm against her forehead.

Won started laughing and said, "All right, ladies, that's about all I can take! I'm outta here! Are you straight, 'Neema? Do you need anything before I leave?"

"I'm fine, Uncle Won. You know I'm in good hands with Mama-Mama," she said seriously.

"Hey! What about me?" cried Lyla.

"Oh, yeah. And you know White Chocolate here is going to take good care of me."

They laughed some more as Won stood and said, "All right then. I gots me a flight to catch. I'll make sure I get back this way real soon to check on you, baby girl. Remember, if you need anything, call me. You still have the numbers?"

She smiled and answered, "Yep!"

"Good," Won said, and gave her a kiss and a light hug. He then stepped over to Mama-Mama, gave her a hug and a kiss also and said, "Do you need anything before I go, Mama-Mama?"

"Go on and catch your plane, Won. We're just fine over here," she happily said.

He smiled at her and said, "Okay, bye, y'all!" As he stepped outside of the house, he couldn't help but wonder if Lyla was serious about becoming a stripper. *She'd make a nice chunk of change,* he thought with a smile on his face.

It was a little after ten p.m. when Taz and the crew made it to their hotel room at the Marriot Courtyard, in downtown Oakland. Taz checked his diamond-studded Cartier wrist-watch and said, "All right, y'all, strap up so we can get this shit over with."

Each member of the crew grabbed a silenced 9 mm pistol from the bag that Taz had pulled out from under the bed in his room. After checking and rechecking their weapons, each one of them gave Taz a nod of their head.

"Y'all good?" asked Taz.

"Yep," answered Red.

"Ready," said Keno.

"Strapped," said Wild Bill.

"Locked and loaded," said Bo-Pete.

"Let's do this," Tari said as she jammed her pistol in the small of her back.

They filed out of the room and went straight toward the stairway that led to the underground parking area. Once they made it to the blue Navigator, Keno said, "It amazes the hell out of me every fuckin' time Won does this shit."

"What?" asked Red as he climbed inside the SUV.

"How he has everything already set up when we get to wherever we have a mission."

Tari laughed and said, "You should be used to it by now, Keno."

"I know, but the shit is kinda on the creepy side for real. I be feelin' like that nigga's gon' pop up any minute and tell us that we're not handlin' our business right or some shit."

Taz laughed as he started the ignition, and said, "Man, would you kill that silly-ass shit?"

Everyone inside of the truck got a good laugh at Keno's expense as Taz pulled the Navigator out of the parking lot.

*****

Back in Oklahoma City, Won was talking on his cell phone as he boarded his flight back to Los Angeles. "Yeah, they should already be there by now. By the time I touch down, they should be back at their rooms waiting to get up outta there in the morning. I'll give you a holla after everything is everything. Remember, if you hear from me in any form other than the norm, then you know what needs to be done next," he said to whomever he was speaking with on the other line.

After he closed his cell phone, he found his seat on the airplane and got himself comfortable. *I got your ass, Pitt! Either way this falls, I got your ass!* he thought to himself as he closed his eyes and began to relax.

Taz made a U-turn and headed back toward the bail bondsman's office and said, "Here we go, y'all. Y'all know the drill. Watch your ass at all times. Tari, I want you right next to me at all times."

"Fuck that weak shit, Taz! Let's do this shit! Stop worrying about me. I'm good."

He smiled at her and repeated, "Right by my fuckin' side, Tee! I ain't playin'!"

"Whatever!" she said as they all jumped out of the SUV with their weapons held down at their sides.

Taz led the way to the back entrance, and like always, the door was unlocked just as Won said it would be. He opened the door slowly and entered the back of the office. He saw the safes, and quickly stepped toward the one on the far left of the room. Tari was right next to him as she began to dial the combination to the safe next to the one he was opening.

Keno and Bo-Pete stood by the door and watched their backs as Red and Wild Bill were opening the other two safes. Each of them had large duffel bags for the drugs as they quickly emptied the safes and filled their bags.

Tari finished emptying her safe first and dragged her bag toward the back door. Keno took the bag from her and carried it back outside to the Navigator. Tari then took his spot as sentry, and waited for the others to finish up.

Taz was next to finish. He slid his bag to Bo-Pete, who grabbed it and took it outside to the truck, while Taz took his place at the door next to Tari.

After Red and Wild Bill had finished emptying the last two safes, they carried their bags past Taz and Tari as they headed toward the truck. Taz and Tari brought up the rear as they followed them out of the office with their guns ready.

Once everyone was inside of the truck, Keno eased out of the parking lot and into the late evening traffic. Mission completed.

By the time Won's flight had arrived at LAX, he received a call on his cell. He smiled as he walked out of the terminal and toward a waiting all-black stretch limousine.

As he stepped inside of the limo, he said to the person who called him, "All right, after they leave, make sure that you hurry up and get everything out of that room. I'm sure Pitt is going to be on the warpath, and he's definitely going to be checking all local hotels and shit. Call me when you're finished." He then closed his phone.

"One down, and Cash Flo, to go!" he said aloud as he reached to his left and grabbed a bottle of XO from the mini bar.

Mama-Mama was asleep, and Tazneema was bored. She knew that she needed time to heal from her wound, but she missed her man. Clifford was her heart, and she knew that he loved her just as much as she loved him. It was so hard to accept the fact that she had lost her child. She prayed hard that Cliff wouldn't be upset with her. *I have to talk to him,* she thought as she went into her bedroom, grabbed the cordless phone from its base and quickly dialed Clifford's home number. She didn't realize that she was holding her breath until she felt a tightening in her stomach. She exhaled just as Clifford answered the line.

"Hello."

"Hi, baby! How are you?" she asked him.

"'Neema?" Clifford asked excitedly.

"Yes, it's me, baby."

"How are you doing? Are you all right? When are you getting out of the hospital? Is the baby all right?"

"If you'd let me get a word in, I'll answer all of your questions! Dang!"

"I'm sorry, 'Neema. Go right ahead."

"Okay. First off, I'm at Mama-Mama's house. I came home from the hospital earlier today. The doctors said that I'm going to be okay as long as I stay off my feet for a few more weeks."

"As to the baby . . . I lost it, Cliff. The baby couldn't withstand the stress of the surgery. The bullet traveled further than the doctors had anticipated, and they had to remove it from my back. I have a real ugly scar on my back now, so I guess I won't be getting any of those special back licks of yours anymore."

He smiled and said, "Baby, I can't wait to be able to lick all over that delicious body of yours. I love you, 'Neema. You know that, right?"

She sighed heavily and said, "Yes, I know. And I love you too, Cliff. But we're going to have to be very careful. Taz wants your head cut off, so we're going to have to keep it on the low-low for a little while, at least until I can talk some sense into him."

"You're never going to be able to talk any sense into Taz, baby. He hates me."

"Trust me, when it comes to me, Taz always lets me have my way. It will be a little harder than usual, but eventually he'll give in and let me do me," she replied confidently.

"Why didn't you tell me he was your father, 'Neema?"

"Why didn't you tell me that you already knew who he was? You actually used to go with Sacha?"

"Not really. We went out a few times and were starting to get close, but your father came into the picture and everything changed. After that, I was real bitter with the both of them because I thought I really loved Sacha. That is until I met you. Once we got to know one another, my feelings for Sacha evaporated with the quickness. It was all about you, 'Neema.

You have to believe me when I say this, 'cause it's so true. I never lied to you when I told you I was in love with you."

"*Was?*"

"That's not what I mean, baby. I love you so much that it's killing me that I can't hold you in my arms through all of this mess."

She smiled and said, "I love you too, Cliff. There's no need to trip. I'm good. Now, let me go before I wake up Mama-Mama. I'll give you a call some time tomorrow, okay?"

"Okay. Tell me. Does Mama-Mama hate me too?"

"You're not on her favorite persons list right now, but don't worry. She's just as much of a pushover for me as Taz is. She'll come around. I love you, baby!"

"I love you too," Clifford said before he hung up the phone.

After Tazneema put the cordless phone back on its base, she smiled as she climbed on her bed. "Cliff still loves me, and I'm not letting anyone get in the way of our relationship—not even my daddy!" she said aloud as she stared at a picture on her dresser of her and her father.

Chapter Seven

Taz and the rest of the crew arrived back in Oklahoma City a little after two in the afternoon. They went directly to Taz's home so they would be able to check their accounts and check in with Won.

Taz smiled as he walked inside of his home and saw Precious and Heaven as they ran toward him with their tongues happily hanging out of their mouths. He rubbed the both of them under their chins as he walked toward his den. The Dobermans knew better than to follow him to the den, so they sat down right outside of the den and watched as the rest of the crew followed Taz.

Tari stopped, knelt next to the dogs and rubbed their chins tenderly and said, "How's my babies been doing? You miss me?" She played with them briefly then stood and went into the den with the others.

Taz grabbed his laptop from behind his bar and set it on the pool table. Once he opened it, he started punching its keys. When his account came onto the screen, he smiled and said, "I have an extra two hundred gees in my account."

"That means there was what, a li'l over a ticket in those safes?" asked Wild Bill.

"Looks like it. Here, check yours and see if y'all have the same in y'all's accounts," Taz said as he passed the laptop to Wild Bill.

Everyone checked their accounts, and they each had two hundred thousand dollars added into their offshore accounts in the Cayman Islands.

Tari smiled and said, "Well, since I don't have a fancy account over in the Islands, I'll have to get at Won and see what he has set up for me."

"Don't trip, Tee. I'm about to get at him right now," Taz said as he pulled out his cell and called Won.

While Taz was on the phone, Red said, "Call that nigga Bob and see what he's up to."

Keno laughed and said, "That nigga is probably layin' up with his broad, gettin' his freak on."

"How the fuck is that nigga gon' be gettin' his freak on with that damn shit bag on his side?" laughed Bo-Pete.

Taz, who was laughing also, said, "Excuse me, O.G., these silly-ass niggas are over here clownin' about that nigga Bob. What it do?"

"Everything is everything out his way. Have y'all checked y'all's accounts yet?" asked Won.

"Yeah, everything is good, all except for Tee. She's wondering where her chips are."

Won started laughing and said, "Tell your li'l snowbunny that I said her ends have been deposited into her credit union account. I know she didn't think I was going to forget about her."

"Nah, she knew you'd have it taken care of. So, now what?"

"Like I told y'all, we wait. When I get work, y'all will be notified. The last leg of this is almost over with, Babyboy. I suspect Pitt is somewhere having a fucking fit right about now," Won said as he started laughing.

"Do you think he'll try to get at you before we're able to move on that other nigga?"

"Nope. If it was that easy, I would have taken him out of the game years ago. You see, by me being a council member, he has to have some major proof to get approval to move against me. And that's something he doesn't have. So, don't worry about me, Babyboy. I'm good. Y'all, stay on point. I'll hit y'all when it's time. Out!" Won said, and hung up the phone.

After Taz closed his cell, he told everyone inside of the den what Won had just told him. "So, I guess y'all can go on to the pad and chill out. When everything is everything, he's goin' to get at us."

"What's up for the weekend? Y'all want to hit the club or what?" asked Bo-Pete.

"I'm wit' it," said Red as he got out of his seat.

"Fuck it! Why not?" added Wild Bill.

"I haven't been to a club in years. It might just be fun. Count me in," Tari said with a grin on her face.

"We move as a unit, so you already know I'm in," said Taz.

As everyone started filing out of the den, Tari stopped Taz and said, "What's up with you and Sacha? Are y'all beefing like that?"

"How do you know that we're beefin' at all?"

"You better go on with that silly shit, boy. You know damn well I can tell when you have something heavy on your mind."

"Have you forgotten that my daughter has been shot recently? And the nigga that did it is still breathing? What? That's not heavy enough for you?"

"Stop lying to me, Taz. You know I know better. Call her and let her know we made it back. That lady loves you, boy, and you know you love her just as much." She kissed him lightly on his cheek and added, "Saying I'm sorry really isn't that bad, macho man!"

He smiled at her and said, "Fuck you, white girl!"

She gave a wave of her hand. "I may be a white girl, but there are a whole lot of sistas out there that wish they had an ass like this one!" she said as she slapped herself on her behind.

Taz started laughing and shaking his head as he watched her leave his home. He stood in his doorway and watched as each of his friends climbed inside of their respective vehicles.

Red pulled out of the driveway in his all-black Chevy Tahoe. Bo-Pete followed in his all-black Navigator. Wild Bill was behind him in his all-black Durango. Keno was behind Wild Bill's truck in his all-black Range Rover, and then there was Tari as she climbed into her all-black BMW truck.

What's up with us with all of this black shit? Taz asked himself as if this was the first time he ever realized that the entire crew drove all-black SUV's as their primary vehicles. Even though he had an S-Class 600 Mercedes and a Bentley Azure parked inside of his four-car garage, he also owned an all-black Denali.

Life was good for them all. They had enough money to live the rest of their lives in extreme comfort. Together, the crew was worth more than a billion dollars. *Won lived up to his part of the deal, so it was only right that they finish this shit for him,* thought Taz as he turned and went upstairs to his bedroom.

Sacha stared at the phone as it continued to ring. She saw Taz's number on the caller ID box, and silently thanked God for letting them make it back safely. She knew he'd call her once he had gotten back, but she just wasn't sure if she was ready to talk to him yet. Since her first doctor's appointment for her pregnancy was in the morning, she knew she would have to speak to him. She took a deep breath, picked up the phone and said, "Hello."

"What up, Li'l Mama?"

"Hi, Taz."

"You still mad, huh?"

"What do you think?"

"Do you still want me to go to the doctor with you in the morning?"

"Do you still want to go?"

"Come on, Li'l Mama. What kind of shit are you on? You know ain't nothin' changed with me. This shit is all on you!"

"I know you're not trying to twist this shit on me, Mister Taz! I'm the only one using some common sense in this crazy shit you have me mixed up in!"

"Mixed up in? You're not mixed up in any fuckin' thing! I told you, my business doesn't have anything to do with you. But, no-o-o! You wanted to know everything about what I do. You just had to know what was what. And now that you do, you're trippin'. You see, that's why I didn't want to tell your ass shit in the first fuckin' place!"

"Stop yelling at me, Taz!"

He took a deep breath to try and calm his nerves, and said, "Look, Li'l Mama. You are my now, my tomorrow, my everything, and I love you more than words will ever be able to truly express. But you gots to let this shit go! I'm gon' do me and finish what I've started. Accept it, 'cause it's not goin' to change nothin' if you don't. If you can't accept this, then you can't accept me and who I really am. Now, what time is your appointment again?"

"It's at ten."

"Do you want me to pick you up, or do you want me to just meet you?"

Sounding real professional, she said, "Yes, Taz, you can meet me at my doctor's office. It's located on the south side, right off of the highway on May Avenue."

His temper rising again, Taz gritted his teeth and asked, "So, that's how it's gon' be, huh?"

"Bye, Taz!" Sacha said and hung up the phone on him.

Taz hung up the phone and quickly dialed another number. When Won answered, Taz said, "Something is really puzzling me, O.G."

"What's that, Babyboy?"

"Earlier you said that Pitt couldn't do nothin' 'cause there would be too much drama behind it without any proof."

"Yeah. So?"

"If that's the case, then how are you goin' to pull off the next demo with Tari doin' her thang on that nigga Cash Flo'?"

"This is the end game, Babyboy. Some of the rules are being changed at this part of the game. Don't worry yourself about the particulars. I gots this. All I'm needing from your end is to make sure that Tari will be put in place so she can do what needs to be done."

"All right. Man, with all of this shit on my plate, I'm just tryin' not to miss shit, you know what I'm sayin'?"

"Yeah, I know. I've just been informed by one of the council members that Pitt is on the fucking warpath. So, I guess he's been notified of his losses out in Oakland. I should be getting a call soon, so I'll keep you posted."

"That's cool."

"All right then. Out!"

"Out!" Taz said. He hung up the phone feeling a little bit better about what was going on. "This shit is crazy," he said to himself as he relaxed back on his bed.

***

Out in Northern California, Pitt, a stocky, brown-skinned man, was sitting at his desk in his plush office right outside the city of Oakland, rubbing his neatly trimmed beard. Though he had a smile on his face, he was currently furious. He couldn't believe that Won had finally made his move against him. He didn't have any proof, but he was positive that Won had his place burglarized. *Won has been putting this thing down for years now. I've always known it, but I've never been able to prove it,* Pitt thought as he sat back and continued to watch the video surveillance tape of his bail bondsman office in East Oakland.

All of a sudden, the screen on Pitt's fifty-five-inch plasma screen went fuzzy. "What the fuck?" he yelled as he raised himself out of his comfortable leather chair. He stepped quickly toward the television and started pushing the buttons on the DVD player. It took close to four, maybe five minutes before the screen resumed back to the footage of the back room of the bondsman's office. "That nigga is good that he had a plug in my shit! How the fuck else would the camera go blank for a few minutes?" he yelled as he went back behind his desk and grabbed the phone.

He lit a freshly rolled Cuban cigar and chomped on it furiously as the phone rang. When the other line was answered, he said, "Cash Flo', we need to meet."

"What's going on now, Pitt? I'm tied up on some very serious negotiations with them dagos out East."

"Fuck that shit! It's Won! Won is the fucker whose been robbing us blind for the last God knows how many fucking years!"

"What the hell are you talking about, Pitt?" asked Cash Flo'.

"Look, I'm on my way down your way. Have some of your people scoop me from LAX in an hour and a half."

"All right, but I hope when you get here you have something solid for us to move on, 'cause if you're wasting my time, Pitt—"

"I know, I know. Kill that shit, Flo'. This is your boy. You know I know the rules to this game. I'll see you in a li'l bit," Pitt said. He hung up the phone and quickly left his office.

As he rode the elevator down to the underground parking area of his office building, his thoughts were of Won. *I don't know how you've been pulling this shit off, nigga, but you fucked up by ever fucking with me. Whoever turned against me in my camp is going to be found. Then I'll have the proof I need to smash your ass,* he thought to himself as he pulled out his keys and climbed inside of his 2006 Jaguar, and sped out of the parking area on his way to the airport.

Chapter Eight

The next morning, Taz met Sacha at her doctor's office. He had to smile when he saw her looking so delicious sitting in the waiting room. She was wearing a lavender Baby Phat jogging suit, with a pair of matching Nike tennis shoes on her small feet. Her shoulder-length hair was looking as silky as ever, pulled back tightly in a long ponytail. Her smooth, brown skin was flawless as always, and at that moment Taz knew that he could never let this woman get away from him. After he was seated next to her, he said, "What's up, Li'l Mama?"

"Good morning, Taz," she said in the same businesslike tone she'd used with him the night before.

"Come on, Li'l Mama. Can't we call a truce? I'm not with the simpin' sucka shit. It's just not in me. I love you, though, so I'm willin' to swallow my pride a li'l."

"A little?" she asked with a hint of a smile on her face.

"Yeah, a li'l," he said as he held up his thumb and index fingers inches apart from one another.

Damn, I love this man! she thought to herself. To him she said, "Taz, I really thought I'd be able to deal with how you live, but I can't. You don't know how terrified I am while you're out of town doing that shit. I can't take it! I just can't!"

"I understand, Li'l Mama. That's why I'm about to get out of this shit. I know you don't believe me, but it's almost over. To be totally honest with you, I don't even have another mission to go on. All I have to do is make sure that a person gets where they need to be. After that, everything is a done deal. The party will be over. I know you don't trust Won or believe that he's goin' to stop needing me for things, but I need for you to believe in me. I haven't lied to you since we've met, and I don't intend on starting either. I'm not goin' to lose you over this li'l shit, Li'l Mama. Whatever it takes to prove it to you, I'm willing to do it. I can't take it without you next to me in my bed at night. It just don't feel right."

Sacha smiled as his words weakened her resolve. "Do you give me your word that after you get whomever where they need to be that there will be no more out-of-town trips?"

"My word, Li'l Mama."

"Do you give me your word that you will not under any circumstances do anything illegal for Won ever again?"

"My word."

"Do you love me, Taz?"

"You know I do, baby. With all of my soul."

"Then don't you ever break the promises you've just made to me. Because if you do, I'll never forgive you. Do you understand me, Taz Good? I'll *never* forgive you!"

"I understand, baby. Now, can I have a kiss or somethin'?"

Just as they were about to kiss one another, the receptionist said, "Excuse me, but you two can go in to see Doctor Moses now."

Sacha smiled and said, "Come on, let's go see about our child."

Taz smiled brightly and said, "I'm right behind you, Li'l Mama."

Mama-Mama was up early as usual, cooking Tazneema a big breakfast.

Tazneema was sitting at the dining room table watching her grandmother prepare what looked like a meal for ten instead of two. She smiled and said, "Mama-Mama, why do you always have to cook so much food?"

"'Cause Mama-Mama loves to cook. Whatever's left over, I'll just take it over to the church so the good Reverend can eat as much as he wants to."

"Hmph! I think you and the good Reverend gots something going on with each other!"

Mama-Mama turned around from the stove, smiled and said, "If we do, you'll never know." They both started laughing as the telephone started ringing.

"I'll get it, Mama-Mama," Tazneema said as she slowly rose from her seat and went into the living room to answer the phone. "Hello."

"Hi, baby! You miss me?" asked Clifford.

Tazneema smiled and said, "You know I do. You shouldn't be calling here, Cliff. What if Mama-Mama answered the phone?"

"I would have asked for someone else, like I had the wrong number. What are you doing today?"

"Nothing but resting. I'm not supposed to be on my feet for at least a few more weeks."

"Man, I wish I could see you."

"Me too. But, look, I have to go. Mama-Mama is in the kitchen making me something to eat. I'll give you a call later on."

"You promise?"

"I promise."

"Tell me you love me."

Tazneema gave a quick peek toward the kitchen and quickly said, "I love you! Bye!" After she hung up the phone, Mama-Mama asked her who was that who had called. "That was Lyla, Mama-Mama," she lied as she walked back into the kitchen.

After the doctor confirmed that Sacha was indeed two months pregnant and in good health, Taz and Sacha left the doctor's office in a very good mood. "Do you want to go get something to eat?" asked Taz.

"Mmmm-hmm. I'm starving," Sacha replied as they stepped outside.

"All right, this is what we'll do. I'll follow you back to your place. Then we'll head on out to Mama-Mama's for some of her good-ass breakfast food."

"How do you know if she's made anything?"

Laughing, he said, "Come on, Li'l Mama. If there's one thing that I know for sure in this world, it's that my mother has been up, since maybe the crack of dawn, cooking something to eat, especially with 'Neema being over there. By the time 'Neema gets back on her feet, she's goin' to be so fat that it's goin' to take a hell of a lot of working out to get that weight off of her ass."

They both laughed as Sacha climbed inside of her car. "In that case, let's go then! You know I'm eating for two now!"

After Taz closed her door for her, he smiled and said, "I'm right behind you, Li'l Mama!"

Tazneema had just finished eating when she heard Taz's loud music thumping from his truck. She smiled and said, "Here comes your son, Mama-Mama!"

"I wish that boy would turn that damn music down. He acts like he's deaf or something," Mama-Mama said as she came out of the kitchen wiping her hands on a dishtowel.

Taz and Sacha came inside of the house, hand in hand. Taz smiled when he saw his mother and said, "What's up, Mama-Mama?"

"What's up with you, boy? Why in the hell do you always have that music of yours up so damn loud?"

"You know I live to gets my bump on," Taz said as he turned toward Tazneema, winked his eye at her and said, "What's up with you? You straight?"

Nodding her head yes, Tazneema said, "I'm good. A li'l bored, but good."

"At least you're bored here at Mama-Mama's instead of that stuffy old hospital room," Sacha said as she sat down next to Tazneema on the couch.

"I know. So, what brought you two way out here?"

"Sacha was hungry, and I knew Mama-Mama had something on the stove, so I brought her over here so she could pig out a li'l," Taz said with a smile on his face.

"Girl, get yourself in this kitchen and come make yourself a plate. I gots plenty of food in here for your butt," Mama-Mama said as she turned and went back inside of the kitchen.

After Sacha followed Mama-Mama into the kitchen, Taz asked Tazneema, "How do you feel about Sacha? Do you really like her?"

"Yeah, she's cool. I see you two are getting deep, huh?"

"Yeah. I've asked her to be wifey."

"For real? That's cool, Taz!"

"She pregnant too."

"What? You mean to tell me that after all of these years you're finally about to give me a li'l brother or sister?"

He smiled at his daughter and said, "Looks like it. I just want you to know that, no matter what, you will always be my baby."

"I already know that, Taz."

"And no matter what changes I make in my life, your mother's memory will forever be in my heart. I've finally found someone who I can love and honor, but the love that I have for your mother is forever."

With her eyes watering, Tazneema said, "I know, Daddy. I know."

"*Daddy*? Where did that come from?" he asked with a smile on his face.

"Shoot, you got me getting all emotional and stuff. It kinda just came out. What? You don't like it when I call you Daddy?"

He smiled and said, "It's been so long that it shocked me a li'l bit. You can call me whatever you like, Babygirl. You know that."

"Since you're in such a good mood, I need to talk to you about something without you going off on the deep end on me, Daddy."

"What's up?"

"I spoke to Cliff last night and this morning. I really need to see him. I love him, and we plan on getting back together when I get back on my feet."

Taz's smile turned to a frown quickly when he heard Tazneema mention Cliff's name. "There is no way in hell that I'm going to allow you to fuck with that nigga, 'Neema! Do you understand me? Don't you fuck with me on this shit! That nigga ain't shit, and there is no fuckin' way that I'm going to let you be with that nigga!"

"You can't stop me! I'm a grown-ass woman! How the fuck are you gon' step in and try to play the *daddy* role now? You passed them duties to Mama-Mama when shit got too rough for you, remember? Now, just because you don't like who I've chosen as my mate, you want to act all 'father knows best,' and shit! Fuck that! I love that man, and I am going to be with him whether you like it or not, *Daddy*!"

Before Taz could respond to Tazneema's outburst, Mama-Mama and Sacha came back into the living room. "What the hell are you two screaming about?" yelled Mama-Mama.

"Your son here thinks he can run my life and tell me who I can and can't see!" screamed Tazneema.

"Nah! Your damn granddaughter has gotten too damn fast for her li'l ass! She thinks I'm goin' to let her be with that nigga, Cliff. I'm tellin' you, Mama-Mama, you need to talk some sense into this girl before I beat some into her ass!"

"Watch your mouth in my house, Taz! Now, 'Neema, you know we don't particularly care for that man. He done wrong in my home and almost took you away from us."

"But, Mama-Mama, it was Taz's fault! If he would have left Cliff alone, he would have never pulled that trigger!"

"So, it's my fault that the nigga shot you, 'Neema? Is that how you truly see it, baby girl?" Taz asked calmly with a hurt expression on his face.

Tazneema stared at her father, and though she knew the words she was about to speak would hurt him, at that point and time she didn't give a damn. She loved her man, and she was going to stand behind him no matter what. "You damn skippy! I don't hate you for it, so you shouldn't hate my man. You have your future wife with you, and y'all have a baby on the way. I'm happy for the both of you, so why can't you be happy for what me and Cliff plan to share with each other?"

"Baby? Wife? What the hell is she talking about, Taz?" asked Mama-Mama.

"Sacha's pregnant, and I've asked her to marry me, Mama-Mama," Taz said quickly. He took a deep breath and told Tazneema, "You can go against the grain if you want to, but just remember, once you step over that line, you're goin' to have to live with that for the rest of your life. I left you in the loving care of my mother because I knew I couldn't give you the balance you would need in this crazy-ass world. Some-times I regret the decisions I've made, and sometimes I know that leaving you with Mama-Mama was the best decision I've ever made. I love you, 'Neema. You're my only child. Please, don't go against me."

Tazneema was shocked . . . shocked because she had never heard her father speak to her in this manner. Her anger overrode all rationality though. She was in love, and she had the right to be with whomever she wanted. And she wanted Cliff. It was as simple as that. "I love you too, Daddy. But I also love my man. Whether you accept it or not, I'm going to keep loving Cliff."

Taz's voice turned stone-cold as he asked, "Are you sure you want to go against the grain, Tazneema?"

"I'm standing behind my man, Taz," she replied just as coldly."

Taz nodded and said, "So be it. When he dies a slow death, I hope you won't hate me."

"If he does die, I will hate you for the rest of my life, Taz."

"So be it."

"You two, stop this nonsense right this minute! Taz, you are not going to do anything to that man! Do you hear me?" yelled Mama-Mama.

"Yeah, I hear you, Mama-Mama. But you and I both know that when my mind is made up, no one is goin' to change it. I'm in no way tryin' to be disrespectful, but that nigga has to die by my hand."

Taz then turned his attention back toward his daughter and said, "I have given you all of the love and financial support any child could hope for. I know my not being around all of the time has hurt you, but it was for your own protection. You don't know me, 'Neema. You don't know what I'm really capable of. I've always sworn that I would never let you see that part of me. But you have now forced my hand, and because of that, you are about to see a part of your flesh and blood that you're going to wish you had never seen. So, warn your man. Let him know that the coldest nigga in Oklahoma City is comin' after his ass." He grabbed Sacha's hand and said, "Come on, let's bounce, Li'l Mama."

As they walked out of Mama-Mama's house, Tazneema cried in her grandmother's lap. "Why? Why can't he let me be happy with Cliff, Mama-Mama?"

"He's your father, baby. All he wants to do is protect you from the evils of this world."

"But Cliff isn't evil, Mama-Mama! He's a good man!" she cried.

"Not in your daddy's eyes, baby. I know my son better than anyone in this world. When he lost your mother, he was on the verge of going crazy. To this very day, I don't know exactly what brought him back to me. I'm thankful to God that he's still here and has done so well for himself. I'm no fool, and I know that he got all of that fancy stuff from doing something illegal. He has taken care of the both of us for a very long time now. I have to respect him for that. You have to respect him for it also. If he doesn't want you to be with that man, then you should listen to your father and not be with him."

Tazneema tried to speak, but Mama-Mama stopped her with a raised hand and continued. "Wait, child, and hear me out first. I understand that you are all grown up and all, but that man hurt you because he tried to kill your father. He tried to take my only child away from me. If he had succeeded in doing that, I would have killed him myself. Do you hear me, baby? I would have committed murder behind the death of my only child. So, how do you think Taz feels about that man shooting *his* only child? Put yourself in his place. How would you feel?"

"I understand his anger, Mama-Mama. When I was lying up in that hospital bed, I was mad at Cliff too. I never thought I'd want to see him again, let alone be with him. But after thinking about it, I realized that I still love him. It's as simple as that. I love him, Mama-Mama. I love my daddy too. I know how cold Taz is. I've heard the stories about how he was a killer, and how everyone around the city fears him. He doesn't know I know, but I know. Even though I respect what he has done for me, he has no right to try and dictate how I live my life. None whatsoever! I love him, that fact is true, but I'm not scared of him, Mama-Mama. If he can kill, so can I."

Chapter Nine

Pitt was picked up at Los Angeles International Airport by a chauffeured limousine. It took the driver less than twenty minutes to arrive in front of a gigantic office building in downtown L.A. Once the driver opened the door, Pitt slid easily out of the limousine and marched inside of the building. He rode the elevator to the twenty-first floor. The door to the elevator was barely open as he squeezed his stocky frame through it. He stepped quickly toward the receptionist, who was staring at him as if he had lost his mind.

"May I help you, sir?" asked the receptionist.

"I'm here to see Cash—I mean Mr. Harris. My name is Pitt."

"Is Mr. Harris expecting you, sir?"

"Call him and find out!" Pitt said arrogantly as he pulled out one of his hand-rolled Cuban cigars.

The receptionist rolled her eyes slightly as she pressed the intercom button and said, "Excuse me, Mr. Harris. There's a Mr. Pitt out here to see you."

"Send him in," Mr. Harris replied over the intercom.

When the receptionist raised her head to speak with Pitt, he had already stepped past her and was on his way inside of Mr. Harris' office. *Prick!* she said to herself as she went back to her work.

Pitt stepped inside of the office and said, "What's up, Cash Flo'?"

"You already know what's up. What do you have to tell me that's so damn important, Pitt? You know I've been caught up with those dagos in the East. On top of that, them bitch-ass Colombians are trippin' too. They are actually trying to up the price on The Network 'cause they feel we're not getting enough work from them. Can you believe that shit? We've been getting anywhere from thirty to thirty-five hundred kilos a month from them, and they say that's not enough! I'm telling you, Pitt, that's one of the reasons I'm about ready to get out of this shit. Anyway, what's the deal with you?"

Pitt smiled at the small man sitting behind the large cherry wood desk and said, "It's that nigga Won. I told you a long time ago that it was that fool. Won has been the nigga responsible for all of those mysterious-ass burglaries and licks the rest of the council have been taking."

"Do you have any proof, Pitt? Because without any solid evidence, we won't be able to move on this. You know that, right?"

"Yeah, I know. I don't have any yet, but I will soon. You see, that nigga has finally fucked with the wrong council member. I knew sooner or later he would try to get at me, but you see my clique is too tight. No one has the heart to cross the Pitt."

Cash Flo' smiled and said, "I thought you told me that you just got hit for a nice chunk."

"I did. Yeah, someone finally got enough nuts to cross me, but that's a good thing. I've set up a meet for my entire crew out in Oaktown. At this meeting, I will find out exactly who it was that crossed me, and in turn, they will tell me the person who put them up to it. Once I get that information, I'm sending a heavy hit squad at that nigga Won."

"Whoa! Hold up a second, bad boy! How do you know that it will be Won that your people give up? What if he had someone else get at them? Then what are you going to do?" Cash Flo' asked.

"If Won was involved, I will get his name sooner or later, Flo'. All I want to know is, do I have your support on this shit?"

Cash Flo' leaned back in his comfortable leather chair and thought about what Pitt had just asked him. He stroked his salt-and-pepper beard slowly as he stared at his longtime friend and business partner. They went back as far as the late seventies, when Pitt was a teenager out in Northern California.

Pitt was known as a hothead sometimes, but only when he felt that he was dead to the right. His position over the years had grown inside of The Network only because Cash Flo' felt he was worthy of the promotions. *If I give him my support on this and he's wrong, there's going to be a war within The Network,* Cash Flo' thought. Then he said, "I'm going to give you my support, Pitt, but only if you're right on this shit. If you're wrong and you go falsely accusing Won, you know what kind of position that will put you in. I won't back you if you're wrong, but if you are indeed correct about Won, then you will have everything you need to deal with the situation accordingly."

"Always got to protect ya neck, huh?"

Cash Flo' smiled and said, "Always."

"Cool. I ain't got a problem with that. I'll get at you when I have that nigga's name," Pitt said as he raised up out of his seat and left the office.

Cash Flo' sat back in his chair and gave some more thought to this situation. *What the fuck would Won have to gain from doing all of this shit? He's already a fucking millionaire a few times over,* he thought to himself. Then, as if a brick hit him, the answer came to him. "Power! If this shit is true, Won's on a fucking power trip!" he said aloud as he grabbed the phone on his desk and started dialing.

By the time Taz and Sacha made it to his house, he was so upset, he could hardly think straight. He went downstairs to his indoor gym and started working out furiously. He did some curls with some lightweight dumbbells to loosen up. Afterward, he went to the curl bar and started repping some heavy weight. After an hour of this, his entire body was dripping wet with sweat, so he went upstairs and jumped into the shower.

While he was showering, he was trying his best to think of a way to get Sacha to tell him where Clifford lived. He knew she wasn't going to tell him, but he had to try to get that information out of her.

While Taz was working out, Sacha chose to stay out of his way. She took the Dobermans outside and let them run around Taz's gigantic backyard. She threw a tennis ball as far

as she could and smiled as both Precious and Heaven ran to
go fight for the ball. Whichever dog got to the ball first would
run and bring it back to her. She did this with them for over an
hour before she finally started feeling a little fatigued.

She brought the dogs back inside of the house and went upstairs to take a shower. When she walked inside the bedroom,
she smiled as she watched Taz get dressed. Her smile turned
into a frown quickly when she focused and saw exactly what
Taz was putting on. He had on a pair of black Dickies pants
and a black sweatshirt. As he tied up the laces to his black
leather Tims, she said, "So, you're about to go hunting, I see."

"Don't fuck with me on this, Li'l Mama. I'm not tryin' to
hear you right now."

"What about the promises you made to me, Taz? Have you
forgotten about them already?"

"Let me see if I'm correct. I gave you my word that I would
not be going out of town to do anything for Won after I finish
up what I have to do with my peoples. I also recall me saying
that I give you my word that after I'm done, I won't let Won
get at me with any more missions or anything illegal. I plan on
standing on every promise that I made to you, Li'l Mama. But
I did not say anything about not dealing with that nigga Cliff.
So, you can't put that shit in this now."

"Dammit, Taz! You know damn well what I'm talking
about! Why can't you leave that man alone? Can't you see that
your daughter really cares for him? You're going to ruin the
relationship you have with your only child because of some
macho bullshit! That's ridiculous, Taz! Let them be. If 'Neema
wants to be happy with him, then give her that opportunity."

Taz stood, clapped his hands a few times and said, "Very
good, counselor! That was a very convincing speech. But you
see, this shit has nothin' to do with being macho. Baby, you
know that I know I am the man. I know that nigga ain't really
worth my time for real. But, you see, he hurt mines, and when
someone hurts mines, I hurt them. It's that simple. As for
'Neema, she went against the grain. So, basically, it's fuck her
too. I love her, and I always will. If she doesn't say another

word to me for the rest of my life, that's on her. I'm doin' what I feel has to be done, period! End . . . of . . . discussion, Li'l Mama!"

"Ooh! You make me so damn sick with this craziness!" Sacha screamed, and went into the bathroom and took her shower.

Taz smiled sadly as he left the bedroom. He went down into the den and called Keno. After Keno answered the phone, Taz said, "I'm about to go huntin', gee. You want to roll wit' me?"

"For that nigga, Cliff?"

"You got it."

"I'm on my way over right now!" Keno yelled excitedly.

"Nah, I'm on my way to scoop you," Taz said before he hung up the phone. He grabbed the keys to his truck and said, "Now, where in the hell do you live, nigga? 'Cause death is about to knock on your front door!"

Chapter Ten

It had been two days since Pitt met with Cash Flo' out in Los Angeles. Pitt was as happy as can be as he walked into the conference room he had rented at the Marriot Hotel in downtown Oakland. Every last member of his team was inside the room. He spoke to everyone as he went to the head of the long conference table. Now was the time to find out exactly who it was that crossed him. "What's up, everyone? Y'all good?" he greeted.

Everyone inside of the room gave a positive response to him as they got themselves comfortable in their seats.

"Good. Now, I know y'all are wondering why I called this emergency meeting, so I'll get straight to the matter at hand. Someone in this room has crossed me, and I'm here today to find out exactly who that person is. There are approximately thirty-six people in this room, not counting myself. And no one is leaving until I find out who gave up the information on the bail bondsman spot. It is now ten minutes after three. At three thirty, my men, Leo and Tru here, will start executing each one of you until someone confesses their wrongs committed against me."

There were several murmurs around the conference room as the members of Pitt's crew stared at Leo and Tru, who had both pulled out silenced 9 mm.

Pitt continued. "Now, I want to give you my word that once the guilty party confesses, he or she will not be harmed. All I want to know is who the person is that made contact with them, and got them to cross that line. Other than being dismissed from this crew, nothing will be done to them." He then raised his right hand and said, "I swear to God! You see, this matter has to be dealt with immediately, because it endangers not only our daily operations, but our safety as well." He stopped talking, sat back in his chair and lit up one of his Cuban cigars. He gave a quick glance toward the clock mounted on the right wall of the conference room and said, "Fifteen more minutes, and the executions will begin."

A tall gentleman dressed casually in a pair of Dockers and a short-sleeved Polo button-up shirt stood and said, "Come on, Pitt. This shit is crazy. Ain't no way you're going to be able to blast everyone in this room and get away with it. This shit is ridiculous!"

"Munk, have you ever known me to give faulty threats?"

"Nah, but—"

"I have this room rented for the rest of the day. We will be long gone by the time Leo and Tru finish handling their business. I really didn't expect to have to go through with this shit, but I see the person who's crossed me really doesn't give a fuck about y'all either. 'Cause if that person did, they would have come forward by now . . . that is . . . unless that person is you, Munk."

Shaking his head furiously, Munk said, "You know I'd never cross you, Pitt. It wasn't me. I swear!"

"Have a seat, Munk, and shut the fuck up then!" Pitt glanced toward the clock again and said, "Twelve more minutes."

After about three more minutes of silence, a petite woman stood up and said, "It was me, Pitt."

Pitt frowned and asked, "Why, Brenda? We've been together for years. I've always made sure that you were eating well from this table. Why would you do me like that?"

Brenda gave a slight shrug of her petite shoulders and simply said, "Greed, Pitt. He offered me a million dollars to give up the bail bondsman spot. He also promised me that no one would be hurt. I figured I'd score me a quick ticket, and all would be well. I knew your losses would be made up eventually, 'cause a nigga like you ain't gon' fall off over some shit like a few kilos of heroin. So, I said fuck it, and gave up the info. True, you've made sure that I have always eaten well, but I don't have a meal ticket stacked in the vault."

"But you do now, huh?" Pitt asked sarcastically.

"Yeah, I do now," Brenda said with her head bowed in shame.

"All right then. Who was it that approached you? I need to know his name and how to get in contact with him."

"The name he gave me was G. I have a cell number right here in my purse," Brenda said as she opened her purse and pulled out a white slip of paper with a telephone number written on it. She passed it to Tru, who had come and stood right next to her. He then went to the front of the conference table and gave it to Pitt.

Pitt sighed heavily, because it hurt him deeply to know that Brenda was the person who had crossed him. She had been with him for a very long time, and he thought she would always remain loyal. *Damn! This some fucked up shit!* he thought. Then he asked her, "Did this G mention anyone else?"

"Nope. All he was worried about was the location of the spot, and security and shit like that. He was on some sneaky shit, but his primary concern was the drugs."

"Is there anything else you're not telling me, Brenda?"

"That's everything, Pitt. I swear to God."

"Come here," Pitt said as he waved his hand for her to come to him.

Brenda walked to the front of the conference table and stood in front of Pitt. "I know saying I'm sorry is worthless right about now, Pitt, but I am. I let my damn greed get the best of me, and I'm truly sorry for that."

Pitt grabbed Tru's silenced 9 mm and said, "You know I have to take you, right?"

"Bu—but you said that I wouldn't be harmed! You swore to God and gave all of us your word, Pitt!" screamed Brenda.

"I'm a criminal just like everyone else in this room, baby. You know my word ain't shit," Pitt said to her before he shot her right between her eyes. Her lifeless body dropped to the floor instantly.

Pitt gave Tru his gun back and said, "Clean up this mess. I'll have some janitors of mine come and get the body in a little bit. Now, as for the rest of y'all, I want y'all to know that you were never in any danger. I knew that the person who was responsible for this shit would come forward before the deadline expired."

"Bullshit, Pitt! You're one cold nigga!" someone yelled from the back of the conference room.

Pitt smiled a deadly smile and said, "You better fucking believe it! You cross me, and you die! It's that fucking simple. This meeting is now adjourned. Get back to getting that fucking money!"

Back in Oklahoma City, Clifford was talking to his homeboys, H-Hop, Astro, and Li'l Bomb.

"So, you got heavy beef with them niggas, big homey?" asked Li'l Bomb.

"Yeah, cuz. That nigga Taz is real salty at a nigga 'cause his daughter's in love with me," replied Clifford.

"Do you think he's goin' to try and take it to the next level, cuz?" asked Astro

"That fool ain't no joke, cuz. I didn't want to tell y'all, but I ain't really got no choice. Taz is the same nigga who killed Do-Low."

"*What?*" all three of the Hoover Crips yelled in unison.

"So, this nigga Taz is the nigga Do-Low tried to jack at the club that night, loc?" asked H-Hop.

"Yeah."

"Cuz, that nigga gots to go!" Li'l Bomb said angrily.

"I'll take care of that nigga, cuz. I'm going to need y'all to help a nigga out with his crew though. Those fools got major chips, so I know they're strapped like out of this world," Clifford said seriously.

"Cuz, we're strapped out of this fuckin' world! Fuck them niggas! How you want to do this?" asked Li'l Bomb.

"They normally go out to the club on the weekends. They don't be slippin', so we gots to make sure that when we move, we move correctly. Let me check into a few things, and I'll get back at y'all."

"All right, C-Baby. You do that, cuz. When the time is right, we gon' smoke all of them fools! For my nigga, Do-Low! Hoover in peace!" H-Hop said seriously.

Clifford smiled and said, "Fo' sho, loco!"

Taz was frustrated. It had been two days, and he still wasn't able to get a line on where Clifford's home was. He even went to his old job and tried to see if he could get the information from one of Clifford's former coworkers, and he still came up short.

When Sacha heard that Taz was at her job asking questions about Clifford, she became infuriated. She called Taz and told him to meet her at her house for lunch. Taz, knowing that she was about to rip him a new asshole, reluctantly agreed.

As soon as she entered her house, she went straight off on him. "How fucking dare you come up to my place of employment and try to find out where Cliff lives! What the fuck wrong with you, Taz? Don't you realize that if anything happens to him now, you're going to be the number one fucking suspect? Are you trying to beat the fucking door down to the pen? What the fuck were you thinking about?" she screamed.

Taz sat down onto her sofa and said, "I guess I wasn't really thinkin' at all, Li'l Mama."

"Taz, baby, you have to let this go. You're letting this completely consume you, and it's eating up your fucking brain cells! I'm not trying to lose you to nobody's jail, baby. Please, let this go."

He shook his head no, and said, "I slipped, Li'l Mama. It won't happen again. I promise. Now, calm down before you make yourself sick or somethin'. That nigga has to die. It's as simple as that."

"I can't fucking believe this shit! You're going to let this man put you behind bars for the rest of your fucking life, and for what? Just because your daughter loves him? You are the dumbest fucking millionaire I have ever met in my fucking life! Get the fuck out of my house, Taz Good!"

"Come on, Li'l Mama! Stop trippin'! Damn!"

"I mean it, Taz! Get the fuck out!" she screamed as she pointed toward her front door.

Taz got to his feet and walked out of Sacha's home feeling like a rookie in the game. *Damn! How did I slip like that?* he asked himself as he climbed inside of this truck.

When Taz made it back to his place, he called Tari and asked her if she was still going out to the club with them.

"Ain't nothing changed, baby. I told y'all I was with it," she said as she closed the door to the nurses' station at her job.

"All right, I was just checkin' to make sure that you was still rollin'. We'll most likely all meet here around ten thirty. We don't normally hit the club until eleven or eleven thirty."

"That's cool. Should I wear something sexy, or something comfortable?"

Taz started laughing and said, "It don't matter, Tee. You know how we get down. Some of us will be fly, and some of us will be on some gee shit. I was thinking about sportin' my new pieces tonight though."

"Yeah? What you got now, 'Mr. Baby Birdman'?"

"Birdman? You got me twisted, Tee. I ain't no Lil Wayne. I'm that nigga, Taz! You know I got the tightest shit around this clown-ass town."

"Whatever! What have you gone and bought now, boy?"

"Last month when me and Sacha were in L.A., she bought me this tight-ass canary-yellow diamond bracelet and ring. So, I took it a step further and had my grill man out in H-Town hook me up a canary-yellow diamond grill to match."

"Top and bottom?"

"Yep! That shit is way tight too. Watch. You'll see later on," he said happily.

"So, what are you wearing tonight? I know it's going to be something real fly since you're going to be flossing all of those yellow rocks."

"Nah. You know I rarely get my floss on like that. I leave that shit to Keno. I'm rockin' a pair of brown Rocawear jeans, with my butter-colored Timbs, and a white tee."

"I swear, I don't understand how you got all of that money and you dress as if you're still out hustling on the block."

"It is what it is, Tee. What? I should be suited and booted every fuckin' day? You know I don't get down like that."

"Yeah, I know. And I also know that you have Armani, Gucci, and every other top-name designer inside of your closet too. Why don't you wear one of those sexy-ass tailormade suits of yours?"

"'Cause that shit is for funerals, weddings and other special events. Not for no fuckin' club in the city. Look, I'll see you later. I got some calls to make and shit."

"Wait! Did you and Sacha smooth things out with each other?"

"Yes . . . and no."

"What did you do now, boy?"

"I'll tell you about it later on, Tee. I gots to go."

"All right, bye." She hung up the phone and went back to work.

Keno, Bo-Pete, Red and Wild Bill arrived at Taz's house a little after ten p.m. They were all dressed casually, in jeans and shirts. They either had Timb boots on, or a pair of Nike by Jordan or Kobe Bryant. With all of their expensive jewelry on, they looked like a group of rappers.

Taz smiled as everyone complimented him on his new canary-yellow diamond grill.

"Damn, nigga! When you bust those pieces?" Keno asked as he walked to the bar to pour himself a drink.

"A few months ago," answered Taz.

"How many carats you got in your mouth now, nigga?" asked Red.

Taz shrugged and said, "About one-twenty, I think. I'm not really sure. I called my grill man out in H-Town and had him hook this up for me."

"You always gots to outshine a nigga, huh?" asked Keno.

"Nigga, ain't no way I can outshine you! You're the number one stuntin' nigga in the city!"

Keno smiled and said, "I know, huh!"

Everyone laughed at his silly-ass.

"Dog, what's up with Katrina? I haven't heard you talkin' 'bout her in a minute," asked Taz,

"We're good, gee. As a matter a fact, she's goin' to be at the club later on. We've been chillin' and shit. She has really shocked me."

"How's that?"

"She's not the normal around-the-way broad. She actually goes to school and is trying to get her degree in literature. She wants to be a school teacher."

"Yeah, that's straight. So, you think she's wifey material?"

"It's possible, my nigga. It's possible."

"What's up with you, Red? Have you hit her homegirl yet?"

"Yeah, I tossed her a few times. She's good too. I told her not to sweat me though, so she's been givin' a nigga plenty of room. I know she'll be in the spot tonight, so most likely she's goin' to be bouncin' up outta there with me."

"I guess that leaves you two. What's crackin' in y'all's sex life?"

Bo-Pete just smiled as he stood sipping his drink.

"Dog, I ain't goin' out like you chumps. I'm a fuckin' millionaire, and I ain't tryin' to get tied down by no broad. I can fuck who I want, when I want, and that's just how I fuckin' like it," Wild Bill said with a smile on his face.

They all started laughing at Wild Bill as he stood and went to the bar and had Keno pour him a drink.

Even though Wild Bill was the smallest member of the crew, he was still considered one of the most dangerous. Taz didn't know if it was because Wild Bill had a complex about his height or what. He was a stone-cold killer. He stood under five foot six inches, and wore a pair of gold-rimmed glasses. He was damn near blind, but when it came to handling his business, he had never let any of them down.

Taz smiled as he looked at his homeboys. He loved each one of them as if they were his blood brothers. *These are niggas that I would die for,* he thought to himself as he sipped on his glass of XO.

Taz heard his front door open and smiled, because he thought Sacha had calmed down and come over to the house. His smile quickly left his face when he saw that it wasn't Sacha who had just entered his home. It was Tari.

Tari noticed the look on his face, smiled and said, "I guess I'm not who you were expecting, huh?"

Taz ignored her and said, "What's good, Tee? Damn! You're lookin' like you tryin' to catch somethin' tonight!"

"Nah, I'm just trying to make some of them sistas hate a li'l bit," she said with a sexy smile on her face.

Tari was wearing a pair of low-cut Apple Bottom jeans, and a cut-off T-shirt that showed off her belly ring. Across the front of her shirt were words in bold lettering that read, "I GOT ASS TOO!" Her long blonde hair was hanging loosely past her shoulders. She was looking extremely sexy, and every man inside the room knew it. *Long legs, sexy blue eyes and a body like a sista, that white girl was right!*

"Well, since everybody's here, y'all already know what time it is," Taz said with a smile on his face.

"Already!" Bo-Pete said, and downed the rest of his drink.

Then in unison, the rest of the group said, "It's time to go clubbin'!"

Chapter Eleven

Clifford, Astro, H-Hop and Li'l Bomb sat parked across the street from Club Cancun's parking lot, waiting to see if Taz and his crew had chosen to come out and have a little fun. *If indeed they did, they would have a big surprise waiting for them after the club let out,* Clifford thought as he watched as the club hoppers started filling up the parking lot.

"What makes you so sure that they're comin' up here tonight, cuz?" asked Astro.

Clifford shrugged his shoulders and said, "It's just a feeling I got, loc. They might not though. I figure it's maybe sixty-forty in favor of them showing up though."

"I hope they do, cuz, 'cause on 107 Hoover Crip, I want that nigga who took the big homey, Do-Low!" Li'l Bomb said seriously from the backseat of the stolen Nissan Maxima they were sitting inside of.

Clifford smiled and said, "If they show, you're going to get your chance, li'l homey. So, let's just wait and see, cuz."

"Didn't you say they all pushed all-black whips?" asked H-Hop.

"Yeah."

"Well, that gots to be them right there, loc," H-Hop said as he pointed toward the small fleet of all-black SUV's pulling into the parking lot of Club Cancun.

Clifford smiled and said, "Yeah, you're definitely going to get your shot at them niggas tonight, cuz!"

Li'l Bomb smiled and pumped a live round into the chamber of his AK-47 and said, "Good!"

Taz and Tari rode together in his truck, while Red rode with Bo-Pete and Wild Bill in Bo-Pete's Navigator. Keno didn't want to ride with Taz because he knew Taz would most likely want to leave the club before he did, so he chose to drive his Range Rover solo.

After they had parked their vehicles side by side in the parking lot, everyone exited their trucks and started walking toward the club's entrance. Since they had a ritual of how they entered the club, Bo-Pete and Wild Bill entered the club first. Three to four minutes later, Red and Keno entered the club. Five minutes after that, Taz led Tari inside. Normally, Bob would have been paired with Red, but since he was laid up, Keno was his replacement, because Taz was going to make sure that Tari was by his side at all times.

Once Taz and Tari entered the club, Taz saw that Red and Keno were posted up on the far left side of the club, while Bo-Pete and Wild Bill were posted up on the far right side. He gave them all a slight nod and stepped toward the bar with two fingers held up, signaling Winky, the bartender to give him his usual drink, a double shot of XO.

Winky passed Taz a brandy snifter with his drink, smiled and asked, "Anything for the lovely lady, Taz?"

Taz turned toward Tari, and she said, "Yeah, give me a Hpnotiq."

Taz smiled and said, "Now, what the fuck you know 'bout a Hpnotiq?"

"Taz, you may think I'm some kind of hermit because I don't do the club scene that often, but I do have friends, and occasionally we go out and have drinks and stuff."

He laughed and said, "My bad, Tee!"

"Fuck you, boy!" she said, and started laughing also.

Taz noticed that Keno had found Katrina, and smiled. "Looks like Keno's girl is here."

"Which one is she?" Tari asked, and sipped her drink.

"The thick one right there with the micro-braids in her hair. The girl standing next to her is her homegirl, Paquita. She's the one Red's been gettin' at."

"The light-skinned one with all of that damn weave in her hair?"

Taz laughed and said, "Yeah."

"Damn! She didn't give that horse a break, did she? She knows she's wrong for that shit!"

"Be good, Tee. Red seems to like her."

"She is kind of cute though. Her body is bangin' too. But she could lose like ten to twelve inches of that damn weave!"

They both started laughing as they watched Keno and Red talking to their lady friends.

Keno smiled at Katrina and said, "So, what's poppin', *mami*?"

Katrina returned the smile and said, "Nothin', *papi*. What's up with you?"

"The same old shit."

"What's up, Red? What? You can't speak tonight?" asked Paquita.

Red smiled and said, "Hah! It ain't like that, ma. What it do? You good?"

Paquita smiled and answered, "I am now."

"I know that's right! Y'all want somethin' to drink?"

"Yeah. I'll have me a glass of Henny," said Paquita.

"Get me an Absolut Peach," said Katrina.

As Red went to go get their drinks, Katrina asked Keno, "So, am I leaving with you tonight, *papi*?"

"It depends."

"Depends on what?" she asked with a pout on her pretty face.

"If you're goin' to be as freaky as I want you to be later on!"

She punched him lightly on his arm and said, "You know you need to quit, with your nasty self!"

He laughed and said, "You know I'm clownin', *mami*. Of course, you're bouncin' with me. I need some sexual healing, and I know you're goin' to look out for your boy."

She smiled seductively and said, "You got that right, *papi!*"

"Ooh, y'all so damn nasty! Y'all need to quit that shit!" Paquita said just as Red returned with their drinks.

"Girl, you the one who needs to quit, 'cause you know damn well you gon' leave with Red and get your freak on too!"

Red gave them their drinks, smiled and said, "I don't know what y'all have been over here talkin' about, but I sure hope you're right, Katrina!"

They all started laughing as they sipped their drinks and enjoyed their evening.

Bo-Pete and Wild Bill were busy on the other side of the club, trying to impress two lovely ladies.

The rest of the evening went by rather quickly to Taz. He was surprised that he was having so much fun with Tari. They danced for a few songs, and continued to laugh and make jokes with one another about any and everything. Taz never realized that Tari was such a clown. She was talking about almost every other female inside of the club, from what they were wearing to the bad weave jobs they had in their hair. That shit was hilarious to him.

What took the cake was when a guy with a jheri curl came up to Tari and asked to buy her a drink. Tari smirked and said, "I already have one, dear," trying to sound extra white and shit. But when Jheri Curl persisted and asked her, did she want to dance with him, she said with plenty of attitude in her voice, "Look, I don't feel like dancing, okay?"

"Damn, baby! I'm just trying to be entertaining!" said Jheri Curl.

Tari burst into laughter and said, "Man, will you get the fuck away from me!"

Jheri Curl was about to say something he was definitely going to regret, but Taz saved him just in time by saying, "She's my peoples, dog. Why don't you go on and let her make it, huh?"

Jheri Curl stared at Taz briefly then said, "Whatever, dog. She ain't all that anyway."

As Jheri Curl was walking away, Tari had to hit him off with one last jab. "I may not be all that, but at least I'm not dripping no damn jheri curl juice all over the fuckin' club either, you fuckin' clown!"

"Come on with that shit, Tee!" Taz said as he tried his best to control his laughter. Seeing that she was a little heated, he said, "Let's shake this spot and go get somethin' to eat. I'm a li'l hungry. What about you?"

"Yeah, I've had enough of this club to last me a minute. What about the others?"

"Let's go get at them and see what's on their plates," Taz said as he led her toward Bo-Pete and Wild Bill. When they made it to where they were, Taz said, "We're about to shake the spot and go get our grub on. What's up with y'all?"

"Ain't nothin' really crackin' in here for me. I'm gon' bounce too," replied Wild Bill.

"Yeah, I'm a li'l tired. Might as well call it a night," said Bo-Pete.

"All right, let's go get at Keno and Red real quick then."

Keno was kissing Katrina on her neck, when Taz walked over to him. Keno smiled and said, "I know that look, nigga. You're about to shake the spot, huh?"

"Yeah. I've had all my fun. We're out. Y'all good or what?"

Keno stared at Red, who gave a shrug of his broad shoulders and said, "Yeah, we're good. We got some shit to take care of after the club is over anyway."

Keno smiled brightly and added, "That's right. We gots shit to take care of."

They all laughed and stared at Katrina and Paquita.

Katrina blushed, slapped Keno on his face lightly, and said, "Stop that shit, Keno!"

Paquita, with no shame at all, said, "You damn right, you got something to take care of tonight, and you better take good care of it too!"

Taz shook his head from side to side and said, "Y'all are made for each other, for real! Watch yourselves," he said as he grabbed Tari's hand and walked toward the club's exit.

As she watched them leave the club, Katrina frowned and said, "I thought Taz was all in love with old girl. What's her name, Sacha?"

Keno laughed and said, "Don't worry about that shit, *mami*. My nigga is always gon' be all right. Now, come here!" he said playfully as he grabbed her by her hand.

Tari had her arm around Taz's waist as they followed Wild Bill and Bo-Pete out of the club. They stopped and inhaled some of the fresh air once they were outside.

Just as they were about to walk toward Taz's truck, Tari suddenly reached under Taz's shirt, pulled out his 9 mm, pushed Taz to the side and screamed, "Watch your ass, Taz!" She then began unloading his weapon at the four guys in dark clothing who were charging them with what looked like assault rifles in their hands.

After Tari started shooting, Bo-Pete and Wild Bill reacted instantly. They pulled out their weapons and started shooting at the men in the dark clothing too.

Realizing that they had lost their advantage, H-Hop, Astro, Clifford and Li'l Bomb began retreating. Even though they had heavier firepower, they were being shot at from one too many angles. Therefore, they weren't able to get a good shot off at their targets.

Taz, who had regrouped quickly after Tari pushed him to the side, knelt on one knee and watched as she, Bo-Pete and Wild Bill handled their business. *Ain't this a bitch!* he thought as he watched the niggas who tried to blast them run and jump inside of a black Nissan Maxima. As they sped out of the parking lot across the street from the club, Tari, Bo-Pete and Wild Bill ran into the middle of the street and stood side by side, and continued to unload their weapons at the Maxima.

Once the car was out of their sight, Bo-Pete came back and checked on Taz. "You straight, gee?"

Taz got to his feet and said, "Yeah, I'm good. Go inside of the club and get Keno and Red."

Bo-Pete went to go do as Taz had told him, while Tari and Wild Bill came to Taz's side.

"What the fuck was that shit, dog?" asked Wild Bill.

"I don't have a fuckin' clue, my nigga."

"You still got beef like that out here in these streets, Taz?" asked Tari as she was breathing heavily.

Shaking his head no, Taz said, "Nah, you know I don't fuck with niggas out here no more."

"Then what the fuck was those clowns doing? Playing? Baby, I think you have some beef and don't even know it. That little fucker with the orange bandanna around his face was aiming that fucking assault rifle right at your head when I spotted his ass."

"Orange bandanna? Ain't that Hoover colors, Wild Bill?"

"Yeah, dog. But we don't fuck with no gang niggas."

"What the fuck!"

Keno, Red and Bo-Pete came outside of the club with their weapons in their hands.

"What the fuck happened out here?" asked Keno.

"Some niggas tried to dump me. Tari saved my ass, gee. Look, let's shake this spot. You know 'the ones' will be here in a minute. I'll get at y'all in the morning so we can look at this shit clearly."

"All right," they replied in unison, and they all went toward the vehicles they came to the club in.

After Tari and Taz were inside of his struck, she said, "I think it'll be safer if we went back to your house and I make us something to eat."

Taz smiled and said, "Ya think?"

Chapter Twelve

Even though Tari handled the situation at the club like a pure veteran, she was still a little shaken by the time they made it back to Taz's home. She went straight into the den and poured herself a stiff shot of XO from the bar. After she downed her drink, she quickly poured herself another one and sat down on the couch. "What the fuck was that all about, Taz?" she asked as she sipped her second drink.

"I don't even know, Tee. We'll try to figure this shit out tomorrow. Right now, I'm taking my ass to bed and get me some sleep," he said as he yawned.

"I thought we were going to eat something."

"I ain't got the energy to wait for you to put somethin' together. I'm out. You can lay it down in here, or you can use the guest room if you want."

Tari smiled and asked, "Why can't I come and sleep with you? You scared of me now that you're all in love?"

Taz returned her smile and said, "You know if we sleep in the same bed what's goin' to pop off, Tee."

"So? I won't tell if you won't."

"I'm engaged, Tee."

"Engaged, yeah, but you're not married."

He took a deep breath, turned toward the door of the den and said, "Come on, you."

Tari smiled as she followed him up the stairs and into his bedroom. She continued to smile as he started to undress. Once he had his clothes off, he got under the bed covers and said, "This is never goin' to happen again, Tee. Do you hear me?"

After taking off her jeans and sliding out of her transparent thong, she said, "In that case, let's make this a night to remember." She slid onto the bed and pulled back the covers from Taz's chiseled body and began to slowly lick him from his head to his feet.

Chills ran all over his body as he tensed when Tari sucked each one of his toes. *Damn, I miss this type of shit!* he thought to himself with his eyes closed tightly.

When Tari finished with his feet, she worked her way up to his crotch area and began sucking his testicles. His dick was so hard that he felt as if he was about to cum any moment.

She left his balls alone for the moment and started sucking his rock-hard dick greedily. The slurping sounds she was making while giving him one of the best blow jobs he had ever had in his life seemed to drive him over the edge.

He grabbed her by her long blonde hair and held her tightly as he came inside of her mouth. After she swallowed every last drop of his cum, she smiled and said, "M-m-m-m-m!"

He shook his head from side to side as he pulled her up toward his face, and they began to kiss passionately.

After Taz felt he had regained his strength, he turned her over and said, "Now, you li'l freak, it's my turn!" He started at her breasts and nibbled on each one of her rock-hard nipples until she moaned with pleasure. He smiled as he licked his way lower. When he made it to her sex, she was so wet and sticky, he felt as if he had just stuck his tongue into some warm milk.

Tari's clit was so hard that it looked like a mini-missile. Taz sucked and nibbled on it, causing Tari to scream out with pleasure. "Oh-h-h-h, Taz! Don't stop! Please, Daddy! Don't you fucking stop!" She screamed as loud as she could as she gyrated her hips and ground her pussy in his face.

When she came, she felt as if every fiber of her body was on fire. "Damn, Taz! I'm cumming! I'm cumming! I'm cumming, baby!"

Her body went limp under his tongue assault. He didn't give her a chance to recoup. He slid on top of her and entered her piping-hot pussy quickly.

She gave a gasp as she felt all of his manhood deep inside of her love box. "Damn, that feels so-o-o good, Daddy! Give it to me, baby! Give it to me!" she screamed as he worked her over real good for close to twenty minutes.

By the time Taz reached his second orgasm, his entire body was covered with sweat. Tari had already cum several times while he was pounding away in her sex.

It's time for the finale, he thought as he quickly flipped her over onto her knees and entered her from behind. Her fat ass was raised high in the air as he rammed himself deep inside of her.

"Here it goes, Tee! Here it goes!" he screamed as he let go a monstrous nut inside of her pussy. After the last tingling sensations had subsided, he slid out of her and fell onto the bed completely spent. "Damn, that was good!"

"Do you miss this pussy, Taz? Do you miss it as much as I've missed this dick?" Tari asked lazily with her eyes half closed.

"Mmmm-hmmm," Taz replied as he closed his eyes and drifted off to sleep.

The next morning, Taz was awakened by his phone ringing. He opened his eyes and groggily answered it. "What up?"

"Good morning, Taz," said Sacha.

Upon hearing his fiancée's voice his head cleared instantly. "What up, Li'l Mama? You all right?"

"I should be asking you that question. I heard about last night, Taz."

"What? From who?"

"Gwen called me this morning and told me that Bob told her that Wild Bill called him this morning and told him what happened at the club last night. What's going on, baby? I thought you said that you didn't have that kind of beef in the city."

"I thought I didn't, but obviously I was wrong. Don't worry about it though. I'll take care of this shit, Li'l Mama."

"Don't worry about it? How can I not worry about it, Taz?"

He smiled and said, "I thought you was mad at me."

"I am. That hasn't changed, mister. But just because I'm mad at you doesn't change the fact that you are my man, my fiancé, the man I plan on spending the rest of my life with. I love you, Mr. Good, and don't you ever forget that."

Her statement gave Taz a tremendous attack of the guilts as he stared at Tari sleeping soundly right next to him in his bed. He climbed out of bed and went downstairs with the phone to his ear as he listened to Sacha talk. "Yeah, I love you too, Li'l Mama. I don't need you all stressed out behind this shit though. I'll deal with it, I promise. My seed needs to be stress-free while he's growing inside of you."

"Your seed needs you to be here when he or she comes out of this womb too, mister."

He laughed and said, "I know. Look, what you got planned for the day?"

"After I get dressed, I'm going over to Bob's house and have breakfast with him and Gwen. You wanna come?"

"Nah, I'm about to get with Keno and 'em so we can try and figure out what the fuck is crackin' with them fools that tried to blast me."

"So, you know who they are?"

"Not exactly, but I do have an idea. Give me a holla after you finished gettin' your eat on. And tell that nigga Bob I said to relax and don't be over there trippin'. We got this shit."

"Is it true that Tari saved you last night?"

Taz smiled and said, "Yeah, she spotted the fools first, pulled my strap from my back, pushed me to the side and started servin' them fools."

"Damn! That sounds like something that happens in the movies!"

"I know, huh? All right then, Li'l Mama, let me go so I can get dressed."

"Okay, baby. I'll call you in a couple of hours. I love you, Taz."

"I love you too, Li'l Mama. Bye," he said, and hung up the phone.

"Do you feel as guilty as I do?" Tari asked, standing behind Taz in the kitchen.

Taz jumped and yelled, "Damnit, Tee! Don't be creepin' up behind me like that! You scared the shit outta me!"

Tari laughed and said, "I'm sorry, scaredy cat! Damn!" She stepped toward the refrigerator and asked, "What do you want for breakfast?"

This shit is crazy! Here we are, standing in my kitchen, butt-ass naked like nothing was wrong with this picture, thought Taz. "Whatever you feel like puttin' together is cool. I'm 'bout to go take a shower and call up Keno."

"All right. You don't want to talk about last night, I assume."

He turned and faced Tari and said, "We did what we did because we will always be close like that. You know I still love you, Tee, and I will never stop loving you."

"But that was the last time, right?"

He smiled at her and said, "Yeah, that was it, baby."

Tari smiled and simply said, "Okay. I'll have something ready for us to eat by the time you finish with your shower." She then opened the refrigerator and bent over as she grabbed some food out of it.

Taz stared at her fat ass and shook his head as he left the kitchen. *Damn, she's fine as fuck!* he thought as if that was the first time he had ever seen her behind. He was still shaking his head as he walked up the stairs to his bedroom.

Clifford was sitting up in his bed talking to Tazneema, when someone called him on his cell phone. "Hold on for a minute, 'Neema. I need to answer my cell real quick."

"Just call me back after you're finished with your call, baby."

"Are you sure? I thought you didn't want me calling over there while Mama-Mama was around."

"I'll explain all of that when you call me back. Go on now," Tazneema said and hung up the phone.

He had a smile on his face as he hung up the phone and grabbed his cell phone. After flipping it open, he said, "Hello."

"What up, C-Baby?" asked H-Hop. "What you doin', cuz?"

"Just sitting here chillin'. What's up with you, loco?"

"Cuz, I was layin' here thinkin' 'bout them niggas last night. It ain't gon' be as easy as I thought it was gon' be to get at them niggas."

"I told you, cuz, them fools ain't to be taken lightly."

"But who was that bitch that was with them? If it wasn't for her, we had they ass!"

"I don't even know, loco. It damn sure wasn't Sacha. She looked like a fuckin' white girl, huh?"

"Yeah, she did. But ain't no snow bunny gon' be dumpin' like that. That bitch almost got us, cuz!"

Clifford laughed and said, "I know, loc. Don't trip. Let's lay back in the cut for minute. That nigga is bound to slip sooner or later."

"I don't know, cuz. That nigga's crew is solid. I think we might have to take that nigga hard. Do you know where that fool stay?"

"Nah, but I can find out. Give me a minute and I'll get back at ya. Tell that nigga Li'l Bomb I said to be patient. We'll get 'em, loc."

H-Hop laughed and said, "All right, cuz. I'll holla."

After Clifford hung up the phone he called Tazneema back at Mama-Mama's house. "Now, what's up with Mama-Mama letting me call the house now?"

"Well, you're still not on her favorite persons list, but she's accepted the fact that I love you, and no matter what, I'm going to be with you. So she's keeping her feelings to herself."

Clifford smiled after hearing that and said, "Hopefully she'll let me show her that I am a good person."

"Don't worry about it. Everything will be all right in time, baby. So, what are you getting into today?"

"Nothing much. I was getting ready to redo my resume so I can try to find me some employment."

"I'm so sorry that you lost your job behind this mess, baby. I wish I would have known that Sacha was going to get you fired. I would have stopped her."

"Don't worry about that. I'll be all right. How are you feeling?"

"Actually, I feel pretty good. I'm so tired of being cooped up in this house. I wish I could do something, but Mama-Mama ain't having none of that. The only time I can get some fresh air is when she lets me go outside to watch her work in her garden, or out back when she dumps some food scraps to the hogs in the hog pen."

"Don't worry, you'll be able to get out and about real soon. I can't wait either, because I'm so-o-o horny!"

Tazneema laughed and said, "Me too! You're going to be in trouble when I get a hold of that body of yours, baby."

"I love you, Tazneema Good."

"I love you too, Cliff. Don't you ever forget that."

"I won't."

By the time Taz and Tari finished eating, Keno, Bo-Pete, Red and Wild Bill had made it over to Taz's home. They were sitting in the den, thinking about the same thing—*What caused them to have a beef with the Hoover Crips?*

"Fuck it! Let's go get at them punk-ass niggas! They ain't nothin' but a bunch of wannabe L.A.-ass niggas!" yelled Wild Bill.

"Yeah, but some of those guys are brutal, Wild Bill," said Tari.

"Eight out of ten brutal men are straight cowards, Tee. They move with force when their numbers are deep. Them niggas ain't built for war for real," Keno said seriously.

"All right, check this shit out. Put some feelers out and see what we can come up with. Keno, you and Red get at Katrina and Paquita and see what they can find out for us. I don't like the fact that we're walkin' around this bitch in the blind. The sooner we find out what's what, the sooner we'll be able to deal with this shit," said Taz.

"What the fuck is it to find out? Them niggas got at us! Let's get right back at they ass!" screamed Bo-Pete.

"What you wanna do, Bo? Just go and blast them niggas up?" asked Red.

"You fuckin' right! If we don't make a move, all they're goin' to do is keep on gettin' at us until they eventually get lucky and pop one of us. I'm tellin' you, dog, we should take the offense and move on them niggas as soon as possible."

"You're right, Bo-Pete. Do them niggas still be over there on Lottie?" asked Taz.

"I guess. How the fuck would I know? But it don't fuckin' matter. Let's go huntin' and see what we can find."

"All right then, we'll move tonight. But today we're goin' to roll through the city and see exactly what we can find out. Cool?" asked Taz.

"I'm with it," said Bo-Pete.

"Me too," said Red.

"Ride or die, baby," replied Wild Bill.

"It is what it is," added Keno.

"Don't think you're leaving me out of this mess!" said Tari.

Shaking his head no, Taz said, "You gots to stay ready for Won's mission, Tee. We can't put that in jeopardy behind this bullshit. You done handled your business, so let us take care of these wannabe drive-by-ass niggas."

"Drive-by? Them clowns had assault rifles, Taz! They ain't playing, and they shouldn't be taken lightly. Go ahead and handle them, but do not for one second underestimate them. If you have to do them, then make sure that they're done," she said in a deadly tone.

Taz smiled at her and said, "Got'cha!"

Chapter Thirteen

Tazneema was horny, and she just couldn't take being away from Clifford any longer. So, after Mama-Mama went to bed for the night, she threw on a pair of sweatpants and a T-shirt, grabbed her purse, and sneaked out of the house. Since her car was still over Mama-Mama's house, it was easy for her to make her temporary escape. She climbed inside of her car and put the gearshift into neutral and pushed her Camry out of the driveway. Once she had her car out into the street, she jumped inside and started the ignition. She smiled as she pulled from in front of her grandmother's home. She pulled out her cell phone and dialed Clifford's number, praying that he was at home. When he answered his phone, she said, "Get ready for me, baby. I should be there in about twenty minutes or so."

"Stop playing with me, 'Neema! Are you serious?" he asked excitedly.

"Yep. I snuck out of the house. I won't be able to stay long 'cause you know Mama-Mama gets up before the crack of dawn. A couple of hours, tops, is all that we'll have."

Clifford smiled and said, "That's a lot of time, baby. Hurry up!"

Tazneema laughed and said, "I'm hurrying!"

As soon as the sun had set, Taz and the crew went hunting. Earlier they had found three different streets where the Hoover Crips were known to hang out, so Taz decided to get at all three locations. He and Keno were inside of Taz's Denali, while Bo-Pete, Red and Wild Bill were inside of Bo-Pete's Navigator. Their destination was the corner of Twenty-third Street and Lottie Avenue. There was a paint and body shop that the Hoovers were known to hang at.

As they drove by the auto body shop, Taz saw a couple of gang members standing in front of the shop, smoking and drinking some Olde English malt liquor. He smiled as they drove down to the next block and made a U-turn with Bo-Pete right behind them. When Taz pulled in front of the gang members, he rolled down the passenger's side window and Keno said, "Hey, homies, y'all want to play with the big dogs?"

"What you say, cuz?" asked one of the young Hoover Crips.

"If you wanna play with the big dogs, you gots to know how to get your man!" said Keno as he pointed his 9 mm at them and shot each one of the Crips twice in their midsections.

Taz pulled away from the curb and made a right turn back onto Twenty-third Street as if everything was completely normal.

Their next stop was a half a mile on Twenty-third Street and MLK. This time when Taz saw the Hoovers standing in a small group, he didn't pass by them by. He stopped right in front of them and jumped out of his truck, followed closely by Keno. They didn't say a word as they started shooting every one of the gang members in their sights. The Crips that were lucky enough not to be hit by Taz and Keno on sight really weren't that lucky, because they ran right into more bullets from Bo-Pete, Red and Wild Bill.

Just as suddenly as the shooting began, it ended. Death was all around the corner of Twenty-third Street and MLK as Taz and the crew sped away onto their third and final destination.

Clifford and Tazneema were lying next to one another, bathed in their own sweat and completely out of breath. After Tazneema had made it over to Clifford's house, they made love until they felt as if they were going to pass out.

Clifford turned onto his side and asked, "Are you all right, baby? I lost control of myself. I hope I didn't hurt you."

She smiled and said, "I'm fine, baby. I have to admit that I kinda forgot about my injuries. I'm sore as hell. I think my shoulders going to be killing me in the morning."

"We shouldn't have done this, 'Neema. I need you back in tip-top shape. I'm sorry, baby."

"Would you be quiet with all of that? I'm a big girl, Cliff. I'll be all right. Now, let me go take a shower so I can get back to Mama-Mama's before she wakes up and realizes that I'm gone," she said as she climbed out of the bed.

Clifford smiled as he watched her sexy body sway back and forth as she walked into the bathroom. He relaxed back on his pillow, completely drained. *That girl is something else!* he thought to himself as he closed his eyes.

Ten minutes later, Tazneema came out of the bathroom wrapped in one of Clifford's towels. She smiled when she saw that he had fallen asleep. Just as she had finished getting dressed, the telephone rang.

Clifford reached for the phone on the nightstand without ever opening his eyes and said, "Hello."

"Them niggas is gettin' at us, cuz!" screamed H-Hop.

"Wha—what are you talking about, Hop?" Clifford asked groggily.

"Cuz, them fools just finished blastin' up two homies on Twenty-third and Lottie! And then they served about seven of the homies on the corner of Twenty-third and Martin Luther King! After that, they caught six more of the homies slippin' on Thirty-sixth at one of the homeboy's bud spots. I'm tellin' you, loc, them niggas are on a fuckin' warpath!"

"How the fuck did they know to get at us? Them fools shouldn't have a clue about who put that work in!"

"Cuz, all I'm tellin' you is that the homies are mad as fuck! We got about twelve homies shot the fuck up!"

"Did anyone get smoked?" Clifford asked as he climbed out of his bed.

"Yeah, the first two homies that got hit on Lottie are dead. Them fools dropped them right on the spot. I'm tellin' you, loc, we gots to hurry up and get at them niggas! They ain't playin', cuz!"

"Calm down, cuz! Where are you now?

"I'm at the pad. When I heard about all of that fuckin' bustin', I got the fuck outta dodge," H-Hop stated wisely.

"I'm about to get dressed and come scoop you, loc. Give me about twenty minutes."

"All right, cuz," H-Hop said, and hung up.

After Clifford hung up the phone, he didn't notice the funny expression on Tazneema's face. He jumped out of his bed and threw on a pair of jeans and a T-shirt. As he was tying his tennis shoes, Tazneema asked him, "Is there something wrong, baby?"

"Huh? No . . . uh . . . kind of, 'Neema. A few of my friends have been hurt tonight. I really need to go check on them."

"You're in a gang, Cliff?"

"Huh? Baby, that's a long story, but to answer your question, not really is the best I can tell at this time. Gang-banging is a part of my past, though. I guess it will always be a part of me. I worked real damn hard to stay away from that part of my life, but here lately it seems like something or some unknown force is trying to pull me back to 'cripping'."

Shaking her head, Tazneema said, "No one can make you do something that you don't want to do, Cliff. It's solely on you, baby. If your heart's not in it, please don't destroy yourself by wasting your time with that craziness."

He smiled as he stepped into her embrace and said, "Don't worry, baby. I won't. I'm just going over to show some support to my people and their families. Go on back to Mama-Mama's, and I'll give you a call in the morning."

After sharing an intense kiss, Tazneema smiled and said, "I'll be back over here tomorrow night at the same time, 'kay?"

He returned her smile and said, "Good!"

After leaving the bloody scene on Thirty-sixth Street, Taz called Bo-Pete on his cell and told him, "Dog, let's split up. We'll get at y'all in the morning. If you have any problems before you make it to the pad, get at me. If I don't hear from either of y'all, then I'll know everything is everything."

"That's straight," Bo-Pete replied before he closed his cell phone.

Keno smiled and said, "That should show them punk-ass niggas that we are not to be fucked with."

"Yeah, it should, gee, but I got a funny feelin' this shit has just gotten started," Taz said seriously.

"What makes you say that, dog? They ain't gon' want to fuck with no niggas they know ain't playin' with they ass."

"If that's the case, then why in the fuck did they get at us in the first place? I'm tellin' you, homie, somethin' just ain't right about all of this shit. I can't put my finger on it, but somethin' just ain't right."

"Everything will be everything, my nigga. Watch. You'll see. Now, drop me off at the pad so I can go scoop Katrina and tap that ass a li'l bit," Keno said, and they both started laughing.

Chapter Fourteen

The next morning, every news channel and newspaper in the Oklahoma City area was focused on the slayings of the night before. Local preachers were seen on television yelling about this sudden gang violence and how it has to stop before the black community is completely destroyed.

Taz watched the news as he sipped on some orange juice. He was waiting for the crew to arrive for their daily workout. Even though they had slacked up lately, he felt that it was time for them to get back to their normal routine. This sudden beef with the Hoovers was really bothering him. He wanted to make sure that they were at the top of their game for this unexpected and unwanted drama. He wasn't trying to go to anyone of his homeboys' funeral, and he damn sure wasn't trying to go to his own.

Sacha called him just before the crew arrived, and started rambling on about the same thing he was watching on television. "Isn't it sad the way these youngsters are out there killing each other, baby?" she asked.

"It is what it is, Li'l Mama. I'm not really concerned with that shit right now. I gots enough on my plate as it is," Taz answered irritably.

"What's wrong with you this morning? Why is your attitude all funky?"

"I just told you, I got a lot on my plate. Why are you trippin'? Look, let me go. The homies just pulled up, and we're about to work out. After I finish with that, I have to go check on some of the IHOPs and some of my rental houses."

"Okay, give me a call when you have some time," she said then hung up the phone.

Since Taz was doing so well financially, he hardly paid much attention to any of the small food chains that he owned in Oklahoma City. He basically let his attorneys and managers take care of everything. He took pride in the fact that between himself, Keno, and the rest of the crew, they all owned a nice percentage of rental property in the Oklahoma City area—over one hundred homes apiece to be exact. Each member of the crew cleared close to two hundred thousand dollars yearly off their rental properties, so money was not an issue with any of them. Unfortunately, the Hoover Crips were.

Once the crew had made it down to Taz's built-in gym and began to warm up and stretch, Taz said, "I'm tellin' y'all, we're goin' to have to watch ourselves now that we've made our move against them niggas."

"Dog, fuck them fools! They ain't gon' try no stupid shit," replied Bo-Pete as he stretched next to Red.

"Yeah, after the demonstration we gave them niggas, they're probably somewhere licking their wounds," Wild Bill said as he bench-pressed some light weight to loosen up his arms.

"Dog, we can't be underestimating these young niggas. Don't forget that they got at us first. Just because we gave them a li'l somethin' doesn't mean that they won't try to get back. All I'm sayin' is to stay on your toes when you're out and about. It's been a long time since we had any beef in town. I ain't tryin' to lose none of y'all. Feel me?"

"Yeah, we feel you, nigga. Now shut the fuck up so we can get our workout on!" Keno said, and everyone started laughing.

Taz smiled and said, "Fuck you, clown!"

They then started their intense workout for the day.

"I'm tellin' you, loc, we gots to get at them niggas!" yelled Li'l Bomb.

"I know, my nigga. That's why I'm trying to find out where that nigga Taz rests his head. A while back I got his tag number, so I gave it to a partner of mine who works for the Highway Patrol. I'm waiting on him to get back at me now. If he can give me that nigga's hookup, we'll be able to get at him at his pad. So relax, cuz. We're going to get them," Clifford said confidently.

"Relax? Cuz, them niggas smoked my nigga, Li'l Lights! If I wouldn't have went back into that shop, I would've been right out there with Li'l Light and C-Rag! They could have got me too! I'm tellin' you, cuz, I ain't really with this waitin' shit!"

"So, what are you going to do? Just ride around the town to see if you can get lucky and catch one of them niggas? I know you're hurting, loco. We all are. You're just going to have to remain calm until we can get something solid to move on."

"Fuck this shit, cuz! I'm outta here! Hit me when y'all know somethin', H-Hop," Li'l Bomb said as he left H-Hop's apartment.

"This is the fucked up part of the game, my nigga. You remember how it goes. Now we have to sit back and bury some more Hoovers. And that shit ain't even cool, cuz," said H-Hop as he lit a cigarette.

"Yeah, I remember, loc. How could I ever forget some shit like that? Believe me, I can't wait until we get them niggas, cuz. I want them dead more than anybody else," Clifford said seriously.

After Taz and the crew had finished their workout, they all went upstairs to Taz's kitchen and raided the refrigerator.

Red pulled some steaks from the freezer and threw them into the microwave to defrost them. "Y'all tryin' to eat some steaks or what?" he asked as he stepped back toward the refrigerator.

"Yeah, hook me up one of those bad boys," Keno said as he sipped on a bottle of Evian water.

"Yeah, me too," added Wild Bill.

"Nah, I'm good. I'm goin' to see if Sacha is down to do lunch. I'm not tryin' to be around you clowns all damn day," Taz said with a smile on his face as he grabbed the phone and gave Sacha a call. When she answered the phone, he asked, "Are you busy, Li'l Mama?"

"Not really. I just finished a meeting with my paralegal. What's up?"

"Do you want to have lunch with me today, or are you still salty with me, boo?"

She laughed and said, "It seems as if I'm always going to be mad with you, Mister Taz. I'm kind of getting used to it. I'd love to have lunch with my boo. What do you have in mind?"

"Let's go get something to eat at the new spot in Bricktown. I think it's called The Daiquiri Zone. I heard they got the bomb hot wings. I know you can't do no drinkin', but Tari told me that their daiquiris are pretty good too."

"That sounds like a winner to me, baby. I might not be able to drink any alcohol, but I can still have me a virgin daiquiri. Do you want me to meet you there, or are you going to come and pick up?"

"Yeah, I'll come scoop you in about thirty minutes. I just finished working out, so let me jump in the shower real quick and I'll be on my way."

"All right, baby, I'll be waiting."

Taz ran upstairs and took a quick shower. After he was finished, he put on a pair of loose-fitting Azure jeans and a fresh white tee. He then grabbed his new Jordan's and slipped them onto his feet. After hitting himself with a few spurts of his D&G for Men cologne, he grabbed his 9 mm pistol and slipped it into the small of his back. He turned and went to his dresser and grabbed his diamond Cartier wristwatch and his long 220-gram platinum chain with a diamond-encrusted Jesus piece and put it around his neck. Last but not least, he put his platinum and diamond grill inside of his mouth. He smiled a sparkling smile and said, "Lookin' like a million bucks, baby!"

By the time Taz came back down stairs, his homeboys were busy munching on their steaks that Red had prepared for them. When Keno saw that Taz was all spiffy he said, "Damn, nigga! You just goin' to get somethin' to eat! Why you get so clean on a nigga?"

Taz laughed and said, "Fool, I'm eating with wifey. She likes it when a nigga is lookin' and smellin' good. Stop hatin', clown!"

"Fuck you, nigga!"

"Look though. After I finish eating, I'm goin' to go check on some of my rental houses on the south side. What y'all got up for the day?"

"I'm goin' to go kick it with that nigga Bob," Red said from the other side of the kitchen counter.

"I think I'm gon' hit the mall up and do me a li'l shoppin'. It's been a minute. I need me a few new outfits," replied Keno.

"I'm tired as a muthafucka. I'm goin' to the pad and lay it down," said Bo-Pete.

"Me too," added Wild Bill.

"All right then, lock up the spot when y'all bounce, and make sure you messy niggas clean up y'alls mess. I'm outta here."

"Dog, have you heard anything from that nigga, Won yet?" asked Keno as he wiped A-1 Steak Sauce from his lips.

"Nah, I ain't heard shit from that fool. He'll holla when it's time though. You better believe that."

"Yeah, I know."

"All right then, my niggas, I'm out," Taz said as he turned and left the kitchen.

By the time he arrived in front of the office building that housed the offices of Whitney & Johnson, Sacha was standing outside looking gorgeous yet businesslike in a brown pants suit. Her shapely figure could be seen, even though her pants were somewhat loose-fitting. She had her long, jet-black hair tied up in a bun. Taz smiled as he pulled in front of her and quickly jumped out of his car and opened the door for his fiancée. She smiled as she climbed inside of the car.

After he had gotten back inside of the Bentley, Sacha asked, "What made you bring the Bentley out today, baby?"

He shrugged his shoulders and said, "I don't know. I was in the mood to roll around with my Li'l Mama in a li'l luxury, I guess." Truthfully, the real reason he chose to drive one of his other vehicles was that he didn't want to take the chance of being seen by any of them Hoover niggas in his truck. He was not about to let anything happen to Sacha. Not if he could help it.

They arrived at The Daiquiri Zone and enjoyed a lunch of hot wings and French fries. Sacha's appetite shocked Taz as he watched her totally devour a plateful of hot wings. "Damn, Li'l Mama! You kinda hungry, huh?"

After wiping hot sauce from her lips, she smiled and said, "You know I'm eating for two, baby."

He laughed and said, "Yeah, I know!" He sipped his strawberry daiquiri. *I normally don't drink sweet fruity type drinks, but this one tasted pretty good,* he thought to himself as he stared at his fiancée.

Sacha noticed him staring and asked, "What?"

He smiled and said, "I want you, Li'l Mama. Do you have to go back to work? Or can you take the rest of the day off?"

She smiled seductively and said, "I've already taken the rest of the day off, baby. I was thinking the same thing as soon as I got off the phone with you."

"Then hurry up and finish off the rest of those wings, so we can go to your spot and work up another appetite!"

Chapter Fifteen

Keno and Katrina were relaxing on Keno's bed, engaging in a little pillow talk. Katrina had just finished sexing the hell out of Keno, and he was as content as ever. She smiled lazily, stretched and said, "I asked around about what's been up with them Hoover dudes, like you asked me to, baby."

"Yeah? Did you find out anything?" Keno asked as he reached and grabbed a Black and Mild cigar off of his nightstand.

"Do you know a guy by the name of C-Baby? He's an original 107 Hoover. He was one of the first ones that started Hoover in the city back in the days. Them L.A. Hoovers liked him and put him in charge of organizing the rest of the guys in the city."

"Is that right? Nah, I don't know no nigga like that. Why? What's up with him?"

"I don't know, but there has to be a connection somehow. Remember that guy that Taz shot in front of the club a few months back?"

"Yeah."

"He was from Hoover."

"What? You bullshittin'!" he asked excitedly.

"Uh-uh, I'm serious. As a matter a fact, he was real tight with C-Baby back in the days."

"So you think this C-Baby nigga has the beef with us?"

"I'm just saying, your boy did kill his homeboy. That has to be it. Why else would the Hoovers be trying to get at Taz? Y'all ain't on no gang-bangin' shit."

"Real talk, baby, that's good lookin'," Keno said as he grabbed the phone and quickly dialed Taz's home number. When Taz answered the phone Keno repeated everything Katrina had just told him and said, "That's got to be the reason, my nigga. You took that fool, C-Baby's dog. And since he's supposed to be an O.G. over there, he has to get back at ya."

Shaking her head no, Katrina said, "Uh-uh, it's not C-Baby whose getting at y'all. He don't even come around no more. He's some big-time lawyer now downtown at Whitney & Johnson law firm. He has the rest of them Hoovers all fired up to look at y'all 'cause he don't get down like that no more. At least that's what I heard."

Taz heard what Katrina had just told Keno and asked, "What did she just say, dog?"

"She said that that nigga C-Baby ain't the one who actually put in the work 'cause he's some big-time lawyer now."

"How the fuck can an O.G. Hoover Crip become an attorney?" Taz wondered aloud.

"Maybe the nigga found Jesus and changed his ways or some shit. How the fuck would I know?"

"She did say that that clown worked at Whitney & Johnson, huh?"

"Yeah. Why?"

"Think about it, nigga. Sacha's a partner at that firm, remember?"

"That's right! I forgot about that shit, dog! This shit is hittin' too fuckin' close to home, Taz. What the fuck is up?"

"I don't know, my nigga, but I'm about to find out. I'll get at ya in a li'l bit. Tell your girl that I said good lookin'."

"Fa' sho," Keno said, and hung up. He then turned to Katrina and said, "You done good, baby, and just for that, I'm gon' break you off some more of this good dick."

She smiled and said, "M-m-m! Is there anything else you want me to find out for you, baby?"

"Not right now, *mami*, but you can find your way back on top of this!" he said as he held his erect penis in his hand.

Back at Taz's house, he was wracking his brains trying to figure out how the pieces to this puzzle fit. All of a sudden it came to him. "Nah! Hell nah! I know that nigga didn't!" he screamed as he grabbed the phone and called Sacha on her cell phone. When she answered, he asked her, "Where are you, Li'l Mama?"

"I'm on my way home. I just left Bob and Gwen at Bob's house. What's up, baby"?"

"Tell me somethin', Li'l Mama. How well did you know that nigga, Cliff when y'all were goin' out and shit?"

"What do you mean?"

"Did he tell you anything about his past?"

Sacha thought about Taz's question for a minute while she drove, and then she said, "Now that you mention it, not really. Why? What's goin' on, Taz?"

"Baby, you're not goin' to believe this shit, but I got a funny feelin' that the nigga Cliff is the reason them Crip niggas tried to get at me at the club the other night."

"What?"

Taz quickly explained to her what Katrina had told Keno. Afterward he said, "But how could that nigga have been caught up with the Hoovers, and then become an attorney and shit?"

Sacha pulled into her driveway, cut off her car and said, "That's easy, baby. As long as he was never convicted of a felony, there would be nothing in his way to stop him from becoming an attorney."

"Well, I'll be damn! And to think I was actually thinkin' 'bout lettin' that clown-ass nigga make it!"

"What are you talking about, Taz?"

"Don't you see it, Li'l Mama? That nigga Cliff is C-Baby! He had that nigga I smoked in front of the club try to rob us. But, on the real, he wasn't just goin' to rob us; he was supposed to smoke me! He wanted to get me out of the way so he could get to you!"

"Come on, baby. That's a little far-fetched, don't you think?"

"Think about it. Cliff's friend from back in the day tries to rob us, and I smoke his ass. Months later, some Hoover niggas try to dump on me at the same fuckin' club. I don't believe in coincidences, Li'l Mama. It all makes fuckin' sense. That nigga tried to have me smoked! He knew that he had to get me out of the way to be able to get at you!" Taz yelled excitedly.

"Calm down, baby. All you have is circumstantial evidence. You still don't have any solid proof against him."

He smiled and said, "There goes that lawyer in you talkin', Li'l Mama. I have all of the proof I fuckin' need. That nigga's a dead man now for real!"

Sacha climbed out of her car, walked inside of her home and said, "Baby, what about Tazneema?"

"What about Tazneema? What about *me*? That fool has tried to take me out—not once, but twice! You want proof, Li'l Mama? All right, I'll give you some fuckin' proof. What's that nigga's telephone number?"

"Why?"

"I'm gon' call him and ask for C-Baby. If he doesn't acknowledge that he's in fact C-Baby, I give you my word, on MiMi's grave, that I'll leave this shit alone and never bring it up again."

"Deal! But what are you going to say if he does or doesn't acknowledge you?"

"I'll just hang up the phone. My number's unlisted, and it won't show on his caller ID."

Sacha smiled and said, "Okay, his number is 427-7023."

Taz clicked over and quickly dialed the number that she had just given him, and then clicked back over to Sacha while the phone rang. The telephone rang three times before it was answered. When Cliff picked up the line, Taz made his voice sound deeper than normal and said, "Can I speak to C-Baby?"

Clifford hesitated momentarily, and then said, "This is him. Who's this?"

Taz hung up the phone in his face and yelled, "I told you! I fuckin' told you, Li'l Mama! That nigga is fuckin' dead!"

Sacha sat down at her dining room table and said, "Shit!"

After Clifford hung up the phone he said, "Fuck! That was Taz! That nigga has figured out my ties with the homies! He's going to try to get at me for real now!" He picked up the phone and called H-Hop. When H-Hop answered the phone, Clifford said, "Cuz, my peoples wasn't able to get a line on that nigga's pad from his tag number. It came back to his mother's house out in Spencer. We have to get them niggas, loc. I think he's about to try and make a move on me."

"What makes you say that, cuz?" asked H-Hop.

Clifford told him about the call he had just received, and said, "That nigga didn't know me by C-Baby, cuz. He has done his homework, loc, and figured shit out."

"How you wanna play this shit, cuz?"

"Whichever way we play this shit, we gots to play to win, 'cause that nigga's going to come at us real hard."

Chapter Sixteen

Pitt was sitting inside of his office with a content smile on his face. He was about to get at whomever this G person was, and after that, he was confident that he would be able to get all of the proof he needed to hang Won's ass. There was a knock at his door and he yelled, "Come on in!"

A short white woman entered his office, followed by Leo and Tru. She smiled at Pitt and asked, "How are you doing, Pitt?"

"Just fine, Vixen, just fine. Did you bring everything you're going to need for this one?"

With a nod of her head, she said, "Yes, I have everything right here. All you have to do is keep this guy on the line for at least thirty seconds, and I'll get a direct line on him. I'll only be able to hold onto him for thirty to thirty-five seconds though. So it's important that you apprehend him as soon as you can, or we'll have to go through this all over again."

"Don't worry, I won't miss. Leo and Tru here are going to make sure that they get him on the first try," Pitt said confidently as he smiled at his two heavy hitters.

Leo was a Samoan who stood a little over six foot, and was very muscular. He kept his long hair pulled back into a tight ponytail. Just by looking into his eyes one could tell that he was not to be fucked with. Pitt liked to refer to Leo as his "personal torpedo" because when Leo hit, he hit hard and fast and caused a tremendous amount of damage.

Though Tru was older than Leo, he was equally as dangerous. He stood at six foot two inches, and was small compared to his partner. His body language made people feel as if he was harmless, but that was not true at all. Tru had executed more men than anyone else in Pitt's camp. And most of his victims died by his hands. Pitt thought that was strange at first, but he quickly understood that Tru got some kind of crazy rush when he killed a man or woman with his bare hands. Pitt really didn't give a damn how the work was completed, just as long as the job was done effectively.

Pitt sat back in his leather chair and said, "All right, Vee, do you."

Vixen smiled and pulled out a small laptop computer. After she turned it on, she started typing what looked like a thousand words a minute. Her fingers were a blur to one's vision as she typed at a super speed. After about six or seven minutes of this, she finally stopped and said, "I'm ready, Pitt. What is the telephone number?"

Pitt grabbed the white slip of paper that Brenda gave him and read the number off it. When he was finished, he said, "Tru, you and Leo head on downstairs to the truck. I'll call y'all and give you directions on where to go get this nigga as soon as Vixen gives me his hookup. Make sure that he remains breathing, Leo. He's no good to me dead."

Leo smiled and said, "Don't trip, Pitt. I got you."

After Leo and Tru left the office, Vixen tapped some more keys on her laptop and said, "All right, this is how this works. I have plugged my laptop to your phone here, and all you have to do is call this guy and keep him on the phone for at least thirty seconds like I said. Once you hang up, I'll have a line on all of his movements as long as he has his cell phone on his person."

"I'm telling you, Vee, this is some crazy shit. This shit is like that TV show, 24 on Fox. Do you ever watch that shit?"

Vixen smiled and shook her head no.

Pitt started laughing and said, "You know what? You're my 'Chloe'!"

"You're what?" she asked with a smile on her face.

"Chloe. You know, the computer geek broad who saves Jack's ass all of the time. She's the best at that shit. As a matter a fact, I think she did some shit like this before for Jack."

Vixen laughed then said, "Okay, Pitt. Are you ready or what?"

He lit one of his hand-rolled Cuban cigars and said, "Yep, I'm ready if you are."

"Make the call," she said as she focused on her laptop.

Pitt dialed the number to the cell phone of the mysterious man named G. The cell was answered on the third ring. "Hello?"

"Yo', let me speak to G," Pitt said in a deep tone of voice.

"Who's this?"

"Is this G?" Pitt asked as he took a quick peek at his platinum watch by Jacob the Jeweler.

"Yeah, this is G. Now, who the fuck am I talkin' to?"

"Check this out, clown. My name is Pitt, and I want to know who put you onto my girl Brenda. If you give me this information, I'd highly appreciate it."

G started laughing and said, "Yeah, I bet you would, dog. But check this out. Fuck you, nigga! You've wasted your fuckin' time gettin' at me, partna!"

"I'm sorry you feel that way," Pitt said as he watched as Vixen gave him thumbs-up, indicating that she had what she needed. He smiled and told G, "I guess I'll be seeing you then, my man."

"Whatever, Mr. Big Man!" G said as he started laughing and hung up the phone in Pitt's ear.

After Pitt hung up the phone, he stared at Vixen as she tapped furiously on her laptop. After she finished, she turned the screen toward him and said, "Right now he's over in Fairfield, out by Travis Air Force Base. He's not moving, so I assume he's at his home right now. Go on and tell your boys to head out toward Fairfield. I'll have his exact address within the next five minutes."

"You mean you can tell me exactly where he lives at?" asked a shock Pitt.

Vixen nodded. "Sure can. You'd be surprised how much I can do with this bad boy right here," she said as she lovingly rubbed the side of her laptop.

Pitt started laughing and yelled, "You *are* my Chloe!" He then called Leo and Tru and told them to head out to Fairfield, which was maybe twenty minutes outside of Oakland. "G, you're about to get the surprise of your fucking life!" he said as he smiled and inhaled deeply on his Cuban cigar.

***

Won had become slightly concerned. *Cash Flo' and Pitt should have called for a meet by now,* he thought as he walked around his luxurious home. He stepped out onto his sun deck overlooking the Pacific and smiled. For as long as he could remember, he had lived the good life. His hunger for power was what kept him motivated to have more. Once he obtained complete control over The Network, there would be no stopping him. It would be as if he owned a nice chunk of the world. "Come on, Cash Flo', don't change up on me now, you old bastard!" he said aloud as he turned and went back inside of his home.

Back in Oakland, Pitt was on the telephone talking to Leo on his cell phone. "The address is 2671 North Williams Avenue. Vixen just told me that he's still at that address right now. How far are y'all from Fairfield now?"

"We've just made it in. We'll be at his place within the next ten minutes," Leo said, and gave the address to Tru.

"All right, call me after y'all got that nigga," Pitt said, and hung up the phone. "All right, Chloe, how much do I owe you for your services this time?"

Vixen smiled and said, "The usual, Pitt. But shouldn't you wait until your boys have grabbed your man?"

"Nah, they'll handle everything. You can go on and have some fun. As a matter a fact, I'm throwing in an extra thousand for your superb work," he said as he passed her an envelope with eleven thousand dollars inside of it.

Vixen accepted the money from him and began to disconnect her equipment from Pitt's telephone line. After she had all of her stuff together, she said, "You know where to find me if you need me, Pitt."

"That I do, babe. Take care of yourself," he said as he watched her leave his office. Just as he reclined in his chair his cell phone rang. "Hello."

"What's going on with you, old boy?" asked Cash Flo'.

"Everything is just fine up here in Northern Cali, baby. What's up with you down there in the South?"

"I'm sitting here wondering why haven't I heard anything from you. But since you sound so fucking happy, I guess it's safe to assume that everything is going the way you want it to."

"Yeah, you can say that. I'm waiting on a call as we speak to confirm that I got that nigga who paid my people to cross me. Once I have him, it won't be long before I give you a call so you can green-light that nigga Won."

"I'll be waiting," Cash Flo' said, and hung up the phone.

Just as Pitt closed his cell phone, the phone on his desk started ringing. He glanced at the number on the caller ID and smiled as he picked up the receiver and said, "Tell me that you got his ass."

Leo smiled and said, "Yeah, we got him. Tru just put him inside of the truck."

"All right, you know where to take him. I'll meet y'all there."

"Cool," Leo calmly replied.

After speaking with Leo, Pitt jumped out of his chair and grabbed his suit jacket. He had a huge smile on his face as he left his office. He went down to the underground parking area and jumped into his Jaguar, and sped out of the parking lot.

It took him under ten minutes to make it to East Oakland. He pulled into the driveway of a house that looked as if it had seen better days. The windows were boarded up, and the grass looked as if it had been scorched for years.

Pitt's Jaguar looked totally out of place in this neighborhood as he climbed out of it and walked toward the front door of the broken-down home. He pulled out his keys, unlocked the front door and quickly stepped inside.

Though the house was a boarded-up wreck on the outside, the inside was a completely different story. Inside of the living room sat a fifty-five-inch plasma screen television equipped with a DVD player. To the far right of the living room was a comfortable-looking sectional sofa. It wasn't all that plush, but it was definitely comfortable. Pitt sat down on the sofa and pulled out his cell phone and called Leo. "Where y'all at?" he asked when Leo answered his cell.

"We're turning onto the street now. I see your car in the driveway right now," replied Leo.

"Good," Pitt said and closed his cell. He went to the front door and watched as Leo pulled into the driveway and parked his truck behind his Jag. Since the sun had already set, it was dark enough for no one to really pay any attention to Leo and Tru as they walked G inside of the boarded-up home in handcuffs.

Once they had him inside of the house, Pitt smiled and said, "Hi, G. My name is Pitt. I'm the guy you got real fly with earlier. I want you to know that what you're about to go through will be very very painful—that is if you choose not to cooperate with us. If you do cooperate, then your death will be swift. Either way, you are going to die today. So, the choice is yours on how you go out. Do you understand what I'm saying, G?"

G, a tall, dark-skinned man, smiled and showed a mouthful of bright white teeth and said, "Since I'm dying regardless, I think I'd rather go out the hard way." He shrugged his shoulders and continued, "I'm kinda funny like that. I've never been with taking the easy way out, ya know what I'm sayin'?"

Pitt smiled and said, "I can accept that. But you are going to tell me what I need to know."

"That remains to be seen, Mr. Big Man!" G replied arrogantly.

Pitt sighed heavily and then told Leo and Tru, "All right, you two, get to work." He then went and sat back down on the sofa and watched as his men began to viciously torture G.

Chapter Seventeen

"I'm tellin' you, Tee, I should have been taken that punk-ass clown out the game! That nigga is actually tryin' to get at me! That fool really doesn't know who he's fuckin' with!" yelled Taz.

"Obviously he does, Taz. If he didn't, he wouldn't have tried to get at you in the first place," Tari replied logically.

"I bet you that that punk-ass nigga wasn't even at the club that night. It was probably some of his li'l homeboys. He don't have no heart like that."

"How do you know that, Taz? There were four of them that night. One of them could have been him. You were on the ground, remember?"

Taz smiled and said, "Fuck you, Tee!"

Tari laughed and said, "I didn't mean it like that, silly. I meant that he could have been there, you know."

"Yeah, but I doubt it. But, look, I gots to have that nigga, and I mean like yesterday. Until I do, I'm makin' sure that the homies stay out of the way."

"Just remember to use your head, Taz. Don't let your emotions control you on this shit."

"I won't."

"I spoke with Won the other day."

"Yeah? What's up with him?"

"I don't know. He sounded sort of strange to me. I don't think things are going the way he planned them to. If that's the case, then he's in a real funky mood."

"I wouldn't know shit about that one. I've never been around him when shit ain't goin' his way."

Tari laughed and said, "Well, I have, and believe me, it's not a pretty sight."

"Oh, well! He'll get it together. You just make sure that you're ready when he does."

"I stay ready, Taz," she said seriously.

"Good. Now, let me roll. I got some shit to check on."

"Be careful out there, Taz."

"I will. Bye!" After hanging up with her, he called Sacha and asked, "Are you ready, baby? It's Friday night, and I'm tryin' to have a pleasurable evening with my Li'l Mama."

"Umm . . . Taz, baby, I kinda invited Bob and Gwen to join us for dinner," Sacha said hesitantly.

Taz laughed and said, "You *kinda* invited them, huh? How can you kinda invite someone out with us, Li'l Mama?"

"You know what I mean! Stop that, baby! They've been cooped up inside of Bob's house since he got back from New York. I thought it would be fun for them if they came and had dinner with us. Are you mad at me, baby?" she asked sweetly.

"Don't even try it, Li'l Mama! That sweet shit ain't gon' make everything all good. On the real though, nah, I ain't mad at ya. I haven't seen my nigga since he made it back anyway. With all of this drama goin' on, I've been too caught up. I'm on my way over, so please be ready when I get there. I'm not tryin' to be sittin' there for forever waitin' on you to finish gettin' dressed."

"I'm not even going to respond to that comment, mister! Bye!"

Taz smiled as he hung up the phone, grabbed his keys and went into his four-car garage. He jumped into his Bentley and hit the garage door opener. As he was pulling out of the garage he saw Bo-Pete's Navigator pulling into his circular driveway. He stopped, climbed out of his car and walked toward Bo-Pete's truck. "What up, my niggas?" he asked Bo-Pete and Wild Bill once he made it to the driver's side of the Navigator.

"Ain't shit. Bored as hell, really. We just came over here to see what you had poppin' for the night," said Bo-Pete.

"I'm on my way to go have dinner with Sacha, Gwen and Bob. What? Y'all tryin' to tag along?"

"Fuck nah! We might as well hit the club and have some drinks," Wild Bill said from the passenger's seat.

"Might as well. We ain't got shit else to do," replied Bo-Pete.

"Dog, why don't y'all get with Red and Keno if y'all gon' hit the club up? You know shit is too hot right now. I don't want them Hoover niggas to have any action at gettin' at any of us."

"First off, fuck them fools, gee! And, second, Keno and Red are doing the same thing you and Bob are doing. They're spending time with their broads. Don't worry about us, gee. We'll be straight. Believe me, when we walk out that bitch, we'll have the straps in our hands cocked and locked!" Bo-Pete said confidently.

"All right, but make sure that you hit me after y'all leave the club."

Wild Bill started laughing and said, "Look at this nigga, all worried and shit! Don't sweat it, my nigga. We gots this."

Taz laughed and said, "Fuck you two niggas! I'm out!" He turned and walked back to his car.

Just like Taz figured, when he made it over to Sacha's house she was still in the process of getting dressed. "Damn, Li'l Mama! Why you always got to do me like this? I told you I didn't feel like waiting forever for you to get ready."

Sacha smiled as she applied the last of her makeup. She came out of the bathroom and said, "You can't rush a woman when she's getting dressed, Taz. That's not polite."

"Polite? Whoever said I was a polite nigga? You better bring your ass on before you get left!"

"O-o-o-h! I like it when you're all tough and demanding with me!" she said as she grabbed her Chanel purse.

Taz smiled and had to admit that his fiancée was looking real damn good. She was wearing the hell out of a sexy black-and-gray dress by Prada, with matching gray pumps. Her hair was hanging loosely past her bare shoulders just the way he liked it. Her cleavage was looking edible to him. "We need to gon' and bounce before I end up changin' our plans for the evening," he said as he stared at the long split that went straight up the middle of her dress.

She smiled and said, "I'll take that as a compliment. Come on, silly. I'm ready."

***

Clifford was on the phone talking to Tazneema, when he got a call from H-Hop on his cell phone. "Hold on, baby," he told her, and then answered his other phone. "What up, cuz?"

"Since we haven't had any luck finding them niggas, me and Li'l Bomb are about to go post up at that club and see if them niggas pop up again. You tryin' to roll, cuz?" asked H-Hop.

"I don't think they'll show, but fuck it, cuz! I ain't got nothing else to get into for the night. I'll be over there in about twenty minutes. It's early, so I know those fools won't be there yet—that is if they come out."

"All right, cuz, see you in a li'l bit."

Clifford grabbed the phone as he set his cell phone on the table, and told Tazneema, "Looks like I'm on my way out, baby."

"Where are you going?" Tazneema asked jealously.

He laughed and said, "I'm about to go have a few drinks with some lawyers I know from another firm. You know, network a little. I am trying to get another job, remember?"

"Oh. I thought you had a hot date all of a sudden. You know I was about to tell Mama-Mama I gots to go stop my man from being naughty!"

They both laughed at her joke. "You don't ever have to worry about anything like that, 'Neema. I'm yours and yours only for as long as you want me."

"Then that means you're mine forever, Cliff."

He laughed and said, "So be it, baby. Give me a call on my cell a little later if you want. You can come on over, and we can cuddle for a little while."

"Cuddle? If I sneak out of this house, I'm not coming way over to your house just to cuddle. I'm coming to get me some, boy!"

He laughed and said, "You are crazy, girl! I love you!"

"I love you more. I'll give you a call later. Bye!" she said and hung up.

Clifford went into his bedroom and put on a pair of black jeans and a blue sweatshirt, and grabbed his car keys. He was off to see if he could get lucky enough to kill Taz tonight.

***

Bo-Pete and Wild Bill were standing outside of the club, checking out their surroundings. Bo-Pete tried to remember every single car parked close to and across the street from them. He wasn't about to let those Crips get a lucky shot at him and Wild Bill.

After they felt comfortable, they put their 9 mm in the small of their backs and entered the club. It felt good to know that they could always enter the club with their weapons. They had it like that. There were no metal detectors for any members of their crew. *That shit was for suckas*, thought Bo-Pete as he stepped to the bar and ordered a glass of Hennessy for himself and Wild Bill.

Taz and Sacha met Gwen and Bob at the Outback Steak-house. While they were enjoying their meal, Taz had a feeling that something was just not right. For some reason, he just couldn't relax. *Bob seems to be back to his old self,* he thought as he watched his homeboy clown with his girl Gwen.

"I'm tellin' you, baby, as soon as they take this bag off, I'm gon' break you off somethin' real proper for the way you been handlin' a nigga," Bob told Gwen with a smile on his face.

"Humph! You need to! I'm sick and tired of having to do all of the damn work, with your nasty-ass!" Gwen said as she smiled lovingly toward her man.

Ever since Bob had made it back from New York, their relationship seemed to have intensified. Gwen was so scared that she was going to lose him, she clung to him tighter than ever now.

Even though Bob was on some "tough man time," he had been just as scared of losing Gwen. He didn't fear the thought of dying. What scared him most was the thought of not being able to be with his soul mate for the rest of his life. He was in love for the first time in his crazy life, and it felt real good.

They laughed and joked for the rest of the evening. After dinner was over, they decided to head over to Bob and Gwen's place for some more drinks. As Taz followed Bob out to his home, he still couldn't shake that funny feeling he'd been having evening. He grabbed his cell and called Keno. When Keno answered his cell phone Taz asked, "What's up, dog? Y'all straight?"

"Yeah, we're good. What's up with you?"

"Chillin'. We just finished eating, and we're on our way over to Bob's spot to chill out for a li'l while longer. You heard from Bo-Pete and Wild Bill?"

"Nah."

"They told me that they were goin' to the club and hang for a minute."

"Is that right? Well, you know them niggas are most likely gettin' their drink on and clowin' with some hoes or some shit."

"Yeah, I know. All right then, my nigga, I'll get at you in the morning."

Keno didn't like the sound of Taz's voice, so he asked, "What's wrong, dog?"

That nigga knows me like a book, Taz thought. "What you mean?" he asked.

"Come on, nigga. You know I be knowin' when somethin' ain't sittin' right with you. What's up?"

Taz sighed and said, "I don't know, dog. I've been havin' this funny feeling all night, like I'm missin' somethin', or that I should be somewhere I'm not."

"Keep your eyes open at all times, dog, and everything will be all good. We're in some stressful times right now. You just mind fuckin' yourself, that's all. Everything's goin' to be everything."

"Yeah, I know. I'll holla," Taz said and closed his cell phone.

As he pulled into Bob's driveway, Sacha said, "Are you really okay, baby?"

Taz shrugged his shoulders and said, "I guess. Come on, let's go on inside and chill with these two clowns."

Sacha laughed and said, "You got that right! I swear they're made for each other. I'm so happy for Gwen. She really deserves to be happy."

"Yeah, I'm happy for my nigga too. I never thought he would have been capable of crackin' a broad of Gwen's caliber. I guess it's true what they say."

"What's that?"

"Love is a muthafucka!" They both started laughing as they walked inside of Bob's ranch-style home.

Clifford, Li'l Bomb, Astro and H-Hop were sitting across the street from Club Cancun, staring at Bo-Pete's Navigator. "Do you think that's one of them niggas' shit?" asked Li'l Bomb as he racked a live round into the chamber of his AK-47 assault rifle.

"It could be, but I don't see any of them other niggas' trucks. I told you, they don't roll unless they're six deep," Clifford said as he let his eyes roam all over the parking lot of the club.

"They might feel that they've handled their business enough to make us lay it down. But you never know. They might be cocky enough to slip, cuz," said H-Hop from the back seat of the stolen SUV they were sitting in.

"Why don't you go on inside and see if you can spot them real quick. Ain't no need for us to be sittin' out here all night for nothin', loc," Astro said.

"All right, I be right back," Clifford said as he climbed out the truck. He jogged across the street and walked inside of the club. He stopped right before he made it to the downstairs entrance. He saw Bo-Pete and Wild Bill talking to a couple of females. He quickly scanned the rest of the club to see if he could spot Taz and others, and once he was positive that they weren't there, he turned and went back outside to the truck with his homeboys. When he got back inside of the SUV, he said, "Them niggas are slippin' tonight, cuz. There are only two of them in there. That nigga Bo-Pete and that li'l nigga they call Wild Bill."

"All right, now we wait. You never know. The rest of them niggas might just show up. If not, then we'll serve them two punk-ass niggas, cuz. That'll let that fool Taz know that we ain't playin!" Astro said seriously.

"I'm with that shit, cuz. I'm gettin' my man tonight. That's on 107 Hoover Crip!" yelled Li'l Bomb.

Back inside of the club, Bo-Pete and Wild Bill were bored. "Dog, we should have went on and hung out with the homies. I'm sick of these fake-ass hoes up in this spot. Ain't none of them wifey material for real," Bo-Pete said as he set his glass of Hennessy on the bar.

"Nigga, I ain't tryin' to find no fuckin' wifey any fuckin' way. All I'm tryin' to do is get me some ass from one of these hoes tonight. You're right though. Ain't nothin' up in this spot worth getting at tonight," replied Wild Bill.

"Let's go shoot some pool up at the Plum Tree. There might be a few hoes up there we can get at."

"I'm with you, my nigga." Will Bill downed the rest of his drink and set it down on the bar next to Bo-Pete's empty glass.

They stepped away from the bar and started walking toward the exit of the club. As soon as they made it to the door, they paused and pulled out their weapons. They then stepped outside of the club side by side, and let their eyes roam quickly all over the parking lot. Neither of them saw anything out of the norm, so they started walking toward Bo-Pete's truck.

The first shot almost hit Wild Bill as he ducked and yelled, "Watch it, Bo! They're on your right!"

Bo-Pete turned to his right and started firing his weapon at the three guys running toward him and Wild Bill. Will Bill was right by Bo-Pete's side, firing his pistol at the Crips attacking them.

Neither the Crips nor Wild Bill nor Bo-Pete were backing down from one another. It was basically a modern-day shoot-out at the OK Coral, the only difference being that they were in the parking lot of Club Cancun. The Crips kept charging Bo-Pete and Wild Bill, and Wild Bill and Bo-Pete kept calmly walking toward the Crips with their weapons spitting fire. The night was lit up with sparks as the gunshots rang out.

They were about six feet from each other when Wild Bill saw Bo-Pete fall to the ground. Wild Bill knew that Bo-Pete had been hit, but he couldn't stop to help him. He knew the only way either of them was going to survive was if he got his man. He aimed carefully and picked off Astro. He hit Astro twice in his chest and quickly aimed his gun again, this time toward Clifford. He missed Clifford by inches. Even though he missed, his last two shots did what he had hoped they would. Clifford turned and started running back toward the truck, and so did Li'l Bomb, because his AK-47 had jammed and he didn't want to take the risk of trying to un-jam it and get himself hit.

While they retreated to their SUV, Wild Bill ran back to Bo-Pete, scooped his gun out of his hand and ran toward the truck the Crips were climbing inside of. He let off three shots at the truck before he felt himself spin and fall to the ground. He rolled over onto his side and fired some more at the fleeing SUV. He slowly got to his feet and staggered over to where Astro was lying in the street and shot him twice in his face. He then stumbled toward where Bo-Pete was lying. He screamed as he knelt next to his homeboy. He held Bo-Pete's lifeless body in his arms as he continued to scream. *"No-o-o-o-o!"*

Chapter Eighteen

Keno was walking to his kitchen when the telephone started ringing. "Who the fuck is this callin' me this fuckin' late?" he said aloud as he grabbed the cordless phone from its base on top of the kitchen counter. "Hello!"

"Dog! Them niggas got Bo-Pete! They got Bo-Pete!" screamed Wild Bill.

"*What?* Where y'all at?"

"I'm in a fuckin' ambulance right now! They're taking me to Baptist! I got hit in my shoulder, but Bo-Pete didn't make it, dog. He's gone! He's fuckin' gone!"

"Look, calm down, Babyboy. Just calm down. We'll see you at the hospital, gee. Go on and let them fix you up my, nigga. We'll be there in a few minutes."

The only response he got from Wild Bill was, "He's gone, dog! Bo's gone!"

Keno hung up the phone and quickly called Taz's cell. After he told Taz what Wild Bill had just told him, Taz said, "I'll meet y'all at the hospital." Taz closed his cell phone and told Bob, "Them niggas got Wild Bill and took Bo-Pete, dog!"

"*What?* Come on, my nigga! Please tell me you're playin'!" cried Bob.

"I wish I was, gee. I gots to go. I'll give you a call when I know more."

"*What?* Nigga, I'm rollin' with you!"

"Nah, stay here and get your rest, dog. I'll get at ya when everything is everything."

With tears sliding slowly down his face, Bob said, "Fuck you! You can't stop me from goin' to the fuckin' hospital! I said! I'm! Rollin'! With! You!"

With tears of his own falling freely, Taz shook his head and said, "Come on, dog, let's bounce then."

Gwen and Sacha both knew better than to say anything. The shit was about to hit the fan, and there was absolutely nothing either one of them could do to stop it.

By the time Taz and Bob made it to Baptist Hospital on the northwest side of town, Red and Keno were sitting in the waiting area of the emergency room.

Red was visibly shaken. His eyes were bloodshot from crying so hard, and the look on his face told all that looked his way that he was in a murderous mood.

Keno sat in his seat with his hands covering his face, trying his best to control his emotions.

When Taz saw the both of them, his heart felt as if it had stopped. He actually couldn't breathe as he sat down next to Keno.

Keno felt his presence, looked up at his homeboy and said, "They got him, dog. He was dead before he made it here. Those punk-ass niggas hit him twice—once in the neck and once in his chest with somethin' real heavy, my nigga. The cat in the ambulance told me they tried everything they could, but his wounds were just too severe."

"Where's Wild Bill?" asked Taz.

"He's in surgery right now. They said he's goin' to be all right. He caught a shell in his shoulder."

"Did you get a chance to holla at him again?"

Shaking his head no, Keno said, "Not since I've been here. When he called me, he told me that them Hoover niggas got at him and Bo-Pete, and that Bo was gone. That's all I know right now, my nigga. They killed one of ours, gee! You know what that means, don't you?"

Taz stared hard at his lifelong friend and said, "Yeah, I know what it means. Are you ready to do this?"

Keno stared at Taz for a moment, and then said, "Yeah, I'm ready. None of this really matters no more to me, dog. We started this shit together, and we gots to end it together. Fuck the world, my nigga! Fuck the muthafuckin' world!"

Taz shook his head no and said, "Nah, fuck them Hoover niggas! Fuck every last Hoover! And that's exactly what we're about to do." He turned toward Red and said, "I've always hoped and prayed that it would never come to this, but we made a pact years ago. If somethin' like this ever happened to one of us, we would ride until the beef was settled. The only way we can settle this beef is to remove every last one of them coward-ass niggas. You know that, right?"

Red stared hard at Taz as if he had lost his mind and said, "Nigga, you don't have to explain shit to me. Let's get this shit started!"

Taz held up his hand, signaling Red to wait a minute as he turned toward Bob. "Dog, you'd be in the way more than anything if you tried to ride with us on this shit. You gots to stand down, dog."

"Fuck that! I made the same pact as the rest of you niggas! This shit bag ain't shit to me, Taz! Don't do this, dog! I gots to roll too!" Bob screamed.

"No, you don't!" screamed Gwen. "All you have to do is bring your ass home with me and let them take care of whatever they have to take care of!" she yelled, tears streaming down her face.

Bob was shocked because he hadn't seen her or Sacha enter the waiting room. He stepped over to where she was standing, grabbed her hand and said, "Gwen, I love you more than you'll ever imagine. Please believe me, because it's so damn true. But nothin' and nobody can stop me from gettin' the niggas who killed Bo-Pete. If I have to die, then so be it. I gots to do what I gots to do."

Before Gwen could respond, Taz stepped behind Bob and began to choke him out. He put Bob in a full-nelson chokehold until he was unconscious. He then gently sat him down in one of the chairs in the waiting room and said, "That was the only way, Gwen. He was goin' to go with us no matter what you said to him."

"I know, Taz, and thank you. Thank you so much!"

Taz turned and told Red, "Grab Bob and take him and Gwen back to his spot. Make sure when you get there that you take all of his weapons. Leave one with Gwen. He's still gon' need somethin' to protect them, just in case them fools find out where he stays." Taz turned back toward Gwen and said, "No matter what, make sure that he doesn't know that you have a weapon in that house. Make him think that we took everything out of there. We're also taking the keys to his truck, your car, and his other vehicles. If y'all need anything, call Sacha and she'll make sure that y'all are straight."

Gwen didn't say anything. She just gave Taz a nod of her head, indicating that she understood what he had just told her.

Taz turned toward Sacha finally and said, "I'm sorry, Li'l Mama. I'm so sorry." Before she could say a word, he told Keno, "Come on, dog. We gots work to do."

Sacha sat down and cried as she watched Taz and Keno leave the hospital. When Gwen tried to help her to her feet, she shook her off and put her face into her hands and cried even harder, and screamed.

Taz was walking down the hallway when he heard his fiancée scream. "Damn! This is so fucked up!" he said as he stopped and faced the door of the emergency room.

"I know, my nigga, but we gots to do what we gots to do," Keno said seriously.

"I know," Taz said as he led the way outside to the parking lot.

Clifford was sitting inside of his car talking to H-Hop. "Cuz, they got Astro! What the fuck are we going to do now?"

"We gon' stay down, cuz, and finish this shit we started. This shit done got real personal, loc. You know Astro was my li'l cousin. Them niggas gots to die! Every last one of them fools ain't gon' be breathing this time next month! And that's on 107 Hoover Crip!" yelled H-Hop.

"It's too damn hot right now, cuz. We're going to have to kick back for a minute."

"Fuck that shit, loc! We about to ride! Fuck the ones and anyone else who tries to get in our fuckin' way! So either you're with us or against us, cuz!"

"I'm with you, you know that. My life is on the line just like everyone else's. Don't waste your breath getting at me like I'm some busta-ass nigga. I'm still 'bout my work."

"All right then, I'll get at you in the morning, loco. The word will be out by then that we got one of them niggas, so you know it's gon' be on."

"Yeah, the word is also gon' be out that they got one of us too. We're going to have to tread lightly at first, loc. I'm telling you, that nigga Taz is about to go crazy on our ass."

"Yeah? Well, there's about to be two crazy muthafuckas goin' at it, cuz. They took my people, loc, and for that they have to die! It's as simple as that," H-Hop said as he climbed out of Clifford's CLS 500 Mercedes Benz.

Taz, Keno and Red had stayed up the rest of the night preparing for what they were about to do. They were downstairs in Taz's gym, checking and rechecking their weapons. Taz owned a heavy arsenal, complete with everything from pistols to assault rifles. Semi-automatic guns to fully automatic ones. Bulletproof vests and enough ammunition to supply a small army.

After they loaded all of the weapons they planned on using, Red said, "It would be best if we waited for the sun to set. That way we'll be able to move a li'l easier."

"Yeah, you're right. Plus, I'm tired as hell," Keno said as he yawned and stretched.

"All right, y'all niggas gon' and bounce. We'll meet back here around six." Taz then called Gwen and asked her, "How's he doin'?"

"He's still asleep, Taz. How are you?"

"Hurtin', Gwen. I still can't believe my nigga is gone."

"I understand. Believe me, I do understand. But, Taz, you have to realize that by retaliating there is only going to be more and more bloodshed. Sooner or later you'll have to feel this pain again, because another one of your friends will get hurt. Then what? You go off on another rampage? That doesn't make any sense. Y'all have too much going on for yourselves to take the risks y'all are about to take. What happens if something happens to you, Taz? Aren't you the least bit concerned for Sacha and the baby? I don't want to lecture you or anything like that, I just want to make sure that you're fully aware of what you're putting at risk. It's not just all about Taz right now. You have your mom, your daughter, your fiancée, as well as your unborn child to think about. You could stop this madness if you chose to. You do know that, don't you?"

"Can I? What about that nigga Cliff? He's the one taking this war to us, Gwen. If it wasn't for that clown, Bo-Pete would still be alive! So, to answer your question, yeah, I know I can stop this shit if I chose to. But that's not the decision I'm making. That nigga has shot my child and lived to talk about it. He's shot at me and lived to talk about it. Now he's responsible for killin' one of my closest friends, and he's *still* fuckin' breathin'! That is unacceptable, and nothin' and no one will stop me from hurting him and every last one of his niggas. I love Sacha and my unborn seed more than anything in this world. But I can't and I won't be deterred from handling this shit the way it's supposed to be handled. You make sure that you keep Bob under wraps for us, 'cause when that nigga gets up, he's gon' be on one for real!"

"Don't worry, I'll handle his ass. Thank you again for keeping him away from this mess. I'd die if I lost another love of my life. I just wouldn't be able to recover from that."

"Yeah, I know. I'm gon' keep it real with you, Gwen. If Bob was in good enough condition to ride with us, I wouldn't have done what I did. Like he said, we all made the same pact years ago. We're goin' to honor that, no matter what. Hopefully we'll be able to put an end to all of this and be able to move on with our lives. Whatever happens has to happen though. And it is goin' to happen as soon as that sun sets. Tell my Li'l Mama I said, no matter what happens, I will always love her."

"I will, Taz. Bye."

"Bye," he said, and went into his bedroom and collapsed onto his bed. While lying flat on his back, he stared at the ceiling as tears slid down his face and said, "We gon' get 'em, Bo-Pete. We gon' get every last one of them bitch-ass niggas, or die tryin', dog! Real talk!"

Chapter Nineteen

Pitt couldn't fucking believe his eyes. No matter what Leo and Tru did to their captive, G, he took it with a scream and a big-ass smile. Though he was in tremendous pain, G refused to give Pitt the information he desired.

"Listen, you fucker! Why are you making this so damn hard on yourself? You're going to die anyway!" screamed a very frustrated Pitt.

After catching his breath from Leo and Tru's torture, G smiled, spit out a mouthful of blood and said, "Watching you sit there and squirm gives me strength, Mr. Big Man. I'm gon' take whatever your boys got to give. You ain't gettin' shit outta me. I'm goin' to my grave, yeah, that's true. But I'm goin' to die with the satisfaction that you never got what you wanted outta me."

Leo slapped the shit out of G and started back with his torturing. He stuck an ice pick straight through the top of G's right kneecap. Leo smiled as he watched G scream over and over. G screamed but he never broke down. That infuriated Leo. He then untied G's hands and pushed him to the floor. With G's feet still tied Leo wasn't worried about him going anywhere, especially with an ice pick stuck in his knee.

"I got somethin' for your ass, nigga," Leo said seriously as he pulled the ice pick out of G's kneecap and put it into his back pocket. He pulled G's pants down around his ankles and told Tru, "Go into the kitchen and grab me one of those pot scrubbers. If this don't break this nigga, then nothin' will."

As Tru went inside the kitchen to get the pot scrubber, Pitt asked, "What are you going to do now, Leo?"

"You'll see," Leo said as he grabbed a bottle of vodka out a bag that he had set on the floor when they first came inside of the house. Tru came back into the room and gave Leo the pot scrubber. Leo smiled and said, "Let's see how you handle a li'l ass-play. Tru, spread that nigga's ass cheeks for me."

"What? Man, I ain't fuckin' wit' dat nigga's ass!" yelled True.

Pitt smiled and ordered Tru, "Do it, nigga. Earn your fucking money."

"Give me some fuckin' gloves or somethin'! I ain't about to be touchin' that nigga's ass! Fuck your money! I don't get down like that, Pitt."

Pitt laughed and said, "I thought you liked to use your damn hands on your victims."

"Fuck you, Pitt!"

They all started laughing as Leo passed a pair of leather gloves to Tru and said, "Here you go, you old soft-ass nigga."

Tru accepted the gloves and said, "Ain't nothin' soft 'bout me, youngsta, and you damn well know it." Tru then slid on the gloves and knelt down next to G and did as Leo told him to. After Tru had spread G's ass cheeks wide open, Leo sat next to him on the floor and began to rub the metal pot scrubber up and down the inside of G's ass.

G screamed louder than he had since he'd been held captive. The excruciating pain that he was absorbing was incredible. He prayed that they would end it for him soon, but he knew in his heart that they were going to keep on until he broke down. He was loyal to Won and he would die before he broke down. Won warned him when he accepted the million dollars for handling his business that it could get dangerous for him. So this was what Won had warned him about. *I guess I'm going to die, but I'm not breaking my promise to Won for nothing,* G told himself just as Leo poured the entire bottle of vodka down G's raw asshole. G screamed as the liquid burned his tortured body. His body could no longer take any more abuse, and went limp as he slipped into a state of shock.

"Ain't this a bitch! What the fuck are we going to do now?" screamed Pitt.

Leo shrugged his shoulders and said, "Man, he's one tough muthafucka, Pitt. We're going to just have to keep working his ass. Sooner or later he will break."

Pitt shook his head and said, "He has to, Leo. He has to."

Just as the sun was setting, there was a knock at Taz's front door. Taz, who had just finished getting dressed in all-black army fatigues, finished tying the laces to his black leather Tims, grabbed his bulletproof vest and walked downstairs to see who was knocking at his door. He smiled sadly when he saw that it was Sacha. He opened the door and said, "What up, Li'l Mama? Where's your key?"

Sacha entered his home and said, "I must have left it at the house, because I can't seem to find it." She focused on what Taz had on and said, "Please tell me that there is something that I can say that will stop you from going out there and doing something crazy tonight, baby."

"Bo-Pete's dead, Sacha. Do you hear me? He's dead! There is no way in this fuckin' world I'm gon' let them niggas get away with killin' my nigga! No fuckin' way!"

"What if they kill you? What if you get caught and go to jail for the rest of your life? What am I going to do then? What is the baby going to do without a father? Think, Taz! Don't do this to yourself! Don't do this to us!" she screamed.

Taz listened to his fiancée's pleas, and it hurt him deeply, but he refused to let her affect his decision. His mind was made up. It was as simple as that. "I ain't gon' die, Li'l Mama, and I ain't goin' in nobody's cage. I will die before I let some shit like that go down. If it's meant for me to go be with MiMi, then so be it. The cowards that did this to my man have to die! Every last one of them!"

Sacha grabbed a hold of her stomach with her right hand and said, "I need to sit down. You're stressing the hell out of me, Taz."

He followed her inside of the den and watched as she sat down on the couch. She stared at him and asked, "So, you're going to completely disregard me and the baby?"

Before he could answer her question, there was a knock at his front door. He turned and went and let Keno and Red inside of the house.

When they returned to the den, Sacha saw that both Keno and Red were dressed exactly as Taz, in all black. Taz sighed as he grabbed a black duffel bag with the weapons they were about to use inside of it. Red went downstairs and came back with the assault rifles, as well as silencers for their pistols.

As Taz screwed a silencer onto his 9 mm, he said, "You should go on home, Li'l Mama. I don't know how late I'll be tonight."

Shaking her head no, she said, "I'm not going anywhere. I'll be here when you get back . . . that is if you make it back."

Taz stepped to her, kissed her on her forehead and said, "I'll be back, Li'l Mama. That's a promise." He turned toward Red and Keno and said, "Let's do this."

Just as they made it to the front door, Taz stopped suddenly as if he had forgotten something. He turned and yelled, "Heaven, Precious! Come!" Both of the Dobermans that were lying down in the living room came running toward their master. They stopped and stood at Taz's feet and awaited for their next command. Taz smiled and said, "Come!" and they followed him, Red, and Keno out of the house.

Once they were all inside of an all-black Suburban, Taz watched as his dogs climbed inside of the truck and sat down in the third back seat. He smiled and said, "They might come in handy tonight. Where did you get this truck, Red? It looks brand-new."

Red turned the ignition and started the Suburban, and said, "A friend of mine at the Chevy dealership owed me a favor. He heard about Bo-Pete, so he looked out. When we're through, I'll give him a call and he'll report it stolen."

Taz nodded and said, "Good thinkin'."

Precious and Heaven were sitting in the back of the SUV, relaxing as if they knew that they were about to go on the kill. Keno smiled at the dogs and said, "Damn, dog! Look at them! It's like they know we're about to go huntin'."

Taz smiled and said, "They do. Let's go."

Clifford was sitting on his bed sweating bullets. *Taz and the rest of his crew are going to come at me hard now. I have to get the fuck out of this house. I know Sacha told them where I live by now,* he thought to himself as he got up and started packing some clothes inside of a gym bag. Just as he finished packing, the telephone rang. "Hello."

"Hi, baby. Whatcha doing?" asked Tazneema.

"I've just finished packing, baby. I was about to call you to let you know that I have to go to Dallas for an interview. I'll be gone for a few days," he lied.

"Interview? Dallas? Why are you trying to get a job way out in Texas, Cliff?"

"Because it seems like they're the only ones willing to pay me what I'm worth. To tell you the truth, I'm tired of the city anyway. It's time for a change."

"But what about me? You're just going to up and leave me?"

"Come on now, you know better than that. Once you're back on your feet, you can come and stay with me."

"What about school? I still have to finish, Cliff."

"That's true. Look, OU isn't that far from Dallas. You could still finish school and come be with me on the weekends. And if it gets too hectic, I can always come up to Norman and spend some time with you during the week. I love you, 'Neema, and nothing is going to stop me from being with you. But I have to get back to work."

"I understand. I just wish that there was someone here that would pay you what you're worth."

"Me too, babe . . . me too. I'll give you a call as soon as I make it to a hotel, okay."

"Okay. I'm going to do a little shopping tomorrow, so I'll call you on your cell while I'm out."

"Out? Mama-Mama's actually letting you go out?"

Tazneema smiled and said, "Yeah. She told me that since I've been sneaking out of the house every other night, I might as well go on out and get ready to go back to school."

"She knew?"

"Yep! And she didn't even say anything about it. That's just how Mama-Mama is. That's why I love her so much," she said with a lot of pride in her voice.

"That's cool. Okay, baby, let me hit the road. I love you!"

"I love you too, Cliff," Tazneema said and hung up the phone.

Clifford grabbed his bag and quickly left his home. For a minute there he actually thought Tazneema had called to stall him for her father. *Shit, I'm fucking paranoid for real!* he thought as he got inside of his car and pulled out of his driveway.

Taz, Red and Keno were driving slowly around 107 Hoover Crips' turf, looking for anyone who even resembled a gang member. Taz saw two Crips walking down the street and said, "There goes the first two. This is how I want to play this. We need to find out where that fool Cliff rests his head, 'cause once we start puttin' this shit down, he's goin' to get spooked and shake the spot. None of this will matter if we don't get the nigga who started it all."

"I feel you. So, what's up?" asked Keno.

"You'll see," Taz said as he turned toward the backseat of the truck and said, "Heaven, Precious." Both dogs raised their heads, jumped over the seats and climbed out of the truck as Keno held the door open for them.

Taz stepped out of the SUV also and said, "Get 'em, girls!" Heaven and Precious took off running in the direction that their master was pointing.

The two young Crips weren't paying any attention to the two deadly Doberman Pinschers as they ran their way. By the time they noticed the dogs, it was too late. Precious attacked the first Crip's leg viciously, and Heaven did the same to the next Crip. They were screaming at the top of their lungs as Taz slowly walked up to them.

"Stand down, Heaven! Stand down, Precious!" Taz commanded. Both of the dogs stopped their attack and watched the two youngsters as they laid flat on their backs, crying uncontrollably. Taz smiled and said, "I'm gon' ask y'all one time, and one time only. Where does your big homeboy, C-Baby, live?"

"Ahhh, cuz, we don't know! That nigga just started comin' around a few months ago!" whined one of the Crips.

"That's on the real, loc! We don't know where that nigga live at!" the other Crip replied.

"You know what? I believe y'all. But y'all are goin' to have to give me somethin', or I'm gon' have to do y'all."

"Come on, cuz. We ain't got no beef with you," said the Crip who had spoken first.

"You see, that's where you're wrong. I got beef with *all* 107 Hoovers. I know y'all know about my homeboy that got smoked last night. So either give me somethin' I can use, or I'm gon' lay y'all down. Or better yet, I'll let my girls here finish y'all off."

"Cuz, all of this shit is because of Li'l Bomb! He wanted y'all dead because y'all did Do-Low!"

"Nah, loc, it was H-Hop too! He wanted to get y'all because of that nigga, C-Baby!" yelled the second Crip.

"All right, where can I find H-Hop and this Li'l Bomb nigga?"

"H-Hop stays out on the north side in the Highland Glen Apartments, apartment 1697, way in the back. You'll know if he's at home because his orange Cutlass will be parked right in front of his apartment building."

"Li'l Bomb should be over on Lottie at the auto body shop right now. That's where he hangs out and serves his bud, loc."

Taz smiled and said, "All right then, that's good lookin'. Now, I'll make this fast so y'all won't feel too much pain," he said as he pulled out his silenced 9 mm.

"B-b-but you said that you wasn't gon' do us, cuz!" yelled the first Crip.

"Ye-yeah, you said we had to give you somethin', loc, and you wasn't gon' smoke us!" cried the other Crip.

Taz shook his head and said, "Y'all are Hoovers, so y'all gots to go." He then shot both of the Crips right between their eyes. He turned and jogged back to the SUV, followed by his dogs.

Once he was inside of the truck and Red had pulled off, he said, "Head over to Twenty-third and Lottie. Park in front of that auto body shop that's across the street from that old steakhouse."

"Gotcha!" Red said, and they headed toward their next destination.

Li'l Bomb was leaning against an old rusty Ford when his eyes grew wide as saucers. He couldn't believe what he was seeing. Two Doberman Pinschers were attacking any and everyone inside of the shop. "What the fuck?" he yelled as he pulled out his nine and tried to get a clear shot at one of the dogs.

All in all, there were seven Hoover Crips in the back of the auto body shop. Every last one of them was running around for their lives as the vicious dogs attacked.

Taz, Red and Keno smiled as they stood on the side of the building and watched Precious and Heaven get busy. Taz frowned when he saw Li'l Bomb pull out his gun and cock a live round into its chamber. He stepped around from the side of the building and started unloading his nine toward Li'l Bomb. Li'l Bomb caught two bullets in his right leg and one in his left arm and he fell to the ground.

Taz yelled for Precious and Heaven to stand down. Both of the dogs stopped their attacks and watched as Red and Keno commenced to shooting every gang member inside of the room. Taz stepped over to Li'l Bomb and asked, "Where does that nigga C-Baby live, li'l nigga?"

Li'l Bomb spit toward Taz's face and yelled, "Fuck you, cuz! I'm Li'l Bomb! I ain't no fuckin' snitch! This is Hoover Crip 'til I die, cuz!"

Taz didn't say another word as he shot Li'l Bomb three times in his face. The young gang member died instantly. Taz turned and saw a female, who couldn't have been more than seventeen years old, cowering behind a beat-up old Chevy. He stepped over to her quickly and asked, "Are any of these li'l niggas related to you?"

The teenager shook her head violently and said, "N-n-no, s-s-sir!"

"All right, this is what I want you to do. Get the hell outta here, and if anyone asks if you were here or anything about what happened here tonight, you bet' not tell them anything about what you saw, because if you do, then I'm goin' to have to come find you. And even though hurting women and children ain't my thang, you would have forced my hand. Do you understand what I'm tellin' you?"

The terrified teenager stared at Taz and said, "Ye-yes, s-sir, I understand."

"Good. Now get outta here!" Taz smiled as he watched the scared teenager run out of the auto body shop without a backward glance. He turned toward Red and Keno and said, "Let's go get that nigga they call H-Hop."

After Clifford had checked into the Westin Hotel in downtown Oklahoma City, he called H-Hop to see if everything was all right around the way. As soon as H-Hop answered the phone, he said, "Cuz, them niggas is tryin' to take the whole fuckin' set out! They done blasted about ten or twelve of the homies already!"

"*What?* When did this happen?" Clifford asked as he sat down on the bed in his hotel room, trying to absorb the news that H-Hop just gave him.

"About twenty minutes ago, cuz. I don't know about you, but I'm up out this bitch, loc. Them niggas are on the war ride for real! I'm about to get outta dodge for a minute," H-Hop said.

Though it wasn't a laughing matter, Clifford laughed and said, "I thought you was about to get your ride on. What happened to that slick shit you was talking, cuz? I told you them niggas ain't playing."

"Yeah, I'm feelin' you now, cuz, 'cause I'm outta here!"

"Where are you going to go?"

"I gots a bitch that stays out in Midwest City. I'm gon' lay it down at her pad until this shit dies down a bit. You know the ones are goin' to be all over the fuckin' place. I ain't got time to be gettin' caught up with them. You know I'm still on paper."

"Yeah, I feel you. What's up with Li'l Bomb? Have you heard from him yet?"

"Nah, but from what I heard, he might just be dead too, cuz. Them niggas went to the auto body shop where that li'l nigga is always at and tore shit up. One of the homies said something about some killa dogs or some shit too."

"Killer dogs? Where the fuck did that come from?"

"Ain't no tellin'. You know how niggas get to stretchin' shit, loc. I ain't waitin' around to find out if it's true or not, though. I'm outta here. Hit me on my celly if you find out anything. We still gon' get them niggas, cuz. It's just goin' to take a li'l longer than I expected."

"All right then, I'll get at you," Clifford said, hung up the phone and relaxed back on the bed. *Damn! Taz is on the warpath. Astro's dead, and Li'l Bomb is probably dead too. This shit has gotten way out of hand,* he thought as he tried his best to calm his nerves.

Timing and a lot of luck was on H-Hop's side. He pulled out of his apartment complex about three minutes before Taz, Red and Keno pulled up to his apartment building. When Taz didn't see H-Hop's car parked in front of his building, he decided enough was enough, at least for the time being.

"Let's take it in, my niggas. That nigga H-Hop gets a pass tonight. We can't keep rollin' around in this 'Burban."

"Yeah, the message has been sent. Them fools know we ain't playin' with they ass no more," Red said as he turned the truck around to leave the apartment complex.

"What are we gon' do now, dog?" asked Keno.

Taz sighed heavily and said, "We goin' to put the homey to rest and let the heat cool down in the city. After that, we're goin' to turn it right back up until we get H-Hop and that nigga Cliff. They have to die before I'll even consider stoppin' this shit."

"You gots that right, my nigga," said Red.

"Listen, after you dump this truck, you need to take the straps we used tonight and get rid of them too. Ain't no need for us keepin' some hot heat. Can you handle it, or do you need some help?"

"I got it, dog."

"Have you heard anything from Wild Bill?"

"Yeah, he's straight. He said they stitched him up and his arm's in a sling. He's good though," said Keno. "But you know that li'l nigga is gon' be on one as soon as he feels up to it."

"Yeah, I know. I can't believe that he's gone, dog. Bo-Pete is fuckin' gone! This shit is too fucked up!" said Taz as he rested his head on the headrest of his seat.

"Yeah, I never thought we'd ever have beef like that out here. It's been so damn long that we had to get at anybody in the city that I just didn't think some shit like this could ever happen, dog," Keno said as he lit himself a Black and Mild cigar.

"They say everything happens for a reason, gee," said Red.

"I wish someone would explain to me the reason why we gots to bury Bo-Pete. 'Cause for the life of me, my niggas, I just can't understand this shit," Taz said as he closed his eyes for the remainder of the ride back to his home.

Chapter Twenty

As soon as Taz walked into his home, Sacha ran into his arms and gave him a tight hug. He scooped her into his arms and carried her upstairs to his bedroom. No words were exchanged as they both undressed and made passionate love for the next few hours.

Just before Taz fell asleep, Red called him and told him that he disposed of the truck as well as the weapons they'd used earlier.

"All right, dog, get at me in the morning so we can start gettin' Bo-Pete ready."

"All right, my nigga. Oh, you better call that nigga Bob. He's pissed! I mean *p-i-s-s-e-d* at your ass!" Red said and laughed.

Taz smiled and said, "All right, I'll call his ass now. Out!"

"Out!"

Taz smiled at Sacha as she snored lightly next to him. He climbed out of the bed, grabbed the cordless phone and took it downstairs with him. When he made it to his living room, he sat down on his sofa and called Bob.

Bob answered on the first ring and said, "Nigga, you ain't shit! How the fuck could you do me like that, Taz? That shit was fucked up, dog! You think I'm a coward or some shit, nigga? Huh? Is that it, Taz? You think 'cause I fucked up in L.A. and in New York that I'm on some soft shit, gee?"

"Calm the fuck down, nigga! Damn! You know damn well I know you're not a coward. I just didn't want you in the fuckin' way. You still fucked up, dog, can't you see that? I'm not lettin' Wild Bill get down with us either, not until he's a hundred percent to the good. So you might as well sit back with your broad and relax, 'cause ain't nothin' goin' down until you're ready, my nigga."

"You know what? Fuck you! Nigga, you can't tell a grown-ass man what the fuck he can and can't do! You think you took all of my straps? You think you took the keys to all of my rides? Fool, I got somethin' for your ass. There are some things about the Bob that you don't know, nigga! Them niggas took my nigga, so I'm takin' some of them! It's as simple as that!" Bob yelled angrily.

"Look, dog, we done put it down for the night. The city is too fuckin' hot for you to go out there right now. All you'll fuckin' do is end up gettin' caught the fuck up. Stand down for at least the rest of the night, my nigga."

"Fuck you, Taz!" Bob screamed and hung up the phone in Taz's ear.

Taz shook his head from side to side as he went back upstairs to his bedroom. *Everything happens for a reason,* he thought to himself as he climbed back in bed with his fiancée.

Gwen had tears falling down her face as she watched Bob put on his black Army fatigues. She knew that nothing she could say was going to stop him from doing what he felt he had to do. She took a deep breath and calmly said, "Bob, can you wait for a minute?"

"Wait for what? I told you, them niggas have to be dealt with, baby, and I'm about to deal with they ass!"

"I understand that, Bob, I really do. I just need you to wait for a minute, because if you're going to go out there and handle your business, then I'm going with you."

Her words stopped him from getting dressed. He turned toward her and asked, "What the fuck did you just say?"

"You heard me. I said I'm going with you. I lost William because I wasn't with him, and there hasn't been a day that has passed by that I haven't wished I was inside of that car with him and my baby. If you have to do this, Bob, then I'm doing it with you. That way if something goes wrong, at least I'll know I was by your side the entire time. And, believe me, there is nothing you can do or say to stop me. I'm going with you!" she stated coldly.

Bob smiled and said, "Are you sure you can stomach what I'm about to put down, baby?"

"I guess I'm about to find out."

"I gots me a straight gangsta bitch on my team, huh?"

Gwen shook her head no and said, "I'm a psychologist, Bob. I'm nowhere near a gangsta. I've made this decision simply because there is no other way for me to be able to deal with this logically. I'm in love with my man, and I'm willing to die before I let him leave me."

He gave her a nod of his head and said, "All right then, baby, let's go."

Tazneema was watching the news with Mama-Mama, listening to all of the killings that had taken place in the last few hours. "Dang! What's going on in this city?"

"Them damn heathens are out there actin' a damn fool," Mama-Mama said from the other side of the room. "That shit don't make no damn sense, killin' each other like that. And for what? A damn gang? Lord, please help these children!"

As Tazneema listened to her grandmother, for some strange reason her father came to her mind. "Have you talked to my Daddy, Mama-Mama?"

Mama-Mama smiled and asked, "Your Daddy? Who is that, girl?" She laughed and continued, "I can't remember the last time I've heard you refer to Taz as your Daddy." She slapped herself on her forehead and said, "Wait a minute! Yes, I can! Just before your boyfriend shot you, you called Taz *Daddy*."

"Would you stop that, Mama-Mama, and answer my question?"

"You know how that boy is, girl. If he don't call me, I don't bother him none. Why? What's wrong with you? You're missing your 'Daddy'?" Mama-Mama teased.

Tazneema shrugged her slender shoulders slightly and said, "I'm just wondering why he hasn't called or come by, that's all."

"Well, why don't you give him a call then?"

"I will. I'll call him in the morning. Right now I'm about to go to bed. I'm a little tired."

"Humph! You bet' not be sneaking out of this house tonight. I know that much. You ain't completely healed yet, girl, and there is too much killin' goin' on out in them streets for you to be wandering around the town for some man."

Tazneema laughed and said, "I'm not going anywhere tonight, Mama-Mama. Relax!"

Mama-Mama didn't respond. Instead she just smiled, because she knew Tazneema wouldn't be sneaking out of the house because she took the keys to her car and had them safely tucked in her bosom.

Bob and Gwen rolled all over the east side of the city looking for Hoover Crips, but all they saw were police cruisers. On almost every other block there was a police car either parked or patrolling the area. "Damn! Taz wasn't bullshittin'! The town is like super fuckin' hot."

"Does that mean we can go back home now, baby?" Gwen asked nervously.

He smiled at his girl and said, "I guess so, scaredy cat. You gave a nigga a pretty good front back at the house, but I knew your ass was scared as fuck."

"I never said anything about not being scared, Bob. I just refused to stay at home and watch you go out and act a damn fool without me by your side," she said with a smile. She turned onto the Broadway Extension, headed back toward Bob's home and feeling relieved.

The next morning, Sacha woke Taz and said, "Baby, get up! The police are at the front door!" she said urgently.

Taz opened his eyes and said, "All right, Li'l Mama, I'm up! Don't panic. Everything is all good." He climbed out of his bed and put on a pair of his pajama pants, slipped his feet into his Nike slippers and went downstairs to see what Oklahoma City's Finest wanted with him this early in the morning. When he opened the front door, he frowned and asked, "Yes, may I help you?"

"Good morning, Mr. Good. May we have a moment of your time please?" asked Detective Bean as he flashed Taz his badge to confirm what Taz already knew—the po-po was in the house.

Taz stepped aside and said, "Come on in." They followed Taz into his living room. He smiled when he saw the look of awe in both of the detectives' faces as they looked around his luxurious home.

"Now, how may I help you two officers this morning?" Taz asked as he sat down on the sofa.

"Detectives," said Detective Bean. "We've had several reports that you and some of your associates have staged a personal war against the Hoover Crips here in the city."

"What? Do I look like a gang-banger, Detective? I think someone is playing with you all. Why would I have a problem with some Crips?"

"Maybe because they shot your close friend, Billy Trent, in his shoulder the other night outside of Club Cancun," said Detective Bean.

"Or better yet, because they also shot and killed your other close friend, Reggie McClelland," said the other detective.

"Come on, Mr. Good. We didn't come way out here to waste our time with you. Please, don't insult our intelligence," said Detective Bean.

"Both of my friends were shot the other night at the club, but what makes you think that those Hoover Crip guys had something to do with it?"

"Would you let us do the questioning, Mr. Good?"

Taz smiled and said, "Go right ahead."

Before either of the detectives could ask another question, they were interrupted by Sacha. She came into the living room dressed casually in a pair of Capri pants with a matching top. She smiled and said, "Excuse me, detectives, but I'm Mr. Good's attorney. If you have any questions for him, I'd prefer for you to go through me."

Detective Bean smiled and asked her, "And your name is?"

"My name is Sacha Carbajal. I'm a partner at Whitney and Johnson."

Detective Bean turned toward Taz and asked, "Is it routine for you to have your legal representation at your home this early in the morning, Mr. Good?"

Before Taz could answer his question, Sacha said, "I'm also Mr. Good's fiancée. Now, may we get to the bottom of this early-morning intrusion?"

"Sure. We have reason to believe that Mr. Good and some of his associates have retaliated on the Hoover Crips for the shooting death of Reggie McClelland and the shooting of Billy Trent. There have been ten homicides committed since that particular shooting outside of Club Cancun. We don't feel that it was a coincidence that every last person murdered was a Hoover Crip."

"So, you have reason to believe that my client was involved, but do you have any proof of this?" Sacha sat down next to Taz.

"We don't have any witnesses, if that's what you mean. Like I just told you, they're all dead. We do have several bullet casings that we retrieved from the crime scenes. Before we go any further, do you happen to own any dogs, Mr. Good?" asked Detective Bean.

Taz smiled and said, "Yes, I do. I have two Dobermans. Why?"

"I was just wondering, because at one of the crime scenes it seems that the victims were attacked by dogs. We'll know for sure once their autopsies are completed."

Taz started laughing and said, "So, you think I brought my dogs along with me to get revenge for my peoples? Come on, man! You gots to be kidding me! Look, you're reaching for straws and shit. I understand that you have a job to do, and I will do whatever I can to assist you. I have nothing whatsoever to hide. I want the guys that did this to my people caught and put *under* the jailhouse. Even though you coming to my home this early in the morning with these wild accusations should offend me, I'm not. So, if that's all, gentlemen, I have a funeral I have to start making arrangements for."

"Do you own any weapons, Mr. Good?"

Taz stared directly at Detective Bean and answered, "Yes, I do. I'm a registered owner of a 9 mm Beretta."

"Would you mind if we took your weapon back down to the station to have our forensics team check it out for any matches on the victims?"

"Just as long as you return it," Taz said as he got up from the sofa and went back upstairs and grabbed his gun. He came back downstairs with the weapon in his left hand and the clip in his right. He then passed the gun to Detective Bean and said, "Here you go."

After accepting the gun from Taz, Detective Bean smiled and said, "We'll be in touch, Mr. Good,"

With a laugh, Taz said, "Yeah, I bet you will. You two, have a nice day."

After the detectives left, Sacha said, "You shouldn't be mocking them like that, Taz. They could cause you a lot of problems if they choose to."

"Problems? Look, Li'l Mama. They don't have shit, and they know I know they don't have shit. Like they said, all of their potential witnesses are dead. They're tryin' to build a circumstantial case against me 'cause Bo-Pete and Wild Bill are my niggas. On top of the fact that somebody has heard a few rumors about our beef, that's it and that's all. They gots nothin', and I'm gon' make sure that it stays that way," Taz said before he grabbed the phone and called Bob.

When Bob answered the phone, he told him, "Look, dog, I know you're salty at me right now, and I understand that, but the shit is thick right now, gee. Them people just left my spot talkin' like they knowin' somethin'. I really need you to stand down, homey, for real."

"Yeah, the spot's hot, my nigga. I went on a run last night and saw that for myself."

"You didn't put anything down, did you?"

"Nah, there was way too many of them black and whites on the block. I came back to the pad and laid it down."

"Cool. We'll finish this, gee, but right now we gots to kick it for a minute."

"What's up with Wild Bill?"

"They should be letting him out of the hospital some time this afternoon. Keno and Red are goin' to scoop him while

I start getting Bo-Pete's funeral together. Might as well get ahead of the game, 'cause ain't no tellin' how long they're goin' to keep the body."

"Yeah, that shit is crazy. You know how homicide gets down. Who's goin' to take care of the body?"

"Temple and Sons. You know they're the best in the city. Ain't nothin' but the best for my nigga. So, get that Armani out, 'cause we're all wearing the same suit we're burying Bo-Pete in."

Bob smiled sadly and said, "Damn! I never thought a day like this would happen to us, gee. We almost made it though, huh?"

"Yeah, almost. All we got now is us, dog, so we'll maintain like we're supposed to. Bo-Pete's family will be set for the rest of their lives. I'm about to get at Won now and have him take care of everything on the financial side, you know, change the accounts over to Bo-Pete's people and shit."

"I'm real tired, gee. Go on and handle shit. Just make sure you keep me in the loop, dog."

"Gotcha."

After hanging up with Bob, Taz called Won. "What's up, O.G.?"

"What's going on, Babyboy?"

"Bad news, dog . . . bad news. Bo-Pete's dead."

"*What?* What the hell happened?"

"It's a long story, O.G., so I'll give you the short version."

After Taz finished telling Won about everything that has happened, he ended with, "So you see, it's really all on me. If I would have laid that clown Cliff down from the beginning, this shit wouldn't be as fucked up as it is now."

"You can't blame yourself, Babyboy. Shit like this happens sometimes. Don't stress yourself out too much behind this madness. I need you to remain focused."

"What's what on that other thing?" asked Taz.

Won sighed heavily and said, "To be honest, Babyboy, I don't even have a fucking clue. I'm still stuck at square one. I'm going to make a few calls today and hopefully find something out."

"All right, get at me when you're ready. But, look, we need you to take care of Bo-Pete's money and shit. Everything goes to his moms and pops, since he didn't have any kids. Can you take care of that for us?"

"You already know that won't be a problem. Get back at me with their names as well as their socials, and I'll take care of everything. Make sure you let them know that there will be absolutely nothing to worry about as far as taxes or anything. But they will never be able to bring all of that money over here to the U.S. Explain to them that whenever they need any money, they will have to do a wire transfer through the Islands and their banks. As long as they do that, they'll be all right."

"All right, O.G. I'm about to take care of that right now. I'll get at you and let you know when the funeral will be."

"Make sure you do that, Babyboy. Out!"

After getting off the phone with Won, Taz turned toward Sacha and said, "I need you to come with me over to Bo-Pete's parents' house. I don't think I can do this solo, Li'l Mama."

Sacha grabbed her man's hand and said, "Come on, baby. Let's go and get it over with."

Taz stood and gave her a tight hug as tears fell slowly down his face. *Damn!*

Chapter Twenty-one

This shit is in-fucking-credible! thought Pitt as he watched once again as Leo and Tru revived G.

They had been torturing G for over four days now, and the man still refused to break. Leo admired his strength, but Pitt was furious.

"This shit has to fucking stop! You have to break this fool, Leo! You fucking have to! If we don't get what I need, we'll never be able to move on that nigga Won!" screamed Pitt.

"I've thought of everything I could possibly do to this fool, Pitt. He's determined not to give up shit. He's not going to be able to hold out much longer. Shit, he should have been dead days ago," Leo said seriously.

When G heard Pitt mention Won's name, he smiled because he knew that once again the old man was definitely going to come out on top of the pile. *Won never loses,* he thought to himself.

Pitt sat in his seat steaming as he tried to think of a way to make G tell him what he needed to know. His thoughts were interrupted by the ringing of a cell phone. He checked his and saw that it wasn't his phone that was ringing, and so did Leo and Tru.

Tru reached inside of G's pants and pulled out his cell and passed it to Pitt, who answered it. "Hello. Hello? Hello?" Pitt smiled as he closed the cell phone and said, "Kill that piece of shit and put him out of his misery."

"But I thought we had to get that info you needed from him first," Leo said.

With a huge smile on his face, Pitt said, "We just did." He went and knelt next to G's tortured body and said, "Just before I kill your man Won, I'll make sure to tell him what a stand-up guy you were."

"Wha-what are you talkin' 'bout?" asked G.

"You know what I'm talking about, nigga. Won! He's the nigga that paid you to get at my peoples! You gave him to me even though you tried not to," Pitt said as he reopened G's cell phone and stared at the number that showed on G's caller ID screen. The number showing was Won's cellular number in Southern California.

"Don't feel bad. It's not your fault. That nigga fucked himself by calling your ass on his cell. He's not that fucking bright after all." Pitt then slapped G lightly on his face and said, "See ya!"

Leo pulled out his 9 mm and shot G once in the back of his head.

Pitt grimaced and said, "Get someone out here to clean up this fucking mess. I gots shit to do."

Tazneema couldn't believe it. She was pregnant again! *Damn! I must be fertile as hell,* she thought as she threw the pregnancy test into the trashcan. She had a smile on her face as she went into her bedroom so she could call Clifford and tell him that once again, she was pregnant with his child.

When Clifford answered his cell phone and heard the good news, he smiled and said, "We're going to make sure that everything turns out like it's supposed to this time, 'Neema. I can't believe that you got pregnant again so fast."

She laughed and said, "Well, it's really not that hard when you have unprotected sex, baby."

"I know, huh? That was stupid of me to say. But you know what I meant. I love you, baby."

"I love you too."

"When are you going to tell Taz and Mama-Mama?"

"As soon as I get off the phone with you. I'm not making the same mistake twice."

"Do you want me to come over? I can hit the highway and get back to the city in a couple of hours."

"Uh-uh. It'll be easier if I take care of this by myself this time, baby. I'll give you a call after I've told them. When are you coming back to the city?"

"Later on this week some time," Clifford lied.

"When is your interview?"

"Hopefully in a day or so. I'll know for sure later on after I talk to a friend of mine."

"Okay, make sure you keep me posted on what happens."

"I will, 'Neema. Bye, baby."

"Bye," she said and hung up the phone. She went into the kitchen, where her grandmother was preparing dinner. She sat down at the kitchen table and said, "Mama-Mama, I'm pregnant again."

Mama-Mama stopped stirring the pot of beans, turned around, faced Tazneema and said, "You had to go and be stupid again, huh? Girl, don't you know you're going to drive Taz crazy? What's wrong with you, 'Neema? Why must you continue to cause problems within this family?"

Mama-Mama had never spoken to Tazneema like this before, and she couldn't believe she'd heard what Mama-Mama had just told her. "How dare you accuse me of causing problems within this family! Just because I'm in love with my man and I'm having a baby by him doesn't mean that I'm causing any problems! You don't like Cliff, I understand that. Your son doesn't like him, I understand that too. What the both of you don't seem to understand is that y'all don't have to like him! As long as I love him, that's all that matters! I'm sick and tired of the both of you and the way y'all treat me! I'm no longer a child, Mama-Mama. The sooner you and your son realize that fact, the better off we all will be! I'm sorry for yelling at you, because you know I love you dearly, but I've had enough of this . . . this craziness! I'm going back to my place in Norman. This house has gotten too small for me now."

Mama-Mama stood in front of the stove and shook her head from side to side as she watched her granddaughter leave the kitchen. "That girl just don't understand. Her daddy ain't gon' let her be with that man, let alone have a baby by him. God, keep my family in Your hands, please. We're definitely about to need You and some of Your divine mercy," she prayed as she continued to stir her pot of beans.

After Tazneema packed her things, she said good-bye to Mama-Mama, jumped into her car and headed to her apartment she shared with Lyla out in Norman, Oklahoma, not far from the campus of OU. While she was driving, she decided she might as well go on over to Taz's house and tell him about her pregnancy while she had the nerve.

When she pulled into the driveway of her father's home, she noticed that her uncles were over there as well. She smiled, because even though they really weren't her uncles, she loved Bo-Pete, Wild Bill, Red and Keno as if they were blood relatives. Ever since she could remember, they had always made sure that she had whatever she needed. She jumped out of her car and went to go face her father's wrath.

Taz smiled at his daughter when he opened the front door and said, "What's good, baby girl? I see you're looking better."

As Tazneema stepped inside she smiled and said, "Yeah, and I'm feeling a whole lot better. How are you? I haven't heard from you in a while, so I decided to come over and see how you were doing," she lied.

"I wish I could tell you that I was fine, but that's not the case, baby girl," Taz said as he led her into the den, where everyone was.

After speaking to Red, Keno, Bob, Sacha, Gwen and Wild Bill, Tazneema asked, "What happened to you, Uncle Bill? Where's my Uncle Bo-Pete?"

Everyone else inside of the room turned and stared at Taz. Taz inhaled deeply and said, "Your Uncle Bo-Pete was killed a couple of days ago, 'Neema. He and Wild Bill got shot coming out of the club."

She screamed and ran into her father's arms and began to cry uncontrollably. "Who did this, Daddy? Who killed my Uncle Bo-Pete?"

As Taz held his daughter in his arms, he knew that he couldn't hold anything back from her. She had to know the truth about the man she loved. He just hoped and prayed that she wouldn't trip the fuck out on him once he told her what happened. He sighed heavily and said, "That nigga Cliff and his homeboys did it, baby girl. They been beefin' with us for over a month now. They tried to get us all one night at the same club, but they got Bill and Bo-Pete. Cliff and his Hoover homeboys."

She pulled from her father's embrace, glared at him and said, "What did you say? 'Cause I know I didn't hear you correctly."

"You heard me, baby girl. That nigga Cliff killed your Uncle Bo-Pete."

"Now, come on, Taz. You don't actually know for sure if Cliff is the actual person who pulled the trigger," Sacha said, trying her best to defuse a situation she knew was about to become volatile any second. She could see it in Tazneema's eyes.

"Even if the nigga didn't actually pull the fuckin' trigger, this entire war is behind him tryin' to take me out so that he could be with my fuckin' child. Go on with that shit now, Li'l Mama. You know damn well all of this shit is behind that nigga."

Tazneema shook her head from side to side and said, "No. I know for a fact that Cliff wouldn't do no crazy mess like this. He doesn't want any beef with you, Taz. He just wants to move on with his life. We've discussed this, and I know he didn't have anything to do with my Uncle Bo-Pete getting killed."

Taz shook his head in disgust and said, "What the fuck you mean, you've discussed this with him? You still been fuckin' with that nigga, 'Neema? Huh? After I told you not to go against the grain, you still been fuckin' with the nigga that has been tryin' to take me out? You gots to be outta your muthafuckin' mind!"

"Taz! Stop it! She's hurting enough as it is!" Sacha yelled as she stepped over to Tazneema who had sat down on the couch next to Gwen.

As tears fell slowly from her eyes, Tazneema said, "I love him, Taz, can't you understand that? On top of that, I'm pregnant again with Cliff's child. I'm having my baby, and I'm going to be with my man," she said.

"*You're what?* Didn't you hear anything I just told your crazy-ass? That! Nigga! Killed! Bo-Pete! You just can't seem to understand what I'm tellin' you. That nigga ain't gon' be around to be no father to no fuckin' baby, 'cause as soon as this heat dies down in this fuckin' town, the hunt will be right back on for his punk-ass! Do you hear me? He's a dead man, 'Neema! *D-e-a-fuckin'-d!*"

"So, it's been y'all who have been shooting all of those gang-bangers around the city? Me and Mama-Mama saw that stuff on the news the other day. All because you think Cliff is the one who killed my Uncle Bo-Pete?" Tazneema asked as she continued to cry.

"Think? *Think?* We're sitting here makin' fuckin' funeral arrangements for your uncle right fuckin' now! And you fuckin' ask me if I *think* that nigga of yours done this shit! You gots to be outta your fuckin' mind! Get this through your fuckin' head right fuckin' now! If you think that nigga will be around to be the father of your child, then you got another thing comin'! I raised you with the help of my mother and the men you see in this room right now, except for my nigga, Bo-Pete—rest in peace—and we can do the same for your unborn seed, 'Neema. But that child will *not* have that nigga Cliff as a father! 'Cause I swear to you, on your mother's grave, I'm going to kill that nigga before the month's out!"

Tazneema stood and calmly said, "If you kill my man, then you might as well kill me too. 'Cause I swear to *you,* on my mother's grave, that if you hurt Cliff, I'm going to try my very best to kill you!" Before Taz or anyone in the room could say a word, she grabbed her purse and left her father's home.

Taz sat down after Tazneema had left and said, "Well, I'll be damn!"

"Don't pay her any attention, dog. She's just too caught up emotionally right now," said Keno.

Taz shook his head no, and said, "Nah, dog, she's my child. I know her like a book. She's gon' ride with that nigga to the end."

"So, what are you goin' to do now?" asked Red.

Taz stared at everyone inside of the room for a full two minutes before he spoke. When he did speak, it was barely audible. "If she goes against the grain, I'll kill her myself. I've dedicated my life to take the very best of care of that girl, and I swore when I buried MiMi that I would always take care of her. But, I swear to God, if she rides with that nigga against me, I'm going to kill her, dog. Real fuckin' talk!"

Chapter Twenty-two

Pitt smiled as he waited for Cash Flo' to answer his telephone. *I'm about to get at that nigga Won something vicious,* he thought to himself as he impatiently tapped his fingers on top of his desk. When Cash Flo' came on the line, Pitt skipped the pleasantries and said, "Damn! What took you so damn long to pick up the phone?"

"What? Man, don't call me, questioning me on how long it takes me to answer my damn phone! What the fuck is wrong with you?" Cash Flo' asked, clearly agitated by Pitt's rudeness.

"Look, I got confirmation that it was that nigga Won who got at me. All I need for you to do is to give me the green light so I can handle my business," Pitt said excitedly.

"First off, I need to hear exactly what type of proof you have, and if I'm feeling that, then and only then will I give you the go-ahead."

Pitt smiled as he told Cash Flo, about G and everything that happened back at his torture house. After he was finished he said, "For a minute there I thought I was going to come up empty, but the cocky bastard called G's celly and made my fucking day!"

Cash Flo' was quiet for a few seconds as he absorbed everything Pitt had just told him. Then he said, "You really don't have all that much on him, Pitt."

"*What?* Come on with that shit, Flo'! You know damn well that's enough to green-light that nigga! You think it's a coincidence that Won would call that fool's cell too, huh? Don't do this shit, Flo'. You and I got that nigga dead bang."

Cash Flo' shook his head from side to side as if Pitt was in the same room with him and said, "You may be right, but I need to think on this shit a little bit more before I give you the green light. I've got to go out to the East Coast to holla at the dagos. They acting like they want a piece of the dope game all of a sudden. They see how profitable it's been for The Network lately, and now they want in. When I get back, I'll have a decision for you, Pitt."

"Decision? You mean you're actually telling me that there's a chance that you might not let me get with the nigga?" Pitt asked angrily.

"Like I said, I'll give you my decision when I get back."

"How long will that fucking be, Flo'?"

"You'll know when I call you, Pitt," Cash Flo' said before he hung up the phone in Pitt's ear.

"I can't fucking believe you, Taz! How in the hell could you forget to call me and tell me about Bo-Pete?" Tari screamed as tears streamed down her face. She sat down on Taz's couch in his living room and cried like a baby.

Taz stepped over to her and tried to console her. As soon as he was near her, he started crying himself. They sat there side by side and cried for over twenty minutes.

Finally, Taz shook it off a little and tried to regain his composure. "Look, Tee, we got all of the funeral arrangements made. All we're waiting for is the homicide detectives to give the go so they can release the body to Temple and Sons Funeral Home."

"Why haven't they done that yet? How long does something like that take?"

"Normally it's about a week or so, but sometimes it takes a li'l longer."

"Okay. So all of this killing I've been reading about in the papers is behind Bo-Pete's death?"

Taz gave her a slight nod of his head and said, "Basically. You know it was that nigga Cliff and his homeboys who got at us that night at the club. If I would have popped that clown right after he hit 'Neema, Bo-Pete would still be alive."

"You can't blame yourself, Taz. Too much shit has been happening around here lately. There's been entirely too much drama going on here in the city. So, I guess it's safe to assume that Cliff is no longer a breathing human being, huh?"

"Nah, that clown is hiding somewhere. We ain't been able to get his ass yet."

"But you intend to, right?"

Taz stared at Tari as if she was crazy and said, "What do you think?"

She sighed heavily and said, "I know. I just can't get over the fact that Bo-Pete's gone. This shit has me really tripping." As her tears started to fall again, she said, "Let me go. Make sure you give me a call whenever they release Bo-Pete's body." She stood and kissed Taz tenderly on his lips and left his home.

"Bitch, not only did I go with him, I was actually about to shoot somebody with him," Gwen said as she held the cordless phone between her shoulder and right ear.

"Stop lying, ho! You know damn well you wasn't going to do shit!" Sacha yelled into the receiver.

Gwen sat down at the dining room table and said, "Sacha, I'm not losing another man that I love. If Bob is determined to go out there and get revenge for his homeboy, then I'm going to be his ride-or-die bitch and be right by his side. If something goes wrong for him, then it's going to go wrong for me too."

"You love him that much, ho?"

"You damn skippy! But, anyway, since nothing happened, I've been praying like hell that he don't want to go back out there. Bitch, I was scared as hell!"

They started laughing, and then Sacha said, "Ho, you are too fucking much! Let me go. I have a court appearance to make. I'll give you a call when I get back to Taz's."

"All right, bitch," Gwen said and hung up the phone.

Bob, who had been listening to Gwen's entire conversation with Sacha, stepped back into his bedroom and sat down on the bed. *That woman really loves a nigga. I can't put her in that kind of situation again. What the fuck was I thinkin' about?* he asked himself as he laid back on the bed and started thinking about Bo-Pete and the past. *This shit has really gotten crazy. Taz is on the verge of losing it. If he's talking about hurting 'Neema, then I know the end of the world is coming. That nigga Cliff has to die, but is it worth Taz and his only child going at it like some killas on the streets?* "Damn!" he said aloud as he closed his eyes and drifted off to sleep.

"I really need to see you, Cliff. When are you coming back to the city?" asked Tazneema.

"I'm not sure yet, 'Neema. What's wrong, baby?"

"I need to talk to you, and it's very important. Where are you staying? I could come out there if I have to."

"What? Come on now, baby. You're in no condition to be making this long drive to Dallas. Why won't you tell me what's on your mind right now?"

"I need to be with you when I talk to you, baby. I have to look into your eyes to make sure that you're not deceiving me."

"Deceiving you? What are you talking about, 'Neema?"

"Do you really love me, Cliff? I mean, am I really the woman you want to be with?"

"Come on, 'Neema. You already know the answer to those questions."

"If I'm the woman you love, then come out to my apartment in Norman. I need you to get here as fast as you can. I'm only three hours or so out of Dallas. You could make it here before midnight if you left right now. I need you, baby. I need you to confirm what my heart already knows."

"And what is that, 'Neema?"

"Are you coming or not, Cliff?" she asked firmly.

He sighed and said, "I'm on my way, baby."

She smiled into the receiver and said, "I'll see you when you get here."

After Tari left Taz's house, Taz went downstairs to the gym and started to work out vigorously. The harder he worked his muscles, the heavier his heart felt. He was trying to punish his body for the mistakes he felt he made. His own daughter was going against him for a man she felt loved her. One of his closest friends had been murdered in the street because he waited too long to handle what he normally would have finished immediately. The only reason he paused on killing Cliff was because of his daughter. *Now look at this shit!* he thought as he pumped his arms up and down, harder and harder. He was bench-pressing two hundred and forty-five pounds of solid iron. The burning sensation he was feeling in his muscles was nothing compared to the hurt he was feeling inside his heart.

He heard a car pull into his driveway and smiled as he racked the weights he'd been lifting. He wiped sweat from his face as he left the gym to head back upstairs. Just as he made it to the next floor, Sacha was opening the front door to his home. He smiled and said, "Damn, Li'l Mama! Where you been? It's almost eleven!"

"I stopped over at Gwen and Bob's, and we ended up going out to dinner. I called you here and on your cell to see if you would want to join us, but you didn't answer either phone. Are you all right, baby?" she asked as she stepped over to him and kissed him lightly on the cheek.

"Yeah, I'm good. I was working out. I left my cell upstairs in the bedroom. Tari came by, and I told her about Bo-Pete. After watching her lose it a li'l, I got depressed all over again and needed to work out some of my frustration."

"I understand. Are you hungry? I could make you something real quick if you want me to."

"Nah, I'm gon' go get me something after I take a quick shower. You go on and do whatever you got to do. I'm good."

"You sure?"

"Yeah, I'm sure."

"Taz?"

"Huh?"

"Go talk to your daughter. You have to put an end to this madness, baby."

He frowned and said, "I know, Li'l Mama. But the only way any of this will end is when Cliff is dead. That fact will never change. He has to die." He stepped past her and went upstairs to the bedroom.

Sacha shook her head from side to side as she followed her man upstairs.

Clifford was a nervous wreck as he pulled into Tazneema's apartment complex. When he'd left his room at the Westin, he drove around the city for close to the hour and forty minutes he needed to pass by before he drove out to the city of Norman. *What if she had Taz over there waiting to take me out? What if the police have gotten her to try and set me up? What if . . . ?* These were the questions going through his mind as he sat in his car and stared up toward Tazneema's apartment. After five minutes of this, he took a deep breath and said, "I love her, and I know she loves me. She would never do anything to hurt me like that. I know she wouldn't." When he made it to Tazneema's front door, he shook all doubts out of his mind and knocked softly on the door.

Tazneema opened the door, smiled and gave him a tight hug and said, "Come on in, baby. Lyla isn't here, so we'll have all of the privacy we need."

Clifford let her pull him over to the couch and sat beside her and asked, "Now, what's so important that you made me drive all of the way back to Oklahoma, 'Neema?"

She stared into his eyes and said, "I wanted to know if you were responsible for my Uncle Bo-Pete's death, Cliff. Did you kill my uncle?"

Clifford was shocked by her abruptness. He was even more shocked at how calm she was. He stared directly back into those deep brown eyes of hers—eyes exactly like her father's—and said, "What? Come on now, baby. Do I look like a killer?"

"Answer my question, Cliff. I have to hear you say it. I have to see it in your eyes, baby. Please, answer my question. Did you kill my Uncle Bo-Pete?"

Still staring directly at her, he said, "No. No, 'Neema, I did not kill your Uncle Bo-Pete."

"Did you have anything to do with him getting killed?"

"No."

"Did you know that your Hoover homeboys have been trying to kill my father?"

"For what?"

"I was hoping you would answer that question for me, Cliff. You see, my daddy has his mind made up that he's going to kill you. He feels that my Uncle Bo-Pete was either killed by you or your homeboys. Either way, he's holding you responsible."

"That's absurd! I don't deal with any of those Hoover homeboys, as you called them. Now, I do speak with some of my close comrades from back in the day, but that's about it. For Taz to even think I'd have something to do with a murder is absolutely ludicrous! I know you don't believe any of this craziness, 'Neema." Clifford stared at her for a minute and said, "You do! You actually think that I'd commit murder!"

Tazneema's heart began to literally melt at that very moment. She smiled at the man she loved more than anything in this world and said, "No . . . no, I don't, baby. I love you. I had to look into those gorgeous brown eyes so I could be sure my heart wasn't leading my brain. I've gone against my father for you, Cliff. I'll never leave your side, baby. Never!" she said and kissed him tenderly.

Clifford pulled from her embrace and said, "What did you mean, you've gone against your father, 'Neema?"

"He swore on my mother's grave that he was going to kill you, baby," she said with a sudden fury in her voice. "So I swore on my mother's grave that if he killed you, then I was going to kill him."

"My God! This is ridiculous! What the hell are we going to do to straighten out this madness, baby?"

She shrugged her shoulders and said, "I don't know. All I know is, I love you. I'm about to have our child, and no matter what, nothing and nobody is going to hurt my man without paying dearly for it. I'm my Daddy's child. If he can kill, then so can I. Now, come on. Lyla won't be back for at least another couple of hours. I want to do it," she said with a sexy smile on her face.

Clifford shook his head and said, "You're something else, crazy girl!"

"But you love me, right?"

As he let her pull him toward her bedroom, he smiled and said, "Yeah, I love you. I love you more than you'll ever know."

Chapter Twenty-three

"So, she went back to her place, huh, Mama-Mama?" asked Taz as he turned his Denali onto the highway.

"Mmm-hmm. You really need to talk to that girl, Taz. She's acting out because she doesn't know any better."

"She's grown, Mama-Mama. I can't make her do anything that she doesn't want to."

"That may be true, but you can still try to talk some sense into her smart tail."

"I'm about to go out to her place now and see if I can do just that, Mama-Mama. I'll give you a call in the morning and let you know if I was able to do any good."

"Make sure you do that," Mama-Mama said before she hung up the phone.

Twenty-five minutes after he had gotten off the phone with his mother, Taz pulled into Tazneema's apartment complex. If he was fifteen minutes earlier, he would have bumped right into Clifford as he left Tazneema's apartment.

Taz jumped out of his truck and walked toward his daughter's place with a heavy heart. He knew she was going to stand firm on what she believed was right. *I hope and pray that I'll be able to convince her to see things my way because, if she doesn't, things are going to get ugly out here in Norman,* he thought as he knocked on her front door.

When Tazneema heard the knock at her door, she immediately assumed it was Clifford coming back for something. She ran to the door with just her thong and bra on. She opened the door and asked, "Did you forget something, baby?"

Taz stared at his damn-near naked daughter and said, *"What?"*

"Oh, shit! I'm sorry, Taz. Come on in," she said as she ran back into her bedroom to put on some clothes.

Taz stepped inside of her neat little apartment and asked, "Where is Lyla?"

"She's out! She should be back in a little bit though!" Tazneema yelled from her bedroom. "What brings you out this way at this time of the night?"

He glanced at his iced-out Cartier watch and said, "I know it's late, but I really need for us to clear the air, baby girl."

She came back into the living room and said, "Look, Taz. I love him, you hate him. He's my man, not your enemy. Cliff didn't have anything to do with shooting at you or my Uncle Bo-Pete's death. I know you don't believe that, but I do. Can you please let this go, Daddy? Please?"

He sat down on the couch and said, "Baby girl, you know I will give you anything in this world. I love you more than words can ever express. You're all of my MiMi that I have left, 'Neema. But I can't and I won't let that nigga make it for the shit he's responsible for. He did it, 'Neema. I swear to you on your mom's grave, baby girl, he did it! He tried to get me, and he done Bo-Pete. For that he has to die. It's as simple as that. I don't want to lose you or the love we have for one another, but if you force my hand, 'Neema, I'll have no other choice but to do me."

"No choice about what? What? You're going to hurt me too, Taz? Are you that cold, Daddy?" she asked sarcastically. "You know what? You don't even have to answer that, 'cause I already know you are. Like I told you when I was at your house, if you get at my man, then expect for me to be getting at you. Now, if you'll excuse me, I'm tired and I'm going to bed now."

"You really don't understand, do you? That shit is crazy! Love's a bitch. I know this, and I realize that you're in love with that nigga. I respect that, just as I respect you for being loyal to your man. But by being loyal to your man, you're not being loyal to the one man who would do whatever it would take to make sure that you're taken care of for the rest of your life.

"I've done more in this lifetime than you could ever imagine, 'Neema. I've robbed, I've killed, and I've hurt a whole lot of people, baby girl. I did what I did to ensure that my only child would always be taken care of. You are set for the rest of your life financially because of the crazy-ass life I've chosen to lead, and you have the fuckin' nerve to stand there and tell me that you'll go against me! You can't even pay your half of the rent for this place! I pay your school bills, this apartment included, your expenses for clothes, food. Hell, I pay every fuckin' bill, you have! Me! Me, 'Neema! I pay for every fuckin' thing! And you think I'm gon' let you talk to me like I ain't shit?

"I could break your fuckin' neck right fuckin' now, and no one would ever know! I can't hurt you, baby girl. You're my blood, and I love you with all of my heart's love. So, for the last time, stay away from that nigga. He's a dead man as soon as I can catch up with his ass. After I do that nigga, if you still want to come get at me, you know where to find me. I'll be waiting for you." Taz stared hard at his daughter for another moment, shook his head sadly and left her standing in her living room with tears falling down her face.

The next morning Taz was lying in bed when Detective Bean called and told him that he could come and retrieve his weapon.

"Why don't you come and deliver it? After all, you did come and get it," Taz said arrogantly.

"I'd prefer for you to come downtown to the station, Mr. Good. I have a few more questions I'd like to ask you," Detective Bean replied.

Taz laughed and said, "You know what? I don't have anything else better to do. I'll be there within the hour." Taz then hung up the phone and took a quick shower. He dressed in his everyday gear, a pair of black Dickies with a white T-shirt. After tying up the laces to his Timb boots, he put his diamond grill in his mouth and draped himself with the rest of his expensive jewelry. He was all smiles as he went into his garage and hopped into his truck. *This shit is going to be fun,* he thought to himself as he pulled out of his garage.

Tazneema tossed and turned the entire night. She couldn't understand why her father was so confident that Cliff was responsible for her Uncle Bo-Pete's death. *Is Taz right? Did Cliff have something to do with it? Or is Taz trying to destroy my relationship with Cliff?* She asked herself all of these questions over and over almost the entire night. By the time she did fall asleep, she was bone-tired.

Now that she was awake, the questions still remained. *Did Cliff have anything to do with all of this mess? I love that man, and he loves me. He wouldn't lie to me. I'm not going to let you fuck up my relationship, Taz,* she thought to herself as she climbed out of her bed and went into the bathroom to take a shower.

Taz was talking to Mama-Mama on his cell phone as he drove toward downtown Oklahoma City. "I'm tellin' you, Mama-Mama, she's so caught up with old boy that she's not listening to me."

"Are you positive that that boy was the one who did this to Bo-Pete, Taz?" asked his mother.

"Yeah, I am. If I wasn't, I wouldn't move on that clown until I was, Mama-Mama. I don't want to cause my baby girl any pain, but I have no other choice. That fool has to go."

"I don't want to be hearing none of that, Taz! I understand that you're hurting, but so am I. That boy was like a son to me. You have a decision to make, Taz, and the sooner you make it, the better off you and 'Neema will be."

"What decision are you talkin' about? 'Cause I already done told you that clown has to go. I'm not changin' my mind about this, Mama-Mama. I love my daughter and she knows it, but if she chooses to go against me, then she has chosen her own fate." Before his mother could respond he said, "Look, I'm at the police station downtown. I'll give you a call later on Mama-Mama."

"What are you doing down there, boy?"

He smiled into the receiver and said, "Nothin'. I'm 'bout to have a li'l fun, that's all."

"Fun? Oh, never mind. I got a funny feeling that I don't need to know what you're talking about. Be good, boy," Mama-Mama said and hung up the phone.

Taz closed his cell, stepped out of his truck and strolled confidently inside of the police station.

After a fifteen-minute wait, Detective Bean came out into the lobby, where Taz was waiting patiently for him and said, "Good morning, Mr. Good. Would you please come this way?"

Taz followed the detective into his office and took a seat in front of Detective Bean's desk.

Detective Bean stared at Taz for a moment and then said, "I know all about you, Taz. I've had some time to do some serious research on you and your past."

Taz smiled and said, "I figured you would. So, tell me, what you think? Pretty interesting stuff, huh?"

Detective Bean laughed and said, "That's funny. Yeah, you're an interesting individual, Taz. There's something that confuses me though."

"What's that?"

"You're a very wealthy man. Not only that, but you seem to have all of the right people behind you and your friends. How did a young man from the streets get into such a powerful position?"

"Sometimes when a person knows the right people, they can make certain dreams become a reality."

"I don't understand."

"I know. It wasn't meant for you to. Look, I'm here for my pistol. Can I have it back or what? I have a busy day planned ahead of me."

Detective Bean reached inside of his desk and pulled out Taz's 9 mm that he had inside of a plastic Ziploc bag. He passed it across his desk to Taz and said, "One more thing, Taz. I know you and your crew did those Hoovers. To be honest with you, I really don't give a damn about those cowards. You live by the sword, you die by it. Just because you missed me on that one doesn't mean you'll always miss me. I'm very thorough. I don't miss too often."

Taz smiled and said, "Neither do I, Detective. Neither do I." He stood. "You have a nice day, Detective." Then he turned to leave Detective Bean's office. He stopped at the door, turned back and said, "I'm curious. Who informed you about me and my peoples?"

It was now Detective's Bean's turn to smile. He relaxed back in his chair and said, "Won's been around for a very long time, Mr. Good . . . a very long time."

Taz kept his poker face intact even though he was shocked as hell when he heard the detective mention Won's name. He smiled at the detective and asked, "Who's Won?"

Detective Bean burst into laughter and said, "Oh, you're good! You're very good, Mr. Good! Have a nice day. And, Taz, stay outta the way. It would be a shame for you to lose all that you've acquired over the years due to something as messy as this."

Taz stared at the detective for a full minute before finally turning and leaving his office. As soon as he was back inside of his truck, he called Won. When Won answered the phone, Taz said, "What's up with this Detective Bean out here in the city, O.G.?"

Won started laughing and said, "He's my cousin."

Taz gave a sigh of relief and said, "Yeah, well, you need to get your peoples off of my fuckin' back."

"I did. Why the fuck you think you had that meeting with him? He gave me a call a couple of days ago, asking me all types of shit about you. I gave him the semi-version of your life, and the rest is history. You don't have to worry about him. He's a teammate."

"You're something else, O.G. You know that?"

"Yeah, I know, Babyboy. That's why my name is *Won!*"

Chapter Twenty-four

Taz, Keno, Red, Wild Bill and Bob were seated at the front of the church, staring at the closed casket that their lifelong friend was lying in. Each one of them was caught up in their own personal thoughts about Bo-Pete at that moment. They were dressed identically in black Armani suits, with black Mauri alligator shoes on their feet. Once Bo-Pete's casket was opened, everyone inside of the church would have noticed that he too was dressed as his closest friends were.

Sacha and Gwen sat in the pew right behind their men. Won was by their side, giving comfort to them both. Even though he too was hurting from this tragedy, he gave the appearance that he was in complete control of his emotions. He couldn't let his pain be seen by Taz and the others. If he did, he felt that Taz would lose it and all hell would break loose.

Just before Bo-Pete's family came inside of the church, Tari came and sat down beside Won. She was dressed in an all-black dress with matching pumps. She gave a nod toward Sacha and Gwen and then reached over the pew and gently rubbed Taz on his shoulders.

Taz turned around and smiled sadly at her, but said nothing. No words could express the pain he was going through at that very moment. Tari saw the pained expression on his face and couldn't stop the sudden flow of tears falling from her eyes. Taz turned back around quickly before he started bawling himself.

Bo-Pete's family was led into the church, and everyone inside of the building stood as the family was seated.

The Reverend's sermon/eulogy was mostly about living right and doing the right thing. At least that's what Taz thought, until the Reverend started screaming and yelling about violence and all of the senseless killings that had been going on all around them lately.

Though the Reverend was bouncing all around the podium, Taz felt as if he was directing his sermon toward him. *I know this clown ain't shootin' his shot at me,* he thought as he continued to stare and listen to the Reverend preach.

Then, as if the Reverend had heard what Taz was thinking, he turned toward him and said, "Greed! Greed is what causes us to get together like this!" He yelled as he stood over the closed casket, "When men start controlling their urges for that almighty dollar, then and only then will we be able to avoid such tragedies as this one here!"

Taz turned toward Keno, shook his head from side to side and whispered, "I can't take too much more of this, dog. I'm goin' out to the truck. I'll be back when it's time for the final viewing." Before Keno could say a word to try to stop him, Taz was on his feet and on his way out of the church.

He was almost to the back of the church when he heard the Reverend yell, "You can't run from your fate! Nor can you run from God! Change! Change is the only way to make things right!"

Taz stopped in his tracks and turned slowly back around so that he was facing the entire church. He saw his daughter sitting next to Mama-Mama and he smiled at the both of them. *I'm not lettin' this preacher man get to me,* he thought as he marched right back to his seat in the front of the church. After he was seated, he stared hard at the Reverend, basically daring him to keep picking on him.

The Reverend noticed and him and quickly directed his gaze elsewhere. After he finished his eulogy/sermon, it was time for friends and family members to say a few words about the deceased.

After a few of Bo-Pete's cousins and other relatives had spoken, Taz took a deep breath and stepped up to the podium. Once he grabbed the microphone, he stared out into the crowded church and said, "I've known Bo-Pete most of my life. We went to school together, we went on our first date with our girlfriends together, and we learned how to become men together. He always used to tell me that I'm too emotional and I need to learn how to control my temper. When this man died, so did a part of me. I'm not an overly religious person, but I do believe there is a God in Heaven. I pray that he forgives me as well as Bo-Pete for our wrongs in life. Because Bo-Pete's wrongs as well as mine coincide as one. Neither one of us should be considered as greedy men." He paused and glared hard toward the Reverend before he continued. "We did what we felt was the right thing to do to take care of our families."

After that statement, Taz let his eyes scan the crowd, until they locked with Tazneema's. Then he continued, "There was nothing in this world that Bo-Pete wouldn't do for me and my family, just as there is nothing in this world I wouldn't do for his. That's not the way of greedy men. That's the love for one another! The respect! The loyalty! The honor! I'd gladly change places with my man lying inside of that there coffin," he said as he pointed toward Bo-Pete's casket. "But I can't. All I can do is live and let his memory give me strength to do the things that I feel I must do. I will do everything that needs to be done. That, I promise you, my dog . . . my brother . . . my friend!" Taz said as he stared at the gold-trimmed mahogany casket. He stepped away from the podium with his face wet with his tears. When he sat back down, Keno wrapped his arms around his shoulders and gave his friend some much-needed support.

Sacha was in tears also as she watched her man speak with so much passion. Gwen too was in tears as she stared at Bob, who was sobbing loudly. Wild Bill and Red, as well as Won and Keno, were all in tears also.

One of Bo-Pete's relatives came to the podium and started singing "Amazing Grace" as the morticians came to the front and opened the casket for the final viewing of Bo-Pete.

When Taz saw Bo-Pete's smooth, chocolate-brown skin look so pale with the makeup the morticians used, he lost it. "*No-o-o-o-o! No! No! No! God, no! Why you take my nigga? Why?*" he screamed over and over.

Keno tried to grab him, but he was too strong for him to hold.

Red stood up and grabbed Taz and said, "Come on, my nigga. Calm down. You're spooking everyone, gee."

Taz took a few deep breaths and gave Red a nod of his head to let him know that he was okay. He then stepped over to the casket and stared at his dead homeboy. "I'm gon' get him, Bo-Pete! You know I got 'em, dog," he said as he bent forward and kissed both of Bo-Pete's cold cheeks. He then turned toward the family, walked over to Bo-Pete's mother and said, "I'm sorry for my behavior, Mrs. McClelland. Please forgive me."

With tears sliding down her face, Bo-Pete's mother said, "There's nothing to forgive, Taz. I know how much you and that boy loved each other. Don't you pay that preacher no mind, ya hear?"

Taz smiled and kissed her on her cheek and said, "Don't worry, I won't." He stepped back, so the family could have their final viewing of Bo-Pete.

After the casket was closed, Taz, Red, Bob, Keno and Wild Bill stepped over to the casket so that they could carry it to the hearse. Even though Wild Bill's right arm was still in a sling, he refused to let anyone stop him from helping carry his homeboy.

Once they had the casket inside of the hearse, they all went and got into their vehicles. Keno drove his Range Rover, Red and Wild Bill had come together in Red's Tahoe, Gwen drove Bob's Escalade, while Taz, Sacha and Won all rode in Taz's Denali.

Taz was climbing inside of his truck when Tazneema ran up to him and said, "Taz, can I speak with you for a moment? Please?"

He stared hard at his daughter and asked her, "Have you changed your mind, 'Neema?"

"No, but—"

Before she could finish her sentence, he stopped her with his hands and said, "Then please get the fuck away from me!" He started the ignition and pulled out of his parking space, leaving his daughter standing there with tears sliding down her cheeks.

Won, who didn't know what the fuck was going on, went ballistic. "What the fuck was that, Babyboy? Why in the hell did you just speak to your child like that?"

"Let's talk about it later, O.G. I'm really not in the mood for it right now."

"*What?*" Won turned toward Sacha and said, "Would you please explain to me what the fuck is going on around here?"

"Later, Won. Just let it be for now, okay?"

"Okay? Hell nah, it's not okay! What the fuck is going on?"

Taz sighed heavily as he told Won everything that was happening with him and Tazneema. He finished just as they pulled into Trice Hill Cemetery.

"You can't—and I mean this, Babyboy—you can't let this interfere with your relationship with your child. There has to be another way to handle this situation," Won said.

"If there is, I haven't thought of it, O.G. What? You want me to let that nigga make it or something?"

Won stared at Sacha for a brief second then to Taz he said, "Why not? You don't have to make it so damn obvious to your daughter. She's in love with the man, Taz, for Christ's sake! Give him a pass until we can think of a better way of handling this situation."

"Fuck, nah! That nigga is the reason we're about to put my nigga six feet deep!" Before Won could say another word, Taz jumped out of his truck and marched toward the hearse to help the others carry Bo-Pete's body to its final resting place.

Won and Sacha met up with Gwen and Tari, and they all walked toward Bo-Pete's gravesite. Sacha knew that there was nothing that could be said to Taz. She hoped and prayed that maybe Won would have been able to talk some sense into him, but all of those hopes went out the window after the conversation she heard during their ride to the cemetery. She knew for certain now that Clifford was going to be buried himself real soon.

After the Reverend finished with his final prayer, Taz and the rest of the crew stood over Bo-Pete's open grave. Each member of the crew said their good-byes in different ways. Bob pulled off his diamond-studded Cartier wristwatch and tossed it on top of Bo-Pete's casket and said, "Watch over us, gee. I love you."

After Bob walked away, Red pulled out a picture of himself and Bo-Pete that was taken when they were vacationing in Cancun, and dropped it onto the casket and said, "You may be gone, my nigga, but you'll never be forgotten."

Keno took one of his two-carat stud earrings and tossed it onto Bo-Pete's casket and said, "This life ain't gon' be the same without you, gee. I love you, homey."

With tears sliding down his face, Wild Bill took off his Presidential Rolex watch and tossed it onto the casket and walked away. He was too choked up to even speak.

Finally, Taz pulled out his favorite Jesus piece and platinum chain and tossed it onto the casket and said, "Hold me down, dog. Hold me down."

They waited and watched until three of the cemetery's caretakers came and started shoveling dirt over Bo-Pete's coffin. Once they were a quarter of the way finished, Taz turned toward the crew and said, "Come y'all. Let's bounce."

"Are we rollin' back to the church to eat with the family?" asked Keno as he loosened his silk tie.

Shaking his head no, Taz said, "Nah. If I get too close to that wack-ass preacher, I just might sock his ass. Let's go to my spot and get faded."

"Yeah, I'm wit' that!" Wild Bill said as he wiped his eyes.

"Bust out the XO, nigga, 'cause it's about to be a long muthafuckin' night!" Bob said as he led the way back toward their vehicles.

As Taz followed the crew back to their trucks, he paused and looked over his shoulder and said, "I got 'em, Bo. I got his ass, gee. Real talk."

Chapter Twenty-five

The remaining crew members, plus Won, Tari, Gwen and Sacha, were having a good time getting drunk and listening to each member of the crew as they took turns talking about something funny concerning their fallen comrade. Katrina and Paquita had been invited to their little get-together also. Taz felt that since they were kind of close to Red and Keno, they were worthy of knowing where he rested his head. Therefore, he welcomed them into his home.

"All right! All right, y'all, hold up. I got one. Do y'all remember when we had those goofy-lookin' twin niggas hemmed up at their dope spot on the east side?" asked Keno.

"You mean them fag niggas from Prince Hall?" asked Red.

"Nah, not them fools. Them niggas didn't give us a fight at all. I'm talkin' 'bout those fools who didn't want to tell us the combo to they shit. You remember, Taz. You was like, 'Fuck it! Let's bounce!' 'Cause we had already popped they weak-ass crew comin' in."

"Oh, I know who you talkin' 'bout. The umm . . . umm . . . what was they fucking names? Oh! Mick and Mike, or was it Mikey and Mike? Some shit like that," Taz said and sipped some more of his XO.

"Yeah, them clowns. Anyway, remember when I got mad and was about to pop 'em?"

"Yeah, and Bo-Pete stopped you."

"That's right! Do you know the reason why he stopped me?"

"'Cause the spot was hot and we had to get the fuck outta there!" Wild Bill laughed from the other side of the room.

"Nah, nigga. That nigga Bo-Pete was cool with them fools. He didn't want to hurt them 'cause he said y'all used to be on the same football team back at John Marshall and shit."

"Yeah, they was, but I wasn't even thinkin' 'bout no shit like that. We was hungry, and we did what we did 'cause that was our thang," Taz said as he sat down next to Sacha.

"I know, but you didn't care if we let them make it or not. Remember how hot Bo-Pete got at me when I told him to take his soft-ass outside to the truck while I pop them clowns?"

"Yeah. That nigga wanted to do you somethin' for real," answered Red.

"That's right. Y'all got into it big time after you smoked them fools. Bo-Pete was mad at your ass for about a month behind that shit," Bob said as he rubbed Gwen's thigh.

"So tell me. What's the point of this story?" asked Won.

"The point is, my nigga was a good nigga. He had a good heart. Me, I was on some Eazy-E ruthless shit. They saw our faces so they had to fuckin' go! But not my nigga Bo-Pete. He felt they wouldn't try to get back at us, so he wanted to give them a pass. That was one good nigga right there for real!" slurred Keno.

The room fell silent for a few minutes as everyone started thinking about how much they missed Bo-Pete. Taz broke the silence and said, "Come on, y'all. Let's go get something to eat. I'm fuckin' starvin'."

"Yeah. Let's hit up one of your spots. At least that way we'll be able to eat for free!" Bob started laughing.

"Look at this clown! All those chips and he wants to get a free fuckin' meal! Niggas will always be niggas!" Red said as everyone started laughing.

Won stepped over to Taz and said, "I gots to be going, Baby-boy. I got a flight to catch out of Tulsa in a couple of hours. Let me talk to you for a minute."

Taz took Won upstairs to his bedroom and started to change clothes. As he was getting undressed, Won told him, "I don't know what's what on this last mission. Shit ain't going according to plan, so I really need for you to stay on point for me. If something goes wrong, I want you to promise me that you will take care of things that need to be taken care of."

After Taz slid into a pair of black Dickies, he asked Won, "What are you talkin' about, O.G.? Don't be gettin' at me with no riddles. That's not for me and you. What's up?"

Won sighed, and for the first time in a long time he showed someone that he was worried. "I don't know, Babyboy. I think Pitt done got the upper hand on me this time. I haven't heard from one of my peoples in a minute, and when I got at him, I could have sworn that Pitt answered his phone."

"So, you think that nigga Pitt got at your peeps?"

"I don't know. I think so though. Flo' is shaking me, and the rest of the council is being real tight-lipped, like they know something is about to pop off. But, look, I'm gon' keep it straight with you. If something happens to me, you will inherit everything that I have. You're like the son I've always wanted, Babyboy, and I love you that much. But you gots to promise me that you won't try to get revenge on any member of the council."

"What are you talkin' about, O.G.? I don't even know who the council is."

"Listen. When everything is everything, you will then understand the meaning of this conversation. You will have a decision to make, and I'm banking on you to make the right one. If something happens to me, Pitt will be responsible. Don't worry about that nigga though. He's a slipper."

Taz smiled and said, "Yeah, and slippers fall."

"Exactly."

"But, on the real, what's poppin', O.G.?" Taz asked seriously.

"It is what it is, Babyboy. Only time will tell how this one is going to fall. You just make sure that you continue to stay ready. If things go as planned, I'm going to need you to be ready. If they don't, you're still going to have to be prepared to handle shit. Remember this—whatever you decide, you will have my blessing. If and when the time comes, you'll understand everything I've just told you. All of the hard work we've put in was for this sole purpose. I don't want to fail. You know I've never lost, but I got a funny feeling I just might lose this one. If that's the case, I want you in the position that I've been striving for all of these years."

"The position of power you told me about?"

"Exactly." Won gave Taz a tight hug and said, "We can't change fate, Babyboy. If it's meant to be, it will be. Always remember, I will always love you and that crazy-ass crew of yours."

"Come on with that shit, O.G.! You're spookin' a nigga. We've already lost Bo-Pete. I don't think I can stand another loss that heavy."

"Losses are a part of life, Babyboy. You can handle it. You're built for the long haul. I knew that the first day I saw you. There's one more thing I want you to do for me."

"What's that?"

"Start thinking things through more thoroughly. You handled the situation with 'Neema ass backward. I realize it was because of your pain and anger behind Bo-Pete. She's your only child, you should have considered her feelings in this mess."

"I did. That's why I waited to deal with that nigga, and look what happened because of me waiting."

"Still, you should have finessed the situation instead of exposing your hand. Now you're on the verge of losing the love of your only child. If something happens to that fool right now, even if it's an accident, there would be nothing you could do or say to prove your innocence to 'Neema. She would blame you, no matter what."

"So, what should I do now, O.G.?"

"Call her and let her know that you love her, and even though you're not feeling dude, you're willing to let this pass simply because you're hurting too damn much behind the loss of Bo-Pete. Explain to her how deeply you feel for her and her well-being. Show your seed that the love you have for her is stronger than any revenge plot. Make sure that you're sincere enough to convince her you're being real with her."

Taz smiled and asked, "And after I've convinced her that I'm sincere?"

"You already know. Smoke that nigga! He has to be punished for our loss. But make sure you have a solid alibi, not only for the people, but for 'Neema as well." They hugged each other again quickly, and Won said, "All right, I'm out. I'll give you a call in a few days if I've learned anything. If you don't hear from me, then that means I've went dark and I'll holla when the time is right. I have to take care of a few loose ends out in Texas, but I will get at you when the time is right."

"What if something goes left? How will I know what's what?"

"You'll be notified," Won said as he turned and left the bedroom.

***

Later on that night after enjoying a pretty pleasant evening with his friends, Taz and Sacha were lying in bed, talking about their future. "Which room are we going to turn into the baby's room, Taz?" Sacha asked as she stretched and slid into his arms.

"It don't matter to me, Li'l Mama. Whichever one you want."

"I was thinking about the guest room right next to us. I want my baby to be as close to me as possible, all of the time."

He laughed and said, "*Your* baby? What about me? Ain't he gon' be mine too?"

She laughed and said, "Why do you keep referring to the baby as a *he*? What if it's a she?"

Taz shook his head from side to side and said, "No way, Li'l Mama! I know for sure it's goin' to be a boy."

"What makes you so positive about that, Mr. Taz?"

"'Cause my son is replacing Bo-Pete," he said somberly.

"Is that the name you've chosen for him if indeed we do have a son?"

"Yep. Reginald Good—li'l Bo-Pete," Taz said with a sad smile on his face. "Do you have a problem with that, Li'l Mama?"

"Nope. I like it, baby. I really do. Can I ask you a question though?"

"You know you can. What's good?"

"When are we going to make this engagement official and do the damn thing? I'm ready to become Mrs. Good."

"You know, I was thinking about that too. Do you want to wait until after the baby is born, or are you ready to make it happen this summer?"

She smiled and said, "This summer is fine with me!" They laughed and shared an intense kiss with one another. Afterward, Sacha said, "Umm, you know you done got me horny with all of that sweet tongue you just gave me."

He pulled at her transparent thong and said, "Well, let's take care of that then!"

Chapter Twenty-six

The next morning when Taz climbed out of bed, he noticed that Sacha had already left for work. He smiled as he thought about her and how freaky she had been during their lovemaking. *That girl be trying to put it on a nigga,* he thought as he went downstairs to get himself something to drink.

As he sipped on some orange juice, he decided to give 'Neema a call and do as Won suggested. He grabbed the cordless phone off the kitchen counter and dialed his daughter's number. When Tazneema answered the phone, he said, "Hey, baby girl. What you up to?"

"Nothing. Just getting ready to go back to school. It feels so strange since I've been out for so long. I have a lot of catching up to do."

"Yeah, I bet you do. You'll be all right though. Look, 'Neema, I'm not goin' to play any games with you. I hate that nigga Cliff. I hate the fact that you fell in love with him also. I hate it even more that you're goin' to have a child by him. But all of the hate I have is nothing compared to the love I have for you, baby girl. I could never intentionally cause you any pain. It took for me to bury Bo-Pete to realize that this shit is just not worth it. Please understand that I'm not changing the way I feel about him, 'cause that will never change, because whether you believe it or not, he did have something to do with the death of you Uncle."

"Taz—"

"No, wait, 'Neema. Let me finish. Like I was sayin', the love I have for you is stronger than any hateful feelings I have for Cliff. Keep him away from me and my home. He's not welcome. Do that, and I promise you that I'll never do him nothin'."

"What about the others? How do they feel?"

"We all love you, and we've all come to this conclusion last night," he lied. "You mean the world to us, and we don't want to cause you any pain. Plus, Keno said he feared for his life 'cause you was wolfin' some high-powered gangsta shit!"

Tazneema laughed as tears of joy and relief slid down her face. "I love you, Daddy! Thank you! Thank you so very much!"

"I love you too, baby girl. Now, gon' and finish gettin' ready for school. If you need anything, give me a holla."

"I will," she said, and hung up the phone feeling real good inside.

After Taz hung up the phone, he smiled because he knew that Won would be proud of how he just rocked his daughter to sleep with his manipulation. Because there was no way in hell that nigga Cliff would still be breathing by the end of the summer. *After me and Sacha do our wedding thang, that nigga is good as dead,* he thought to himself as he downed the rest of his orange juice.

Keno slapped Katrina on her thick behind and said, "Girl, you better get your ass up! You're goin' to be late for work."

She rolled to the other side of Keno's California king-sized bed and said, "Come on, boo. Let me sleep a li'l longer, 'kay?"

Keno laughed and said, "For real, for real, I don't give a damn if you never went to work again. It ain't like you need the money. Fuckin' with me, you straight."

His statement made her open her eyes. She turned and faced him and asked, "What does that mean, Keno? You trying to take care of me or something?"

"Yeah, it's time for a nigga to settle down and start a family and shit. You with somethin' like that?"

Katrina smiled and happily asked, "Are you trying to wife me, Keno?"

He returned her smile and said, "Do you wanna be wifey?"

She frowned and said, "You can't answer a question with one, Keno!"

"Yes, I'm tryin' to wife you. Will you marry me, Katrina?"

"Yes! Yes! *Yes!*" She screamed as she rolled into his arms and kissed him passionately. "I love you, Keno! I love you so much!"

Keno didn't know how much he had actually cared about Katrina until that very moment, because he said the three words he never thought he would ever tell a woman. "Yeah, *mami*, I love you too. So, you gon' quit your job and shit now?"

She pulled from his embrace and said, "Uh-uh. I'm going to finish school and keep on working. What I look like, just living off my man? I'm gon' bring something to the table too. I'm a *real* woman, Keno. Not some leech."

Keno laughed and said, "*Mami*, if I thought you were anything less than a real woman, you would have never gotten as close to me as you have. My wifey don't have to do no work if she don't want to. I'm in a position to make sure that your every dream can come true. Your every want and desire can and will be fulfilled. All you have to do is tell me what you want, *mami*. Real talk."

Staring deeply into Keno's brown eyes, Katrina said, "I believe you, baby, but all I want from you is your love and devotion."

"You got that, *mami*."

"What about the game, Keno? Are you going to stop hustling?"

Keno laughed and said, "Hustling? What makes you think I'm a hustler?"

"Come on, baby, don't play me like that. Look at all of this," she said as she waved her arms around Keno's bedroom. "This big-ass mini-mansion you're living in, the fat Range Rover, the six hundred and all of them expensive low riders that you have in your garage, not to mention all of the expensive jewelry and stuff. I'm not lame to the game, baby. I just want you to be smart enough to get out while you're way ahead of it, that's all. I don't want to become your wife just to lose you one day to jail, or like Bo—well . . . you know what I'm saying."

Keno pulled her toward him and said, "Listen to me, *mami*. I'm not goin' to nobody's jail, and I don't plan on leaving this earth anytime soon. You don't ever have to worry yourself about none of that craziness. I'm here for as long as you want me to be. As for the hustling, that shit is funny. I don't get down like that. I'm a legit businessman. I have more shit than I can even begin to explain." He jumped off the bed and stepped quickly toward his dresser. He opened one of the drawers, pulled out a black bankbook, went back to the bed and handed it to Katrina and said, "Look at this, *mami*, and tell me if you think a hustler could do it this big."

Her eyes damn near popped out of their sockets when she saw the seven figures inside of Keno's bank account. She was speechless as she saw how much money he earned yearly.

"You see, *mami*, I ain't no damn hustler. Everybody out there thinks we're dope boys or some shit like that. They're so far off that it's crazy, and that's exactly how we like it. Let niggas in the streets think we're dope boys or whatever. As long as we keep everyone in left field, we'll always stay one step ahead of the game. So, don't worry about a thang. Once you become wifey, everything in my life will finally be complete. You with that?"

"Am I! Come here!" she said as she pulled his face to hers and kissed him deeply.

After their kiss, he asked her, "So, are you goin' to work today? Or are we going to go get your wedding ring?"

She smiled and said, "Yeah, I'm going to work. You're going to go get my wedding ring, baby. I want you to pick what you want me to have on this finger," she said as she wiggled her ring finger in front of his face.

"Your wish is my every command, *mami*," he said as he started laughing. *Damn! This love shit feels pretty good,* he thought to himself with a smile on his face.

Katrina frowned and asked, "What's so funny, Keno?"

"I can't believe I just said some corny-ass movie shit like that."

She playfully slapped him on his face and said, "That was not corny, Keno. That was the sweetest thing you've ever said to me."

"Yeah, it may be, but that was still some corny-ass shit," he said as he quickly ducked another blow from his fiancée. He grabbed her around her waist and pulled her close to him and said, "I'll be as corny as I wanna be for you, *mami*, 'cause you're about to be wifey."

With a bright smile on her face, Katrina said, "That, I am, baby. That, I am."

After Katrina had gotten dressed and left for work, Keno called Red and told him what he had done.

Red started laughing and said, "Nigga, stop lyin'! I know you didn't! Not you!"

"I did it, dog. As a matter a fact, I'm about to get dressed and go pick her out a tight-ass wedding ring right after I get off the phone with your ass," Keno said proudly.

"That's cool, my nigga. Congratulations."

"Thanks. What you got goin' on for the day?"

"Shit. I might go scoop Paquita up and take her out to lunch or something. Other than that, my plate's empty. We need to be gettin' back on our regular schedule for real. We haven't worked out in a minute."

"Yeah, I know. But with Wild Bill out of commission and Bob still laid up, I guess Taz just ain't been feelin' it, ya know?"

"Yeah, this shit is crazy, dog. I still can't believe all of the shit that's happened. Bo-Pete's gone, dog. He's fuckin' gone!"

"I know. All we can do now is finish what we started, and live on for him, gee. His peoples is straight, so it ain't like he didn't bless the game."

"That's one way you can look at it. But from my eyes, I'm like, why didn't the game bless my nigga? Bo-Pete didn't deserve that shit, dog."

"I feel you. But, look, I'm in a pretty good mood right about now. I'm not tryin' to get back all depressed on the day that I've officially surrendered my playa card. I'll holla at ya later, my nigga. I'm about to go buy a wedding ring."

Red laughed and said, "My bad, dog! Gon' and do you, my nigga. Get at me when you've finished handlin' your business."

"Out!" Keno said and hung up the phone and went into his bathroom to take a shower so he could start his day.

***

After Taz finished getting dressed, he called his mother and explained his conversation with his daughter. When he was finished, Mama-Mama said, "Humph! She believed all of that, huh?"

Taz smiled into the receiver and thought, *I can fool my daughter, but I damn sure can't fool my Mama!* But to her he said, "Why wouldn't she? I meant it, Mama-Mama. I want nothing but the best for 'Neema. You know that."

"Yes, I do know that, but don't you think for one minute that I believe you're not going to do something to that boy! I know you better than you think, Taz Good! You are not the type to let things go. And if your silly-ass daughter was thinking straight, she would be able to see through the bullshit you're pulling her through. I have one question for you, what are you going to do after you finally do whatever you have planned for that boy, Taz? And don't you dare lie to me, boy!"

He laughed and said, "Whatever's goin' to happen won't be my fault, Mama-Mama . . . at least that's how it's goin' to look."

"Mmm-hmm. I figured that much. Bye, boy! I got my food on the stove."

"Bye, Mama-Mama," Taz said and hung up the phone laughing.

After taking a quick shower and getting dressed, he called Sacha at work to see if she wanted to go out to lunch with him. Sacha's receptionist told him that she was out of the office and that she would be back around one. Since it looked like he was solo for the day, he picked the phone back up and called Bob.

Bob answered the phone on the first ring and said, "What's really good, my nigga? You must have read my fuckin' mind, 'cause I was just thinkin' 'bout your ass."

"Yeah! What's poppin', gee?"

"Please—and I mean *please*—come and rescue me from this overbearing woman of mines! She's driving me fuckin' batty in this house, dog!"

Taz started laughing and said, "Yeah, well, that's good for your ass. Gwen needs to stay on top of your ass."

"That's the fuckin' problem! She won't get off a nigga! She's turned into some kind of fuckin' sex maniac! I'm tellin' you, gee, I'm not even fully healed, and she's tryin' to fuck my brains out! You know a nigga loves the pussy and all, but damn! A nigga needs a fuckin' break sometimes!"

Taz heard Gwen in the background scream, "What kind of man runs from some good pussy, Taz?"

Taz laughed so hard that tears started forming in his eyes. "Damn, my nigga! It's like that?"

"You fuckin' right, it's like that! Come and get a nigga, dog. You're the only one she'll let me bounce with. She said I'd run over Red, Keno or Wild Bill and get into some shit. She's comfortable if you come scoop me though. For some reason she feels you can control 'The Bob'."

"All right, look. Get dressed, and I'll be over there in about thirty minutes. We can go get somethin' to eat and go check out a few rental houses out in Midwest City. I checked my e-mails a li'l while ago, and saw that a few new listings have been posted."

"That's cool, gee. Anything, and I mean *anything,* to get me away from this house is fine with me!" Bob said, relieved.

"You scared-ass nigga! You better hurry up, Taz, 'cause I might just change my mind and pull out my whips and handcuffs!" yelled Gwen in the background.

Taz hung up the phone and was in tears as he grabbed his keys and went into the garage.

Taz and Bob had just left from checking out their fourth rental house out in Midwest City. They were now on their way to get some lunch when Taz got a call from Sacha on his cell phone. "What's good, Li'l Mama?" he asked when he answered it.

"I just got back to the office, and I saw that you called. Why didn't you call me on my cell?"

"I didn't want to disturb you. I thought you might have been busy or somethin'. Have you had lunch yet?"

"Nope. I was hoping you'd take me somewhere so I could get my grub on. I'm starving."

"You're always starvin', Li'l Mama." Before she could reply, he said, "I know, I know. You're eating for two."

She laughed and said, "You got that right, buddy! So, are you taking me and your child to lunch or what?"

"Yeah, I'll feed you two. Better yet, you three! Bob is with me. We've been out in Midwest City checking out some rental houses that recently came up for sale."

"Bob? Where's my girl at? Don't tell me he done shook my nigga!" Sacha said, trying to sound as 'hood as she could.

Taz laughed and said, "Nah, she let him roll with me for a li'l while. Really, it was more of an escape for Bob. Your girl has been tryin' to fuck him to death."

"*What?* Never mind. Forget I asked."

"I'll put you up on it in a li'l bit. We'll be there in about fifteen minutes. I'm gettin' on the highway now."

"Hurry up. I want me some ribs from Tony Roma's."

"All right, greedy. I'll be there in a minute," he said, and closed his cell phone.

Taz, Bob and Sacha were enjoying their meal of barbeque ribs, baked beans and potato salad, when Red called Taz and told him about Keno asking Katrina to marry him.

"Is that right? That's way out. I'd never think that nigga was the marrying type," Taz said as he continued to munch on his rib tips.

"Yeah, I know, but it looks like that nigga is for real. When I talked to him earlier, he told me that he was on his way to go pick her up a ring and everything. That nigga is definitely serious. I got Wild Bill with me now. We're about to roll over to that nigga's spot and check out how much money he done spent on his future wifey."

"Y'all niggas are that bored, huh?"

"Yeah. It ain't shit else to do. I was tellin' Keno earlier that we need to get back to working out and shit too. We've gotten way off schedule."

"I know. Let's get together around seven and get back on it."

"That's straight. Did Won speak about finishing up everything while he was here?" asked Red.

"Yeah. He told me to make sure that we stay ready. He also told me that he thinks things may have went left on him."

"What? What's up with that?"

"I'm not knowin', really. I'll put y'all up on it when we get together for our workout. Ask that li'l nigga, Wild Bill, if he can put any weight on that sore shoulder of his."

After Red asked Wild Bill Taz's question, Taz heard Wild Bill say, "Fuck you, nigga! I can still out-bench your ass with a weak shoulder!"

Taz laughed and said, "Now that's what I'm talkin' 'bout! All right then, my niggas. I'll holla in the morning. Tell that nigga Keno I said he will be gettin' clowned when I see his ass. I ain't forgot how he tried to clown me when I told him I asked Sacha to be wifey."

Red started laughing and said, "All right, dog. I'll—*What the fuck!*"

"What's up, gee?" Taz asked with alarm.

"Somethin's wrong, dog! Keno's front door is wide the fuck open, and there's a body layin' in the doorway, my nigga! Hold on for a minute," Red said as he and Wild Bill jumped out of his truck and ran toward Keno's front door.

When Taz heard Red scream, "Ah, hell nah! Hell nah!" He knew that he had lost another close friend. Fuck!

Chapter Twenty-seven

After Taz and Bob dropped Sacha off back at her job, Taz drove like a bat out of hell toward Keno's home.

"I'm tellin' you, dog, we gots to put an end to that nigga Cliff! He's fuckin' tryin' to kill all of us!" Bob yelled from the passenger's seat.

"He's dead, dog! That nigga is dead to-fucking-night! I can't believe this shit! How in the fuck was he able to find out where Keno's spot was?"

"Do you think ol' girl might have put them niggas up on it?"

"Nah, Katrina don't strike me as a broad like that. But we'll still check into it later though. I ain't puttin' nothin' past nobody right now," Taz said as he pulled into the long, circular driveway that led to Keno's mini-mansion.

Police cars, as well as an ambulance, were parked in the driveway as they climbed out of Taz's truck. Taz saw Red talking to Detective Bean, and quickly rushed over toward them. Once he was standing in front of the detective, he asked, "Where's the body? I want to see my nigga!"

"This is a crime scene, Taz. You'll do more damage by trying to take a look at your friend," Detective Bean said as he stood in front of Taz.

Taz frowned at the detective and whispered through clenched teeth, "Where is my homeboy's body?"

Detective Bean sighed heavily and said, "Follow me."

Taz, Red and Bob followed the detective toward the front door of Keno's home. There were several police officers, as well as other detectives standing and moving around.

Taz stepped to the doorway and saw a body covered with a white sheet. He stepped to the body, knelt next to it and pulled the sheet back. Tears fell slowly from his eyes as he stared at

Keno's dead body. He could see one of the bullet-holes that had killed his man. Keno had been shot three times at close range with a small-caliber pistol. He could tell because of the size of the bullet-holes. After wiping his face, he replaced the sheet over Keno's body, stood and stepped out of the house.

Wild Bill, who had been on his cell trying to get in contact with Katrina, saw Taz walking toward his truck and said, "Dog, what the fuck are we gon' do now?"

Taz stared at Wild Bill for a moment then said, "Right now, I'm goin' home, gee. Y'all take Bob back to his spot for me. I need to be by myself for a li'l bit."

Before Wild Bill could say anything in response, Taz saw a blue Nissan Maxima pull into the driveway. Katrina jumped out of her car and ran toward the front door of Keno's house, screaming, "No-o-o-o-o! No-o-o-o! He asked me to marry him today! God, no-o-o-o! We're getting married!"

With tears sliding down his face, Taz said, "Go take care of her, gee. I gots to get the fuck outta here." He turned and stepped quickly to his truck and left the scene of a crime that had just broken his heart.

Taz drove from Keno's home straight to his mother's house out in the country. As soon as he walked inside of the house, Mama-Mama took one look at him and knew something was wrong. She stood and asked, "Who's been killed, Taz?"

Taz stared at his mother with tears falling from his eyes and said, "Keno. That nigga done killed my man, Mama-Mama! Out of all of us, that nigga killed my man! Please, Mama-Mama! Please tell me that you know where that nigga lives!"

Mama-Mama sat back down on the couch and shook her head sadly as she said, "I've never known where that boy's house is. And if I did, you know I wouldn't tell you, Taz. You have to let this stuff go, boy."

"Let it go? *Let it go?* How in the hell can I let this go when that nigga keeps on killin' my niggas? That man has to die, Mama-Mama! Can't you see that?"

Tears started falling from Mama-Mama's eyes as she fully understood what her only child was telling her. She couldn't believe Keno was dead. She'd practically raised him along with Taz. "Oh, Lord, please stop this madness!" she prayed aloud.

Taz went and sat down next to his mother, wrapped his arms around her and gave her a tight hug. "I'm sorry for yellin' at you, Mama-Mama, but it feels as if I'm losing my mind. I can't take too much more of this. I've got to put an end to that nigga, and the sooner the better."

"But what about 'Neema? You know what this is going to do to that girl, Taz."

"Yeah, I know, but what about the rest of us? Sooner or later, that nigga and his Crip homeboys are going to get lucky and get me, Bob and Wild Bill. I'm tellin' you, Mama-Mama, this is the only way. That man has to die!"

Sacha went to Taz's house after she got off of work, and went straight into his den. She turned on the television and watched the news as the reporter talked about Keno's murder. She sat down on the sofa and said a silent prayer: *Please, God, don't let Taz get too crazy behind this.* As she prayed, she knew that her prayer was in vain, because there was nothing and no one that could stop Taz from getting his revenge for Keno. That thought scared her more than anything in this world. She grabbed the phone and called Gwen.

As soon as Gwen answered the phone, she said, "Bitch, you do know that all hell's about to break loose, don't you?"

"Yeah, I know, ho. Them niggas are 'bout to go crazy," Sacha said as she relaxed back on the sofa.

"Do you know what happened?"

"Uh-uh. Me, Taz and Bob were having lunch at Tony Roma's when Red called Taz and told him that something was wrong at Keno's house. Taz dropped me off back at the office and left to go over to Keno's. I just came home and turned on the TV and saw that they don't have a clue as to what happened to him."

"Humph! Them TV people might not know what happened, but I do! Them Crip niggas did this shit! Bob is going to go so crazy behind this shit!" Gwen yelled, totally frustrated.

"Bob? Ho, Bob's not going to be half as bad as Taz is. The shit is really about to hit the fan. I can't believe this shit either."

"Believe it, bitch, 'cause it damn sure is true!"

After sitting and talking to his mother for a few hours, Taz decided that it was time to get at Tazneema, so he grabbed the phone and called his daughter. When she answered the phone, he said, "What's up, baby girl?"

"Hi, Taz," Tazneema said as she sat down on her bed.

"I'm not goin' to waste time with this, 'Neema. There's somethin' I need to tell you, and you're not goin' to like it."

"What's wrong now, Taz?"

"Your Uncle Keno was found dead at his house this afternoon."

"Wha-what are you saying? Wh-who did this?" Before Taz could answer her questions, she slapped her hand over her mouth and screamed into her palm. She knew what her father was about to say, and she didn't want to hear it. "Please, Daddy! Don't tell me that you think Cliff did this to my Uncle Keno!"

Taz inhaled deeply and said, "He did. I know what I told you about tryin' to accept that nigga, 'Neema. At that time I meant it. But now, shit has changed. That nigga won't stop until he has all of us lying side by side up at Trice Hill. He's got to go," he said, and hung up the phone in his daughter's ear.

Tears were streaming down Mama-Mama's face as Taz gave her a kiss on her salty cheek and said, "I'll talk to you later, Mama-Mama."

Mama-Mama was too choked up to speak. She gave him a nod of her head and watched her only child as he left her home, on his way most likely to commit a murder.

As Taz was leaving his mother's house, Tazneema was calling her man to warn him. Clifford answered his cell and listened to her as she screamed at him. "You have to stay out there in Dallas, Cliff! My Daddy is going to kill you if you come back to the city!"

"What are you talking about, 'Neema? Calm down!" Cliff said as he got off of the bed in his hotel room at the Westin in downtown Oklahoma City.

"Someone has killed my Uncle Keno, and my Daddy thinks that you are that someone!"

"What? That's preposterous! You know damn well I'm not even in the city right now, 'Neema!" Cliff lied.

"I know, but my father doesn't."

"Well, why didn't you tell him?"

"He didn't give me a chance to. He hung up on me before I could tell him. Just make sure that you stay where you are until I can get a chance to talk to him, okay?"

"That's bullshit! I'm sick and tired of this shit! I'm on my way back to the city now. I'll give you a call when I hit Norman."

"Please, Cliff! Stay where you are, at least one more day. Give me a chance to talk to my Daddy."

"No, 'Neema, it's time we put a stop to this madness right now," Cliff said, and he hung up the phone. He grabbed his keys, wallet and cell phone as he left his hotel room. As he was riding the elevator down to the lobby, he dialed H-Hop's cell phone number. "I can't believe that nigga got at Keno!" "Clifford said to himself as he waited for H-Hop to answer his phone. When he got H-Hop's voicemail, he left him a quick message: "Get at me, cuz. We gots to talk. Hit me on my cell," he said, and closed his cell phone. *This shit is about to get hectic real quick like,* he thought as he stepped off of the elevator.

By the time Taz pulled into his driveway, Sacha was a nervous wreck. She just knew that he would be out hunting for Cliff all night long. She gave a sigh of relief when he walked into the bedroom. She jumped off of the bed, ran into his arms and said, "Taz, baby, I'm so sorry. I'm so sorry about Keno."

He held on tightly to his fiancée and said, "It's real fucked up, Li'l Mama . . . real fucked up!" He gave her a kiss on her forehead and said, "Come on, let's lay down for a minute." He pulled her back toward the bed and slipped off his Timb boots.

Once they were comfortable, he said, "I've been driving around the city for the last few hours, thinking about all types of shit. This shit with Won, what's happened to Keno, you, and everything else that's been goin' on in my crazy-ass life. I'm tellin' you, Li'l Mama, I'm a cursed nigga. Everyone that comes into my life seems to always end up getting hurt."

Shaking her head no, Sacha said, "That's not true, baby. It just seems that way because of Bo-Pete and Keno's untimely deaths. You're not cursed, you're just going through some rough times right now, that's all."

"Rough times, huh? Li'l Mama, in less than a month I've lost two of my closest friends—two men who were like brothers to me. I lost one woman who I loved more than anything in this world because of my arrogance and stupidity. Can you imagine how it feels every time I look at Tazneema and see her mother's features? Can you imagine how it feels to know that I'll never be able to tell my niggas how much I really loved them? Can you imagine how my relationship is going to be with my daughter after I kill the nigga she's about to have a baby by? Can you? Huh? You can't sit there and tell me I ain't cursed, Li'l Mama. The life I chose to live has caused all of this pain! All of this is my fuckin' fault! I accept that, because that was the hand I was dealt. I'm not a quitter, nor am I ever goin' to let another nigga beat me at this gangsta shit. So, the first thing in the morning, I want to go down to your office and redo my will. I have one already written through your firm. I want to make a few changes just in case somethin' goes left."

"What are you talking about, baby?"

He stared deeply into her eyes and said, "Won has always taught me to be ready, and that's exactly what I'm doin' now. I'm stayin' ready for whatever."

"But why?"

"'Cause I'm 'bout to go all the way out, Li'l Mama. All the fuckin' way out!" Taz said as he turned flat on his back and closed his eyes.

Tears slid down Sacha's face as she watched the tears slide slowly down the face of her man. *Damn!*

Chapter Twenty-eight

After riding through his old neighborhood a few times looking for H-Hop, Clifford decided to go on and head out to Tazneema's apartment. He left word with a few of his homeboys to tell H-Hop to get with him as soon as possible. As he drove toward Norman, he was still wondering where the hell H-Hop was. More importantly, how in the hell did he get at Keno? "Damn! We gots to hurry up and smash that nigga Taz now! If we don't, he won't stop until I'm a dead man," he said aloud as he made a right turn into the City of Norman.

Tazneema was so happy to see her man that she didn't know what to do. She grabbed Clifford around his waist and led him into the bedroom.

Lyla was sitting at the kitchen table studying as they went into Tazneema's bedroom. "Damn, that was rude! She didn't even have time to stop and let that whack-looking clown speak! The dick can't be that good!" she said as she went back to her studies.

Inside the bedroom, Tazneema and Clifford were kissing each other as if this would be their last time ever being intimate with one another. After a few minutes of this, Clifford pulled from her embrace and said, "Whoa! What's gotten into you, 'Neema?"

"I love you, baby, and I'm so scared that my Daddy is going to hurt you. Why couldn't you do as I asked you and stay out in Dallas?" she said as she sat down on the end of the bed.

Clifford sat next to her and said, "Because, I haven't done anything, 'Neema. Why should I hide from Taz when I have absolutely nothing to hide for? Whomever killed Keno has nothing to do with me."

"Are you sure? Are you positive that it wasn't some of your old homeboys, Cliff?"

"I can't honestly say that right now, but I am looking into it. I'll know for sure after I talk to my homeboy, H-Hop. As of right now, I'm speaking from my gut, because I don't feel that any of my people had the resources to be able to get at someone like Keno. So relax, baby. Everything is going to be all right."

"How can you say that and be so sure, Cliff? Haven't you understood anything I've told you? Taz is going to try his best to make sure that you no longer exist. He's not playing, baby, and he damn sure doesn't give a damn about how I feel anymore. My Uncle Bo-Pete, and now my Uncle Keno . . . I'm positive he's about to go on a rampage. Any and everybody who gets in his way is going to be in some serious trouble."

"I understand what you've told me, 'Neema, but what can I do? Run from your father for the rest of my life? I haven't done anything to him or any of his friends. Once I've found out for sure whether or not any of my homeboys had anything to do with this mess, I'm going to put an end to this craziness."

"How are you going to do that, baby?"

"I'll call a meeting with your father and explain the situation to him."

Tazneema started laughing and said, "You have to be playing, 'cause ain't no way in hell Taz is going to go for some shit like that. Do you really understand what kind of man my Daddy is? You obviously don't, because if you did, you would know that trying to arrange a meeting with him would be like you signing your own death certificate!"

Clifford smiled and said, "I'm no fool, 'Neema. Nor am I trying to put myself six feet under anytime soon. When it's time for us to meet, we'll meet somewhere I'll know I'll be completely safe. I still have some powerful friends in the city, baby. They'll make sure that I'm protected while I present my case to Taz."

"If you say so, baby. Just please, don't think for an instant that he's going to let you make it, 'cause I could hear it in his voice, he wants your head."

"Don't worry about that mess. I got it under control," he said as he pulled her into his arms again. After sharing another intense kiss, he smiled and said, "Is it cool if I spend the night with you, baby?"

Tazneema smiled, pulled off her T-shirt and slid back onto her bed and said, "I was hoping you'd say that. Now, come here and give me some of that big old thang!"

Red, Wild Bill and Bob came over to Taz's home early the next morning, feeling defeated. The pain of losing yet another close friend was weighing heavily in their hearts. Taz let them inside and led them into the den.

Precious and Heaven were lying in front of the pool table when the four men entered the room. Taz smiled at his beloved Dobermans and said, "Go play!" Both of the dogs jumped to their feet and silently left the den.

Bob smiled and said, "I don't think I'll ever get used to how them dogs understand you so well, gee. That shit is crazy for real."

"It cost me a grip and a lot of time with them, but it was well worth it. They'll never let me down, dog," Taz said as he sat down on the sectional sofa. "All right, we already know who did this shit, and we already know why. What's fuckin' with me is, how in the hell did they get that close to Keno?"

"Yeah, I've been thinkin' the same shit," said Red. "I mean, the Ones said he was tapped three times in the back of the head. How the fuck could someone other than one of us get that close to him? I called Katrina's job. She arrived at work exactly when she said she did, so that scratches her, gee. Who else could get close enough to him to be able to tap him in the back of the dome? That's the million-dollar fuckin' question."

"Fuck it! It's done, dog. Our nigga is out. We gots to lay the rest of them fools down now. Them niggas ain't playin', so we might as well turn this shit right back up until we get our man," Wild Bill said angrily.

"I agree. Them niggas gots to go, dog," added Bob.

"We might as well get onto that nigga, H-Hop. He's our best bet at gettin' at Cliff. Once we take them two, this shit should be over. Them other youngstas ain't tryin' to let this shit carry on."

"How can you be so fuckin' sure, Taz? Them niggas might be ready to ride or die for their losses too. Fuck this shit! Let's take it to every last one of them niggas! Fuck Hoover! They all die!" screamed an emotional Bob.

"Come on, my nigga. I'm feelin' your pain, but we can't be stupid with this shit. We know who the beef is with, and we're goin' to take it to they ass. But overdoin' it won't do any of us any good. It'll only hurt us in the long run. We gots to play this shit smart. Let's get onto that nigga, H-Hop's spot later on tonight and see if we can get a line on where Cliff rests his head."

"Yeah. So once we find that out, we can take that nigga's head smooth off!" Red said menacingly.

"Exactly!" Taz said as he stared at his friends.

Clifford woke up when he heard his cell phone beeping, indicating that he had messages on his voicemail. He slipped out of Tazneema's bed and put on his boxer shorts and pants. He tiptoed lightly into the bathroom and closed the door so he wouldn't wake either Tazneema or her roommate, Lyla. After he relieved himself, he opened his cell and checked his messages. He had three, all of which were from his homeboy, H-Hop. He quickly dialed his apartment number and waited for him to answer his phone.

After the fourth ring, H-Hop finally answered. "What's up, cuz? Why the fuck are you callin' me this fuckin' early?" he asked.

"Where the fuck have you been hiding, cuz? I've been trying to get at you to see what's what with this shit."

"What's what with what? What the fuck are you talkin' 'bout?"

"Listen. My girl told me that her daddy is on the hunt for me, loc. We gots to hurry up and out that nigga, cuz. We can't be wasting no more time on his homeboys. We gots to get that nigga Taz. He told my girl that there is nothing and no one that's going to stop him from getting at me, so you know he's going to try and get at the homies again."

"I know, huh? Where you at, cuz?"

"I'm out here in Norman at my girl's pad."

"Nigga, you layin' up with that broad?"

"I'm good out this way."

"How the fuck you know she ain't called that nigga Taz and told him you over there?"

Clifford laughed and said, "That's the last thing I gots to worry about, cuz. 'Neema loves my dirty drawers. She'd never do me dirty like that, cuz."

"Nigga, you slippin'."

"As long as she never finds out about what we did to that nigga, Bo-Pete, she'll always be in my corner. I'm telling you, she'll go against her daddy for me, cuz. She loves me that fucking much. That's why we gots to hurry up and handle that nigga."

"Whatever, cuz. Look, get at me later so we can come up with somethin'. I'm about to lay it back down. That bitch I was chillin' with out in Midwest City damn near sucked a nigga dry. I gots to get me some fuckin' rest!"

"All right, cuz. I'm going to stay out this way until the sun sets. Then I'll come over to your pad. I'm about to go get me some early-morning pussy real quick, then I'll lay it down for a while."

H-Hop started laughing and said, "Cuz, you just as gone for that young broad as you say she is over your ass."

"Yeah, loco, you might be right. I do love her. I really don't want to hurt her or cause her any kind of pain, but her daddy gots to go," Clifford said seriously.

"You fuckin' right, cuz! I'll holla," H-Hop said, and he hung up the phone.

After Clifford closed his cell phone, he tiptoed out of the bathroom and back into Tazneema's bedroom. He didn't notice that Tazneema's roommate, Lyla, was standing right outside of the bathroom door.

***

After Red, Wild Bill and Bob left, Taz went upstairs and watched Sacha as she got dressed for work. He smiled as he saw the slight lump showing in her stomach. *Damn! I'm about to be a daddy again! This shit has got to stop. I can't keep livin' like this,* he said to himself as he continued to watch his fiancée.

Sacha turned, and for the first time she noticed that he was watching her. She said, "Are you all right, baby?"

"Yeah, I'm good. I'm just sittin' here thinkin' about how my nigga won't ever get to meet his future nephew."

She smiled sadly and said, "You mean his niece?"

Taz returned her smile and said, "Nah, I meant what I said, his nephew. Come here, Li'l Mama."

Sacha stepped over to where he was sitting, sat down on his lap and gave him a hug. He put his right hand on her stomach and began to rub it lightly and said, "I love you, Li'l Mama. When everything is everything, I think it's time we got the fuck outta the city and try somethin' new."

"Something new like what, baby?"

He shrugged his shoulders and said, "I don't know. I was thinkin' about some shit that Won got at me about. What do you think about movin' out to the West Coast?"

"California?"

"Yeah. You think you could do somethin' like that with me?"

"Baby, I'll go wherever you want me to. As long as I'm with you, I have no doubt that I'll be taken care of and completely happy."

"But what about your career? You haven't even been a partner at your firm for a full year yet."

"I don't care about that anymore, baby. All I want is for you to be happy with me. I can get a job, or even open up my own firm once we're settled out West. So don't let me stop you from making whatever decisions you need to make. I'm behind you one hundred percent." They kissed each other passionately. Then Sacha pulled from his embrace and said, "Now, let me go. I have a court appearance at ten."

He smiled and said, "All right, Li'l Mama. I got some calls to make and some more shit to handle later on. If I'm not here by the time you get off, hit me on my cell. It might just be a late one for me tonight."

She stared at her man and said, "Be careful, Taz."

Taz stared right back at his heart and soul and said, "All the time, Li'l Mama. All the time."

Tazneema got up a little after nine a.m. to find Clifford sound asleep right next to her. She smiled as she thought about their early-morning sex session that they had a couple of hours ago. She climbed out of bed and went into the bathroom to get ready for her ten o'clock class. By the time she finished showering, she felt as if she was ready to take on the world.

That feeling changed quickly after she had a discussion with Lyla. As Tazneema was leaving the bathroom, Lyla came up to her and urgently said, "Come into my room for a minute. I know something that I think is very important to you."

Tazneema followed her roommate into her bedroom and watched as she closed the door behind them. "What's got you all spooked, girl?" she asked as she sat down on Lyla's bed.

Lyla took a deep breath and said, "Girl, you know I know how much you love Cliff, right?"

"Yeah, and?" Tazneema asked, slightly agitated.

"You know I would never do or say anything to hurt you, right?"

"Stop with the fucking questions, Lyla, and tell me what you have to say."

"All right. Dang! This morning, I was on my way to the bathroom, and I saw that the door was closed. I had to pee bad, so I waited outside of the door for whomever was in there to finish. I heard Cliff talking to someone on the phone. I looked at the bottom of the door and didn't see the phone cord, so I assumed he was on his cell phone. Anyway, he was talking to someone, and he told them that, and I quote, 'As long as she never finds out about what we did to that nigga, Bo-Pete, she'll be in my corner, cuz.' He then started talking about hurting your father."

"*What?* Are you sure, Lyla?"

"Come on, *T!* It might have been early in the morning, but I know what I heard. He said something about how he really loves you, but your daddy has to go. He kept saying 'cuz' a lot, like he's a gang member or something. Just before he hung up the phone, he said that he was about to go get some early-morning pussy, then he was going back to sleep for a while. Did you two do it this morning?"

"That's none of your business, girl!"

"I mean, if you did do it, then you know what I'm telling you is the truth. Your boyfriend is out to hurt your father, *T*. What has Taz done to Cliff?" Lyla asked with a puzzled look on her face.

Tazneema wanted to cry. She wanted to let her tears wash her face, not because she was physically hurting, but because she was ashamed of herself. She actually believed Cliff and all of his lies. She went against her flesh and blood for that man. Though she tried her best, she wasn't able to control her tears as they slowly slid down her face. She stared at her friend and said, "Tell me again everything that you heard, Lyla. Don't skip anything. This is very important." Tazneema wiped her eyes and listened closely to every word that her roommate said. Her pain had now turned into anger as she thought about her father. *I went against the grain, Daddy, and I'm so sorry!* she thought as she continued to listen to Lyla as she told her about Clifford's early-morning telephone conversation.

After Sacha left for work, Taz grabbed the phone and called Won out on the West Coast. He knew it was early out there, but he needed to talk to his O.G. When Won answered his phone, Taz wasted no time in telling him about Keno's murder. After he finished, he took a deep breath and said, "We're handling this shit tonight, O.G. I gots to have this fool before he hurts someone else close to me."

"Yeah, you need to handle this as soon as possible. I didn't think that clown was that 'bout it," Won said as he wiped his teary eyes.

"To be honest with you, neither did I. Look, I just wanted to put you up on everything. Don't trip. I gots this end."

"I know you do, Babyboy. Make sure that you take care of yourself, and remember what we talked about."

"Yeah, I got you. Is everything cool on your end?"

"As of right now, things are good. I'll know more soon. Cash Flo' is out on the East Coast taking care of some business. That nigga Pitt has been laying low, so that tells me that he's waiting for some reason or the other. Don't worry about me though. You just do what needs to be done. If you ever get at me on this line and I don't answer, that means either I went dark, or I'm no longer breathing. Either way, you will be notified of the next phase of the game."

"Come on with that shit, O.G.! I'm not tryin' to hear that shit!"

"It is what it is, Babyboy. I love you. Out!" Won said, and he hung up the phone.

Taz hung up the phone and called Tari at her job at Mercy Hospital. She screamed so loud that he thought she was having a heart attack after he told her what had happened to Keno. He tried his best to calm her down, but she kept screaming over and over, "No! No! No! No!"

Finally, one of her coworkers took the phone from her and came on the line. "I'm sorry, but Tari is having problems right now. Can she call you back?" asked the coworker.

"Tell her that Taz said to call him as soon as she's regained her composure."

"I'll do that, sir," she said, and hung up the phone.

"You're a dead man, you punk-ass nigga!" Taz said aloud as he got up and went into the kitchen to get himself something to drink.

Just as he was pouring himself a glass of orange juice, his cell rang. He went back into the den and grabbed his phone, flipped it open and said, "Yeah!"

"Taz, I need for you to take me to Tulsa today. I have to get out of this city for a while," said his mother.

"When do you want to leave, Mama-Mama?"

"I just got off the phone with Christy and Derrick. They told me that I could come stay with them for as long as I liked. I don't plan on being out there for too long 'cause I want to be here for Keno's funeral."

"All right, Mama-Mama. Go on and get yourself ready. I'll be out that way in an hour or so."

"Okay, baby. Bye," Mama-Mama said before hanging up

Taz sat down and thought about having to make funeral arrangements for Keno for the very first time. He couldn't believe that he was going to have to do this shit all over again. All of the sudden, he slapped his forehead, quickly grabbed his cell and redialed Won's number. When Won answered, Taz said, "I forgot to ask you if you could take care of Keno's ends for me, O.G. He don't have any family other than us though. I think he has an aunt somewhere out in Cali, but I'm not sure."

"Don't panic, Babyboy. I got you. I'll have all of his ends transferred into your account. That way, if you find his peoples you'll be able to look out for them."

"That's good lookin', O.G."

"You know I gots y'all. Now, let me bounce. Out!"

"Out!" Taz said, and closed his cell phone. Just as he was setting his phone down, it began to ring. He reopened it and saw that it was his daughter calling. He sighed and said, "What the fuck does this crazy-ass girl want?" He took a deep breath and prepared himself for another argument with his only child. "Hello."

"Daddy, we need to talk," Tazneema said seriously.

Taz pulled the phone away from his ear and stared at it as if it had done something to him. *Daddy? I know she don't think she's goin' to be able to sweet-talk me outta not taking that nigga Cliff!* he thought. But to his daughter, he said, "What's good, 'Neema? What do we need to talk about now?"

Tazneema stared at Clifford's sleeping form and said, "I can't really talk about it right now, 'cause I'm late for class," she lied. "What will you be doing later on?"

"I'm about to take Mama-Mama to Tulsa. She's goin' to spend a few days with Christy and Derrick. She's trippin' off of what happened to Keno."

Tears welled into Tazneema's eyes as she said, "I am too, Daddy. I am too. I want you to know that I'm so sorry for not believing you. I should have known better. You have never lied to me. I should have never gone against the grain. Please forgive me, Daddy!"

Taz pulled the phone away from his ear again, because he knew he was really tripping out now. He put the phone back to his ear and asked his daughter, "What's brought on this sudden change of heart, baby girl?"

"Mama-Mama always told me that whatever goes on in the dark will always come to the light sooner or later."

"Yeah, yeah, I understand all that. What does that got to do with this situation, 'Neema?"

"You were right and I was wrong, Daddy. Just leave it at that."

"All right, I'll accept that. Now, does this mean you'll assist me and tell me where that nigga Cliff lives?"

Tazneema stared at Clifford as he continued to sleep soundly and said, "Yeah, I'll tell you, Daddy. Call me when you get back from Tulsa."

"You understand what's goin' to happen to him, don't you, 'Neema?"

"Yes, Taz, I understand perfectly. As you and my uncles like to say, 'It is what it is'."

He smiled into the receiver of his cell phone and said, "Exactly!"

Chapter Twenty-nine

Pitt was all smiles as Cash Flo' gave him what he'd been waiting a very long time for—permission to murder Won.

"I've spoken with no one about this, Pitt. I thought it would be better this way. So if you miss, you're on your own. You know Won is not to be taken lightly. The only reason why I'm giving you the green light is because I feel that Won is up to something, and that something just might jeopardize my position within The Network. So, handle your business, Pitt. Efficiently and effectively."

"Gotcha," Pitt said, and hung up the phone. He then pressed the intercom button on his desk and told his secretary to call Leo and True and tell the both of them that he wanted to see them as soon as possible. He then relaxed in his chair and smiled. *I got your ass now, Won. It took me over fifteen muthafuckin' years, but I got your ass now!* he thought as he fired up one of his Cuban cigars.

"Cliff, would you mind meeting me out at Mama-Mama's house later on?" Tazneema asked as she slipped on a pair of loose-fitting capri pants.

"Why? What's up, baby?" he asked lazily as he stretched and climbed out of bed.

"I'm putting an end to this stuff today. The only way I'll be able to do that is if I can convince Mama-Mama that you didn't have anything to do with the death of my uncles. Mama-Mama's real old-fashioned. She believes that if a person can look another person in the eyes and deny the charges that are against him, then he's either telling the truth or is a very good liar. If you come over there with me and help me present your case, I truly feel that we'll be able to get her on our side. And, believe me, we need her on our side."

This woman really does love me, Clifford thought, and then said, "What time do you want me to be there, baby?"

As Tazneema was putting on her Nike running shoes, she said, "I'll be out of my last class by two. Then I'm going over to my Daddy's house to talk to him before I go on over to Mama-Mama's house. So, meet me there around four."

"Are you sure you want to go over to your father's alone? I could go with you, 'Neema."

And you'd be a dead man as soon as you stepped through the fuckin' door, you slimy bastard! she thought to herself as she grabbed her school bag. "No, I have to talk to him alone, baby. If you came with me, all there would be is a bunch of yelling and arguing. Once we have Mama-Mama on our team, we'll all meet and talk this thing through. I feel that's the best way to go about this situation."

Cliff stepped over to where Tazneema was standing, gave her a hug and said, "Whatever way you want to handle this, baby, is fine with me. The sooner we get this mess cleared up, the sooner we can move on with our lives." He then gave her a soft kiss on her lips and went into the bathroom to get dressed. If he'd suddenly stopped and turned around, he would have seen the look of complete disgust and contempt Tazneema had on her face.

"That's right, Mama-Mama. 'Neema agreed to tell me where that fool lives," Taz said as he continued to put Mama-Mama's bags inside of his truck.

"What made her change here mind about this, Taz?"

He shrugged his shoulders and said, "I don't know. I'm just glad she did. Now I can put an end to all this shit."

"Watch your mouth, boy!" Mama-Mama scolded.

"Sorry about that, Mama-Mama. But you know what I mean. That man has caused us all nothin' but grief since he came into our lives."

"Lord knows what you're saying is the truth, Taz. But taking that man's life is another sin that you're going to have to answer for one day, baby. God is a loving and forgiving God, but you're pushing Him, baby, pushing Him real hard."

After making sure his mother was comfortable inside of his truck, Taz started the ignition and said, "Whether God forgives me or not will have to be determined at a later time, Mama-Mama, 'cause that nigga Cliff gots to go."

Mama-Mama closed her eyes and said a quick prayer for her only child: *Please keep Your hands on my son, Lord. He's only doing what he feels is right. Though You and I both know he's about to commit a sin against one of Your Commandments, please don't abandon my baby. Please watch over him for me, Lord!*

Sacha was sitting inside of her office, talking to Gwen on the telephone. "Ho, I'm telling you, this shit is really about to get off the hook. Taz hasn't even been acting angry about Keno's death. That tells me that he's at the point of no return. Cliff and the rest of his homeboys are in some very deep shit."

"That's putting it mildly, bitch. Bob is so mad, that he hardly slept at all last night. I had to give him one of my top-notch blow jobs to drain him for him to close his eyes for a little while."

Sacha started laughing and said, "You nasty ho! You would have done that whether he was mad about Keno or not!"

"I know that, bitch. What I'm saying is, my baby is real fucked up too behind this shit. If Taz is going to go crazy, you better fuckin' believe Bob is too."

"And so are Red and Wild Bill. I just hope and pray that nothing else happens to any of them. God forbid someone else loses their life behind this craziness."

"The only one who's about to bite it now is that nigga Cliff. If your man don't kill him, then it's going to be mines, Red or Wild Bill that does. Either way, he's outta here," Gwen said seriously.

"You ain't never lied, ho. Let's hook up for lunch later on, 'kay?"

"I might as well. I'm not trying to be around this house all damn day by myself. Meet me at the Red Lobster on Northwest Expressway around noon."

"I'll see you then. Bye, ho!"

"Bye, bitch!" Gwen said, and hung up the phone.

After Taz dropped off Mama-Mama at his cousin's home in Tulsa, he quickly got back onto the highway and headed back toward the city. His only thoughts were on how and when he was going to kill Cliff. *I want to punish that nigga real slow,* he thought as he drove in silence. *Nah, better yet, I might feed his ass to the hogs out at Mama-Mama's house while he's still breathing. That nigga has to feel the type of pain I'm feeling behind losing my niggas. Yeah, nice and slow. That nigga is goin' to die nice and slow!*

By the time Tazneema had gotten out of her last class, she was hyped for what she was about to do. *That nigga fuckin' lied to me all this time. He took complete advantage of me and my feelings for his punk-ass. I forgave the bastard for shooting me. I continued to love that man even after my father and uncles warned me to leave him alone, and he crossed me like I was nothing to him. Humph! Well, now, nigga, you're nothing to me. I'm my Daddy's daughter, you coward muthafucka! You cross a Good, then you die, you bitch-ass nigga!* Tazneema thought as she climbed into her car and headed out to her father's home.

She prayed that Taz wouldn't be home when she made it to his house. If he was, that would interfere with her plans. She crossed her fingers as she got onto the highway.

When Taz made it into the city limits, he picked up his cell, called Red and told him to get with Wild Bill and Bob and meet him at the Outback Steakhouse in Edmond. After hanging up with Red, he called Tari at work. He was told that she had taken the day off, so he quickly hung up and called her at her house. She sounded so weak and weary when she answered the phone, he felt as if he was being stabbed in his heart. He took a deep breath and said, "What's good, my snow bunny?"

"Hi, Taz. What are you up to?"

"Shit, I just got back from taking Mama-Mama out to Tulsa so she could visit with some relatives. I'm on my way to the Outback to meet with the homies. Why don't you meet us out there? We gots some shit to discuss."

"I'm really not in the mood, Taz. I can't get Keno off of my mind. It hurts, Taz, it really hurts!"

"I know, Tee, but you gots to shake this shit off for the time being. We're about to bring the end game to that nigga, and I know you're wanting to be a part of that."

Shaking her head no as if Taz was standing in the same room with her, she said, "No, Taz, I don't. This stuff has to end, I know, but I don't want any part of it."

"I understand."

"Have you heard from Won? I've tried to call him, but I keep getting his voicemail."

"Is that right? I spoke with him earlier, and he told me that if I called and didn't catch him, then he went dark and he'll be in touch."

"Is everything all right with him?"

"To tell the truth, Tee, I don't even know."

"Great! That's fucking great! Look, I'm about to try to get some sleep. I've been up all night looking at old pictures of us all. I'm so depressed I feel as if I'm losing my mind, Taz."

"Do you want me to come out there and kick it with you for a li'l while, Tee?"

"Go on and take care of this madness first. After everything is everything, then come and spend some time with me. I need to get some sleep right now. Don't worry about me. I'll be all right by the time you get out here."

"All right then, Tee. I love you."

Those words put a smile on her face as she said, "I love you too, Taz." After she hung up the phone, she grabbed her 9 mm pistol, jacked the chamber back and watched as the single bullet popped out of the chamber.

Taz would never know that he had called just in time to save Tari's life.

Tazneema smiled as she jumped out of her car and ran toward the front door of Taz's home. She pulled out her keys and quickly opened the front door. She saw Heaven and Precious as they watched her punch in the security code to the alarm system. After the alarm was deactivated, she stepped over to the Dobermans and said, "Hey, babies! You guys miss me?" Both of the dogs began to rub their wet noses against her open palms. After playing with them for a few minutes, she said, "Okay, guys, protect me." Heaven's and Precious's ears became alert as they silently stepped away from her.

Tazneema then went downstairs to her father's indoor gym, and went directly toward the equipment closet, where he kept all of his weapons. He didn't know she knew about his arsenal. *Hell, he doesn't know that I know a lot of things about his lifestyle!* she thought to herself as she grabbed a small .380 pistol and a full clip of bullets. She snapped the weapon back and slid a live round inside of its chamber. She smiled and put the gun inside of her purse, quickly closed the door to the equipment room and went back upstairs.

She went into the kitchen and saw that the dogs' water bowls were empty. After refilling them, she went and grabbed a bottled water out of the refrigerator and left her father's home, ready for the next phase of her mission.

Tru and Leo arrived at Pitt's office an hour after Pitt's secretary had summoned them. Once they were seated, Pitt said, "All right, this is how it's going to go down. That nigga Won is about to try to shake the spot, but I gots eyes on his ass, so it's all good. We're about to catch a flight down south to L.A. and handle his punk-ass real quick like. It's a must that I get some information from that nigga before we out his ass. Once I got what I need and he's done, you two will have another mission to complete."

"And what's that?" asked Leo.

"I want y'all to fly out to Oklahoma City and out Won's li'l country-boy crew. Those country muthafuckas are the niggas that have been putting down all of those licks against The Network."

"How did you find out about them?" asked Tru.

Pitt laughed and said, "Money can get you whatever you want in this world, my nigga. I learned that from that nigga Won. Not only do I know the names of those niggas, I know where the daughter and the mother of the head nigga reside. I want them bitches to pay for even thinking that they could get away with fucking with The Network. So, come on. We gots a flight to catch."

Back in Oklahoma City, Taz was the first to arrive at the Outback Steakhouse. He was seated and had just ordered himself a glass of XO when Red, Bob and Wild Bill entered the restaurant. After they were seated, Taz told them what Tazneema had told him. "I wanted to wait until we were all together before I made the call to her to get the address on that clown-ass nigga."

Wild Bill smiled and said, "We're here now, nigga! What the fuck are you waitin' for? Make the call!"

Taz laughed as he pulled out his cell phone and called his daughter's cell. When she answered her phone, she said, "Hi, Daddy."

"What's up, baby girl? You good?"

"Yep, I'm just fine."

"That's cool. I need that address, 'Neema. It's time for me to handle this shit."

"Okay. Can you meet me at Mama-Mama's in about an hour?"

"Yeah, I can do that. Is everything all right?"

She smiled and said, "Everything is everything, Daddy. I'm your daughter, and whether you know it or not, you taught me well."

Taz raised his eyebrows as he stared at his cell phone. Then he asked, "What exactly is that supposed to mean, 'Neema?"

She laughed and said, "You'll see, Daddy. Just make sure that you meet me at Mama-Mama's house in one hour."

After she hung up the phone, Taz told everyone what she had just told him. When he was finished, Bob said, "Dog, you don't think she's goin' to try to do some shit to you, do you?"

Taz took a sip of his drink then said, "For her sake, I hope not."

Chapter Thirty

As Tazneema waited for Clifford to arrive, she began to have doubts about what she was about to do. *I should just wait for my Daddy to get here and let him handle this mess. I'm no killer,* she thought as she stared at the gun she held in her hand. Before her doubts could totally consume her, she heard Cliff's car as it pulled into Mama-Mama's driveway. She took a deep breath, put the gun back inside of her purse and set her purse back down on the coffee table. She then went to the front door and watched as he climbed out of his Mercedes 500 CLS.

Cliff smiled at her as he strolled confidently toward her. When he made it to the door, he said, "Hey you!"

They shared a kiss, much to Tazneema's dislike. She pulled away from his embrace and said, "Come on inside. Mama-Mama went to the store. She ran out of something. She's cooking dinner."

"That's cool. You know I love your grandmother's cooking," Cliff said as he entered the house and took a seat on the sofa. "So, have you had a chance to talk to her yet?" he asked.

She shook her head no and said, "I was waiting for you to get here so we could do it together. It's very important that we convince her that you had nothing to do with my uncles getting killed." Tazneema stared at him hard after she made that comment. She wanted to see if he was really that good a liar, as well as a cold-blooded killer.

Cliff smiled a confident smile and said, "There's no need for convincing when you're telling the truth, baby. Your grandmother will know that we're not lying to her. The truth is exactly what it is . . . the truth. I didn't have anything to do with either of your uncles' murders, baby. It's as simple as that."

This nigga is really good, Tazneema thought as she said, "I'm glad that you're here now, baby. Now we can put this mess behind us." She checked her watch and thought to herself, *Taz should be on his way right about now. Either I'm going to handle my business now, or leave it up to my Daddy.* She shook her head as she made her decision. *This is for my uncles!* She reached inside of her purse, pulled out the .380 and pointed it directly toward Clifford's head and said, "You're a fuckin' liar and a coward, Cliff! You did kill my Uncles, and you're still plotting to kill my Daddy! How the hell can you tell me that you love me and still hurt me this way? Answer that for me, Cliff, before I kill your sorry-ass!"

Cliff jumped out of his seat when he saw that Tazneema was dead serious, and said, "Come on, 'Neema, baby! You know damn well I didn't have anything to do with killing your Uncles! Hell, I wasn't even in town when Keno was killed! That should be enough proof for you right there! Come on, baby. Put the gun down so we can wait for Mama-Mama to get back so we can talk this out."

She laughed and said, "Nigga, Mama-Mama is out of town. The only person we're waiting on is my Daddy. And you and I both know what's going to happen to your ass when he gets here. You might not have killed my Uncle Keno, but that wouldn't have stopped one of your gang-banger friends from doing it. Either way, it's *your* fault, Cliff. And to think I loved your sorry-ass!"

"*Loved?* Come on, 'Neema. You know you still love me. Just like you know damn well that I didn't do what you're accusing me of. You've let your father's influence over you finally get the best of your judgment. You know me. You know I'm no killer, baby. Come on, let's talk this out sensibly."

For some reason, Clifford's words irked her to no end. She felt ashamed—ashamed of being manipulated, used and made a complete fool of. These feelings caused a fury to swell inside of her so cold that she didn't even realize that she was pulling the trigger to the pistol that was gripped tightly in her right hand. She shot Clifford seven times right in the middle of his chest. Her first shot was what killed him though. It was a direct hit to his heart.

As he fell back onto the sofa, he had a look of shock on his face as he grabbed his chest in an effort to stop the flow of blood that seeped from his body. He died with his right hand over the hole in his heart.

Tazneema calmly went and checked his vital signs to make sure that her job was complete. Afterward, she got to her feet and pulled Clifford's body onto the floor. "Mama-Mama would kill me if I'd gotten any blood on her sofa," she said aloud as she went into the hallway closet to get a sheet to cover Clifford's dead body.

Just as she returned to the living room and put the sheet over the body, she heard Taz's truck pull into the driveway. She quickly stepped to the door and smiled as she watched her father and her three Uncles come running toward the door with their weapons in their hands.

When Taz made it to the front door, he asked, "Where's that nigga at, baby girl?"

Tazneema stepped aside so that Taz and her Uncles could enter the house. She said, "There he is, Daddy." She pointed toward Clifford's covered body and continued. "I went against the grain, Taz, but I fixed my mistake."

Taz stared at his daughter in disbelief and asked, "What the fuck have you done, 'Neema?"

She smiled at her father and said, "What I had to do."

Red went over to the body, pulled the sheet back and said, "Well, I'll be damned! She done got the bastard!"

Bob started laughing and said, "Like father, like daughter for real!"

"Shut the fuck up, Bob! This shit is fucked up!" Taz yelled as he turned back toward his daughter. "Get the hell outta here, baby girl! Take your ass back to Norman, and don't you dare mention this shit to nobody, do you hear me?"

Now that the realization of what she'd actually done had sunk in, she became very nervous all of a sudden. "Are you going to take care of this, Daddy?" she asked in a voice that was of a little girl instead of an eighteen-year-old young lady.

Taz nodded and said, "I've taken care of you all of my life, baby girl, and I'm not about to stop now. Go on and let us take care of this shit. I love you, Tazneema."

She smiled and said, "I love you too, Daddy." She grabbed her purse and left the house without so much as a good-bye to any of her Uncles.

Red smiled and said, "Well, at least this clown-ass nigga is out of the way."

"Yeah, you're right. Come on. Let's take care of this fool. Then we can go get at that other nigga, H-Hop," Taz said as he grabbed Clifford's body and lifted him onto his broad shoulders.

"So, that nigga gots to go too, huh?" asked Wild Bill.

"You fuckin' right! He's the last piece to this fucked up puzzle, dog. Once he's done, it's a wrap."

"What are we goin' to do with this fool's body?" asked Bob.

Taz smiled and said, "We gon' feed him to the hogs."

"Da-a-a-a-amn! That's fucked up!" Wild Bill said with a sadistic smile on his face.

Taz carried Clifford's body outside to Mama-Mama's back-yard and set it down right beside the hog pen. He turned toward Red and said, "Look. This is how we're goin' to get down. After we dump this nigga to the hogs, you and Bob go take his car somewhere in the city and dump it. Me and Wild Bill will go sit on that nigga, H-Hop's spot. If we can get his ass, then we'll move on him. If not, I'll get at y'all later on. Either way it falls, at least we're more than halfway through with this shit."

"Yeah, thanks to 'Neema," Red said with a smirk on his face. "That's straight crazy, gee. We couldn't get to this nigga, but 'Neema could."

"It was easy for her, though. She had a line on the fool. That nigga was slipping, because he was in love and didn't see it comin'. Oh, well! It's a done deal now. Here," Taz said as he went into Clifford's pants pocket and pulled out the keys to his Mercedes. He passed them to Red and said, "There should be some gloves in the garage. Go check and see. That way, y'all won't leave any prints on that nigga's shit. Now, help me throw this piece of shit to the hogs."

"Gladly," Red said, and helped Taz throw Clifford's lifeless body over the fence and into the hog pen.

Mama-Mama's four humongous hogs squealed loudly as they began to tear into Clifford's dead flesh.

***

Tazneema was scared, yet she was calm as she drove toward her apartment in Norman.

Just as she was passing the City of Moore, she decided to make a quick stop. She got off the highway exit and headed toward Tari's home. When she pulled into Tari's driveway, she smiled when she saw her peeping out of the living room window. She quickly cut off her car and went to the front door.

Tari smiled when she opened the door, and said, "Well, well! What a lovely surprise! How are you doing, baby girl?"

They shared a brief hug, and Tazneema said, "I'm fine, Tee. I was on my way back to my place and I thought I'd drop by to holla at you for a minute."

"Come on in here, girl, and tell me what's on your mind."

Tazneema followed Tari inside of her home. After they were seated in the living room, Tazneema said, "Ain't too much going on. I just wanted to talk to you for a few, that's all."

Tari smiled at her and said, "Mmm-hmm."

"Mmm-hmm what?" Tazneema asked with a smile on her face.

"Girl, you're just like your father. Whenever you two have something on y'all's mind, y'all get to talking about how you just want to talk for a little bit. So save it, 'Neema, and spit it out. What's on your mind?"

Tazneema smiled again, shook her head from side to side and said, "I don't want to have this baby, Tee. Could you take me somewhere so I can get an abortion?"

"Whoa! Are you sure about this?"

"I'm positive. I don't want to have anything that will remind me of that sorry, lying-ass nigga Cliff!" she answered angrily.

"Watch your mouth, young lady! You know how I feel about that *N* word!"

"Sorry, Tee," she said sheepishly. "Anyway, will you take me to get one?"

"Does your father know about this?"

"Nope. But do you really think he'll mind?"

"I guess not, huh? All right, let me make a few calls, and I'll get back to you in a day or so."

"Thanks, Tee. I knew I could count on your help," Tazneema said sincerely.

"I have one more question though. How is Cliff going to feel about you killing his child?"

Tazneema stared at Tari for thirty seconds, and finally said, "Ask my Daddy."

Chapter Thirty-one

Taz and Wild Bill were sitting inside of Taz's truck in front of H-Hop's apartment building. Taz smiled as he pulled out his cell phone and quickly dialed Red's cell. When Red answered, Taz asked him, "Where are y'all at now?"

"We just left Arcadia. We're on our way back to the city now. What's good?"

"That nigga H-Hop's car is parked in front of his spot. We're about to go on and do this nigga. Do y'all want us to wait for y'all or what?"

"Nah, go on and do that clown and get this shit over with, gee."

"I'll get at y'all when we're on our way back to my spot," Taz said, and closed his phone and said to Wild Bill, "Let's go do this bitch, gee."

Wild Bill smiled as he checked to make sure that he had a live round chambered in his 9 mm, and said, "You know it!"

They jumped out of the truck and calmly walked toward H-Hop's apartment building. When they made it to H-Hop's apartment, Taz put his ear to the door and listened. He heard some rap music playing, and he could tell someone was walking around inside. He glanced toward Wild Bill and gave him a nod, directing him to kick in the door.

Wild Bill, though small in height, was a very powerful man. He stood in front of the door and gave it a solid kick right next to the doorknob.

Taz stepped inside of the apartment with his gun pointed directly toward H-Hop, who was standing at the open refrigerator door. The shocked look on his face told Taz all he needed to know. *This clown-ass nigga is alone, and he's about to die alone,* he thought as he slowly stepped toward the kitchen.

Wild Bill stood at the door and kept an eye out for any unwanted company.

When Taz made it to the kitchen, he told H-Hop, "You already know what time it is, so turn around and drop to your knees, nigga."

Realizing that he had been caught slipping, H-Hop inhaled deeply and said, "Fuck you, cuz! I may be 'bout to die, but I'll be damned if I'm gon' go out like a coward! Do what you got to do, cuz, 'cause I ain't gettin' on my knees for no nigga!" he screamed defiantly.

Taz admired him for his courage. For that, he decided that he would at least let his family be able to have an open casket at his funeral. Instead of shooting him in his face like he had originally planned, he smiled as he shot H-Hop twice in his heart. He then turned and left the kitchen without a backward glance. As he made it to the door, he told Wild Bill, "It's over, my nigga. Come on, let's get the fuck outta here."

Pitt, Leo and Tru's flight arrived at LAX, and they were picked up by some of Pitt's people in Southern California. Once they were inside the back of the limousine, Pitt asked the driver, "Has that nigga Won left his home?"

"No, sir. He's been home the entire day," the driver answered as he eased the limousine into the heavy Los Angeles traffic.

"All right, this is what I need you to do. Make the call to my associates and let them know that I said they have the green light to proceed, but not to take any action against Won. He is not to be harmed. Secure his home until we get there."

"Understood," the driver said, and picked up his cell phone and did as he was told.

Pitt sat back in his seat and smiled. "By the time we make it to Won's home, everything should be secured. When we get there, I'll get the information I need. After that, I'm going to enjoy killing that bastard."

"What? I thought that was our job," said Leo.

"Yeah! Since when did you start gettin' your hands dirty?" asked Tru.

"Won is a major player within The Network. He has been for a very long time. Even though he let his thirst for power blind him, he's still a man of respect and tremendous integrity. He played the game his way. But he underestimated another man with the same amount of integrity though. He has to die by my hand, and my hand only," Pitt said, and fired up one of his Cuban cigars.

Back in Oklahoma City, Taz and the rest of the crew were all sitting in his den, replaying the day's events.

"I still can't believe that 'Neema did that nigga, dog," Bob said as he sipped his Absolut Vodka and cranberry juice.

"Yeah, that shit is crazy. But it is what it is. Now, all we have to do is put my nigga to rest properly and try to move on with our crazy-ass lives," Taz said, and downed the rest of the XO he had in his glass.

"What about Won? Is this shit over with him or what?" asked Red.

"To be honest, dog, I don't even know. All we can do is sit back and wait on that one, gee. The last time we spoke, he told me that I'd be contacted one way or the other."

"One way or the other? What the fuck is that supposed to mean, my nigga?" asked Wild Bill.

Taz shrugged his shoulders and said, "Your guess is as good as mine, dog." Before he could say anything else, he heard Sacha as she came into the house. "Look, let's get together tomorrow and work out. We might as well try to get back on our regular routine."

"Dog, what about Bo-Pete and Keno? Shit ain't never gon' be regular no more," Bob said somberly.

"I know that's right, gee. But you know what I mean. Right now, I'm about to chill with wifey and let her know that everything is everything. I can't be havin' her stressed the fuck out while she's about to have my second shorty."

"All right then, 'Foolio!' We'll see you in the morning," Red said, and he led the rest of the crew out of the den and out of Taz's home.

After the crew was gone, Taz poured himself another shot
of XO and went upstairs to the bedroom. He smiled as he
entered the room and saw Sacha sitting on the edge of the
bed, taking off her stockings. "Damn, you look sexy even when
you're doing the simplest things!"

She smiled and said, "I don't feel sexy. I feel tired and
hungry."

"Do you want me to make you something to eat, or do you
want to go get something?" he asked as he stepped to the bed
and sat down next to his fiancée.

Sacha smiled and said, "I've already ordered a pizza. It
should be here any minute."

"A pizza? You and your cravings! Well, I guess pizza it is
then."

Sacha stared at her man for a full minute then asked him,
"What's on your mind, baby?"

He returned her stare and simply said, "My niggas. I'm
never goin' to be able to tell either one of them how much I
really loved them. They're gone, Li'l Mama. They're gone," he
said as he wiped a tear from his eye. He sipped the drink in
his hand and continued. "It's over, Li'l Mama. That nigga Cliff
and his homeboy have been dealt with. It's over."

She let his words register deep within her before she spoke.
"I don't know whether to be happy or upset, baby. I'm glad
this mess is finally over with, but I'm sort of upset because of
the pain Tazneema is going to have to endure once she finds
out about Cliff's death."

Taz smiled and said, "Don't worry about her. She'll be
good. As a matter of fact, I need to call her to make sure she's
straight. She's had a pretty busy day today."

"What do you mean by that, Taz Good?"

Taz started laughing, and told her exactly what had happened earlier at his mother's home.

Sacha couldn't believe what she was hearing. When he was
finished, she stared at him to see if he was really telling her
the truth. After staring into his brown eyes for a couple of
seconds, she shook her head from side to side and said, "Well,
ain't that something! But what about the baby, Taz?"

He shrugged his shoulders and said, "Let's see." He picked up the phone and dialed his daughter's apartment.

Pitt was smiling as he climbed out of the limousine, followed by Leo and Tru. The limousine driver was talking to some of Pitt's hired help as Pitt was led into Won's vast estate. Pitt's team had been able to secure all of Won's security with very little difficulty. Since Won's mansion was so secluded, it wasn't difficult at all for his people.

As Pitt entered Won's home, he was amazed at how calm he felt. Victory was his, and he was loving every second of it. The leader of Pitt's team led him into Won's office, where Won was being held.

When Won saw Pitt, he smiled and said, "I was wondering when you'd arrive, Pitt. I guess I've finally lost, hmm?"

Pitt smiled and said, "Yeah, you finally lost the game, old boy. Look, I'm not going to take a whole bunch of time with this, Won. There're some things I need to know before we can finish up this mess."

"And what is that?" Won asked as he calmly relaxed back in his chair.

"Where's the work, Won? I want to know exactly where the drugs are at. I know you didn't dump them. If you had, I would have gotten your ass years ago. So, the only other possibility is that you got all that work stashed real fucking good."

Won smiled and asked, "Are you sure about that, Pitt? I move more work across the board than anyone else in The Network. It could have been real easy for me to move it without tipping my hand."

"But you didn't' do that. You stashed it until you got ready to make your power move. That's what all of this shit is about, you and your fucking power trip. So stop playing games and give me the information I need, Won."

"Or what? You're going to kill me?" Won started laughing and continued. "That's funny, 'cause I can only assume that you're here to do that anyway."

"I'll tell you what. I'll spare your li'l clique in Oklahoma City if you just go on and give me the whereabouts of the work. It's either that, or they all die—even that pretty li'l daughter of your boy Taz," Pitt said with a devious smile on his face.

With his poker face intact, Won asked, "Taz? Who's that?"

Pitt laughed and said, "Good! Very good, Won, but not good enough. I've done my homework thoroughly. That country-ass clique you got has robbed The Network. For that they have to go. If you do me this justice, I can find it in my heart to let them make it."

Won sighed heavily and said, "What guarantees do I have that you'll honor your word, Pitt? I could give you the information you desire, and you could still kill my peoples. I might as well take the location of the drugs with me to my grave."

"I swear on my mother's grave, as well as the oath we both took when we helped form The Network so many years ago, that if you give me the location of the work, your people in Oklahoma City will be spared. That's about all I can do for you, Won. Like you said, you are about to die," Pitt said seriously.

Won shrugged his shoulders slightly and said, "I guess I'm going to have to take your word on this, Pitt. The work is out in Austin. My people out that way have it secured in a warehouse. I'll need to make a call to let them know that everything is good, or they'll never let you get near that warehouse."

Pitt smiled brightly, gave a nod of his head toward the telephone that was on Won's desk and said, "Make the call."

Won grabbed the phone and quickly dialed the number to his main man out in Austin, Texas. When the line was answered, Won said, "Hey, Charlene, what's good? Is Snuffy around?"

"Yeah, here he is, Won," Charlene said, and passed the phone to her man, Snuffy.

Snuffy accepted the phone from her and asked, "What it do, big homey?"

Won laughed and said, "Not much. Look, I need for you to pass along what you got put up for me. My people will be contacting you soon."

"What? Are you serious, big homey?"

"Very. It is what it is, Snuff, so make sure you take care of this for me. My people's name is Pitt. Give him everything he asks for. Your account has already been taken care of, so you and Charlene will be straight."

"I gots you, big homey, and don't worry. You know I'm gon' handle my end of this shit for you."

Won simply said, "I know you will," and he hung up the phone. He reached across the desk, grabbed a pen and a piece of paper, wrote down Snuffy's number in Austin and passed it to Pitt and said, "There you go. All you have to do is give him a call and make the necessary arrangements."

Pitt put the piece of paper into his wallet and said, "Thank you, Won. You're a top-flight nigga all the way." He then pulled out a chrome 9 mm with a silencer attached to it and asked, "Have you taken care of your affairs, Won?"

Won stared directly into Pitt's eyes and said, "Everything is in order. I'm ready for the next part of the game. I'll see you when you get there."

Pitt smiled sadly and said, "I won't be coming for a minute, but hold me down, baby." He pointed his gun at Won and shot him three times in the heart.

Won took all three shots with three grunts, reclined back in his chair and died with what looked like a smile on his handsome face.

"Even in defeat the cocky bastard has a lotta class. Come on, you two. We gots more shit to handle," Pitt said.

"Are you really gon' let them fools in Oklahoma make it?" asked Tru.

Pitt showed that devious smile again and said, "Fuck, no! Them niggas gots to die. You know my word ain't shit!"

"But you put it on your mom's grave and shit," Leo said with a frown on his face.

"That bitch never gave a damn about me, and I damn sure ain't never gave a damn about her. As for that oath shit, nigga, this ain't no *La Cosa Nostra* shit. This is The Network, the Black Mafia for real! We do shit how we want to do shit. I'm at the top of the pile now. I can do or say whatever the fuck I want to. First, we're going to Austin to secure that work with my peoples in San Antonio. Then we're going to hit Oklahoma City, so you two can earn some of this muthafuckin' money. Now, come on. Like I said, there's work to be done!"

Chapter Thirty-two

Three days after Won's murder, Taz was sitting in his den talking to Bob, when he received a call from one of his attorneys at Whitney & Johnson. "What's good, Peter?" he asked as he relaxed on his sectional sofa.

"I just received some papers marked 'Urgent,' along with a DVD for you from a law firm out in L.A."

"What's it about?"

"From what I've read, it looks like a will for a William B. Hunter."

"William B. Hunter? I don't know anybody by that name. Are you sure it's for me, Pete?"

"Positive. Whoever he is, or was, made sure that the attorney in L.A. sent this to me. Are you busy? If not, why don't you come on down and check this out?"

Taz checked the time on his watch and said, "All right, I'll be there in about thirty minutes. Is Sacha around?"

"Yes. I just saw her heading to the boss' office."

"Good. Let her know that I'm on my way down there, and that I want her to join us for this meet."

"Will do, Taz. See you in a little bit," Peter said, and hung up the phone.

Taz set the phone down and told Bob, "Dog, some shit has come up. I'm gon' need you to get with Red and Wild Bill so y'all can go make the funeral arrangements for Keno. Detective Bean called me this morning and told me that they were releasing the body today."

"All right, I got you. What was all of that about?"

"I'm really not knowin'. I'm about to find out though. Give me a holla after y'all made all of the arrangements."

"Bet!" Bob said as he followed Taz out of the house.

***

By the time Taz made it to Whitney & Johnson's law firm, Sacha was waiting for him inside of Peter's office. He smiled as he stepped inside and said, "What's good, Li'l Mama?"

"Hi, baby." Sacha stood and gave him a kiss.

Taz reached across Peter's desk, shook his hand and said, "Now, tell me exactly what the hell is goin' on here, Pete."

Peter once again explained how he had received the paperwork and the DVD that was sitting on his desk. Afterward, he said, "If you don't know who this William B. Hunter is, then I guess we need to watch this DVD in order to figure this mess out, Taz."

"Put it in then. I got a heavy plate today, and I don't have any time to waste."

Peter inserted the DVD into his portable DVD player, pressed the play button and turned it so that Taz and Sacha were able to look at the screen. As soon as Taz saw a picture of Michael Jordan slam-dunking a basketball over John Starks of the New York Knicks, he inhaled deeply and said, "Stop it!"

"What's wrong, Taz?" asked Peter.

"I said stop it, Pete!"

Peter did as he was told. He sat back in his chair and stared at Taz with a puzzled look on his face.

Sacha knew that something was terribly wrong, because Taz's smooth brown complexion seemed to pale right before her eyes. She put her hand on his shoulder and asked, "What's wrong, baby? Do you know who this person is now?"

Tears fell slowly from his eyes as he nodded his head yes.

Pitt, Leo and Tru arrived at Austin's Bergstrom International Airport a little after five p.m. Pitt had arranged for a vehicle to be waiting for them when they arrived in Texas. As usual, there was a stretch limousine parked in front of the arrivals terminal. The limousine driver was standing at the rear door of the limo, holding it open for Pitt and his men, who got inside of the car.

Once the luxury vehicle pulled away from the curb, Pitt pulled out his cell and called Snuffy. As soon as Snuffy answered the phone, Pitt said, "This is Pitt. I'm in town. When and where can we meet so we can handle what needs to be handled?"

"I'm out in San Antonio right now, but I'll be back in a few hours. Does it matter whether it's daylight or not?"

"Not really. I just need to check and make sure that everything is there. After that, it's all about transporting really."

"All right then, check this out, gee. Why don't you go get a room and hit me after you're checked in and shit. I'll make some calls and see if my girl Charlene can come and scoop you up and take you over to the warehouse."

"I'd prefer to deal with you rather than your girl."

"Hold up, partna! Charlene is my ace. She rolls with me on everything. Won told me to take care of you, and that's exactly what I'm gon' do, ya dig? You ain't gots to worry 'bout wifey. She's with the team."

"Whatever!" Pitt replied sarcastically.

"Like I was sayin', after you get checked in, hit me back up and I'll see what we can do about making everything go down tonight."

"All right. I'll call you after I get to a room," Pitt said, and hung up the phone on Snuffy. He then leaned toward the front of the limousine and asked the driver, "Are there any decent hotels around here?"

The driver smiled and replied, "Yes, sir, there's an Ameri-Suites right up the street on Ben White Boulevard."

"Good. Take us there and then you can be on your way. I'll give you a call when your return is needed."

"Yes, sir," the driver said as he navigated the huge car toward the Ameri-Suites Hotel.

Taz sat in the chair inside of his attorney's office in a daze. He couldn't believe that Won was actually dead. He shook his head sadly and said, "Look, I'm sorry for yelling, Pete. This shit is just too much for me. Do me a favor though."

"Anything, Taz. You know that," Peter said from behind his desk.

"Do what needs to be done with the paperwork. I trust you and your judgment completely. Right now, I've gots to get up outta here. I need that DVD though. If need be, I'll get it back to you. I have a feelin' that what's on it was meant for my eyes only."

"Of course, Taz. Anything you say. I'll give you a call in a couple of days, after I've taken care of everything."

Taz stood and said, "Thanks, Pete." After shaking his attorney's hand, he turned toward his fiancée and said, "I gots to go get some air, Li'l Mama. Can you come join me for a minute?"

Sacha checked her watch and saw that she had a few minutes to spare before going to her court appearance. She smiled and said, "I have ten minutes before I have to run over to the courthouse, baby."

"That's cool. Come on," Taz said, and led her out of Peter's office. Once they were outside of the building, he stopped by his truck and said, "This is too fuckin' much, Li'l Mama! Too fuckin' much! I feel as if I'm losin' my fuckin' mind!"

Sacha put her arms around her man and held him tightly for a moment then said, "It's Won, isn't it? Won is William B. Hunter."

Taz sighed heavily and said, "Yeah. Yeah, Li'l Mama. Another loved one of mines is gone. Won is resting in peace."

"But how?"

With a shrug of his shoulders, he said, "Ain't no tellin'. He knew somethin' was goin' to go down because he's been warning me for a minute now."

"Warning you?"

"Basically lettin' me know that I'm goin' to have to prepare to take on somethin' new."

"What does that mean, baby? You're confusing me."

"I'll know more after I look at this," Taz said as he held up the DVD in his right hand. "I expect to be told everything that I'm goin' to need to know on this here DVD. So let me bounce. We'll go over everything when you come home later on."

"Okay, baby," she said, and gave her man a hug and a kiss. "I love you, Taz."

He smiled and said, "I love you too, Li'l Mama." He watched as she went back into the office building. Then he turned and climbed into his truck.

Once he was comfortable, he inserted the DVD into his DVD player and said, "Screens one and two, please!" The DVD player was then activated by his voice command. The picture of Michael Jordan slam-dunking the ball over John Starks showed on the two front TV screens inside of the truck. As Taz pulled out of the parking lot and into the light mid-morning traffic, the two screens slowly changed into a picture of Won.

Later that evening, after Pitt had checked into the Ameri-Suites Hotel and had gotten himself comfortable, he called Snuffy back and told him where he was staying. "Do you know where it's at? It's not too far from the airport."

"Yeah, you're about ten minutes away from where we're going to meet in the morning," Snuffy said as he smiled at his wifey, Charlene.

"In the *morning!* I thought we were going to do this shit tonight!"

"Man, ain't no way in hell you're going to be able to move that much shit this late at night."

"Who said anything about moving it tonight? Look, you're doing way too much damn thinking. All I need is to see the product and make sure that everything is everything. After that, everything else will be taken care of. So, you need to come and pick me and my peoples up and take us to wherever this fucking warehouse is!"

"All right then, big-time! Calm down! My bad! Like I told you, you're about ten minutes away from the warehouse off of Highway 71. I'm like twenty minutes from you now, so give me ten to fifteen minutes then come outside of the hotel. How many people you got with you, boss?"

"There's three of us total."

"That's cool. Be looking out for me and wifey. We'll be in a red Escalade."

"Hurry up!" Pitt said impatiently, and once again hung up on Snuffy.

Fifteen minutes after hanging up in Snuffy's ear, Pitt, Leo and Tru were standing outside of their hotel, still waiting for Snuffy and his wifey. Just as Pitt was pulling out his cell phone to call Snuffy again, Leo said, "Here comes a red Escalade now, Pitt."

Pitt turned and smiled when he saw the red truck had come to a stop in front of them. His smile brightened at the sight of a tall, brown-skinned woman with legs that seemed to never stop, and an ass that could make a grown man cry.

Charlene stepped up to Pitt and said, "Would you like to sit up front with my man, or would you like to ride in the back with your friends?"

"Yeah, the back's cool. That way, I can keep my eyes on you!" Pitt said flirtatiously as he followed Charlene back to the truck.

Once everyone was inside of the vehicle, Snuffy pulled away from the curb and said, "What it do, boss?"

"Everything is everything, my man. How long has the product been at this location?"

"Won used to have a lot of shit brought here every other month or so. It's been a minute since he's gotten down like that though. This is his main spot in town. No one knows about it but me and my baby. Ain't that right, boo?" Snuffy asked Charlene.

Charlene smiled and answered, "That's right, baby."

"Do y'all know exactly how much work is there?" Pitt stared at Charlene.

The both of them started laughing, and after they seemed to regain their composure, Charlene said, "Baby, ain't that much countin' in the fuckin' world! Won always told us to make sure that we kept everything in order for him, and that's exactly what we did. What we look like, tryin' to count all of that damn dope?" she said.

Snuffy pulled into the parking lot of a large warehouse and turned off the ignition to the truck. He then said, "Here it is, boss. The building is locked tighter than a virgin's twat. Here're the keys to the two locks, as well as the security code to the alarm system." He then passed the keys and a piece of paper with the alarm code written on it to Pitt.

After Pitt accepted it from Snuffy, he said, "All right, why don't you let your girl take me inside and show me the work? I'll leave my boys here with you."

Snuffy shrugged his shoulders and said, "Go on with the man, *mami*. The quicker we get this over with, the quicker we can go do us, ya feel me?"

Charlene smiled at Snuffy and said, "I got you, baby." She grabbed her purse and stepped out of the truck, followed closely by Pitt. She led the way to the warehouse, and when they made it to the main entrance, she told Pitt, "You gots the keys, baby. Open it up."

Pitt stepped in front of her, unlocked both of the locks on the door, and stepped inside. He saw the control panel for the alarm system blinking on his right, so he quickly stepped over to it and punched in the seven-digit code to deactivate it. He smiled when he saw that the alarm was deactivated, and asked, "Where's the fucking lights?"

"Over to your left," Charlene said as she pulled a silenced 9 mm out of her purse and took aim exactly where she figured Pitt would be standing when the lights came on.

When Pitt turned on the lights, he almost pissed on himself when he saw Charlene pointing her gun at him. "What the fuck is that for, Charlene?" he asked nervously.

"You don't know? Nigga, did you really think that you could kill Won and get away with it?"

"Come on with that shit! Won ain't dead! What the fuck is wrong with you?" he lied convincingly.

Charlene started laughing as she shook her head from side to side. She then said, "You are somethin' else, Mister Pitt!" She quickly glanced down at her watch then said, "Since we got a li'l time until Big Junior gets here, I'll break it all down to you real quick like."

"Who the fuck is Big Junior?"

"He's Won's only living relative. He's the man who's going to take your life."

"*What?* Come on with this shit, Charlene! Stop playing!"

"Playing? That shit is too funny right there, for real! But check it. When Won called my boo and told him to turn over everything to you, that was the code that you were to be killed. We were to kill whoever came to get this work. Won was prepared for you years ago, buddy. It really hurts me to know that he's no longer with us, but it makes my heart feel real good to know that me and my man did our part just as he expected us to."

Pitt stood in front of Charlene with a look of disgust on his face. He couldn't fucking believe it. That nigga Won had still beaten him. Before he could say another word to try and talk Charlene out of this mess, his eyes grew as wide as saucers when he saw Leo and Tru being led inside of the warehouse by Snuffy and two other men.

Snuffy smiled and said, "Baby, these Cali boys is somethin', ain't they?"

"Uh-huh. I just got finished explaining to Pitt here what Won told us about him."

"Good. Let's get this shit over with," Snuffy said coldly.

"Wait! Don't you realize that I can make the both of you richer than either of you ever imagined? I'm the second in charge of The Network! Whatever you ask of me, I can give it to you. Don't be stupid, Snuffy. You'll be able to have whatever you want."

"If I let you go?" asked Snuffy.

Pitt bobbed his head up and down and said, "Yes, if you let me go."

Snuffy and Charlene started laughing, and so did the other two gentlemen who had remained silent up until that moment.

"Dog, don't you realize that Won has already made it possible for me and Charlene here to have anything we want in his world? Why would we want to have a plug with the second-in-charge of The Network, when I'm about to have a direct link with the number one man of The Network?"

"What? Cash Flo' would never fuck with any of you guys! I'm telling you, you gots to listen to what I'm saying here!" Pitt yelled.

"Cash Flo'? Who the fuck is Cash Flo'?" asked one of the men who had accompanied Snuffy when he brought Leo and Tru into the warehouse. "Taz is about to be the next head of

The Network. My Uncle Won planned on taking over himself, but since thangs went left for him, it's meant for Taz to be the man. You kilt my Uncle, and for that, Mister Pitt, you gots to die by my hand!" Big Junior said as he smiled at Pitt.

Big Junior stood a little over six foot three inches, and was fucking huge. He could easily pass for a defensive lineman or a lean-ass linebacker. His muscles rippled all through his white tee.

Pitt looked as if he had already been shot by one of the guns aimed at his heart. "Ta-Taz! That country nigga in Oklahoma City?"

Big Junior nodded his head and said, "Yep! In a few weeks, he's about to take complete control of The Network."

"Never! Cash Flo' won't stand for that shit!"

Big Junior shrugged his huge shoulders and said, "If you say so. But check this out. We got thangs to do, and I'm sure Snuffy and Charlene have made plans for the evening."

"That's right, dog. Me and wifey tryin' to go get our freak on!" Snuffy said with a laugh.

Big Junior pulled out his silenced 9 and said, "Oh, I almost forgot. Uncle Won told me to tell you that he'll be waitin' for you in hell!"

Before Pitt could speak, Big Junior shot him two times in the head. He died instantly.

Snuffy turned toward Leo and Tru, and in his best Tony Montana impersonation, he asked, "You two want a job?"

Both Leo and Tru nodded their heads up and down eagerly, grateful their lives were being spared.

Charlene laughed and said, "Quit giving these niggas false hopes." Then she shot Leo and Tru right between their eyes. Their bodies fell to the floor instantly. She smiled at Snuffy and said, "Come on, 'Tony.' Let's get out of here!"

Snuffy smiled and asked, "But what about them?"

Big Junior said, "Don't trip. Major gots some of y'all's peoples from the twenty-one on their way to handle the cleanup. Let's ride!"

***

With tears sliding down his face, Taz stared at Won's image and listened to what he had to say. Won had a sad smile on his face as he spoke to the camera.

"If you're watching this DVD, Babyboy, then I guess I've finally lost the game. Don't worry, though, 'cause if I lost, then that means you've won. Listen, and make sure that you do exactly as you're told, if, in fact you do decide to roll with what I'm about to propose to you.

"Pitt was able to pick up the pieces, and he obviously got to me before I could get to him. So, that means that by the time you get to watch this DVD, he too should have come to his demise. You will be receiving a call from my peoples with confirmation of this act. You then will also be notified of the position of power that is awaiting you out here on the West Coast.

"As you can see in my Will, I've left everything I have to you and Tazneema. But that's not all. I would be very pleased with you if you took over and became the head man of The Network. Everything is in order. All you have to do is give my man Snuffy the word that you have agreed to be the next head of The Network. After that, Cash Flo' will be eliminated, and the position of the most powerful Black criminal organization in the U.S. will belong solely to you. I know this is a shock to you, Babyboy, but take your time before deciding which way you're going to go. I designed this for the both of us. Either it was going to be me or you who ran The Network.

"Since I've come to my demise, I'm hoping that you'll carry on my dream and take this position. If not, I still want you to know that I have always loved you as my son, and I will forever be watching over you. . . ."

Won paused and stared at the camera then said:

"Follow your heart on this one, Babyboy. Out!"

The picture on the screen faded out slowly into another picture of the great Michael Jordan, only this time it was a picture of him standing with all six of the NBA championship trophies that he'd helped the Chicago Bulls win during his stellar career.

By the time Taz made it back to his house, he watched Won's DVD three more times. He couldn't believe what he had done for him. Now, the questions remained. What the hell was he going to do? Should he take the position as head of The Network? Or should he leave all of that shit alone and try to move on with his crazy-ass life? A decision had to be made. He just didn't know what the fuck he was going to do. *Life's a bitch, ain't it?* he thought as he climbed out of his truck and entered his home.

Chapter Thirty-three

It was the night before Keno's funeral. Taz was glad that Wild Bill, Red and Bob had decided not to have a wake. *I don't think I would be able to go through seeing my nigga in that coffin more than once,* Taz thought as he relaxed on his bed.

For the last few days, Taz kept himself busy by going over all of the financial matters of Won's estate. Won left him and Tazneema over sixty million dollars, including his big-ass boat and properties all over the West Coast. Everything was to be divided evenly between the two of them. That put a smile on Taz's face as he thought about how Tazneema was going to react when she found out that she was now an extremely wealthy young lady.

His smile quickly turned into a frown when he thought about her having that nigga Cliff's child. He reached and grabbed the phone and gave his daughter a call. When Tazneema answered the phone, she sounded a little funny, so he asked, "What's up, baby girl? You all right?"

"Not really, Daddy, but I'll be fine. I just need to get some rest, that's all," she said as she held onto her stomach.

"What's wrong? You sick or something?"

She took a deep breath and said, "I just got back home from having an abortion, Daddy."

"You what? What made you do that, 'Neema?"

"I didn't want to have that man's child. He was the devil, Daddy. I couldn't see myself bringing a child into this world that could possibly have that man's lying ways inside of him or her."

"Why didn't you tell me? I could have gone with you."

"I had Tari take me. I didn't think you'd be too comfortable with me going through that process."

"Are you sure you're okay? Do you need me to come out there?"

"I'm fine, Daddy. Tari's here, and she refuses to leave until I've eaten something and have fallen asleep. So relax."

Taz smiled and said, "Whatever, baby girl! Put that white girl on the phone."

Tazneema smiled and said, "You are too crazy, Taz! I'll see you tomorrow."

"All right, baby girl," Taz said somberly as he thought once again about having to attend his best friend's funeral in the morning.

Tari accepted the phone from Tazneema and said, "Don't you start with me! She made me promise not to tell you about any of this. It was her decision to make, Taz," she said seriously.

"Would you be quiet, snow bunny? I ain't mad at you or her. On the real, I'm kinda glad she did it, but a part of me wished she didn't. Does that make any sense?"

Tari laughed and said, "Yes, it makes perfect sense, silly! You're human, Taz. Don't worry though. The doctor told us that everything went fine. She's going to feel a little sluggish for a few days, but she's going to be A-okay. How are you doing?"

"I'm good, I guess. What about you?"

"I'm trying my best to accept all of this death. It's hard, baby . . . it's real hard."

"Yeah, I know."

"Why didn't Won want us to bury him properly? That was so damned unfair of him."

"You know he always had to do things his way. He requested to have his body cremated and his ashes spread out over the Pacific, so I had his attorneys take care of everything. Do you want to fly out to Cali with me to take care of the ashes?"

"I need a vacation, so why not? Can we do some thangs while we're out that way?" she asked devilishly.

"Tari!"

"All right! Damn! Can't a girl at least try?"

They both laughed.

"All right then, I'll see y'all tomorrow. I'm about to chill out for a li'l bit. Sacha should be here any minute."

"Tell her I said hello. I'll talk to you later," Tari said, and hung up the phone.

As if on cue, Sacha came into the bedroom, followed by Heaven and Precious. When Taz saw them enter the room, he smiled and said, "What's good, Li'l Mama?"

After slipping out of her pumps, she said, "Not much. Just tired as hell." She climbed onto the bed next to him, put her head on his chest and asked, "How are you holding up, baby?"

As he slowly stroked her long, jet-black hair, he said, "I miss him, Li'l Mama. I miss my man so much, it's killin' me slowly. I don't know how in the hell I'm gon' be able to look at him in a fuckin' casket. I don't think I'm gon' be able to take that shit."

Sacha closed her eyes as she listened to Taz speaking with so much pain in his voice. Her heart rate seemed to increase as she thought about all of the pain she had caused the one man that she would gladly give her life up for. For the thousandth time, she tried to convince herself to tell Taz the truth about how Keno was killed, but she just couldn't bring herself to do it. She couldn't tell her man, her fiancé, her heart, that she had killed his best friend because Keno had murdered her twin brothers so many years ago. Taz loved her, she was confident of that fact. But she wasn't willing to put their love to that ultimate test. This secret was going to have to go with her to her grave.

She raised her head, looked at her man and said, "Don't worry, baby. I'll be right by your side. I know it's going to be hard, but you know he's in a much better place now. He's with Bo-Pete and Won, and you know all three of them are watching over you."

Her words put a sad smile on his face as he thought about all three of his friends. "Yeah, they'll be watching over us all."

Before he could continue, they were interrupted by the telephone ringing. Sacha reached over Taz to answer it.

"Hello . . . May I ask who's speaking? . . . Just a moment please," she said. She handed the phone to Taz and said, "It's someone named Snuffy from Austin, baby."

Taz accepted the phone from her and said, "I was wondering when he was goin' to call." He put the phone to his ear and said, "What's good?"

"Everything is everything, my man. Do you know who I am?"

"Yeah, I know. I've been expecting your call."

"Do you have an answer for me yet? Or do you need some more time?"

"I have a question."

"Holla at your boy then."

"Has Cash Flo' been taken care of yet?"

"Do you want the grimy details?" Snuffy answered as he rubbed Charlene lightly on her left breast.

"Nah, I'm good. I just wanted to know. So, everything is all on me now, huh?"

"Yep. So, what's it gon' be, gee? Do you want to accept this position or what?"

Taz stared at Sacha as she rested her head on his chest and asked, "Can one man handle that much power?"

"Won felt that you could handle it, and I've never doubted that man in all of our years dealing with one another, gee. And I'm not about to start now. I think you can handle it," Snuffy said seriously.

Taz took a deep breath before answering Snuffy's question, because he knew it would change the direction of his life, as well as everyone else's around him. Wild Bill, Red, Bob, Sacha, Tari, Mama-Mama, Tazneema and Gwen's as well. If he moved to the West Coast to run The Network, they were all coming with him. There was no way in hell he would have it any other way.

"Yeah, I'm with it, Snuffy. I gots to carry the torch for my man. Won wanted it this way, so I gots to roll with my nigga's wishes. It wouldn't be right if I didn't."

"Exactly! I'll notify the rest of the council. When do you want to have our first official meeting?"

"What? You're part of the council?"

Snuffy smiled and said, "Dog, that was me and my wifey Charlene's blessing for being loyal all of these years. We would have gladly given our lives up for Won, dog. Now, that same loyalty belongs to you, Taz. We'll die for you if we have to. Real talk."

"That's good lookin'. Check it. Set it up with everyone else for next week out in Cali. We'll take Won's boat out and spread his ashes over the Pacific like he wanted. Afterward, we'll put the wheels of this ride in motion."

"Gotcha!" Snuffy said, and he hung up the phone.

After Taz replaced the cordless phone back on its base, Sacha looked up into his eyes, smiled and asked, "So, we're going to California, baby?"

Taz smiled at his fiancée and said, "Yeah, we're all moving to the Wild, Wild West!"

Sneak peek . . .

Gangsta Twist 3

Coming soon 2015

Chapter One

Akim Novikov and his long time comrade Alexander Sokolov both stood and watched as Akim's private jet slowly taxied toward the runway to make its departure from Moscow's Domodedovo International Airport to the United States, Los Angeles, California to be exact. The twenty-one hour flight would make one stop before arriving at LAX and their new business associates would be back safely to their home. Akim smiled, turned toward his comrade and spoke in Russian. "Well my friend, it looks as if we now begin this new business arrangement with Taz and The Network. I'm confident this should prove to be very profitable for us and all parties involved."

"You should be confident, you've put a tremendous amount of time and effort into this decision to deal with Taz. It's been over six years now and we've missed out on a lot of money in America because of you and your patience with this man. My question for you is, why did it take you this long to make contact with Taz? You have told me numerous times how you trusted Won totally. If that was the case I figured you would have made contact with Taz and put everything in motion years ago."

As they turned and began to walk toward the airports exit Akim's smile seemed to brighten when he spoke. "That was my dear deceased friend Won's request. He wanted me to sit back and be patient and watch Taz from a distance to make sure he was in fact ready to do the type of business that Won and I had planned on doing. Won was never one to jump into anything without being absolutely positive things would come out in his favor. Even in death he prepared for everything to work in Taz's favor. He wanted to make sure Taz was in fact ready to take on such a tremendous responsibility being the

leader of The Network. After six years of watching Taz lead
The Network to soaring profits I felt it was time for us to help
him soar even higher. Just as Won predicted Taz is a leader
in every sense of the word. The power given to him by Won
made him a man with enormous resources. Those resources
accompanied with the intelligence and ruthlessness Taz has
displayed over these past six years has shown me that he is
more than ready to embark in our very profitable business
ventures. Taz is not a man to be taken lightly, I respect that
and I am anxious to see how this evolves."

Once they were inside of their chauffeured limousine
Alexander asked, "What about the rest of the council, you
know they aren't going to accept what Taz will tell them about
the drugs?"

"This is true comrade. Taz loathes drugs, the council knows
this. The Network's primary profits come largely from the
distribution of drugs. The fact that drugs have made The
Network very rich is secondary to Taz. He possesses the power
to take The Network well beyond their current position. Taz
will make sure this transition within the business dealings of
The Network will go smoothly."

"And if there's any problems?"

Akim smiled. "Then we will assist our American comrade."

"This should prove to be very interesting."

"That indeed comrade, that indeed," Akim said as he
relaxed in his seat and lit a cigarette.

Taz, Wild Bill, Red and Bob made themselves comfortable as
the G-5 smoothly lifted off the ground and was airborne headed
home. It had been a long, tiring week spent in Moscow. Taz
smiled as he thought about the fun they had while in Russia.
Partying with Akim and Alexander had been something he
hadn't expected. Those Russian mafia guys sure know how
to kick it. Shit, he still had a slight hangover from all of that
Vodka he drank while partying with them. What surprised him
most was how they handled their business. No word games or
beating around the bush with Akim, he got straight to the point
and laid down the rules and what he expected from Taz and
The Network. Taz respected that. Now it was time to bring this

to the attention of the council to see if they will agree with the decision he made while in Russia. He really didn't care but he had to do it the politically correct way. So far he chose to never throw his weight around the council and for that they seemed to have more respect for him. Again, this was something he really didn't care about, as long as his crew was with it and by his side he would do whatever he wanted to. Won left him in power and he was determined to make the best of this, not only for Won but for everyone that was important to him. His crew, Red, Wild Bill, Bob, and Tari. His family; his wife Sacha, his mother Mama-Mama, and his children, Tazneema and his twin sons, Keenan and Ronald. Every move he made was for the well being of his loved ones and Won's memory. He was winning so far and it felt real good. Real good!

In six years Taz used the influence Won left him to hook The Network up and take their criminal enterprise to an international level. Won had a game plan and he secured contacts for Taz with some very serious criminal organizations. Sicilian mobsters, South American drug cartels, Cuban drug lords, Asian gangsters and finally the Russian mafia. Originally Taz wanted to remove the drugs from The Network but he saw that would be basically impossible because the distributions of narcotics was where the majority of The Network's money came from. So he bided his time and waited patiently. He even made some stronger moves to help the drug trade elevate for The Network through Won's connection with the Orumutto family in California. The money earned from their X-pills was enormous. So far every move Taz made has been the right move and that gave him the confidence to make this next move with the Russians. Weapons Arms dealing. The money they would make in arms dealing with the Russians would surpass all of the drugs they dealt ten times over. He knew he could be greedy and make these moves with the Russians and keep the drug trade The Network ran intact and everything would be good. But that's not what he wanted; he still loathed drugs and wanted no part of it any longer. At the next quarterly council meeting he was going to present his plan of removing The Network from the drug game all together. Not only did he dislike drugs or selling them, he felt that it was too risky of a business to continue with. It was only a matter of time before things got wicked. Yes, they were not the average street level drug dealers, but that didn't matter to him, he wanted a peace of mind and as long as The Network was involved with drugs he would never have that. Sooner or later the DEA or the FBI would catch wind of certain people and when that happened the snitching would begin. That meant murder would come into play because he knew without a doubt he would order the death to anyone he even thought was running their mouths. Though every move that has been made thus far under his leadership had been calculated to a tee didn't mean every move had been made right. To him they had been extremely lucky and luck runs out sooner or later. It was time for The Network to switch shit up. Time for the drugs to stop. If the council didn't agree with what Taz was going to propose then there was going to be some serious issues, issues that would most likely make Taz use his position of power, and that meant a division within. *Oh well,* Taz thought as the jet reached its cruising altitude. He reclined in his seat and wondered what his wife and sons were doing at home. He yawned and closed his eyes and began to doze as the rest of the crew was doing.

By the time Taz woke up Wild Bill was arguing with Red about who had the most money between Diddy and Jay-Z. For the life of him Taz couldn't understand how two men in their early forties could have such a childish argument. But these were his lifelong friends and nothing they did could ever destroy their friendship. He sighed and said, "Will you two fools shut the fuck up, acting stupid and shit."

Red, the biggest man of the crew at a little over six-two smiled at Taz and said, "You know how this little man gets to tripping when he's wrong gee. Everyone knows that Diddy has way more money than Jay."

"Little man? Nigga, I can still out bench your big yellow-ass any day any time, so kill that little man shit fool!" They all started laughing because Wild Bill was extra sensitive when it came to his height. Any reference toward how small he is sets him off instantly. Red knew this and used this tactic frequently to piss his friend off. Wild Bill, the smallest member of the crew at five-seven was extremely strong, his muscular physique was something he was very proud of, that and his long perm hair that he refused to cut. Even after Taz and Red decided to cut their long braids for a more conservative businessman type look. Wild Bill laughed at them both and told them that he was like Sampson, his strength came from his hair. Another one of his funny moments.

The next member of the crew was Bob. Bob was another comedian of sorts. Over the last few years since becoming a father he had calmed down considerably with some of his wild antics. His wife, Gwen had a lot to do with this transformation. They were a perfect match for each other. She was the only person other than any crew member who could keep Bob in check when he got to tripping. Bob was five-eleven, dark skin with a four inch knot right in the middle of his forehead that made him the brunt of a lot of jokes over the years. Only from the crew though several men and woman have been punished for trying to clown Bob about his knot, he did not play with that at all. Though his wild days seemed to have been behind him Bob was still just as dangerous as the rest of the crew.

Taz also at five-eleven was the head of the crew in a way but chose to lead by example. He tried to make all of the right decisions when it came to his friends. They were a crew, but they were friends forever in his eyes and he loved them all like brothers. They had been reduced to a four man crew when originally they were a six man crew before losing two of their close friends in a beef with some Hoover Crips in their home town of Oklahoma City. That beef nearly destroyed Taz and his relationship with his daughter Tazneema. Taz and the crew went all out to get revenge for their friends' murders. Bo-Pete and Keno. In memory of their friends each crew member put portraits of Bo-Pete and Keno tattooed on each side of their chest. So no matter what as long as they were still breathing their friends would always be with them. Taz took it a step further when he found out that his wife Sacha was having twins he chose to name both of his sons after his fallen friends. Ronald Michael Good was Li'l Bo-Pete and Keenan

Mitchell Good was Li'l Keno. Sacha chose the middle names. The crew was composed of four men but the total members of the crew were five because of Tari, Taz's ex-lover. Tari was a drop dead gorgeous white woman that had held Taz down for many years after they were first introduced by Won, Taz's mentor/father figure. Their lives took a major turn because of Won and because of those turns they were now on a private jet returning to America from Russia.

"All right clowns chill, we need to talk some business for a minute here. I thought we would wait until we got back home but since you fools have so much energy we might as well handle this now," Taz said seriously. Each member of the crew sat up in their seats and gave Taz their undivided attention. "So, you all heard what has been proposed by Akim and Alex. You know I am on board with it because I want to move The Network in a different direction away from the drug game. We don't get our hands dirty directly but if anything ever went left we could all be caught up in some heavy federal conspiracy shit and I am just not trying to go out like that over some damn dope money. You know how I feel on that shit. Your thoughts?"

Bob reclined in his seat and spoke first. "If you're with it Taz then I trust your call. I mean you've made every move the right move since you've become the man over The Network. You've taken us just as far as Won figured you would. You know I feel the same as you do when it comes to the dope game. I say let's roll with these Russians and get this money with the gun thing."

Taz laughed and said, "Gun thing, huh? It's bigger than that my nigga, but I feel what you're saying. We'll be participating in some heavy arms dealing. Not just some guns, this will be some major army type shit. Missiles, rocket launchers, automatic assault rifles as well as pistols, silencer and such. This move will bring us way more money than the percentages we collect from the council of The Network. It will also solidify The Network as major players internationally."

"I agree with Bob dog, I feel we should continue to trust your judgment because every move you have made has been on point," said Red.

"I agree too, but I do have some concerns," said Wild Bill.
"Talk to me gee."
"The drugs have been the main get down for The Network
since the beginning. That's how Won has always ate and
made the moves he was able to make. He kept all of the right
connections and did his thang major with the dope game. The
entire council except for you have a direct hand with the ho
game. True, you collect a large percentage for all the drugs as
the rest but it's mostly how they eat. By making this move you
would be taking from them what they have been dependent
on for decades. Two things can come from this, one, they
could roll with it and be willing to make this change. Or two,
they will not want to make that move in fear of change. Fear
of the unknown makes people hesitant, dog. Especially when
you're talking about some heavy figures like what they bring
in quarterly. I personally feel that if they choose not to roll
with you on this it will cause problems within The Network.
That will then cause someone to die because if I even feel like
someone in that council is thinking about bringing you any
harm I will take their head off myself. Real spill."

Taz gave him a nod and placed his right palm over his chest
where the tattoo of Keno's face was and said, "Love my nigga.
I feel every word you have spoken. Now let me break it down
to you as I see it and feel it. The percentage that we collect, not
just me dog, whatever I get I split with you guys evenly. That
will never change. Yes, I am the head of The Network, but
we are a crew and that comes before anybody and anything."
Each member gave a nod and placed an open right palm over
their chest. "Now, I know that change will be something that
won't be easily accepted within the council that is why I will
propose an extra incentive for this move. I will give them one
year, one year to get full profits from their drug moves. I will
concede my percentage during that year. That means they will
make over sixty–seventy million dollars during this last year
of drug activity. But when that year is over The Network will
sever all ties with all drug businesses. I think this tactic will
make that fear of the unknown a tad bit better to deal with."

"Maybe. But have you given thought about how it will affect the others involved with the drug business? I mean you got the Orumutto fool with the X-pills. You got Jorge Santa Cruz from the South American drug cartel in Buena-Ventura. It's bigger than the council, my nigga. This shit could cause a major war with you pulling The Network out. You would be taking money from more than just the council members," Wild Bill said logically.

Taz sat and thought about those words for a few minutes then said, "You've made a good point with that Bill. I can make the decision over the council whether they're with it or not because though it's a vote I have the authority to overrule all and make it happen. I didn't give much thought to what you pointed out though. That's why I love this crew, we will never let each other miss a thing. Five minds are better than one. This is what I intend to do. I'm going to have Sacha set up the next Network quarterly meeting out in Miami. Have her pick a real fly resort so we can kick it and have some fun while handling the business out there. In the mean time I think we will be doing some more international traveling. Columbia to get at Jorge is a must because you know he don't play no phones or e-mails at all."

"Miami because of the Cuban?" asked Bob.

"Exactly."

"Are you trying to bring them in on the business with the Russians?" asked Red.

"No. I will offer them some serious action on the weapons though. You know they will definitely want some action on them with all of the beefs they go through yearly. I think if I do this right I can avoid war with them."

"I feel you, but I feel that one of them ain't going to be with it," said Wild Bill.

Taz shrugged his shoulders and said, "Then that's the one that will get rolled on."

Wild Bill smiled and said, "Real spill."

"Okay, this is how we'll work this, we'll keep this close to our vests until we've spoken with Jorge Santa Cruz, Danny Orumutto and Señor Juarez in Miami. Then we'll proceed from there with the council."

"I wanna go home, I miss the City, gee. Can we add that trip into this mix?" asked Red.

Laughing, Wild Bill said, "Nigga, you need to dead that weak shit and go on and wife Paquita and bring her ass out west with the rest of us. You know you just wanna go back home because of her!"

Red gave Wild Bill the finger because he knew he was right on target with that jab.

"I was thinking the same thing actually. I need to see Mama-Mama and Tazneema. You already know the white girl is gonna want to know the business. So this is what we'll do. Before we bounce to make the meeting needed we'll go back home and chill for a week, check on the businesses and our rental properties out there and relax a little bit before we roll out. Agreed?"

"Agreed!" the rest of the crew answered in unison.

"One more thing Taz?" asked Wild Bill.

"What up?"

"Didn't you give the Russians a year on the guns, I mean arms dealing thing?"

Taz gave Wild Bill a faintly mocking smile that Sacha says he had become known for and answered honestly. "I told them that I would deal with them whether or not The Network's council was with it. So, yeah dog, I gave them the green light."

"I thought so. That's why you not really tripping on a war with any of these clowns. What we packing with The Network combined with the Russian mob we got enough power to handle shit."

Taz gave his friend that smile again and said, "Exactly."

Chapter Two

Sacha Good was all smiles as she watched her twin sons slept soundly in their beds. She was amazed at how much her sons looked like her twin brothers who had been murdered almost twenty years ago. When she watched her sons she was so filled with mixed emotions at times that she didn't know whether if she wanted to smile or cry. She missed her brothers so much it hurt. She loved her sons so much she knew there was nothing in the world she wouldn't do for them. She did what she had to do to avenge her brother's death and she felt no remorse for it at all. Killing Keno gave her the most satisfying feeling she had ever felt in her life. She could close her eyes and remember ringing his doorbell waiting for him to come to the door while she had her hand inside of her purse as if it was yesterday and not six years ago. She remembered the strange calm that came over her when she saw Keno open the door with a surprised look on his face.

"What's up Sacha? Everything straight with Taz?" Keno asked with a puzzled expression on his face.

"Everything is fine Keno. I came over because I wanted to talk to you about all this violence. You're the closest to Taz and if anyone can talk him out of something you're the man who can do it. I understand you guys need to get revenge for Bo-Pete but this has to stop before I lose the man I love more than anything in this world. I want my baby to have a father around, Keno. I need your help."

Relieved, Keno sighed and said, "Come on in and let's talk, Sacha," he turned and started walking followed closely by Sacha.

Sacha stopped, turned, closed the door and asked, "I hope I'm not interrupting anything, Keno. I know you and Katrina been doing it real tough lately."

"Yeah, we good. You ain't in the way though, I was just about to go out and do some shopping. Ring shopping," Keno said with a smile.

"Ring shopping? Wow!"

"I know, huh. Never thought I'd be the one to wife a female. Come on let's go in the den so we can chop it up."

Sacha smiled as she pulled out a small .380 caliber pistol and shot Keno three times; two in the back of the head and once in the back of his neck. She then stood over his dead body for a moment to make sure he was dead then said, "That was for my brothers you bastard. I hope you burn in hell." She then calmly put her gun back inside of her purse, pulled out a scarf and wiped the door knob, then opened the door and left with the door wide open.

That had taken place six years ago and to this very day she was so afraid of what Taz would do to her if he ever found out she was the person who murdered his best friend, not the Hoover Crips in Oklahoma City who he had been beefing with at the time. She was more than afraid, she was terrified. So terrified she made sure no matter what, Taz was never able to spend time alone with her parents. When they were married she made sure she kept them apart or Taz was never alone with either of them. Taz knew nothing about her brothers let alone they had been murdered. She didn't want him to find this out and start to put two and two together. He was no dummy and it wouldn't take him long to realize what she'd done. Living with this constant fear in the back of her mind was maddening at times; there was nothing she could do about it but continue to live and try to enjoy the life she had with her husband and her children. Taz had given her a good life, no worries at all. She had everything she ever wanted materially and had become an intricate part of Taz's businesses both legally and illegally. She smiled at that thought; she called herself the unknown member of The Network. That always got a good laugh from Taz. But he agreed because he knew she would always give him solid advice and that made her feel even better knowing her husband trusted her like that.

They started Good Investments Inc., in Oklahoma City and moved west so Taz could take control as the head of The Network. She gave up her partnership at Whitney & Johnson, a prestigious law firm in Oklahoma City, to follow her husband to the west coast where they now lived on a beautiful estate located in the most prime section of lower Bel Air through East Gate. On just under one acre, the property showcased expensive park-like grounds with a large flat grassy yard that Taz loved because there was plenty of room for his beloved Dobermans, Precious and Heaven to roam around and be comfortable. The interiors are classically proportioned with elegant formal rooms on a grand yet intimate scale which Sacha totally loved. Hardwood floors and paneling gave it an even more expensive feel. The master bedroom featured dual baths and walk-in dressing rooms to give them the space they needed because Sacha was well known for her shopping binges and clothes was a top priority, so gigantic closet space was a must. Seven more bedrooms, a gym for Taz and his crew to get their work out on, and a entire wing of the estate solely for the twins. Play rooms and their video games along with all of their many, many, toys completed their dream home. The property is set back from the street behind gates with a spacious motor court and three car garage that housed Taz's Ferrari and Bentley as well as her brand new seven series BMW. Everything about their home even the location was perfect. It was within minutes of UCLA Medical Center, one of the best hospitals on the west coast and within walking distance to the famous Bel Air Hotel and Country Club. Everything a couple from the country would just love. For the first few years living lavishly absolutely fascinated Sacha, now she was used to it and had become a well known socialite within the Bel Air community. She even talked Taz into attending certain social events from time to time. Her motives behind this were to solidify them as a legitimate power couple living amongst so many other ultra-rich people. Taz was proud of her every move because so far everything had worked out perfectly for them.

Good Investments Inc. was doing quite well in Oklahoma City so the legitimate money continued to flow, but the main money came from the illegal moves from The Network. Taz made anywhere from seventy to a hundred million a year tax free and it was Sacha's duty to make sure that money was properly handled as well as laundered. A task she had taken seriously by completing several online courses for accounting and being taught the ropes by Won's financial advisors Taz had introduced her to when they first arrived in Los Angeles. Tazneema, Taz's daughter, along with Tari ran the day to day operations of Good Investments Inc. Which basically consisted of making sure all of their properties and businesses were running smoothly and looking for new ways to invest the millions they were making? Over twenty-five fast food chains; Subways, IHOPs, Popeye's Chicken, and several McDonalds and Burger Kings. That added to over three hundred and fifty rental homes around the Oklahoma City area, the Good family along with the crew were doing quite well financially. Quite well, indeed.

Sacha gave her sons a kiss while they slept peacefully and left their room quietly. By the time she made it to the bedroom she decided she wanted to do something instead of being stuck in the house bored all night. She missed Taz. The thought of him made her smile, he was on his way home and that meant she would be able to get her hands on her handsome husband. *Mmm, yummy*, she thought as she slipped out of her jeans and top. She only had a pair of boy-shorts and bra she stepped to the dresser and grabbed her cell and called her best friend Gwen. When Gwen answered the phone Sacha said, "What's up Mommy? What are you doing?"

"Nothing much Mommy. Playing *mommy* for real, just put Bob's two kids to bed," Gwen said laughing. "Now I'm bored wishing Bob's ass was here so I could put this pussy on that knot and get freaky."

"That's so crazy because that's exactly what I had on my mind too."

"What? Since when have you wanted to get freaky with my husband's knot Mommy?"

"Shut up! You know what I meant. This week long trip to Russia has me missing some Taz."

"I know that's right. But all of that will be over in the morning right?"

"Mm-hm. They're supposed to be home around ten or eleven a.m. Mommy. So, what you got up for tonight?"

"Nothing. Done playing mommy for the night so I was going to take me a long hot bath and watch some TV so I can be well rested when Bob gets back. Because as soon as his black ass walks in that door we are fucking right there in the foyer!"

"Nasty ass."

"At least I ain't fake with it, 'cause you know damn well you feel exactly as I do!" They both started laughing. They had been best friends for so long they knew each other inside out.

After Sacha met Taz she introduced Gwen to Bob and their love connection shocked everyone. They were a match made out of true opposites; Gwen, the highly intelligent psychiatrist and Bob, the wild man of the crew. They seemed to be opposites but in reality they were the perfect yin to each other's yang. It was love at first fuck for them because they were two of the most insatiable human beings Sacha ever met. Bob complimented Gwen and did so much for her in so many different ways. Whereas Gwen did equally as much for Bob. They were married right after Sacha and Taz and soon after were blessed with two beautiful kids; a boy, Bob Junior and a girl, Gwendolyn who Gwen affectionately called Bob's kids. It had been a good six years for them as well and Sacha thanked God every single night for Gwen's happiness. She'd been through way too much pain with the loss of her first husband and son, William and Remel in a tragic accident over ten years ago. Now, that tragedy was stored in the back of their minds as the continued to live and try to make the best out of their lives together.

Gwen was just as dedicated to her man as Sacha was to Taz. She also became more involved with the business side of things as well. Though Bob's role with everything wasn't as intense as Taz's, Gwen made sure she did her part to help out when called upon. Like Sacha she left her thriving private practice as a psychiatrist to live and be by her man's side on the west coast. As soon as they made it to California Bob made his first purchase which was some beach front property in Malibu for his bride. Their home was so lovely that Sacha tried her best to find a reason to get out there at least twice a week. The Malibu residence was located one hundred and fifteen feet from the beach. The property is known as one of Malibu's original beach front residences. The Hacienda style home had been meticulously restored with three bedrooms including an oceanside master suite, top of the line finishes, controlled private entry, Crestron products and walls of glass doors. Gwen's personal touch to it made the home warm and inviting. Though much smaller than Sacha and Taz's estate it was worth more than seventeen million dollars. With Bob being a millionaire himself he felt it was nothing to make sure he kept his family in the very best home. Gwen was in heaven and loved the life she had stumbled into with Bob. She was his bride, best friend, and his ride or die and would do whatever it took to make sure they made all of the right moves together. Where Bob liked to get emotional at times

Gwen was the calm more calculated of the couple and would bring the thinking to the equation, which made them a hell of a part of the entire crew. The crew was all one big happy family, everyone played their part. And together they were all winning, big time.

Both Sacha and Gwen stood five–five and could pass for sisters. Sacha was the thicker of the two with a bronze skin tone that gave the impression that she was from the islands somewhere. Long silky hair passed her shoulder with some firm C-cup sized breasts to bring heavy emphasis to her small hips. Taz loved her shapely ass and constantly reminded her it was her ass that drew his attention to her at a club in Oklahoma City six years ago. Gwen, with her boob job C-cups was just as easy on the eyes as Sacha. Though two kids had put some weight on her thin frame she packed a nice ass herself. Hazel eyes with a light brown skin complexion. She was everything Bob had ever dreamt of having for a wife.

Before either of the best friends had children they used to refer to one another as bitch and ho affectionately. Sacha being the bitch, and Gwen being the ho. After they each gave birth they decided that type of terminology was too graphic for mother's to be calling each other so they chose to stop calling each other bitch and ho and now called one another Mommy. Taz thought it was funny but it stuck with the women and that's how they referred to one another.

"All right Mommy, how long will it take for you to make it this way?" asked Gwen.

"What are you talking about?"

"If you don't quit that, you know damn well no one knows you better than I do. You're bored and you want to do something. Since you have the live in maids and what not you can move around and I can't. So that means you want to come out here and kick it for a little while, which is cool with me because I'm equally bored. I'll break out some XO and fry up some hot wings and we can go kick it on the deck out back, sip and eat while watching the gorgeous Pacific. I swear no matter how long we stay out here I'll never get tired of this ocean view Mommy, that's real."

"I know that's right Mommy. I'm on my way! Get to frying up them wangs!" Sacha hung up the phone laughing as she went into her walk-in closet to get dressed in something comfortable for the drive out to Malibu to kick it with her best friend for a few hours.